Evelyn Hood Omnibus

By Evelyn Hood

EVELYN HOOD OMNIBUS

Pebbles on the Beach
Another Day

EVELYN HOOD

WARNER BOOKS

A *Warner* Book

This omnibus edition first published in Great Britain by
Warner Books in 2001

Evelyn Hood Omnibus Copyright © Evelyn Hood 2001

Previously published separately:

Pebbles on the Beach
First published in Great Britain in 1995 by Little, Brown and Company
Published by Warner Books in 1996
Reprinted 1996 (twice), 1998, 1999

Copyright © Evelyn Hood 1995

Another Day
First published in Great Britain in 1996 by Little, Brown and Company
Published by Warner Books in 1997
Reprinted 1997 (twice), 1999

Copyright © 1996 by Evelyn Hood

The moral right of the author has been asserted.

A CIP catalogue record for this book
is available from the British Library.

ISBN 0 7515 3170 7

Printed and bound in Great Britain by
Mackays of Chatham plc, Chatham, Kent

Warner Books
A Division of
Little, Brown and Company (UK)
Brettenham House
Lancaster Place
London WC2E 7EN

www.littlebrown.co.uk

Pebbles on the Beach

To Una and Malcolm,
for putting up with me through thick and thin

1

'Lachlan!'

Trace horses dragging a loaded cart up Mearns Street from the docks to the nearby sugar refinery clattered by just as Elspeth shouted her cousin's name across the width of the playground, ironbound wheels and hooves rumbling and sparking over the cobblestones.

The figure leaning against a tenement wall opposite the school gates, studying a newspaper, didn't move. Frustrated, Elspeth put two fingers to her lips in the way Thomas and Lachlan had taught her years before, and blew a piercing whistle that cut through the chill autumn air.

This time Lachlan looked up at once, his young face splitting into a huge grin as he saw her at the bottom of the school steps. He wasn't the only one to look in her direction; all through the playground and in the street beyond the railings heads turned. Women gossiping to each other from the tenement windows opposite the school, most of them with their arms comfortably folded on cushions or blankets protecting them from the stone sills, gaped and craned to see where the noise had come from.

'Elspeth Bremner! Kindly remember that you're a young lady and not a steam whistle down at the shipyards!' snapped the teacher who had just emerged on to the steps, and Elspeth whirled guiltily, the movement whipping her skirt against her long thin legs.

'Yes, Miss Scott, sorry, Miss Scott. It's just th–that—' She was stammering in her excitement at seeing Lachlan right there in Greenock, when she had thought him to be in some army barracks in England, '—that's our Lachlan over there. He m–must have come home on leave and I didn't know about it—'

The woman's face softened. 'In that case, run along – but don't you ever let out that dreadful noise in my hearing again.'

'Yes, Miss Scott, thank you, Miss Scott.' Elspeth set off at a run across the playground, weaving around the loitering groups. Her schoolbooks, held together by an old belt, were clutched to her chest, and the thick brown plait that hung down her back bounced against her spine with every step.

The headlong rush didn't stop until she was through the gate and across the street, letting the bundle of books fall unheeded on the pavement, running straight into Lachlan's open arms, being swung up into the air and round in a circle.

'I didn't know you were coming home!' she said breathlessly as he put her down.

'Neither did I till yesterday. God, Ellie, ye've put on weight! Ye were just a wee scliff of a thing when I last saw ye.'

'I'm older now.' She prodded him in the stomach. 'You've got fatter yourself.'

'Och, that's the stodge they feed us in the army,' Lachlan McDonald said, then glanced over Elspeth's shoulder. 'Hello, Molly.'

'Hello.' Molly McKibbin's round face was strangely blotchy. She looked, Elspeth thought, surprised, as though she was coming down with something. 'You dropped your books, Elspeth.'

'I didn't drop them, I threw them down.'

'Without looking? They could have landed in some old man's spit,' Molly said self-righteously, turning the bundle over and examining it carefully.

'They're fine.' Elspeth knew that her voice was too sharp,

2

but with good reason. It was true that she and Molly always walked home from school together, but surely today, with Lachlan arriving so unexpectedly, Molly should have had the tact to leave the two of them on their own. Elspeth reached for the books, but Lachlan stretched a long arm out beyond hers, and got to the shabby strap first.

'I'll carry them. I'll take yours as well, if you like,' he added, and Molly promptly handed over her own armful of books, simpering foolishly.

'You've both shot up while I've been away,' he teased, and Molly's simper became a silly little giggle. Best friend or not, Elspeth could have slapped her.

'What's that on your face?' she asked instead.

Molly's hand flew up. 'Where?'

'Your cheeks are all blotchy – and your neck, too. Big red blotches all over. Have a look at yourself in that shop window there.'

'Stop teasin' the lassie,' Lachlan told her, amused. 'It's nothin', Molly, just a wee bit red – from the wind, mebbe. It's cold enough. Come on, I've only got till tomorrow and I don't want to spend my leave standin' here.'

Behind their wire-framed spectacles, Molly's eyes shot a look of pure venom at Elspeth, who gave a bland smile in return.

'Where's your uniform?' Elspeth slipped her hand possessively into Lachlan's free arm as they turned towards home, leaving Molly to trail behind them.

'Ach, I couldnae wait to get out of it and intae my own clothes. It's scratchy, and it doesnae fit me properly. They never do.' Then, squeezing her arm against his side, 'Happy birthday, Ellie.'

'You remembered?'

'Of course I remembered, that's why I'm here. I said to the Sergeant-Major, "Listen, sir," I said. "Our Ellie'll be thirteen years old next Thursday, so I'd be much obliged if ye could see yer way tae stoppin' the war for a couple of days so's I can go home and taste a bit of that dumpling my mum'll be making for her."'

'You did not!' Molly gasped from Elspeth's other side.

'Of course he didn't, don't be daft!'

'But I would have, if he hadnae come up with the idea himself before I even got a chance tae speak tae him.'

'I wish it was longer than just till tomorrow!'

'Aye, well, I've not quite managed tae see the Kaiser off yet, so they need me tae go back and finish the job properly. Then I'll be home for good. Here – try my jacket pocket.'

Elspeth slipped her hand into the nearest pocket, as she had often done on cold days in the past, before the war. The familiar warmth of his body against her fingers, the confident swing of his hip, brought back comforting memories. She had missed Thomas, the first of the two brothers to go off to war, but Lachlan had always been a special favourite. When he was called up, only weeks after his seventeenth birthday, she had cried herself to sleep for several nights after he left.

Her fingers encountered a tiny glass bottle; she drew it out and gave a gasp of delight.

'It's toilet water! Oh, Lachlan—!'

He flushed. 'Well, ye're growin' up now, aren't ye? I thought that'd please ye more than sweeties.'

Molly pushed in between them, so close that she tramped on Elspeth's heel. 'It's bonny,' she agreed, her voice hushed with awe as she peered at the pretty little bottle with a delicate spray of lavender pictured on the label. She reached out an avaricious hand, but Elspeth pulled her own hand back and opened the bottle to allow the light fragrance of lavender to tickle at her nose. She flipped the bottle deftly over then upright again, then dabbed her wet fingertip below each ear.

'Can you smell it, Lachlan?'

He sniffed, his nose cold against her earlobe. 'Aye, but I'd as soon smell dumplin'. Come on, I'm hungry!'

Ignoring the silent plea in Molly's eyes, Elspeth refastened the bottle and put it into her pocket. Tomorrow after school she would let Molly have a dab of lavender, but not today. This was her birthday, her special day, and she wanted to keep its joys to herself for a little while, at least.

The three of them reached the top of the slight hill leading up from the school, and Elspeth stopped, as she usually did, to drink in the view. So did Lachlan; she had known he would, in spite of his claim to be hungry. Like her, he loved any view of the River Clyde.

The rest of Mearns Street ran down the hill that Greenock was built on. From where they stood, the tenements on either side, dropping away below them, framed the width of the River Clyde and the soft green hills on the far side. At the bottom of the street could be seen a clutter of cranes in one of the shipyards fringing the river all along the Greenock shore.

Today, both the September sky and the river below it were grey, but that didn't bother Elspeth, nor, she knew, would it concern Lachlan. The Clyde fascinated them both in all its moods, at all times of the year.

'It's grand tae taste this air again, and see the hills,' Lachlan said after a moment. 'They don't have a lot of hills in England.'

He drew in a deep lungful of air and Molly, standing demurely on his other side, did the same. 'Wee bizzum!' Elspeth thought resentfully, for normally Molly fussed and fretted impatiently when Elspeth stopped at this point every day. Peering round Lachlan, she glared at her friend, who smiled sweetly back at her.

She got her revenge a few short minutes later, when they reached the corner of Roxburgh Street. 'See you tomorrow then, Molly.'

'Eh?'

'This is where you turn off for your own house,' Elspeth said slowly and clearly, as though talking to a small child, taking

5

Molly's books from Lachlan and handing them back to their owner. 'Unless you've moved and not thought to tell me?'

Embarrassment spread the blotches over poor Molly's face until they joined together to create a full blush. 'Oh. I didn't realise we were here already.'

'I'll see you tomorrow morning, then.'

As the two of them crossed Roxburgh Street, leaving the other girl behind, Elspeth took Lachlan's arm again, hugging it tightly against her side. He wasn't going to be home for long and she wanted to make the most of this short, precious moment together. In the evening the neighbours would crowd into the small flat to greet the returned warrior and hear about his experiences, which meant that there would be little enough private time to spare.

Lachlan's mother, she knew, would feel the same way. Flora McDonald, fair though she was in most things, had always favoured her sons more than her daughters.

'What's the army like, Lachlan?'

'Ach, it's OK.'

'Have you done any fighting yet?'

'We've just been trainin' so far,' he said vaguely. 'How's school?'

'It's OK,' she mimicked, and he gave her a friendly punch on the shoulder.

'Don't you be so cheeky tae one of His Majesty's brave soldiers! Just a year to go, eh?'

Elspeth hesitated, then decided to let him be the first to hear her news. 'Miss Scott said this morning that she thinks I should stay on for another year.'

'Oh? So we've got a clever-clogs in the family, have we?'

'It's not just me – Mattie's done well too, in spite of having to be off so much.' Mattie, Lachlan's sister, was in the class above Elspeth's. She suffered from asthma and was at home that day, recovering from an attack. Mattie should have left school the previous June, but her parents had agreed to let her

6

stay on for an extra year, to make up for the time she had missed.

'Right enough, ye write a grand letter. Half the lads in the unit look forward tae your letters arrivin'.'

'You don't show them to anyone else, do you?' Elspeth asked, alarmed.

'Why not? Reading them makes me feel as if I'm back home again, and they're funny, too. The other lads enjoy them. But ye'd not want tae stay on at the school, would ye?' asked Lachlan, who had been desperate to leave school as soon as possible and join his father in one of the shipyards.

'I think I would. I like school, and Miss Scott says I could get a better job if I stayed on longer. She says that mebbe I could learn to be a teacher myself.'

'God, imagine havin' a teacher in the family! Have ye told Mam?' It would never occur to Lachlan to mention his father first. Henry McDonald was an easy-going man, happy to leave the family decisions and the family budget in his wife's capable hands.

'I've not told anyone yet, except you. D'you think Auntie would agree?'

Although Flora McDonald and her husband were the only parents Elspeth had ever known, Flora had always insisted on her calling them Auntie and Uncle.

'I don't know, Ellie. Mebbe she will. The war'll be well over by then, surely, and that means that Thomas and me'll be back home, so that'd help with the money. Mind you, I've still got my apprenticeship tae finish.'

'I thought that with Rachel earning a wage now, and Mattie out of school by then—'

Elspeth's voice trailed away. Flora and Henry McDonald had been good to her as it was, taking her in when her mother, Flora's dearest friend, died giving birth to her. But they had their own family to worry about, and they might not be prepared to support her for longer than they had to.

They were at the spot where Regent Street cut across Mearns Street now, the corner where their tenement building stood. 'I've got something else for you,' Lachlan said as they stepped into the spotless close with its tiled walls and scrubbed stone floor, edged all the way from the pavement to the top landing with white pipeclay. 'I came across it on the train and thought ye'd like it.'

'Something you found? A kitten?' Elspeth asked doubtfully, following him up the first flight of stairs. Flora refused to allow any pets in her house, not so much as a canary, on the grounds that it might aggravate Mattie's asthma. A kitten would only cause trouble.

'Wait and see.'

The tenement consisted of a ground floor with three floors above. There were six sets of stairs to climb before the flat was reached, and three half-landings where the stairs took a bend. Each half-landing was lit by a window set with a mosaic of coloured glass. Elspeth loved these windows, for on sunny days the colours spilled over the stone stairs in a fallen rainbow.

The kitchen, which also served the family as living room and dining room, was cosy and welcoming as usual, warmed by a small coal fire as well as the heat from the gas stove. Today, the whole flat was rich with the smell of the dumpling Flora always made to celebrate a family birthday. Rachel, her oldest, was setting the table, assisted by Mattie, still pale and drawn from her bout of asthma. Rachel worked as a laundrywoman and seamstress in a large estate a little further along the coast, and as luck would have it, she had that afternoon off.

Flora McDonald was in her usual place by the stove, but it was the young man busy at the sink by the window, dressed only in a pair of khaki trousers, who caught Elspeth's eye as soon as she stepped into the room.

'Thomas!' She threw herself at him, regardless of the water spraying from his face and hands as he swung round from the sink.

'Steady on, Ellie,' he spluttered, at the same time returning her hug enthusiastically, while Flora, her face flushed with heat, her hair detaching itself strand by strand from the loose bun at the back of her head, snatched up a towel and began dabbing at the two of them.

'For goodness' sake, lassie, ye'll soak the place with yer carrying on!'

'Lachlan, why didn't you tell me?'

'I wanted tae surprise ye. She thought I'd brought her a kitten, Tom.'

'It's as well ye didnae, for it'd have gone straight out again,' his mother told him. 'Take this towel, Thomas, and let me get back tae my stove.'

'Mebbe ye'd've preferred a kitten, Ellie.' Thomas towelled himself vigorously.

'I'd rather have you two home any day of the week!'

'That reminds me—' He hung the towel up by the sink and fumbled at the khaki tunic hanging over the back of a chair, finally withdrawing a small cardboard box, slightly squashed. 'Happy birthday, Ellie.'

Inside the box, pinned to a small square of card, was an oval brooch made of polished pebbles. The centre and largest stone was dark and glossy, while those set around it were red and green, pale blue and the soft pearly grey of the sky and the River Clyde on a still, mild autumn day.

'As soon as I saw it, I was minded of the times we've collected pebbles along the beach,' Thomas explained as Elspeth stared in silence at the brooch. Then diffidently, 'D'ye like it?'

She found her voice, though it was only a whisper at first. 'Oh, Thomas, it's beautiful!'

'It is that,' Rachel agreed as she and Mattie came to look. Then she sniffed at the air. 'What's that smell? It's like – flowers.'

'Don't be daft,' Lachlan said swiftly as Elspeth, suddenly remembering the toilet water, cast a guilty look at Flora, who didn't approve of lip colours, perfume, powder or scented soap. 'How could ye have flowers at the top of a tenement?'

He glared at his sister, who grasped the message in his brown eyes and sniffed again, loudly. 'It's gone now – my nose must've gone funny for a minute.'

'Pin it on for me, Thomas.'

He did as he was bid, his fingers damp and cool against Elspeth's chin. 'There. It looks nice.'

She reached a hand up to caress the little brooch. It was the first piece of jewellery she had ever owned. And Lachlan's gift was the first scent she had ever had, apart from the illicit bottles of rose-water she and Mattie sometimes made from crushed rose petals in the washhouse during the summer.

Looking from Thomas to Lachlan, she loved the two of them with all her heart, for today, her thirteenth birthday, they had combined to remind her that from that day on, she was grown-up.

2

'So neither of ye knew that the other was comin' home on leave?' Henry McDonald pushed his empty plate away an hour later and leaned back in his chair, stretching strong, sinewy arms above his head. After a thorough wash in the sink to remove the grime of the shipyard, he smelled of carbolic soap, and his greying curly hair, still damp, stood up in a spiky halo round his broad moustached face. His two sons and two daughters had all inherited his curls instead of their mother's straight hair.

'Not a bit of it. The first I knew was when Lachlan here got out of the next carriage when we reached Glasgow.'

'Does a twenty-four-hour leave not mean they're going to send you abroad?' Rachel wondered aloud. Her brothers exchanged brief looks, and for a moment a chill seemed to threaten the room's warmth before Lachlan said casually, 'Mebbe it does, and mebbe it doesnae. They never tell us much about their plans.'

'That's what happened when they let Bob Cochran home for twenty-four hours,' Rachel persisted.

'How's Bob doin' these days?' Thomas wanted to know.

'Fine, the last letter I got.'

'It must be serious if ye're writin' tae each other,' Lachlan said.

'She sleeps with his letters under her pillow,' Elspeth said.

11

Unlike the house servants on the estate, Rachel didn't live in. The three girls shared one tiny bedroom, Rachel with a cot of her own, the two younger girls squeezed into a bed little larger than a single, but not as broad as a double bed.

'Does she now?'

Rachel's pretty round face went pink. 'I do not! Don't listen to her, Thomas, Ellie's just a wee liar,' she flared, but Mattie came to Elspeth's rescue.

'You do so. And you keep his photograph under the mattress'

'Here, here – no fightin' when we're all together at last,' Flora ordered. 'Clear the plates, Elspeth.' She waited until fresh plates, spoons and a large jug of custard were on the table before carefully bringing the rich, round, steaming birthday dumpling to the table. Amid a murmur of anticipation, she picked up a long sharp knife and cut into it, releasing a further gout of steam and the mouth-watering aroma of currants and raisins and treacle.

A second cut parted the first generous soft slice from the dumpling, and as it was skilfully flipped on to a plate Elspeth's heart quickened as she noticed the gleam of white paper against the moist brown interior. It was the custom, on special occasions like birthdays and Christmas and Hogmanay, to wrap silver threepenny bits in paper and bake them in the dumpling.

Normally the first slice would have gone to Elspeth, since it was her special day, but instead Flora laid the plate before Thomas, her first-born and favourite.

He immediately handed it across the table. 'Here ye are, Ellie – it's your birthday after all.'

With the tip of a spoon she dug into the slice, withdrew the tiny bundle, and opened it, the paper hot against her finger tips, to disclose a shining silver threepenny piece.

'Lucky you,' Mattie said. 'Think of the sweeties you can buy with that.'

'Or a nice bit of ribbon,' Rachel suggested.

'Far better tae put it away – the time might well come when ye'll be glad of it,' Flora put in, but Elspeth shook her head to all the suggestions.

'Uncle Henry, could you drill a wee hole in it for me, so that I can hang it on a bit of wool round my neck?'

'If ye want, hen,' her uncle agreed amiably, ignoring his wife's scandalised tutting.

'Ye're never goin' tae spoil a good thrup'ny piece by turnin' it intae a necklace, lassie!'

'It won't be spoiled. I'm going to keep it always, to remind me of today, with all of us together again.'

'Ye'll forget all about that the minute ye go intae the corner shop and see those jars of raspberry balls and liquorice straps,' Thomas told her.

'I won't.' She looked round the table at the only family she knew, and contentment surged through her. At that moment, life was perfect, she thought – then happened to meet Flora's eye.

In the older woman's glance she saw, not for the first time, a distant expression that made her feel that she was being singled out, set aside from the others round the table. Elspeth had seen that look several times during the past thirteen years; when she was a small child, it had set her off into inexplicable bouts of frightened tears which Flora, all at once her usual motherly self again, had soothed away. Now there were never tears, just a numbing, bewildering sense of being different, a chill reminder that she didn't really belong to the only family she had ever known.

'The army cooks can't cook as well as you do, Mum,' Thomas said just then, and Lachlan, his mouth full of warm, spicy dumpling, mumbled enthusiastic agreement.

Flora smiled, and the moment of uncertainty was gone as though it had never existed.

Elspeth could think of no reason for her aunt's flashes of hidden resentment. But she knew, from experience, that they would come again; always, like today, when she least expected them.

'It's not fair!'

'It's perfectly fair – and don't use that tone of voice tae me, lady,' Flora snapped, hanging Mattie's school blouse on the clothes horse to air and lifting the next garment from the pile waiting to be ironed. 'Ye've already had an extra year at the school tae set ye up for the future.'

'Mattie's had two extra years!'

'Mattie's already missed out on a lot because of her bad chest, and she's just as clever as you. Ye're not the only one with brains in this house, remember that. When she came this afternoon tae speak tae me about it all, Miss Scott could dae no more than agree with me. We cannae afford tae keep two of ye – d'ye not think Mattie deserves her chance just as much as you dae?'

'Y-yes, but—'

'There ye are, then.' Flora thumped the iron down on its end. 'We can just about manage with one of ye stayin' on, but not both. Anyway, fluff an' dust bothers Mattie's lungs, and it'd be more difficult tae find work for her than for you. So – it's only right that she's the one who gets tae stay on at the school.'

Tears crowded behind Elspeth's eyes, and she had to blink hard to hold them back. She had dreamed of becoming a teacher, had let herself believe during that extra year of schooling that it was going to happen. The sudden shock of hearing that her dream had crumbled to dust was more than she could bear. She made one last appeal. 'Uncle Henry—?'

'Now don't go encouragin' the lassie, Henry,' Flora warned at once. 'Ye know as well as I dae that one of them'll have tae go out tae work.'

Henry McDonald shifted uncomfortably in his chair, lowering the newspaper he had been holding before his face. 'I'm sorry, lass, yer auntie's right. We cannae afford tae keep the

14

two of ye on at the school, with the lads both still away.'

'I know,' Elspeth said wretchedly, 'I know.'

'My heart's broken for the lassie,' Henry said when she had gone out of the room. 'Did ye see the way the light just went out of her eyes there?'

His wife smoothed the iron over his work shirt. 'She's too quick at wantin' her own way, that one. And she's old enough tae know that we all have tae deal with disappointment from time tae time.'

'I know, but—' He bit the words off, but it was too late. The iron was banged down so hard that the sturdy table shook, and Flora whirled to confront him, hands fisted on her hips.

'But what, Henry McDonald?'

He rattled the newspaper noisily, trying to find the right words. 'Sometimes I feel you're a wee bit too hard on that lassie, Flora.'

'Too hard on her? You're sayin' that tae me, who took her in when her own grandmother would have nothin' tae do with her? Me that raised her when I'd more than enough tae do carin' for my own bairns? Don't haver, man,' Flora said witheringly. 'I'm hard on them all – I have tae be. We've not got the money tae spoil any one of them, as ye well know.'

'Aye, but – it's just that sometimes I feel ye're harder on Ellie than the others, and I cannae think why, when I mind how you and her mother were closer than sisters—' His voice died away as he looked up and saw the rage in his wife's eyes and the colour rising in her face.

'Sometimes ye've got a nasty tongue on you, Henry, and a nasty mind, accusin' yer own wife like that!'

'I didnae mean anything by it,' he protested. Henry McDonald was a strong man, afraid of nothing. All the men who worked with him in Lithgow's shipyard respected him and thought highly of him. They would have been amazed if they had seen the way he seemed to shrink into his chair before his wife's anger. 'I just thought—'

15

'Aye, well, thinking's no' bringin' more silver intae the house, is it? If I was as soft as you are, we'd all of us be in the poors' hospital by now,' Flora said scathingly, and returned to her work, attacking the shirt with the heavy, hot iron as though Henry was inside it.

Prudently, he went back to his paper. Flora was a good wife, but he knew from experience that he'd do best to hold his tongue, rather than bring even more scalding anger down on his head.

In the privacy of the small bedroom, Elspeth sat on the edge of the bed she shared with Mattie and revelled in the luxury of a good cry for a full five minutes. Her shoulders shuddered as she gasped and sniffled and wept for the future she had wanted so much, and had lost for ever. She would have enjoyed a good loud, babyish bawl, but instead she wept quietly, determined not to let her aunt and uncle hear her grief. Fat tears poured down her face and dripped off her chin, some trickling between her lips to lie salty on her tongue.

Lachlan's comment on her thirteenth birthday kept coming back to her: 'The war'll be well over by then, surely, and that means that Thomas and me'll be back home, so that'd help with the money.'

But almost a year later the war was still going on, and Lachlan and Thomas, both over in France now, hadn't been home since her birthday. Although their mother never spoke to anyone, not even Henry, of any fears she may have harboured for them, more silver glittered through her fair hair than ever before, and her mouth had tightened.

At last the tears began to ease off and Elspeth's wet face started itching unpleasantly. She scrubbed her hands over it, smearing tears over her cheeks, then got up and washed them away, dipping a face cloth into the chipped bowl of cold water that stood on the tallboy, then drying her face on the well-worn towel drooping from a nail in the wall.

She was just in time; as she put the towel down the door to the flat opened and Mattie, who had been packed off on an errand, passed the bedroom door on her way to the kitchen.

Elspeth peered into the foggy mirror that stood on a rickety table at the window, and saw that her eyes were pink-edged. Dropping to her knees by Rachel's bed, she pulled out the cardboard box that held the older girl's good shoes, lifting them out then scooping up the sheet of cardboard below. This was where Rachel kept her secret hoard of powder, lipstick and perfume, bought out of the few pennies the girl was allocated from her weekly pay packet, and well hidden from her mother.

Elspeth opened the little box of powder with fingers that shook in their haste, and dabbed the puff round her eyes. She put it back exactly where she found it, then replaced the cardboard and the shoes before pushing the box well out of sight beneath the bed.

Referring to the mirror again, she saw to her horror that now clumps of powder stuck to her lashes, which were still damp, and that the skin round her eyes was thick with the stuff. Hurriedly, she smoothed the surplus powder away with the tips of her fingers, then used her handkerchief to wipe up the grains that had fallen on the table. Mattie came in just as she finished.

'What're you doing?'

'Nothing. Just thinking.'

Mattie's nose wrinkled. 'What's that smell?'

'What smell? '

'It's—' Mattie sniffed again. 'You've not been at Rachel's perfume, have you?'

'Of course not!'

'You know what she's like if she thinks we've touched her stuff.'

'I told you – I've not touched it!'

Mattie hesitated, then sat down on the bed she and Elspeth

17

shared, linking her fingers tightly on her lap. 'Mam says that Miss Scott came to visit her today.'

'I know. She told me.'

'Imagine, a teacher coming to the house to talk about you and me, and in the holidays too.' There was awe in Mattie's voice, and Elspeth fully understood why. Teachers belonged in school, not in houses; it had never occurred to either of them that teachers had any other kind of existence. For all the two girls knew, Miss Scott might well be hung up in the classroom cupboard out of school hours, waiting patiently with the boxes of chalk and shelves of books for the next school day to begin.

'Did Mam tell you what's been decided?'

'Yes.' They were both silent, then Elspeth went on, her voice sharp with accusation, 'I didn't know you wanted to be a teacher.'

'I didn't, till Mam said that Miss Scott said that I was clever enough. With me being off school so much, I never thought—' Mattie's voice trailed away, and her fingers writhed in her lap, getting into such a tangle that Elspeth began to wonder if the girl's hands could ever be separated again. 'Ellie, it's not fair that you have to be the one to leave.'

'Yes it is.' Hard though it was to say the words, Elspeth recognised that Aunt Flora had right on her side. Mattie was just as clever as she was, and the girl had been off so often during the past ten years that if the days at home were added up she must have missed at least a year's education. And Mattie was Aunt Flora's own daughter, while Elspeth wasn't.

'I feel terrible about it, Elspeth.'

'Aunt Flora's right, they can't pay for us both. I'll enjoy going out to work,' she lied. 'I'll try for a job in an office. Mebbe I'll learn how to typewrite, and do book-keeping.'

The thought of it cheered her up a little. She had always thought that working in an office would be interesting. She might even turn out to be good at it.

Mattie smiled at her gratefully. 'I'll tell you all about

everything I learn. I'll show you all the books I have to read, so that you'll know all about how to teach.'

'And I'll tell you all about my office work.' For a moment, Elspeth felt better about everything. Peering into the mirror again, she was relieved to see that the puffiness had begun to fade from around her clear blue eyes.

Then, as her aunt called the two of them through to help her with the evening meal, realisation hit her. The summer holidays would be over in another five days, and two weeks after that she would be fourteen, a birthday that marked the end of her schooldays.

Panic swept over her, and as she followed Mattie into the kitchen she felt as though she was falling, and there was nothing to hold on to.

Flora McDonald, a trained seamstress, had dressed her family almost entirely by her own efforts, using a large heavy sewing machine that was her pride and joy. She had even made most of the clothes her husband and sons wore, and had taught the three girls to sew as soon as they were old enough to be trusted with needle and scissors.

The skills Rachel had learned from her mother had led to a position with one of the wealthy families living on the hill above the town, and Elspeth, too, had shown talent. In her constant eagerness to please her aunt and justify the day Flora had taken her in, she had worked hard and learned well, and by the time she was in her teens she was making most of her own clothes. To her dismay, her own diligence turned out to be her undoing, for as the school summer holidays drew to a close, Flora announced that she had arranged an interview for Elspeth with the sewing-room supervisor at Brodie's, the town's largest department store.

Her plea to be allowed to seek work in an office had been turned down flat.

'Office work indeed! What next? Yer poor mother and me

were seamstresses, and that's what you'll be too. Brodie's is the best store in the town – ye're very lucky, gettin' an interview there. When ye've got a man and bairns of yer own tae clothe ye'll be glad of the trainin' Brodie's'll give ye,' Flora said, and would hear no more about offices.

Elspeth, who had never been inside Brodie's in her life, gazed around, fascinated, as she followed her aunt through the entrance and found herself in a world she had never known existed. Despite the hardships of the war, the counters scattered throughout the ground-floor area seemed to her to be well stocked with rolls of ribbon and lace, buttons, hooks and eyes, and banked rainbows of sewing thread in little display boxes.

'Don't dawdle, Elspeth.' Flora tossed the words over her shoulder as she hurried towards the stairs. 'We're expected, and I'll not have them thinkin' ye're a poor timekeeper.'

Up a flight of stairs they sped, to another open area, this time set out with men's and children's clothing. The third floor held women's clothes; Elspeth caught a glimpse of gloves on one counter, petticoats on another, as Flora stopped to ask directions, then the two of them went through a door and into a narrow dark corridor, quite unlike the spacious areas they had just left.

'First door on the right,' Flora muttered, fidgeting along the corridor and pausing before a door that almost vibrated with a humming sound from the other side of the panels. It sounded to Elspeth as though a lot of sewing machines were being operated within the room.

'This'll be it,' Flora muttered, tapping tentatively with her knuckles. They waited for several long minutes, but there was no answer.

'They'll not hear you for the noise,' Elspeth ventured. 'You'll just have to go in.'

'Ye don't just walk intae strange rooms – ye wait tae be told!' Flora snapped, and they waited in vain for another few minutes before, clearly remembering the passing of time, she gave an anguished little whimper and steeled herself to open the door and reveal a large, stuffy room. An enormous table holding an impressive number of sewing machines, all in use, took up most of the space. A few of the machinists flicked a brief glance at the newcomers, then returned to their work. One of them, a pretty, red-haired girl, smiled and winked at Elspeth. A tall, cold-eyed woman examining the output of one of the machines finally noticed them, and straightened up.

'Yes?'

'We've got an appointment with Miss Buchanan – about a job.' Flora, unusually nervous, stumbled over the words.

The woman surveyed them both for a moment as though amazed that two such ordinary people should dare to approach her, then said shortly, 'This way.'

They followed her in single file along the edge of the room to a doorway that led into a tiny office, with only enough room for a cluttered desk and two chairs. 'Miss Buchanan is with a client at the moment,' the woman told them. 'I'll inform her of your arrival when she's free. What name shall I say?'

'Flora Mc— I mean, Elspeth Bremner,' Flora almost whispered. Elspeth had never known her aunt to be so cowed; the woman's nervousness started to affect her, and her knees began to shake. As soon as they were alone Flora pounced on her, brushing imaginary fluff from her best woollen coat, setting her beret straight, whirling her round to tweak at the thick dark brown plait hanging down her back.

'Stand straight, for any favour! Speak out when Miss Buchanan asks ye anythin', but don't talk unless ye're invited tae. And don't fidget!'

The inspection over, Flora sat herself down on the small plain chair at their side of the desk, drumming her fingers on her knee, while Elspeth pulled her shoulders back and stared at a crack on the wall behind the desk, wishing that she hadn't turned out to be so good with a needle.

The drumming of the sewing machines on the other side of the wall reminded her of the little she had been able to glimpse of the sewing room as she and Flora were whisked through it. The only windows she had noticed were small, and ran along the upper wall area on one side of the room, so that the girls working at the machines couldn't see out. Her heart sank, and she wanted to run from the room and from the building. Only the thought of what Aunt Flora would say and do to her kept her in her seat.

They waited in silence for a further ten minutes, both jumping when the door finally opened and Miss Buchanan arrived, small and elderly, slightly stooped and with a permanent frown tucked between eyes magnified by her spectacles.

'Mrs – er—' She fluttered a hand towards Flora in greeting, then withdrew it and edged in behind her desk, leaving Flora with her own hand outstretched. 'And – um,' she added, settling herself into her chair.

'It's about the interview,' Flora said too loudly, her cheeks pink with embarrassment as she sank back into her own seat and folded her hands together. 'You said you'd see Ellie – Elspeth – about a post.' She was speaking, Elspeth thought, surprised, as though her mouth was full of wee pebbles that slowed and restricted her speech.

'Oh yes, I did agree to consider her for employment in our workshop.' Miss Buchanan's small hands sifted through a pile of papers on the desk before emerging with a sheet of notepaper bearing Flora's careful handwriting. 'What age is she?'

'Almost fourteen,' Flora offered as Elspeth opened her mouth to reply. 'Fourteen in September. She'll be leaving school then.'

'And you want to be a seamstress?' Miss Buchanan's artificially large eyes studied Elspeth, who opened her mouth to reply, and was forestalled.

'She's very good with her needle. I taught her myself. Her mother and me were both seamstresses in Glasgow,' Flora

22

PEBBLES ON THE BEACH

contributed, rummaging in the depths of her worn shopping bag and bringing out a piece of snowy linen, carefully folded. She opened it to reveal two pieces of embroidery. 'These are the lassie's own work.'

Miss Buchanan opened a drawer and took out a pair of thin gloves. Slipping them on she studied the material, holding it close to her eyes to examine the fine stitching. Laying it down again, she took off her spectacles, which dangled from her neck by a ribbon. Immediately, her eyes became small and insignificant. She studied the work again, this time holding it almost at arm's-length, then, sounding surprised, she commented, 'This is quite good.'

'Oh yes.' Flora's nervousness had vanished for the moment; her voice was clear and firm and smug, for all the world, Elspeth thought, resentful at not being allowed to say a word on her own behalf, as though she had done the work herself.

'As you probably know, we now have a large ready-to-wear department, and most of our seamstresses' work involves making alterations in our ready-to-wear stock for our customers,' Miss Buchanan told Flora, as though Elspeth was invisible. 'We do a certain amount of dressmaking for our special clients, but that work, of course, is only undertaken by our most talented seamstresses. Few girls attain that standard.'

'I'm sure Elspeth'd be able to reach it, in time,' Flora snapped back, and Miss Buchanan's brows rose.

'As to that, Mrs – only time will tell.' For the first time, she looked at Elspeth studying her carefully. 'Would you like to work here?'

'I'd prefer to work in an—'

'She would.' Flora said swiftly.

'I believe that she might fit in here quite well. We'll give her a three-month trial, Mrs – er—'

Ten minutes later it had been arranged between the two women that Elspeth should start work the week after her birthday. 'What d'ye think ye were doin'?' Flora hissed in her

23

normal, unpebbled voice as soon as they were back among the shoppers again. 'For a minute there I thought the woman was goin' tae say ye were too cheeky for the job.'

'I only wanted to ask if there was any work in the offices.'

'There isn't. It's not everyone that gets tae work at Brodie's, for they're very particular. Ye're lucky ye've been accepted as a seamstress, so let's have no more nonsense about offices. Yer mother'd be pleased,' she added as an afterthought as they descended the stairs.

'I might as well not have bothered going to the interview myself,' Elspeth wrote to Thomas that evening. 'It was a bit like being sold at a cattle market. Maybe I should be grateful that Miss Buchanan didn't insist on opening my mouth and having a look at my teeth, the way they do with horses.'

3

Elspeth's final day at school was one of the worst she had ever known. Usually, the 'leavers' lolled about on their last day, doing nothing, eyed enviously by those still bound to the classroom. But Elspeth worked hard, savouring every moment.

'This is the last time I'll walk into school – the last time I'll hang my coat up on this peg – the last time I'll sit in this seat—' The litany kept ringing through her mind, each 'last' clanging like a bell summoning mourners to a funeral.

When the real bell rang to mark the end of the day, she lingered at her desk, making a business of emptying it, until there were no more corners left to study in search of an errant eraser or a missing pencil.

'Come on,' Mattie said impatiently from the doorway.

'I'm coming.' Elspeth closed the desk – 'this is the last time I'll close this desk' – and followed her cousin from the room, her hands hanging uselessly by her sides. There were no books to carry, for they had all been handed in for some other pupil to take home and study in future.

Miss Scott stopped her in the hallway. 'Good luck, my dear. I'm sorry you weren't able to stay on any longer.'

'Yes, Miss Scott, thank you, Miss Scott,' Elspeth mumbled to the teacher's sturdy shoes, unable to meet the sympathy that she knew would be in the woman's eyes.

'Come back and see us. We'd like to know how you're getting on,' Miss Scott said, then, mercifully, she let them go, and for the last time, Elspeth walked out of the school door, down the steps, across the playground. Molly, a few months older, had left joyfully at the beginning of the summer holidays, and was working in a bakery in West Blackhall Street.

'I wish it could have been you staying on instead of me,' Mattie said by her side.

'No you don't, you want to stay as much as I do.'

'You're right. I suppose I meant that I wish we could both have stayed.'

'No, Aunt Flora's right – you've not been at school as often as me because of your chest.'

'That doesn't help to make me feel any better about it.'

'Nor me,' Elspeth thought as she walked out of the school gates for the last time.

Working in the sewing room at Brodie's wasn't as bad as Elspeth had feared. For one thing, she was allowed to pin up the long brown plait that had been a temptation all through her schooldays to boys who pulled it in the classroom and sometimes in the street. She hinted at getting it cut, but Flora wouldn't hear of it.

'Ye've got lovely hair, just like yer mother's, rest her soul. It'd be sacrilege tae cut it off. One day ye'll thank me for no' lettin' ye dae it!'

There was also the pleasure of taking a wage packet home every Friday. True, it had to be handed over to Flora unopened, just like Uncle Henry's and Rachel's wages, but at least she was earning her keep, instead of being an added burden. The fourpence handed back for her own use each week was a fortune compared with the twopence spending money she had received before.

The small, high windows in the workroom couldn't provide enough ventilation for the number of women and girls there, so the place was airless, and noisy with the continual whirring of the machines, but once the strangeness of everything and

26

her shyness among people she didn't know wore off, Elspeth found that she was good at the work, and took pleasure in getting the occasional word of grudging praise from Miss Arnold, well known for her high standards and sharp tongue.

'If they'd left the men at home and just sent her tae fight the Jerries instead,' muttered Lena Stewart, who worked on the machine opposite Elspeth's, 'she'd've cut the legs from the lot of them with one sentence and saved us a lot of bother.'

Elspeth was surprised into a giggle, quickly disguised as a cough as Miss Arnold's cold eyes swept in her direction. Nobody was allowed to talk during working hours, but she discovered on her first day that there was always a certain amount of conversation going on, sometimes in whispers and murmurs hidden by the continual sound of the machines, sometimes by means of signals, or silent mouthing and lip-reading.

'Everyone needs tae talk,' said Lena, the redhead who had winked at her on the day of her interview. 'It's not natural tae expect women tae keep their mouths shut for hours.'

She was very pretty, with the type of looks that would have caused Flora MacDonald to tut disapprovingly. Her curly red hair continually escaped from the ribbons that were supposed to hold it back from her face, and she was well rounded, her creamy skin dusted with freckles. Her brown eyes sparkled, and even without artificial colouring her mouth was full and red.

Lena, Elspeth had quickly discovered, was a rebel, dressing in bright clothes despite Miss Buchanan's insistence on muted colours for her staff, and talking when she was expected to be quiet. She only kept her job because she was an excellent seamstress.

'Are ye stayin' in for yer dinner?' she asked when Elspeth's first morning's work ended and she was following the other girls out of the room – not through the door leading from the store, but through another, smaller door at the back of the room which led to narrow wooden stairs.

'I'm going home. I only live in Mearns Street.'

'Ye should bring a piece and eat with the rest of us.' As they reached the bottom of the stairs, Lena gestured towards an open door in front of them. Peeping in, Elspeth saw a large room with benches set at long tables. Men and women were settling down at the tables, unwrapping packets of sandwiches.

'The nobs have a place of their own upstairs,' Lena explained. 'Counter staff and floorwalkers and the like. This is for folk like us and the packers and carters. There's hot water and milk and mugs, and ye bring yer own tea and sugar in wee screws of paper.'

Elspeth, hurrying home through a drizzle of rain, liked the idea of sharing her midday break with Lena and the other girls, but when she suggested it to Flora, her aunt was horrified.

'Eating down in the basement with the carters and all? Ye don't know what ye might catch! Ye're better off with a good hot dinner here.'

'But I don't have much time – it would surely be better for me to eat something at the store instead of running home and running back and mebbe being late.'

Flora put a bowl of soup before her. 'I ate my dinner with Mattie. I can see tae it that ye're not late back.'

'That's another thing – I get out later than Mattie, and that means you've got two dinners to see to. If I stayed at work there'd only be hers.' A fresh shower, hurling itself against the window, gave Elspeth further ammunition. 'And winter's coming in, Auntie Flora. I might catch cold running to Mearns Street then back, and if I did I'd have to stay home, for Miss Buchanan and Miss Arnold would never let me cough and sneeze over the customers' clothes.'

'Aye, well, there is that,' Flora said slowly. 'But I hope I'd not be expected tae make up pieces for yer dinner – I've got enough tae see tae in the mornings as it is.'

'I'll do my own. I'll get up earlier.'

To her joy, Flora gave in, and Elspeth spent her midday

breaks in the canteen, drinking scalding-hot tea out of a tin mug that would have sent her aunt running for the disinfectant if she had known of it, and eating her sandwiches at a wooden table. At last, she began to feel like one of the crowd.

It was during those midday breaks that she discovered that Lena was a singer. Every time a music-hall company came to Greenock Lena was in the audience, treating her fellow workers the following dinner-time to an impromptu concert of every song in the programme. She had a good memory, and only needed to hear a song once to recall tune and lyrics.

Her voice was lovely, strong and confident when the song required it, or so sweet and pure that even the gruff carters could be seen to buff a tear away with the back of a hand when she sang a ballad or lullaby.

'It's what I like doin' best,' she confided to Elspeth. 'I sing in our local pub on a Saturday night, and at gatherin's.' Then, her eyes glowing, 'One day I'm goin' tae sing on a proper stage, like the Hippodrome or the King's Theatre. D'ye go there?'

Her eyes widened when Elspeth admitted that she had never been inside a theatre. 'But they're so bonny, with crimson velvet curtains tied back with gold ropes, and pillars right up tae the ceilings, and folk on the stage with beautiful clothes. There's lovely scenery on the stage too – come tae the Hippodrome with me on Saturday night.'

'I can't. My Aunt Flora doesn't like theatres.'

'I'm no askin' yer Aunt Flora,' Lena pointed out. 'I'm askin' you.'

'But I'd have to ask her, and she'd say no.'

'Don't tell her, then. Say ye're goin' out with a friend – it wouldnae be a lie.'

'She'd find out anyway,' Elspeth said, but finally agreed, after much coaxing, to ask her aunt's permission.

Flora's reaction was just as she had predicted. 'The theatre? Indeed you'll go tae no such place, milady.'

29

'But it's with one of the girls at the store.'

'I don't know what her mother's thinking of, lettin' her watch folk cavorting about on a stage.'

'Her mother's dead. She lives with her father.'

'There ye are, then – there's no woman in the house tae guide her. No wonder the poor lassie's goin' wrong. That'll no' happen tae you – ye're just out of the school and still a bairn.'

The unfairness of it stung Elspeth. 'How can I still be a bairn when I'm old enough to earn my own keep?'

Her aunt's head snapped up, eyes blazing. 'I'll tell ye how – while ye behave like a bairn ye'll be treated like one. The very idea,' she clucked like an agitated hen, 'answerin' me back after all me and yer Uncle Henry've done for ye!'

'I didn't ask you to take me in!'

Flora's patience snapped. 'Ye cheeky besom, ye!' she railed. 'Times like this I think we should have left ye tae yer Grandma Bremner. She'd've packed ye off tae the orphanage, and I don't see *them* lettin' ye stay on at the school for another year!'

No matter how hard Elspeth worked at holding her tongue and keeping the peace, Flora managed time and time again to overturn her attempts to be a dutiful foster daughter. The argument raged on, ending, as sometimes happened, with Flora ordering her out of her sight, and Elspeth running off to Granjan's tiny kitchen, tears of frustrated anger running down her cheeks.

'I never mean to upset her, but I keep doing it!' she sobbed, and Janet Docherty, Flora's mother, hauled herself out of her chair and crossed the faded rag rug to pat her bowed head.

'Yer Auntie Flora's awful hard tae please at times. It's just her nature, she doesnae mean tae sound as hard as she does.'

'I know, but I don't make things any better when I answer back. Why can't I stop myself?' Tears dripped from Elspeth's chin and made damp circles on her woollen skirt. She was huddled into a chair with her knees drawn up to her chin and her arms wrapped around them.

'If it was that easy for folk tae hold their tongues, there wouldnae have been any wars,' Janet pointed out, then, as the sobbing eased to a sniffing, hiccuping stop, 'Feelin' better now? Here—' A clean dishtowel was thrust into Elspeth's hands. 'Dry yer face, pet, an' I'll put the griddle on. Pancakes and a cup of hot tea'll make the world look better.'

Janet Docherty never threw anything away if she could get some use out of it. Greaseproof papers that had wrapped squares of butter were neatly folded and stored in a drawer once the butter was finished; now she produced one and ran it over the large black iron griddle to grease it. A paper spill from a vase on the mantelshelf was lit at the fire and used to light a ring on her small gas cooker, then she lifted the griddle by its hooped handle on to the ring to heat.

'You're awful good to me, Granjan,' Elspeth said gratefully, scrubbing at her eyes with the dishcloth.

'Ye're a good, obedient lassie and we all need a bit of comfortin' now and again.' Janet took a bowl down from a shelf and collected flour and an egg and milk.

'If I was good I wouldn't anger Aunt Flora so much.'

'Ach, Flora gets het up too quickly. She always did, even as a wean,' said Flora's mother cheerfully, measuring flour into the basin. 'Wash yer face at the jawbox now, and fill the kettle for me.'

After obediently splashing her face with cold water at the tiny sink set below the window, Elspeth dried it before filling the kettle, while Janet whipped the contents of the mixing bowl into a creamy, pale golden liquid. Scooping a spoonful up, she dropped it on to the heated griddle, which started to sizzle. The soft dough spread to just the right size, then halted, bubbles forming on its surface, as Janet dotted the large griddle with more spoonfuls. Then she started flipping them over deftly with a fish slice, disclosing the golden-brown cooked side of each.

Nobody could make pancakes as swiftly or as well as

31

Granjan, Elspeth thought contentedly, setting the table and opening the window to fetch a pat of butter from the larder, a small wooden box with a mesh door to let air in, fastened to the windowsill to keep any meat and milk and butter stored inside it fresh and cool. Her stomach gave an unladylike rumble as she turned back into the room and smelled the delicious aroma of fresh-made pancakes.

Although her own children had been raised to call Janet Gran, Flora had tried hard to make little Elspeth address her mother as Auntie Janet. 'She's got a gran of her own, it would-nae be right tae let her call you gran too,' she had said when Janet protested.

'Ach, away wi' ye – there's nothin' wrong with her havin' two grans, like most bairns. Yours'd have two if Henry's mother was still livin', God rest her.'

'It's not right,' Flora had insisted stubbornly. Elspeth, only just over a year old and confused by this sign, the first she received, that she wasn't one of Flora's children, had found her own compromise and began calling Janet Granjan, to the old woman's secret delight. Flora, frustrated in the face of the child's determination, had given in and let the name remain.

Now, while they ate, Elspeth told Granjan about Lena. 'She's a good seamstress, but she's awful casual about her work.' She bit into a pancake, and Janet clucked, shaking her head.

'I hope she's not leadin' ye intae bad ways, lassie.'

'Oh no, I'm doing well. Miss Arnold set me to sewing some lace on a petticoat yesterday, and it's not everyone that's given work like that. She says I've got a deft touch. It's lovely material, Granjan – so soft and silky. Wearing it must be like wearing a sunbeam.' She stopped to wipe melted butter from her chin, then giggled. 'Imagine walking round all day wearing a sunbeam under your clothes.'

'Ye're awful like yer mother,' Janet said without thinking. 'She could jump from sorrow tae laughter in the blink of an eye too. Not that she was often sad, even when things were goin' against her. Maisie always saw the good side of life – and of folk.'

'Am I really like her?' Elspeth was greedy for all that she could glean about her mother.

'I've told ye often enough. Ye've got her hair, and her bonny face.'

'But not her eyes.'

'Did Flora say that?' Janet asked, taken by surprise.

'She's like Grandmother – neither of them ever tells me about my mother. I wouldn't know anything about her if it wasn't for you, but you never say I've got her eyes, Granjan.'

'Ye're gettin' altogether too sharp for yer own good, young lady. Watch out ye don't cut yerself.'

Elspeth nibbled at her pancake, then said, 'I've got his eyes, haven't I?'

'Whose?'

'My father's.'

Janet poured a second cup of strong tea for herself. 'I never saw him, so I cannae tell,' she said shortly, her discomfort so obvious that Elspeth, much as she longed to ask more questions, changed the subject.

'Thomas thinks I should take evening lessons in typewriting and shorthand.'

Janet set the teapot down with a thump and stared at her. 'What on earth for?'

'Because I want to work in an office, only Aunt Flora won't let me. Thomas said in his last letter that there's no reason why I shouldn't try to learn office skills, so that I could mebbe use them one day.'

'Don't you let him unsettle you, pet.' Janet Docherty's voice was uneasy. 'Ye're a seamstress, and that's an end of it.'

'He's not unsettling me, he's just saying that one day I might decide to do something else. He's learned to drive in the army, did you know that? He says he didn't realise how

33

interesting engines were. He might be thinking of a change himself one day.'

'Thomas is doin' very well as a gardener. And anyway, who's tae pay for those evening lessons he's got ye talkin' about? Not Master Thomas, I'll be bound.'

'I'd pay for them myself. I'm saving up already, for I like the idea,' Elspeth said eagerly. 'I'll mebbe learn book-keeping as well, if I can afford it.'

'Now don't go rushin' intae anythin',' Janet warned. 'Here – have another pancake.'

'I wish Grandmother was more like you,' Elspeth said, doing as she was bid.

'Tuts, lassie, it'd be a dull world if we were all alike.'

'But I should be closer to Grandmother than I am. After all, she's my real mother's mother. D'you think she'd really have sent me to the poors' hospital if Aunt Flora hadn't taken me in?'

Janet, about to sip her tea, spluttered into the cup and almost choked. Elspeth hurried out of her chair and round the table to pat her on the back. 'Sit down, sit down, I'm fine,' Janet gasped when the coughing fit was over. 'God save us, child, what gave ye an idea like that?'

'Aunt Flora says that's what Grandmother would have done. That's why I was crying so hard when I got here.' Elspeth, who had gone back to her pancake, put it down again, her appetite fading as she remembered the anger in her aunt's face, the pain of the words she had hurled.

'What a thing tae say tae a bairn!'

'I'm not a bairn any more, Granjan, I'm a working woman, old enough to know the truth.'

'And how can Flora have any notion of what Celia Bremner would've done?'

'She didn't take me in when my mother died. Surely that shows that she didn't want me,' Elspeth said round a lump in her throat that wasn't for her, but for the helpless baby she had once been.

'Only because Flora wouldnae hear of anyone but herself takin' ye in. Wasn't she yer poor ma's best friend? Does that not show ye how much she wanted ye?'

'Yes, but – Grandmother doesn't have any photographs of my mother in her house, nor anything that belonged to her. I don't think she'd have taken me if Aunt Flora hadn't wanted me.'

'Now ye're just haverin',' Janet said sharply. 'And we'll have no more of it. Eat up that pancake, and stop fiddling with it. It's time ye were getting back home.'

4

A large red hand suddenly imposed itself between Elspeth's eyes and the table, whipping her exercise book away before she could do more than give a squeak of surprise at the interruption. She had been so involved in writing the letter that she hadn't noticed anyone approaching.

'What's this ye're scribblin' at – a letter tae yer sweetheart?' The ginger-haired messenger boy danced round to the opposite side of the table, waving the book.

'Give it back – please.'

'In a minute. Let's see, now. "Dear – er – dear L-lachlan,"' he read aloud, struggling over the words like a small child learning to read. 'Who's Lachlan, yer fancy man?'

'My brother.' Elspeth stood up and reached for the book, her face burning with embarrassment as a few people sitting at the long table looked on, laughing. 'Give it back.'

The boy pursed his lips. 'If this Lachlan's yer brother, what's yer sweetheart's name, then?'

'I don't have a sweetheart.' Elspeth, unused to being the centre of attention, felt humiliating tears stabbing at her eyelids, and wished that she could just crawl under the table and hide.

'A bonny lassie wi' no young man of her own? Tell ye what, I'll give it back if ye'll promise tae come tae the pictures with me tonight,' the lad suggested, smirking.

'Just give it back.'

'Aw, come on – a wee visit tae the—' he began, then it was his turn to yelp with shock as a hand skelped lightly across his ear, while at the same time its partner whipped the book away from him.

'Stop yer nonsense, Johnny Crawford, and leave the lassie alone,' Lena Stewart ordered, handing the exercise book back to Elspeth.

'What d'ye think ye're doin', you? That was sore!'

'Ach, away ye go, I scarce touched ye. Ye'll get a lot worse than that from the Boche if ye're ever old enough tae go and bother them,' Lena teased. 'Away and play with yer pals, and stop pretending tae be a man when ye're nothin' but a wee laddie.'

The boy's face went scarlet as an elderly carter shouted from further down the table, 'Ye're right there, Lena hen – he's that young he's still walkin' all bandy-legged!'

'Bitch!'

'Here, here – another word out of ye and I'll learn ye what a proper slap feels like,' Lena told him sharply, and he subsided, slinking away, crimson to the tips of his ears. 'Don't let the likes of him bother ye, he's just tryin' it on. He's fancied ye ever since ye started workin' here.'

'Lena!'

'Have ye never noticed the wee glances and the wee smiles? Ach, there's no harm in him, but ye could do better for yerself. Why not come tae the dancin' tomorrow night?' Lena coaxed, not for the first time. 'There'll be plenty of men there, and there's somethin' about a uniform and a foreign accent that can set a lassie's heart racin'.'

The deep-water area off Greenock, known as the Tail o' the Bank because it marked the end of a vast mudbank, was always busy with warships these days, and the townsfolk had become used to sharing their streets with foreign seamen in unfamiliar uniforms, speaking different tongues. The local people held concerts and dances for these young men so far from home, and in turn they provided plenty of company for local girls with sweethearts in the services. Lena and most of the others who worked in the sewing room attended the dances.

'You know Aunt Flora won't let me.'

'Why not?'

'She says I'm too young.'

'Ye're old enough tae earn a wage,' Lena pointed

'That doesn't make any difference to her. I don't really want to go to dances anyway.'

She was grateful when Lena shrugged and accepted her decision without any further attempt to get her to change her mind. She had no wish to cause further trouble with Auntie Flora by sneaking out behind her back. One way or another she was certain to be found out, and then there would be another row. In any case, she was intent on saving every penny she could so that she could pay for evening classes.

Although she spent very little on herself, the tiny hoard of coins kept in an old tobacco tin in her bedroom never seemed to grow. She had borrowed a book on book-keeping from the lending library and worked on it in her spare time, but it was difficult, on her own, to grasp the finer points of crediting and debiting and cross-referencing.

Once, sent along to the accounts office to deliver a note from Miss Buchanan, she had looked enviously at the confident young woman sitting at a desk before a large, solid typewriter, tapping briskly on the keys. She longed to try her hand at typewriting.

Reaching the bottom of the page, she awoke from her daydream to find that her pencil had written, 'Yesterday when I was typewriting to Mattie' instead of 'talking to Mattie'. Vexed, she began to tear the sheet out neatly.

'What's wrong?' Lena wanted to know.

'I wrote the wrong word.'

'Scribble it out, then. I've tae dae that all the time when I'm writin' tae George.' Lena's young man was in the navy.

'I don't like pages with mistakes scribbled out, it looks untidy. I'll do it over again at home.' A glance at the large clock on the wall showed that it was almost time for the loud bell that summoned the sewing girls and the carters and cleaners and packers and messenger boys back to work. The counter and office staff ate their sandwiches upstairs, in a room next to the offices.

'Ye're awful fussy,' chimed in one of the other seamstresses, leaning on Elspeth's shoulder so that she could have an upside-down look at the unwanted page. 'Ye should see the letters I write tae my young man – they're that untidy, he sometimes says he cannae make out what I'm sayin' tae him.' She hesitated, then asked diffidently, 'Would ye mebbe write tae him for me, Ellie? It'd please him tae see a tidy letter for once.'

'I couldn't do that.' Elspeth was shocked at the idea. 'It wouldn't be your letter then, and that's what he'll want more than anything.'

'What he wants is tae be able tae read what I'm tellin' him. He says that when ye're in a shell hole with all that mud, and the bullets flying around, ye don't want tae have tae keep peerin' at a piece of paper, tryin' tae make out what it's sayin'. Anyway, I'd tell ye what tae write. I just want it put down nice. Ye could do it in the dinner hour tomorrow,' the girl added eagerly.

'I don't know—'

'If she writes a letter for anyb'dy, Cora Simpson, she'll write one for me,' Lena broke in jealously. 'She's my friend more than yours, and I don't like writin' either. I only do it because George is desperate for letters.'

'I'd pay ye, Ellie,' Cora said at once. 'I'd give ye a penny tae dae it for me.'

Lena knocked the girl's arm off Elspeth's shoulder. 'And I'd pay her tuppence, so there!'

'I haven't said I'll do it yet,' Elspeth protested as the two girls glared at each other. She couldn't believe that anyone would be silly enough to pay to have something done when they were perfectly able to do it themselves.

'If ye do, it'll be for me, because I'm yer friend.'

'But I asked first!'

As they wrangled, Elspeth put aside the absurdity of writing other people's letters, and started to consider the benefits. If she wrote the two letters, she would be able to add thruppence to the money she was putting by to pay for her evening classes.

'I'll do them both,' she announced, 'for a penny halfpenny each. One tomorrow and one the day after – you can toss a coin to pick which one I write first.'

And to her astonishment, both girls agreed.

Cora won the toss. It was strange, writing someone else's letter at their dictation. At first, Elspeth, who had done well in grammar at school, found herself wanting to make corrections, much to Cora's indignation.

'Listen, it's my letter tae my lad,' she snapped. 'Just write what yer told – and I'll have an extra page of that book when ye're finished, so's I can write my own wee private bit tae him. He'll just have tae put up with my own scribbling for that bit.'

Once Elspeth settled to writing down the dictation, the way her class had been taught in school, the work came easily, and two days later the tobacco tin in her drawer at home was richer by three pennies. To her astonishment, once the others who ate their midday meal in the basement room caught on to what she was doing, a few more girls asked her to write letters for sweethearts and fathers and brothers away at the war. Then one of the carters asked if she would write to his daughter, married and living in Stirling.

'Her mother was the one that always wrote tae her, once a week without fail.' He took off his cap and scratched his bald head. 'Since the wife died our Betty expects me tae keep up with the letters, but I was never a letter-writer, and it comes awful hard.'

'She just wants to know what's been happening to you and the neighbours, now that she's not here to find out for herself,' Elspeth suggested, and he nodded.

'I know that, lass, and that's the sort of things I talk about all day tae my horse. It's easy with the horse, but when it comes tae puttin' it all down on paper for our Betty I'm tongue-tied. Ye'd be daein' me a right favour if ye'd see tae it for me.'

Then an elderly cleaner timidly asked her to write a letter to the factor about rainwater pouring in through her kitchen window.

'When I'm in front of them, all they see's an auld woman no worth botherin' about, but a letter in a nice hand's different. It's more—' She searched for a word, and beamed when Elspeth suggested, 'More businesslike?'

'That's it, hen – ye've the right way with the words. Will ye dae it for me?'

'Tell me what you want to say.' Elspeth drew the exercise book towards her. 'I'll write it down, then I'll do a proper letter tonight and give it to you tomorrow.'

When word that the factor's men had repaired the window went round the store, Elspeth was inundated with requests. She spent her evenings writing letters, and once or twice had to call on Mattie for assistance in return for helping her cousin with her homework.

'Imagine people paying to have letters written for them, when they could manage for themselves,' she wrote to Lachlan and Thomas. 'I'm getting to know as much about this town as the journalists who write in the *Greenock Telegraph*. Only they know about the important things, while I know about varicose veins and who's had a baby and how someone's Uncle William's come down with the bronchitis again. It's just as well that I can keep secrets.'

'It'll bring you out of your shell, and high time too,' Lachlan wrote back, while Thomas's letter said, 'You're discovering that everyone has some talent that's needed by others, Ellie. It's called supply and demand, and if you're wondering how I know such high-flown things, it's because I've learned a lot myself, mixing with so many different folk. That side of the war's interesting, but I'd give anything to be back home, waking in the morning and knowing that I'm going to be working in the Bruces' nice garden without having to duck every time a Boche shell comes screaming past. They don't have gardens here, only mud.'

'It's a lot of nonsense,' Flora announced when she discovered what was going on. 'Folk should see tae their own letter-writin'.'

'You rely on Ellie to do most of the writing to Thomas and Lachlan,' Mattie pointed out, and earned a cuff on the ear for her disrespect.

'That's different, milady, and well ye know it. I've got more than enough tae see tae as it is. I'd certainly not go askin' a stranger tae write letters for me. And I'm not so sure that it's right for ye tae take money for doin' it, Elspeth.'

'They want to pay their way,' Elspeth explained hurriedly, anxious in case her aunt put a stop to the letter-writing and the money she was earning towards night school. 'I don't ask to be paid.'

'Ye should be proud of the lass, Flora.' Henry's voice came from behind his newspaper. 'She works all hours at that writin' she's daein', and she surely deserves tae be paid for it.'

Flora frowned and muttered, but to Elspeth's relief she raised no further objections. Sometimes, but only sometimes, Flora McDonald listened when her husband spoke.

By January 1918 Elspeth had saved up enough money to start evening classes twice a week in typewriting, shorthand and book-keeping at Greenock Higher Grade School.

On the other three evenings and at weekends she was kept busy coping with the demand for letters, which grew until she had to rise half an hour earlier in the mornings to fit them all in.

Typing and shorthand and book-keeping satisfied her love of order and neatness, and from the start she enjoyed evening classes, getting even more pleasure out of them than she had done from day school.

She quickly realised, too, that office work brought far more satisfaction than machining a neat hem on a skirt, or even stitching the pretty petticoat Miss Arnold entrusted to her one day with the comment, 'You're one of our more careful seam-stresses, Elspeth. I can trust you not to make a mess of this.' Sewing had always been part of her life, but office skills brought a fresh challenge, one that she took on with enthusiasm.

Shorthand, a written language that could never be spoken, fascinated her. She took great pleasure in her newfound abil-ity to cover a page with its crisp, swift hooks and strokes and curls, then translate the symbols back into real words. In book-keeping, she loved to see lists of figures growing on the pages of her cash-book, each amount neatly ranged beneath the fig-ure above, each corresponding with a figure on another column, another page.

She particularly enjoyed sitting at a typewriter, tapping on the keys and watching the letters forming on the paper that moved regally upwards, line by line, from the carriage. Sometimes the teacher tapped out the alphabet on the black-board with a cane, and the whole class was supposed to hit the correct keys to the rhythm she was setting. When the exercise worked, the sound of the keys all crashing together to the beat of the cane was music to Elspeth's ears, and it set her teeth on edge when slower girls missed the beat and threw the rhythm out.

Most of all, she treasured the knowledge that her precious evening classes were being paid for by money she herself had earned. She was doing what she had always wanted to do, and she hadn't had to turn to anyone else for help.

She envied those classmates who had already gained entrance into offices, and had been sent to night school by their employers.

'One day,' she told Mattie, her only confidante apart from her letters to Thomas and Lachlan, 'I'm going to work in an office. If you're determined enough, you can do anything.'

5

When Elspeth first started her evening classes, she didn't say a word about them to Grandmother Bremner, in case they turned out to be a mistake and she had to accept failure and give up. But by May they were going so well that she felt free to talk about them on her monthly visit to the old lady. Grandmother, she felt sure, would be pleased to hear that she had even managed to pay for them herself, and was beholden to nobody.

Celia Bremner lived near Bogstone railway station in Port Glasgow, a shipbuilding town adjacent to Greenock. The tenants in the row of tenements in which she lived were envied by others, because the railway line, which the tenement faced, had been built above the shore road to Greenock. The line was flanked on one side by a sheer drop of at least thirty feet to the shore road, and on the other side by Grandmother's street, which ran parallel to the line, but a little above it. This meant that the tenement windows had an excellent view of the Clyde, looking right over the railway line and even over the shipyards beyond to the open stretch of water and the soft green hills on the opposite shore.

The Bremners were, as Grandmother often told Elspeth, of good stock. Looking at Celia Bremner, erect as a soldier on parade, pride stamped into the hard lines of her face, Elspeth had no reason to doubt her words. During her regular visits to the house, which had started after Celia Bremner was widowed, the old woman always sat in an upright, heavily carved chair, her lower arms laid along the wooden armrests, her hands, twisted with rheumatism, curving precisely over the polished knobs at the ends. She and the chair fitted each other so well that as a child Elspeth had wondered if the chair had been specially made to her grandmother's measurements, and had supposed that somewhere in the house stood a series of identical chairs, starting with a small one made for her grandmother when she was a child, then ranging in size to the imposing adult chair standing now by the fireplace.

Grandfather Bremner, who had, as far as Elspeth knew, never set eyes on her, had been paymaster in one of the sugar refineries; a man, according to his widow, who had been looked up to by his staff and highly regarded by his employers.

Elspeth's secret hope was that if she did well enough at night school, her grandmother might be willing to put in a good word for her at the office where her grandfather had once worked.

She began by talking about the letters she was writing for other people, and was interrupted before she could get to the part about the night school classes.

'I trust you're not asked to write anything vulgar or sensational in those letters?'

'Oh no, Grandmother. Just news of what's happening in the town and with the soldiers' families.'

'In that case I believe your grandfather would have approved,' Celia Bremner said in her dry, flat voice. 'We should all use our God-given talents, and your ability to write comes from him. He himself wrote excellent letters.' Her glance travelled briefly to the mantelpiece, where a photograph of herself and her late husband stood in an elaborate carved wooden frame.

Every item of furniture in Celia Bremner's three-roomed house was carved. Wherever the eye landed it was met by a profusion of balls and claws, bunches of grapes, climbing vines, and formal flowers, all in a state of suspended animation, as though some wicked witch had cast a spell over them and stopped the flowers just at the point of opening, the leaves when they were about to toss in the wind, the grapes at the moment before they were plucked.

Even the photograph of Grandmother and Grandfather Bremner looked as though it had been frozen in time, Elspeth thought, following the old lady's gaze. He, richly moustached but balding, his eyes staring coldly through the glass, sat in a chair – surely a photographer's chair, since it was plain, with no sign of any carvings – his wife on her feet, slightly behind him, one hand firmly planted on his shoulder as if to show that he was hers and nobody else's, her sculpted hair glimpsed beneath a feathered hat.

Studying the photograph, Elspeth found it hard to imagine her grandparents in any other, less formal pose, sitting eating their dinners, for instance, or sleeping in the large carved bed in the bedroom. It was certainly impossible to imagine them talking, laughing, moving freely.

She wondered what it must have been like for her mother to grow up with these two people. From what Granjan said, Maisie Bremner had been a happy young girl, full of fun. Perhaps, thought Elspeth, feeling an itch on her calf and unable to scratch it in front of Grandmother Bremner, that was why there were no photographs of Maisie on the mantelpiece. Even a pictured image of her might hint at too much movement, too much liveliness, in this immaculate flat where the only thing allowed to move was the pendulum of the grandmother clock in the corner of the living room. Even that was strictly regulated to make sure that it didn't recklessly drop or add a second.

Deciding that a respectable interval of time had been given over to contemplation of her grandparents' portrait, she moved tentatively towards the core of her news. 'I enjoy writing letters. I'd like to work in an office one day – like Grandfather.'

47

To her surprise, her grandmother's nostrils flared and her already stiff back stiffened further. Her large-knuckled hands gripped at the armrests.

'Offices are not suitable workplaces for respectable women!'

'But a lot of women work in offices now, Grandmother.'

'That's between them and their consciences,' the old woman rapped out, eyes flashing. 'If this letter-writing is going to lead to such foolishness on your part, Elspeth, I trust that your Aunt Flora has the sense to put a stop to it at once. You're fortunate in having found a good position as a seamstress with a reputable firm, and with diligence, you may do very well for yourself there. I'll not have any more talk of office work from a granddaughter of mine, d'you hear me?'

Elspeth was completely taken aback. She had no idea what she had done to deserve this outburst, but instinct told her that retreat was the safest option. 'Yes, Grandmother.' The itch was worse now, nagging and niggling, demanding to be scratched. She shifted slightly in her chair in an attempt to relieve it.

'Don't twitch, child, it's unladylike. I expect it means that you want your tea,' Celia said reprovingly. 'Very well, you may go to the kitchen and fetch the tray.'

Elspeth, disturbed by her grandmother's sudden change of mood, was only too happy to leave the room. Clearly, there was no question of talking about her night classes now. She felt sure that if the old woman knew about them, she would put a stop to them.

Despite her rheumatism, Grandmother Bremner kept her kitchen, like the rest of the house, spotless, with never a thing out of place. The kitchen was actually a scullery, a walk-in cupboard barely large enough for the gas cooker, sink, and closet it held. The kettle, sitting over what Granjan called 'a wee peep of gas', was ready, pluming subdued little puffs of steam into the air.

With some difficulty, for the scullery was so small that

there wasn't room for even one person to bend down when the door was closed, Elspeth indulged in the luxury of clawing at her calf until the itch was subdued, tears of relief coming to her eyes. She was sure that another minute of sitting in the living room while the itch grew to monstrous proportions would have set her screaming.

The itch finally gone, she warmed the teapot then emptied it into the sink before, mindful of her grandmother's wishes, measuring a precise half-spoonful of tea into the pot from the elaborately painted caddy with its picture of Queen Victoria. After pouring boiling water into the pot she refilled the kettle from the kitchen tap.

A tray had already been set with cups and saucers, plates, milk jug and sugar bowl. Elspeth added the teapot, covered it with the knitted cosy Grandmother always used, and took four biscuits from the biscuit barrel on the shelf, laying them neatly on the blue leaf-shaped plate already on the tray. Back in the living room she put the tray down on the small table between their two chairs and poured tea, first putting in the correct amounts of milk and sugar.

They had their tea in silence, because Grandmother didn't believe in talking while taking refreshments. Sipping at the pale liquid, which she found tasteless compared to the sturdy, strong brew she was used to at home, Elspeth wished that she was back there, practising her shorthand and book-keeping, and perhaps writing two letters that she had promised for Monday morning.

She wished, too, and with all her heart, that Grandmother Bremner was more like Granjan. The two women were like chalk and cheese. Both had given birth to one child, a daughter, and both were widowed, but that was as far as any resemblance went. Granjan was small and plump and cosy, with twinkling grey eyes and a ready sense of humour, while Grandmother was tall and bony, with a long unsmiling face and cold blue eyes. Both wore their hair in a bun, but there

49

again, they were quite unlike each other. Granjan's hair was grey, and always making attempts to escape from captivity; Grandmother's was pure white and drawn back tightly, enhancing the skull-like look of her face. Grandmother spoke very properly, articulating each word clearly, while Granjan chattered on in the local dialect, saying 'tae' and 'ye' instead of 'to' and 'you' and scarcely bothering with word endings like 'th' and 'ing'.

On leaving school, Granjan had worked in Boag's factory, where the bags from the many sugar refineries in Greenock were washed and prepared for re-use, while Grandmother had obtained a position as lady's maid in one of the big houses in Largs, a residential town further along the coast, where many of the wealthy manufacturers from Glasgow had built seaside homes.

Both women had given up work when they got married, Granjan to a labourer at Caird's shipyard, Grandmother to an ambitious wages clerk in one of Greenock's sugar refineries.

Granjan, forced to become the breadwinner within two years of her marriage, when her husband, still in his twenties, was crippled in an accident at the yard, had taken work wherever she could find it, as a cleaner and washerwoman. Widowed in her mid-thirties, she still paid her way by washing for women who could afford to pay someone else to see to their laundry.

Grandmother's husband had achieved the position of paymaster before his death, leaving his widow with enough money to continue living in the comfortable flat they had shared, and to cover her frugal lifestyle. It was once she was on her own that Celia Bremner had acknowledged the existence of her dead daughter's illegitimate child, insisting on monthly visits. Flora had taken Elspeth to Port Glasgow in the early days, leaving her at the door and waiting for her in the street an hour later. As soon as Elspeth was old enough, she started making the visits on her own, although as far as she could tell, her grandmother didn't derive any more pleasure from their meetings than she herself did.

When they had finished tea Elspeth removed the tray and carefully washed and dried the fragile fluted cups, then put them away in the cupboard. As always, her grandmother took advantage of her absence to visit the lavatory.

Unlike most residents in the three towns – Port Glasgow, Greenock and Gourock – strung together along the banks of the Clyde, Grandmother was fortunate enough to have an indoor lavatory. While this was a blessing to be envied, Elspeth was aware that as far as Grandmother was concerned it was more of a curse if anyone else happened to be in the flat, as it meant that they could hear the cistern flushing.

She had learned early in her visits to remain quietly in the scullery until the noisy rush of water had ceased and the old woman had had enough time to settle herself carefully back in her chair, as though she hadn't moved from it at all. Celia Bremner hated to let anyone know that she did anything as common as using a lavatory.

Elspeth often wondered how her grandmother would have managed in the Mearns Street tenement, where all the tenants on one landing shared the privy on the half-landing below, and the folk on the ground floor had their privy in the back yard. She was sure that Grandmother Bremner would rather have burst than admit that she was prey to the same physical actions as other human beings.

Waiting in the scullery until it was time to return to the living room, Elspeth recalled her own sense of shock on hearing from Molly McKibbin, one of a large family, about how men and women made babies. It had been then, and still was, very difficult to think of Auntie Flora and Uncle Henry indulging in such goings-on in the large kitchen wall-bed they shared, but quite impossible to fathom out how the couple in the photograph on Grandmother's mantelpiece could ever have conceived her mother.

Even now that she was older and had had Molly's scarlet-faced, giggling whispers confirmed by some of the girls in the sewing room, she couldn't believe it of her grandmother. Surely a woman who hated to have it known that she had to answer calls of nature like everyone else would never have permitted herself to get involved in that way with a man!

'I hope you've not chipped any of my china.' Celia's cold, creaky voice brought her back to the present just when her thoughts were threatening to get completely out of control.

'No, Grandmother.' She returned to the living room, hoping that her expression carried no hint of the impure thoughts she had been having. 'I was just dusting the biscuit barrel.'

'And how is everything in the sewing room?' Celia Bremner asked when they were facing each other across the fireplace again.

'Very well, thank you, Grandmother. Miss Arnold allowed me to hand-stitch a hem on a petticoat last Thursday, and she was pleased with it when I'd finished.' In her enthusiasm at the memory of Miss Arnold's grudging praise, Elspeth hitched herself slightly forward in her chair. 'It was beautiful material, lovely to touch—'

'Sit up, girl, you're slouching. I'm glad to hear that you're giving satisfaction. You get your sewing ability from me, of course – when I attended Miss Hope Childes, I was well known for my delicate stitching,' Celia said firmly, giving no credit at all to the hours of hard work Flora McDonald had put into teaching Elspeth and her own two daughters how to sew.

'Miss Arnold says that she might let me do some more work for clients who have their clothes made for them.'

Her grandmother inclined her head. 'You could do well for yourself, then.'

The clock in the corner gently chimed the half-hour, and Elspeth sighed inwardly. Thirty more minutes must pass before she was free to make her excuses and go.

'Thomas wrote to me last week,' she volunteered. 'He's in Belgium now. Lachlan's still in France, and we don't hear so much from him just now. I hope he's all right. Thomas says things are just as bad as ever before.' She looked down at her hands, and tried hard not to let her voice shake as she went on, 'I'm so worried about the two of them. I couldn't bear it if they didn't come back home.'

'They're doing their duty by their king and country,' Celia Bremner said implacably. 'You must fix your mind on that, and accept whatever the Lord may choose to send.'

Elspeth was startled by the sudden jolt of anger that ran through her. She longed to ask why anyone should accept without protest a war that was killing hundreds and thousands of ordinary young men like Thomas and Lachlan, but she didn't dare. Instead, she folded her lips together to contain her fury, and waited for the clock to chime four times and release her.

When it finally, grudgingly, did so, she held back until she had rounded the street corner and was well out of sight before starting to run, rejoicing in her freedom and the pleasure of stretching her limbs after having to sit so still in the claustrophobic room she had just left.

6

Spring made little impact on the cobbles and slabs of Greenock's streets and back yards, though flowers and trees and bushes could be seen stirring with life in the town's parks and in the wealthier townsfolk's gardens and the countryside beyond. Most of the residents, though, marked the arrival of the spring season by the soft green shading on the hills at the other side of the Clyde.

In the battlegrounds of France and Belgium there was even less indication of the release from a long, cold, wet winter. Elspeth gathered from Thomas's letters that the rain had eased somewhat, and smoke from the guns drifted across blue skies, but the mud was still there. In one letter he wrote about spending a night in the ruins of a big house, similar to the house his employers, the Bruce family, had in Gourock, describing graphically the glassless windows, the odd scrap of wallpaper still clinging here and there to what remained of a wall, a door hanging askew on one twisted hinge.

'It was hard to believe that it had once been a cosy home where a family had lived,' he wrote. 'I wonder where they are now, and what's become of them? We thought we were in clover when we arrived, because almost one entire room was left standing, complete with a fireplace and a bonny ceiling, with carving all round. We gathered up wood and lit a fire, only to discover that the chimney had fallen in, so we were driven out of the place by clouds of smoke. We were so pleased at being able to sit at a real fire in a real fireplace that we hung on for as long as we could, until we were all wheezing and coughing, the tears running down our faces.

'I managed to find time to go out into the grounds before we left. It reminded me a lot of the Bruces', for this place had a kitchen garden and a rose garden and once it had had some bonny box hedging and statues on the terracing, all broken and destroyed now. All the glass was gone in their greenhouses, of course, but I did find a pot with a hyacinth blossoming in it, a lovely deep blue flower. I cleared the broken glass from it and moved it to a sheltered spot. Maybe after the fighting is over and the folk come back to rebuild their house, the hyacinth will still be there, waiting for them. It was good to think that all this destruction can't entirely kill Nature off.'

As Elspeth had told her grandmother, Lachlan's letters to her and to his parents had become sporadic. When he did write, his letters were short, and tended to be filled with memories of the past: 'Do you remember that day we all walked over the hills to Loch Thom and had a picnic?' or, 'I was thinking this morning about the time Thomas and me went to Gourock and hired a boat and rowed out into the river so far that we thought we weren't going to get back before the hire time was up.'

She knew from what the other girls in the sewing room said that men on active duty often clung to thoughts of home. One of the carters who had fought in the Boer War in South Africa told her that it was important to soldiers to know that everything was the same at home, just waiting for them to return and slip back into the place they had left.

'Not that anything's ever the same,' he said, scratching his bristly chin, 'for the man himself's bound tae be changed by the things he's seen an' heard an' done. But even so, he needs tae believe that his real life's still waitin' for him back home. That's what keeps him goin'.'

*

In the summer, as the tide of battle slowly began to turn in the Allies' favour at last, a War Office telegram arrived at the McDonalds' flat. Lachlan had been wounded, and was in hospital in France.

To Elspeth, who had become increasingly superstitious about both Thomas and Lachlan, and had taken to lying awake night after night, fretting over them, the news was welcome. The war had dragged on far longer than anyone had at first believed possible, and by now almost every family she knew had lost a young man in the fighting, or had had word of wounds received in battle.

So far this hadn't happened to the McDonalds, and she had got it into her head that Thomas and Lachlan had escaped harm for too long while men were injured and killed all around them. Some form of blood sacrifice, she had begun to believe during those long dark sleepless nights, might have to be made before they could be truly safe.

Now she saw Lachlan's wound as just such a sacrifice, an omen that both he and Thomas would survive and return home safely when the war was finally over. She was even relieved for Lachlan's sake, happy to know that for a little while, at least, he was distanced from the fighting and able to rest in safety and without fear.

But when she tried to express these thoughts to Flora, who had almost fainted away at the sight of the War Office envelope, her outraged aunt was in no mood to listen.

'All I know is that my poor laddie's lyin' hurt and in pain in some foreign hospital, with none of his own there tae see tae him,' she snapped. 'I see nothing tae be happy about – and neither would you, if ye'd the sense God gave ye!'

Once again, Elspeth thought in despair, biting her tongue to prevent herself from trying to explain and thus annoying Flora even further, she had caused trouble without meaning to. Would she never learn to keep her opinions to herself?

She was already feeling low that summer. The evening

classes had ended, and wouldn't begin again until September, and as Mattie's school was also closed there was no homework to study with her.

More orders for letters were coming in, and her savings for the next evening-school session were growing, but she missed working on the typewriter, and found a sewing machine a poor substitute. She begged a large sheet of cardboard from a local shopkeeper, and carefully, working from memory, drew out on it a typewriter keyboard. Working on it helped to keep her fingers supple, but at the same time she missed the crisp tapping of a real typewriter's keys.

August brought some excitement to the sewing room. Catherine Bruce, the elder daughter of the family for whom Thomas worked in peacetime, was engaged to a young captain in the Scottish Rifles, and when he was sent home to recuperate from wounds, the couple decided to marry before he went back on duty. The bride's mother, Mrs Lorrimer Bruce, was insistent on a proper church wedding complete with bridesmaids. There was also to be a full trousseau for her daughter's honeymoon, brief though it must be, as the groom was to rejoin his unit by mid-September.

Because the war and the lack of time made it difficult for the trousseau to be made in Glasgow, as would have happened in peacetime, Brodie's store was pressed into service. The sewing room suddenly became a whirl of activity, with all the seamstresses enlisted to help meet the deadline. Even the 'plain' sewing women, who normally only dealt with alterations to ready-made clothes, were given something to do for the wedding.

Miss Buchanan rushed about like a dandelion ball caught up in a whirlwind, her arms filled with sketches and patterns and materials, and Miss Arnold, two bright spots of colour high on her normally pale cheekbones, seemed to be everywhere at once, instructing, checking, criticising, while at the same time soothing her near-hysterical superior.

'This is a great honour for the department,' she told the staff at least once every day. 'We must show Mrs Bruce that we can do as well as any big Glasgow store.'

'The gentry won't even let a war deprive them of their bit of show,' Lena said with a sniff as they all stitched and cut and trimmed.

'What's wrong with a nice dress and jacket?' one of the other women wanted to know. 'That's what my sister wore when she married her sweetheart a few months ago. It's the marryin' that counts, not the show.'

'When ye're a nob, it's the show that counts more than the marryin',' Lena retorted disparagingly. 'What I'd like tae know is, where did they get all this lovely material? It's hard tae find stuff like that nowadays.'

'I heard that a lot of it comes from Mrs Bruce herself,' one of the other girls ventured. 'She put it by before the war began, just in case it was needed for somethin' like this.'

'God! The rest of us makin' do with what we can find, and the likes of the Bruces even hidin' away good cloth!' For a moment Elspeth thought that Lena was going to explode. Her face went red and her hair seemed to give off flashes of light. She opened her mouth to speak, then bent over her work, almost choking with suppressed anger, as the door opened and Miss Arnold swept back in to urge her staff to further efforts.

Elspeth didn't object at all to the hustle and bustle, because the hard work gave her something to do and took her mind off the loss of the evening classes. She enjoyed handling the beautiful materials chosen for the trousseau, and loved the sight of all the colours spilling across the worktables, brightening the drab room.

Once, when she was sent to the fitting rooms with a lawn petticoat she had just finished, a beautiful garment trimmed with pink ribbons and lace, she caught a glimpse of the two Bruce sisters.

Catherine Bruce, the bride-to-be, was a pretty young woman with soft dark hair framing a round face. She was standing before a full-length mirror, garbed in a crimson silk underdress beneath a sequined net overdress in the same colour. Two of the seamstresses were on their knees beside her, working on the hem, while Miss Arnold watched critically, her back to Elspeth, who hesitated at the door, unwilling to interrupt.

She had never seen a more beautiful dress, but the wearer's brows were drawn together above dark-lashed green eyes, her full small mouth turned down at the corners in a sulky pout.

'I still don't like the neckline. It doesn't look right.'

'I think it very flattering, Miss Bruce.' Elspeth had never heard Miss Arnold speak in that soft, soothing voice before. 'Just your style.'

'That's very well, but you're not the one who has to wear it, are you?' the girl snapped without taking her eyes off her own reflection. Elspeth saw Miss Arnold's back stiffen, but when the woman replied it was in the same quiet, reasonable voice.

'If we change the neckline, we change the entire style of the dress, madam.'

'For goodness' sake, Kate, stop fussing. It's lovely, and you know it,' a new voice cut in, and for the first time Elspeth, spellbound up to now by the beauty of the dress, noticed the girl sitting in the corner. Clearly this was Catherine Bruce's sister, for there was a strong family resemblance; but while the bride was pretty, the other girl was breathtakingly beautiful. Her hair was hidden beneath a turban striped in two shades of green, the darker shade an exact match for her wide, clear eyes, and a dark green feather swept up from it. Her silk suit, also in dark green with a lighter shade picking out the lapels, cuffs, and facing, was cut in a severe military style, and her small, narrow feet wore soft green kid button boots. Her face was less rounded than her sister's, almost angular, with a small yet soft mouth.

'It's all right for you, Aileen, all you need is one

bridesmaid's dress. I wish Mother had come with me,'
Catherine Bruce fretted, turning back to the mirror.

'So do I,' her sister agreed, then the lovely green eyes discovered Elspeth. 'Someone's waiting to speak to you, Miss
Arnold,' she said, and the supervisor turned.

'What do you want, Elspeth?'

'You asked for this, Miss Arnold.'

'Yes, I did. Run along now,' Miss Arnold said briefly, taking the petticoat and turning back at once to her client.

The bridesmaids' dresses, Elspeth knew, were to be in pale
yellow muslin, cut straight across from shoulder to shoulder
and trimmed with silver and yellow roses. Aileen Bruce would
look beautiful in hers, she thought, hurrying back to her
work.

As the wedding date approached, Miss Buchanan, clearly
convinced that the clothes would never be ready in time,
worked herself into a frenzy.

'If she's not careful, one of these days she'll go whizzin' out
the door and bump intae hersel' coming back,' Lena remarked
during a midday break in the basement. 'Either that, or she'll
run right up her own arse by accident. We used tae have a dog
that was forever chasin' its own tail – it never did catch it, but
she's in danger of catchin' hers.'

'I wish she'd just keep out of the way and stop telling us to
leave what we're doing and go on to something else,' Elspeth
complained. She was working on another petticoat, one with a
lot of tucking in the bodice that required careful and time-
consuming work, and twice that morning Miss Buchanan had
tried to make her stop what she was doing and turn to another
garment.

If it hadn't been for Miss Arnold's cool efficiency, Miss
Buchanan would have got the entire sewing room into such a
tizzy that work on the wedding clothes could well have
descended into chaos. She took to following Miss Buchanan
around, calmly and quietly countermanding her superior's

conflicting orders and ensuring that one garment was finished before work started on the next.

'It's Miss Bruce that's the real problem.' Lily, one of the women who had been in the fitting room the day Elspeth took the petticoat in, leaned across the table. 'Talk about fussy – she doesnae like any of the things she ordered. Keeps wanting them all tae be changed, and she should know better than anyb'dy how little time we've got left. She's spoiled rotten, that one, thinks money's all that matters. Thank goodness her man comes from Perth – the folk up there are welcome tae her.'

'Remember that she's tae stay with her mother till the war's over,' someone else cautioned. 'We'll not get rid of her until her husband's back home for good, so let's hope nothing happens tae him.'

'I can see the day he'll wish something had,' Lily sniffed. 'Courtin''s one thing, marryin''s another. I should know – it wasn't until my man went off to the fighting that I realised what a pain in the neck he is. Once Miss Catherine's new husband's got her all the time he might wish he'd never proposed.'

'The sister seems to be quite nice,' Elspeth offered, and Lily shrugged.

'She's decent enough. Mind you, she's been away at some posh boarding school, so she's mebbe learned a few manners there. Once she's been under her ma's wing for a year or two she might be just as bad,' she said, then, coaxingly, 'Elspeth, ye wouldnae have the time tae write me a wee letter tae the factor, would ye? He's tryin' tae tell me I'm still owing my share of those roof repairs, and I know I'm not. But I cannae seem tae put the words down the right way.'

Preparing the trousseau in time for the wedding date began to resemble being in a locked room with the walls slowly moving in to crush the life out of its occupants. As the wedding day approached, the seamstresses worked almost every evening until quite late. Miss Buchanan tottered continually on the verge of apoplexy, while Miss Arnold's controlled serenity was magnificent to see.

It was just as well that there were no evening classes, for Elspeth would have had to miss them. She had been put almost entirely on to fine work that couldn't be done on a machine, and her fingers were red and stiff, the skin rough from plying a needle, her back aching with tension after long hours bent over the worktable. At home, she had to work into the night and get up early in the morning to keep up with her letter-writing as well, but she was determined not to let it fall behind, for it had turned out to be a lucrative sideline.

Between the letters and overtime in the sewing room, her savings had grown considerably and she now had enough to ensure another year at night school, even though she had given a percentage of her overtime earnings to Flora.

To her surprise, her aunt was reluctant to take it. 'Ye've been workin' hard, lassie, with never a word of complaint. Ye deserve tae keep it,' she said, but Elspeth insisted, constantly aware of the debt she owed Flora and Henry McDonald, and anxious to do what she could to repay them.

Secretly, she dreamed of buying them a nice house one day, and furnishing it throughout, to show them how grateful she was for all they had done for her, and to make up for all those occasions when she had inadvertently annoyed Aunt Flora.

One evening when the seamstresses were working late on the last part of the wedding trousseau, a list of the clothes completed went missing, together with two essential patterns. Everyone stopped work and the sewing room was searched, but it was nowhere to be found. Miss Buchanan had had to go home at dinner-time with a severe headache, and as it was her habit to scoop up every piece of paper she could find during her dashes into the sewing room to interrupt and harangue her long-suffering workers, Miss Arnold searched her tiny cubby-hole, but came back empty-handed.

Elspeth and Lena, who had both just finished the work they had been doing, were despatched to the main office, where a copy of the list was kept in case of emergencies, while the overseer continued to hunt for the patterns.

'Mr James Brodie's still on the premises, so he'll be in his room, off the accounts office. He'll know where the list is. Remember to speak clearly, don't gabble, and don't stare at the floor when he speaks to you. I don't want him to think that we employ mindless idiots in the sewing room. And remember that the staff call Mr James "sir",' Miss Arnold cautioned, and the girls, their minds seething with instructions, obediently scurried off up the narrow stairs to the top floor, where the main office and accounts department were housed.

'Why send two of us?' Elspeth wondered as they went.

'So that we can keep each other out of mischief.' Lena was bounding ahead. 'It's great tae get out for a few minutes, isn't it?'

There was no reply when they tapped at the door of the main office. After waiting for a moment or two, Lena nudged Elspeth in. The room was empty, and so, they realised after tapping at the inner door, was the small office belonging to Mr James Brodie, manager of the store, and son of the owner, who had retired.

'Now what do we do?'

'Wait here. There's no sense in goin' back empty-handed,' Lena advised. 'The lights are on and the door's not been locked, so he can't be far away. He'll have gone tae the privy.' She stood in the middle of the main office, turning slowly, taking everything in. 'It's awful tidy, isn't it?'

'That's because they don't have patterns and cloth every-where.' The office's neatness delighted Elspeth. The high desk along one wall was swept clear of books and papers, pens were laid in the grooves provided and the inkwells were free of stains. All the drawers and cupboard doors were closed, and neat rows of files filled the shelves that lined another wall.

'It's brighter here during the day than it is in the sewing room.' Lena indicated the skylights let into the ceiling. 'I wish we'd some daylight, I hate workin' under the electric light all the time.'

Elspeth didn't hear her. Her eye had fallen on the small table in the corner, with the unmistakable shape of a typewriter filling out its protective dust cover. Envy and longing flooded her mind and her fingers started to itch. She edged over to the table to run her fingertips over the cover, then, after a quick look at the door leading to the corridor, she whipped it off to reveal the typewriter itself.

'Here – what're ye doin'?'

'Just looking.' Her eyes devoured the machine greedily; it was high and shining and solid, the round keys, each with its letter or number clearly stamped on it, as mouthwatering to her as a glossy heap of liquorice allsorts would have been to a hungry child staring in through a sweetshop window.

Her fingers yearned to touch those keys, her ears longed to hear them at work. Several sheets of paper lay by the machine, white and untouched as a fresh snowfall, waiting for letters to be tapped briskly across their pristine surfaces. It was almost too much to bear, being so near a typewriter again and not being able to touch it.

'Mr James can't be at the privy,' she said without taking her eyes from the machine. 'He'd have been back by now.'

'My dad can spend hours in our privy,' Lena said from behind her. 'He suffers terrible from constipation, and when he manages tae go it takes a while. The neighbours have tae pee intae buckets when that happens. Here, what're ye doin' now?' she added in alarm as Elspeth drew out the chair tucked in beneath the desk.

'Just looking.' Elspeth sat down and let her fingers rest on the keys. A shiver of pure pleasure ran through her, and she knew that she couldn't leave things at that. She had to try the typewriter, to find out whether, during the summer, she had lost her recently learned skills.

'Keep an eye on the corridor,' she said, reaching for a sheet of paper and rolling it into the machine.

'Elspeth Bremner! You'll get us both the sack!' Although she could be a rebel in the sewing room, Lena was intimidated by the office, a room she had never been in before.

'I'll not be a minute. Just watch the corridor and tell me if you hear him coming.'

Beneath her fingers the keys leapt into life. 'The cat sat on the mat,' she typed, then ran the carriage back to start a new line. 'The quick brown fox jumped over the lazy dog' was followed by a swift, sure alphabet, every stroke true and clear like a run of notes on a piano.

'That's clever! Where did ye learn tae dae that?' Lena asked in wonder, coming to lean over the desk.

'I've been going to evening classes.' Elspeth hadn't told any of her workmates about her studies for fear of being laughed at, but now, with her ability clear for all to see, she didn't mind talking about it. She ran off another alphabet, her wrists at just the right angle, her fingers skimming over the keys, her eyes fixed on the paper and not the keyboard. Her teacher would have been proud of her, she thought, tossing the carriage back with a flick of the wrist to begin a new line.

She was so taken up with the joy of touching a typewriter again that she didn't even register the fact that Lena, who was supposed to be keeping watch, was in fact standing beside her, equally entranced. Neither of them heard the footsteps in the corridor, or the door opening behind them. When someone suddenly stepped into their line of vision and a male voice, as crisp and sharp as the tap of the keys on the paper, asked, 'Just what do you think you're doing?' the two girls jumped and squealed.

65

7

James Brodie's long, handsome face was grim, his brows drawn into a frown as he surveyed the two young women trembling before him. 'Well?'

Lena, gasping like a landed fish, her hand pressed tightly to her heart, was for once lost for words. Elspeth, suddenly aware of the enormity of her actions, stood up slowly.

'I – we – Miss Arnold sent us for a copy of Miss Bruce's wedding list, Mr – s-sir.' The words stuck in her throat, on her tongue, behind her front teeth, and it was difficult to get them out. Mindful of Miss Arnold's orders, she lifted her chin when all she really wanted to do was to hide her face against the linoleum on the floor.

The eyes surveying her were frosty, and so was his voice when he said, 'Did she ask you to fetch the list, or to type it out?'

'You werenae here, sir.' Lena finally found her voice, and her wits. 'We were waitin' for ye.'

'You were doing more than waiting.'

Elspeth swallowed hard. 'I – I was just trying out the type-writer – sir.'

'But you're a seamstress, not a typist.'

'She goes tae the night school,' Lena said eagerly. 'She knows how tae work it.'

'Then she'll know how to leave it as she found it, won't she?

And while you're doing that, I'll find this list you're supposed to be fetching.'

Silently, cheeks burning and mouth trembling, Elspeth rolled the sullied sheet of paper from the machine and laid it down on the desk before lining the carriage up properly. In a futile attempt to erase her crime, she used her clean handkerchief to wipe the surface of the keys before replacing the dust cover. By the time she had finished, Mr James had returned from his own small office. He handed the list to Lena.

'Take that to Miss Arnold, and tell her—' He stopped, looking from one flushed face to the other, then said ominously, 'Never mind, I'll tell her myself. I'll have that, young woman, it's my property.'

Elspeth had picked up the used sheet with some idea of removing all traces of the sacrilege she had just committed. Scarlet with mortification, she laid it in the outstretched hand.

'Now you can go back to where you belong,' the manager said dismissively, and the two of them crept out and along the corridor, running down the stairs as though the devil was at their heels, not stopping until they were back on the level where the sewing rooms were situated.

'Sweet Jesus, I near died when I saw him standing there,' Lena gasped, clutching at the banisters with her free hand.

'You were supposed to keep watch for him!' Elspeth blazed at her, fighting back tears of humiliation. It had been the worst moment of her whole life.

'I wouldnae have heard him even if I'd been at the door. It's unnatural for a grown man tae be so light on his feet. Anyway, it's all your fault for touchin' the thing in the first place. I wasnae doing anything wrong – it was you,' Lena said virtuously.

'D'you think he'll tell Miss Arnold?'

'He's sure tae. Did ye see the look on his face? He was ready for throwing us out of the place there and then.'

'What'll we do?' Elspeth wailed. 'What'll Aunt Flora say if I'm turned off?'

Her distress cooled the older girl's anger. 'Ye'll get another position, surely.'

'But it was her that got me this one! She'll say I've let her down again – I'm always doing it! Oh, why couldn't I have kept my hands to myself?' Elspeth wrung the offending hands, in such a state that Lena put an arm about her.

'Don't fret, hen, it'll all work out somehow. Come on, we'll have tae get back tae Miss Arnold, she'll be in a state about this precious list of hers. Don't say anything tae her, what she doesnae know won't hurt her – and no doubt she'll hear about it soon enough. There's one thing,' she added consolingly as they went along the corridor, 'at least yer typewritin' was nice and neat. He cannae accuse ye of doin' it badly.'

Fortunately, Miss Arnold, who had found the missing patterns just before they returned, was less harassed by the time they arrived back in the sewing room. She took the list from Lena, then looked from one to the other. 'You took a long time.'

'Mr James was in the – wasnae there,' Lena said smoothly. 'We had tae wait for him tae came back.'

The supervisor peered more closely at them. 'You're both looking flushed. What have you been up to?'

Elspeth, in the grip of her own private terror, stared dumbly back at her, but Lena was ready with another glib answer. 'We ran down the stairs, 'cos we knew you'd be waiting.'

'Well, you've wasted enough time away from your work. Elspeth, I want that skirt I left by your machine hemmed, and Lena, you can stitch the ribbons on to that camisole,' the supervisor ordered, and bustled off to the cutting room.

Elspeth sank thankfully into her chair and picked up the skirt. It was just as well that she had to machine instead of sew by hand, for she was shaking so much that she couldn't have threaded a needle. As it was, it took all her concentration to guide the material through the machine in a straight line.

*

Normally, when she got home from working overtime, she was as hungry as a horse, but that night she couldn't touch her supper.

'I hope ye're not sickening for something,' Flora fretted. 'I've got enough on my mind worryin' about our Lachlan without you falling ill as well.'

'I'm fine.'

'You don't look it,' Rachel said, eyeing her.

'I've got a sore head. It's all that sewing. I'll go to my bed early.'

'I'll be glad when this wedding's by.' Flora removed her untouched plate and covered it with a clean cloth. 'I'll put this in the oven, mebbe yer uncle'll be glad of it when he gets back from his meetin'.'

Elspeth lay sleepless, racked by guilt and wishing that she had never gone near the typewriter. When Mattie came to bed, tiptoeing about in the dark, trying not to waken her, she pretended she was asleep. A little later, Rachel came in with a candle and was about to light the gas mantle when Mattie hissed. 'Leave it, you'll wake Elspeth.'

Rachel sighed gustily, but did as she was told, though she would have been better to light the mantle, as she kept falling over things in the candle's weak light, yelping and muttering and loudly hissing, 'Shush yourself!' each time Mattie tried to quiet her.

At last she settled down, and soon both she and Mattie were breathing slowly and evenly, with the occasional fluttering snore. Elspeth lay awake, listening to the movements of her aunt and uncle, and the sounds of the tenement – the faint gurgle of water in the pipes, the clump of heavy footsteps on the stairs, the wailing of a child startled awake by a nightmare. She heard Mr McAllister from the flat below returning late from the pub, raising his voice in song then shouting at his wife and being shouted at in return.

Gradually, all the noises eased off as the tenement settled

down for the night. Then there was only the occasional plaintive toot from one of the many ships out on the river, or the melodious sound of a church clock striking the hours and half-hours.

Elspeth was still awake, feverishly going over and over those few moments of temptation in the office, wishing that she had pushed her hands into her pockets, or even cut them off, rather than allow them to touch that typewriter. One hand sought the little silver threepenny bit she had found in her birthday dumpling more than a year earlier, clutching it tightly. True to his word, Uncle Henry had drilled a hole in it for her, and she had worn it round her neck ever since, day and night. One of the first things she had bought with her earnings had been a fine chain to replace the piece of wool it had hung from. It had helped her in moments of stress, but tonight, not even the feel of it biting into her palm could comfort her.

The thought of having to tell her aunt that she had been turned away from the good, respectable job that had been found for her set her moving restlessly in the bed. Mattie, sound asleep, gave a moan of protest as an elbow jabbed into her back, and Elspeth made herself lie still, picturing the look on Flora's face when she heard the dreadful news.

The next two days, busy as they were, dragged by. Every time Miss Arnold or Miss Buchanan came into the sewing room Elspeth cringed, her heart thumping so hard that it was like a drum beating in her ears. She scarcely ate a thing, and it was all she could do to concentrate on her work, and on the letters she wrote during the midday meal break.

Lena, on the other hand, behaved as though nothing had happened, talking when she was supposed to be concentrating on her work, chattering like a budgie during their breaks, laughing and joking with the carters and the errand boys.

'Ach, he'll have forgotten all about it,' she said airily when

Elspeth wondered aloud when retribution was going to fall on them both. 'If he'd meant tae tell on us he'd have done it right away. Besides, we didnae steal anythin', or break anythin', did we?'

'I touched the typewriter, and spoiled a sheet of paper.'

'With the money he has, he can afford tae lose a hundred sheets of paper. And it'll teach you tae keep your hands tae yourself in future, miss. Now stop worryin' about it,' Lena ordered. 'Ye're like a wee ghost. Ye'll make yerself ill if ye don't watch out.'

Flora already thought that Elspeth was sickening for something, and had made her take a spoonful of her favourite cure-all, brimstone and treacle. For once, Elspeth had swallowed it down without protest, for she knew that she wouldn't feel better until she had received some form of punishment for what she had done, and if Mr James Brodie had indeed decided to let them off this time, the nasty-tasting medicine would do instead.

When nothing had been said after three days, she allowed herself to relax, trying to push the shameful episode to the back of her mind so that she could concentrate on the last frantic whirl of getting the trousseau finished.

To everyone's surprise, they managed it. Mrs Bruce and her daughter gave their grudging approval to the garments that had been made in a very short time, Miss Buchanan stopped behaving like a whirling dervish and Miss Arnold permitted herself a slight smile as she congratulated the seamstresses on their hard work.

There was even a small bonus payment made to each of the women. Elspeth used hers to buy a little brooch for Aunt Flora, some tobacco for Uncle Henry, ribbons for Rachel, and a new pen for Mattie.

'Ye should have spent it on yerself, lassie,' Flora said, surprisingly, when the gifts were handed out. 'Ye've worked hard and almost made yerself ill intae the bargain.'

But Elspeth, still suffering from guilt over what she had done in Mr James Brodie's office, had no desire to spend a penny of the money on herself, or even to put it into her savings. As she saw it, she was buying back a clear conscience by spending her bonus on others. She bought a small poke of raspberry balls for Granjan, who doted on them, and since she couldn't think of a gift for Grandmother, she went out into the countryside on her way to visit the old lady and picked a bunch of flowers.

Celia Bremner's eyebrows shot up at the sight of the pale pink wild roses and red campion. 'What's this?'

'I thought you'd like them, Grandmother. The fields are looking pretty just now, and I wanted you to see what's growing there.'

'Unexpected gifts,' said Grandmother shrewdly, 'are usually the sign of a guilty conscience. Have you been up to something, child?'

Elspeth's mouth dropped open, and she felt the beginnings of a blush warm her face. 'No, Grandmother.'

'I hope not. Very well, you may put them in the small glass vase you'll find at the back of the middle shelf above the sink. And bring a tray cloth with you, to put under the vase. Flowers drop petals and make a mess. It'll be easier to gather it all up if it falls on the cloth.'

Filling the vase and drying it carefully before arranging the flowers in it, Elspeth wished that she hadn't bothered picking them. She was sure that under Grandmother's baleful stare the poor things would wilt and die earlier than they might have in anyone else's house. She wondered if this was the way her grandmother had treated her mother, and if so, how Maisie had managed to be as bright and happy as Granjan said she was. Elspeth was sure that if she herself had had to grow up in Grandmother's house she would have wilted away very quickly.

Carrying the vase carefully back into the living room, a

clean tray cloth draped over one arm, she was grateful to Aunt Flora for having taken her in, instead of leaving her to her grandmother's tender mercies.

On the day of the Bruce wedding, the last Saturday in August, Mattie, Lena, Elspeth and Rachel walked to Gourock to see the bridal party emerge from the church. It was a beautiful day – 'It wouldnae dare tae be anythin' else, for the Bruces,' Lena said scornfully – and the bride's white satin dress, embroidered with silver threads, shimmered in the sunshine as she and her groom emerged from the church's cool darkness and paused on the top step.

An awed murmur rose from the women clustered round the gate. Many of them were pale and thin, grey-faced from over-work and worry and lack of nourishment. In the main, the clothes they wore were shabby, and most of them carried small children and had toddlers whining impatiently round their skirts. Marriage had done little for them, and yet, Elspeth thought, taking a moment to note the way their tired, dull eyes brightened and softened at the sight of the newly married couple, they still loved to see a wedding, and still clung to the hope that for someone else it would turn out to be the roman-tic, happy-ever-after story they had dreamed of for themselves as young girls.

'Would you look at that dress,' Rachel sighed, eyeing the panels of embroidered lace draping into points at each side of the mid-calf-length skirt.

'And the veil,' Mattie marvelled, as a light breeze caught the fragile lace, causing it to drift round the bride's head. 'Isn't it bonny? Was it made at Brodie's too?'

'I heard it was her mother's,' Lena informed her. 'Italian lace. It must've cost a fortune just on its own.'

As the rest of the wedding party came out to join the bride and groom, the women at the gate crowded closer, peering through the bars at the beautiful clothes, the smart hats, the

73

jewellery sparkling at the women's throats and ears and wrists and fingers.

The precious stones were no doubt real and very beautiful, but Elspeth, putting her hand up to caress the pebble brooch Thomas had given her, wouldn't have exchanged it for all the diamonds and rubies and pearls and sapphires adorning the Bruce women and their guests. The minister, moving here and there among the guests in his sober black robes, looked like a crow socialising with a flock of peacocks.

The five bridesmaids were as pretty as a bunch of daffodils as they grouped together in their yellow muslin gowns. Wide-brimmed straw hats in the same shade as the dresses were tied under their chins with long pale gold ribbons.

As one of them stepped aside from the rest to talk to a tall young man in naval uniform, she took her hat off to reveal the pale gold rose nestling against the crown. She turned to smile at the women clustering round the gate, and Elspeth recognised her as Aileen Bruce, the girl she had seen in the fitting room. Her hair, black as ebony, was cut short and clung to her small, neat skull.

Lena's eyes were on the naval officer. 'Ooh, he's a bit of all right! Lucky her, with him for a sweetheart!'

One of the women standing beside them let out a cackle of amusement. 'That's not her sweetheart, that's Ian, her brother. I should know, 'cos I used to work in Mrs Bruce's kitchens before I got married.'

'Which of them's *his* sweetheart, then?' Lena wanted to know, and the woman shrugged.

'Don't ask me. When I worked there he was only a lad at school, but even so, every girl who came tae the house made eyes at him.'

'I'm not surprised.' Lena clutched at the railings, almost forcing her body through them in her attempt to watch Ian Bruce as he moved with his sister through the throng on the gravel sweep before the church. 'He's lovely!'

'I wouldnae mind a few hours alone with him,' one of the other women said, and there was a squeal of laughter when Lena wriggled her shoulders and retorted, 'You're slow – I'd only need a few minutes!'

Hooves clattered on the road behind them as the carriages that had been waiting a short distance away came up to form a line at the gates. The elderly horses that drew them – all the young, fit horses had been commandeered for the war effort – had been groomed until their coats shone, and flowers had been pleated into their manes and tails. Ushers crunched down the gravel drive to open the gates, and the onlookers fell back to form a guard of honour on the pavement as the wedding party prepared to leave for the reception at the Bruces' large house.

Elspeth raised herself on tiptoe and craned her neck to take in everything she could. Seen close to, the wedding dress and veil were the loveliest, most fragile things she had ever seen. A thousand points of light blazed from the small tiara on the bride's dark head, and the cloudy veil was so fine that it surely must have been spun by angels from happy dreams, she thought, lifted into a rare and unexpected transport of poetic fantasy by the colour and excitement of the occasion.

The bridegroom, a thin-faced young man smart in the uniform of an army captain, walked with a very slight limp, a relic from the wound which had sent him home from France for a few months and made this summer wedding possible. The limp and the uniform added to the romance of the occasion, and a faint sigh of sympathy rippled across the onlookers as he handed his bride into their carriage. Its seats were covered with white satin, and flowers were scattered here and there among the rich snowy folds.

Aileen Bruce dipped a slim hand into her brother's pocket and brought out a small paper bag. Hurrying after the newly-wed couple, she sprayed a fountain of rice over them just as they were getting into their carriage. The women crowding the pavement on both sides of the open gates squealed and laughed as stinging pellets of rice fell among them, and Aileen laughed back at them before gathering up her skirt and springing nimbly into the second carriage, followed by the other bridesmaids.

Mr and Mrs Bruce, he in top hat and tails, she in powder-blue silk with a cluster of deep blue feathers pinned to the brim of her hat, were ushered into their carriage by their son, who then stepped up to sit beside them, looking neither to right nor to left. Viewed from close quarters, he was the handsomest man Elspeth had ever seen, even on the cinema screen. Lena clutched at her wrist as he passed by, her nails digging into the skin, and hissed dramatically, 'I'd die for a man like that, so I would!'

After the guests had swept away in their carriages, a small group of men and women who had followed the others out of the church and had hung back during the general movement to the carriages, came down the drive, accompanied by the minister. The four women were in nursing uniforms, and some of the men also wore uniform – the dark blue of the navy, or army khaki, with two in the lighter blue of the air force. Others were in civilian clothing. Some wore slings, some had crutches, one was missing an arm, his empty sleeve neatly pinned up.

One or two members of the small group bore no outward sign of wounds, but like many of the women on the pavement, they were gaunt and stamped with the marks of suffering. One young man, who had a tearing, rasping cough that sounded as though he was shredding his lungs, pressed a large handkerchief to his mouth every time an attack started, as though ashamed to be associated with such a harsh sound.

The onlookers fell silent, knowing that these were some of the men living at the Bruces' big house, part of which had been turned into a convalescent home for wounded military. Some of the women on the pavement reached out to touch a shoulder or a hand, or called, 'Good luck tae ye, laddies,' or

'Bless ye,' as, with the help of the nurses, the men boarded a wagon that had halted at the church gate.

When the wagon had departed and the church gates were closed the girls strolled silently back to Greenock, each caught up in her own thoughts. Glancing at them, reading their expressions, Elspeth was certain that Rachel was thinking longingly of the bride's clothes, and Lena of the bride's brother. Mattie looked as though she was musing over the pleasure of being involved, even briefly and from the sidelines, in something out of the ordinary.

Elspeth herself, as they walked home, started composing her next letter to Thomas, who, as he worked for the Bruce family and hoped to continue working for them when he was finally free of his war duties, would surely want to know all about the wedding. She was also thinking of the convalescent men she had just seen, and about Lachlan.

8

Although at first it was understood that Lachlan's arm wound was not serious, he was still in a French hospital at the end of August. His letters, dictated to one of the nurses there, were very brief, merely informing his worried parents that he was recovering and being well looked after. There were no letters for Elspeth, nor did she expect any under the circumstances.

She herself wrote to him every week, as usual, making her own letters as cheerful and amusing as she could, avoiding any reference to his wound, or to the likelihood of him being sent back to his battalion when he was fit again.

Flora continued to fret about her younger son. 'If it's takin' so long for him tae get better, how can it only be a mild wound?' she repeatedly asked her family, who knew no more than she herself did. 'It must be worse than they're lettin' on. It's gone gangrenous, that's what's happened. He'll have tae have it cut off, and what'll become of him then? How can he work in the shipyards with only one arm, tell me that? Or mebbe they'll not cut it off in time, and he'll die, out there in that hospital where he doesnae know anyone, and they don't even talk the same language as he does—'

'Come on now, lass,' Henry would interrupt at this point, his voice rough with his own worry. 'If he was as bad as that they'd tell us. Anyway, there'll be army nurses and doctors there, as British as he is. Who d'ye think writes his letters for him? A Frenchie nurse couldnae do that, now, could she? He'll be fine, you wait and see.'

Thomas, still in Belgium, did his best to find someone who knew about his brother's battalion and could tell him what might be happening to Lachlan, but with no luck. There was nothing to do but wait and worry and hope.

By the end of September the tide of war had firmly turned in the Allies' favour. The Germans were being swept back all along the Western Front, yielding yard by yard at first, then mile by mile. This meant that Thomas, in Belgium, was now in the thick of it all, and between fretting about him at war and Lachlan in hospital, Flora, weakened by worry, fell victim to the Spanish 'flu that swept across Europe, killing hundreds of people already battered by years of deprivation and suffering because of the war.

In Flora's case, it was so bad that she had to be taken into the Greenock and District Combination Hospital. Without her, the small flat immediately began to resemble a yacht at sea, suddenly deprived of sails and keel and tossing helplessly on the waves. The three girls did their best to keep things going, but without Flora at her usual place in the kitchen, there was a frightening sense of uncertainty about the place.

Nobody was allowed to visit the ward where Flora lay with other 'flu victims, in case the visitors themselves caught the infection. The nurses and doctors, it was said, were going down like flies themselves.

Henry, a strong and confident man in the shipyard, collapsed like a deflated ball, and spent all his time at home sitting gazing into the fire, scarcely hearing a word that was said to him, his pipe, usually puffing tobacco smoke into the air, empty and clenched between his teeth.

'It's like looking at a whipped dog,' Mattie said nervously one evening as the three girls sat in their tiny bedroom. They had taken to spending most of their time there, because they felt like interlopers, sitting in the kitchen with Henry and his silent grief.

'He's hurting, and he doesn't know what to do about it. If he could just see her it might help him.'

'It wouldnae do her any good, though, would it?' Rachel said. 'It'd only make her feel worse, that long face of his hanging over her bed. She'd be certain that she wasn't going to survive.'

When Granjan moved in and took over her daughter's responsibilities, things became a little easier. No matter how worried she herself might have felt about Flora, she didn't show it in the slightest. Instead, she bustled round the kitchen, cooking delicious meals, chattering cheerfully, bullying Henry out of his trance and on to his feet.

She found all sorts of odd jobs for him to do, fastening down a corner of linoleum in the hall that had been threatening for months to trip up unwary feet, tightening drawer handles, whitewashing the kitchen ceiling.

'Now's yer chance tae get things done,' she would say, almost forcing a brush or a hammer or a screwdriver into his hand, nagging him to his feet when all he wanted to do was sit and stare into the fire. 'Think how pleased Flora'll be when she comes home tae find everythin' done. Ye know how much she hates a mess – best see tae it all while she's tucked up in her hospital bed, not knowin' a thing about it.'

She made him paint the woodwork throughout the small flat and re-paper the kitchen, searching Greenock and Port Glasgow herself for paint and paper, scarce commodities. With the help of the three girls she herself scrubbed the rugs and polished the linoleum and washed the curtains and cleaned the windows.

'We've got tae get it all done before Flora comes home,' she kept saying, and gradually, in the face of her persistence, Henry and the girls began to think of the time when Flora was well again, instead of wondering if that day would ever come.

At night, Elspeth lay in bed long after Mattie and Rachel

had drifted off to sleep, praying for Flora's recovery, suffering agonies of guilt over the number of times she had upset and annoyed the older woman, wishing that she could have been a model foster daughter, worthy of all that had been done for her, and that she herself had been struck down instead of Flora.

She even promised herself that she would never again upset Flora, if only she could recover and come home. Knowing all too well from bitter experience how easy it was to do or say the wrong thing without even knowing that in Flora's eyes it was wrong, she was uncomfortably aware that she would probably not be able to keep those promises.

It was so difficult, she thought, to live by other people's standards.

When she woke up one morning with a sore throat and aching joints, she was convinced that her prayers had been answered, and that she had been given the chance to bear Flora's illness in her place. But it turned out to be ordinary influenza, and after a few days of Granjan's nursing, she was up and about again, though pale and shaky.

By that time, Flora was on the mend, and had been moved into an open ward. Elspeth had to stay behind when the others visited her, in case, in her own enfeebled state, she re-infected herself or her aunt. Mattie and Rachel were awed by their mother's fragility.

'I've never seen her like that before, all pale and thin and just lying there, with her hair down in two plaits,' said Mattie.

'I have,' Rachel told her. 'When you were born.'

Henry, who stayed on by his wife's side when the others left, looked more like his old self when he got back. 'She gave me dog's abuse when I told her we'd been paintin' and paperin' the place. Said I should've waited until she was home tae see what I was up tae. That's your fault,' he accused his mother-in-law.

'Indeed it is not, it's yours for waggin' yer silly tongue,' she snapped back, a gleam in her eyes. 'She's quite right when she says ye should've known better – better than tae go tellin' her!'

'Ach, she got it out of me. I was never good at keepin' anythin' from Flora.'

'That's the best way for a married man tae be,' his mother-in-law told him drily. ''Specially if it includes his wages. It saves a lot of quarrelling.'

'It didnae save me from a tellin'-off. The whole ward was listenin', tae. I didnae know where tae put my face.'

'That shows she's getting better.' Janet, who only reached halfway up Henry's waistcoat but matched him in width, craned up towards his chin, sniffing loudly. 'I didnae know they sold beer in the hospital.'

He reddened and retreated to his usual armchair, picking up his pipe and reaching for his tobacco pouch.

'Ach, I met some o' the lads on my way home and went for a wee drink with them.'

'That's another thing ye don't want tae go tellin' Flora when ye visit her tomorrow night,' Janet said, grinning at the girls, who beamed back. After almost two weeks of sucking at an empty bowl, the man of the house was filling his pipe again. Flora McDonald was going to recover, and all was well with her household.

A few days later Elspeth returned to the sewing room, which was almost empty because many of the women, including Miss Buchanan, were off with 'flu.

'But not Miss Arnold,' Lena said sadly after getting a lecture from the overseer for chattering when she should have been working. 'There's not an influenza germ that'd dare tae touch her.'

'I notice you didn't get it,' Elspeth pointed out, and her friend grinned.

'The devil looks after his own. Any word about your Lachlan?'

'He's been moved to a hospital in England.'

Lena's brows rose. 'What for?'

'I don't know. The letter just said that he'd been moved, and they'd let us know when he was coming home.'

'That means he's finished with the fightin'. My dad says it'll all be over soon, so they'll surely not send him back now.'

'I suppose not.' Elspeth knew that she should be happy for Lachlan, safe in Britain and away from the front line. Wasn't this what she had wanted for him? But as she settled some material beneath the sewing machine, she wondered, as they were all wondering at home, why Lachlan was still in hospital, and why they hadn't been told more about his condition.

Flora, who firmly refused to go to a convalescent home, returned to her family, pale, thin, still weak, but determined to take up her usual everyday life as quickly as possible. She inspected the decorating that had been done during her absence, and grudgingly admitted that it 'wasn't too bad'.

'It was mebbe as well tae get it seen tae, with our Lachlan comin' home soon,' she decided, sinking into a fireside chair. 'Mattie, put the kettle on, I've been parched for a decent cup of tea these last few weeks. I cannae be doin' with being ill. It's all a nonsense.'

A nonsense that had claimed victims throughout the town, including two in their tenement, an elderly woman who lived alone on the ground floor, and a three-month-old baby, the first child of a couple on the second floor, conceived during her father's last leave from the Royal Navy.

Flora had fully recovered her strength by the time the war finally came to an end in November. That evening, Greenock held one big street party, and Elspeth, Rachel and Mattie wandered round the packed town, enjoying a sense of freedom that they had never known before. Hundreds of thousands of men and women on both sides had lost their lives during the struggle, and proper mourning for them would come later, but for that evening, all people wanted was a chance to mark the end of the conflict.

From the shipyards and from the vessels moored at the Tail o' the Bank came the clamour of sirens, and in the town itself everyone who could play a fiddle or an accordion or even a penny whistle had brought it along. Cars and buses and tram-cars, nudging their way slowly and patiently along the streets, tooted their horns or clanged their bells, while those hanging out of the windows had plenty of time to shake hands with the people all around before passing on their way.

Groups of women and children and old men leaned on every tenement windowsill, calling down to the crowds below. Folk were hugging and kissing total strangers, talking and laughing with them like old friends, drinking and dancing together. Here and there, couples had opted out of the crush and could be seen closely entwined in shop doorways and close-mouths, oblivious to everyone else.

They met Lena and some of the other girls from the sewing room, arm in arm with a group of foreign seamen, most of the men clutching bottles of beer. When they were introduced, Lena's escort, a young giant of a man with a thatch of black curly hair, insisted on kissing all three of them. His mouth was wet and rubbery, and tasted of drink, and it was a relief when he and Lena moved on and Rachel, Mattie and Elspeth were able to scrub at their mouths with handkerchiefs.

'I don't know how Lena can enjoy kissing the likes of him.' Mattie's face was wrinkled with distaste. 'It was terrible! I think he tried to put his tongue in my mouth, too.'

'He did not!' Elspeth was scandalised at the very thought.

'Either that, or he'd three lips. If that's what kissing's like, I'm not going to bother getting myself a boyfriend.'

'Bob doesn't kiss like that at all,' Rachel put in quickly. 'It must be because that man's foreign.'

'Oh, so Bob's kissed you, then?' Mattie winked at Elspeth as her sister blushed deeply. Until now, Rachel had refused to admit that she and Bob were anything but good friends.

'If you must know, he kissed me goodbye the last time he was home on leave. And he's asked me to marry him.'

'Rachel!' The two younger girls stopped and eyed her with a new respect.

Rachel preened and simpered, enjoying her moment in the limelight. 'I haven't said I will, so don't you go telling Mam when there's nothing at all to tell.'

'But you'll say yes, won't you? When he comes home from the army?' Elspeth thought it was all very romantic.

'I might – and I might not, so not a word,' Rachel cautioned, and they both crossed their hearts, then Elspeth, looking beyond Rachel, said in astonishment, 'Granjan! What are you doing here?'

'Celebratin' the end o' the fightin', same as you.' Janet Docherty was bright-eyed and flushed with excitement. One arm was closely linked to her neighbour, Mrs Begg, and from the elbow of the other dangled the shiny black leather handbag only brought out on special occasions. It was bulging, as usual, because Janet made a point of taking everything of importance with her when she went out, just in case she got knocked down and taken to hospital, and needed her personal papers. 'Bein' old doesnae mean we cannae have a celebration, does it, Teenie?'

'I'm just glad I lived tae see the day,' Mrs Begg confirmed, dipping her head up and down energetically. With her small sharp eyes and her long thin nose, the gesture made her look like a bird drinking from a puddle. 'Though we'll no' be out too long. The town's too crowded for my liking.'

'Ach away wi' ye, it's just grand tae see all the folk so happy,' Janet chided her. 'How's Flora? Are Henry and her not out in the streets too?'

'My dad went to have a drink with his mates, but Mam's at home,' Rachel explained. 'She says she's happy just sitting on her own, thinking about Thomas and Lachlan coming home soon.'

'Aye, right enough, it's grand tae think that we'll get them back again,' Janet agreed. 'Come on now, Teenie, we'd best be off and let the lassies enjoy themselves,' and the two elderly women forged on through the crowds.

A group of people were dancing in Cathcart Square; for a while the girls stood and watched, then they too were pulled into the dance. Elspeth's partner was a burly man in civilian clothes, probably a shipworker who, like Uncle Henry, had been excused military service because he was needed in the yards. As they revolved under a streetlamp, she saw that beneath a bushy moustache his grinning mouth revealed tobacco-stained teeth. His hands were hot and damp as they clasped hers, spinning her round and round until her feet were almost lifted from the cobbles.

'Don't worry, hen, I'll no' let ye fall,' he bellowed, seeing the panic in her face. It was a relief when the music ended and she was able to stop, one arm looped about a lamp standard because the square was still whirling about her head.

'Here – this'll steady ye,' the man said, pushing an opened bottle under her nose.

'No – no thank you.' She tried to pull back, but the bottle followed, nuzzling insistently against her mouth.

'Go on, a wee drop'll no' hurt ye.'

'I don't want it.'

'Let's have another dance, then,' he wheedled as the accordionist started up again. He tried to draw her back on to the cobbles, a hand about her waist, but she clung to the lamppost, shaking her head.

'It's time I was getting home.'

'On a night like this? The war doesnae end every day, hen. We'll dance the night away an' have somethin' tae tell our grandweans, eh?'

'I have to go,' Elspeth insisted, breaking free, backing away from his clutching hands. There were so many people about that it was easy to plunge back into the crowd, away from him. That same crush, however, made it impossible for her to find Mattie and Rachel. She worked her way round the square in search of them, then, deciding that the task was impossible, she began to struggle out of the square, along Hamilton Street. There was no fun in being out on her own; she might as well make for Mearns Street and home.

It had been possible to walk along the crowded streets when there were three of them linked together, forging a path through the crush. Alone, Elspeth found, it was a different matter. She kept getting forced back by the sheer numbers moving towards Cathcart Square, drawn by the jaunty music. It seemed to be a matter, as Flora McDonald tended to say on a busy day, of one step forward and two steps back all the time.

Once, when a drunken French sailor unexpectedly scooped her up and whirled her round above the heads of the passers-by, she thought that she glimpsed Rachel on the other side of the road.

''Ello, pretty mademoiselle,' the young man yelled above the general noise as he set her down again. He attempted a gallant bow, but his feet betrayed him, sending him stumbling side-ways. His friends, roaring with laughter, caught him before he landed among a sea of feet, and carried him off with them, while Elspeth, beginning to lose her nerve now that she was on her own, launched herself off the edge of the pavement and across the road.

9

When she got to the opposite pavement Rachel was nowhere to be seen. Elspeth struggled on in the direction of home, then realised after a few stumbling steps that she had turned round without being aware of it and was heading back to Cathcart Square. She started to retrace her steps, only to run into the man who had danced with her earlier.

'There ye are, hen, I've been lookin' for ye. Come on, just a wee dance—'

He got a firm grip on her wrist this time, and started towing her back in the direction of the accordion music, pushing his way through the crowds. Elspeth pulled back, but couldn't break his grip. A gap cleared to one side of her, and she wrenched herself towards it in the hope that her change of direction would catch him by surprise, only to find that she had made a mistake. Her sudden sideways lunge had taken them to the inside of the pavement, and instead of pulling her onwards, he now crowded her against the wall of a tenement building.

'D'ye no' want tae dance?'

'I want to go home!'

'A wee kiss first, eh? A wee kiss tae celebrate a great day—'

'No!' She tried to wriggle away, but she was pinned between his large body and the wall. He clamped his arms round her, at the same time shuffling along sideways like the crabs she had sometimes seen on the shore when she played there as a

88

child. Elspeth couldn't understand what he was doing until the wall suddenly dipped away from behind her and she staggered back a step or two before coming up against another solid obstruction. He had eased her into the doorway of a shop, out of the way of the people flocking past.

Elspeth, panicking, kicked out at him and tried to push him away. He laughed at her, crowding her more closely against the shop door.

'I like a lassie wi' spirit,' he said, then kissed her hard, pushing her lips against her teeth, forcing her head back until it was jammed against the door. It was as though he was trying to force his own face right through hers. She was sure that he was going to succeed, and the bones of her face were going to give way. Mattie had been right about Lena's boyfriend kissing her with his tongue as well as his mouth. This man was doing the same, and disgust and revulsion almost choked her.

One of his hands managed to insert itself between their bodies, crawling like a spider over her until it reached her breast, where it fastened hungrily. A year earlier, he would have had nothing to clutch, but since the summer her body had fleshed out, maturing at what seemed to Elspeth to be an incredible and embarrassing speed. Before then her measurements had been more or less the same from shoulder to thigh, but now her waist had slimmed down, while her breasts and hips had rounded out.

She tried to scream, but he was pinioning her mouth with his own, and it was difficult enough to breathe, let alone shout. Even if she had been able to make any sound it was unlikely that anybody would have heeded; there was so much noise in the street that even a loud yell could have gone unnoticed.

He was pushing himself against her now in short, rhythmic thrusts, while one knee tried to intrude between her legs.

The separate, onlooking part of her mind suddenly fled, unable to tolerate what was happening, and sheer terror gripped Elspeth. She couldn't breathe, she was at the mercy of this man she had never met or seen before. She was going to die, her mind screamed at her. She was going to die, either of suffocation or from what he was about to do to her.

Her understanding of the sexual act had always been sketchy, made up as it was by only half-believed information from her schoolfriend Molly, giggling comments overheard in the sewing room, and magazines and novelettes she and Mattie had smuggled into their bedroom. The foster-sisters had mulled over what they knew of the subject frequently, and between them had tended towards the romantic side, with the men always honourable and respectful towards their women-folk.

Now, as the stranger's knee managed to prise her legs apart and his hand tightened painfully on her left breast, Elspeth knew that she and Mattie had been wrong in their assumptions. Love wasn't as essential as they had thought – there was a physical relationship too, one that had nothing to do with tenderness or respect, but everything to do with hurting and perhaps even killing.

The noise that had been beating in her ears since she had ventured on to the streets began to fade, the glow of the gas streetlights to dim. She closed her eyes tightly to shut out the face pressing against hers, and flashing lights seared the inside of her lids.

The man lurched back slightly, releasing her mouth and breast, moving his hand downwards. She felt his knuckles pushing painfully into her stomach as he apparently fumbled with his belt. Sucking air into her starving lungs, Elspeth made one last bid for freedom, lurching towards the pavement with its continual flow of passers-by. He reached out a long arm and wrapped it about her, hauling her back against the door, moving his body so that it formed a blockade between her and the people only a matter of a yard away in the street.

'Hold still, ye stupid bi—' he started to say, then suddenly grunted, lurching hard against her so that the air she had managed to drag into her lungs was forced out again by the weight of his body.

'Ye dirty midden, ye,' a familiar voice yelled. 'I'll teach ye tae put yer mucky hands on my grandwean, Johnny Lafferty!'

The man pulled back, spinning to face the street. 'Ow!' she heard him yelp as a well-aimed blow from Janet Docherty's best handbag landed on his nose. He tried to retreat sideways along the shopfront, hands thrown up before his face to protect it from the blows raining on him. 'For God's sake, missus!'

'Keep God out o' it, foul-tongued blasphemer that ye are!' Janet was smaller than he was, but she managed to keep aiming blows at his face by bouncing like a rubber ball with each swing of the bag. Mrs Begg, bleating, 'Oh dear, lassie, oh dear!' put her arms about Elspeth, who was sagging at the knees.

Despite the noise in the street, Janet's outraged yells and the howls of the man now cowering against the shop front attracted attention. A small crowd gathered to watch and laugh, their backs forming a wall around which the rest of the revellers flowed.

'The dirty bastard was tryin' tae attack my grandwean,' Janet informed them between blows. 'And her only a wee bit of a lassie!'

'I didnae ken she was yer grandwean,' the man wailed, then, appealing to the onlookers, 'I didnae ken!'

'Mebbe no', but ye must've kent she was someone's grandwean, ye filthy pig, ye! An' you a grown man wi' a wife, God help her, an' six weans of yer ain!' said Janet, and aimed another blow at him. Because he had lowered his arms in order to appeal to the crowd, her best handbag landed fairly on his nose, and he yelped like a beaten dog.

The onlookers were all on Janet's side. 'That's right, missus, you show him,' a man shouted, while others jeered at the drunk, and a woman screeched, 'I ken him tae – a worthless piece o' scum that's nae use tae his wife except for fatherin' more and more bairns on the poor sowl!'

'Mercy me,' said Mrs Begg in distress, doing her best to cover Elspeth's ears.

'Here's a polisman, missus,' someone called out. 'Hand the rascal over tae him.'

Janet stood back, the first white-hot rush of anger spent. 'Ach, let him run tae his hole, stinkin' rat that he is,' she said with sudden dignity, and the crowd, respecting her right to decide, stood back to let the man go, then melted away as the policeman approached.

'Are ye all right, pet?' Janet asked anxiously, gathering Elspeth from Mrs Begg's arms, then, as Elspeth nodded, beyond speech for the moment, 'Here, Teenie, you take her on that side and I'll take her on this, and we'll get her out of here.'

'Are ye taking her home tae her mammy?' Mrs Begg asked above Elspeth's bowed head as the three of them struggled along towards Nicolson Street.

'Have ye lost the wits God gave ye, woman? Can ye see our Flora's face if we take the bairn back lookin' like this? We'll take her tae my house and get her tidied up first.'

Back in Granjan's cosy little flat in Nicolson Street, Mrs Begg made tea while Janet washed Elspeth's face and hands and combed her hair, talking soothingly as she worked.

'Thank goodness I caught a sight of ye when ye were tryin' tae get away from that drunken lout. No sense frettin' over what didnae happen, is there? Ye've got a split lip on ye, hen.' She dabbed gently at Elspeth's mouth. 'But that's easy explained tae yer Auntie Flora – ye'll no' be the only one in Greenock tonight tae walk intae a lamppost in all that crush.'

'I've got a wee bit of whisky in my kitchen cupboard. Will I fetch it and we can put some in her tea tae help her get over the shock?' suggested Mrs Begg, who lived across the landing.

'And take her back tae Flora smellin' of drink? For goodness' sake, Teenie! She'll be fine, won't ye, pet? All she needs is a good strong cup of tea with plenty of sugar in it.'

She was right. By the time the cup was half empty Elspeth was feeling more like herself, though Granjan was still seething.

'That Johnny Lafferty's always been a midden, so he has.'

'He was drunk, he didn't know what he was doing.' Now that the nightmare was over Elspeth felt a shred of pity for the man who had so quickly turned into a whining child under her grandmother's relentless attack.

'The man's never sober. That poor wife of his has a lot tae put up with!'

'Where d'you know him from, Granjan?'

'From here. He lives up above.' Janet Docherty glared up at the ceiling. 'I should push the handle of my broom clean through right now an' hope it'd come out right where he's standing. I'd do it too, if it wasnae that I feel so sorry for Liza. She's got no chance of a decent life with him, and most of her bairns'll probably grow up tae be like their wastrel of a faither, then she'll have even more heartbreak.'

She shook her head in sorrow, then went on briskly, with a change of tone 'Now – finish yer tea, and Teenie and me'll see ye back home. Flora'll be frettin' about ye, specially if Rachel and Mattie are home already. Mind, now, all ye need tae tell her is that ye met up with some friends, then got pushed intae a lamppost by accident in the crush. And put that man out of yer mind, hen. There's plenty of fools like him in the world, but with any luck ye'll never meet up with another of them. If ye do, and yer as close tae him as ye were tae Johnny, take my advice and bring yer knee up like this – see? It fair takes their mind off any further ill-doin'.'

'Janet!' Mrs Begg screeched as Granjan demonstrated by lifting one plump knee up sharply, almost overbalancing.

'Ach, stop yer scrakin', Teenie Begg. Lassies should know these things. That's what saved me more than once in my own young days. Come on, then, pet, time you were home. And I'd be grateful,' Janet added as she helped Elspeth on with her coat, 'if ye'd no' let on tae yer Auntie Flora that I used the word "bastard" in front of ye. It was all said in the heat of the moment, hen.'

Elspeth had always thought that once the war was over, every-thing would get back to normal, but instead, life went on as usual for several months. There was still a shortage of food and clothing, and most of the men were still away from home. Women still did men's work in the factories and shipyards, and on the buses and trams as clippies and drivers.

Round about Christmas time the foreign ships began to depart from the river and the first of the Greenock men returned home. Among them was Bob Cochran, Rachel's sweetheart. Rachel went about with a permanent smile on her face, but Bob, never a chatterbox, had become even more morose during his time away. When he did speak it was usu-ally to complain about the way the soldiers had been treated by officers who knew nothing, but thought they were superior just because they had been brought up in posh houses and went to posh schools.

His other complaint was about conditions in the shipyard where he had taken up his former job.

'What did we fight for, tell me that?' he would demand, sit-ting opposite Henry in the McDonalds' kitchen, his booted feet sprawled across the rag rug. 'What did we risk our lives for, and live in muddy water up to our knees for? Tae build a better world, they told us.' A contemptuous jerk of his close-cropped head towards the hall door indicated that 'they', the officers and shipyard owners and others of their ilk, existed somewhere outside the tenement. 'But what's better about it, tell me that? I'm no' paid any more than I was before I went away. I'm no' treated any better. A land fit for heroes? That's not what I'd call it!'

'He's an awful moaner, isn't he?' Mattie said in disgust when she and Elspeth had escaped to the bedroom, Elspeth to write letters, Mattie to do her homework. 'I don't remember him making such a fuss about everything before. He was quite nice then.'

'He's got a right to be angry, I suppose.' Elspeth was curled up at the head of the bed, trying to get as close as she could to the gas mantle, which didn't give out much light. Mattie was sitting on Rachel's bed, beneath the other mantle. 'He must've had a hard time of it, and then he comes home to find that things are no better than they were before.'

'I'd think more of him if he made the best of it,' Mattie said flatly. 'I don't know what Rachel still sees in him. He looks so – hard, doesn't he? Mebbe he'll look better when his hair grows back.'

They collapsed in giggles, remembering Bob's first visit to the flat after leaving the army. Before going off to war, he had had a fine head of light brown hair, thick and soft, but to Rachel's dismay he had come home for good with his hair cropped even more ruthlessly than army regulations demanded, so close to his scalp that the skin shone through. The shaven head, accentuated by his thick, short neck and powerful shoulders, gave him a menacing look.

'Och, Bob, why did you let them cut your nice hair so short?' Rachel had asked, running her hand over the stubble. Then she pulled her fingers back sharply as her beloved said, 'Nits.'

'Nits?' Rachel almost screamed the word, wiping her hand hurriedly on her skirt, while Henry stopped in the act of knocking out his pipe, and Flora gasped. Head lice were common in the Greenock tenements, but Flora had worked hard to keep her own children's heads clean, combing their hair with a special close-toothed comb every day, washing their heads with strong-smelling coal-tar soap that they all hated. To the McDonald household, nits meant dirt and squalor.

'We was alive with the wee bu—' Bob shot a look at Flora and suddenly remembered where he was, '—blighters in the trenches. If we hadnae had our heads shaved we'd've been too busy clawin' at ourselves tae shoot back at the Jerries.' Then, as Rachel moaned softly, 'Ach, don't make such a fuss. I've been well scrubbed wi' disinfectant since then. They're all gone – and the body lice tae. What else can ye expect?' he went on as Rachel retreated from the arm of his chair, shuddering. 'We was crowded together for weeks on end in these trenches, never findin' the time tae change our clothes, let alone clean them.'

A sneer brushed across his mouth as he surveyed the horror in the faces around him. 'Ye know a pal's really a pal when ye've shared nits an' fleas with him,' he said, then the sneer changed to a hoot of derisive laughter.

'D'you think Thomas and Lachlan'll have their hair all cut off too?' Mattie said when the girls' giggles had died down. Without being aware of her actions she ran a pencil through her own brown curls, using it to scratch at the scalp beneath.

'How should I know?'

'You write to them both.'

'Nits aren't the sort of thing you ask about in letters. I see that Aunt Flora's bought in some extra-strong soap, and another bottle of Jeyes fluid,' Elspeth said, then she and Mattie shuddered in unison.

10

Thomas arrived home in the middle of February, a week after his twenty-third birthday. His brown hair had been cut short, but not nearly as short as Bob's. It clung round his scalp in curls, and his boyish body had filled out, not with fat, but with muscle. There was a new awareness in his eyes, too, but apart from that he was the Thomas they all knew well, still cheerful, happy to be back, with none of Bob's bitter resentment at the war that had torn him from home and family.

'It wasnae a picnic, and I'd not want tae go through it again,' he said as he enjoyed his first home-cooked meal, 'but a lot more had it worse than me, losing their lives or bits of their bodies, or their homes and everything they had in life. And I'm talking about civilians too, not just soldiers. Those poor souls in France and Belgium that saw their towns and villages turned into battlefields – it'll take them a long time tae get back to a normal life.'

He waited until the meal was over, and the neighbours who had crowded into the flat to welcome him back had eventually returned to their own homes, before telling his family that he had visited Lachlan on his way home.

Flora was overjoyed. 'How is he? How's his arm?'

'It's fine, Mam, all mended, and only a wee scar to show where the bullet went in. Lucky for him it didnae do any permanent damage. His arm'll mebbe never be as strong as it used tae be, but there won't be much difference.'

97

'Than why isn't he home? He'll do far better here than in any hospital where there's nobody of his own blood tae comfort him. I would've gone tae visit the laddie, but what with the influenza and yer dad needin' me here tae see tae his meals for him when he comes in from—'

'Mam, will ye just wheesht a minute and listen tae me?' Thomas asked quietly, but with a gravity in his voice that brought all their heads swivelling round in his direction.

'There's more tae it than they said, isn't there?' Flora's clenched fist went up to her mouth. Above it, her eyes were anguished. 'I knew they werenae tellin' us the truth of it!'

'Flora—' Henry reached across from his own chair to put a large hand on his wife's knee. 'Just dae as the laddie asks, and give him the chance tae tell us what's amiss wi' Lachlan.'

Thomas looked from one face to the other. 'He's fine, in his body,' he said at last, carefully. 'But in his head—'

'He was wounded in the head as well?' Rachel asked sharply, while Flora whimpered into her fist, her free hand finding and clutching Henry's fingers.

'Just in the arm, and I've already said that that's fine. It's inside his head I'm talking about. He'd a hard time of it in France, with all the noise and the business of seeing laddies he knew and fought beside being injured or killed. It's all been too much for him.'

'Shell shock.' Elspeth didn't know she had spoken until they all looked at her.

'That's what the hospital folk said. It's somethin' that can happen tae a soldier.'

'How did you know what it was called, Elspeth?' Henry asked.

'One of the girls I write letters for, her lad's cousin had it. He'd to come home early from the war. He's getting better now,' Elspeth added swiftly to her aunt.

'I don't understand.' Mattie's thin face was puzzled. 'How can he be shell-shocked if a shell didn't hit him?'

'It's the noise,' Thomas explained. 'The noise all the time of those big shells screamin' past day and night, sometimes for days on end without any stop tae it. Ye've no idea of the noise unless ye've lived through it.' He paused for a moment, then said, 'It's a wee bit like standin' in a very big railway station, with trains runnin' through every platform, one after another, never stopping, never givin' yer ears a rest, even when they're dingin' wi' the noise and ye'd give anythin' ye had tae get a bit of peace and quiet, only nothin'll make it stop.'

He paused, looked at his family's perplexed faces, and shrugged. 'I don't have the words tae explain it any better. It's like something in a nightmare. The place where Lachlan was based was very bad for the shellin'. If he hadnae been shot in the arm, I don't know what would've happened tae him. He'd mebbe have gone mad, poor soul.'

'By the sound of it, he has.'

The words were no sooner out of Rachel's mouth than Thomas rounded on her, jumping up from his chair to grab her shoulders. 'Our Lachlan's not mad,' he said vehemently into his sister's startled face. 'And don't ever let me hear ye say that about him again!'

'Here—' Henry cut in sharply, getting to his feet. 'No need for that!'

As they all stared at Thomas in astonishment, his hands fell away from his sister's shoulders, and he stepped back, his Adam's apple lurching visibly in his throat as he gave another gulping swallow.

'I'm sorry, Rachel. I – I didnae—'

'You frighted me!' Rachel's pretty face was red with shock and embarrassment.

'I'm sorry,' Thomas said again. 'It's just that – Lachlan's not mad, and I'll not hear anyone sayin' it. Nobody.'

Henry took his son by the arm, drawing him to his own armchair. 'Sit down here, lad, by the fire, and tell us more about what's ailin' him.'

Thomas resisted the hand on his arm, moving back to the table, where he sat down. 'You sit in yer own chair, Da, I'm fine here.'

'What's wrong with Lachlan?' Flora had scarcely noticed the interruption.

'He's a wee bit confused, Mam. He's spent so much time under fire that he can't grasp the fact that it's all over and he's safe. He jumps at the slightest noise. He – he cries a lot,' Thomas said, and Mattie and Elspeth stared at each other. Men didn't cry. Crying was for bairns and small children. They couldn't imagine Lachlan, who found a laugh in everything that happened to him, even the bad things, in tears.

'He'll get better, though?' Mattie's voice was very small, and Thomas reached across the table to give her hand a reassuring squeeze.

'Of course he'll get better, given time. The nurses and doctors are working with him. They're very kind tae him, you need have nae fear about that. He's well looked after.'

'Not as well as he would be in his own home. I want him back here,' Flora said firmly.

'When he's a bit better I'll—'

'Never mind when he's a bit better, I want him home now. He's my son, and I want tae look after him myself!'

'Mam—' Thomas began, but she ignored him.

'Are ye tryin' tae tell me they won't let him out? Is it a hospital or a prison he's in – tell me that?'

'It's a hospital, and of course they'll let him out, but should we not give them a wee while longer with him?'

'We've been without the two of ye for near enough four years, and we want ye both back here, where ye belong!' Flora insisted.

She was adamant, refusing to settle for anything less than a firm promise that Thomas would write to the hospital the next day, and travel back down to England within the week to bring Lachlan home. At last, worn out from a long day of travelling and talking, he gave her that promise, and the family all went to bed.

In the narrow lobby Elspeth asked fearfully, 'Thomas, is Lachlan going to be all right?'

'Of course he will, but it might take longer than Mam thinks.' There was no gas lighting in the boys' tiny room, and in the glow of the candle he carried, Thomas's face was drawn with tiredness, his eyes deep black pits. 'We'll all have tae be very understandin' with him.'

'We will be. Get a good night's sleep, you look as if you need it.'

He smiled slightly. 'I've learned tae sleep in all sorts of places at all sorts of times. Don't you worry about me, I'll be snoring as soon as my head touches that pillow.'

On the following day Flora made Thomas write to the English hospital. He posted the letter on his way to Gourock to see Mr Bruce, his former employer, about getting his old job back.

All that day in the sewing room Elspeth fretted about him. The men working in factories and shipyards had been assured of their own jobs back when the fighting was over, which meant that Lachlan would be able to return to the shipyard. But Thomas, employed by one man instead of a company, couldn't be so sure of returning to his old employment. He might have to seek work elsewhere, in a job market in turmoil, with returning servicemen expecting to be reinstated at once, to the resentment of some of the women who had kept the shipyards and factories and shops going by taking over men's work. They had worked on the buses and trams, even carrying sacks of coal on their backs, and had enjoyed being independent at last, and earning decent wages.

Now many of them were rebelling against a return to their kitchen sinks and dependency once again on their menfolk. Many women whose men either didn't return or were too badly wounded to work were terrified of losing the wages they had become accustomed to, and ending up with their children in the poors' hospital.

As Miss Buchanan refused to allow what she called 'unnecessary adornments' among her workforce, Elspeth couldn't wear Thomas's little pebble brooch at work. She kept the silver threepenny bit hidden beneath her blouse, and several times that day she felt for its outline, wishing on it for Thomas.

When she got home that evening he was in the kitchen, peeling potatoes for his mother and grinning from ear to ear.

'He's not only willin' tae have me back, he's goin' tae buy himself a motorcar, and I'll have the job of looking after it and driving him and his family around as well as helping in the gardens,' he announced proudly. 'It's a good thing I learned tae drive in the army.'

'Here, give that knife tae Elspeth, now she's home, and let her see tae the potatoes,' Flora fussed, but Thomas shook his head.

'Elspeth's been workin' hard all day while I've been enjoying myself, getting to know Greenock again. I can see tae them.'

'It's not seemly, a grown man doing a woman's work!'

'Mam, in the army we'd tae turn our hands tae everything. If I'd a pound for every potato I've peeled in the past four years I'd not need to work ever again. Imagine,' he exulted, wielding the knife so vigorously that peelings flew all over the kitchen and Flora, always a thrifty housewife, was driven to the point of apoplexy, 'me, drivin' a fine car and gettin' paid for it!'

Two days later a letter arrived from the English hospital, advising against taking Lachlan away so soon. Flora's mouth tightened as she read it. 'He's been in hospitals quite long enough. It's time he was with his own folk.'

'Mam, the doctor's working with Lachlan just now, and if we give him a wee while longer—'

But Flora would have none of it. 'Write back, Thomas, and

tell them ye're on yer way there and they've tae let our
Lachlan go.'

Thomas's eyes met Elspeth's, and his shoulders lifted in a
faint shrug. 'Aye, Mam, if that's what ye want.'

As he didn't have to start working for Mr Bruce until the
following Monday, he left for England early the next day, taking with him money that Flora had somehow managed to
scrape together to pay for the train fares. That day and all during the next, as her sons travelled homewards, Flora worked on
their room, hauling the narrow beds out from the walls, scrubbing the floor, polishing the small window and washing down
the woodwork. She even managed to whitewash the ceiling and
put some cream paint on the walls.

They were due home on Saturday, which meant that all the
members of the family would be free to greet them. When
Elspeth got back from the department store, breathless and red
in the face from running all the way, Mattie was pacing the
pavement outside the close, so wrapped up against the chill
February air that only her red nose could be seen peeping
from the scarves wound round her head. Elspeth could hear
the breath whistling in the other girl's lungs.

'What are you doing out on a cold day like this?'

Mattie coughed wheezily into a mittened hand. 'Mam's
been beating every cushion in the house, and my chest got so
bad with the dust I had to get out of the place.'

'But she knows you can't take the dust! She shouldn't be
beating cushions while you're home.'

'She can't see past Lachlan just now. She's so desperate to
get things nice for him that everything else's gone clean out of
her head. Go on up and see if the place is clear.'

Elspeth could smell the dust in the air as soon as she walked
into the flat. Flora, down on her knees, giving the shining
brass tongs and poker and hearthbrush an unnecessary final
polish, looked as though she hadn't stopped working all
morning.

'There ye are, at last. Put the kettle on, will ye? My throat's dry. Did ye see our Mattie on yer way home? I was wantin' her tae give me a hand, but she's been out half the morning.'

'She's outside in the cold wind, because the dust from the cushions brought her asthma on again.'

For a moment, Flora had the grace to look slightly ashamed, then she rallied. 'I couldnae have the place lookin' like a midden when Lachlan's coming home after all these years!'

'Aunt Flora, this house is never a midden, it's as clean and as neat as a palace.' Elspeth lit the gas ring under the kettle, then took a cup and saucer out of the cupboard.

'Ye can cut some bread and bring out the cheese, and we'll have somethin' tae keep us going.' Flora glanced at the clock and sucked her breath in. 'Would ye look at the time! Yer uncle and Rachel'll be home any minute. Fetch Mattie up and she can give ye a hand gettin' things ready for them.'

'She can't come up yet, Aunt Flora. I can still smell the dust in the air, it'll only make her chest worse.'

'Of course it won't – she's growin' out of the asthma, she's not as bad as all that,' Flora snapped. She had always gone out of her way to help Mattie during her bouts of asthma, sitting up at nights with the girl without a word of complaint, boiling kettles to create steam and making bread poultices to ease her daughter's chest. Now, guilt at having made Mattie ill in her eagerness to get everything ready for Lachlan brought a sharp note into her voice. 'Go down and fetch her.'

'She'll only start wheezing again as soon as she comes in. You'll need to wait until the dust—'

'That's enough, miss!' Flora McDonald snapped, her cheeks, already flushed with activity, flaring with added colour. 'Do as I say!'

Arguing would only have added fuel to her anger and precipitated yet another row between them, so Elspeth held her tongue and did as she was told. On the first landing she stopped and unbuttoned her coat so that she could fumble in her skirt pocket. She brought out some coins she had been paid that morning for writing two letters, balancing them thoughtfully on her outspread palm. They had been intended for the old tobacco tin used for saving money to pay for her evening classes, but today Mattie's need was greater than her own.

With a small, regretful sigh she slipped the coins into her coat pocket and continued on down the stairs.

Mattie was still pacing, her nose redder than before. 'Can I go up?' she asked eagerly when Elspeth appeared.

'The dust's still in the air. Aunt Flora says we're to buy three meat pies and have our dinner at Granjan's,' Elspeth lied, drawing the coins from her pocket. 'She gave me the money for them.'

Mattie's eyes brightened. 'I'm starving,' she admitted. 'And freezing.'

'Come on, then.' Elspeth linked arms with her and the two of them set off, walking as quickly as Mattie's breathing would allow. Aunt Flora was going to be awful angry, Elspeth thought as they went. The trouble she would get into when they returned would be well deserved for deceiving both her aunt and her cousin. But on the other hand, she couldn't have let Mattie go back up into the dusty air of the flat, or hang about any longer on the windy pavement.

11

For once, the angels were on her side. When she and Mattie, the latter breathing more easily now, returned to Mearns Street later that afternoon, Granjan was with them.

'Ye don't think I'm goin' tae let our Lachlan come back home from the war without his granny there tae greet him,' she had insisted, and Elspeth was happy to agree, knowing that Flora wouldn't make a fuss about her deception in front of Granjan.

The place was spick and span and dust-free, and Bob Cochran was waiting in the kitchen with the rest of the family, dressed, as they all were, in his Sunday best. He got up to let Granjan have his seat by the fire.

'Where have you two been?' Flora wanted to know.

'At Gran's,' Mattie answered cheerfully. 'We bought meat pies and had our dinner with her.'

'It was a kind thought, Flora hen,' Janet Docherty chimed in. 'The three of us had a good gossip, and all the dust's cleared out of the lassie's lungs now.'

Flora's eyes narrowed as they met Elspeth's. She opened her mouth to speak, but just then Mattie, at the window, shrieked, 'I see them – I see them!'

'Where?' There was a rush to the small window, and Mattie narrowly escaped being knocked into the sink by the crush of bodies at her back.

'There, look, coming up the hill.'

'It's them all right.' Bob's height gave him the advantage of being able to see over everyone else's heads. 'That's Thomas, carrying the suitcase, and the other—' He paused, then said, his voice puzzled, 'The other's surely Lachlan.'

'Now sit down, the lot of ye, and I'll go tae the door on my lone.' Flora's voice, trembling with anticipation, rang out over the excited chatter. 'Mind that the laddie's no' been well, and don't all rush at him at the one time.'

As the others did as they were bid, almost falling over each other in their haste to take their places, Elspeth craned across the small sink to look down at the street. She saw Thomas walking slowly towards the tenement building, a suitcase in one hand, the other holding the arm of the man who walked by his side, head bent, huddled into his coat.

Often in the past she had waited at this same window, watching for Lachlan returning from the shipyard. Despite the hard day's work he had just finished, he always ran up the hill effortlessly, craning to look up at the kitchen window, waving to her with both arms sawing through the air above his head. It had become a ritual for the two of them.

But if Lachlan was indeed Thomas's companion today, he was walking like a feeble old man. Some of the joy of seeing him again began to seep away, to be replaced by anxiety, and an eerie sense of dread.

It seemed a long time, long enough for them to exchange puzzled glances before they heard Flora opening the door and saying tremulously, 'Oh, Lachlan!'

When she finally came into the kitchen tears were trickling unashamedly down her face, and her smile was almost a grimace. 'Here he is, at last!' she announced, then, turning back to the door, 'Come on in, son. Everything'll be all right now ye're home.'

Lachlan came in hesitantly, stopping in the doorway as he took in the crowd waiting for him in the small kitchen. For a moment Elspeth thought that he was going to turn and go out again, then she heard Thomas say, low-voiced, 'Go on, you're doing fine,' and Lachlan McDonald, home from the war at last, stepped into the kitchen.

The greetings died in their throats. His head was down, his eyes fixed on the floor or on his hat, which was clutched between hands that turned it round and round unceasingly. His light brown hair was much longer than Thomas's, and untidy, as Lachlan's soft fine hair had always been, but the shine had gone from it and it hung lank and lifeless.

'Well, well.' Henry McDonald, swallowing back his shock at first sight of his younger son, got to his feet and moved to clap the young man's shoulder. Normally his large, strong hand landed on backs and shoulders heartily, but this time it paused for a fraction of a second in mid-air as Lachlan flinched, then landed gently, more of a caress than a clap. 'Welcome home, son,' Henry said, his voice gruff. 'Come on in and sit down – here, sit in my chair, near the fire.'

'He'd be best at the table, Da,' Thomas said swiftly, managing to reach round his brother's painfully thin figure to pull a chair out for him. He eased Lachlan out of his coat and into the chair, talking cheerfully all the time, his eyes, moving from one person to the next, carrying clear warning that Lachlan must be treated gently.

They all understood. One by one, they offered a few words, a touch of the hand. As Lachlan's pale, drawn face bobbed up at each of them through a ragged fringe of hair, his lips curved in a forced smile and he spoke their names – 'Mattie . . . Rachel . . . Elspeth . . . Gran' – in a slow, puzzled way, as though surprised to see them there. After each naming he ducked his head down again, pushing his chin against his chest as if he was afraid of drawing too much attention to himself.

Thomas stood behind and slightly to one side of him, his hand on Lachlan's stooped shoulder; now and again a quiver ran through Lachlan, and each time that happened Elspeth saw his brother's hold on his shoulder tighten very slightly in reassurance.

When they settled themselves round the table to eat, Thomas, beside Lachlan, talked cheerfully and continuously, though he himself looked exhausted, his face grey and his eyes heavy with strain. Every now and again he sprinkled his chatter with, 'Isn't that so, Lachlan?' or, 'Didn't we, Lachlan?' And each time Lachlan gave a quick, shy nod, and a muttered 'Aye.'

'We thought we'd never get here, didn't we, Lachlan? The train was busy, and it crawled all the way. I think myself it was an English train, with no liking for coming over the border, for it seemed tae get even slower after that. We were luckier than some, though, weren't we, Lachlan, for we found seats beside each other, and the hospital had given us a packet of sandwiches, so we didnae starve.'

It was painful to watch Lachlan's terror and the efforts he made to keep it under control. It was as though he was with hostile strangers, Elspeth thought, rather than his own bloodkin, the people he had grown up with. She wanted desperately to put her arms around him and hold him close, safe from the world. But she sensed that even a touch of her hand might send him into a panic.

Watching the way he pushed the food around his plate, it was clear to her that he should have stayed in the hospital until he was more able to face the world. She looked round the table, seeing the tears in Mattie's and Rachel's and Granjan's eyes, the stunned horror on Henry's face, and, even worse, the mingled incredulity and distaste on Bob Cochran's coarsely handsome features, and experienced a rush of anger at Flora for having insisted on dragging her son home with no thought to how he might feel about it.

Flora herself was clearly determined to make the most of the situation. Like Thomas, she talked cheerfully, pretending that everything was all right, even laughing now and again, a harsh, forced laugh that made Lachlan jump.

'D'ye not want yer nice mince?' she asked him, as though he was a child, when every other plate had been emptied and Lachlan's reduced to an unappetising congealing mush of meat, gravy and mashed potatoes. 'I made it specially for ye. It was always your favourite – mind how much ye liked it?'

'I think he got enough to eat on the train, Mam.' Thomas picked up the cold plate and handed it to her. 'They gave us a lot of sandwiches, didn't they, Lachlan?'

It was the same with the dumpling and custard. Scarcely a spoonful went into Lachlan's mouth, although Granjan and Elspeth, in an attempt to draw attention away from him, started up a conversation about nothing in particular, glaring at the others until they took the hint and joined in.

A few minutes later, glancing back at Lachlan, Elspeth was horrified to see a large tear drop from his lowered face into the yellow and brown soup he had made of his pudding. It was followed by another, then another.

'Thomas—' she began, just as Lachlan's shoulders began to shake and a muffled whimper escaped from his throat.

'I think it's time we went tae our beds,' said Thomas swiftly, getting to his feet. 'It's been a long day, and I'm tired out. You must be too, eh, Lachlan? Come on, old son,' he added gently, and his brother allowed himself to be eased to his feet and turned towards the door.

'I'll help ye,' Flora and Henry said at the same time, but Thomas shook his head.

'We'll be fine. We'll see ye in the mornin', eh?'

When the door had closed behind them, the people left at the table stared at each other blankly. Mattie began to weep, and Elspeth felt the tears she herself refused to shed forming a solid ball of grief in her throat.

'Mattie, stop behavin' like a daft wean!' Flora's voice was over-loud. 'We're all home together at last, and there's nothin' tae cry about! Ye'll take a cup of tea now, Mam?'

But Granjan excused herself, saying that it was time she was off home. Bob immediately offered to walk back to Nicolson Street with her, and Rachel said that she'd go too. Elspeth got the impression that Bob couldn't wait to get away from the flat.

Once the three of them had gone, Flora sent Mattie and Elspeth off to bed, announcing that she would wash the dishes herself. Although it was still early they went without argument.

'That's not our Lachlan at all,' Mattie burst out as soon as they were alone in the bedroom. 'What's happened to him?'

'I don't know.' Elspeth spoke with difficulty round the great lump of tears in her throat. 'But whatever it was, it must have been terrible.'

'Bringin' him home was a nightmare,' Thomas admitted to his family the following morning. Lachlan was still asleep, and the rest of them had gathered in the kitchen. 'It was hard for him tae be outside the hospital, with crowds of folk in the streets and the railway station, and in the train. Times I'd tae coax him every step of the way, and once when a train whistle blew he threw himself under a bench and I'd the devil's own job getting him tae come out again. We nearly missed our train over the head of it.'

His lips twisted in the ghost of a grin. 'I've never seen our Lachlan move as fast as that in my life. It gave one or two other folk a shock, too. The rest of the time he was clutching my arm so tight it felt as though it had been caught in a vice.' He rolled up his shirtsleeve to reveal the bruises made by Lachlan's fingers on his muscular, hairy arm.

He himself still showed some of the previous day's exhaustion, having had his sleep interrupted each time Lachlan awoke and cried out in terror at finding himself in unfamiliar surroundings.

'But he doesnae need tae be scared of anything now,' Flora fretted. 'He's home, in that room he's slept in ever since he was old enough tae spend a night away from my side.'

111

'I know, Mam, but Lachlan's not the laddie he used tae be,' Thomas tried to explain patiently. 'The things that happened tae him in the war have changed him. He's coming tae folk and things he used tae know like a stranger, seein' them for the first time. We must give him time tae get used tae being home again. The Sister at the hospital told me he took time tae settle in there, and the same'll have tae happen here.'

'But you haven't changed, Thomas, and Bob didn't change.' Rachel's pretty face was twisted with the effort of trying to understand. 'Why should Lachlan?'

'I've seen it happen tae more than one poor soul. Mebbe it's because they're more sensitive than the rest of us, mebbe it's because they were in the worst of the fighting, or mebbe a mixture of the two. There's no discredit tae them, for at times we all saw things that no human being should have tae see.' Thomas paused, his warm brown eyes darkening with bleak memories. Then he blinked, shrugging himself back to the present.

'It was easier for me, for we were moving on, over the French border and through Belgium, fightin' as we went. We'd a job tae do and we were able tae get on with it. But there was a time when Lachlan's unit was pinned down under fire for days on end, then more time spent advancing a wee bit, then being driven back again, then tryin' tae advance again. And they suffered heavy losses.'

'What can we do for him?' Flora wanted to know.

'Just – accept him, Mam. Don't try tae push him intae gettin' better. The doctor I saw says it's best just tae treat him gently. Let him know he's not on his lone, and leave him tae work things out in his own time.'

'I don't know how long the shipyard'll keep his job open for him,' Henry said doubtfully.

There was a note of suppressed irritation in Thomas's voice when he answered. 'Then he'll have tae find a new job when he's able, Da.'

'Will he ever get back to himself?' Mattie asked.

'Of course he will, given time.'

Elspeth, glancing at Thomas, saw the flicker of doubt that crossed his face as he spoke, and a shiver ran through her.

As Thomas had said, the Lachlan who had come back to them after the army finished with him wasn't the Lachlan they had known. It was as though some stranger had put on Lachlan's body as he might have shrugged on his jacket. It didn't quite fit, it didn't look right, and yet in some eerie way it was still undeniably Lachlan.

It was hard for them, but hardest of all for Lachlan. He spent most of his time huddled in Flora's armchair by the fire, or in his tiny bedroom, occasionally with a newspaper in his lap, though he rarely read it. He jumped at sudden noises or movements, and responded timidly and haltingly when spoken to, searching for the right words, his voice often tailing away in mid-sentence. At night, in the grip of nightmares, his screams frequently woke the entire household, and the neighbours too.

Used to working in the constant din and clatter of machinery in the shipyard, Henry McDonald tended as a result to speak loudly at all times, and to move about noisily at home. After startling Lachlan into a fit of hysteria when he barged noisily into the kitchen on his return from work on the day after the boy's arrival home, he had to work hard at learning to change his ways.

That first day alone in the house with Lachlan was bad for Flora. He panicked when he saw her getting ready to go to the shops, and was equally panic-stricken when she suggested that if he didn't want to be left alone, he could go with her. Finally she had to take her coat off, and stay at home. As it was her custom to shop each day, there was nothing in the house for that night's dinner. When Mattie arrived home from school she was sent back out again to buy pieces of fried fish for the evening meal, and Flora suffered the humiliation of seeing her family eat their first shop-cooked meal.

After that, Janet Docherty came every morning to sit with her grandson while Flora went to the shops. The old woman's placid nature was good for Lachlan; when she was there he relaxed more than he could with his mother, who watched him anxiously all the time, trying to anticipate his every need.

'Ye don't need tae treat the laddie as if he's made of fine china, Flora,' Janet tried to explain to her daughter. 'He'll no' break. It's just as if he's had a blow tae the head—'

'It's nothin' like that at all, Mam!' Flora swatted the words aside impatiently. 'It wasnae his head that got hurt, it was his arm – and what I'm sayin' is, how can a bullet in anyone's arm make them go the way our Lachlan's gone? Tell me that.'

'I didnae say he'd been hit on the head,' Janet said patiently. 'I'm just sayin' it's like a blow tae the head, and – wheesht for a minute, will ye, and let me explain,' she added as Flora opened her mouth to protest. 'If ye get a hard knock on the skull, ye feel all dazed and out of place for a minute, don't ye? Mind that time ye fell off the wash-house roof that ye'd no right tae be on in the first place, and ye felt dizzy for a whole day after it? That's the way poor Lachlan's feeling right now, with all that's been happenin' tae him.'

'But he's not just been like that for a day, has he? It's been months, from what we've heard, and there's no betterment.'

'Aye, well, as far as he's concerned, the fallin' off the wash-house roof business must've happened tae him time after time, day after day, and nob'dy knew, so it just kept gettin' worse and worse. The longer it went on and the worse it got, the longer it'll take him tae get over it,' Janet ended triumphantly. 'D'ye see?'

Flora sniffed. 'There's a queer difference between fallin' from a wash-house roof and bein' in a war,' she said, and Janet, realising that she wasn't going to best her daughter, held her peace and went back to her knitting.

Elspeth, who had come home for her midday meal, as she now did two or three times a week to see how Lachlan was, had been listening to the exchange, but for once she had the sense to keep out of it and avoid bringing Flora's wrath down on her head. But she was impressed by the old woman's grasp of the situation.

'How did you manage to work out all that about the washhouse roof, Granjan?' she wanted to know as the two of them went out of the close together, Janet heading back to her own home and Elspeth bound for the sewing room.

'Ach, there's nothin' tae it, hen. Christ did that sort of thing all the time in the New Testament tae explain things tae the folk, and if it's good enough for Him it's good enough for me,' Janet said breezily, adding, 'Mind you, I don't know if He'd've managed with his wee stories so well if a lot of the folk listenin' tae Him had been like our Flora.'

12

It was difficult to explain to friends and neighbours just what had happened to Lachlan. Normally when a soldier returned from the war, everyone in the tenement where his family lived, and sometimes everyone in the entire street, flocked to welcome him back and hear about his experiences. Lachlan had always been popular with young and old alike, and quite a few people were offended when asked not to come to the house on his return.

'Their experience of men getting hurt in the war's kept to bullet wounds or sword slashes, or coughing their lungs up from the gas,' Thomas explained to Elspeth. 'They can understand amputation and death, but not someone being hurt in the head without anything actually smashing through his skull.'

'You said there were a lot of soldiers hurt like Lachlan.'

'Aye, but some of them are still in hospitals, where Lachlan should still be, and there were some poor devils couldn't take it any more and took their own lives, while others' – Thomas stopped short, then went on cautiously, watching her from the corner of his eye – 'others were killed for it.'

'What d'you mean?'

'Shot as cowards, or as deserters.' Thomas's voice was so matter-of-fact that for a moment she couldn't take in what he was telling her. When she did, she gaped at him in horror.

'Killed by their own side, you mean?' There was something about the unexpected sight of blood and flesh normally kept

116

tidily where it should be, beneath intact skin, that made the onlookers' stomachs twist and knot in sudden revulsion. Elspeth had experienced it at school more than once, when a child tripped and cut its head open, or someone tore an arm on one of the spiked railings that surrounded the playground. She felt it now.

'That couldn't happen!'

'I've seen it, Ellie.' The bleak, dark look was in his eyes again. 'There was one in our own unit, a decent enough laddie, just seventeen years old. We could all see that it was gettin' tae him, but the officers wouldnae listen when some of us tried tae tell them. The way they saw things, a soldier had tae be brave all the time, else he was lettin' his king and country down. I sometimes wondered how the King himself would've managed if he'd been there instead of safe at home. Anyway, one day this poor lad couldnae take any more. We were goin' intae battle, and he threw his rifle away and started crying like a bairn. Crying for his mam, he was, with his eyes squeezed shut and his mouth open and the tears and the snot runnin' down his face.'

'What happened?'

'They arrested him, and held a court martial as soon as they could. Then they found a bit of wall that was still standing and they stood him up against it with a blindfold round his eyes, and they shot him. He wasnae the only one it happened tae, but he was the only one I knew as a comrade.'

Elspeth felt sick. 'Did his parents know?'

Thomas's shoulders had hunched as he relived the experience. Now they straightened, and he went on polishing his shoes for work the next day. They got muddy, working in the Bruce gardens, but Thomas liked to start the day with clean shoes, and he always scraped off all the mud and polished them every evening.

'They were told he died in the line of duty. At least they never knew the truth of it, and there's not one man in the unit that'd tell them different if he was tae meet up with them. So now ye know why our Lachlan's one of the lucky ones, in spite of what he's goin' through just now. That's why I'll do anything I must tae get him better. I'm not lettin' the army destroy my brother the way they destroyed that laddie and all the others, pushing them intae a hell they couldnae handle, then punishing them for allowin' it tae get tae them.'

It was difficult for Elspeth to explain about Lachlan to the girls at work. They all knew that her foster brothers had come back safely from the war, but nobody could understand why, with his arm wound fully healed, Lachlan showed no signs of returning to the shipyard.

Lena, who had an eye for the opposite sex and had tried on several occasions to coax Elspeth to agree to a visit to the local Hippodrome in a foursome – the two of them, Thomas, and Lachlan – couldn't understand it at all. 'If he's got the right number of arms and legs and he's not even lost his sight like some poor buggers have, why's he ill?' she wanted to know. 'What else can be wrong with him?'

'It's his head—' Elspeth began, then, realising that they would all think she was talking about a head wound, she amended it to, 'I mean, inside his head.'

'Ye mean he's a daftie?' one of the girls suggested, and Elspeth rounded on her.

'I do not! Our Lachlan's a clever lad – everyone knows that!'

'Aye – clever enough tae pretend that there's somethin' wrong with him when there's nothin' at all,' Betty Jardine sneered. 'If you ask me, he's just swinging the lead.' Betty's brother and one of her cousins and the young man she had been walking out with had all been killed during the war. She and her family had suffered badly, and because of this she was treated more gently than usual by the rest of the girls, though she was sharp-tongued and carping by nature, and before her tragic losses she had been thoroughly disliked.

'He's not! How dare you say such a thing about our Lachlan!' Elspeth was furious, and close to tears with frustration.

'What else is there tae say?' Betty shot back, and there was a murmur of agreement round the large table. Elspeth stopped her sewing machine and half rose from her seat, sheer rage closing her mind to everything but the need to punish Betty for the terrible things she was saying about gentle, suffering Lachlan. Just then Miss Arnold walked in, her presence putting a stop to what might have become a nasty confrontation, and the girl sitting next to Elspeth grabbed her skirt and hauled her back down to her chair.

'Just as well,' Lena said during the midday break. 'That Betty's got sharp fingernails on her, hen. Ye might've got the worst of it – and lost yer job, too.'

'I'll not have her saying such things about our Lachlan,' Elspeth muttered sullenly, but she was secretly relieved that the overseer had arrived when she did.

She had only once in her life been involved in a fight, and that had been a shoving and hair-pulling playground clash with another six-year-old who had tried to steal her new pencil-case. Even now the memory of it made her face burn with shame. She vividly recalled the humiliation of being made to stand in front of the entire class afterwards, the shocked outrage in her teacher's voice as she said, 'Elspeth Bremner, I never thought I'd see you behaving like a guttersnipe!' The final word, spoken with the utmost contempt, had hurt her far more than the two strokes of the belt the teacher had then delivered on her small, wincing palm.

A month after she started work, two of the women from the packing department had come to blows in the basement room during the midday break, kicking and clawing, dragging at each other's hair, screeching like harlots, and eventually rolling on the ground, with a crowd gathered round them, yelling encouragement. Elspeth had stayed well back, the sound of the fight stirring unpleasant memories of her own single lapse.

Both women, eventually separated by a floorwalker drawn to the scene by the noise, had been dismissed on the spot. The very thought that the same thing could have happened to her if Miss Arnold hadn't come in when she did made her cringe, and resolve to say nothing in future about her home life, or Lachlan.

He had been damaged as cruelly as any man blinded or crippled in the war. The real tragedy of it was that in Lachlan's case, nobody could see the wounds.

Although it was only April, the sun was warm on Thomas McDonald's back as he raked and smoothed the gravel of the long curving driveway leading to Overton, the Bruces' house. Occasionally he stopped to stretch and ease stiffened muscles, leaning on the long-handled rake and taking a moment to look about him.

One side of the drive was bordered by a wall of rhododendrons a good twelve feet high. In a month's time they would be studded with crimson and pink and white flowers, each as large as a dinner plate. Where Thomas stood, almost at the top of the drive and near the point where the gravel opened out into a great forecourt in front of the graceful grey-stone mansion, the opposite side of the drive was a smooth grassy bank topped by a row of peony bushes. They had already started blooming, each individual blossom made up of hundreds of tight-packed velvety crimson petals. Beyond, in flowerbeds dotted over the smooth green lawns, the last of the daffodils and tulips could still be seen, and in the woods edging the estate, where he had been working the day before, he had seen stretches of bluebells beneath the trees. Thomas loved this place, and had clung to the memory of it during the war. To him, the gardens of Overton represented peace and serenity and an assurance that while they were there, nothing totally evil could happen.

Returning to his work, he thought of Lachlan, sitting at

home day after day, and longed to bring him to this place with its wide sweeps of smooth green lawn, the walled kitchen and rose gardens, and the lily pond. Surely in gardens like these, with grassed paths leading between flowering bushes to secret little glades, each holding a surprise – a sundial, a huge stone urn filled with flowers, a statue, a graceful gazebo to rest in – his brother's troubled mind would mend.

Thomas believed in the healing power of the open sky and the sight and smell and touch of growing things. He had tried to persuade Lachlan to walk with him to the open land behind Greenock, where they had once played as boys, but Lachlan had lost his nerve once he got to the street, and bolted back to the flat.

It would help if Lachlan could be transported most of the way in the handsome dark blue car now standing in a former carriage-house at the rear of the Bruce house. But Mr Bruce wasn't the kind of man to permit his car to be used for the benefit of his chauffeur-cum-gardener's brother.

Thomas's mouth was dry; he looked up at the sun, and estimated that soon it would be time to go round to the kitchen for a cool glass of lemonade, unless Ina brought one out to him before then.

Ina, one of the Bruces' housemaids, had shown her interest in him from his first day back after the war. She was a pretty girl, with large blue eyes and fair curly hair, and Thomas had been happy to start walking out with her.

Hooves crunched along the drive from the double gate and Thomas moved to the verge and kept working. To his surprise the horse stopped instead of passing by.

'Hello. I thought you were the chauffeur now.'

Startled, he looked up at the girl sitting straight-backed in the saddle.

'I'm a gardener as well, Miss Aileen, when the motorcar's not needed.' The smart grey chauffeur's uniform, complete with gloves and peaked cap, was kept in a small room off the kitchen, so that he could change into it when the car was required.

'Isn't gardening a comedown after driving the car?'

'Not for me, I like working in the garden just as much as I like driving.'

'D'you like horses too?'

Thomas glanced at the handsome chestnut she rode. 'Yes, miss.'

'In that case,' Aileen Bruce said hopefully, 'would you mind very much taking Cavalier round to the stables for me? I should do it myself, but I've stayed out too long and we have guests arriving soon. I must go and change or my mother'll be furious.'

'Of course, miss.' Thomas laid the rake down carefully on the grass verge and went to the handsome chestnut cob, taking the reins in one hand and running the other down the animal's soft nose. The girl slipped from the saddle with ease to stand beside him, her own hand caressing the horse's neck. The other took off her brown leather peaked cap to reveal sleek black hair cut close to her neat skull.

'He's beautiful, isn't he?' She spoke easily, as though Thomas was a friend rather than one of her father's employees. 'I should stay with him until he's been unsaddled and rubbed down and settled into his stall – it's a poor rider who doesn't look after her mount, you know – but I daren't upset Mother. Give my abject apologies to Alfred, and tell him I promise it'll never ever happen again.'

'Yes, miss.' Thomas glanced down at the girl, a good head smaller than he was, and suddenly the world shifted abruptly on its axis. He had often seen her in the gardens, a pigtailed schoolgirl, but while he was away she had become a beautiful woman, and this was the first time he had ever been so close to her. He stared, unable to help himself, at her perfect face, the vivid green, thick-lashed eyes looking up into his.

She blinked, then glanced away from him and back at the

horse. 'Thanks,' she said, then, as though she could no more help it than he could, she looked into Thomas's eyes again.

They might have stood there forever, if a voice hadn't called her name. Wrenching his eyes from her, looking over her head, Thomas saw his employer's wife standing at the top of the steps.

'I'd better go – thanks again,' Aileen Bruce said, and set off at a run across the great sweep of gravel to the house. The scarlet jersey she wore with fawn riding breeches made an exotic splash of colour against the grey walls, and a shaft of sunlight on her black hair made it gleam like a blackbird's wing as she followed her mother into the house.

Thomas watched until she had disappeared, then ran his free hand through his own hair, which had grown longer since he came home from the army, and had fallen into its usual casual waves. He clicked his tongue at the horse and gave its warm silky neck a final caress before leading it round the side of the house, towards the stables.

'We'll never manage it!'

'We will, Aunt Flora.' Elspeth put another pin into the paper pattern, and slid the muslin cloth carefully along the table so that she could reach the next stretch of pattern.

'We'll have to manage, for I'm not letting Annie Cochran outdo me.' Rachel emphasised her words by stabbing at the air with a large pair of scissors.

'I don't know why ye didnae just insist on waitin' till the end of the year, like we agreed,' her mother lamented, pushing back a strand of hair that had come loose from the bun at the back of her head.

'Because I want to get married, and it's a long time till the end of the year.'

'Aye, well, ye'll find that marriage lasts a long time too,' Flora muttered. Her face was red and shiny, for it was a lovely day outside, and the kitchen was hot. They had tried opening the window, only to close it again because the refreshing breeze had riffled the cream-coloured muslin Rachel had chosen for her wedding dress, making it impossible for them to cut it out.

Rachel paid no heed to her mother. 'Anyway, it means that we'll have a nice wedding breakfast in a hotel, instead of all crowding in here.'

'Da's not pleased about that – there's no drink sold in the Anderson Waverley Temperance Hotel,' Mattie put in from the window, where she was perched on the draining board, stitching a broad brown ribbon round a straw hat.

'It'll not do him any harm tae drink lemonade for once,' Flora told her, adding, 'If we ever get there.'

Bits of ribbon and material lay all over the kitchen. It was as bad, Elspeth thought, pinning another section of pattern and material together, as the time the sewing room at Brodie's were all trying to get Catherine Bruce's wedding trousseau ready.

Ever since Bob Cochran had come home from the war he and Rachel had been saving and planning for their wedding on New Year's Eve, the traditional date for Scottish marriages since it enabled the happy couple to start both a new year and a new life together. But at the end of April Bob's parents had suggested that since his sister Annie was marrying in May, there should be a double wedding, followed by a joint reception in the back hall of the Anderson Waverley Temperance Hotel in West Blackhall Street. The booking was made possible because Archie Cochran, Bob's father, was a leading member of the local temperance movement.

With very little time in which to prepare for the wedding, life in the McDonald household had become chaotic. By some miracle, Bob had managed to find a two-roomed flat to rent down by the river, and he and a band of helpers, including Thomas and Henry, were working there at that moment in an effort to make the place habitable in time.

'Where's the light brown thread?' Flora asked, and they all stopped what they were doing to hunt for the elusive bobbin.

When it was finally located under a pile of ribbons, she dislodged Mattie from the draining board so that she could get enough light to see as she threaded her needle.

'I'm tellin' ye,' she said again, her eyes crossing as she tried to fix them on the thread wavering close to the needle's eye, 'we'll never manage it.'

'We will so, Mam.' Now that she was almost a married woman, Rachel felt bold enough to defy her mother. 'We will.'

They did. And, thought Elspeth as she stood in the hotel's back hall watching Rachel dance past on Bob's arm, her pretty face glowing with happiness and excitement beneath the bell-shaped brim of her straw hat, it had been worth it. It was a lovely wedding, marred only by Lachlan's absence. Thomas had volunteered to stay at home with him, but Flora wouldn't hear of it.

'Ina'll be expecting you to take her, and Mam's already said she'll keep Lachlan company, so that's that decided.'

'Of course, we all know why the Cochrans were so eager,' Elspeth heard Flora murmur now as the other happy couple whirled past on the small dance floor. 'They had tae get their Annie married off quickly. Would ye look at the size of her?'

'Ach, Annie was always a plump lassie,' Henry said placatingly. Seeing him glance at the glass of lemonade in his hand before taking a tentative sip, Elspeth nudged Mattie's elbow and both girls stifled giggles. Clearly, Henry McDonald was missing his usual glass of beer, and wishing that his daughter's new in-laws weren't in the temperance movement.

'Don't talk nonsense, Henry – Annie Cochran was solid all over before, not just in front.' Flora tugged at her new gloves. 'She's either gone too far too soon with that young man of hers, or the fat's slipped.'

She brushed a piece of thread from the skirt of the dark green suit she had bought just before the war. It was a bit tight for her now, and as it was a heavy winter suit she was hot, but she couldn't bring herself to take the long jacket off, for she was tormented by the suspicion that the skirt fastenings, unable to hold her in place any longer, might give way, treating the wedding guests to a glimpse of her petticoated hip bulging through the gap.

'It'll mebbe be our Thomas's turn next, him and Ina,' she added, spotting her elder son's fair head among the dancers. 'If they get married, mebbe Mr Bruce'll give them a nice house on the estate.'

13

'Which of you,' Miss Arnold asked from the door of the sewing room, her voice so cold that the words might have been carved from ice, 'is the girl who apparently had the audacity to touch the typewriting machine in the accounts office?'

Elspeth felt as though someone had hit her hard and unexpectedly in the stomach with a rolling pin. The material she was holding dropped from her fingers; her mouth dried and her face flamed as a shockwave ran through her entire body.

Lena, too, was stunned into blushing confusion by the question, coming as it did so long after the crime had been committed. Before she could prevent herself she turned and looked at Elspeth, but even if she had been able to hide her reaction, it would have made no difference, since the culprit's guilt was so obvious that every eye in the room, including Miss Arnold's, was on her.

'I—' Elspeth started to speak, but no sound came out. She cleared her throat and tried again. 'It was me, Miss Arnold.'

'And when was this?'

'When we were working late on Miss Bruce's wedding clothes. You sent me to the office—'

'I sent— I did no such thing!'

'Yes you did.' Elspeth was too caught up in the need to explain to realise that she was not only contradicting Miss Arnold, but implicating her. 'It was when we were busy with

127

Miss Bruce's trousseau, and you sent me to ask Mr James for a list.'

The woman's face crimsoned. 'For a list – not to make free of the office and touch things!'

'She didnae dae any harm.' Lena rushed to defend her friend. 'You sent me as well, Miss Arnold, and I saw what happened. She just touched the machine, then Mr James came in and—'

'That's enough! Get on with your work. As for you, Elspeth Bremner, you're to go at once to Mr James's office!'

Elspeth's knees were so weak that she could scarcely walk along the corridor. She swallowed convulsively several times, blinking hard to clear her sight, which had misted over. How could Mr James do this to her? How could he be so cruel, waiting for months before deciding to punish her for her lapse?

Then a far more frightening question crowded into her head, obliterating her anguish over James Brodie's betrayal. What was Aunt Flora going to say?

By the time she reached the accounts office she had made up her mind that when the ordeal to come was over she would walk out of the department store with her head high – then run away somewhere, anywhere. She couldn't face Flora and tell her that she had been dismissed for bad conduct, with no reference to show to a future employer.

In the accounts office the typewriting machine, the cause of Elspeth's shameful downfall, sat smugly on its table in the corner, shrouded by its dust cover. A young man and an older woman were sitting on tall stools at the high sloping desk running along the opposite wall, each writing in large ledgers.

The woman twisted her head over her shoulder. 'Yes?'

'I'm—' Elspeth swallowed hard, then tried again. 'I'm to see Mr James. I was sent from the sewing room.'

The young man looked up, his gaze sweeping her from top to toe.

'Oh, yes,' the woman said, and to Elspeth, the words had an

ominous sound. Everyone, it seemed, knew about her crime. 'He's expecting you.' She nodded at the closed door leading to the inner office. 'Knock on the door first, and wait till he tells you to go in.'

Wiping her palms nervously down the sides of her serviceable blue skirt, Elspeth approached the door, knocked tentatively, waited for a moment, then knocked again.

'It's all right, he only bites on Wednesdays,' the young man said. She turned, surprised, to be met by a wide grin.

'You've got enough to do without poking your nose in where it isn't wanted, Graham Adams!' the woman snapped, just as a voice shouted, 'Come in!' from the office.

Elspeth, faced with the choice of confronting James Brodie again or showing abject cowardice and running away, grappled with the door handle and almost plunged forward into the lion's den without giving herself further time to think.

'Yes?' The man who had caught her tampering with the office typewriter looked up from his crowded desk.

'You wanted to see me, Mr James? Elspeth Bremner,' she added as he stared blankly at her.

'And what did I want to see you ab—?' he began, then recognition came into his eyes. 'You're the one I found typewriting that night.'

'Yes, sir.'

'Your friend said you went to night school?'

'Yes, sir. I've been studying for eighteen months. Typewriting and shorthand, and book-keeping,' she added, since he seemed to be expecting her to go into detail.

'And what does a seamstress want with book-keeping and all the rest of it?'

'I – I want to work in an office one day,' she said, then shied back nervously as he got up and surged round the desk towards her, dislodging a pile of papers as he went. He and Elspeth both caught at it as it prepared to launch itself into space, then Mr Brodie took a sheet from the top.

'This'll do.' He opened the office door. 'Follow me, Elspeth Bremner.'

She did, and together they surveyed the covered typewriting machine, until Mr James said impatiently, 'Well? It's a good machine but it hasn't learned to uncover itself yet, so take the cover off, sit down and put some paper into it. Now,' he went on when she had done as she was told, 'make it type something.'

'What, sir?'

'Anything – I just want to see if you know what you're doing.'

'The cat sat on the nat,' Elspeth typed, then, professional pride overcoming fear, she pushed the carriage back and corrected her mistake. 'The cat sat on the mat,' the second line said, with confidence. As her fingers recognised the familiar, pleasant sensation of keys yielding beneath them, the third line appeared. 'Peter Piper picked a peck of pickled peppers.'

'Now try copying that.' The paper he had brought with him was thumped down beside the typewriter. Elspeth picked it up and looked at it, appalled. It was a long handwritten list of materials, complete with measurements and prices which would, she knew, have to be laid out in neatly spaced columns.

'What's the matter?' James Brodie asked from above her head. 'Do they only teach you quotations and nursery rhymes at the night school?'

'No, sir, but – I'll need more paper.'

'Then take that one out, and put another one in,' he said, exasperated.

'Excuse me, Mr James, I think the lassie would do better on her own, without anyone standing over her,' the woman at the desk suggested.

'Hmmpphh. Very well, Elspeth Bremner, bring the copy to me when you've finished it – and I'll expect to see it before the sun sets and the moon comes up,' the manager said, and stamped back into his small office, shutting the door noisily behind him.

When a fresh sheet had been rolled into the machine, Elspeth, grateful that she had reached tabulating in her studies, set up the machine, and began to type.

Ten minutes later she laid the typed sheet on James Brodie's desk, with the original list beside it. He picked them both up, comparing them line by line, while she waited, hands linked. In spite of her confusion and bewilderment, she had enjoyed typing again, and the need for concentration had soothed her.

'Very good,' he said at last. 'Go back to the sewing room now, and tell Miss Arnold that I'd be grateful if she would allow you to begin tomorrow morning at half past eight sharp.'

'Begin?'

'Begin,' he repeated, then, eyebrows raised, 'Did she not tell you?'

'Tell me what – Mr James,' she added hurriedly.

He laid the papers down. 'What d'you think you're here for?'

'To be dismissed, because I typed on the typewriter that time.'

'Well, well,' James Brodie said thoughtfully. 'Isn't that a bit of malice?' Then, just as Elspeth opened her mouth to assure him that she had intended no malice at all, but had only wanted to try the typewriter, he returned to the business in hand. 'The fact of the matter is, Miss Bremner, my typist has fallen ill and I need someone to take her place until she comes back. I recalled being told that you were taking lessons, and so I asked Miss Arnold to send you along. You may go now – and remember, half past eight, and not a minute later. There's a lot to be done.'

She ran all the way home from work that afternoon, bursting into the flat to announce that she was to leave the sewing room and work in the department store office and be a real typewriter, for a little while, at least. Mattie and Rachel were delighted for her, and when he came home, Thomas picked her up and swung her about the room.

'Good for you, Ellie!'

Uncle Henry joked about Elspeth running her own office next, and Auntie Flora said that Elspeth had done well – then launched into a lecture about the need for her to mind her manners and do as she was told and not make a nuisance of herself in the accounts office.

'She's not going tae make a nuisance of herself, Mam.' Thomas was brushing his shoes, and preparing to meet Ina on her evening off. 'They need our Ellie's talents – she'll do well for herself, just wait and see.' Even Lachlan smiled and hugged her and said how pleased he was. Then, putting the tip of a finger against the little silver threepenny piece at her throat, 'It's brought you luck right enough.'

'It has,' she agreed, and wished that she could find some way of bringing a little luck to Lachlan, who sorely needed it.

It wasn't until that night that she remembered Mr James's comment about malice, and told Mattie.

'I thought he meant me, touching the typewriter when I shouldn't have, but now I'm thinking it was Miss Arnold he was talking about, not telling me why he wanted to see me.'

'Jealous old cat,' Mattie said absently, peering at a textbook. The single cot had been taken out of their room when Rachel married, giving them a bit more space. Mattie was studying, sitting on her haunches at the end of the double bed, while Elspeth herself, leaning against a pillow propped against the bedhead, was writing letters, using her drawn-up knees as a desk.

'It's all water under the bridge now. No harm was done, after all.' Elspeth put the writing pad aside and eased herself on to her knees, her face alight. 'The important thing – the wonderful thing – is that I'm going to get to work in an office!'

'Until the real girl comes back, just,' Mattie cautioned.

'Even so, I'm going to be able to type all day long.'

'And this time,' Mattie cast her work aside too and bounced

up on her own knees, taking Elspeth's hands in hers, 'you're going to get paid for it!'

It had been cloudy all day, threatening rain, but not following the threat through until early afternoon, when Thomas, giving a final trim to the box hedging round some herbaceous borders, felt the first drops on the back of his neck. He ignored them, and worked on, but within minutes the rain was falling hard and fast, soaking him, and there was no sense in continuing.

The nearest shelter was a small hexagonal summerhouse in the nearby rose garden; Thomas pulled up the collar of his thick working shirt, and ran, skidding slightly on the wet paving stones between the rose beds. He cleared the three steps up to the summerhouse in one stride, threw open the double doors with their diamond-shaped panes of coloured glass set into the top sections, and catapulted into the little building.

Something already inhabiting the space within moved and gave a shriek of fright. Before he could stop himself, Thomas, too, gave out a sharp, startled cry, then felt like a complete fool as he saw Aileen Bruce crouched against the opposite wall, green eyes wide, one hand pressed to her mouth and the other to her heart, a handful of rosebuds scattered on the floor round her feet.

For a moment he stared at her dumbly, unable to believe that she was really there. Ever since the day he had spoken to her in the drive, Thomas had been unable to get the girl out of his mind. He saw her occasionally, on the tennis court, or out riding, or sitting a short distance behind him as he drove her and her parents. He had developed a strange sixth sense where she was concerned – when she was nearby he knew it, even before he actually saw her.

Once, when she was gathering flowers for the house, he had cut off a spray of lilac that was difficult for her to reach. He would never forget the light, sweet touch of her hand against his as she took the spray, the wide smile as she thanked him.

'Thomas! I thought – you came barging in like—' She gave a nervous giggle. 'I feel such a fool.'

'So do I.' In his dreams over the past months he had rescued her several times from runaway horses, or saved her from drowning. In reality, he thought grimly, sick with humiliation, he had gone crashing into the summerhouse and scared the life out of her. Desperate to get out of the confined space and go somewhere where he could slam his fist, or at least his stupid head, against the good solid trunk of a tree, he muttered an apology and turned to the door, just as the shower settled in and rain started drumming hard on the wooden roof just above their heads.

'Wait – you'll get soaked out there. There's room for us both.' She moved forward to stop him, then gave an exclamation and bent to pick up a rosebud. 'Oh, the poor thing, I've stepped on it.'

'Let me, miss, some of those thorns are wicked.'

'They can draw your blood just as easily as mine,' she objected as he knelt to gather the roses.

'I'm used to thorns.' He picked the flowers up and laid them carefully in the trug she held out to him.

'You must think I'm empty-headed, screaming and giggling like that,' she said, sitting down on the bench and settling the trug by her side.

He wanted to tell her that he thought she was the most beautiful, most wonderful woman he had ever met. Instead, he cleared his throat and said, 'Not at all, Miss Aileen. I've seen plenty of men during the war yelling because they thought a shell was going to get them, then laughing like idiots with the relief when it didn't. I've done it myself.'

'You were in the war? So was my brother. He enjoyed it.'

No doubt he had, Thomas thought grimly. Ian Bruce, an arrogant, handsome young man with never a glance or a word for the servants, was employed by a firm of lawyers in Glasgow, and lived in the city, driving to Gourock most weekends in his own smart two-seater car. When he was at home during the summer there were tennis parties, either on the Bruce court, which was kept in immaculate condition for them, or at friends' courts.

Ian Bruce, Thomas thought, would have been an officer. True, some of the officers had suffered just as much as their men, but others – and he had a feeling that Bruce was one of them – had never really had to face the realities. Aloud, he said bluntly, 'There's not much pleasure in killing and being killed.'

'Tell me about your war.'

He could have told her about the mud and the misery and the naked fear. He could have talked about the helpless certainty at times that the war would never ever stop, that he and those with him would spend the rest of their lives struggling with the enemy for a few hundred square yards of ground that for some unknown reason mattered tremendously to both sides.

He could have told her about the times when all he had wanted was to feel the impact of that final, fatal bullet, and get it all over and done with; about what it was like to see close friends screaming and dying.

Instead, his words underlined by the rain hammering on the roof, he told her about Lachlan, and what the war had done to him.

She listened without interruption, her green eyes luminous in the summerhouse's dim light. 'That's – terrible,' she said, when he had finished. 'That poor young man. My brother made it all sound like a bit of a lark. I'd no idea what it was really like.'

Thomas came back to earth with a jolt, cursing himself all over again for his stupidity. Her brother had probably tried to protect her from the truth, and he had come lumbering along and told her things she should never have heard.

'It was a bit of a lark, quite a lot of the time,' he lied. 'I expect your brother made a better job of it than I did.'

'I expect,' said Aileen Bruce shrewdly, 'that his war was easier than yours. What's going to become of your brother? Will he get better?'

'I don't know,' Thomas said honestly. 'I keep telling the rest of them that he'll be fine, but it's been so long now that I'm not sure. The nightmares have almost gone, but he's not got any of his confidence back.'

'Would a doctor not be able to help?'

'No!' He spoke so fiercely that she jumped. 'He's had his fill of doctors and nursing. I should have insisted on him staying in that hospital for a while longer instead of bringing him home because my mother wanted it. They might have made a difference then. But it's too late now tae think of ifs and buts. If we were tae send him back tae hospital now it would only make him think we'd given up, or that we don't want him. Besides, it'd more likely be the asylum now than the hospital, and I'm not having our Lachlan put intae that place.'

He stared down at his hands. 'Mam – my mother – she's beginning tae treat him as if he was a bairn again, and that's not good for him. The other day I caught her running a brush through his hair. Next thing we know she'll be dusting him, as if he was part of the furn—'

He halted, realising that something was missing, and glanced up at the roof. 'The rain's stopped.'

They made for the door at the same time, reaching out for the latch simultaneously, so that his hand landed on hers.

'I think, miss—' he started, just as she began, 'Perhaps we should—' Then they both stopped, laughing. She was so close that he could smell her skin, fresh and flowery, like a summer's day. He began to remove his hand from hers, but just then Aileen turned her own hand round so that their fingers became entwined. The trug fell to the floor for the second time, and her other hand came up to touch his face lightly, then moved over his shoulder to the nape of his neck, while his arm reached around her waist, drawing her closer.

Ina kissed boldly, her mouth open and her tongue teasing his, but Aileen Bruce's kiss was chaste and innocent, and all the sweeter for that.

It was a short kiss, but long enough for Thomas's entire life to change for ever. When they separated and he looked down into her face, he saw her eyes filled with the things he himself wanted to say. He bent towards her again, then a voice calling some distance away broke the embrace and sent them springing away from each other.

'I'm – I'm sorry, Miss Aileen, I had no right—'

The hand that had cupped the nape of his neck touched his mouth, stopping the words. 'I wanted you to kiss me,' she said, then, with sudden urgency, 'You must go. I'll find you tomorrow.'

Blessed by the rain, the garden smelled fresh and faintly perfumed, like her skin. Thomas, dazed by what had just happened, and by the strength of his own reaction, blundered out of the summerhouse and through the bushes, heedless of the light sting of branches against his face, and the soaking he got from them.

He reached the place where he had been working just in time; as he retrieved the shears from under the bush where he had stored them, Aileen and her brother met at the other side of the tall beech hedge a few yards away from him.

'I've been looking for you everywhere,' Ian Bruce said irritably. 'Where have you been?'

'Picking roses. I took shelter in the summerhouse.' Her voice, Thomas thought, stirring to the memory of her mouth beneath his, was like little bells chiming.

He bent his head over his work just as the two of them turned the corner and came towards him.

'If you wanted flowers,' Ian Bruce said shortly, ignoring the figure kneeling at the side of the path, 'you should have asked one of the gardeners to get them for you. That's what they're there for.'

'I'm quite capable of doing things for myself,' she retorted, then they were past, and Thomas looked up as they went through an archway of green and out of sight, Ian Bruce carrying the basket of rosebuds, his free arm about his sister's shoulders.

The thought came to him that while Ina fitted snugly in his arms, Aileen Bruce belonged in them. He knew what his grandmother would have said if she had known what had happened in the summerhouse: 'It'll all end in tears!'

Maybe so, but he had never been happier in his entire life than he was at that moment.

14

The typewriter clacked nonstop, turning out a continuous flow of lists, letters, and memorandums to the many departments housed within Brodie's store. As the days flew past, Elspeth's confidence grew and her initial shyness eased off. James Brodie was a fair employer, a man who put in a decent day's work and expected the same of his staff. He didn't hover over them all the time as Miss Arnold and Miss Buchanan did in the sewing room, nor, if he was in a bad mood, did he vent it on them. Wilma Morgan, the older woman, was a sharp-eyed clerkess who ruled over the accounts office, but was friendly enough as long as she was given the respect she considered due to one who had worked there for ten years. Graham Adams, still serving his apprenticeship as a clerk, was a cheerful nineteen-year-old with ambition.

'If I play my cards right, I'll be the boss in here, in time,' he bragged to Elspeth when Wilma and Mr Brodie were out of the office.

She pressed the tabulating key, and the large heavy carriage sped on its way, then crashed to a standstill at the correct place. 'D'you think so?'

'The way I see it, once the old man dies and Mr James inherits the store, he won't want to be stuck here day in and day out. He's got no choice just now, for his dad expects him to do as he did. He never missed a day at his desk himself, until the bronchitis got worse and he had to stay at home.

Imagine owning a place like this and sitting behind a desk like one of the staff!'

He had swung round on his high stool and was leaning back against the sloping desk, his elbows hooked nonchalantly on the ridge that prevented the heavy ledgers from sliding off. 'Once Mr James owns the place, I reckon he'll want to have more time for yachting. He's got his own boat at Gourock – takes it out every Saturday afternoon, and does some racing in it, too. He'll want a second-in-command here, and that'll be me.'

He jabbed at his own chest confidently with a thumb. 'So keep in with me, Elspeth, and you could do well for yourself.'

'I'm not going to be here for long. The typist'll be back one of these days, then I'll have to go back to the sewing room.'

'I can still do you some good there, for Mr James's manager would be in charge of all the departments.'

Elspeth rolled a sheet of paper out of the typewriter and put a fresh sheet in. 'I won't be here by then. I don't want to spend the rest of my life as a seamstress. I want to work in an office.'

'I could arrange that for you, when I'm in charge.' He paused; although she was concentrating on her work, he knew that he was running his eyes over her, a habit of his that she disliked intensely. 'Have you got a sweetheart?'

'My aunt says I'm too young.'

'What age are you, then?'

Lena would have come up with a pert return, or slapped his face for his cheek. Elspeth merely answered the question. 'I'm fifteen.'

'A bit young, but still, I'm not particular,' Graham said magnanimously. 'I'll take you out tonight, if you like.'

'I'm visiting my grandmother tonight.'

'Tomorrow.'

'I'm helping my Aunt Flora to do the weekend cleaning.'

'When, then?'

He was smirking confidently, appearing to think that Elspeth would be flattered by his attentions. Instead, she merely found his persistence irritating. What with the excitement over her temporary move to the office, worry about Lachlan, and her letter-writing she had enough to think about.

'I don't know.'

Graham's eyes hardened and his mouth turned down at the corners. 'I'll not wait around for ever.'

'I'd not expect you to,' she retorted, just as Wilma's heavy tread could be heard in the corridor outside. Graham spun round to the desk, snatching up his pen.

'Damn!' he muttered, and Elspeth glanced up to see a large blot of ink, dislodged from the pen as he grabbed it, spread itself over the page he had just completed.

Then Wilma was in the room, wailing over the mess he had made, and suddenly Graham, reaching for a sheet of blotting paper, protesting that it had been an accident, seemed a far cry from being Mr James Brodie's manager, and lord of all he surveyed.

Although Elspeth, as an office employee, could have eaten her midday sandwiches in the upstairs canteen, she continued, despite Wilma's obvious disapproval, to join Lena and the others in the big basement room. For one thing, she knew that soon she would have to return to the sewing room, and she had no wish to annoy the women there by appearing 'snobby', and for another, her letter-writing was still in demand, and she depended on the money she earned from it for her night-school classes.

She had thought that once the war was over her talent for writing letters would no longer be of use, but she was wrong. As well as the usual formal letters voicing complaints or asking advice, girls who wanted to keep in touch with soldiers and sailors who had been in the town during the war sought her assistance, and once the returning brothers and cousins heard of her skills they, too, contacted her, eager to keep in touch with young women they had met elsewhere, but unable to put together the things they wanted to say.

Elspeth, who had long since passed the stage of being embarrassed at requests to write about love and longing, and had in fact become famed for her ability to write love letters, sat patiently, exercise book in one hand and pencil in the other, while her clients blushed and stammered and said, 'Ach, just tell him I love him, and I cannae wait tae cuddle him again,' or, 'Can ye put down somethin' nice about her bonny face in the moonlight, and how I'll never forget that night when we – tae hang wi' it, just say that night, she'll know what I mean.'

The pennies and halfpennies filled her tobacco tin to capacity, and were exchanged for sixpences, then shillings, then half-crowns. Only Thomas knew how much she had saved, and he advised her to keep her own business to herself.

'But it seems underhand, not letting Aunt Flora know.'

'There's nothing wrong with it. You pay your wages into the house the same as the rest of us, and anything extra's yer – your own business,' said Thomas, who had been working hard on improving his speech since donning a chauffeur's uniform. 'You might need something some time, and be glad of the money.'

He urged her to open a bank account, and after she had approached the bank door three times then turned away again, unable to walk into such a place on her own, he went with her, handsome and reassuring in his smart grey chauffeur's uniform.

As they stepped back on to the street, the bankbook clutched in Elspeth's hand, Thomas said, 'I'm fetching Mrs Bruce in ten minutes. There's time to give you a lift back to Brodie's.'

Sitting in the deep, comfortable seat beside him, gliding through the streets with the mingled smell of leather and Mr Bruce's cigars tantalising her nose, was like glimpsing heaven. She had just begun to imagine herself a titled lady, dressed in the best Brodie's had to offer, on her way to take tea with the Provost's wife, when Thomas broke the spell. 'I'm worried about our Lachlan. He's not gettin' any better, is he?'

'He still needs time,' Elspeth offered, but without much

conviction, for she knew what he meant. Lachlan, who had always had some artistic skill, had taken to drawing, first on the margin of newspapers with a stub of pencil he had found, then in a blank exercise book Mattie had given him, together with a better pencil.

At first the family had looked on his new hobby as a step forward in his recovery, but all the drawings turned out to be of men in battle, some yelling defiance at the enemy as they charged, bayonets fixed on their rifles, others screaming in agony as they writhed on the ground. They were appalled by the pictures, drawn with such ferocity that the pencil dug deep into the paper.

'Mebbe we're treatin' him the wrong way,' Thomas fretted. Glancing sideways at him, Elspeth saw that his face was bleak with worry. 'Mam treats him as though he's a bairn again, and he's content to let it happen. Mebbe he needs to be pushed into doin' more for himself, instead of havin' things done for him.' He turned the wheel, easing the big car round a corner. 'He's only just gone into his twenty-first year – his whole life's still in front of him. Times I lie awake at night worryin' that he'll spend it just the way he is now.'

'But if we try to push him, could it not make him worse?'

'Mebbe, but being kind to him isn't making him any better, is it?' Thomas said in despair as they reached the corner of the street where the department store stood. 'I'd best let you out here, so's nobody in the store sees you.'

Standing on the kerb, watching Thomas drive off, Elspeth decided that one day she would like to have her own car and her own chauffeur. Patting the pocket that held her new bankbook, she felt that by opening a bank account, she had just taken the first step to future affluence.

'I will not have it!'

Elspeth, who had just stepped into the flat, halted as she heard the words booming from the kitchen.

She recognised the voice – one she had never expected to hear in Mearns Street.

'There's nothin' wrong with the lassie workin' in an office,' Flora rapped back. 'What d'ye think she'll do, Mrs Bremner – help herself tae one of the clerks?'

Elspeth opened the door on a gasp of outrage from her grandmother to see Flora McDonald and Celia Bremner facing each other across the kitchen table. Flora was red in the face, and two bright red blotches stood out on Celia's sallow cheekbones.

'You're a bad besom, Flora Docherty,' Celia hissed, using Flora's own name, as was the custom among local women. 'I never liked our Maisie going about with you – it's no wonder she went wrong!'

'It wasnae me that did for Maisie, and well you know it,' Flora almost shrieked. 'If anythin' harmed that poor lassie, it was growin' up with all the bitterness and vindictiveness in that house of yours. Oh, she told me about it – she had tae tell someone!'

Celia gave a strangled cry, her hands forming themselves into claws. For a moment Elspeth, still transfixed in the doorway, thought that her grandmother was going to throw the table aside and launch herself on Flora, then another voice broke in, high and desperate.

'Stop it!'

She hadn't even realised that Lachlan was in the room until he cried out, for he wasn't in his usual chair by the fire. Instead, he huddled in the corner between the sink and the wall that held the curtained bed-recess, his thin body pressed against the wall as though trying to force its way through the plaster and bricks. His face was ashen, and his body shaking so much that water splashed over the edge of the cup he clutched tightly in both hands.

'Stop it,' he said again through clenched teeth, his voice thin and raw. 'Stop it, stop it, stop—'

'It's all right, Lachlan, all right.' Elspeth erupted into the room, pushing past her grandmother, and squatted down beside him, talking soothingly, trying to take the cup from him. As his fingers began to relax, a ship's siren suddenly blared out from the river below. It was too much for him. He gave a short, high, animal-like scream and his body jerked at the sudden noise. Cold water slopped over Elspeth's hands, soaking through her gloves, and Lachlan's fingers spasmed, tightening round the cup until she feared that it might break.

Then Thomas was pushing her aside, raising his brother to his feet, coaxing him away from the wall and out of the room, talking in the low, soothing voice he always used for Lachlan.

Celia Bremner watched him go, her face frozen in a grimace of astonishment and distaste. 'What in the world's wrong with the laddie?' she wanted to know when the two young men had gone from the room.

'I told you, Grandmother, it's what happened to him in the war. He can't help it.'

'He should be in the infirmary – or the asylum.'

'You hold yer tongue!' Flora almost spat the words at the old woman. 'There's nothin' wrong with my laddie that a wee bit of peace and quiet cannae cure. Ye've said yer say, Mrs Bremner – now ye can get out of my house.'

'Elspeth, you will come with me. This is no place for any granddaughter of mine.'

Elspeth felt as though the ground had been pulled from beneath her feet. Panic caught her heart and squeezed it painfully as she backed away from her grandmother, groping with one hand for the sturdiness of the wall at her back. Her fingers caught instead at the bed-curtains, gathering a handful of the material.

'I don't want to,' she heard herself saying.

'It's not a question of what you want. I'll not have my own flesh and blood living in this house.'

'Ye never wanted Ellie before, so why should ye have her now?' Flora wanted to know. 'I'll not let you waste her life the way ye wasted poor Maisie's.'

'You have the nerve to say that to me, when your own son's no better than—'

'Mam!' Thomas's voice was like the crack of a whip. He moved quickly from the door to intercept his mother, who was on her way towards Celia Bremner. 'Sit down, Mam, I'll deal with this.' His mother's body stiffened, like that of a small child unwilling to be put in a seat, but Thomas's youthful strength won, and Flora had no option but to sit down. Then he turned to Celia. 'Mrs Bremner, I think you should go home now.'

She eyed him warily, moving back a step. 'Elspeth—'

'Elspeth's staying here for the moment. If she wants to live with you, she'll make her own way.'

'She'll do as her grandmother tells her!'

Thomas's face was like stone, though his voice was still low and reasonable. 'Elspeth's old enough tae earn her keep, and she's old enough tae make up her own mind. Not one person in this house'll try tae influence her, one way or another. You have my word on that. Now – I'll walk with you down tae the tram stop, and see you on your way.'

Celia summoned up the last of her strength. 'Elspeth, I'll expect you in Port Glasgow!' With one last, scathing look at Flora, she made for the door, but by that time her fingers were trembling so hard that they fumbled helplessly with the handle.

Thomas reached round her to open the door. 'I'll not be long,' he told the others as he followed Celia out. 'Ellie, look after Lachlan.'

As the outer door closed, Flora slumped in her chair. She, too, was shaking, her face grey and old. 'Elspeth, see tae Lachlan.'

'Aunt Flora, why is my grand—'

'Do as yer told!' Flora snapped, summoning such a steely edge to her voice that Elspeth fled at once from the room.

Lachlan was sitting on his bed; when she sat down beside him, her arm against his, she could feel him trembling.

'It's all right, Lachie, it was just my grandmother in a temper.'

'I don't like folk shouting,' he whispered through white lips.

'I know. I don't either.'

'She was shouting about you, Ellie. What've ye done tae make her so angry?'

'I've not done anything. She's just awful strict, like a teacher.'

'She told Mam that ye've tae go and stay with her.'

Elspeth felt a shiver run through her at the thought of living in the cheerless house she could scarcely bear to sit in for even two hours.

'I'm not going.'

'Good.' Lachlan took her hand in his. He was like a child, Elspeth thought sadly, remembering how she had always looked up to him in her own childhood, always longed to be as grown-up as he was.

She started talking about times they'd had as children, and about her work, and gradually he relaxed. She heard Thomas return eventually, going directly to the kitchen. Then Mattie and her father came in and the small flat grew fragrant with the smell of the midday meal. And still she talked, until, at last, Thomas appeared in the doorway.

'It's dinner-time.'

Lachlan went off cheerfully enough, while Elspeth lingered to ask, 'How's Grandmother?'

'I went all the way back with her, to be on the safe side. She was in an awful state, poor old soul.' A faint smile touched the corners of his mouth. 'She wouldn't talk to me. I had to sit at the back of the tram and pay my own fare. I think she was glad enough to have someone keeping an eye on her, but she'd have died before she'd admit it. Don't say anything to the rest of them,' he added as they went through the hall. 'Mam won't want them to know what happened.'

15

Flora refused to discuss Celia Bremner's visit, and Elspeth was left puzzling about what she had overheard, and trying to make sense of it. Finally, she ventured to speak to Granjan about it.

'It's no business of yours or mine, pet.'

'But it is my business,' Elspeth said, exasperated. 'The quarrel was about me. I thought Grandmother would be pleased about me wanting to work in an office like my grandfather. But when I mentioned it she was so sharp that I didn't even dare to tell her I was going to night school. What have I done wrong?'

'Nothing at all,' Janet Docherty hastened to assure her. 'It wasnae you who did wrong.'

'Who did, then?'

Janet sighed. 'I suppose ye should know – but not a word tae anyone. If Flora knew I'd told ye she'd be ragin'.'

'Not a word, I promise.'

'It was yer grandfather.' Granjan spoke as though every word was being dragged out of her. 'It seems there was this woman worked in the same office as him, and he – liked her.'

Elspeth gaped at her. 'He fell in love with another woman while he was married to Grandmother?'

'It happens tae folk sometimes – but not often,' Granjan added hurriedly. 'Marriage is marriage, and nothin' should come between man and wife. But I'll admit that Celia Bremner was never what ye'd call a warm, lovin' sort of woman.'

'Did she find out about it?'

'If she didnae know before he went off, she must have known then,' Janet said drily. It was almost too much for Elspeth to take in.

'You mean he ran away – with this woman?' Her voice rose to a squeal, and Janet winced.

'For any favour keep yer voice down – the neighbours'll hear.'

'But Grandmother said he died.'

'So he did, as far as she was concerned.' Janet bent stiffly to pick a piece of fluff from the carpet. 'Marriage is important tae a woman, Ellie. There's a certain respect in havin' a ring on yer finger an' bein' called Missus. There's as much respect for a widow, but little for a deserted wife.'

'Folk must have known, surely.'

'Of course they did. The whole place buzzed with it, and I felt that sorry for Celia – not that she was a woman who'd let anyone sympathise with her. The gossip soon died down, the way gossip does. As tae her sayin' he died – he might well have by now, for all folk know. An' give the man his due, he saw tae it that she wasnae left destitute.'

Elspeth sat silent, trying to understand the new picture Granjan had painted of Celia Bremner. She was such a proud woman, and she must have suffered greatly over her husband's desertion.

'Was it just after that that she started wanting to see me?'

'I believe it was, hen.'

'She wants me to go and live with her,' Elspeth said, and shivered. 'But I can't. I'm sorry for what happened to her, but it doesn't make her a different person.'

'We all have our own lives, and nobody else can live them for us. You do whatever's best for you,' Janet told her. 'But whatever you do, mind what I said – not a word about this tae a soul!'

*

As the day for her usual monthly visit to Port Glasgow drew near, Elspeth was in a quandary. She had decided, after the quarrel, never to visit her grandmother again, and the decision had been a relief, for she hated the duty visits. But Granjan's story had made her feel guilty about turning her back on her maternal grandmother, who had already lost her husband and her daughter – or, rather, driven them both away from her.

She was still unsure when the day came, and was taken aback when Flora said after the midday meal, 'Is it not time ye were gettin' ready tae go tae yer grandmother's?'

'You want me to go, after what happened between the two of you?'

Flora glared. 'That has nothin' tae dae with you doin' yer duty by her. She's yer own flesh and blood.'

'I'll come with you, Ellie,' Mattie volunteered as Elspeth hesitated, and her mother rounded on her.

'Ye'll do no such thing, lady. Elspeth's old enough tae tend tae her own business.'

Apprehension settled in a solid lump behind Elspeth's ribs as she prepared for the visit. By the time she reached her grandmother's door it had become a hard, jagged boulder. She banged the polished brass doorknocker the way she had been taught, loud enough to be heard, but not loud enough to annoy Grandmother, then stepped back, hands folded protectively across the part of her stomach where the boulder lay.

After a moment she heard movement behind the door, then it opened to reveal Celia Bremner, as erect and as awesome as ever.

'It's you,' she said, as she always did. Then, moving back, 'You'd best come in.'

The visit went along its usual lines, with not a thing said about Celia's visit to Mearns Street. In the kitchen, the teatray was set out as usual, as though there had been no question of Elspeth staying away.

After tea, instead of waiting in the kitchen until

Grandmother emerged from the lavatory, Elspeth tiptoed into the living room to study the photograph more closely. Surely that balding, respectable man behind the protective glass couldn't possibly have had a sweetheart, she thought, but a more intensive study showed that in actual fact he was quite a good-looking man.

Noting afresh the possessive hold his wife had on his shoulder, Elspeth began to understand why he had felt the need to escape. Then the cistern was flushed, and she fled, mouse-like, back to the kitchen, reaching it just in time.

Flora sank into a chair by the table and fanned herself with one hand. 'That washhouse was like a furnace today,' she said, then, as she always did when she returned to the house, 'Put the kettle on, Elspeth, I could do with a cup of tea.'

Thomas, studying a book at the table, put a detaining hand on Elspeth's wrist as she moved past him to the cooker. 'Lachlan,' he said blandly, 'put the kettle on, will you?'

Lachlan, who had been idly gazing into space, stared. So did his mother.

'What?'

'Elspeth's been helping you with the washing, Mam. She's just as tired as you are, and I'm tryin' to read this book about car engines. Lachlan's not doing anything.'

'But Lachlan's—'

'—as able as any of us to make a cup of tea,' Thomas said evenly. 'It's time he was doing something round the house.'

Flora went red. 'Don't talk nonsense. Elspeth, do as you're told.'

Thomas's fingers tightened. 'Sit down, Elspeth, and let Lachlan see to it.' His brown eyes flashed a clear message at her, and she sank into a chair, her heart thumping, and her palms clammy.

'I'll make it myself,' Flora said icily, but Thomas's free hand caught at her sleeve as she started to rise.

'He can manage, Mam. He's a man, not a bairn.'

'He's not well!'

'And he'll not get well if you keep fussing over him. It's gone on long enough. You heard me, Lachlan,' Thomas told his brother, his voice suddenly hard. 'Get up and put the kettle on.'

Lachlan, who had been looking wide-eyed back and forth between his mother and brother during their argument, did as he was told. Seeing his hands shake as he filled the kettle, Elspeth longed to get up and do it for him, but didn't dare.

'Now put the cups on the table,' Thomas said, his voice crisp and hard. An officer's voice, Elspeth suddenly realised. The voice of authority, one that Lachlan had been trained in the army to obey automatically.

Step by step, keeping one hand on his mother's wrist, Thomas talked his brother through the ritual of making tea. Uncertainly, moving like an old man, Lachlan did as he was told, while Flora sat motionless, her mouth so tight that it could scarcely be seen, her eyes like icy pebbles.

When the time came for Lachlan to pour boiling water from the kettle to the large shabby tin teapot, his hands were trembling so much that Elspeth was convinced that he was going to scald himself. She half rose from the chair, then as Thomas said her name very quietly, forced herself to sit down again.

After Lachlan had placed a cup in front of each of them, he began to take his own tea back to his chair, where he took all his meals, a towel tucked into the neck of his shirt by Flora. Thomas's voice halted him. 'Sit at the table with us, Lachlan.'

The young man hesitated and half turned, his eyes pleading. 'Here, beside me,' Thomas said implacably, drawing out a chair, and Lachlan obeyed.

It was more like a funeral than four people enjoying a cup of tea. Thomas talked about car engines, while Flora stared at the table, making no attempt to drink her tea, and Lachlan, after trying to lift his cup two-handed and being forced to put it down again because his trembling hands threatened to splash hot liquid all over the table, gave up the attempt.

Elspeth, glancing over at him, saw that he was weeping silently. She put her own cup down, determined this time to do something about his misery, but just then he got to his feet and left the room, scrubbing one sleeved arm over his face in a heartbreakingly childish gesture.

'Are ye satisfied now?' Flora hissed at her first-born as soon as Lachlan had gone. 'D'ye not think the poor laddie's got enough trouble without you bullyin' him? Wait till yer father—'

'Sometimes, Mam, we have to be cruel to be kind.' Thomas got up with an abrupt movement and went to the door.

'Where d'ye think ye're goin'?'

'To Lachlan.'

'Leave him – ye've done him enough harm!'

'It's me he needs. Sit down, Mam, and drink your tea.'

'I don't want it!'

'When we behaved like that, you called it cutting off our noses to spite our faces,' Thomas said, and left the room. Flora scraped her chair back from the table, poured her tea down the sink, and began to scrub the potatoes for the evening meal, the water flying in all directions a testimony to her inner fury.

The next morning Thomas, who had until then been helping Lachlan to dress and undress, got his brother up half an hour earlier than usual, and stood over him while Lachlan laboriously dressed himself.

Flora tutted when he appeared in the kitchen with his shirt buttons in the wrong buttonholes. 'Lachlan, will ye look at yerself, laddie! Come here till I sort ye out.'

Lachlan started to move obediently towards her, but Thomas, coming into the room at his back, stopped him.

'Leave him be, Mam. Look, Lachie—' He hooked a finger into the loop of shirt on Lachlan's thin chest caused by an

153

unused buttonhole. 'You've missed one. You'll have to undo them all and start again. From the top now, and work your way down.'

From then on, the battle for Lachlan was under way. Flora's fingers itched every time she saw her son with his braces twisted or his shoelaces untied, but Thomas continued to push his brother into looking after himself, and saw to it that Elspeth and Mattie and his father did the same.

At first, Lachlan's struggles were painful to see. Often he was in tears of helpless frustration, but gradually, the tears gave way to bouts of anger, mainly directed against Thomas, who shouted back at him, goading him on.

'He never used to lose his temper,' Elspeth said nervously after Lachlan had stormed off to bed following a particularly bad flare-up.

'It's time he learned, then.'

'Thomas, are you sure you're doing the right thing, treating him this way?'

'It's that, or seeing him turn into a helpless invalid.' Thomas pushed his thick fair hair from his face, but, as usual, it fell back across his brow as soon as it was released. 'And what'll happen to him then, Ellie? Who's going to care for him when Mam's gone? D'ye want to see him put into the asylum or the poors' hospital, or left to walk the streets because he can't fend for himself? I know I'm hurting him, but it's like thawing out someone who's been frozen. It's sore, but if he isnae thawed out he'll die. That's what's happening to Lachie.' He caught at her wrist, shook it slightly. 'And you've got to help me, for none of the rest will.'

Picking up Lachlan's discarded sketch book he leafed through the pages, then gave a short laugh. 'Take a look at that.'

The battle scenes concentrated now on one soldier. In every sketch he was injured and suffering, and in every sketch he bore a clear likeness to Thomas.

'The man's got talent,' Thomas commented drily.

He didn't let up for a moment, and as the days and weeks went by, Lachlan began to show unmistakable signs of improvement. Tormented by his brother's jibes about grown men who let their mammies look after them, he began to shrug his mother's hands away when she tried, in Thomas's absence, to do something for him.

Looking at the expression on the older woman's face each time that happened, Elspeth sympathised with her, for she was only trying to do what she saw as the best for Lachlan. She herself felt ashamed of the times she had answered Aunt Flora back and been difficult, and tried to be kinder and more understanding.

Unfortunately, Flora, wounded to the core by what she saw as Lachlan's rejection, interpreted Elspeth's overtures as pity. She became even more irritable with the girl than before, and gradually, Elspeth's good intentions flew out of the window, the two of them reverting back to the uneasy relationship they had known for years.

Flora's bitterness over Thomas and Lachlan was eased when Rachel plucked up the courage to tell her that she was expecting a child.

'There's just one thing,' the girl went on nervously. 'It's due in January.'

Flora, as used to mental mathematics as any housewife forced, week after week, to make the money available go as far as possible, did a swift calculation in her head, then glared at her daughter. 'A seven-month bairn?'

'Eight months, Mam.'

'Don't quibble with me, lady, it's still too early. Some of the neighbours might be daft, but they're no' fools. No wonder ye were so keen tae take up the Cochrans' offer of a double weddin'!'

'What with Bob coming back safe from the war, and all . . .' Rachel's words faded under her mother's look, then she made one more try, 'At least we're not as bad as Annie Cochran and her man – their bairn's born already.'

'Just because she just made it tae the kirk in time, it doesnae excuse what you did. After the way I've tried to bring you up well,' Flora foamed, 'here ye are, giving yer father and me a showin' up before the whole street.'

'It happens to other folk,' Rachel protested tremulously.

'But it's never happened to us. If this is a lassie ye're carryin', wait and see how you feel if she comes tae you with the same tale. Ye'll not be so pleased about it then.'

Tears were shimmering in Rachel's eyes now. 'Don't be like that about it, Mam, Bob's bad enough without you starting on me.'

'What d'ye mean? Is he not pleased about the bairn?'

Rachel sniffed. 'He doesnae want a family so soon. He says I should have been more careful.'

'He what?' Flora's maternal instinct flared up. 'The cheeky monkey! It takes two tae make a bairn, just you tell him that from me! And when it comes, it'll be a lot bonnier than that wee red-faced greetin' thing his sister Annie's got. All my bairns were bonny.'

'Does that mean you're not angry with me, Mam?'

Flora had gone too far to draw back now. 'Aye, well, what's done's done,' she conceded, 'and it'll be nice tae have a grand—' She broke off as the door opened and Thomas walked in.

'Thomas?' She glanced at the clock. 'What are ye doin' here at this time of the day?'

He was in his chauffeur's uniform, the peaked cap tucked beneath one arm. 'Ma – Mother, I've brought Miss Bruce to visit you,' he said awkwardly, just as Aileen Bruce, in a beige silk dress under a long deep green linen jacket, came into the kitchen at his back.

Her smile, as she advanced on Flora, a slim hand extended, was radiant. 'Mrs McDonald – I've been looking forward to meeting you.'

Flustered, Flora and Rachel scrambled to their feet.

'Where's Lachlan?' Thomas asked as Aileen's soft, cool hand met Flora's rough and reddened fingers.

'In his room. Thomas—' Flora said as he went into the hall, then belatedly remembered her manners. 'This is my eldest, Rachel. Ye'll have a wee cup of tea, Miss Bruce?'

Aileen beamed at Rachel, who smiled shyly in return, one hand trying to tidy her hair unobtrusively. 'It's very kind of you, but we're hoping to take your other son for a drive.'

'Our Lachlan?' Flora signalled to Rachel to scoop up the cups sitting on the floor by the two fireside chairs.

'I thought he might enjoy a run to Loch Thom. It's lovely up there.'

'Ye'll take a seat, at least.'

'Thank you.' Aileen Bruce sank gracefully into a chair by the table and, apparently unaware of the tension in the room, chattered easily until Thomas returned with Lachlan, who, much to his mother's relief, had put on a jacket and tie and brushed his hair. His brown eyes were wary, and he was rubbing his hands nervously down the sides of his trousers.

'Here we are.' There was a forced cheerfulness in Thomas's voice. 'Miss Bruce, this is my brother Lachlan.'

Aileen's wide smile broke over Lachlan, making him blink. 'How do you do? I'm sorry you've not been well. Thomas tells me you're feeling better, though.'

'H-how d'ye do?' He shook her hand as though it was made of porcelain.

'I hope you'll come out with us for a wee run.'

'Of course he will,' Thomas said heartily. 'We'd best be on our way – we'll not be long, Mother.'

16

Lachlan was still out when the rest of the family arrived home, and the flat was spotless, for Flora had spent the rest of the afternoon, with Rachel's help, cleaning every inch of it. But there was no evening meal waiting for them.

'I'm not havin' that Bruce lassie findin' us sittin' eatin',' Flora said firmly. 'She'll not catch me unawares twice. Ye'll have tae wait until she's been and gone before ye eat. Henry, away tae the wee room and change intae yer best clothes. I've left them out for ye.'

'Put on my good clothes on a weekday? The lassie's flesh and blood the same as the rest of us,' Henry protested, his stomach rumbling. 'She knows that we eat, there's no shame in her seein' us doin' it.'

'That's not what I think – and for goodness' sake do somethin' about that noise,' Flora snapped as his empty stomach protested again. 'D'ye want tae shame me entirely?'

Hurt and hungry, he took himself off to the pub, announcing that he would buy a pie to keep body and soul together. Flora, her mouth a thin, tight line, started to clean the spotless sink.

'D'ye think she will come back?' Mattie asked hopefully. 'I wish I'd been home earlier to see her!'

Flora, plying a washcloth energetically, sniffed. 'There was nothin' tae see, just a wealthy lassie who'd no business to be here.'

'It was nice of her to think of taking Lachlan out,' Mattie protested. 'Most posh folk are too neb-in-the-air tae come near a tenement.'

'Not Miss Aileen,' Elspeth said. She, too, was disappointed at missing the girl's visit, but at least she could claim to have seen her at close quarters before. 'She was in the fitting room at Brodie's once, when she and her sister were having clothes made for the wedding. I thought then she would be nice to know. D'you not mind, Mattie, when we went to see her sister comin' out of the church after she got married? Miss Aileen was the chief bridesmaid.'

'Oh, yes – a bonny girl, she was, with black hair and a lovely smile.'

'There's more tae folk than a nice smile and clothes that cost enough tae feed a workman's family for a week,' Flora interrupted. 'Dust that skirtin' board if ye've nothin' else tae dae, Mattie. And Elspeth, take a dry mop over the hall linoleum.'

To the girls' disappointment, Lachlan came home alone shortly afterwards, glowing with fresh air and exercise. Aileen and Thomas had taken him over the hills to Loch Thom, the town's reservoir.

'It was grand tae see the grass and the water again, and hear the birds,' he said with an enthusiasm Elspeth hadn't seen since his last war leave. 'We'd a right good walk round the water's edge, the three of us. She's kind, that Miss Aileen. Mam, Thomas says tae tell ye he'll get somethin' tae eat at the big house. He'd tae take Miss Aileen home, then tonight he's drivin' her mother and father.' His eyes swept the empty, polished table. 'Have I missed my dinner?'

Flora's dread of another visit from Aileen Bruce turned to insult because the girl hadn't returned to see the result of all her polishing and scrubbing. 'There's cold meat, and I'll fry up some cold boiled potatoes,' she said shortly. 'That'll have tae dae ye for once.'

*

Thomas didn't come home till late, tiptoeing into the dark, silent hall. When his duties as a chauffeur kept him at work in the evenings, he always went straight to bed without disturbing the sleeping household, but tonight the kitchen door opened to reveal his mother's silhouette.

'In here.'

The kitchen was dimly lit by one gas mantle, and Henry's snores wafted from behind the curtains closing off the wall-bed. Flora had changed into her long-sleeved, throat-to-ankle nightdress, with a large shawl over it. Her grey hair, released from the bun she put it up in every morning, hung down over her shoulders, giving her a vulnerable look. But there was nothing vulnerable about her voice.

'Well?' Thomas asked when they were confronting each other.

'You know fine!' his mother told him, low-voiced, mindful of her sleeping husband. 'Bringin' that lassie intae my kitchen without warning and giving me a right showin'-up!'

Thomas had changed out of his chauffeur's uniform and back into his own clothes. 'Mam, the kitchen was spotless. It always is – there was no need for you to be ashamed of it.'

'But she's used tae a lot better than this, isn't she?' Flora glanced round the small room where the entire family ate and washed and spent their spare time. Ever since Aileen Bruce had stepped into it, she had been looking at it through different eyes, seeing what she imagined Aileen had seen – a crowded little room with handmade rag rugs laid on linoleum that was kept spotlessly clean, but was also faded from all those scrubbings, and cracked in places.

'That doesnae mean that there's anything wrong with the place. She's a nice lassie, Mam, she didnae come here to look down on us.'

'Why did she come, then?'

'To take Lachlan out, and to meet you. She's heard all about you and the rest of the family from me.'

Flora pulled the shawl more tightly about her body. 'Since when does a gardener talk about himself and his family tae his employer's daughter?'

He flushed angrily, his patience almost spent. 'I'm a chauffeur as well as a gardener—'

'Fancy names don't change folk.'

'—and sometimes I've to drive Miss Aileen places,' Thomas forged on, refusing to let the jibe get to him. 'She's interested in folk – where's the harm in that?'

'There's plenty harm when a man workin' for a lassie's father looks at her the way you did today.'

His flush deepened. 'What d'you mean by that?'

Flora put her hands flat on the table, grunting a little at the pain in her stiff wrists, and looked hard at her elder son, the first-born who had always meant more to her than any of the others.

'Ye know fine what I mean. Stop yer nonsense now, Thomas, before ye make a fool of yerself.'

Their eyes met and locked, then Thomas turned and walked out of the room.

Lachlan, worn out by excitement and unaccustomed exercise, was sound asleep, and didn't stir as Thomas undressed and slipped into bed. Tired though he was himself, he lay awake in the darkness.

'Your mother doesn't like me,' Aileen had said as they drove back to Gourock after dropping Lachlan in Mearns Street. She had moved into the front seat, close enough for him to smell the scent she always wore.

'Of course she does! Who could dislike you? Lachlan thinks you're an angel come down from heaven,' he told her, grinning. They had reached a quiet stretch of road, and he drew the car in to the side and stopped. 'You'll have to get into the back now. You can't let your parents see you sitting beside the chauffeur.'

161

She put a hand on his arm, preventing him from getting out. 'And what do you think about me?'

'You know what I think,' Thomas said hoarsely, and as though it was the most natural thing to do in the world, she came into his arms, her mouth hungry for his. He kissed her, quickly and softly at first, then hard, with passion. She responded just as passionately, and he crushed her even closer, heat racing through his body.

Ever since that first kiss in the summerhouse they had been meeting when and where they could. At first the excitement of their secret trysts had been enough, but over the past few weeks their feelings had deepened.

Now, as they drew apart, he said, 'I can't bear the thought of you going away for a whole month.'

'Neither can I, but they wouldn't dream of letting me stay behind.' She reached up and traced his eyebrows with the tip of one finger. 'We'll write to each other, every day.'

'Where can we send the letters?' Thomas asked in despair. 'There's nobody we can trust. You'll meet someone, and fall in love and forget about me – and mebbe that'd be for the best.'

'No!' It was a soft, urgent cry, followed by a rain of butterfly-light kisses on his chin and mouth.

'That's what's going to happen sooner or later, Aileen. I don't see your parents letting you marry their chauffeur.'

'There must be some way!'

Thomas doubted it. He had known from the start that nothing could come of their feelings for each other.

'We have to go,' he said reluctantly, opening the car door. 'They'll be wondering where you are.'

After tucking her tenderly into the cool recesses of the back seat, he resumed his place behind the wheel, taking a moment to glance at the river, lazy and mirror-like beneath the blue, sunny sky. Downriver, the surface was gashed by a passing ship on its way up the Clyde to deliver its load in Glasgow, passing a trim, brightly painted passenger steamer taking day trippers round the islands scattered thickly at the mouth of the river. The disturbed water at the wake of both vessels broke into white ruffles that spread slowly, in long rolling waves. Eventually, those waves would break on the banks.

On the far side, dolls'-house-sized dwellings could be seen, the hills rising behind them soft and green and peaceful.

'I love you, Thomas,' Aileen said softly from the rear of the car as he eased it back on to the road. He smiled at her in the mirror.

'I love you too,' he said.

Now, remembering their stolen moments, Thomas tossed restlessly in the dark of the night, wishing with all his heart that he could have turned the wheel just then and taken the car safely over the surface of the river and on to the far shore, then up into the rich, placid green hills beyond, driving forever with Aileen, never to be found by anyone.

In August, Theresa McCabe, James Brodie's typist, was well enough to return to the office, and Elspeth was sent back to the sewing room.

She was apprehensive about her reception, worried in case the other seamstresses would accuse her of being 'posh', or having airs and graces after spending time as an office worker, but thanks to her decision to continue spending her midday breaks with them, and her friendship with Lena, there was no trouble from the others.

The only person who caused her grief was Miss Arnold. 'I hope this won't be beneath your dignity,' she would say scathingly when giving Elspeth work to do, or, 'You'll be sure to let me know if you think this will ruin your hands, won't you? We never know when Mr James might need your invaluable assistance again.'

'Pay no attention,' Lena advised. 'She's jealous because she cannae do anythin' but sew, and she's not all that good at it. Well, she's not,' she protested as the girls huddled round the table greeted this sacrilege with gasps. 'When does she ever do any sewin' herself?'

'She worked on Miss Bruce's trousseau last year,' one of them volunteered.

'Only plain sewin', though. She got where she is by makin' up tae Miss Buchanan. I'll grant ye she's quite good at organ-isin', but when it comes tae plyin' a needle or usin' a machine we're all better than her. Mebbe we have tae put up with her behaviour, but we don't have tae be frightened by it.'

'Miss Buchanan'll be getting retired in a few years,' some-one pointed out. 'Then Miss Arnold'll get her job. You should try tae get Miss Arnold's place when the time comes, Lena.'

'Me? I'll be long away by then. I'll be on the halls, see if I'm not,' Lena said haughtily.

Following her friend's advice, Elspeth swallowed hard when Miss Arnold's tongue lashed at her, and trapped her own tongue between her teeth to hold back the retorts that so swiftly came to mind. Gradually, as the weeks went by, the woman grew tired of baiting her, and life settled back to normal.

Unable to believe what her casual passing glance had revealed, Elspeth spun round, almost bumping into a fat elderly man, and hurried back to the small shop window.

It badly needed cleaning, and the space beyond it was crowded with the richly varied collection to be found in any pawn shop, but the typewriter in the middle of the clutter stood out like a precious stone in a box of costume jewellery, large and black and solid, its great carriage scarcely demeaned by the bracelets and necklaces that had been looped around it.

She put down the bag containing the exercise book she used to list details of letters to be written, and cupped her hands against the glass to cut out the sun's reflection. Peer as she might, she couldn't see a price ticket.

She straightened up and turned to the shop door, then had

to lean against the window instead as her legs suddenly went weak. For a moment she doubted if she had the strength to take the few steps needed to reach the door, but as she stood there, quivering with excitement, the bell jangled as a woman went in. The thought that she might be enquiring about the typewriter, might even buy it, gave Elspeth the energy she needed, and she followed the woman in so closely that she narrowly avoided being hit in the face as the door swung back.

She trembled in the background, relaxing slightly when the woman produced a vase from her shopping bag and began to haggle with the thin, stooped man behind the counter. The two of them argued comfortably for some time while Elspeth shifted from foot to foot and tried to choke back a sneeze as dust tickled at the back of her nose.

At last, client and pawnbroker reached agreement. Money was handed over and the woman hurried out, while the pawnbroker gathered up the vase and carried it off into the back shop, tossing, 'I'll no' keep ye a minute, lass,' over his shoulder.

After a moment, the bell above the street door jangled and a young man came in, brushing past her to duck round the edge of the counter.

'Can I help you?'

'Th-that typewriter in the window – is it for sale?'

'The Underwood? Yes, it is, the man who pawned it didn't come back for it.' He pulled a ledger from beneath the counter and flipped through it. 'Nine shillings.'

Elspeth did a swift sum in her head. 'I could manage three shillings and sixpence just now, and pay the rest up, if that would be all right.'

'Is it for yourself?'

'Yes. I can type,' Elspeth said quickly in her own defence. 'I'm attending night school, but it's not on just now.'

'Have a look at it, while I ask my uncle.' He cleared a space on the narrow counter, then, after a tussle, managed to heave the typewriter out of the window. As he went into the back shop, Elspeth caressed the typewriter keys gently, dizzy with the thought of owning such a machine.

The young man returned and thrust a sheet of paper at her. 'You'll want to try it out,' he said, and watched with interest as she rolled the paper into the carriage, lined it up, and dashed off the first thing that came into her head. Rolling the paper out of the machine, she studied the result.

'The t's not working.'

He came round to her side of the counter to look over her shoulder. '"Wee sleekit cow'ring tim'rous beastie",' he translated, with some difficulty. 'You're a Burns fan?'

'It's a good poem for practising.'

He tested the keys, then announced, 'That one's sticking. I can oil it for you, and dust it.' Then, straightening up as the older man came through from the back shop, 'What d'you think, Uncle George? Can the young lady buy it in instalments?'

'Well—' The pawnbroker scratched at his chin, the rasping of fingernails against beard-stubble loud in the small claustrophobic space.

'It's been sitting in the back shop for long enough,' his nephew urged. 'Not many folk in this town are desperate to buy a typewriter.'

The pawnbroker glared. 'It's a valuable machine.'

'I'd not expect to take it away until the money's all paid up,' Elspeth put in hurriedly.

'And when'll that be?'

'I'll put something towards it every week, and it'll be paid up by the end of the year – earlier, if I can manage it.'

With almost two-thirds of the asking price still to be found, it was a reckless commitment, but she couldn't afford to ask for longer. She might lose the typewriter altogether, and when would another chance come along? She would make every saving she could, and add in the little she got back from Auntie Flora each week.

'How can I be sure ye'll no' lose interest and stop payin'?

This is a valuable piece of machinery, ye know.'

'If I do stop you can keep what I've paid so far.'

She remembered another barrier to her ownership, and drew a deep breath. 'I've not got the three and sixpence on me, but I'll bring it in tomorrow.' Her whole body was tense with urgency; she felt her mouth trembling, and put a hand up to hide this sign of weakness.

'Come on, Uncle George, it's a fair offer,' the young man urged, and his uncle, after deliberating, nodded creakily, as though the decision he had just come to hurt physically as well as emotionally.

'As long as I get the first payment tomorrow. If I don't, or if ye miss a week, the machine goes right back into the window, mind. Kenneth, I'll hold you responsible.'

Elspeth almost wept with relief. 'I don't know how to thank you!' she said when the pawnbroker had shuffled back through the curtained doorway at the side of the counter.

'For a start, you could give me your handkerchief.'

'My – what?'

He grinned down at her. He had a nice face, round and cheerful. His hair was dark, and his brown eyes crinkled at the corners when he smiled. 'The typewriter needs cleaning – you've smeared dust all over your face.'

'Oh!' Luckily her handkerchief was still spotless and unused. She gave it to him and he wiped her chin and cheek carefully before returning it to her.

'That's better. I'll put it away in the back shop for you, and get it into working order. I'll need your name and address for our books.'

'I'll type it for you,' Elspeth said proudly. 'But you'll have to fill in the t's yourself.'

'Miss Elspeth Bremner,' he read aloud when she had finished, then, holding out his hand, 'Kenneth Monteith.'

'How do you do?' She felt colour rising to her cheeks as they shook hands.

'Are you planning to use the typewriter to start up in business for yourself?'

'Oh no, I'm a seamstress – but I'm going to work in an office one day,' she explained as he raised his eyebrows. 'I write letters for folk, sometimes business letters, so a typewriter of my own would be useful.'

He was about to say something else, but his uncle called on him from behind the curtain. 'Well,' he came round the counter to open the street door for her, 'I'll see you tomorrow, when you make your first payment. Good afternoon, Miss Bremner.'

Her feet skimmed the pavement as she went home. She couldn't believe that at last she was going to have her very own typewriter! She could write letters on it, and maybe papers for Mattie. She was on the threshold of a new life, and the possibilities ahead were endless.

17

There was very little left in her bank account once she'd taken out the deposit for the typewriter, but that couldn't be helped, she thought, hurrying to the pawn shop with the money. She peered in the window as she passed, but the typewriter had gone.

To her relief, Kenneth was behind the counter. 'It's all right, it's in the back shop,' he reassured her as soon as she went in. 'I started working on it today.'

After checking the money and entering the amount into a ledger, he wrote the date and amount on a small card and handed it over. 'This'll help you to keep the payments in order. I've put the full amount at the top,' he explained, then, diffidently, 'I was wondering – there's a good film on at the Central Picture House this week, and I don't like going on my own. Would you care to come with me?'

Elspeth, aware of a sudden warmth in her face, could have wept. Kenneth Monteith would soon begin to think that she was a red-faced clown at this rate. But this was the first time a young man had ever invited her out, apart from the Brodie's messenger boy, and Graham in the office. She hadn't taken either of them seriously, but Kenneth was different. He had been very helpful about the typewriter.

'Yes,' she heard herself say, though she was sure that she hadn't definitely made her mind up. He grinned, showing strong white teeth.

'Tomorrow night? I'll call for you at half past six.'

'I'll meet you outside the Central at quarter to seven,' she said hastily, explaining to Mattie later, in the privacy of their room, that she wasn't at all sure what Aunt Flora would have to say about a gentleman caller.

'She might not let me go at all. It's safer to let her think I'm going out with Lena and the others.' She had been permitted to attend the cinema once or twice with girls from work.

Mattie wrinkled her nose. 'I couldn't be bothered walking out with a young man just now – not when I'm getting ready to go to college.'

'We're not going to start keeping company, it's only a visit to the pictures.' There were times, Elspeth thought, when Mattie had a bit of an opinion about herself. She had left school now, and soon she would leave for Glasgow to start her teacher-training course. In the meantime she had found work during the summer months as a sales assistant in a Gourock dress shop. Since starting the job, a distinct loftiness had crept into her manner.

'He's taking me to the Central Picture House,' Elspeth told her importantly. The Central in West Blackhall Street was one of Greenock's newest and most impressive cinemas.

'D'you like him? I'd need to like someone an awful lot to let them take me to the pictures.'

'He's nice enough, but I'm only going because he's been so kind about the typewriter. Anyway,' Elspeth added honestly, 'I fancy seeing the inside of the Central.'

Fortunately, Kenneth was already waiting outside the picture house when she arrived, so she didn't have to stand around in the open, where one of the girls from the sewing room might have spotted her. To her embarrassment, he insisted on paying for both seats, and buying her a small box of liquorice allsorts.

'You're saving for that typewriter, remember?' he said as they stopped to admire the large fireplace in the foyer, a special feature of the Central.

'I know, but you'll not earn much in that wee shop.'

'I'm fine, don't worry about me. I don't work for Uncle George all the time, just in the holidays,' he said casually as they headed towards the auditorium. 'I'm going back to Glasgow in October to start my second year at the university. I'm hoping to be a doctor.'

They were going up some stairs, and Elspeth tripped over her feet and almost fell flat on her face. Wait till Mattie heard about that, she thought gleefully when she had recovered. And Aunt Flora. To think that she, Elspeth from the sewing room, was going out with a university student – and a future doctor!

She had scarcely recovered from that shock when they entered the auditorium. For a moment, she stood still, looking around. It was magnificent, with its chandeliers and decorative ceiling and plush tip-up seats and uniformed attendants. They took their seats just in time, and as the film flickered on to the screen, Elspeth, glancing round the dark auditorium, saw that some of the young men had their arms about their girls' shoulders.

She sat primly upright, wondering what she should do if Kenneth put his arm about her. He had bought her ticket, and given her sweets, so it would surely be rude to push him away. On the other hand, she wasn't certain that she wanted to be hugged. Fortunately, she didn't have to make the decision, for Kenneth was too engrossed in the film to make any overtures.

Glancing sideways at him, she decided that she liked his profile. His nose was straight and not too long, and he had quite a nice-shaped chin. She offered him a sweet, but he was so engrossed in the cowboys and Indians racing across the screen that he didn't notice, and finally she had to tap him on the elbow, making him jump.

'Liquorice allsort?'

'Oh – thanks.' He fumbled in the box, found a sweet, and turned back to the screen.

Elspeth relaxed into the soft plush seat and began to concentrate on the film herself. She became so involved in it

171

that towards the end, when a fearsome Red Indian warrior, tomahawk in hand, suddenly hurtled down from a tree and on to the hero's back, she yelped and jumped. To her horror, the sweets still left in the box she held shot out of it and all over the floor, rattling against the seats in front. A few heads turned, and there was a low ripple of amusement.

'Oh!' She tried to duck down so that she could scoop up some of the sweets, which were rolling around the carpeted floor, but Kenneth's hand came out of nowhere to stop her.

'Just leave them.' He didn't take his hand away again; it felt warm and comfortable and not in the least threatening. Under its touch, she relaxed again, and they sat companionably together for the rest of the film. When it ended with the heroine running into the hero's arms and resting her trusting head on his manly shoulder, it felt quite nice to be holding – or being held by – a man's hand. Elspeth felt a sisterly bond between herself and the heroine, who now had THE END running across the face lifted for the hero's kiss.

But when the lights went up again she was brought back to the present with a bump. 'Oh, look—' She stared in dismay at the sweets dotted about their feet, then squeezed down into the narrow space between the rows of seats and started gathering them up.

'Don't bother,' Kenneth said above her head. 'We can't eat them now.'

'I can't leave the place looking like this!'

'They've got folk who come in and clean it.'

'But they'll think I'm an awful slitter, leaving such a mess!'

'They won't know who did it.' He drew her to her feet. 'Mind you, we'd better get out quickly, before they come in and catch us at the scene of the crime.'

Her face was burning. 'You're laughing at me!'

'Mebbe just a wee bit. But I like your sense of what's right.' He glanced beyond her, and added, 'We'd better go, there's folk wanting out.'

Turning, she saw that there were indeed some people waiting patiently for her to get out of their way. Scarlet now with embarrassment, she snatched up her coat and moved on, feeling a liquorice allsort squash beneath her foot as she went.

'It was a terrible waste of good sweeties, after you spending your money on them,' she lamented as they stepped out on to the street.

'We'd eaten most of them anyway.' He took her arm and steered her round two drunken men who were staggering along the middle of the pavement. Again, he maintained the contact.

It was dusk when they reached Mearns Street. Elspeth wondered if he expected to be invited up to the flat, but he stopped at the close-mouth, touching her pebble brooch lightly with the tip of a finger. 'I like your brooch.'

'It was a birthday present from my brother Thomas, during the war. We used to collect pebbles together by the river, and he bought this to remind me about that.'

'I like the river. Mebbe we could take a walk down there some night?' Kenneth looked down the hill to where the Clyde could be glimpsed between tenements. The lamplighter came into sight, using his long pole to open the gas lamps. Just a touch of the pole against the wicks within turned them into soft golden globes of light.

'This is a lovely time of the evening,' Kenneth said quietly, looking down at her. 'Your eyes are like very deep, dark pools in this light.'

'Are they?' Nobody had ever talked to her like that before; she hoped that he couldn't see the colour warming her face.

'In daylight, they're so blue. You've got beautiful eyes,' he said, then, 'Before the lamplighter gets this far—'

With an unexpected movement he whisked her up the step and into the dim close. A hand beneath her chin tipped her face to his and he kissed her, his lips first brushing hers, then claiming them, just like the couple on the cinema screen.

'Goodnight, Elspeth,' he said a few moments later. 'Mebbe

we could go out for a walk tomorrow evening?'

'I'll look into the shop on my way home,' she promised, then she was alone, breathless with happiness at the realisation that in spite of the liquorice allsorts, he wanted to see her again. She leaned against the close wall, her mouth soft and a great sense of wellbeing flooding through her, and smiled dreamily at the opposite wall until the lamplighter suddenly invaded the close.

'Aye, lassie,' he said heartily, brushing past her on his way to the lamp at the foot of the stairs. 'A grand night for it, eh?'

'For what?' she asked, still dazed.

Soft gas light filled the close. The lighter, an elderly man, turned and winked at her.

'For bein' alive,' he said, and went on his way, while Elspeth fled upstairs, her mouth still tasting Kenneth's lips, her nostrils filled with the fresh soapy smell of him.

Kenneth was returning soon to Glasgow, but he and Elspeth made the most of the time that was left, seeing each other every day. Because he couldn't afford the cinema or the theatre often, they walked along by the river, or over the hills at the back of the town, sometimes talking, sometimes silently enjoying being together.

Like Elspeth, Kenneth was ambitious. He didn't find her yearning to work in an office at all strange, and with him, she felt that she could be herself, saying whatever she wanted without being laughed at, or accused of trying to get above herself.

He took her to his home in Gourock for tea, and his parents made her welcome. She plucked up the courage to invite him to Mearns Street, where, to her delight, he fitted in well. They all liked him, even Flora, once she had recovered from the shock of realising that Elspeth was walking out with a young man who was clever enough to become a doctor.

He and Granjan took to each other at once, and even

Grandmother approved. 'A civil young man,' she told Elspeth in the kitchen when she took Kenneth with her on her monthly visit. Then, delivering the highest accolade, 'Your grandfather would have been pleased.'

The best part of it was that Kenneth understood about Lachlan. He knew about shell shock, and admired the way Thomas was working to rebuild his brother's confidence.

'It'll take time,' he told Elspeth, 'just as it would if he had broken his leg badly. The hard thing is that in Lachlan's case the damage doesn't show, so folk don't know how to deal with it.'

Lachlan continued to improve. The drawings of Thomas being hurt and killed were a thing of the past; now he sketched the views from the windows, covering page after page with drawings of cranes and ships in construction, and the water and hills beyond. The nightmares that had plagued him, and the entire family, night after night were easing. He nerved himself to go out more, especially down to the shore, where he could sit for hours on end looking at the water.

'The river's not afraid of anything,' he explained to Elspeth. 'It just goes its own way, and it takes its own time, and it always gets where it wants to be. The river knows what's best for it.'

A week before Kenneth was due to leave, he and Elspeth went on an afternoon picnic with Mattie, Thomas and Lachlan. Because the shore at Greenock was lined with ship-yards, they took a short bus ride along the coastline to Largs, a handsome residential town popular with holiday-makers. It was the first time Lachlan had been in a bus since the war; sitting behind him, Elspeth saw his thin shoulders tense with the effort of keeping his nerves under control as the vehicle rattled along. Kenneth, beside her, leaned forward.

'Look at the water, Lachlan,' she heard him say. 'Just keep watching it and we'll soon be there.'

Lachlan's fair head immediately craned to the right, and the tension eased from his back. When they descended at Largs Pier, his eyes were bright with triumph at having broken through another barrier.

They found a sheltered pebble beach beyond the town, with rocks scattered here and there, useful as seats or back-rests. The long, low green shape of the Greater Cumbrae, one of the Clyde islands, lay across the water. Its small town, Millport, was also popular with holiday-makers and day-trippers, and passenger steamers were to be seen regularly plying between the island and Largs.

They paddled in the cold clear water, then ate the sandwiches and ginger beer they had brought with them. Afterwards, Mattie wandered off along the beach in search of shells and Lachlan perched on a rock, his eyes on the river. Thomas tossed pebbles into the water while Kenneth propped his back comfortably against a rock and opened a book he had brought with him.

Elspeth waded into the river again, braving the agony of walking without shoes over the pebbles, gasping as the water enfolded her feet in its cold grip. Her long brown plait swung over her shoulder, the golden hairs glinting in the sunlight. She found a half-submerged rock and leaned against it, watching her bare toes shimmering beneath the surface, then looking up as a passenger steamer passed quite close, tiny arms waving from the crowded rails. A gust of wind almost dislodged her straw hat; she pinned it down with one hand and waved back with the other, then as a slightly larger wavelet broke against her calves, she kilted her skirt higher and made her way back to the beach.

'I've been thinking,' Kenneth said lazily, watching her drying her feet, which were as scarlet as lobsters from the water. 'Why should that typewriter be sitting in the back shop, when you could be using it?'

'But I've not finished paying for it yet.' She handed back the clean handkerchief he had loaned her. Thomas flipped a round, flat pebble into the water and it bounced twice before disappearing beneath the surface.

'I know, but I've got work to do for the beginning of the university year. You could type it out for me if you had the machine – I'd pay you for it.'

'I couldn't take your money!'

'Of course you can,' Thomas said shortly. 'The very best money is the money you can get out of other folk's pockets and into your own. Or so I'm told.'

Kenneth looked puzzled, and Thomas grinned back at him, cold-eyed.

'What I mean is, Kenneth, we all need money, don't we?'

'That's what life's about.'

'I thought your life was going to be about making sick folk well,' Thomas said at once, and Kenneth flushed.

'It is, but I'll have to get paid for it. How else can I live?'

'There's your answer, Ellie.' Thomas sent another pebble into the air with a flick of the thumb. This time it bounced four times, and was quite far out before it sank. 'Folk need money to live, and you've as much right to live as anyone.'

'You earn a wage yourself,' Kenneth's voice was defensive, and Thomas laughed.

'Aye, but I'm only paid enough to enable me to exist.' He started to prise a large stone out of the ground. 'While the man that employs me lives very comfortably because he has a lot more money than me.'

The stone came free, and he held it up, gesturing around the beach with his other hand. 'Suppose this big stone's that man, and the rock our Lachie's sitting on's a man with even more wealth. But when you look all around, what d'ye see?'

His free hand dropped, to indicate the beach around them. 'Wee pebbles, all over the place. These pebbles are us, and all the folk like us. They're necessary, because without them there's no beach, but most folk don't realise that. Most folk think the pebbles don't matter, 'cos there's so many of them, and they're only wee.'

He scooped a handful of pebbles up and tossed them towards the water. They hit the surface with a series of soft plops. Then he hurled the stone viciously after them. It crashed into the river noisily, throwing up spray.

'Pebbles don't make enough noise tae be noticed, but the big stones do, because they're important – important enough to throw their weight around,' said Thomas, then scrambled to his feet, rubbing moisture from his hands.

'So take the lad's money, Ellie. Take all the money you can get. The more you earn, the bigger the pebble you'll be – and the more folk'll take notice of you, and see you as a person,' he said, then strode off along the beach, leaving them to gape after his retreating back.

'What's bothering him?' Kenneth asked, his voice subdued.

'I don't know. He's been like this for weeks. It's not like Thomas at all,' Elspeth fretted.

Kenneth shrugged. 'Whatever it is, it's not our worry. What I was saying is, I've been working in the pawn shop to earn money to help me through university. And it would help me if you'd type some of the papers for me.'

'What would your uncle say?'

'I've spoken to him about it, and he agrees. He's a businessman – he realises that if I pay you to do work for me, you can pay him what you owe on the typewriter sooner than you expected. And that suits him.'

18

Kenneth brought the typewriter to Mearns Street the next evening, trundling it through the streets on a handcart, then carrying it up the stairs to arrive, red-faced and breathless, at the McDonalds' door.

They all crowded into the small bedroom to watch as the typewriter was settled carefully on to a sturdy little table that he had brought from the pawn shop.

'A present from the management,' he explained casually.

Elspeth, shaking with excitement, settled herself on the side of the bed, because there was no room for a chair, and sent her fingers flying deftly across the keys. Listening to their admiring exclamations as she explained the workings of the machine, she glowed. Perhaps she wasn't going to be a teacher, like Mattie, or a doctor, like Kenneth, but this was something that she, and nobody else in the room, could do. She felt important, and gifted.

Kenneth, hunkered down on his heels by the table, his elbows on its edge, caught her eye, and gave her a warm, conspiratorial smile. She beamed back at him, remembering that she owed it all to him. If he hadn't coaxed his uncle to trust her, she might not have got the typewriter, her most precious possession.

Flora had wanted her younger daughter to continue living at home while studying at teacher-training college, travelling by train to Glasgow each morning and returning in the evenings.

But Mattie, suddenly ready to spread her wings, had argued that this was quite impossible; as well as being costly, it would give her little time to study.

To her relief her mother finally gave in. The headmistress of the school Mattie and Elspeth had attended was consulted, letters – typed by Elspeth – were sent out and replies received, and Flora and Mattie spent a nerve-racking day in the city, inspecting a recommended hostel for young women. When they arrived home, Flora flustered and Mattie giddy with excitement, it had all been arranged.

On Mattie's final evening at home, neighbours and friends flocked to the flat to wish the fledgling teacher well. Even Bob, who didn't often visit now, came with Rachel, who wore the dress that had been made for her wedding. It would soon have to be put aside, Elspeth thought, noticing how the skirt, which had hung so neatly back in May, was now tight over the girl's swelling pregnancy.

'Have you noticed the bold Bob?' Thomas murmured to her during the evening. 'That's never ginger he's drinking.'

'Of course it is. Bob's temperance.'

'I'm not so sure.'

It was true that Bob had changed. He was restless, and louder than usual, and she noticed that he had developed a habit of passing a hand over his lips, as though they were parched, although he had a glass in his hand every time Elspeth saw him.

She didn't have time to wonder at Thomas's words, because just then Kenneth, who was also leaving for Glasgow the following day, sought her out.

'It's too crowded in here, I'm going out for a breath of fresh air. Come with me.'

'You'll look out for Mattie, won't you?' she asked as they went through the close to the back yard. 'She'll mebbe feel lost in such a big city on her own.'

'I'm going to be busy, but I'll do what I can. Elspeth, Uncle

George was wondering if you'd look in at the shop tomorrow to have a word with him. I've told him that you might be willing to look after his books.'

'Me?'

'You've been taking book-keeping at night school, haven't you? It'd be good for you get some practice at it.' He put an arm about her. 'You're shivering. Here—' He drew her to where the wash house used by all the women in the tenement bulked against the tenement wall. The door was never locked; the interior smelled of bleach and soda, soap and wet clothes, but at least they were out of the chill night wind.

Kenneth was a silhouette against the small window, his breath warm on her cheek. 'I've done what I can with his books during the summer, but he needs someone to see to things properly. And he'll pay you fairly, I've seen to that too. Will you do it?'

'I'll have a word with him about it.'

'Good,' he said, then he kissed her, and suddenly she felt quite tearful at the thought of being without him. She clung to him in the soap-smelling gloom. 'I'm going to miss you!'

'I'll be home for the New Year.'

'But that's months away yet!'

Kenneth kissed her again, and she returned the kiss with passion, running her fingers through his hair and over the nape of his neck. She knew that he liked that.

'Oh – Elspeth!' he whispered, nuzzling at her neck then her shoulder, his mouth hot through the barricade of her woollen jumper.

Whether it was because of the darkness, or the small space they were enclosed in together, or because his kisses were more passionate than usual, she couldn't tell; she only knew that her stomach was churning, her knees so weak that she was grateful for the support of the big brick boiler against her back. She had heard from Lena and the other girls in the sewing room about love and passion, and had seen it on the cinema

181

screen, but nothing had prepared her for such a sense of elation. She wanted to blend right into Kenneth, to be part of him and for him to be part of her . . .

For a long moment it was wonderful, then the sudden waft of cold air against her stomach when he began to unfasten her blouse brought her back to earth. His hands were sliding over her bare shoulders, his fingers slipping under her bodice to touch her breasts, his body shuddering against her. A strange, pleasant thrill was running through her own body, but at the same time a tingle of doubt flared in her mind.

'Kenneth—'

He didn't hear her, and she had to struggle inelegantly to push his hands down to the comparative respectability of her skirt waistband.

'What is it?' He sounded strange, as if he had just wakened from a sound sleep. 'Oh, Elspeth, please!'

Please, her aroused body begged along with him, but her brain, which had started to function again, said otherwise. Mind and body, longing and common sense – it was like being in a whirlpool. She wanted whatever was happening between herself and Kenneth to go on, but at the same time she knew that it was wrong.

'We'd better not,' she said, squirming away from him, pulling the edges of her blouse together, pushing buttons through buttonholes with nervous haste.

'But I'm going away – can we not just love each other a wee bit so that we've got something to remember?'

'Not like this.' Now that the heat was slowly draining from her, she knew that this wasn't the way she had imagined it would be. Not in the wash house, with the smell of soda and harsh yellow soap.

'Come on, Elspeth—' As he reached for her, light from the small window glinted off the whites of his eyes, and she suddenly realised that in the dark, he could be anybody. For all she knew, Kenneth might have been spirited away somehow, and his place taken by someone – or something – else. Memories flooded back of the man who had dragged her into the shop doorway during the street celebrations at the end of the war.

'Leave me be!' Spurred on by her over-strong imagination, she squirmed away from him, pushing at him frantically, then ran to the door. Her sense of direction had gone, and she panicked when her outstretched hands came up against the brick wall instead of the rough wooden door. She fumbled to her right, found planks beneath her fingers, and burst out of the wash house into the chill darkness.

'Elspeth!' Kenneth caught at her arm and turned her round. And there he was, clearly seen in the light spilling through a ground-floor window; Kenneth, her Kenneth, with his hair tousled and his round face perplexed.

She fell against him, half laughing. 'Kenneth, it's you!'

'Of course it's me, who else could it be? What's wrong with you?'

She sucked in a deep breath, smoothing his jacket with her hands. 'I'm sorry, Kenneth, I just – I had to get out into the fresh air.'

He said nothing, but moved back slightly, so that her hands dropped away from him.

'I have to go, I told my parents I'd not be late home.'

'Kenneth, don't be angry with me—' she began, then jumped away from him, startled, as Thomas spoke from the darkness of the close.

'Elspeth, it's time you were back in the house.'

'I'm just going.' Kenneth brushed past him without another glance at Elspeth.

'What was going on?' Thomas asked as Kenneth's footsteps disappeared along the close.

'Nothing was going on! What did you have to go creeping about like that for?'

'I saw you from the landing window, bursting out of the washhouse. What were the two of you up to?'

'Doing the washing, what d'you think?' She flung the words at him, pushing past him to reach the stairs. He had ruined everything. Because of him, Kenneth had gone, without giving her a chance to explain. She was so angry that she could have hit him.

He caught up with her on the first landing, stopping her and spinning her towards him with his hands on her shoulders. 'Ellie, you're still only a bairn.'

'I'm old enough to look out for myself!'

'You're not. No harm to Kenneth, he's a decent lad, but he's older than you, and he knows more about the world. Don't try to grow up too soon, Ellie,' he said, 'There are bad things as well as good things in it, and once you've taken the final step you can't change your mind and go back to being a bairn.'

'Leave me be!' She pulled free and ran up the stairs, away from him.

In bed later, Mattie clung to her, her tears on Elspeth's neck just where Kenneth's mouth had been, and just as hot. 'What if I don't like it, Ellie? What if I'm a dunce after all, and nobody wants to be my friend, and I'm all alone?'

'You'll be fine. You're clever, and of course folk'll like you. If you get too homesick, we're only a train ride away. You'll be fine,' Elspeth said again. 'Anyway, what about me, left here while you and Kenneth are in Glasgow? I'm going to be lonely without you.'

'But you've got Mam and Dad and Lachlan and Thomas.' Mattie sniffed. 'I'll not have anyone I know!'

By the time Mattie was soothed into sleep, Elspeth was wide awake, her mind filled with the scene in the washhouse. In the safety of her bed, her body tormented by the memory of Kenneth's touch, she wished that she hadn't pushed him away. She moaned softly as she recollected how his fingertips had brushed against her breasts. Would he forgive her for the way she had treated her?

Then she imagined herself having to tell Aunt Flora that a

bairn was on the way. The very thought of such a scene cooled and calmed her burning, restless body. Maybe she had done the right thing after all. Maybe one day she would be glad that she had done the right thing, hard though it had been.

With that thought held firmly in her mind, she fell asleep at last.

George Monteith was standing behind the counter when Elspeth went into the pawn shop after work the following evening. His presence more than anything else brought it home to her that Kenneth was far away in Glasgow now, and for a moment she knew a great sense of loss.

The pawnbroker invited her upstairs to his kitchen, a room furnished with a fireplace, gas cooker, table, chairs and sideboard, but with shelves holding a wide variety of items, all sporting pawn tickets, lining the walls. He laid the books before her on the kitchen table, together with an old tin biscuit box adorned on the lid with a splotched and faded picture of a basketful of kittens, and crammed with pawn tickets and scraps of paper. Each time the bell jangled in the shop below he scurried off, leaving her to find her way through the maze of paperwork.

Elspeth was appalled at the size of the task she had been asked to take on. George Monteith's idea of financial dealings was to scribble all his transactions down on scraps of paper and toss them into the biscuit box. His ledger was shamefully bare and neglected, with nothing balancing.

At first, she was inclined to make some excuse and get out of the place as quickly as she could, but on the other hand, the challenge interested her, and she had some idea in her head that by helping his uncle, she could make up for her childish behaviour towards Kenneth the night before. By the time she returned home, she and the pawnbroker had come to an agreement.

Flora was horrified when she heard that Elspeth was to do

Mr Monteith's books. 'I don't care if he is Kenneth's uncle, he's still a pawnbroker,' she said in outrage, 'and I'll not have you standing behind the counter of that pawn shop. As tae what your grandmother'd have to say if she heard – I've no wish tae have her round here again, makin' more accusations against me!'

'Aunt Flora, it's not going to be like that at all. I'll call in at the shop every Friday evening to collect the books, then bring them back here and work on them over the weekend. I'll hand them back in on Monday morning on my way to work. There's no shame in it,' Elspeth coaxed, horrified at the prospect of having to admit to Mr Monteith that her aunt had forbidden her to do his books. That was no way for a book-keeper to behave!

'Well, ye can give it a try,' Flora said at last, grudgingly. 'But if anyone talks about seein' you goin' intae a pawn shop, it stops at once, d'ye hear me? I've no wish to have folks thinkin' we're havin' tae pawn things in order tae eat.'

From then on, Elspeth was so busy with the task of organising Mr Monteith's books at the weekends and letter-writing in the evenings that she had very little time to miss Kenneth.

She wrote to him, apologising for her behaviour on his last evening at home. His reply was somewhat cool, but she kept writing, and gradually his own letters, never very frequent or very long, took on more warmth, and she felt that she had been forgiven.

Thanks to her work for Mr Monteith, the typewriter was fully paid for by October, and each morning when she woke and saw it sitting by the bed, she glowed with the pride of full ownership. Her bank account, sorely depleted by the money she had had to pay for the typewriter, began to flourish once more.

By the time Mr and Mrs Bruce and their daughter returned from their holiday in the south of France, Thomas, who had tormented himself during their absence with thoughts of

Aileen laughing and talking and dancing with other men, had resigned himself to the fact that he had lost her.

When she came home, he told himself during sleepless nights, he would learn that she had been promised to some handsome, confident, wealthy man. After all, that was what her parents wanted and expected. That was what she had been born to, and the sooner he accepted the truth the better. At least, he tried to tell himself, he had known more happiness with her than he had ever dreamed of. He would always have that to remember. But such thoughts were cold comfort. Aileen was the woman he wanted, and there could never be anyone else.

Ian Bruce, who had returned to Scotland before his parents and sister because of business commitments, went with Thomas to collect them from the station, travelling in state in the back of the car because it wouldn't have occurred to him to sit beside the chauffeur.

When the train came in, Thomas went directly to the guard's van to collect the luggage. By the time he emerged from the station with a porter and began packing the cases into the trunk the family were seated.

After making arrangements to have the rest of the luggage brought to the house in a hired cab, together with the valet and lady's maid who had accompanied their master and mistress on holiday, he took his place behind the wheel and drove from the station, his ears straining to catch Aileen's voice. Every laugh, every word she spoke, squeezed at his heart. Opening the car door at the house, he stared stiffly ahead like a sentry on duty, then glanced at her, startled, as she paused and said, 'Hello, Thomas.'

'Welcome home, Miss Aileen.' He tore his eyes away from her almost at once, afraid of staring, almost choking with anger as he heard her brother say clearly as he accompanied her up the steps to the front door, 'If you must chat with a servant, Aileen, at least use his surname.'

187

Although he had glanced at her only briefly, the image of her, cool and slender in a lemon jacket and skirt that emphasised her perfect golden tan burned in his mind's eye for the rest of that day and all through the night. He woke up the next morning with it strong and clear in his brain.

She came into the garage that morning when he was polishing the car, touching his shoulder lightly and making him jump.

'Miss Aileen—' One glance over her shoulder showed that she was alone, and he added, low-voiced, 'You're not supposed to be in here—'

She was dressed for riding, in a green shirt that emphasised the colour of her eyes. 'I had to see you.' The words sent a jolt of astonished joy through his entire body. 'I've missed you so much, Thomas. I wrote every night, then tore up the letters because I had no way of sending them to you.'

He swallowed hard, scarcely able to believe her. He had worked so hard at convincing himself that her feelings for him would have died by now. 'I – I thought you'd have found someone else.'

'How could you think that?' Her eyes caressed his face. 'How could you doubt me?'

'I – you must have met so many men while you were away.'

'I did, but I wasn't interested in them. I don't want anyone else, surely you know that by now? Oh, Thomas—'

She reached up to touch his cheek, her fingers sending the blood racing round in his veins. He wanted to pull her into his arms and hold her and never let her go; instead, he put his own hand up to cover hers, trapping it against his face for a few joyous seconds before lifting it away.

'You must go. What if someone comes in?'

'Where are you going to be later?'

'I'm taking your father to Glasgow. We'll not be back till late afternoon.'

'Tonight, then.'

'There's a dinner party tonight.'

'After dinner. I'll pretend to have a headache and meet you in the summerhouse.'

Someone walked past the slightly open garage door. 'You must go,' Thomas said again, in a panic.

'Nine o'clock,' she whispered, and left, not bothering to peer out first to see if the coast was clear, but leaving confidently, as befitted someone who had legitimate reasons for going into her own father's garage.

A few minutes later, Thomas, weak with relief at the knowledge that she still cared, heard her horse's hooves clattering on the cobbles outside. Hungering for another sight of her, he left the car and moved to the door to see her go by, straight-backed as ever, her small hands confident on the reins. He watched until she had ridden round the corner of the house and out of sight, then, about to turn back into the garage's gloom, he saw Ina standing by the kitchen door opposite, a basket of washing on its way to the drying green balanced on one hip.

He had put a stop to his meetings with Ina after he first kissed Aileen in the summerhouse, suddenly unable to bear the housemaid's kisses and caresses. It hadn't been easy, for since Rachel's wedding the girl had become very possessive, constantly urging him to agree to marriage, and Thomas couldn't explain to her why he no longer wanted to walk out with her. Finally, he had precipitated a quarrel over nothing, and told her that they were finished. Ina had taken it badly, and hadn't spoken to him since.

Now, she gave him a long, bold, cold look, then her eyes narrowed and she swung away with a toss of the head.

Thomas returned to his work, his joy over the meeting with Aileen suddenly tempered with apprehension. There had been something about Ina's calculating, knowing look that chilled him to the bone.

189

19

Although Elspeth missed Mattie, having the bedroom to herself meant that she could type without disturbing anyone. Lachlan took to coming in to watch her at work and to marvel at her skill. He was still quiet and withdrawn, but much more independent than he had been since coming home from the army. His father had hoped to get him back to his old job, but the continual noise in the shipyards still panicked him.

When, in the middle of September, Elspeth heard that there was a vacancy for someone in the packing office at Brodie's, she suggested it to Lachlan.

'It's not much, just packing up things that customers have ordered, ready for the carters. But it'd be a start. What d'you think?'

Lachlan, sitting on her bed, plucked nervously at the corner of the quilt, thinking for a while.

'I cannae go on like this all my life, can I?'

'It would be good for you to get out and about again. There's not many in the packing room, and I'd be near to hand. We could go to work together, and walk home together too.'

He looked up at her, fear in his eyes, but determination in the set of his mouth.

'I'll try.'

As luck would have it, Miss Arnold was off with toothache the next day, and Miss Buchanan busy with a client, so Elspeth was able to slip out of the sewing room and go to the office, where Theresa McCabe rattled efficiently at the type-writer and Wilma and Graham worked at the big desk.

Wilma raised her brows when Elspeth asked if Mr James was free. 'What d'you want to see him about?'

'I'll tell him that.'

Wilma gave an offended sniff, but got down from her stool and tapped on the office door, closing it behind her when Mr James called to her to go in. She returned in a few minutes and said sulkily, 'He'll see you.'

James Brodie's greeting was more welcoming. He shook Elspeth's hand, and waved her to a chair before asking, 'What can I do for you?'

She told him about Lachlan's shell shock and how he couldn't return to the shipyard because of the noise and the bustle of the place. Then, twisting her fingers nervously in her lap, she ventured, 'I've heard there's a position free in the packing department. I think he could do that.'

'Do you? And what does he think?'

'He'd like to try for it. He needs to do something, Mr James, before it's too late,' she added, trying hard not to beg.

He pursed his lips for a moment, then to her great relief he said, 'Bring him with you tomorrow morning and I'll have a word with him.'

She fretted half the night in case Lachlan's nerve failed him at the last moment, but the following morning, pale and tense, dressed in his best, he walked with her into the store. She took him to the office but then had to go to the sewing room. It wasn't until after work, when she got home, that she found out that he had been given a month's trial.

After all they had been through with Lachlan, it was as if he had gained a place at Glasgow University. Flora and Henry could scarcely conceal their elation, and Thomas, who had finally emerged from the moodiness that had dogged him for a full month and reverted to his usual cheerful self, slapped his brother on the back and insisted on taking him out for a drink.

191

When they returned, he tapped on Elspeth's door.

'You did well.'

She twisted round from the typewriter to look up at him. 'D'you think he'll be all right?'

'I don't know – it's up to him now. But at least you've got him this far,' he said, then let her get back to her typing.

As well as the letters she was commissioned to write, Mattie and Kenneth were correspondents now, just as Thomas and Lachlan had been during the war. Mattie's letters were long and enthusiastic; she was settling in well at college and in the hostel, making friends and enjoying her studies. Kenneth's letters were usually brief reports on the subjects he had studied that week.

To his family's relief, Lachlan settled into the packing department quite well. At first, going to work was a daily trial, but having made the initial effort, he refused to let himself give in and stay at home.

'If I give up now, I'll not go back,' he told Elspeth tersely one morning when he looked so strained that she tried to persuade him to stay at home. As the days grew into weeks she saw the tension easing from his mouth and eyes, and knew that he had broken through yet another barrier.

Night classes had started again, and thanks to her own typewriter and her work with Mr Monteith's books, her typing and book-keeping abilities had improved. She was even allowed, in the typewriting class, to take over the beginners now and then while the harassed teacher dealt with the more advanced pupils.

'You're good at helping them to understand,' the woman commented one evening. 'Have you thought of teaching typewriting yourself, once you get your diploma?'

'Oh, no.' Elspeth was taken aback by the very idea, but the teacher was serious. 'I think you should. You have the right approach.'

Elspeth almost danced her way home that night. She was still set on working in an office, but if nothing came of that, there was now teaching to consider. Gradually, her ambitions were coming closer to being realised.

In October, a few weeks after Elspeth's sixteenth birthday, Thomas came home, grim-faced, and told his parents that he had lost his job.

'You can't have!' Flora's lips were suddenly ashen, and one hand clutched at her chest. Because her own father had been unable to support his wife and child due to poor health, Flora, who had had a harsh childhood despite all her mother's efforts to be the breadwinner, had grown up with a terror of unemployment. 'What did ye do wrong?'

'I did nothing wrong. There was a difference of opinion between me and Mr Ian. He's an arrogant bastard, that one,' Thomas added bitterly.

'What d'ye mean, a difference of opinion? What was it about?'

'Nothing that concerns you, Mam.'

Flora gave an animal-like whimper. 'For God's sake, man, ye lose yer job and say it's none of our concern? D'ye know how many men are bein' turned off these days?' Her voice began to rise. 'D'ye know how hard it is tae find work?'

'I'll manage.' Thomas, Elspeth saw with concern, looked grey and ill. 'I'll find another place.'

'How d'ye expect tae find another position just like that when ye werenae able tae stay in the one ye already had?' Flora almost shouted at him. 'Are ye goin' tae get a good reference from Mr Bruce?'

Thomas looked away from her searching glance. He was her favourite, and there was little he could hide from her.

'Well – are ye?'

'No.'

'No – and how can ye, if ye quarrelled with his son! Can ye no' keep yer tongue quiet when ye're around yer betters, ye daft fool?'

Thomas was stung into rounding on her. 'A man like Ian Bruce isn't my better!'

'Is he no'? Whatever sort of man he is, he's got money, and what d'you have, tell me that? Not even a job!'

'Don't get yerself all upset, Flora.' Henry put a hand on her arm. 'The laddie's got a good head on his shoulders, he'll find somethin' else.'

'Ye think so?' Flora shrugged his hand from her arm and whirled back to Thomas.

'It's her fault, isn't it? That lassie ye brought home with ye – Bruce's daughter?'

His eyes blazed at her. 'Leave it, Mam – I'm going out.' He turned to the door, but before he could open it Flora was on him, clutching at his jacket, hauling him round to face her. 'Don't you walk away from me! It was her, wasn't it?'

'Who?' Henry asked, bemused.

'That Bruce girl – that lassie he brought here tae my house!' She flailed at Thomas with her fists, forcing him to duck and wrap his arms about his head in self-protection.

Elspeth and Lachlan and Henry watched open-mouthed, too stunned by the suddenness of the attack to intervene. They had never seen Flora in such a state before; her face was crimson, her eyes wild, her hair escaping from its pins. Her voice was a harridan's shriek, the words pouring from it as she belaboured her son.

'Dirty, filthy midden that ye are, runnin' after yer master's daughter,' she screeched. 'An' she's no better, flauntin' herself before decent folk! I saw the way ye looked at her that day! I told ye, didn't I? I told ye she'd bring harm on ye!'

'That's enough, Mam!' Thomas had been forced back against the door; now he straightened up, suffering the blows, grappling with her until he managed to catch her wrists. His own face was distorted with rage. 'I'll not have ye foul-mouthin' her!'

Henry, coming to his senses, caught his wife round the waist

194

and dragged her away from Thomas. 'For God's sake, woman, d'ye want the neighbours tae call the polis? Leave the laddie be!'

'Look at the guilt in his face. Ask him if I'm no' right,' Flora panted. 'It was her that cost him his place – let him try tae deny it!'

'I'm not denying it,' Thomas said steadily. 'I love her – and she loves me.'

'Oh aye – it's love that made her stand by and let ye lose yer place, is it?'

'She knows nothing yet about what's happened,' Thomas flared back at his mother. 'She's away for a few days. It was Ina – she found out and told Mr Ian, and he went to his father.'

'Godsake's, man,' Henry groaned. 'Have ye no sense at all? You and Mr Bruce's daughter – how could ye think there was any future in that?'

'I knew there was no future to it, Da, but I cannae help my feelin's—'

'Can ye no'?' Flora stormed. 'Look at the shame yer precious feelin's've brought on us, ye—' Henry's grip on her had relaxed, and all at once she lunged forward, one arm lifting above her head, then swinging down to deliver a hefty open-handed slap across Thomas's cheek. The sharp crack of it rang through the room, then Flora, her rage spent, slumped back against her husband, sobbing, while Thomas put a hand to his reddening cheek. He stared in disbelief at his mother, then turned to the door.

'Come back here, Thomas, and let's get this business sorted out,' his father said.

'I'll come back when I get work, and not before. I'll not be a burden on anyone.' Thomas flung the words over his shoulder, just before the door closed behind him. A moment later, the outer door slammed.

Flora's knees gave way and she would have slid to the floor if Henry hadn't caught her and bundled her into a chair. 'What's goin' tae become of him now?' she whimpered, raising a face that was wet with tears, and aflame with angry red blotches now, as though she herself had been hit repeatedly.

'He'll survive, the way we all have tae.' Henry's voice was old and bleak. 'Ellie, ye'd best make yer auntie a cup of tea.'

Turning in a daze to do as she was told, she saw Lachlan standing in one corner, stooped over as though in pain. Elspeth's heart seemed to drop down through her ribs; this was the way Lachlan had been just after the war, before Thomas started dragging him out of his trauma.

Henry had noticed him too. 'Come on, son, sit over here,' he said, his voice gentle as he eased his son to a chair. 'It's nothin' tae get upset about.'

'How could Thomas do it?' Flora wailed as Elspeth made tea. 'Upsettin' his own brother, too, with never a thought of what he's been through already.'

Elspeth's blood boiled along with the kettle on the stove. If anyone had upset Lachlan it was Flora herself, with her venomous attack on Thomas. She bit the accusation back with an effort, saying instead, as she put a mug of strong, sweet tea into the older woman's icy hands, 'It's over now, Aunt Flora. Don't upset yourself.'

Flora glared up at her, looking like a witch with her untidy hair and narrowed eyes and blotched face. 'What d'ye mean, it's over? There's our Thomas out of work and the whole town'll be tattling tomorrow about what he's been up to with his employer's daughter—'

'He's not been up to anything,' Elspeth was stung into protesting. 'He said he loved her, but that doesn't mean that they've – they've—' She bit her lip, remembering that although she had been earning a wage for two years now, in Flora's eyes she was too young to know anything about what could happen between men and women.

'Love?' Flora gave a contemptuous laugh. 'Ordinary folk like us were never meant tae fall in love! Yer poor mother found that out the hard way – and it was me that was left tae raise the result. I'm not havin' my Thomas goin' along that road!'

'Flora, that's enough,' Henry barked from where he stood over Lachlan.

Despite the warmth of the room, a chill descended over Elspeth, as if someone had just dropped a flexible sheet of ice on her from above. Without a word, she poured out tea for Henry and Lachlan.

Thomas didn't come home that night. Flora, distraught, sent Henry out to look for him, and he came back at midnight to report that Thomas was staying with his grandmother.

'He says he'll come back when he's got a job, and not before.'

'Now look what's become of us.' Worry and exhaustion had taken their toll on Flora, dimming her anger to a feeble spark. 'That lassie's cursed this house!'

'For pity's sake, Flora,' her husband said wearily, 'She's done nothing of the sort. Now let's get tae our beds – we've got work tae see tae in the mornin'.'

On the following evening Elspeth and Lachlan hurried along to Granjan's little flat as soon as they could get away without rousing Flora's suspicions.

'Thomas isnae in,' the old woman said as soon as she opened the door. 'Come on in, the two of ye.'

'How is he?' Lachlan asked anxiously as they followed her into the kitchen.

'In a right state when he arrived here. He'd a good drink in him, and he's still in a right takin'. He cannae see past that Bruce lassie.'

Elspeth looked round the little room. 'Where did he sleep?' There was only the wall-bed, where Granjan slept.

'On the floor, wrapped in a quilt an' with a cushion under his head. He'll sleep there again tonight, for he's determined not tae go back home without a wage packet. Flora's in a terrible takin'.'

'She's been here?'

'Oh aye, most of the day. She's torn between wantin' Thomas home an' wantin' him dead. Ach, she doesnae mean it, though. She dotes on that laddie – on all her bairns,' she added hurriedly, a hand on Lachlan's fair head. 'The trouble with Flora is that she's never learned how tae love folk. She punishes them instead.' Janet Docherty sighed. 'I don't know how that came about, for she had plenty love herself as a bairn. Never be scared tae tell someone if ye love them, Elspeth, even if they let on they don't want tae know. It's the greatest compliment ye can give tae another human bein'.' Then, as the outer door opened, 'Mind what ye say, he's feelin' as tender as if he's been run over by the horse as well as the cart.'

Thomas, pale and drawn, stopped in the doorway when he saw the two of them. 'What are you doing here?'

'We came to see how you are.'

'I'm fine.'

'There's a pot of soup waitin' for ye.' Granjan bustled to the cooker. 'I got a nice bit of flank mutton tae taste it, so there's a good mutton stew as well.'

'I don't want anything to eat.'

'Of course ye do. Ye cannae seek work on an empty stomach.'

'Plenty have to,' Thomas said shortly.

'Aye, poor souls, but I've no intention of lettin' my own grandwean do that – not while I'm alive. Ye'll have a drop of soup too?' she asked Elspeth and Lachlan, who both hesitated. They had already eaten, but the broth smelled good.

'Come on,' Janet coaxed. 'Lachie can do with a bit more fat on his bones, and I'm sure you could manage a wee taste, Elspeth.'

As they squeezed round her little table, Elspeth marvelled at the difference between mother and daughter. Flora was always jumpy and on edge, while Janet was so serene. It would be better for Thomas, she thought, to spend time with his grandmother while his unseen wounds healed. When Lachlan tried to persuade his brother to return home with them, she said firmly, 'I think Thomas is fine here, for the time being.'

He smiled gratefully at her. 'I'll come back when I've got another job, Lachie.'

'When'll that be?'

'Soon, I can promise you that.'

When they rose to go, Granjan announced that she would go with them to visit Flora. As she and Lachlan set out along the road, Thomas detained Elspeth at the close-mouth.

'I've made a terrible mess of it all, Ellie,' he said wretchedly. 'I should never have let it come tae this!'

Elspeth thought of Aileen Bruce as she had seen her in the fitting room at Brodie's and at her sister's wedding. 'She's very bonny.'

'Aye,' Thomas said huskily. 'Why did Ina have to show such malice? Ian Bruce was fair pleased to find out something against me. He was there, in his father's study when I was sent for – I could see the gloating in his eyes.'

'Are you sure it was Ina?'

'She saw us talking once, not long ago. She must have been watching ever since, following one or the other of us. I should have ended it long since, but I kept wanting just one more meeting. Mam's right, I was a fool!'

'Will you try to see her again?'

'No. The damage is done, best leave it at that and not make things worse.' He rubbed his hand hard over his face. 'You'd best go.'

Hurrying along the darkening road after the two figures, one dumpy, the other tall, ahead of her, Elspeth wished that she could have stayed with Thomas. He was strong for others, but vulnerable in his own grief. She wanted to comfort him, but knew at the same time that the comfort he really needed could never be his.

20

It wasn't an easy time to find work. Men were being laid off everywhere, and there was always a crowd waiting down at the docks in the hope of finding even a few hours' paid employment.

Thomas went out every morning and came back every evening, worn out from trudging round the streets. His ability to drive and his skill with engines stood him in good stead; a week after being turned away by Mr Bruce he found work in a small garage run by Forbes Cameron, a man with a deep interest in motorcars and enough money to set up his own business.

Even though he was bringing a pay packet home again, things weren't the same between Thomas and his mother. In the past, he had been the only member of the family able to tease Flora without giving offence; she usually wrangled with him amiably, or, if she could think of nothing to say, reached up and boxed his ears. Now, mother and son were civil to each other, but too much had happened for forgiveness on either side, and the special bond between them had vanished.

Nor could Elspeth forget what Flora had said to her that night. She had always known that she wasn't really part of the McDonald family, but it had never been made so cruelly clear before. She wished that she could find some way of striking out on her own instead of being beholden to the McDonalds.

Early in November, Brodie's typist had to take time off work because of illness in the family, and to her delight, Elspeth was asked back into the office. This time she took over the task confidently, impressing Mr Brodie with her ability to rattle away on the typewriter instead of pecking nervously at the keys.

She was more confident, too, in the way she handled Graham Adams when he started pestering her to go out with him.

'I've got a young man,' she told him loftily. His face dropped, and dropped even further when he discovered that Kenneth was studying to be a doctor. He made one more feeble try: 'If he's away in Glasgow studying, there's no harm in you finding someone to keep you company in the meantime.'

Elspeth whisked a sheet of paper out of the typewriter and rolled another in. 'I couldn't do that. He's very jealous,' she lied, and he said no more.

Rain rattled against the windows as the hands of the clock on the kitchen mantel shelf reached nine o'clock. Flora, who had been throwing surreptitious glances at the clock for the past half-hour, put her darning down. 'Where's that laddie got tae?'

'He'll be working on an engine, Aunt Flora,' Elspeth said, though she herself was becoming concerned over Thomas's absence.

Flora got up and opened the oven, letting the smell of overheated food into the room. 'He'll be more able tae heel his boots with this than eat it, the time it's been waitin' for him!'

Thomas's new job meant erratic hours. He had thrown himself into it feverishly, often working past his official stopping time.

Flora's complaints about the number of times she had to reheat his evening meal only met with a cool gaze and an indifferent, 'I'm not bothered whether the food's burned or cold, Mam – I'm not even bothered whether you make it or not,' that frustrated and frightened her.

'He's never as late as this,' she said now, picking up the sock she was darning, then tossing it down and giving her husband a firm dig in the ribs. He woke with a start from his comfortable doze.

'Henry, that laddie's never back yet – away tae the garage tae see if he's still there.'

Henry McDonald stretched and yawned. 'He'll have stopped in at a pub tae have a drink with some of his pals.'

'Not without comin' home first tae change out of his workin' dungarees. Our Thomas'd never stand in a pub covered with oil and filth. Not like some I could name,' she added with a sniff and a meaningful look at her husband.

'I'll go,' Lachlan offered, just as the knocker rattled.

Elspeth reached the door first, to find a policeman standing on the mat.

'Is yer daddy in, hen?'

The door across the landing had opened a crack; respectable tenements were never visited by the police, and there would probably be an ear pressed to every door the man had passed on his way up.

'Come in,' she started to say, but Flora was already pushing past her to scoop the officer in and shut the door against eaves-droppers. Henry, alerted by hearing a strange voice, appeared at the kitchen door, his shirt open to show his semmit, his braces looped at his waist.

'What's amiss?'

The constable drew his helmet off and tucked it under his arm as he made his way along the short, narrow hall into the kitchen. 'Mr McDonald? I've got some bad news for ye,' he said ponderously. 'It's yer lad, Thomas. We found him an hour since, in a back court. Someone's given him a right beatin'.'

Flora sagged heavily against her husband, just as she had done on the night she and Thomas had had their bitter quarrel. 'Is he – will he—'

'He's been taken tae the Infirmary, missus,' the man told her. 'They'll be able tae tell ye more when ye get there.'

'I'm going too,' Elspeth and Lachlan both said as soon as the policeman had left, but Flora shook her head.

'We cannae all rush there – they'll no' let a crowd of us in.

Better for you two tae stay here and we'll go on our own.'

They had two long hours of waiting before Flora and Henry returned with the news that Thomas was going to be all right.

'There's no bones broken, but he'll be kept in for a few days, just so's they can keep an eye on him. He's in a terrible state, the poor laddie.' Flora's face was streaked with tears, her eyes red.

'Someone gave him a right hidin',' Henry confirmed.

Elspeth opened her mouth to speak, but the words wouldn't come out. It was Lachlan who said, 'But who'd do that to our Thomas? Was it money they were after?'

'And him in his dungarees and covered with oil? Even in the gaslight anyone could see that he'd no' have money on him,' Flora snapped. 'The polis think he was mebbe mistaken for someone else.' Then, wringing her hands, 'What a thing tae happen – a polisman at our door! What'll the neighbours think?'

When Elspeth went to the Infirmary the following evening she didn't recognise any of the men in the beds at each side of the long ward. It was only when he called her name that she found Thomas.

Tears came to her eyes as she reached the bed where he was propped against pillows, with one arm strapped against his chest. His face was a mass of bruises, and both eyes were half shut. 'Oh, Thomas!'

'Now don't start greetin', Ellie,' he said with difficulty through swollen lips. 'Mam's done enough for the whole town. She cried so hard they almost had to change the bed when she left last night, and she was at it again this afternoon.'

Elspeth blinked rapidly to hold the tears back. 'Your face looks like the map of Europe that used to hang on our class-room wall.'

Thomas started to laugh, then winced and stopped abruptly. 'You should see my ribs – they're a world map; but it's not as bad as it looks. My arm's strapped because they put the shoulder out of place.'

She took his left hand in hers. 'There was more than one man?'

There had been two men at least, one stepping out of a close right in front of Thomas, another moving swiftly up behind him. After beating him unconscious they had apparently dragged him through a nearby close and into a neglected back court.

'I'm just lucky someone happened to come into the court and find me, else I'd have lain all night,' he finished.

Elspeth's palms stung; looking down she realised that she had doubled her hands into such tight fists as she listened that her nails were digging into the tender skin, leaving angry red crescents. 'Who would do such a thing?'

Thomas, exhausted with telling the story, slumped back against the supporting pillows. 'Ian Bruce might have the answer to that. I've seen him passing the garage a few times. I think he wanted me to know he was keeping an eye on me.'

'But you've not seen his sister since you lost your job.'

He began to shrug, then stopped as pain flickered across his face. 'He must think I'm still a threat to the family. He'd not find it hard to get men to do his work for him.'

'Did you tell the police?'

'Can you see them accusing Ian Bruce of having an ex-employee beaten?' Thomas asked drily. 'There's no sense in telling them anything.'

'If his sister knew—'

'Leave, it, Ellie. How's Lachlan?'

'He wanted to come with me, but as soon as we walked in the hospital door he started shaking. He'd to turn and go out again – he was awful vexed about it.'

'Tell him I'd not want him to force himself. I'll be home in a day or two. And don't you fret yourself, Ellie, I probably deserved what I got, playing with fire the way I did.'

'Nobody deserves to look like that.'

The words rang in her mind for the rest of the night, and

were still with her in the morning as she walked to work. Just because the Bruce family had money, it didn't give them the right to hurt folk.

The typewriter rattled ferociously that morning as she fumed over the injustice of what had happened to Thomas. Aileen Bruce was surely as responsible as he was for the love that had grown between them, and to Elspeth's mind, Aileen should know just what her brother had done in her name.

She thought of going to the Bruce estate and confronting the girl, but common sense prevailed. If she went to the door and asked to see Aileen she would almost certainly be refused admittance. If the girl's brother happened to be there, she might even put herself into danger. Anyone who could pay people to do what had been done to Thomas would think nothing of hurting a woman. A letter would have a better chance of reaching Aileen.

She had never before done her own work during office hours, but this was an emergency, she told herself, putting a blank sheet of paper into the typewriter. It didn't take long to do, for her fingers flew over the keys, and it was finished and in an envelope without anyone noticing. During the midday break she used some of her precious letter-writing money to bribe one of the messenger boys to deliver it during his rounds.

That evening, Flora came back from the Infirmary in a towering rage that spilled out in a flow of words as soon as the outer door closed behind her. Elspeth and Lachlan heard her squawking in the hall even before the door flew open and she stormed in, with Henry at her back, trying to placate her.

'The lassie was just visitin', Flora.'

'Visitin', d'ye call it? Well, I call it humiliatin'!'

'Miss Bruce came tae the hospital tae see our Thomas,' Henry explained to Lachlan and Elspeth as his wife paused to draw breath.

She wrenched the long pin from her hat. 'She'd no right! Walkin' intae the ward with a bunch of flowers that must have cost a month's wages! Everyone in the place stopped talkin'.' She whipped her hat off and stabbed the pin back into it fiercely for safekeeping. 'It was the silence and the look on our Thomas's face that made me turn round. And there she was, marchin' right past us as if we werenae there, lettin' the flowers fall over the bed and on tae the floor, and takin' his hand for all the world tae see—'

'She was cryin', poor wee lass,' Henry put in.

Flora glared at him. 'I was near cryin' myself. I've never seen such an exhibition! If one of my lassies ever behaved like that in public she'd feel the back of my hand, I can tell ye.' The witch-like, venomous look that Elspeth had seen on the night Thomas lost his job blotched the woman's face again. 'I didnae know where tae look—' All at once, she started to weep.

'Come on, hen,' Henry soothed, easing his wife into her chair. 'Best leave her,' he said over her head to the other two. 'It's Thomas bein' hurt an' all.'

It was more than that, Elspeth thought as she and Lachlan crept from the room. It was the realisation that Thomas was lost to her, now and for ever.

When Thomas came home a few days later, his face still bruised and swollen, Flora's wrath had not abated.

As a result, mother and son had another quarrel, even more vicious than the last, and again it ended with Thomas leaving home. His employer, who already thought highly of his abilities as a mechanic, let him sleep on a cot in the garage office. Ian Bruce found out, too late, that far from keeping Thomas away from his sister, his actions had forced Aileen to choose between Thomas and her own family. She chose Thomas, braving her family's wrath, accepting without flinching her father's refusal to help her in any way.

She ignored Thomas's protests too, and when he found a two-roomed flat to rent, she insisted on selling her personal jewellery in order to buy furniture for their new home.

Flora, just as proud and determined as Mr Bruce, also refused to forgive them, mainly because the story had gone through the town like wildfire and the gossips had had a wonderful time discussing it all.

'She's a snob in her own way, is our Flora,' Janet Docherty told Elspeth. Janet herself had infuriated her daughter by taking a liking to Aileen and refusing to turn her back on the young couple.

When they married at the end of November, only Elspeth and Lachlan and Janet were present. Watching Thomas and his bride standing before the minister in the empty, echoing church, Elspeth thought of Catherine Bruce's fine wedding at the end of the war. Aileen could have had a wedding day like that, with no expense spared, but the happiness on her lovely face as she turned to leave the church, her hand tucked under her husband's elbow, showed that in her own eyes she had made the right choice. Despite the fading yellow and blue and purple bruises still discolouring his face, Thomas, too, was glowing with joy.

It was very hard for Aileen, used as she was to servants seeing to her every need, to settle to such a different life, but she was determined to make her marriage work, turning to her husband's grandmother for help in learning the basic skills of running her new, tiny home.

'It's no' the lassie's fault that she's been brought up tae money and servants,' Janet said. 'As long as her and Thomas make each other happy, what does it matter where they were born and raised? Mind yer hair, pet, it's too bonny tae burn.'

The two of them were in Janet's little kitchen a week after the wedding. Elspeth, making toast at the fire, obediently pushed her long plait back over one shoulder. She always put it up for work, but let it hang free at other times. She had been considering having her hair cut short, but Flora still refused to allow it. Turning the slice of bread on the long toasting fork and thrusting it back towards the glowing coals, she said, 'They say in the sewing room that Mrs Bruce has taken to her bed with the shock of what's happened.'

'Ach, that's just a ploy rich women use tae hide away from folk till the fuss dies down. I daresay poor Flora'd enjoy doin' the same, but she'll just have tae thole it till the gossips get tired. It's a strange world, right enough – the rich don't like tae see their bairns marryin' the poor, and a lot of ordinary folk like Flora don't like tae see the poor marryin' the rich.'

Janet put the teapot on the table and covered it with the woollen cosy Elspeth had crocheted at school, then came to sit by the fire, turning up the hem of her skirt so that her plump legs, richly decorated with varicose veins, could bask in the heat. 'Folk have short memories where scandal's concerned. Another week and they'll have found somethin' else tae whisper about.'

She was right, as usual. With no more fuel to keep it going, the gossip about Thomas McDonald and his new bride died down as the year drew to its close. When Mattie returned home for Christmas and New Year she had blossomed and matured, put on some much-needed weight and gained an air of confidence that startled her family. Contrary to Flora's conviction that her younger daughter would die of asthma within weeks of arriving in smoky, industrial Glasgow, the childhood ailment didn't bother Mattie as often now.

Warned by Elspeth's letters, she said nothing about Thomas and Aileen. Neither did Flora, and the others knew better than to mention Thomas's name. But as soon as she and Elspeth were in their bedroom on Mattie's first night home, propped, as usual, at either end of the bed, she asked, 'What's happening with Thomas? There's a new pinched look about Mam – I didn't dare say his name.'

'They're both fine, and very happy. You must go and see them.'

'I'll go tomorrow. Will they not be coming to see the new year in with the rest of us?'

'I don't think Aunt Flora'll allow it,' Elspeth said, and Mattie's eyes clouded.

'But it's Ne'erday! Everybody's with their own folk at Ne'erday, to start the new year off!'

'She's set her face against accepting Aileen.'

'I never thought she'd turn away from Thomas,' Mattie said wonderingly, then, 'Well, you and me and Lachlan'll just have to go and see them after the bells, for I'm not going to leave my own brother without his family at a time like that, whatever she says. She'll be busy with all the neighbours then anyway.'

'Tell me about Glasgow, and college.'

Mattie's eyes brightened. 'It's grand, Ellie! Teaching's the right thing for me – the only thing. I was born to it.' She adjusted her pillow, which had started sliding down. 'Kenneth's been kind, he kept an eye on me at the beginning, and I see him now and again, but I'd have managed anyway. He said to let you know he's coming home tomorrow. Studying's not as hard as I thought it would be, and I can't wait to get into the class-rooms.'

She talked for a while about her life in Glasgow, and Elspeth drank it all in, wishing that she, too, could have had the opportunity to go to the city.

Mattie's yawns became more and more frequent, and finally she stretched her arms, then slipped beneath the blankets. 'I'm getting sleepy – I'll tell you more tomorrow. Lachlan's looking much better – that work you found for him's doing him good.'

'It's not much, but it's a start. He's been helping out with painting some of the departments, too, and Mr Brodie's talking about giving him more responsibility.'

'All we need now,' Mattie said drowsily, 'is for Mam to stop being so silly about Thomas and Aileen, and everything'll be all right.'

Kenneth was waiting outside the department store when Elspeth left work the following evening. She wanted to run to him, but hesitated, recalling their last meeting, and its sudden end when Thomas came across the two of them in the back court.

He, too, looked awkward; he held out his hand, and Elspeth shook it, aware that Graham Adams and Lena and some of the other girls from the sewing room were nearby. Lachlan, who usually walked home with her, had prudently disappeared.

To her relief, Kenneth drew her hand through his arm as they walked away. 'You've done a grand job with Uncle George's books. He's fair delighted.'

'It was good practice for me.'

He laughed. 'A challenge, more like. Anyone who can get *his* affairs into order must be clever.'

Pride and pleasure warmed her, and she relaxed a little.

That evening he took her to the cinema, and kissed her on the way home.

'I've been thinking, while I was away, about that last time – in the wash house,' he said awkwardly. It was as well that it was dark in the corner where they stood, for Elspeth felt her face burn at the memory. 'It was wrong of me, to try to—'

'I shouldn't have made such a fuss.'

'I shouldn't have—' He stopped, then said, 'I forgot that you're still very young. It'll not happen again.'

'Never?' She tried to get a teasing note into her voice in an effort to lighten the situation. She had missed him, and now she wasn't entirely sure whether she was relieved or disappointed at his words.

'Well – not till you're older, and I'm further on with my studies,' he said firmly, then put an arm about her and turned her towards the lighted street. 'Come on, it's too cold to be standing here. D'you think your Aunt Flora would be willing to offer me a cup of tea?'

21

Despite her family's arguments and pleas Flora obstinately refused to invite Thomas and Aileen to Mearns Street for New Year, so after midnight on Hogmanay, Lachlan and Mattie and Elspeth and Janet left the house shortly after the church bells and the ships' sirens out on the river had noisily welcomed 1920.

'I don't like leaving Mam on her own at New Year,' Lachlan said as they gained the street at last, having been stopped all the way down the stairs by neighbours wishing them a happy new year. As, traditionally, first-footers couldn't go into anyone's home empty-handed, he was armed with a bottle of whisky.

'It's her own choice,' said Mattie, who was carrying a lump of coal, denoting good wishes to the house they were going to enter, and wrapped in newspaper to save marking her hands or her coat. Elspeth's gift was a black bun – a rich fruit cake – that she had baked herself. When Thomas and Aileen came to the door their callers were arguing over who should go into the house first.

'It has to be you, Ellie,' Mattie was saying as the door opened. 'Your hair's not all that dark, but it's darker than ours.'

Thomas, his face split by a huge grin, put one arm about Aileen and reached his free hand out to draw them into the house. 'I've got my own luck-bringer,' he said, 'and nobody here's got hair as dark as hers, so come in, the lot of you. And welcome!'

To mark the new year, Lena had persuaded Elspeth to accompany her and her latest young man to the music hall at the Hippodrome Theatre.

'D'you not want to go on your own with Drew?' Elspeth had asked doubtfully when the outing was first proposed.

'I do not,' Lena said bluntly. George, the naval sweetheart Lena had been writing to when Elspeth first met her, had vanished from the scene almost as soon as the war was over, and since then Lena had changed escorts several times. 'I'm tired of lookin' at Drew, but he's too thick tae take a hint. That's why I want you tae come too, so's I'm not stuck with him all evening. I can scarce get tae the privy in our back court without him trailin' along at my back. Bring yer sweetheart, and Mattie and that nice shy brother of yours that works in the packin' room. He's got bonny eyes.'

'Bonny eyes or not, he's too quiet for you.'

Lena winked. 'I can be quiet and shy when I want tae be. Go on and ask him. Ye neednae fret, I'll not affront ye.'

Mattie agreed enthusiastically, and to Elspeth's surprise, both Kenneth and Lachlan accepted the invitation. When Thomas and Aileen heard what was afoot they announced that they wanted to go too, so there were eight of them in the third row that night, much to Drew's annoyance.

Lachlan, who insisted on sitting at the end of the row in case it all got too much for him and he had to leave hurriedly, glanced frequently and nervously round at the crowded auditorium and up at the boxes flanking the stage. Once or twice Elspeth, sitting next to him, thought that he was going to lose his nerve and make a bolt for the exit, but he stayed where he was, and when the lights went down and the crimson plush curtains swept open to reveal the three lines of chorus girls ready to sweep into 'Put on your Ta-ta, Little Girlie', she felt him relaxing in his seat.

It was an enjoyable evening. The comedians were exceptionally funny, the dancers and acrobats exceptionally lithe, the soprano and baritone of an exceptionally fine quality. The problem came towards the end of the evening, when it was announced that Miss Dolly Burnett, the popular soloist, had had to cancel her appearance because of illness, and someone else was taking over her spot in the programme. An ageing lady in a flouncy pink shepherdess costume then appeared onstage, and the orchestra struck up.

Almost as soon as the substitute raised her wavering voice in song the audience became restless. Murmurs rippled from all directions, and to her horror Elspeth heard Lena say clearly from further along the row, 'That reminds me, Drew, I forgot tae put the cat out before I left home.'

The applause at the end of the first song was sparse, and when the poor woman launched into a second melody, trying to achieve notes that her voice couldn't possibly reach, catcalls and jeers began to be heard from the gallery. The noise grew until the orchestra wavered into nervous silence, and the singer, crimson with mortification and anger, was forced to stop. The Master of Ceremonies rushed on to the stage to appeal for order.

'Ladies and gentlemen, this lady has very kindly agreed to step in at short notice. The least you can do is to give her a hearing.'

'We have,' Lena bawled back at him, bouncing to her feet and ignoring Drew's attempts to pull her back into her seat. 'Now the least she could do's tae stop givin' us an earache!'

The audience applauded, and Elspeth cringed back against her seat as the Master of Ceremonies glared down at the row where they sat.

'If you can do better, miss,' he said crushingly, 'you're welcome to try.'

Lena needed no further invitation. 'Right,' she yelled back, 'I will!' and jumping to her feet she started to push her way along the row towards the aisle.

The man's jaw dropped. 'This is a music hall, not a street

party. Please return to your seat, miss!' He danced at the edge of the stage, his arms making distracted, shooing motions.

'Away with ye, man,' someone bellowed back from right behind Elspeth and Lachlan, making them both jump. 'Ye asked if the lassie could dae better – let her have a try at it!'

The call was taken up across the auditorium and in the gallery as Lena continued to forge towards the aisle. When she reached it, she stopped and turned, taking Lachlan's face in her hands and smacking a hearty kiss on his astonished mouth.

'Wish me luck,' Elspeth heard her say beneath the audience's applause, then she was on her way up the steps to the stage. Glancing down the row, Elspeth could see Drew, red-faced with rage, leaning forward to glare at Lachlan, who was too dazed to notice.

Seemingly undaunted by the lights and egged on by the crowd's noisy encouragement, Lena marched to the centre of the stage. As she knelt to have a brief discussion with the orchestra conductor, the Master of Ceremonies hustled the bewildered shepherdess into the wings, shrugging and murmuring in her ear.

'I expect he's telling her that they might as well let Lena make a fool of herself,' Kenneth said, applauding vigorously with the rest of the audience as the conductor had a quick conference with his musicians, and Lena straightened up to face the auditorium, whipping off her felt hat and loosening the ribbon that kept her long red hair under control.

As it fell in curls over her shoulders the spotlights caught it, turning it into a burst of brilliant colour that distracted attention away from her plain dark coat and heavy practical shoes. Then the music started, the applause died down, and Lena began to sing.

She had chosen a song that began with a serious verse; as the introduction was played she stood alone in the centre of the large stage, head up and face solemn, her hands meekly before her, one holding her hat, the other her ribbon. Her voice was clear and sweet, reaching the high notes without effort. At the end of the verse, she held the final note for several beats, then paused, her eyes sweeping boldly over the waiting audience, before suddenly swinging into a saucy chorus, deepening her voice as she slapped the plain felt hat back on her head, this time at a cheeky angle, and began to dance along the front of the stage.

'My darling daddy never ever puts sugar in his tea,' she sang, then, winking at her listeners, ''cos my sugar daddy says his only sugar's me—'

As cheers and whistles broke out around her, Elspeth stared, dumbfounded, at this new Lena, who was behaving as if going on to a stage was a common occurrence. It was as though she had been born to it.

The applause at the end of the song was tumultuous, and when Lena made to leave the stage, the audience roared for more. This time she sang, 'Poor Butterfly', standing straight and still, her hands clasped before her; her voice, sweet and pure, bringing a lump to Elspeth's throat. She wasn't the only one to be moved – the noisy audience had fallen into attentive silence as soon as the first notes rose from Lena's throat, and now there were a few sniffs from somewhere behind Elspeth, and the occasional gruff clearing of a throat. She glanced at Lachlan, and saw that he was totally absorbed in the lone figure on the stage, his lips parted and his eyes shining.

The applause was again deafening when the last wistful notes faded away, with some members of the audience on their feet. Lena beamed at them, knelt to whisper to the conductor, then announced with a cheeky grin, 'One more song and that's all ye're gettin'!' For the final song, she completely changed her style again, swinging into a pert rendering of 'I Can't Find My Way Home'.

When the song ended, she blew kisses to every part of the theatre, then to the orchestra, before picking up her hat and hair ribbon and walking demurely to the steps. The Master of

Ceremonies appeared as she got there, and they spoke briefly before she continued back down to her seat.

'Thanks for the luck,' Elspeth heard her say to Lachlan, putting a hand on his arm as he stumbled to his feet to let her brush past him.

As the party made their way to the exit after the show they were halted time and again by people crowding round to speak to Lena. She shrugged off their praise modestly, but her pretty face glowed.

'I've always wanted tae dae that,' she said when they finally grouped together on the pavement.

'You were wonderful!' Mattie's voice was awed. 'I could never do what you did tonight.'

'Och, it's easy. Ye don't pay any heed tae the audience, ye just think about the songs and enjoy singin' them.'

'An' make a right exhibition of yerself,' Drew said sourly, glaring at Lachlan, who hadn't said a word but couldn't take his eyes off Lena. 'Come on, it's time we were gettin' home.'

'I've tae go round tae the stage door first. That man wants a word with me.'

'Aye, an' I can imagine what it is,' Drew snarled. 'I'm goin' tae no stage door. I've had enough of a showin'-up tonight as it is!'

'I never said you were goin' with me,' Lena snapped back at him. 'I can manage fine on my own.'

He stared at her wordlessly, then turned on his heel and stamped away. Watching him go, Lena shrugged.

'Good riddance tae bad rubbish.'

'D'you want us to go with you?' Thomas offered as she turned away.

'No, I'll be fine.' She tossed the words over her shoulder as she headed for the side street where the stage door was located.

On Monday morning, she arrived at Brodie's department store to give in her notice. That night she went onstage again at the Hippodrome, and a week later, when the company finished its Greenock booking, Lena left town with them, telling

Elspeth before she went that both Miss Buchanan and Miss Arnold had prophesied a terrible future for her.

'They seem tae think I'll either end up as a white slave or starvin' in a garret,' she said, amused. 'I told them that anythin's better than dyin' of boredom in a sewin' room.'

'It's like a fairy story,' Elspeth marvelled, and Lena shrugged.

'It's just a matter of doin' what ye want tae do. Mind that when yer own time comes. Anyway – it was your Lachlan that gave me the good luck.'

She winked, just as she had winked on the Hippodrome stage. 'He might be quiet, but he's a lovely laddie,' she added, then she was gone.

As Lena's sudden decision to go on the stage meant that the sewing room was short-handed, Miss Buchanan demanded Elspeth's return from the office.

'As it happens, I'm expecting Miss McCabe back next week,' James Brodie said when he broke the news to Elspeth, 'so you would have been returning to the sewing room then in any case. But Miss Buchanan tells me there's a fairly large order in, so she can't wait.'

'I could do some work for you in the evenings, if I can take it home with me,' Elspeth offered, astonished by her own audacity. 'I've got my own typewriter there.'

His brows shot up. 'Your own typewriter? How did that come about?' She felt colour rise to her face as she explained, finishing with, 'It's old, but it's in good order.'

'But you shouldn't have to work in the evenings as well, my dear.'

'I don't mind. I don't go out much anyway,' she told him truthfully. Kenneth and Mattie had returned to Glasgow, and time was hanging on her hands.

He agreed, and each evening after that she went along to the office to collect the evening's work before going home. She was able to fit it in because the demand for her letter-writing skills

217

had finally begun to ease off, though there were still several requests each week.

The work she had to do for Mr Brodie was easy compared to making sense of Mr Monteith's erratic book-keeping on crumpled scraps of paper. That task had seemed at first sight to be quite impossible, but Elspeth, determined not to let it defeat her, had worked hard, thankful, as the little bits of paper spread over the typing table, then the bed, and finally the floor, that she now had the room to herself and there was nobody there to complain.

Mr Monteith's writing was deplorable, his methods haphazard, but as time went by she had begun to read and decipher the scribbles more easily, and to grasp his strange logic. Gradually, the muddle had been transferred from torn-off scraps of papers and used envelopes into the large ledger. She had bought a smaller book and tethered it to the counter, persuading Mr Monteith to enter each transaction in it, rather than using bits of paper. He grumbled at first, but finally gave in.

It had occurred to Elspeth that most local folk took their most precious possessions into Mr Monteith's shop on a Monday morning, redeemed them on Friday, and pawned them again on the following Monday. Once James Brodie's typist had returned to work and Elspeth had more time in the evenings, she drew up a list of the items going through the pawnbroker's hands each week. When it was completed to her satisfaction she started listing the unclaimed or longer-term items stored in the back shop and the flat above, sneezing as the dust tickled her nose.

The listing meant that she spent far more time in the pawn shop than Aunt Flora would have allowed, had she known about it, but fortunately Flora was too wrapped up in her new grandchild to notice what Elspeth was up to.

Rachel's little girl, named Mary, after Mary Pickford the film star, was born less than two weeks after New Year. Once she was back on her feet, Rachel seemed to spend almost as much time in her old home as she had before she was married. Flora had no objection, for it meant that she could spend hours with her little granddaughter on her lap, cuddling her and crooning to her.

'Who's gran's best wee dumplin'?' she would say with a gentleness that amazed her family. 'Who loves her old granny?' Watching her joy in the baby, Elspeth saw another side to the woman she always thought of as sharp-tongued and difficult to please. Clearly, Aunt Flora loved babies, and it was easy to see, now, why she had taken her friend's orphaned child in with no thought to the cost of another mouth to feed.

'Mr James sent for me.' It was strange, Elspeth thought, to be visiting the office she had come to think of as her own work-place. Her eyes strayed to the typewriter, now under Theresa McCabe's control.

'I'll tell him you're here.' Wilma squirmed down from her high stool, saying as she went to the inner office, 'This is the lassie that did the typing while you were off, Theresa.'

'Oh aye?' The typist looked Elspeth up and down, then sniffed, clearly finding her wanting. It was a relief when Wilma reappeared, holding the office door open for Elspeth then closing it behind her.

To her astonishment, James Brodie reached over the desk and shook her hand. 'I wanted to thank you for the work you did in the office, and at home. And' – he held out an envelope – 'to give you this.'

Puzzled, she opened it, and her eyes widened as she saw that it held two crisp one-pound notes.

'But – I'm not due any wages till the end of the week.'

'That's from me, to express my appreciation.'

'Mr James, I can't take money I've not earned.'

'Of course you've earned it,' he said firmly, ignoring her outstretched hand. 'You'll have to learn to value your own skills – that's what business is all about.'

She didn't dare show the money to Aunt Flora, who had always warned the three girls about taking gifts from men. According to her, that was the swiftest way to hell. Surely, Elspeth thought as she left the office, Mr Brodie wasn't that sort of man. But Aunt Flora might not agree.

On the following day, she put the money into the bank.

At the end of January, a postcard arrived from Lena, addressed to Lachlan and bearing a view of Glasgow's George Square. According to the few words scrawled on the other side, Lena was appearing onstage in one of the city's theatres. Flushed with excitement, for he never received any post, Lachlan read it again and again, studying the photograph until Flora told him tartly that he'd wear it away with his eyes.

'I don't know what that lassie's thinkin' of anyway, sendin' cards tae a respectable house,' she added sourly. 'I don't like a son of mine gettin' messages from a woman who flaunts hersel' on the stage in front of goodness knows who.'

'There's nothin' wrong with goin' on the stage,' Lachlan retorted sharply, reducing his mother to open-mouthed astonishment. It was unheard of, even before the war, for him to answer her back.

When another card arrived a month later, this time from Aberdeen, he seized it and bore it off to his bedroom, refusing to discuss it with anyone, though he reported proudly to Elspeth later, 'She says she's doin' fine, and she's askin' after you. They're off to Dundee soon; she says she'll send me a card from there.'

But there were no more cards. As the weeks passed and Lachlan's eager anticipation turned to disappointment, Elspeth became furious with Lena for letting him down. There was nothing she herself could do about it, though, other than deciding that if Lena ever returned to Greenock she would have a few things to say to her.

22

Thomas, wearing trousers and a vest, opened the door to Elspeth.

'I've just arrived home,' he explained hurriedly, 'Aileen's cut herself, and I'm washing the dirt from the garage off my hands so that I can see to her.'

In the kitchen, fragrant with the smell of simmering broth mingled with an undercurrent of stew from the oven, Aileen was sitting on a chair by the stove, one hand nursing the other, a clumsy bandage wrapped about one of her fingers.

'I'll see to it,' Elspeth offered, but Thomas, already back at the tiny sink, shook his head.

'I can manage.'

Aileen smiled apologetically. 'It's just a wee cut where the knife slipped when I was peeling potatoes. I'm so clumsy – it's nothing to fret over.'

'You never know with cuts,' her husband insisted, reaching for the towel while Elspeth picked up the knife that Aileen had dropped and got on with the work of peeling the potatoes, noticing that the girl had cut the peel thick, taking a fair portion of the potato with it. Flora McDonald would have been mortified if she or any of the girls she had raised had indulged in such wastefulness.

Elspeth liked spending time in the little flat, and called in often. Although Thomas and Aileen couldn't afford much in the way of furniture, their love and joy in each other permeated their home, turning it into a warm, welcoming place. Aileen, determined to be as good a wife as she could, worked hard at learning how to look after her new home; the small room was neat and bright and welcoming, the table set, the fireplace swept, the fire well tended.

The only untidiness was unavoidable – Thomas's oily working dungarees, which were lying on a sheet of newspaper in the corner. He himself washed them every Saturday, Elspeth knew, refusing to allow Aileen to take on the heavy, daunting task.

'How's Lachlan doing?' he asked as he tossed the towel down and knelt before his wife, carefully unwrapping the bandage.

'He's working late at the store this evening, helping with some painting.' Elspeth noticed that although Aileen had filled a pot with water in readiness for the potatoes, she hadn't yet put it on to the stove to heat, thus slowing down the cooking process.

'I want to do everything right for Thomas. He's given up so much for me,' Aileen had told Elspeth once, ignoring the fact that she herself had given up even more. She hated to let Thomas see the mistakes she made, although he never found fault.

Now, Elspeth signalled silently to Aileen with the pot before putting it on the stove, and the girl, understanding, gave an imperceptible nod, her green eyes flashing her gratitude. Just then Thomas's fair head dipped swiftly to let his lips brush the tiny cut on Aileen's work-roughened hand. Elspeth looked away quickly, feeling that it was wrong to spy on such special moments between man and wife.

Aileen was showing signs of strain, she thought as she began to cut the potatoes into quarters. A little worried frown was settling in between her brows, and there was an air of tension about her. It couldn't be easy for someone from her background to have to deal with the daily grind of trying to make a small wage stretch as far as possible.

'You'll stay for your dinner?' Aileen invited when the bandage was firmly in place and Thomas had freed her to join Elspeth at the stove.

'I'm expected at home. I just looked in to see how you were.'

'We're both fine,' Thomas said cheerfully, replacing the towel he had been using on its nail beside the window. He hesitated, sniffing the air, then pulled back a corner of the window curtain. Elspeth heard an intake of breath from Aileen as he turned, holding out a small bowl containing a deep blue hyacinth. Its delicate, haunting fragrance began to spread over the room.

'Aileen, pet, I told you we cannae afford to spend money on—'

'I didn't buy it,' Aileen interrupted, fingers twisting nervously at her apron. 'It was a gift. Ian brought it.'

Thomas's jaw dropped and his brown eyes widened. 'Your brother was here?'

'Just for a minute, to see how I was. He brought the wee plant.'

'From the greenhouses,' Thomas said, then swallowed hard. 'To remind you of everything you've turned your back on.'

'It isn't like that at all.' She stepped forward and put her hands over his, so that they were both cradling the bowl. 'He came because he just wanted to see me.'

'And he saw you in this tiny room that's all I can give you.' His shoulders slumped, and his voice was bleak with humiliation. 'Did he ask you to go back home with him?'

'I am home! He's my brother, Thomas, you're surely not going to forbid me to see him now and then, are you?'

'I'd never forbid you to do anything, you surely know that.' Then, with a visible effort, he forced a smile. 'I'm not complaining, lass, of course your brother'll want to see you. It was just – a surprise, that's all.'

'I wish Ian Bruce hadnae come back into our lives,' he told

Elspeth, low-voiced, as he accompanied her to the close-mouth a few minutes later. 'I'd never deny her, but I don't trust the man.'

'He can't come between you and Aileen,' she tried to reassure him. 'You're man and wife, and she'd not turn her back on you now.'

'I know, but—' Thomas sighed, then said, 'The man's a troublemaker.'

Ian Bruce visited his sister regularly from then on, though never when Thomas was home. Elspeth herself found him lounging in his sister's flat when she called one day. She slowed as she saw the smart sports car outside the close, circled enviously by a group of wide-eyed children giggling at their reflections in the gleaming scarlet paintwork. On the nearby street corner loitered the inevitable group of men unable to find regular work. They stared enviously at the handsome automobile that had cost more than a year's wages and muttered amongst themselves, hawking into the gutter.

Elspeth hesitated. She would have turned and hurried away, but she had promised to buy some meat for Aileen on her way home from work, and she had no option but to deliver it.

The girl looked worried when she came to the door, then smiled when she saw Elspeth waiting in the close. 'Come in and meet my brother,' she said, and Elspeth, who had intended to hand the parcel over then leave, was drawn into the kitchen.

She had only glimpsed Ian Bruce, in full uniform at his elder sister's wedding, and had thought then that he was the most handsome man she had ever set eyes on. Close to, out of uniform and in an open-necked white shirt, dark blazer and white trousers, he was like a Greek god. As he rose to his feet and took her hand in his cool, firm grip, his closeness set her pulse fluttering. He knew it – she could tell by the lazy amusement in the green eyes gazing down on her.

'You'll have some tea, Elspeth?' Aileen asked.

She recalled the reason for her visit, and withdrew her fingers hurriedly from Ian's. 'I can't stop, I'm just handing this in.'

Aileen unfolded the parcel and studied the piece of flank mutton, her brow wrinkled. 'How did you say I should cook it?'

'Wash it, then put it into the soup, to get the flavour,' Elspeth gabbled, aware of Ian Bruce's presence only inches away. 'Then take it out before you serve the soup, and put it on two plates with boiled potatoes and some carrots. That way you'll get full use from it.'

Aileen's hand flew to her mouth. 'The soup! I was doing the vegetables when Ian arrived.'

They lay in a small pile on a chopping board, onions and carrots, turnip and potatoes and a halved leek.

'There's still time. I'll see to the meat while you finish the vegetables.'

'How delightfully domesticated,' Ian Bruce drawled, as the two of them set to work.

'Oh, I've learned a lot,' Aileen told him proudly. When the vegetables were in the pot she dried her hands and reached for her purse. 'I'll pay for the meat now, Elspeth, before I forget.'

Glancing at the young man, Elspeth saw his mouth tighten as he watched his sister scrabbling in the small purse, then counting coppers carefully out on to the table. As Elspeth scooped them up and straightened, his gaze moved away, travelling round the room that was so unlike the grand house he and his sister were used to. His lip curled, and suddenly despising him for his dislike of the home Thomas had provided for Aileen, Elspeth stuffed the money into her pocket.

'I must go. Don't bother to see me out,' she added as Aileen moved towards the door.

'I'm sure your friend can manage to find her own way,' Ian agreed, detaining his sister with a hand on her arm. 'Sit down

225

and have a rest. I hate to see you working like a skivvy.'

Outside again, Elspeth almost ran along the street, wondering how she could have been charmed, even for a moment, by the man who had had Thomas beaten unconscious as punishment for loving his sister. She, too, wished that Ian Bruce hadn't come back into Aileen's life.

But Aileen welcomed his visits. 'We were always close, and I've missed him more than I've missed my parents,' she confided to Elspeth the next time she called.

'After what he did to Thomas?' Elspeth's voice was sharper than she intended, and Aileen flushed.

'He knows he did wrong, and he's sorry about it. He even went to the garage to apologise, but Thomas wouldn't speak to him. But mebbe one of these days' – her face brightened – 'I'll get the two of them together. And Ian's trying to persuade my parents to change their minds. One day everything'll be all right.'

'I can't see your parents being happy about the sort of life you lead now.' Elspeth hated to throw cold water on the girl's hopes, but she felt that Aileen was expecting too much.

'They might, and so might Thomas's mother, now that—' Aileen stopped, a hand flying up to her mouth, and said guiltily from between spread fingers, 'Thomas wanted to tell you when we were all together. I'm going to have a child.'

'Oh, Aileen!' Elspeth hugged her. 'I'm pleased for you – for both of you.'

'So are we, and now I've spoiled it for Thomas. You'll not let on, will you?'

'I won't,' Elspeth promised, and managed to be convincingly surprised and delighted when she heard the news officially a week later. Thomas was almost bursting with happiness and pride.

'I'm going to work every hour I can to get somewhere better than this before the bairn comes,' he said exultantly, and when Aileen protested, 'There's nothing wrong with it, we'll manage fine,' he shook his head, hugging her tightly to him.

'I want to do more than manage.'

'And all I want is for our families to be happy for us, and for that to happen soon.' As she rested her head against her husband's chest, Aileen's lovely face was determined.

Outside, it was May; great clumps of golden broom splashed across the hills above the town and the sun's rays sparkled on the river beyond the dockyards, turning the water into a vast treasure chest filled with diamonds. But inside the Infirmary the long ward looked drab and dreary. Here and there, where the sunlight managed to squeeze through the tall, narrow windows, small pools of light dappled a locker top or a sheet.

Celia Bremner lay very still, as she had since being admitted, her bony hands folded on the stiff coverlet, her grey head scarcely denting the snowy pillow. Her eyes were closed and her mouth slightly open, the breath rattling unevenly in and out of her lungs. She hadn't fully recovered consciousness since being brought into the Infirmary after a neglected cold turned to pneumonia. Occasionally she moved, or muttered something unintelligible; once or twice she had opened her eyes and gazed vacantly around before lapsing back into her coma.

During the ten days her grandmother had been in the Infirmary, Elspeth had visited every evening and on Saturday and Sunday afternoons as well. Flora had accompanied her on one occasion, but this was the ward she had lain in during her influenza attack, and the memory of it made her fidget restlessly, anxious to get back home. Lachlan still had a morbid fear of hospitals, but both Thomas and Aileen had gone with her once or twice; as had Mattie and Kenneth during brief visits home at Easter, but preoccupied as they were with the thought of approaching exams they had both been poor company.

Granjan, who had declared from the first that visiting the

sick was no task for a young lassie to tackle on her own, was Elspeth's favourite companion, sitting patiently and calmly by the bed, occasionally reaching out to pat Celia's hand.

'Poor soul,' she murmured now from the opposite side of the bed, 'She'd hate tae know she's been brought tae this.'

A bell tolled in the corridor beyond the ward, and all down its length visitors began to get up and file out. Elspeth, with one last look at the grey, stern face on the pillow, rose and followed Granjan, guilty at the feeling of relief that always came over her as she stepped through the ward doors.

'Best go afore me, for I'm slow on stairs,' the old woman advised the people just behind her on the landing, adding carefully as the two of them waited for the flow of visitors to ease to a trickle, 'Have ye given any thought, pet, about yer grandma mebbe not gettin' better?'

'I know she's very poorly,' Elspeth said doubtfully. She couldn't imagine a world without Grandmother, couldn't imagine the still figure they had just left allowing herself to die.

'She is, poor woman. Best tae be prepared, just in case.' The stairs were clearing now, and Granjan gripped the rail firmly, taking the steps one at a time. When they reached the foyer she headed towards a nearby bench, as she always did. 'I'll just sit here for a wee minute tae catch my breath.'

Someone called Elspeth's name and she turned to see a girl who had attended the typewriting and shorthand classes with her.

'Peggy, what are you doing here?'

'Visiting my dad, he's had a bad turn again.' The girl looked tired and tense, and Elspeth recalled that she kept house for her father, who had a weak heart. 'He'll be all right, they say. Home again next week. What about you?'

'My grandmother's got pneumonia. How are you? Are you working?'

Peggy, who had been one of the star pupils in the typing

class, shrugged. 'Just in the early mornings, in a bakery. It's the only way I can bring in some money and see to Da as well. He can't be left on his own all day, so there's no hope of working in an office. They all want someone who can be there all the time.'

'I did some typing in Brodie's accounts office, but I'm back in the sewing room again.'

Peggy sighed. 'It's a terrible waste of all that learning we did, isn't it? I keep tellin' myself that mebbe one day I'll get to use a typewriter again, if my fingers are still up to it by then . . .'

Walking home with Granjan, Elspeth felt guilty about the typewriter sitting in her bedroom. At least she had her own machine, and some work to do on it, unlike poor Peggy.

Celia Bremner died a few days later, without regaining consciousness, and was buried in the same lair as her daughter. Flora, Henry, Granjan and Lachlan attended the funeral, and so did Thomas and Aileen. When she heard about the coming baby, Flora had finally given in and admitted her elder son and his wife into the family circle, though she was still somewhat stiff and formal with them both. Life was too short to bear grudges, Elspeth thought as she watched her grandmother's coffin being lowered into the ground.

As the undertaker's men withdrew the cords and stepped back, she suddenly felt completely alone. Cold and grim though she had always been, Grandmother had at least been of her own flesh and blood. For all Elspeth knew, her father and grandfather had both died long ago. She shivered, wishing that Kenneth could have been beside her. He, at least, was hers in some measure. She tried to console herself, as the minister's voice droned out the final words of the service, with the thought that he would be home for the summer in only two months' time.

23

A few days later she turned the key in the door and stepped nervously into Grandmother's flat, Rachel crowding in behind her.

'It's lovely!' the older girl breathed, staring at the carpeted floor and the large walnut coat-stand with its carved panels and decorative mirror. Celia Bremner's everyday coat and hat still hung on their usual hooks, and a long umbrella, neatly furled, waited in the stand for a hand that would never again lift it.

The flat was filled with her grandmother's presence, and she wouldn't have been at all surprised if the old lady had suddenly appeared at the parlour door. Crossing the hall and reaching out to open it, she was glad that she had thought of asking Rachel to help her to start clearing the place.

'I'm afraid that there is very little money involved,' the lawyer had said, sitting at his paper-littered desk and peering at Elspeth over the top of his half-moon spectacles. 'Your grandmother had a little money of her own, and used it frugally, but there's not much left. The proceeds of the sale of the furnishings will go to you, Miss Bremner, as sole surviving relative – that is, after my legal fees have been settled.'

'Sole survivor? Are you certain of that?'

'Of course,' the man said abruptly, and Elspeth swallowed hard, the nails of one hand digging into the palm. It had to be said. Everything had to be above board.

She swallowed again, then said, her voice little more than a whisper, 'My grandfather—'

The lawyer's bushy eyebrows shot up. 'You know of your grandparents' – er – situation?'

'I had heard something—'

He looked at her as though she had just shouted his own innermost secrets to the whole town, then said stiffly, 'Your grandfather died several years ago, Miss Bremner. As the family lawyer, I can assure you that you are indeed your grandmother's sole surviving relative.' Then he had changed the subject, and she didn't dare ask him for further details.

Elspeth had put the emptying of the flat off for as long as possible, but now time was running out and it had to be done so that the factor could rent the place to new tenants. Granjan would have helped, but stairs made her breathless, and Flora had made it clear that she had no wish to become involved.

'Never mind that nonsense about no' speakin' ill of the dead – I didnae like the woman and she didnae like me, so I want nothin' tae dae with her possessions,' she had said bluntly. 'I cannae abide that house anyway, it was always cold and unforgivin'.'

Rachel, on the other hand, seized the chance eagerly when asked to help, confessing that she loved seeing other folks' homes. Flora had agreed to take wee Mary off her daughter's hands for a few hours, and had borne the baby off to visit Granjan.

Although Elspeth had called at the house once a month for years, she had only seen the hall and kitchen and bathroom and parlour, and had never set foot in her grandmother's bedroom, with its vast wardrobe and double bed and marble-topped washstand complete with floral ewer and basin, or in the smaller bedroom that had once belonged to her mother. While Rachel exclaimed over the large sideboard and the slippery buttoned-leather *chaise-longue* in the parlour, Elspeth tiptoed into the smaller room, holding her breath, hoping desperately that she would come across something that had belonged to her mother.

But to her disappointment the small bed had been stripped bare and the single wardrobe was empty and smelled strongly of mothballs. The plain yellow ewer and basin on the wash-stand were bone dry, and the tallboy drawers only held spare blankets which also reeked of mothballs. Every trace of her mother had been swept away. It was as if she had never existed.

'I wish I'd a room like this for wee Mary,' Rachel said wistfully from the doorway, then, briskly unfastening her jacket, 'Well, we'd best get on with it.'

The grandmother clock in the living room chimed the half-hour just as she spoke, underlining the shortage of time available, and Elspeth reluctantly stripped her own jacket and hat off and donned the apron she had brought with her.

They worked hard all morning, opening drawers and cupboards, clearing shelves, sorting some forty years of Celia Bremner's life into various piles. The flat had been rented, and Elspeth was pleased about that, for she herself could never have lived in it. But once piles of clothes and sheets and towels and boxes filled with old-fashioned underwear and clothes and shawls and gloves and ornaments and cutlery and dishes and pots and pans began to litter the floor space, blurring the edges of the flat's former identity, she changed her mind. If it had been left to her, she could have given it to Thomas as a fitting home for his wife and coming baby.

The clock chimed again, and she closed the bottom drawer she had been emptying and went through to the kitchen, where Rachel was clearing out cupboards.

'We'll have a wee cup of—' she began, then stopped, staring. 'Rachel, where did you get that?'

Rachel, stretching up to a high cupboard, looked blankly at her over one shoulder. 'What?'.

'That bruise on your arm.'

232

Rachel immediately dropped her arms and stepped away from the cupboard, tugging one sleeve down. 'I don't know what you're talking about.'

'Yes you do.' Elspeth caught at the other girl's wrist, and after a brief struggle managed to push the sleeve up to reveal a nasty yellowing bruise on Rachel's upper arm. 'There.'

'Och, that? I banged my arm against the close wall.' Rachel put her free hand nervously to her throat, and Elspeth's eyes followed the movement.

'Did you bang your chest against it too?' Before Rachel could move, Elspeth drew the neck of her blouse aside to reveal another bruise marring the creamy skin.

'I just – I—' Rachel pulled back. 'It's nothing.'

'Rachel—'

'I deserved it,' Rachel said defensively, then, sudden tears filling her eyes. 'Let it be, Ellie!'

'I'll do nothing of the sort. Does Aunt Flora know about this – and Uncle Henry?'

Rachel flew into a panic at mention of her father's name. 'Don't tell him, Ellie, for God's sake! He'll go for Bob, then Bob'll go for me and—'

Elspeth picked up the kettle. 'Sit down, I'm going to make some tea.'

'But there's still a lot of work to do!'

'Never mind the work, just sit down. We'll have some tea, and then,' she added over her shoulder as she wrenched at the tap and began to fill the kettle, 'I want to know what's going on – all of it, Rachel.'

Half an hour later, when Grandmother's teapot, which for the first time in its existence had been filled to the brim with strong dark tea instead of the pale liquid it had normally held, had been emptied, the whole sorry story of Bob Cochran's brutality had been spilled out.

'He doesnae mean it,' Rachel said for the fourth or fifth

time, her face puffy and wet with the tears she had shed. 'It's the drink – he's not used to it.'

'But Bob's teetotal.'

'He used to be.' Rachel took a moment to blow her nose and dab at her eyes. 'It was the war – it changed Bob just as much as it changed Lachie, only nobody knew it at the time because there was nothing to see. He worries about things – whether he's goin' to be turned away from his work, and what'd become of us if he was. He even worries in case there's ever another war and he has to go away again. And then he has to have a drink to stop the worrying, then another. And when he comes home wee Mary's crying bothers him, though she can't help it, poor lamb, and one thing leads to another.'

'What about his parents? Do they know he's drinking?'

Rachel's body quivered. 'They found out. Now they'll have nothing to do with him, or me. They won't even look at my poor wee M-mary . . .' The tears began to flow again.

'You have to tell Uncle Henry, Rachel. He'd not let this happen to you if he knew.'

'I daren't, because of what he'd do to Bob. And Mam says—'

'You've told Aunt Flora?' Elspeth asked, astonished. 'She knows about this?'

'I had to tell someone.' Rachel had worked her way through both her own handkerchief and Elspeth's. As more tears streamed down her face Elspeth delved into a drawer and found a tray cloth.

'Here, take this.'

'I can't,' Rachel protested, trying to push it away. 'It's far too bonny – look at the nice stitching!'

'Go on – Grandmother'll never know the difference now. What were you saying about Aunt Flora?'

Rachel mopped at her face. 'She says I have to deal with it myself.'

'What?'

Rachel sprang to her mother's defence. 'She's had enough to worry about with Lachlan, then Thomas and Aileen. And she's right – Bob's my husband, and I married him for better or worse. It's up to me to stop him from drinking and h-hitting me.'

'How?'

'Well—' The tears welled again, and Rachel refolded the tray cloth to find a dry spot. 'If I was a better wife to him, he'd not hit me.'

'Did she say that?' Elspeth asked, outraged, then, as Rachel nodded, 'That's terrible!'

Rachel reached across the table and clutched at her hand. 'Promise me you'll say nothing to anybody!'

'But Rachel—'

'Promise!' the girl insisted, and Elspeth chewed her lower lip for a moment, then said reluctantly, 'If that's what you want.'

'It is.' Rachel gave her nose a final blow, and got up to splash cold water on her face. 'It's helped, just talking about it – now, let's get on with the work.'

It took two weeks to clear the house, working at weekends and in the evenings. Every time Elspeth thought she had finished at last, she discovered another drawer stuffed with half-finished knitting or sewing or boxes of buttons.

When it was done, she gave all the bed linen and napery to Rachel, urging her to sell what she didn't want, and spend the money on herself and Mary.

'Don't let Bob take it for drink.'

'I can't stop him,' Rachel said listlessly. She had lost all her confidence, Elspeth realised, and wondered why she and the rest of the family hadn't noticed the change in the girl before. 'If he sees me buyin' stuff we can't afford on his wages he'll want to know where the money's coming from.'

'Then put it aside, to use when you need it.'

'He'll only find it,' Rachel said, and in the end Elspeth sold the linen and napery herself to the owner of a small second-hand shop, and banked the money for Rachel.

Granjan and Aileen also benefited from the flat clearance, but Flora refused to accept anything. Celia Bremner's clothes, together with the small household items left, were collected by a charity happy to get them, and Elspeth called in an auctioneer to take the furniture and carpets off her hands.

Taking a final look round on the day the furniture was to be removed, she discovered that a small drawer tucked away in her grandmother's large mothball-smelling wardrobe refused to shut flush with its framework. After struggling with it for a few moments, she pulled it clear and knelt to feel in the space behind it. The blockage had been caused by a few letters without envelopes, tied together with a piece of string.

Replacing the drawer, which now slid smoothly into place, she sat back on her heels and loosened the string, which had been tied in a neat bow. The pages, released, fell across her lap like dead leaves, and she gasped as the word 'Whore!' seemed to fly up at her from among them. It was scrawled across one of the sheets in a large, angular hand, written so viciously that here and there the pen had broken through the paper. It was repeated on every sheet, almost obliterating the cramped copperplate writing beneath.

The doorknocker crashed on to its brass plate in a way that would have set Grandmother's eyes flashing. Elspeth jumped, then hurriedly gathered the pages up and thrust them into her pocket as she went to let the auctioneer's men in.

Their loud voices and the tramp of their feet across wood and linoleum banished the last trace of Celia Bremner from the house she had lived in for so long. When they had gone, taking the furniture with them and leaving only its imprint on the papered walls, the flat was large and echoing, a place that Elspeth had never been in before.

She closed the door behind the last man and took the letters out of her pocket, moving into the parlour to hold a sheet up to the light from the window, squinting at it until she managed to make out the words, 'My dearest Robert.'

Her eyes flew automatically to the mantel shelf where her grandparents' photograph had stood. Now it was packed into a box under her bed in Mearns Street, together with the few pieces of jewellery she had come across. It was only then that she realised that there had been no trace of her grandfather in the flat either, apart from the photograph. Celia Bremner had wiped both daughter and husband from her life. Everything apart from a few letters written to her grandfather, Elspeth discovered as she strained to decipher the faded writing on the pages in her hand, and even they had been defaced until it was almost impossible to make much out.

As she grew accustomed to the writing, she realised that she was looking at love letters, signed with the name 'Ann'.

Time was passing; she pushed the letters into her pocket and got on with the task of sweeping the floors and making sure that everything was clean and neat for the new tenants.

Leaving the flat for the last time, she walked to the factor's office in Port Glasgow to hand the key in, then squandered a few pennies on a tram ride back to Greenock, too tired for once to walk home.

There was nobody in the flat when she got back. Flora would no doubt be at Rachel's, Lachlan often visited Thomas and Aileen on a Saturday afternoon, and Henry would be at the bowling green with his cronies. In the kitchen, she pulled the letters from her pocket, recalling the story Granjan had revealed about Robert Bremner leaving his wife, eloping with a colleague. At the time Elspeth had struggled to put the tale out of her mind, fearful that Grandmother's sharp eyes might bore right into her skull and discover what she knew. She had succeeded so well that she had almost forgotten it, until reminded by the letters.

Somehow, her grandmother had got hold of them, and had kept them hidden away, perhaps taking them out to read now and then, tormenting herself, stoking the flames of bitterness, nursing her hatred and keeping it alive. Even when the man was dead – and surely the lawyer must have informed her that she was then, truly, widowed – she had kept the letters, refusing to let the matter end.

This, Elspeth thought with horror, was the woman whose blood ran in her own veins. She vowed there and then that she herself would never, ever bear a grudge, or allow bitterness to warp her life as it had warped Celia Bremner's. She lost all desire to decipher the letters further; even lying in her hand they seemed to radiate a pain that she couldn't bear.

Instead, she crumpled them into the empty grate, then took the big box of matches that always stood on the mantel shelf and struck one. Afterwards, she crushed the ashes into powder which she swept up and took down to the midden in the back court, watching with relief the last grains fall from the shovel.

Now the letters were where they belonged, out of harm's way at last.

24

As Elspeth went back upstairs, she paused on the final landing where the colours from the stained-glass window lay like a spilled rainbow on the stone floor. The letters Celia had kept hidden all those years had suddenly become linked in her mind with the present; a thought occurred to her that surely couldn't be right. And yet . . .

She ran up the last flight of stairs, anxious to make the most of the little time she had left to herself in the empty flat. In the kitchen, she drew aside the curtains hiding the wall-bed and went down on her knees to scrabble in the space beneath the bed. Flora McDonald kept a large biscuit box there, right at the back, a box that nobody, including Henry, was permitted to touch.

Elspeth's groping fingers found it, and she drew it out into the open, prising the lid up and riffling hurriedly through Flora's most precious possessions – her marriage certificate, her children's birth certificates, letters written by Thomas and Lachlan during the war. She had reached the bottom of the box and begun to think, with relief, that she had been mistaken, when her fingers touched a slim bundle.

For the second time that afternoon, Elspeth drew a well-kept secret from its hiding place. This one, like the letters in Celia Bremner's flat, was tied with string; she had no need to unfasten it, for one glance showed that it held half a dozen postcards, bearing pictures of various Scottish towns and addressed to Lachlan.

Flora was the first of the family to return home, arriving just after Elspeth had returned the box to its proper place and closed the curtains. She retained the small package of postcards, and as soon as her aunt came in she silently laid them on the table.

Flora's eyes almost bulged as they took in the postcards, and her mouth worked silently for a few moments before she managed to speak.

'Where did ye get these?'

Elspeth swallowed hard. She had done a terrible thing, but surely right was on her side. 'I went looking for them and I found them. They belong to Lachlan, Aunt Flora, not to you.'

Again, Flora McDonald's mouth worked for a second or two before she said, 'I'll not have any son of mine gettin' involved with a woman that earns her livin' on the stage!'

'There's no harm in the postcards – you saw how pleased he was to get the first two.'

'Oh, I saw all right – why d'ye think I held the others back? He's had enough hurt, without her givin' him more.'

'Hiding the cards didn't save him any pain – he was hurt at the thought that Lena had forgotten about him.' Elspeth pushed the postcards across the table. 'Give them back, Aunt Flora. Tell him they must have been held up somewhere and they all arrived today.'

'I should've put them in the fire when they first came!'

'If you burn them now I'll tell him about them.'

'So this is what it's come tae? After all I've done for ye, this is the thanks I get?' Flora pulled her hat off and thrust the hatpin through it savagely, then attacked her jacket, wrenching buttons from buttonholes. 'Have I not had tae suffer enough shame over Thomas as it is? I'm not lettin' our Lachie go the same way. This is a respectable family!'

Exasperation flared beyond caution. 'It'll not be a family for much longer if all you worry about is what the neighbours think. Thomas and Aileen are happy together – surely that's all that matters!'

'She's not the right woman for our Thomas.'

'You thought Bob Cochran was the right man for Rachel, and look what's happened to her.'

'There's nothing wrong with Rachel's marriage,' Flora flared.

'I've seen Rachel's bruises, Aunt Flora, and heard about Bob's drinking and the way he treats her. She's told me that you know all about it, yet you've done nothing to help her.'

'Mind yer own business!' Flora McDonald slammed both hands down hard on the table. Seeing the rage in the woman's face, Elspeth thought she had gone too far. She took a step back, clutching at a chair for support.

'Ye've been nothin' but a troublemaker since ye left the school,' Flora hissed into the space between them. 'Sidin' with Thomas when he came between me and Lachlan, sendin' that girl tae the Infirmary when Thomas was hurt – oh, I knew your hand was in it somewhere, madam, for ye cannae keep out of other folk's business, can ye?'

She hauled open a drawer in the dresser, and fumbled through it, then extracted an opened letter and tossed it on to the table.

'Here's another thing ye can poke yer neb intae. This came yesterday, and I was tryin' tae find the right time tae tell ye about it, but ye might as well read it for yerself,' she said coldly. 'Go on – read it!'

Slowly, Elspeth drew the letter from its envelope. It was from Mattie, and ran along the lines of the letters Elspeth herself received from the girl, telling about her progress at a school she was teaching in as part of her training. Puzzled, Elspeth looked up at her aunt, who stood watching her closely. Her face was hard and unforgiving.

'Try the next page,' she ordered.

At first, Elspeth's eyes ran along the close-packed lines without taking in the words, then she blinked, focused, and started again.

'There's something you should know, Mam,' Mattie had written. 'I need to tell someone before I come home for the summer, because I don't know what to do about it. Kenneth and I—'

Elspeth read to the end, a paralysing chill descending on her and numbing her body until she had no physical sense of her feet on the floor or her fingers holding the letter. Just as she finished, the outer door opened and Henry's tuneless whistle was heard in the hall. Flora scooped up the postcards with one hand, reaching the other across the table to pluck the letter from Elspeth's unresisting fingers.

'One word from you about Rachel,' she hissed, 'and you're out on the pavement – d'ye understand?'

Then Henry was in the room, filling it with noise and movement as usual, quite unaware of the tension between his wife and their foster child.

It was easy enough for Elspeth to slip out of the kitchen and out of the flat without arousing comment. She sped down the stairs; once outside she started to walk quickly, not thinking of where she was going.

Sickened by the ugly scene in the kitchen, she wished that she had never thought of looking for Lachlan's postcards. Then, remembering the sudden radiance in his face after Lena had kissed him at the theatre, and when he received the first postcard, she knew that he had been cruelly wronged, and deserved her help. Lena's fondness for him was probably too fragile to last, but Lachlan was entitled to know that at least she had cared enough to keep in contact, and hadn't forgotten him so soon.

But she had had to pay a bitter price for defending him. 'Kenneth and I—' The words sang mockingly in her head as she walked. Kenneth and Mattie. Kenneth being kind to Mattie at Elspeth's request, helping her to settle into her new life in Glasgow.

Their meetings must have continued, first of all by chance, then by arrangement and choice. Kenneth and Mattie, falling in love, planning to marry when he had gained his degree, and at a loss as to how to break the news to poor Elspeth.

'Could you tell her for me, Mam?' Mattie had written. 'Do it as gently as you can. I don't know how I'll face her. Kenneth's working in Glasgow for most of the summer, so he'll not be home for long. I won't either, I'm coming back early to be with him.'

Aunt Flora had certainly found a way of breaking the news, and at the same time had found a way of punishing her foster daughter for having dared to interfere in family business.

Elspeth wondered if Kenneth had tried to go further than kisses and cuddles with Mattie. If so, how had Mattie responded? She was older than Elspeth, and probably more worldly-wise since moving to Glasgow. Instead of panicking as she, Elspeth, had done in the wash house that night, Mattie might have given Kenneth what he wanted, and given it gladly.

Turning a corner, Elspeth was astonished to see the garage where Thomas worked only yards along the street. She looked round, down over the rooftops to the sun-blessed river below. Without noticing, she had climbed almost to the inland edge of the town.

Thomas was working on a car in the yard. Alerted by her footsteps on the cobbles, he looked up. 'Ellie?' At once, his expression changed. 'Has something happened to Aileen?'

'No, of course not. Why should it?'

'You looked so serious.' He reached for a rag and wiped his oily fingers, then glanced at her again. 'If it's not Aileen, what is it?'

'Nothing, I was just passing.'

'Nobody just passes along this street.' Thomas came round the bulk of the car he was working on. 'What's wrong?'

The concern in his voice was her undoing. She felt her face melt as though it was made of candle grease, and Thomas's figure, as he came towards her, shimmered as tears filled her eyes and began to spill over.

'Come on, I'll make us a cup of tea.' He put a firm hand beneath her elbow.

'Your work—' she protested as he began to lead her over the cobbles towards a door.

'I can take a few minutes off, and Mr Cameron's not here this afternoon, so you don't need to worry about him.'

He urged her through the door and she stopped in her tracks, staring round at the small, filthy kitchen.

'This is terrible!'

'It serves its purpose,' Thomas said blithely, pulling a chair forward and filling the kettle at a squeaky old tap. 'We only use the place for making tea now and again.' Then, as she continued to stare round in horror, 'Never mind the state of the place – sit down and tell me what's bothering you.'

At his reminder, her misery came flooding back. She collapsed into the chair, not caring about her skirt, and poured out the story of Kenneth and Mattie while salty tears trickled, one after another, down her cheeks.

'Well, well – Mattie and Kenneth.' Thomas pushed a mug of tea into her hand. 'Drink that down, now.'

She did as he was told. The tea was very sweet and very hot. The first tentative sip burned its way down into her stomach, and the second set up a glow that began to thaw out the numbed feeling. She looked gratefully at Thomas, who was propped against the sink, cradling his own mug in both hands. Dirty and oily though it was, his face was kind and concerned and his sympathy was so obvious that she felt that if she had reached out a hand she could have touched it.

'How do you really feel about it?' he asked, taking her by

surprise. She opened her mouth to reply, then sipped at her tea instead, giving herself time to think about the question.

Kenneth had never said much in his letters, and he had certainly not made any declarations of love. The letters had eased off over the past month or so, but she had been too busy visiting Grandmother in hospital then clearing out her house, to notice. She had assumed that in the summer, when he came back from the university, everything would go on as before.

'I want him to be mine, not Mattie's,' she said at last, slowly. Then, tipping her head back to look up at Thomas, 'But mebbe I only want him because now he's Mattie's.'

'D'you want to spend the rest of your life with him?' Thomas probed, and smiled when she replied, irritably, 'I don't know – I'm too young to think of the rest of my life.'

'You're right there – you're still far too young to tie yourself down. And no matter what age you are when the right one comes along, you know about it when it happens. Take my word for it – and let Mattie have Kenneth, if she wants him so badly.'

'I'd not want to keep him against his will – but it hurts,' she admitted candidly, 'knowing that he prefers someone else to me.'

A smile pulled at the corners of his mouth, and was quickly subdued. 'I know, Ellie. It's happened to me too, and it always hurts. But that's the way life is sometimes.' Then a frown puckered his brow. 'But I don't understand why Mam let you read the letter without giving you any warning. She didnae need to be so cruel.'

Again, Elspeth opened her mouth then closed it. She had promised Rachel that she would say nothing about Bob's ill-treatment, and if she was to tell Thomas about Lachlan's postcards being kept from him, it would probably do the new and fragile relationship that he and his mother had started to build no good at all.

'What is it?' He was watching her closely. 'You're gasping

like a baggy minnow that's just been scooped out of a pond.'

She got up and eased him aside so that she could rinse out the empty mug. 'I was cheeky to Aunt Flora, so she gave me the letter to punish me.'

'You must have been awful cheeky to deserve what you got.'

'I was,' she said shortly, and he had the sense to leave it at that.

As they left the kitchen, Elspeth to return to Mearns Street, Thomas to get back to his work, she put her arms about him and hugged him closely. He smelled of cars and oil and, faintly, of the soap Aileen kept by her kitchen sink.

'Here—' he protested, surprised and embarrassed.

'I don't know what I'd do without you, Thomas.'

'Ach, away ye go and let me get on with my work,' he said gruffly. Even so, he returned the hug for a moment before opening the door and shooing her out into the yard.

Going back down the hill, she felt warmed and healed by that moment of contact with another person. The coming baby was very fortunate to have such loving parents as Thomas and Aileen, she thought, then pushed the thought away hurriedly because it reminded her of her own situation, orphaned and, as far as she knew, without kith or kin.

When she got back to the flat Elspeth went straight to her own room and peered into the small mirror on the wall. The tea, the talk with Thomas, and the walk home had cleared all traces of tears, though her mouth had a downward twist. She forced a smile at her reflection, pulling a comb through her hair at the same time, and vowed to herself that she would never let Flora McDonald know how much Mattie's letter had hurt her.

When Lachlan tapped at the door a few minutes later she was ready to face him, her hair neat and her smile pinned firmly in place.

'Look!' He was almost incoherent with pleasure. 'Postcards

from Lena, lots of them from all over.' He began to spread them across the bed, reciting, 'Dundee, Inverness, Fort William, Perth, Paisley, Ayr. They must have been stuck somewhere, then they all arrived together. You can read them,' he offered magnanimously.

Although she felt that she had had more than her share that day of reading other people's letters, Elspeth did as she was bid. Lena's spelling left much to be desired, but her enthusiasm spilled across the small space allowed for messages. She seemed to be having a wonderful time, and pleasing audiences everywhere the troupe went. Each card, Elspeth noted, ended with a casual, 'Love, Lena.'

'They're lovely, but Lachlan, Lena's always been a bit' – she searched for the right phrase, but could only think of – 'generous towards folk. She treats everyone the same way.'

'You're worried in case I believe it when she sends her love,' he said in a surprisingly matter-of-fact voice, gathering the cards into a neat stack. 'I don't, but it's great tae have a friend. For a wee while there I was so shy and scared that I was like a wean again. I thought I'd never feel comfortable with anyone outside this house. Now I feel differently, and Lena's helped.' He gave her a slightly embarrassed smile. 'When the cards stopped I was a bit hurt because it was so sudden, but I got over that. If they stop again, it won't bother me.'

Flora was unusually quiet that evening. Throughout the evening meal, she slid sidelong glances at Elspeth, who was deliberately cheerful and carefree. It was, she thought later when she had escaped to her room, a performance that would surely have won her a place in the troupe that Lena worked with.

25

By unspoken agreement, a truce was decided between Elspeth and Flora, with neither making any further reference to the ugly quarrel they had had. But as far as Elspeth was concerned, the harm had been done, and the animosity she had sensed in her foster mother, even in babyhood, had been brought into the open. Nothing, she thought, absently fingering the little pebble brooch pinned to her blouse, would ever be the same again.

Mattie and Kenneth both wrote to her, their letters arriving on the following Saturday morning. They lay unopened in her pocket until the afternoon; she finally opened them on the beach where she and Kenneth had often picnicked with the others, and where she was free to settle her back against a rock and read with only the seagulls for company.

Both were short and apologetic, both spoke of fighting against their growing feelings for each other, and losing. They both expressed a hope that Elspeth would be able to understand, and to forgive.

She stared out across the water, seeing the two of them in her mind's eye, writing their letters together, comparing words and phrases. The waves washing almost to her feet echoed their sighs of relief when they finally signed their names, folded the single sheets of paper, and sealed them into envelopes. She pictured them walking together to a postbox, slipping the letters into its waiting mouth, then hurrying away, fingers entwined, thankful that the difficult task was over, and free, now that they had confessed, to enjoy their love.

She wanted to cry, but there were no tears left. Instead, she tore the letters up, tossing the shreds of paper to the breeze, which then committed them to the water. She had had enough of letters that had been kept and agonised over – the past was past, and only the future mattered.

As the time for Mattie's return from Glasgow drew near, Elspeth sought for ways and means of keeping herself too busy to think about the summer she had once looked forward to. Mr Monteith, well pleased with the work she had done for him, had told her several weeks earlier about a friend of his, a second-hand furniture dealer in Port Glasgow, who could do with some help with his paperwork. Elspeth put on her best hat and coat and paid a visit to the man, coming home with an armful of books to work on.

Lachlan offered to take Elspeth to the pictures on the day of Mattie's arrival, and was surprised when she refused.

'But Kenneth'll be coming as well, for his tea, and Mam'll probably make a fuss of them both. You'll not want to be there when that's going on.'

'I have to be there. I have to face the two of them sometime, Lachie, and it might as well be now.' Even to her own ears she sounded very cool and grown-up, although her stomach was full of butterflies.

He scowled. 'I think our Mattie's got a cheek, parading him in front of you.'

'She's got every right to bring her fiancé to her own home.'

'Are you telling me that you don't mind?'

Elspeth had never lied to Lachlan or Thomas, and wasn't going to start now. 'I minded a lot when I first heard, but I've got used to the idea now. I'd not have wanted Kenneth to stay with me against his will. And I'm going to be here when Mattie brings him home.'

'Oh, all right – but if you feel that you want to get out of the place, tip me the wink and I'll think of something.'

When the moment came, it was hard for her to see the happiness in Mattie and Kenneth's faces and to hear Flora making such a fuss of the two of them. But Elspeth had worked hard to prepare for the ordeal, and she managed to deal with it calmly, congratulating them both and admiring the engagement ring Kenneth had given Mattie. That made it official, she thought, gazing down at the small diamond. There was no chance now of Kenneth changing his mind and asking her to take him back.

Lachlan hovered around Elspeth protectively all afternoon, giving Kenneth a curt nod when he arrived, then eyeing him coldly across the table during the meal. Henry, too, tended to sympathise with her, but Kenneth and Mattie both looked so guilty each time they caught Elspeth's eye that she found herself making a point of being nice to them both.

As the rest of the family were there as well – Granjan and Thomas and Aileen, Rachel and wee Mary – things were easier for Elspeth. The kitchen was so crowded that it was easy for her to avoid the happy couple after greeting them.

Flora, glowing with pleasure and triumph at the good marriage her younger daughter was making, found herself eclipsed somewhat when Thomas announced at the table that his employer, Forbes Cameron, had decided to buy a partnership in a larger garage in Gourock.

'He's going to spend most of his time there, and I'm to run the Greenock garage for him,' he said proudly. 'I've not been there long, but he's pleased with my work and says he couldn't find a better man for the job. I'm to get in another mechanic to work under me. And it means more money, so' – he put an arm round Aileen, sitting by his side – 'we'll be able to afford a better flat before the bairn arrives.'

As the two girls were going to bed that night, Mattie tried to explain, as she had in her letter, that she and Kenneth hadn't intended to fall in love. Elspeth, who couldn't face the prospect of another discussion about the matter, broke in almost at once.

'Mattie, Kenneth and me were just friends, nothing more. I don't mind about what's happened.' She wasn't sure whether that was a lie or not. She was still hurt, but at the same time she was aware of a faint sense of freedom. 'He cares more for you than he ever did for me, and there's nothing else to be said about it.'

Mattie's eyes, which had been sliding away from Elspeth ever since she arrived, brightened. 'You're awful generous, Ellie.'

'I'm just being sensible,' Elspeth told her briskly, then, longing to change the subject, 'It's good news about Thomas, isn't it?'

Celia Bremner's furniture was sold not long after Mattie and Kenneth returned to Glasgow, raising more money than Elspeth had expected. She would have liked to spend it on the others, but realised that in view of the tension between herself and Flora, that would not be wise. Instead, she bought small gifts for Granjan and Rachel and wee Mary, and a pretty scarf in different shades of green to match Aileen's eyes.

'I'm so glad to see you!' the girl welcomed her when she called with the gift. 'Thomas is working late again, and I'm tired of my own company.'

The note of complaint in her voice, unusual for Aileen, put Elspeth on the defensive. 'He's trying to make a success of running the garage on his own, so that he can earn enough to give you and the bairn a good life.'

· 'I know, but—' Aileen hesitated, then said slowly, 'Has he told you that Ian's offered to give us a loan until things get better?'

'Your brother? Thomas would never agree to that!'

'Thomas,' his wife said shortly, 'has more pride than he can afford. I don't see why we shouldn't accept – Ian's my brother, after all, and he only wants to help. It would make such a difference to us, yet Thomas refused to even discuss it.'

'Can you blame him, after what happened?'

Aileen flushed. 'That was ages ago, and Ian's done everything he can since then to make up for it. It's Thomas who's being difficult now. You'd think he'd want what's best for both of us. For a start, we could move out of this place and into something with more room.' She threw her hands out to indicate the small kitchen that she had so lovingly painted and furnished less than a year ago, then said with sudden hope, 'Would you speak to him, Elspeth? He thinks highly of you, and he'd listen to you. You could explain to him that Ian only wants to help us.'

'But I couldn't interfere in Thomas's life,' Elspeth said wretchedly, then, as Aileen opened her mouth to argue, she held out the small package. 'Grandmother's furniture's been sold, so I brought you a wee gift to celebrate.'

To her relief, Aileen brightened at once, exclaiming with delight over the scarf then tying it round her neck and admiring herself in the small wall mirror.

Thomas arrived just then, his eyes suddenly wary as he stepped into the room and saw the pretty green scarf about his wife's throat.

'Is this another of your brother's wee presents? Aileen, I've told you—'

'Elspeth gave it to me. I suppose that's acceptable, since she's a member of your family, not mine?' There was a sharpness in Aileen's voice that Elspeth had never heard before, and she wished that she had left before Thomas's arrival.

He flushed scarlet beneath the streaks of dirt and oil from the garage. 'I'm sorry, Ellie, I didn't realise,' he said, then as he looked again at his wife, the wariness fled and he smiled. 'The colour matches your eyes. You look lovely.' He moved to hug her, but she backed away.

'Don't get oil all over it. I wish you'd wash at the garage, Thomas, and not walk through the streets looking like that.'

'I told you, if I take the time to heat water on the gas ring, a customer's sure to arrive while I'm doing it, then I'm trapped for another half-hour.' He poured hot water from the kettle on the range into a basin and snapped open the metal fastenings holding the shoulder straps of his dirty dungarees. 'It's best to just lock up and go while the place is empty. As for walking home like this, a wee bit of dirt's a badge of honour. There's plenty of poor souls in this town that'd give anything they had for the chance to get their hands dirty from work.'

He stepped out of the overalls and tossed them on to the newspaper waiting in the corner for them, then reached for the harsh yellow soap by the sink and began to wash.

'I'd best go and let you have your meal in peace,' Elspeth said, but Thomas, dousing his face, spluttered through a veil of water, 'Wait a bit, Ellie, I want to ask you about something.'

'What did you buy for yourself?' Aileen wanted to know.

'A new pair of gloves.' Now that the angry flush had left the other girl's cheeks, Elspeth saw that there were shadows beneath her slightly slanted eyes, and the corners of her mouth were drawn down. The baby was showing now and increasing weight had robbed Aileen of her usual grace; as she picked up a jug and went to rinse Thomas's hair she put her feet down heavily, moving with the sway-backed walk of pregnancy.

Her blouse and skirt strained tightly over her rounded belly, so that the hem at the front of the skirt was dragged up, giving the garment an uneven look.

Elspeth felt a stab of pity for the girl. If she had married her own class, she would have been pampered throughout this pregnancy, not allowed to lift even a finger. She would have worn clothes specially made for the occasion, cut skilfully to conceal her swelling figure. Instead, she was denied the luxury that was hers by birthright, forced to cope as best she could. It was little wonder that she was tired and irritable.

'How would you like me to make you a new dress?' she offered impulsively. 'Something loose and more comfortable.'

Aileen handed Thomas a towel and he buried his head and face in it. 'Could you?' Her eyes lit up, the weariness and stress vanishing. For a moment she was pretty and carefree again, then her eyes clouded. 'How much would the material cost?'

'Whatever it is, we'll find the money,' Thomas put in quickly from the folds of the towel. 'It's well past time you had a new dress.'

'Don't worry about the cost – we get remnants for nothing at work, and there's a lovely piece of silky material lying in the sewing room just now, a nice bluey-green that would suit you.'

It wasn't true. Miss Arnold didn't allow the girls in the sewing room to take even the smallest scraps that were left over from their work. As Lena used to say, the overseer wouldn't have given her nail-clippings away free. But Elspeth had been admiring the piece of blue-green material on the remnants counter at Brodie's that very day. It wouldn't cost much, and she could use some of Grandmother's money.

'I'll bring the material in tomorrow, on my way home from work,' she promised. 'We can decide on the style once you've had a look at it.'

Aileen nodded eagerly, her face radiant, as Thomas turned from the sink, running his fingers through his wet hair. 'I'm looking for a favour from you as well, Ellie.' He looked embarrassed. 'With me being in charge of the garage now, it means that I've to balance the books and send out the accounts. I've never in my life had to see to that side of things – I just handed my pay packet to Mam and she handed back my spending money. It was much the same in the army. And Aileen here has no more idea of working with money than I have, though' – he shot a proud look at his wife – 'I've never seen anyone make a few coppers go further than she can.'

Aileen coloured, and said quickly, 'I'm learning, but I can't deal with ledgers and payments and all that sort of thing. I'm still finding out about the cost of vegetables and washing soap.'

'So I thought mebbe you could show me how to do the books,' Thomas went on. 'I'll try to learn from you so that I can take them over myself soon.'

He was running a comb through his hair now; it clung to his skull, combining with his newly scrubbed face to take years off his age. He and Aileen, Elspeth thought as she looked from one to the other, both looked too young to shoulder all the responsibilities and worries that crowded in on them. At that moment, she felt older than either of them, though she was several years their junior.

'Of course I will. Can you bring them home with you tomorrow? I'll have a look at them after I've measured Aileen for the dress.'

Studying the ledgers and cash-books spread before her, Elspeth could see that although Forbes Cameron had known what he was about, Thomas didn't. His financial dealings since taking over the garage reminded her of Mr Monteith's book-keeping.

'I've not got the time to do it all properly as well as getting on with my own work,' he explained anxiously, watching as she riffled through the notes he had made. By his side, Aileen caressed the dress material Elspeth had bought that morning from the remnants counter.

'To tell the truth, it would take too long to sit down and teach you how to keep your own books, but I could see to them for you if you want, and teach you what I can when you've got the time. I could type out your bills properly while I'm at it.'

His eyes lit up. 'That would be grand! How much will you want for it?'

She thought fast, guessing that any money he paid her would have to come from his own wages.

'You've got an office at the garage, haven't you?'

'It's not much – a room with a desk and a gas ring and a paraffin heater.'

'Could I move my typewriter in and work there? I think Aunt Flora's getting tired of the noise the typewriter makes,' she hurried on as Thomas raised his eyebrows. 'If I could use your office I'd do your books in place of paying rent – unless you think Mr Cameron would object.'

'He'll not bother his head about it. But it's not a very cosy room, Ellie.'

'That'll make me work faster, so that I can get away to somewhere more comfortable.'

'In that case, you've got a deal.' Thomas took her hand and shook it vigorously. 'I'll collect the typewriter from Mearns Street tomorrow.'

26

The garage workshop had at one time been the stable and carriage-house of a sturdy Georgian family home on the hill above Greenock. As the town expanded the garden had disappeared beneath cobbled streets and small factories, but the house still remained, its brickwork badly in need of repointing, its high, wide windows either boarded up or so dirty that it was impossible to see through them, its once-handsome front door dingy and permanently sealed.

The only usable entrance to the old building was the kitchen door, which opened from a cobbled yard where horses had once been led out to be yoked to carriages. The upper floor and the attic had been closed off, and only the front two ground rooms were in use, one as a storeroom, the other an office of sorts.

Thomas was right, Elspeth discovered at first sight of the room. It was the most cheerless place she had ever seen. Large and high-ceilinged, it had once been a drawing room, but now the timbered floor was scuffed and scored, faded paper hung dismally from the walls, and the mouldings on the ceiling could scarcely be seen in the dim light from a filthy window. The enormous fireplace lurked against one wall like the mouth of a dark and dismal cave, and the furniture consisted of a few chairs, a paraffin stove, a large sideboard piled with books and papers, a sagging *chaise-longue* that looked as though it had crept into the house to die, and a dusty table where Thomas set down her typewriter. The bulky machine, which had dominated her little bedroom, suddenly seemed small and quite forlorn in the middle of the long table.

'I told you it was cheerless,' Thomas said from behind her as she gazed round. 'Are you sure you want to work here?'

'I'm quite sure. At least I can make as much noise as I like without disturbing anyone,' she added wryly as a loud crash came from the direction of the yard.

'I'd better go and see what Joe's up to,' Thomas said hurriedly, and left.

Now that she was alone, Elspeth took time to study the place more closely, noting the dust that lay everywhere, and the grime on the windows, cutting down considerably on the amount of light in the room. At least something could be done about that. Tiptoeing across the hall, a square, gloomy place with a curved stairway leading up into total darkness, she found that the room at the other side was filled with bits of machinery. She hurriedly closed the door after one brief glance and returned to the office, wiping her dusty hands on her handkerchief.

'I hope you're not going to start fussing,' Thomas said anxiously when he returned to find her rubbing hard at the table with a rag she had located. 'It's only an office, mind.'

'I know, but nobody could work in there the way it is. All that dust'll ruin the typewriter. Don't worry, I'm not going to expect you or Joe to start painting and papering.'

Rachel willingly agreed to help, and the two of them spent the following weekend scrubbing and sweeping and climbing precariously on to chairs in order to knock down spiders' webs with mops lashed to broom handles. They wrapped themselves in huge aprons and swathed their heads in scarves to protect their hair against the dust. Baby Mary slumbered in her perambulator in a safe corner of the yard.

'It's been a bonny house,' Rachel said breathlessly, balancing on the windowsill and rubbing hard at the glass. 'Imagine living in a place like this, with nice furniture, and flowers outside the windows instead of just the street and folk passing by.'

'And a servant to come and turn the pages of your book for you,' Elspeth agreed from the sideboard, where she was sorting through the books, shaking each one vigorously to clear the dust from it. She was enjoying Rachel's company. They had never really known each other before, for Mattie was nearer Elspeth's age and Rachel had always been the older sister, contemptuous of the two younger girls. Now, Elspeth discovered that Rachel was a good companion, with a sense of fun she had never demonstrated before.

As the other girl stretched up to the top of the window, Elspeth noticed a few bruises on her arms. Clearly, Bob was still ill-treating his wife. But she had the wit to say nothing, taking her frustration and anger out instead on a fragment of wallpaper dangling above the sideboard, wrenching it savagely from the wall. It came away with a satisfactory ripping sound, showering her with grit.

'Ellie, what're you doing?'

'It might as well be off as hanging there.' Elspeth stepped back to look at her handiwork, refastening the scarf round her head. 'If we brush over the plaster it'll look better than the way it was.'

'Let me.' Rachel deftly stepped from the sill to a chair, then caught at another drooping piece of wallpaper and tore it free. 'It feels good, doesn't it?' she said with enthusiasm. When she laughed, Elspeth noticed, she looked years younger.

Half an hour later, when Thomas glanced in to see how they were getting on, there was a small pile of paper in the middle of the floor.

'You don't mind, do you?' Elspeth asked, noting Rachel swiftly tugging her sleeves down to ensure that the finger-shaped blue marks on her arms were hidden. 'The walls looked worse with the paper than they do without it.'

He shrugged, and handed over two mugs of strong tea. 'As long as you get my books into order I don't care what you do.'

Their throats were clogged with dust, so they went out into the yard to drink their tea, Rachel going at once to the perambulator to look at her daughter. Six-month-old Mary, oblivious to the noise from the workshop, was sound asleep on her back, one arm thrown above her head, long dark lashes brushing her plump cheeks.

Joe, the man Thomas had hired when he took over the running of the garage, came over to admire the baby. He was a cheerful man in his forties, a marine engineer who had lost his job as a seaman after an accident damaged one leg. Although he could no longer shin up and down the narrow metal ladders of an engine room he was well able to cope with garage work, and enjoyed dealing with cars and motor bicycles instead of ships' engines.

He touched the baby's half-open hand very gently with the tip of one finger, taking care not to dirty her white skin. 'That's a right bonny wee lassie ye've got there, hen.'

Rachel smiled shyly, then said when the man had gone back to work, 'I wish she'd been a laddie.'

'Why?'

'Women don't have much of a time – not women like us, anyway.'

'Are things still bad?' Elspeth ventured, and the older girl shrugged.

'They're no worse, and I suppose I ought to be grateful for that. Never marry for love, Ellie, it doesnae buy food or pay the rent, and it only makes folks bitter in the end.' She bent to draw the blanket gently round her slumbering daughter. 'I'm going to try to teach her that when she's older.' Then, straightening, she said suddenly, bleakly, 'I'm expecting again, Ellie, but don't say a word to anyone till I tell Mam. She'll want to be the first to know.'

'What does Bob say?'

'It's not something I'm in a hurry to tell him. I'll have to pick my time.'

'He'll be pleased, surely.' And surely, Elspeth thought, he'd be kinder to Rachel when she was carrying his child.

Rachel's mouth twisted wryly. 'I was daft enough to think he'd be pleased when I fell with Mary, but that's when the trouble started. To him a bairn's just another mouth to feed and one less drink. That's why I'm hoping this'll be a wee laddie – he might take that a bit better.'

'Why don't you do sewing for folk to make more money, since Bob's drinking most of his wages?'

'I couldn't,' Rachel said at once, startled.

'Yes you could. You earned your living by sewing before you married, and you're good at it. Look at the bonny wee clothes you've made for Mary. There must be neighbours who can't sew – you could offer to help them.'

'They'd not be able to pay me.'

'Money's not the only way to pay for things. They could look after Mary for an hour and let you get some time to yourself, or mebbe give you a few scones, or – there are lots of ways folk can help each other,' Elspeth pointed out. 'If any of your neighbours does cleaning for someone with money, she could mebbe mention your name, then you might get work from people who can afford to pay.'

'I'll think about it. We'd best get back to work.'

'You should have told me about the bairn,' Elspeth said as they rinsed their mugs in the kitchen. 'I'd not have let you climb up on the windowsill or the chairs.'

Rachel threw her a sidelong look from the corner of her eye. 'Why else did you think I was so keen to do it?' she asked, and went back to work.

With the layers of dust removed and daylight filtering in through the cleaned windows, the office, while still shabby and neglected, was at least usable. Elspeth started working there the following weekend, relishing the space she now had.

In her bedroom, papers had been strewn over the bed and

the floor, but here the table was large enough to accommodate them all. It was satisfying, too, to hear the crisp tapping of the typewriter keys and the crash of the returning carriage echo in the large room, knowing that Flora wasn't going to bang on the door to tell her to stop the noise.

It didn't take her long to put the garage books into order. She did Mr Monteith's work there too, as well as Mr Leslie's, the shopkeeper who had heard of her skills from Mr Monteith. Normally, she would only have been able to work in the office on a Saturday morning, but Thomas, in his eagerness to do his best for Aileen and their coming child, often worked into the evenings from Monday to Saturday, and always spent part of every Sunday at the garage, making it possible for Elspeth to put in longer hours than she had expected.

He was driving himself too hard, but her attempts to tell him that were brushed aside.

'It's only rich folk who deal with stocks and shares that make money without getting off their backsides,' he said contemptuously. 'And I'd not want to earn my bread that way, by the sweat of other men's foreheads. If I don't make this place a success Mr Cameron'll close it down, then where'll we be – me and Aileen and the bairn?'

'And where'll Aileen and the baby be if you make yourself ill?'

'Stop girnin' at me, Ellie,' he said, irritated. 'I've got enough on my mind as it is.'

She held her tongue after that, though she continued to worry about him, and about Aileen. She was busy in her spare time making the new dress she had promised Aileen, and she had met Ian Bruce more than once at the flat. Aileen was always animated when her brother was there, and it was clear that he adored her. Surely, Elspeth told herself, it was only natural for Aileen to want to keep in touch with the only member of her family who, at the moment, would have anything to do with her. But at the same time she had the uncomfortable feeling that Ian Bruce was encouraging Aileen's growing dissatisfaction with her surroundings.

Once, rounding the corner on her way to visit, she was in time to see Ian Bruce handing his sister into his car. It was a cool, breezy day and the green scarf Elspeth had given Aileen was tied around her head. Her thickening figure was enveloped in a warm fur coat that Elspeth had never seen before – presumably a garment brought from the wardrobe she had had to leave behind when she walked out of her parents' mansion to marry Thomas.

Neither of them noticed Elspeth; as the red car roared past her, she saw that all Aileen's attention was fixed on her brother.

'I love Thomas, and I'd not want to be away from him,' she said to Elspeth a few days later. The new dress was almost completed, and Elspeth was kneeling at her feet, pinning up the hem. 'But I'm so tired of having to do without and count the pennies. If he'd just let Ian help us, things would be much easier, and we'd have more time together. Ian's sure that once the baby's born Mother and Father will come round. And there's no reason why Father shouldn't buy Thomas a garage of his own.'

'Thomas would never allow that, Aileen,' Elspeth said carefully, and the skirt twitched in her hand as the other girl shrugged.

'He could, if he'd give up this stubborn pride of his.'

When the dress had been taken off, Aileen opened a drawer and showed her a lovely pair of gloves, soft and beautifully made. 'Ian gave them to me, to wear at the baby's christening.' Her eyes shone as she stroked the material with work-reddened hands. 'Don't tell Thomas – I'm going to hide them away until the time comes.'

She had asked Elspeth to buy some mince on her way to the flat; when she opened her purse to pay for it, Elspeth saw that there was more money in it than usual. Remembering Thomas's boast about his wife's ability to make a pound note go a long way, she wondered if Ian Bruce was giving his sister money.

There was nobody she could talk to about her suspicions, not even Granjan, in case she inadvertently let a word slip out in Flora's hearing. So Elspeth held her tongue and tried to assure herself that once the baby arrived Aileen would revert back to her former self.

The garage books gave an impressive picture of Thomas's ability to run the place. Once she managed to sort out the paperwork she found that business was brisk, although she already knew that from the number of people who called in at the garage every day, and from the telephone calls.

Before her arrival, Thomas had dealt with the telephone, which stood in the kitchen. Now it was Elspeth's job to answer it when she was in the office. At first, unused to the machine, she had been nervous.

'Ellie, I've got enough to do without running in here every time the telephone rings. It's only a machine,' Thomas told her impatiently. 'Machines are made for folk's convenience – no need to be afraid of them!'

Stung by his words, she had made herself master the instrument, and within a week had become used to it, though she was thrown into alarm when one of the callers barked, 'Tell McDonald to come to the phone,' as soon as she answered.

There was so much authority in the voice that she obeyed, and had reached the kitchen door before realising that nobody had the right to order her around like that. She returned to the machine.

'Please.'

'What?'

'C-courtesy costs nothing,' she said, then tried to force the nervous quiver from her voice. 'You could have said please.'

There was an exasperated sigh, then the man at the other end of the line asked, 'Will that bring McDonald to the phone any faster?'

'It will.'

'In that case – please.'

'If you'll just hold on, I'll go and get him,' Elspeth said primly, and went to call Thomas from the workshop.

He came into the office a few minutes later. 'What did you say to that man?'

Elspeth finished the entry she was making before looking up. 'The man on the phone? He was impertinent, so I made him say please, that's all.'

'Ah. I don't think anyone's ever made him say that before.'

'I wasn't impertinent back to him. If he says I was, he's lying.'

'He didn't,' Thomas said, and turned to go.

'Who is he?'

'Forbes Cameron, the owner of this place,' Thomas said, and returned to his work.

Forbes Cameron strolled into the office the following weekend to introduce himself.

'And to apologise for my boorishness on the telephone,' he added, and Elspeth flushed.

'I didn't realise it was you.'

'That shouldn't make any difference. You were quite right, I behaved badly. My only excuse is that I'm so used to working among men that I've lost my manners. I'm sure my mother would wholeheartedly agree with you that it was time someone pulled me up about it.'

He was a stocky, broad-shouldered man, a few years older than Thomas. Dark hair that looked as though it had been brushed that morning, but had then found a way of breaking free, topped a square, tanned face. His eyes were grey, and his mouth wide above a determined chin. She knew from what Thomas had said that Forbes Cameron had been born into money and had travelled extensively. He was a racing-car driver and yachtsman.

He glanced around the room, then back at her. 'I never realised what good lines this room has before.'

'It just needed cleaning.'

'It needs more than that.' He looked at the wall behind her, covered here and there by wallpaper, but mainly showing the bare plaster. 'It needs re-papering, for a start.'

'It's not worth papering an office.'

'Painting, then. What colour would you like?'

'There's no need to—'

'Blue? Yellow? Purple? Tell me what you think.'

Elspeth studied the walls. 'If I was doing it, I'd choose a soft shade, mebbe a parchment colour, mebbe a bit lighter than that.'

He strode over to where her coat hung on a nail. 'Come into the town with me and choose something. We'll get a decent coat-stand while we're at it.'

'But I'm in the middle of some work.'

'Give yourself an hour off to choose paint.'

'The room's fine as it is.'

'It's my room, and I say it needs painting. So—' She was scooped from her seat and being helped into her coat before she knew what was happening. Ten minutes later the two of them were choosing paint.

'What about the doors and skirting boards and window frames?' Forbes Cameron asked when she had opted for a pale fawn shade.

'It's too beautiful to be covered, even though it's all marked.'

'Varnish, then, with some treatment first,' he decided briskly. 'Now come and have a cup of tea, and tell me about yourself.'

'This is ridiculous,' she protested as they sipped tea in a small tearoom.

'Not at all; you deserve a proper office, especially after you've done such excellent work on our books.'

266

'You've seen them?'

'I call in every week to keep an eye on things. McDonald tells me you've refused to take any money for the work.'

'Thomas has enough to do with his wages. He lets me keep my typewriter in the office, and do work for other people there in return for what I do for the garage.'

'Nevertheless, it's me who should be paying you, not McDonald. I've been very lax about that. We'll arrange proper payment on the way back, and I'll see that the room's painted during the week, so that it's all ready for you by next Saturday.'

But by the following Saturday a freshly painted office was the last thing on Elspeth's mind. Three days after she met Forbes Cameron, Ian Bruce's handsome red car spun out of control on the hill road to the Loch Thom reservoir, smashing into a stone wall.

Ian and his passenger, his sister Aileen, both died immediately.

A clerk from Mr Bruce's lawyer's firm called at Mearns Street, where Thomas was staying with his parents, to inform him of the arrangements Aileen's father had made for the double funeral.

The family, at their evening meal, sat in awkward silence as the man, his bowler hat tucked beneath one arm, talked to Thomas. When he had finished he left, politely refusing Flora's flustered offer of a wee cup of tea.

'Ye'd've thought they'd've had the decency tae call at a better time – and to consult ye,' she raged when the man had gone. 'They've not even invited ye tae the house, and you their son-in-law!'

'Leave it, Mam,' Thomas told her brusquely. He had scarcely spoken since hearing the news.

'But she was your wife, an' carryin' your bairn—'

'The lassie I was married to's gone, and so's the bairn that never was. No point in quarrelin' over what's left. Anyway, she was a Bruce more than a McDonald.' He got up from the table, pushing his chair back noisily, and left the kitchen. A moment later the outer door shut.

'Now where's he goin'?' Flora wailed.

'Probably back to the garage, Mam,' Lachlan said.

'But he's already put in his day's work, and scarcely touched his food. If he's goin' tae insist on workin' every hour of the day an' night he'll have tae eat tae keep his strength up!'

'Leave it be, Flora, the laddie needs tae go through this in

268

his own way,' Henry said with a rarely heard ring of authority in his voice. 'Don't fuss him.'

She glared, then went over to the sink, leaving her own plate half-full, and began to crash dishes about. 'I don't know – ye'd think he'd talk tae us about it, or even cry if it takes him that way. But this is no' like our Thomas at all.'

'He'll be all right,' Elspeth tried to assure her, though she too was worried about the way Thomas had completely withdrawn from everything and everyone since his wife's death.

'Come and eat yer own food,' Henry added.

'I don't want it.'

'Sit down and eat, woman!' He all but shouted the words. Elspeth and Lachlan glanced at each other, then dipped their heads over their own plates. Although there was nothing wrong with the food, it was as interesting as cardboard to Elspeth, and she was sure that Lachlan felt the same way. They were both making a show of minding their own business in order to avoid the confrontation that seemed inevitable. Henry McDonald, Lachlan had once told Elspeth, could be a feared dictator at work, but he had always been content to let his wife rule the house, until now.

The confrontation didn't come. Flora flounced away from the sink and sat down, picking up her fork and knife.

'It's as if he doesnae care,' she muttered to the cooling, congealing mince and potatoes and carrots.

'Of course he cares – can ye no' see it in his eyes? He cares so much that he cannae speak for the pain of it.'

'Then why doesnae he let his own folk comfort him?' Flora asked, a tremor in her voice, 'When I think of that bonny wee thing, no more than a child hersel' – and how could he say she wasnae a McDonald, when they were wed in front of a minister and her own family's had nothin' tae dae with her since? It's us should be buryin' her, not them!'

'Flora—' Henry said quietly, with real steel in his voice this time. To Elspeth's relief the woman subsided.

Thomas hadn't set foot in the flat he shared with Aileen since hearing about the accident. He had moved into his parents' house at once, unable to return to his home, sending his father to collect clothes for him. He had insisted on working at the garage as usual, and when he was at Mearns Street he sat alone in the tiny room he once more shared with Lachlan, or in the kitchen making a pretence of reading the newspaper. He had aged overnight, and his brown eyes, normally lively and bright, were dull pebbles set in bony hollows.

Neighbours calling to express their sympathies were met with a set, withdrawn expression, and he usually left the kitchen or even the flat when outsiders called, letting his mother do the talking for him.

As a result of this, Elspeth knew, the neighbours were muttering to each other that he was too stuck-up for his own good and no longer interested in his own folk after marrying one of the gentry. She wanted to shout at them that it wasn't true, that Thomas should be left in peace to grieve in his own way, but she couldn't. That would only have incensed Aunt Flora, and made matters worse.

The funeral service was held in the grand church Catherine Bruce had been married in not long before the end of the war. Aileen's flower-bedecked coffin lay beside that of her brother, almost exactly where she must have stood on that long-past wedding day in her pretty yellow bridesmaid's dress.

As Thomas led his family in, an usher scurried up to tell him in a discreet murmur that there was a place for him in 'the family pew'.

'I wasn't welcome in their company when she was alive, and I see no reason to sit with them now,' Thomas said in a low, clear voice and ushered his family into a row halfway up the church while the man retreated, red-faced.

Flora wanted to sit by her bereaved son, but he had paid no heed, and as church was no place for an argument, she had to submit to his wishes, following Janet Docherty to the end of the empty row while the others huddled nervously in the aisle, anxious to be seated as quickly as possible and out of the view of the rest of the congregation.

Thomas chose the seat by the aisle for himself, looking straight ahead and seemingly oblivious to the stares and murmurs as the mourners coming down the aisle recognised him as Aileen's husband. He seated Lachlan beside him, then came Elspeth and Mattie, who had arrived that morning from Glasgow to attend the funeral. Rachel, who was having an uncomfortable pregnancy and looked pale and drawn in her borrowed black coat and a hat that didn't suit her, sat between Mattie and Bob.

As they waited for the service to begin, Flora fretted about Thomas's refusal to sit at the front of the church. 'They'll think he's snubbin' them,' Elspeth heard her say in an agitated whisper, loud enough to set heads in her vicinity turning.

'It doesnae matter any more what they think, does it?' Henry retorted gruffly, and Elspeth could positively hear Flora's withering glare as she subsided.

Many of the people pouring into the church were young, presumably Ian's friends – and former friends of Aileen's, thought Elspeth, though not one of them had visited her after her marriage. Forbes Cameron paused by Thomas, who got to his feet and shook hands with his employer and with the elderly couple by his side before the trio moved on to take their places elsewhere in the church.

The sombre organ music and the heavy scent of the massed funeral flowers had given Elspeth the beginnings of a headache by the time Mr Bruce and his daughter and son-in-law arrived, Catherine's face hidden by heavy veiling. She was the Bruces' only surviving child, Elspeth realised as the three of them walked down the long aisle, and she pitied these people who in their arrogance and insensitivity had turned their backs on Aileen in the final year of her life. For all their money and all their pride, the Bruces were still parents, and this must be a terrible day for them.

As soon as the family was seated the minister began to speak at length about the tragedy of two premature deaths. He talked about Aileen without once making reference to her marriage, her husband or her unborn child. Slipping a glance at Thomas, Elspeth saw that his profile could have been carved out of stone. Not a muscle twitched, not an eyelid flickered, even when the service finally ended and his wife's coffin was carried out, so near to him as it went by that he could have reached out and touched it. Mr Bruce and his daughter and son-in-law, walking behind the coffins, passed Thomas without a glance.

As she rose to make her way out of the church Elspeth saw some of their neighbours from Mearns Street sitting at the back, together with others who were probably Bruce servants.

Outside, the sun was shining, oblivious to the fact that today of all days the sky should have been overcast and weeping cold rain. As the McDonalds hesitated on the gravel drive, clustered in a knot for mutual comfort, Forbes Cameron brought over the elderly couple he had escorted into church, introducing them as his parents. They, at least, were friendly, and Elspeth, who had noticed with concern that Flora had begun to look pinched and shrunken and was clinging to Henry's arm for support, was relieved to see the woman expand a little under Mrs Cameron's kindly warmth. Just like a little Japanese flower, she thought, remembering her childhood, when she had loved to watch tiny dried-up flakes of apparently colourless paper blossom into bright flowers when dropped into a cup of water.

The usher who had spoken to Thomas in the church arrived by his elbow again to inform him that there was a place for him in one of the leading cars.

'Thank Mr Bruce,' Forbes Cameron told him blandly, 'and explain that Mr McDonald and his family are travelling with us.' Then he swept them off to where three handsome black limousines, each with a uniformed chauffeur, waited in the long line of cars.

In the cemetery, Thomas took hold of Elspeth's arm as she stepped out of the car. 'Stay with me,' he said; startled, for it was the first thing he had said to her since hearing of Aileen's death, she allowed herself to be drawn along with him through the crowd of mourners to where the two coffins waited beside the open graves.

In death, as in life, the Bruce family believed in their right to own land. An elaborate wrought-iron fence defended the considerable area set aside solely for their dead; each well-tended grave was watched over by a handsome headstone, and in the middle of the lair a marble memorial soared above the heads of the gathered mourners, the names of all those buried within the fence inscribed on its four smooth sides.

'Hold your head high, Ellie,' Thomas murmured as they took their places on the opposite side of the graves from Mr Bruce and his daughter. She did as she was bid, raising her head, topped by a wide-brimmed, high-crowned black straw hat, on the long stem of her neck, proud to be standing by Thomas, who, although his black suit hadn't cost a fraction of the money that most of the mourners had clearly paid for their funeral clothes, seemed to her to be the most elegantly dressed man there. Aileen, she thought with tears aching in her throat, would have been proud of him.

Arm against arm, they stood motionless during the short-ened version of the church service, separating only when Thomas stepped forward to take hold of one of the cords to help lower his young wife and their unborn child into their final resting place.

Ian Bruce had been buried first, his father and brother-in-law throwing handfuls of earth in on top of his coffin. As the undertaker's men took over the cords, smoothly lowering Aileen to the bottom of the grave, Thomas stooped and gathered a firm fistful of soil from the pile nearby, then held his arm out over the void, opening his fingers to let the earth patter down in a final salute to his wife.

It was hard not to gape when the funeral party went into the Bruce house. Although she had known that the place would be sumptuous, Elspeth was unprepared for the massive hallway they passed through after entering the house.

'It's almost big enough to hold our entire tenement,' Mattie murmured at her side as they stepped through the front door, staring at the huge staircase rising to the next floor. The fireplace in the vast drawing room was as broad as one of the kitchen walls at Mearns Street. Looking around at the paintings, the furniture, the wide, high windows opening on to a terrace where flower-filled stone urns stood, Elspeth felt her heart break for Aileen.

No wonder the girl had been suffocated in the tiny flat that was all Thomas could provide. No wonder she had been so pleased to make contact with her brother, and so eager to urge Thomas to take advantage of an offer that would have given them a larger home.

Mrs Bruce, her face grey and old against her black dress, her eyes filled with a sorrow that would never leave her, put in a brief appearance once the mourners were gathered. Supported by a uniformed nurse, she spoke to a few people, but neither she nor her husband or daughter came near Thomas. If it hadn't been for the kindness of Forbes Cameron and his parents, the McDonalds would have been completely isolated.

The Camerons fussed over Flora in particular, making certain that she had enough to eat, seeing to it that her cup was refilled, although Elspeth could tell by the flickering of Flora's lashes as she sipped carefully at the fragile china cup that the weak tea it held wasn't to her liking.

Standing close to her mother as though for protection, Rachel kept an anxious eye on Bob, who had eagerly accepted a glass of whisky and drunk it swiftly. Flora hadn't noticed, but Henry did, frowning in puzzled disbelief. Now Bob's eyes thirstily watched the silver trays of glasses being carried round the room by immaculately uniformed maids. His face was flushed, and he continually plucked with one finger at the collar of his shirt, or tugged his jacket down. Like Rachel, he must have borrowed his funeral clothes from a more affluent neighbour, for they were too tight for him. When one of the trays moved in his direction his fingers trembled and the tip of his tongue flicked across his lower lip, but somehow Henry, clearly realising that his son-in-law had broken the teetotal pledge made as a child, managed to step between Bob and the crystal glasses half filled with amber liquid.

Watching Bob's suffering, Rachel's misery, Flora's discomfort and Thomas's stoic indifference to his surroundings, Elspeth longed to sweep them all away from the magnificent house which had been the cause of so much heartache. None of them deserved to be treated like this. It was a relief when Forbes Cameron suggested leaving.

'We've been here for an acceptable length of time, and I see that some other people are preparing to go. My mother's tired, and I'm sure that you are too, Mrs Docherty.'

Janet was the only member of the group to have been at her ease, taking in her surroundings and the fine clothes of the women in the room with swift, birdlike glances that carried not a sign of envy. 'I'm f—' she began, then, with a look at her daughter, who was beginning to wilt again, she amended it to, 'I'm fair exhausted, tae tell ye the truth. Would ye mind if we went home, Flora?'

Mrs Bruce had long since retreated from the room. They made their farewells to Mr Bruce, who held each hand limply for a second and made murmuring noises, gazing past their heads, then Cameron saw them into the limousines, which were magically waiting before the door when they went out on to the steps.

Elspeth rode with Rachel and Bob, who were taken straight

home because Rachel was worried about wee Mary, being cared for by a neighbour. She arrived back at Mearns Street in time to see the garage owner assist Flora on to the pavement, under the interested stare of half the street, and bow over her hand before she summoned up the last of her strength and swept regally into the close.

'Such a nice man,' she said when they had gained the kitchen, stripping her hat and gloves off. 'A real gentleman. Elspeth, for pity's sake put that kettle on, I'm parched for a decent cup of tea. That was nothin' but coloured water they were pourin' out of they silver teapots.'

'They're a right gutless lot,' Henry grunted, sinking into a chair and easing his shoes off. 'I'd like tae see them try tae manage a decent day's work in the yards – it'd kill them off before they got properly started. Here – what was Bob Cochran doin', drinkin' whisky?'

'He wasn't,' Flora said at once.

'I'm no' daft, woman, I know whisky when I see it. He'd have had more if I hadnae worked it so that we both got lemonade the second time.' He wrinkled his face up. 'It meant I'd tae do without more whisky mysel', and it was the best I've ever tasted, tae.'

'The lemonade was made from real lemons,' Elspeth said in an attempt to make peace.

'Lemonade?' Henry snorted. 'The only decent drink in this country's the one made with grain and good Scottish water, and I'd tae miss out on my share because of that eejit our Rachel married.' Mention of Bob reminded him of his earlier question. 'And what happened tae the pledge he signed?' he demanded to know.

'Where's our Thomas?' Flora jumped up from her chair and her husband waved a carefully polished black shoe at her.

'Will ye stop jumpin' about like a flea on a dog?'

'He didn't come upstairs,' Lachlan reported. 'He said he wanted a bit of a walk.'

'There ye are, then, he's fine.' Henry relaxed into his chair, wriggling and stretching his stockinged toes. 'An' there's Elspeth made yer precious tea for ye. Now for pity's sake will ye put yer backside down on that chair and drink the stuff?'

Flora, having achieved her main aim and taken his mind off Bob, did as she was told, for once.

28

'Never bother with me, lassie,' Janet Docherty said that evening, poking the coals in her grate into a blaze. 'I've been tae more funerals than you've had hot dinners, and though this was one of the hardest tae thole, I'm old enough tae accept whatever the good Lord chooses tae throw at us. It's Thomas that's needin' a friend tonight, poor soul.'

'He doesn't want anyone.' Elspeth had gone round to Janet's flat to keep the old woman company.

'Aye he does, it's just that he hasnae realised it. His mother's nae comfort, for she fusses too much, and we all know she never wanted that marriage in the first place. With all the goodwill in the world, Flora'll no' be able tae stop hersel' from remindin' him time and again that she's been proved right after all. But you're different, lassie. It was you he chose tae stand by him at her grave. Seek him out, Elspeth. Don't push intae his grief, but let him know ye're there if he needs someone.'

When Elspeth knocked on the door of the flat Thomas had lived in with Aileen, there was an empty, desolate echo to the sound. Convinced that he wasn't sitting inside, refusing to answer, she went back out to the pavement, thinking hard. It wouldn't be his way to seek solace in the noisy, smoky atmosphere of the town's pubs, and if he had gone walking in the country above the town or along by the river, there was no hope of locating him. There was only one place she could try before conceding defeat.

To her disappointment, the garage and workshops were dark and silent. Without hope, she threaded her way round the hulking shadows of vehicles parked in the yard, sliding her feet cautiously along the cobbles at each step, wary of banging her shins or ankles on the pieces of machinery that usually littered the place.

The back door to the house was unlocked, creaking open eerily to reveal a pitch-black cave beyond. Elspeth hesitated. There was a box of matches on the gas stove only a few steps to her left, and candles on the shelf above, but the thought of reaching out into the dark, fumbling for the shape of the cooker and perhaps encountering something else – a hand, a face – was unnerving. Forcing her imagination under control, she proceeded as best she could without seeking light that might attract attention from a policeman passing by on his patrol, and cause further bother.

Gritting her teeth, she inched forward, her outstretched fingers identifying the back of a wooden chair, the corner of a cupboard. Her eyes had become accustomed to the darkness now, and by the time she reached the door leading to the hall she could just make out the outline of the kitchen furniture in the very faint grey light from the window behind her.

The hall was a deep black well. She stood still for a while until her eyes again became accustomed to her surroundings, breathing in the smell of damp and dust and metal and oil that permeated the house. There was a new, sharper smell too, which she puzzled over briefly before identifying it as the smell of paint from the newly decorated office. When her straining eyes finally found the fan-shaped wedge of grey that was the window above the sealed front door, she began the perilous journey across the hall towards the office, lifting each foot elaborately high, then putting it down gently, quietly, on the wooden floor she couldn't see.

She was halfway across, by her own reckoning, when she heard sudden movement from above. She had been trying hard not to think about the staircase to her right, leading up into unknown territory, but now she spun round to face it, her heart leaping into her mouth.

'Thomas?' Her voice, squeaky and trembling, startled her, and she clapped a hand to her mouth. There was no reply, and she didn't dare call again. She wanted desperately to run back through the kitchen and out into the comparative safety of the yard, but she knew that if she panicked now she would lose all sense of direction, with little chance of finding the back door quickly, so she made herself stand still, breathing deeply to calm her racing heart, refusing to accept the sudden picture that had flown into her mind of Thomas on the upper floor, swinging from some hook in the ceiling.

Mice, she told herself – the noise would just be mice, making free of the abandoned rooms. She had seen their droppings on the ground floor, and some of the paperwork piled on the old desk when she first came to the office had been nibbled by tiny teeth. There were rats, too, about the yard.

She was no stranger to rats and mice and cockroaches, for the working class and the poor always shared their lives with such creatures. She had little fear of them, apart from a dislike of their way of appearing suddenly, without warning, and on the whole she accepted their right to exist. But now, alone in the dark, she felt that their presence was menacing. This was their time of day, their territory rather than hers.

All had fallen quiet upstairs, and she told herself firmly that now she had come this far it was better to continue rather than to retreat.

At last she gained the office door and opened it, wrapped in the smell of fresh paint as she stepped inside. Mercifully, the moon was shining on the front of the building, and there was more light in here, enough for her to make out the comforting shape of the desk she worked at, and the smaller hump that was her covered typewriter. She started towards them, then spun round, giving a muffled yelp, as Thomas said from behind her, 'Who is it?'

'Oh – Thomas!' He was sitting on the sagging old couch that stood against the wall opposite her desk. In her relief she wanted to rush into his arms, but managed to hold herself back.

'I came looking for you.' Her voice was still weak and shaky. 'We were worried – nobody knew where you'd gone.'

'You surely knew I'd be all right – or did you think I was going to kill myself?'

'Of course not,' she lied.

He moved, and the *chaise-longue* creaked. 'I'd not do that,' his disembodied voice said. 'It'd be too easy. I just needed to be on my own, to think about things.'

She waited, letting the silence between them gather, then at last he said, 'I was going to ask you. Ellie – would you see to the house for me? I can't bring myself to go into it, and I'd not want to ask any of the others.'

'Of course I will. What d'you want me to do with—'

'Get rid of it all,' he interrupted harshly. 'Everything. I don't want anything from it. The rent's paid up for another two weeks, that should give you enough time. Here's the key.'

She could see well enough now to cross the room quite easily. His hand was cool and dry, the metal key warm as it passed from his fingers to hers. She slipped it into her pocket and retreated to the desk, sensing his need to be on his own.

After another long silence he spoke again, bleakly. 'I did a terrible thing, marrying Aileen. If it hadn't been for me she'd be alive today, probably wed to some man who could have given her everything she deserved.'

'Don't be daft, Thomas McDonald!' The words rushed hotly to her lips. 'Aileen came to you of her own free will, and she didn't regret one minute of it.'

'Ellie, you saw that house today – the servants, the comfort of it all. Who'd willingly walk away from that?'

281

'It was when I saw the house that I knew how much she must have loved you, to give it up for you. And I understood why,' Elspeth said passionately. 'There wasn't an ounce of warmth in that place, while your wee house was brimming over with love and happiness. As for the folk I saw today – they didn't deserve someone like Aileen. There was no – no joy in them.'

'Would you expect them to be joyful on a day like this?' he asked sarcastically.

'You know fine what I mean. They were all wrapped up in themselves. What sort of folk would turn their backs on a lovely lassie like your Aileen just because she insisted on going her own way?'

'Mam did.'

She swatted the words impatiently into the dark shadows of the room. 'Aunt Flora's always like that when she's defied. Anyway, she'd come round to accepting your marriage. Don't be hard on her, Thomas – she's suffering torments over the way she treated the two of you when you first married. I doubt if Mr and Mrs Bruce feel as bad as she does.'

There was a pause before he spoke again. 'Mr Bruce's lawyer offered me money. I got the letter yesterday. One thousand pounds, he'll pay me, if I'll sign a bit of paper promising I'll make no claim on the Bruce family.'

Elspeth almost choked with outrage. 'That's insulting!'

'It's the only way they know. They think that even people can be bought, especially people like us.'

'Pebbles on the beach.'

'What?'

'That's what you said, one day when we were all on the beach at Largs. You said that ordinary folk are like pebbles, too many and too small to be noticed.'

'I don't mind saying it, but it's true. I went to the office and told the man that I'd not take a penny from the likes of the Bruces, not even if I was starving in the gutter. The only way to get respect from folk like that is to show them that you're as good as they are. That's what I'm going to do, Ellie. I'm going to work even harder for Aileen than I did when she was here. I'm going to show the Bruces and the whole town that given time I could have provided her with everything she w⌐nted.' His voice was low and level, but intense. 'I'll make my own thousand, then another thousand, and another. I'll make them admit that they were wrong about me, even if I have to ram bundles of notes down their throats to do it!'

Elspeth shivered though the room wasn't cold. She felt as though someone had just walked over her grave.

'Don't become bitter, Thomas.'

'Of course I'm bitter! Can you blame me? If I hadnae been so opposed to her seeing her brother she wouldnae have gone off with him in his car. We'd had words about it just the day before.'

She thought of the day she herself had seen Aileen drive away in Ian Bruce's car. There had probably been other times that neither she nor Thomas knew about.

'But she must have been in her brother's car hundreds of times before she met you. The accident could have happened at any time.'

'You're talking nonsense.'

'I know,' she said wretchedly, confused by her own clumsy attempts to reason with him. 'It's hard to find the right words. I'd do better if I was putting them down in a letter.'

He laughed, an unexpected barking sound. 'Mebbe you should write to me, then,' he said, his voice suddenly weary, 'Come to me, Ellie.'

When she did as she was told he drew her down on to the couch, putting an arm about her and holding her close. 'Are you cold?'

'No, it's warm enough.'

'You don't need to find the words.' His breath was warm against her ear. 'Just wheesht for a wee while, and let me listen to them for myself.'

283

Timidly, she put her own arms around him. He was so tense that it was like wrapping her arms round the trunk of a tree. They sat in silence for a long time, long enough for his body to relax gradually, until he was leaning quite heavily against her. She wondered if he had fallen asleep. The couch was lumpy and uncomfortable, thrusting small hard fists into the softness of her buttocks, but she didn't want to move in case she disturbed him. Instead she stayed still, inhaling the clean soapy smell from his hair, listening to his breathing, feeling the slow steady thump of his heart echoing against her own ribs. The street outside was silent, for this was an industrial area and not many people had occasion to pass through it at night. Once, she heard a scampering above her head, but with Thomas close beside her there was no need, now, to be afraid.

Finally, when she was almost asleep herself, he stirred and straightened and sat upright. 'You'd best go home, Ellie. Mam'll be wondering where you are.'

Her arms were stiff and numbed. She moved her fingers surreptitiously. 'Come back with me.'

He was still so close that disturbed air brushed her cheek when he shook his head.

'I'm staying here tonight.'

'But—'

'I'll be fine. Come on, now.' He rose and pulled her up from the couch. The life was just beginning to come back to her hands, and they felt as though they were clad in thick woollen gloves. Thomas led the way, sure-footed, through the hall and kitchen with Elspeth clinging as best she could to the back of his jacket. In the street he said, 'Tell Mam I'm fine, and I'll look in on her tomorrow. You'll manage home all right?'

'Yes.'

His hands cupped her shoulders, his lips touched her cheek. 'Thanks, Ellie,' he said 'You're a grand sister.' Then, turning her about to face the empty street, he gave her a little shove. 'Go on, now.'

Pins and needles danced all the way up and down her arms. She welcomed the sensation, because it promised eventual normality, something that had been lacking in her life ever since Aileen's death.

At the corner she stopped and looked back. Thomas's hand was a tiny pale movement against the darkness of the building behind him as he waved.

She waved back, and set off for Mearns Street.

29

Elspeth walked in through the main entrance of Brodie's department store and across the carpeted floor to the elegant lift provided for those paying customers who declined to use the staircases. Patrick, the lift operator, gaped as she stepped in and said, 'The top floor, please.'

'Lassie, what're ye doin'?'

'I'm going to see Mr James.'

Patrick peered out, glancing furtively from right to left. 'But ye cannae use the lift. It's for the gentry!'

'I can do as I please. Will you get on with it, or do I have to see to the buttons myself?'

Alarm flared into his eyes. 'Don't you touch they buttons, Elspeth Bremner! This is my lift and I'll be the one tae—' He broke off as two well-dressed women stepped into the silk-lined lift, and asked, with a noticeable change of accent, 'Which floor, moddom?'

'The third,' the older woman ordered curtly.

'The top,' Elspeth said just as curtly, adding after a pause, 'Please.'

The woman glared, and settled her fox-fur more comfortably on her shoulders, while Patrick, shrugging helplessly, slid the door shut and set the lift in motion.

'Are ye sure?' he asked plaintively as the two women stepped out at the third floor, leaving behind them the powerful scent of expensive perfume too lavishly applied, and an undertone of perspiration. It was May, and too hot for fox-furs.

'I'm sure.'

'It's mair than yer job's worth, lassie, usin' the customers' lift.'

'I'm not bothered.' She had been awake half the night, fretting over the news she had heard that evening, and by morning she had decided on a course of action. It was too late, now, to change her mind. She had already used the main entrance, and the lift. She might as well go the whole way.

It had been over a year since she had worked in the accounts office, but little had changed. Wilma and Graham still laboured over huge ledgers at the sloping desk, and Theresa McCabe typed busily in her corner, though the brisk clatter of keys slowed and stopped at Elspeth's entrance.

'I want to talk to Mr James,' she told Wilma.

'He didn't ask to see you.'

'I know that. It's me that wants to see him.'

The typewriter keys stopped altogether. Graham gaped and Wilma bristled. 'He's dealing with this morning's post. Try again in an hour.'

'I must see him now. It's very important.' The anger that had been burning in Elspeth for the past fifteen hours or so gave her voice a crisp edge. Wilma hesitated, then slipped down from the high stool.

'I'll see what he says.'

'You're looking well, Elspeth.' Graham's eyes travelled slowly down her body.

'Am I?' She had decided not to wear her usual working skirt and blouse today; instead, she had on her best blouse, striped in different shades of brown, and a fawn pleated skirt beneath a smart brown jacket she had made herself. The pebble brooch was pinned to the jacket's lapel, and beneath the blouse's high collar her lucky silver threepenny piece nestled against the hollow of her throat.

The typewriter keys rattled again as James Brodie himself opened his office door and ushered Wilma out.

'Miss Bremner – come in. Take a seat,' he invited, closing the door behind her.

She shook her head. 'I'll only be a minute. I believe you've taken on a new typist?'

'That's right, Theresa's leaving to get married. I was surprised you didn't apply for the job yourself,' he went on, taking the wind out of her sails. She stared, then rallied.

'I would have, if I'd known. I only heard about it last night, when I met a girl I knew from my typing class and she said she'd applied and been unsuccessful.'

It was Brodie's turn to be taken aback. 'But you were the first person I thought of when Theresa said she was going. Miss Arnold told me that you'd decided to stay on in the sewing room.'

Elspeth's knees suddenly went weak, and she sank into the chair she had just declined. 'She told you that?'

They stared at each other for a moment, then James Brodie said slowly, 'It seems that you've been deceived. I'm very sorry, my dear. I would have been happy to give you the position, but unfortunately it has already been filled.'

'Elspeth Bremner, d'you know what time it is?' Miss Arnold squawked as soon as Elspeth went into the sewing room. 'And just what d'you think you're wearing? You know that you girls aren't allowed to—'

'I'm late because I've just been along to see Mr James about the typist's position, Miss Arnold.'

The woman flushed, then rallied. 'Without asking me to arrange an appointment for you? You'd no right to burst in on Mr James like that!'

'And you'd no right to tell him that I wanted to stay in the sewing room instead of applying for the typist's job without consulting me first.'

There was a concerted gasp from the listening women round the large table, and the usual muted roar of sewing machines in operation faltered, then died.

Miss Arnold's face was almost purple. 'Miss Buchanan and I discussed the matter fully and agreed that you're of more value to Brodie's in this department. You're a good seamstress, and a lot of work's gone into training you. In a few years you could mebbe even become supervisor.'

'I won't be here in a few years, Miss Arnold, or even a few minutes,' Elspeth told her, and turned towards the door.

'Stop,' the woman shrieked. 'I'll not have such insubordination!' Then, as Elspeth put a hand on the handle, 'If you persist in this nonsense, Elspeth Bremner, you needn't think you'll get a reference from Miss Buchanan!'

'I won't require one. I'm going to set up in business for myself,' Elspeth said, and walked out of the sewing room for the last time, closing the door on a babble of excited voices.

Flora McDonald was beside herself with rage when she heard the news. 'After all the trouble I went to tae get ye that position! How could ye dae it? Ye'll never get work as a seamstress in the town again once word of this gets out. What have I done tae deserve this?'

The cold anger that had seized Elspeth when she first heard of the position she had lost through deceit still held her in its grip.

'It was you that wanted me to be a seamstress, Aunt Flora, not me. I'm seventeen now, old enough to make up my own mind. I've been thinking about it all, and I'm going to set up my own business, doing typing and book-keeping for folk like Mr Monteith who can't afford to employ someone all the time.'

'Are ye wandered in yer head, lassie? How could the likes of you manage that? Ye're too young, for a start!'

'I don't think I am.'

'And where would ye go? Not in my bedroom, I'll tell ye that!'

'I think I already know of somewhere,' said Elspeth, refusing to let anything her aunt said affect her. She had burned her boats, and now the only way to go was forward.

At Christmas Forbes Cameron, stammering like a schoolboy, had invited Elspeth to dinner at the large house where he still lived with his parents. Surprised, but somewhat flattered, she had accepted, and had enjoyed herself. Mr and Mrs Cameron were kindly people, as she had discovered at Aileen's funeral, and Forbes himself was an entertaining and considerate companion. They had been meeting each other ever since, a relationship that had almost caused a quarrel between her and Thomas.

'I've nothing against the man – he pays my wages – but he's a good ten years older than you are,' he said baldly.

'Does that mean that he's not to be trusted?'

'No, but—'

'Mebbe it's me you don't trust?'

'Don't be daft,' Thomas said, exasperated.

'I'm not a child, so don't treat me like one.'

'I know you're not, but even so, you'd be better with someone more your own age.'

'Like Kenneth?' she asked sarcastically.

'Oh – go your own way, you'll do that anyway. There's no reasoning with you, Elspeth Bremner,' he snapped, and stormed out of the garage office.

As it happened, she and Forbes were going to the theatre in Largs the day she left Brodie's for good, then having supper in a small restaurant.

Prudently, she waited until the meal was almost over before putting her plan to him.

'The old house? My dear girl, it's in a terrible state – you couldn't set up this business of yours in a place like that.'

'It's neglected, but the building's still sturdy. At least let me have a look at it. Please, Forbes – I've got to find some way of earning my living quickly, and this is my chance to do what I've always wanted.'

'Have you really thought about this idea of yours, Elspeth? You're young to start up in business, and it's not that easy.'

'Why does everyone keep going on about my age? Seventeen isn't all that young, and there are times when I feel much older than that. I know of two girls from the typing and book-keeping class who'd probably be glad to come in with me. Neither of them has been able to find work in an office.'

'Do they have money to invest in the idea?'

'No, but they've got office skills, and that's what I need. Peggy has a sick father who can't be left on his own for too long at a time, and Kirsty's got a baby to care for. I could offer them working hours to suit their domestic responsibilities, and there must be a lot of small businessmen like Mr Monteith who could do with typists and book-keepers but can't afford to employ somebody. With two more typists, I could go out to look for new clients. I'll need to buy another two typewriters and some office furniture, but I got my own machine in a pawn shop – I might find others there. And there are good second-hand furniture shops.'

'What about financial support while all this is happening?'

'I've still got the money from the sale of my grandmother's furniture, and I've been saving what I've made working for Mr Monteith and Mr Leslie.'

'And if this venture of yours fails?'

'Then I'll have to admit defeat and look for other employment for myself. I know enough about keeping accounts by now to put an end to it before I run myself into trouble. But it will work – I know it will.' She leaned across the table in her urgency to convey the strength of her feelings for this new venture. 'I want this too much to let it fail.'

'You're taking on an awful lot, Elspeth,' said Forbes

Cameron, who had always relied on his parents' financial support in any venture he attempted.

'I'm not afraid of hard work. Please, Forbes?'

'You look so beautiful when you're enthused about something that it's very difficult to deny you anything,' he said wryly. 'I suppose there's no harm in having a proper look at the place.'

'Oh, thank you! I'll go tomorrow morning – I'm trying to keep out of Aunt Flora's way anyway, in case she starts on about finding another job for me.' she said happily.

It wasn't until she was getting ready for bed that night that she recalled his exact words. At the time she had been too intent on persuading him to let her explore the old house to pay much attention. Now, she peered wide-eyed into the mirror in an attempt to find out why he had described her as beautiful.

The ends of her long brown hair, freed from its plait and fresh from a good brushing, caught the gaslight as it swung about her face. Her blue eyes were clear, but quite ordinary, and her nose and mouth weren't too large or too small. She smiled at her own reflection, and decided that, again, her smile was ordinary.

'You're certainly not beautiful, miss,' she told her mirrored self. 'But you'll do. You'll have to – you're all I've got.'

True to his vow, Thomas had devoted himself to making the garage a success after his young wife's death. Under his single-minded supervision, it had already gained a reputation for excellent service and fair dealings.

Business had done so well that Joe, Thomas's assistant, had been promoted to the position of foreman, and two more mechanics taken on to enable Thomas to concentrate on the sales side. At his suggestion, Forbes had agreed to move into the area of car sales, and to this end the workshops had been expanded and improved and the original garage frontage removed to add a forecourt. During the work, Forbes had had the outside of the old house refurbished and painted.

Car engines were still dear to Thomas's heart, and when Elspeth arrived at the garage on the following morning she found him in his dungarees, working on an engine. She waited, trying to curb her impatience, until he was free, then explained her new plan to him.

His first reaction was a scowl. 'Is this going to mean a bunch of women traipsing through my yard and getting in the way?'

'The front door could be opened up for our use.'

Thomas grunted, then wiped his hands on a rag. 'I suppose you wound Cameron round your little finger?'

'I just asked him if I could have a good look at the house, and he agreed.'

'It's his house,' Thomas said, and called to one of the mechanics to take over.

'The keys to the upper rooms are here somewhere,' he said vaguely, rummaging in a kitchen drawer while Elspeth hovered, trying not to fidget. She had been waiting for so long to realise her dream, and now it was so close that every second's delay was unbearable.

She looked around the kitchen in an attempt to take her mind off her own impatience. She had managed to improve it, scraping years of grease from the gas stove, replacing the cracked linoleum with a remnant piece, clearing and cleaning the cupboards. Now that the garage covered car sales as well, the other downstairs room had been cleared and painted and turned into a proper office where Thomas, in a smart suit, could deal with possible buyers.

He had changed a lot since Aileen's death. Long, bitter months of grief had aged him, but not altogether unkindly. Though his first youth had gone he had taken on a new maturity that suited his lean features. The laughter in his eyes had given way to solemnity, and his body, used now to long hours of hard work and little rest, had a whip-like strength.

In recent months Elspeth had noticed sudden interest flickering into the gaze of more than one woman accompanying a husband or sweetheart to the garage to buy a new car from Thomas McDonald. A few of them had even found ways of making opening advances, but Thomas, steadfastly following his vow to show the Bruces that he was as good as they were, paid them no heed. He had moved his possessions into the old office in the garage house, refusing to give in to his mother and move back to Mearns Street permanently.

'Mam would expect everything to go back to the way it was before,' he told Elspeth. 'She can't understand that life can never go back, only forwards. I couldn't abide her fussing, anyway.'

Because she understood what he meant, and never fussed over him, Elspeth was one of the few people Thomas trusted now, and the affection that had been between them since she was a baby had strengthened.

'Here they are.' He waved a bunch of keys at her, then made for the inner door. 'Let's get this nonsense over with, then I can get back to my work.'

Elspeth kept close behind him as he led the way upstairs to a large, dark landing and unlocked the first of the three doors.

'Hold on.' He paused at the threshold and stamped hard on the floor. There was a scuttling, rustling sound, then silence.

'Mice – mebbe rats.' He crossed the room to wrench at the wooden shutters nailed across the windows.

'I'll get a cat – or a dog, if necessary,' she told him lightly, though she paused on the threshold for a moment before venturing in.

'What about the cockroaches?'

'Jeyes fluid and a scrubbing brush.'

Thomas grunted something, and pulled once more at the shutters, which gave way, dust and grit showering to the floor like a hail storm. The room was revealed, large and handsome and empty.

'It's just like the downstairs rooms. Once the windows are cleaned and the walls painted—'

'And the spider's webs cleared away,' Thomas put in, moving to the other window.

'—and some furniture installed,' she went on, ignoring the interruption, 'it'll make a fine office.'

The second room held the sagging remains of a metal bedstead and the third door, situated above the kitchen, led to a bathroom complete with a huge, stained claw-footed bath.

'Oh, look at this!' Elspeth, brought up in a house with a privy on the landing, was delighted. She tried to turn one of the taps in the cracked hand-basin, but it was too tight for her. After a brief struggle Thomas managed to loosen it, and a trickle of rusty water emerged. Elspeth pulled experimentally at the chain hanging above the privy, and it came away in her hand.

'It'd need a lot of work.' Thomas's voice was heavy with disapproval.

'But it would be worth it.'

'Ellie, you're daft!'

Standing in the ruins of the bathroom, dust streaking her face, cobwebs in her hair, the rusty cistern chain dangling from her fingers, she laughed. 'Mebbe I am, but it'll all work out – just you wait and see.'

It was the busiest summer Elspeth had ever known. Kenneth and Mattie came back to Greenock for the summer holidays, which meant that Kenneth spent a lot of time in the Mearns Street flat. Seeing the two of them together didn't trouble Elspeth a bit. She was too involved in her own life to mourn any further over what might have been.

When she wasn't at the garage, working on books for the clients she already had or chivvying the workmen upstairs, she was tramping the streets, calling in at every small business she could find – not only in Greenock, but in the neighbouring towns of Gourock and Port Glasgow. By the time the building was ready for scrubbing brush and broom she had invested some of her savings in two more second-hand typewriters and found a dozen employers, enough to get her new business off to a start.

When the time came to prepare the upper floor before furnishing it, Peggy and Kirsty, her future employees, arrived to help with the cleaning. So did Rachel, who had given birth to a second daughter, Pearl, in February. This time Elspeth insisted on paying her for the hours she put in.

'But I'm already making something from my sewing,' Rachel protested.

'That's got nothing to do with what you're doing for me.'

'It's thanks to you, for it was your idea in the first place, and you're looking after it for me.' They had agreed that the safest thing was for Rachel to admit to Bob that she was earning a certain amount – most of which he took from her to spend on drink – while she handed over the rest to Elspeth, who banked it along with the money from the sale of Celia Bremner's napery and bed linen.

'I'm still going to pay you for the work you do here. I just wish you could use a typewriter, for I could have taken you on in the office,' Elspeth said, struck to the heart by the older girl's wan, tired face.

'Even if I could type, it wouldnae work, not with the bairns still so wee,' Rachel said wistfully. 'It'd be nice to have something different to do with my life, though.' Then, squaring her shoulders and taking up a broom, she added, 'But Mam's right – I've made my bed and I must lie in it.'

The two of them were alone in the big room that was going to be the office. Kirsty and Peggy were scrubbing out the smaller room, and Mary was playing in the hallway with Sandra, Kirsty's little girl. Pearl, the baby, had been fed, and settled down in a blanket-filled box in a corner.

'It depends who's lying beside you,' Elspeth said, though

she wished she could say much more, and to Thomas and his father. Bob was still violent towards his wife, and Flora still refused to acknowledge what was happening, let alone tell Henry.

'Ellie! Don't be coarse! And mind your tongue in front of the weans,' Rachel added as Mary and Sandra scampered through the room.

'I'm just saying what I think.'

Forbes Cameron followed Elspeth's progress with keen interest.

'Let me start you off with a loan,' he suggested one day, finding her at the downstairs desk frowning over columns of figures and chewing the end of her pencil.

'I wouldn't dream of it. This is my idea, and I'll not risk anyone else's money.'

'Does that mean that you think there's a danger of failure?'

'Of course not.'

'Make it an investment, then. Call me a shareholder and start paying me dividends at the end of your first year.' Then, when she still hesitated, he suggested, 'If you don't like that idea, I could offer a reduced rent for the first year instead,' and went on to name a very low sum.

She squinted at him suspiciously. 'What benefit would you get out of that?' In her opinion, the suggestion smacked of charity.

'The pleasure of helping you to get started, for one. And for another,' he went on hurriedly as she opened her mouth to refuse, 'I'd insist on a more realistic rent after that, to make up what I lost in the first year. And I'd want the chance to get first refusal if or when you decided to sell shares to raise more money.'

'But you've already put a lot into getting the house put to rights. You shouldn't be thinking of spending even more on me.'

'But I've already made an investment of my own. If your business should fail, you'd get nothing back, while I'd still have the house, in better condition than ever before. I could recoup all my outlay by renting the upper floor to someone else.'

Elspeth studied the page before her. Her savings had dwindled quite frighteningly, and soon there would be wages for Peggy and Kirsty to take into consideration. She couldn't afford to be too proud.

'I accept,' she said at last, and he beamed.

By the time she celebrated her eighteenth birthday the upper floor was ready. Three sturdy desks, made for her by Peggy's brother, a carpenter, had been set up in the larger of the two upper rooms to hold the typewriters. Two cupboards bought from a second-hand shop were ranged along one wall, and a polished brass sign – Forbes' birthday gift to Elspeth – engraved with the words 'Bremner Office Agency, First Floor' had been fastened by the front door, which was now in use again.

Forbes held a party to celebrate the opening, inviting a number of guests, including all Elspeth's clients. His parents were there, as were the McDonalds – Lachlan and Henry bursting with pride at Elspeth's achievement, Flora torn between possessive pride and embarrassment. She had been shocked at first by Elspeth's 'walking out', as she put it, with Forbes, agreeing with Thomas that the garage-owner was too old for her, but he had soon charmed her doubts away.

'You know what she's hoping for, don't you?' Lachlan said now, nodding at his mother, deep in conversation with Mrs Cameron. 'You wed to a wealthy man and Mattie wed to a doctor. That'd give the folk in Mearns Street somethin' tae talk about.'

She laughed, and shook her head. 'If that's true, she'll have a long wait on my part. I'll be too busy with my business to think of marriage for a good long while.'

Lachlan himself was doing well in the maintenance department at Brodie's store, and still corresponding with Lena. It was his hope that soon she would appear onstage in Greenock.

'Come on, Elspeth, time to declare the agency open.' Forbes called from the hall, and the crowd of guests parted to let her through. Dazed with the sudden realisation that she had achieved her ambition, she walked between them to the foot of the stairs.

The scissors crunched through the ribbon, it fluttered away on both sides, and the dream she had held close to her heart for the past four years had come true.

30

In January, almost exactly two years after leaving Greenock, Lena Stewart returned to appear for a week in the King's Theatre.

Lachlan was beside himself with excitement when he received the news. At the family's traditional New Year's Day dinner his happiness helped to mask the fact that the annual meal, once a landmark in the McDonald calendar, was quieter than usual. Janet was there, but Thomas had refused to join them, and Mattie was spending the day with Kenneth's parents, much to her mother's disappointment. Rachel had brought her daughters to Mearns Street, but Bob wasn't with her, to Henry's surprise. Flora and Rachel had both had a difficult time fobbing off his questions. Between that, and Lachlan's constant talk about Lena's return, Flora was noticeably irritable before they even sat down at the table.

'Ye'll mebbe get a surprise,' she informed her son crustily. 'She'll have got too high-and-mighty for the likes of you. Ye'll not likely see hide nor hair of her off the stage.'

'You're wrong there, Mam,' he told her breezily, helping himself to another slice of bread and winking at wee Mary, who doted on him. 'I'll see quite a lot of Lena, for she's arranged for me to work as a stage hand in the theatre during her week there.'

Soup spoons clattered against Flora's best china bowls all

300

round the table, and he smirked as everyone stared at him, enjoying the sensation he had caused.

'She's what? Well, ye can forget that, for no son of mine—' Flora began, but he interrupted her.

'It's already arranged, Mam, and I've said I'm doin' it. I've been to see the stage manager at the theatre and it's all agreed.' Lachlan dunked his bread in his soup, something Flora abhorred, and took a mouthful.

'And not a word tae us about it?'

'Leave it, Flora,' Henry advised quietly. 'Lachie's a man now, old enough tae join a circus as the elephant trainer if he chooses. Now – take yer soup before it gets cold. You too, Rachel.'

Rachel had been staring down at her bowl, the spoon drooping from her hand. She jumped, and began eating again, while her father watched her, his brows knotted with concern.

'Are ye ailin', hen?'

'Of course she's not ailin',' Flora snapped.

'She looks awful pale,' Henry said, and Janet nodded.

'I think so too.'

'And so would you look pale if ye'd two weans under yer feet day and night. I'd as soon do a day's labourin' in the shipyards as look after weans.'

'Will ye give the lassie the chance tae answer for hersel'?' Henry asked in a rare burst of impatience, then, as Flora's mouth clamped into an offended line, and she got up and collected in the plates that had been emptied, 'Ye're no sickenin' for somethin', pet, are ye?'

Rachel shot a sidelong look at her mother, then said, 'I'm fine, Da. It's this weather, I've never liked the winter.'

'It's not the winter, you've been looking poorly for a while now.' Elspeth was unable to keep silent any longer.

Despite the fact that not everybody had finished the first course, Flora banged a huge bowl of potatoes down so hard on the table that the cutlery jumped and jangled, and Mary, sitting on a pile of cushions to enable her small face to peep over the table, and tied into her chair for safety, burst into tears. Her sister, on Rachel's lap, immediately followed suit.

'Now look what ye've done!' Flora accused her husband, while in the ensuing rush to comfort the children Rachel whispered to Elspeth, 'Leave it be, for pity's sake!'

By the time the little girls had been calmed, Henry, waiting impatiently for the main course, was too hungry to remember what had caused all the fuss.

Forbes had tried to persuade Elspeth to spend the day at his parents' home, to meet some friends of theirs.

'My mother will be disappointed if you don't. You know how much she enjoys your company.'

'I can't let Aunt Flora and Uncle Henry down, not when Mattie and Thomas are both staying away.'

'But it's not as if they're really your family, is it? Not your own flesh and blood,' he added as she stared at him, puzzled.

'For goodness' sake, Forbes, they're the only family I've ever known!' On occasion, she thought with irritation, Forbes was capable of displaying a grating insensitivity towards others. 'If it comes to that, you and your parents aren't my family either.'

'Mebbe that'll change by next New Year,' he murmured, drawing her into his arms, his mouth seeking and finding hers. The anger ebbed as she closed her eyes and let her body blend with his, parting her lips against the moist warmth of his mouth.

She was very fond of Forbes, she thought, returning kiss for kiss. He had done so much for her, and had become a dear friend as well as a pleasant companion. He had never tried to force himself on her as Kenneth had, so long ago in the wash house, but his kisses and caresses were exciting and desirable, and Elspeth felt that one day quite soon she would want more from him than this chaste loving.

She hadn't as yet decided what she would do when that day

came, but the thought of it warmed her. She was a woman now, no longer a naive girl.

Although she wasn't the star of the music hall her company staged in Greenock, it was Lena that most of the folk in the audiences came to see. When the Master of Ceremonies introduced her as Greenock's own songbird, the storm of applause made the chandeliers high above the auditorium tremble and tinkle.

Elspeth gripped Forbes' arm as the curtains parted and Lena stepped forward, hands outstretched to receive the adulation of her public. The gasp that greeted her appearance could be heard even above the applause. She wore a sea-green gown, cut low in front to reveal her smooth white throat and the shaded hollow between her full breasts. Skilful draping along the top of the bodice enhanced the swell of her bosom, while below the tiny waist the skirt hugged her hips and thighs, then swirled into deep frills. The sleeves were long and tight, and hundreds of sequins caught the light with every movement she made, so that her entire body shimmered. Her red hair was caught up in an intricate pile of curls, with a large bejewelled Spanish comb thrust into them at the back.

Graciously, she acknowledged the applause from every corner of the theatre, then waited, still and erect, until it had ebbed away completely before giving the orchestra conductor a nod.

She had come a long way since her first impromptu appearance on the stage two years before. The voice that filled the theatre was stronger now, clearer and more confident. As before, she slid from one mood to another without effort, singing a ballad then swooping to the wings to collect a cloak and umbrella before launching into a comedy number that was greeted with howls of approval. Then came a slow, sad song that brought a catch to her listeners' throats.

'Didn't I tell you she was good?' Elspeth asked Forbes,

clapping until her hands stung as Lena finally left the stage, blowing expansive kisses to her ecstatic audience.

'You did, and you're right. She'll go a long way,' he predicted.

When she and Lachlan finally arrived in the hotel where they had arranged to meet for supper, Lena walked the length of the dining room like royalty, halted at almost every table by people who had been at the theatre earlier and wanted to congratulate her. She had changed into a narrow, ankle-length deep brown velvet dress, sleeveless, with a silvery silk-chiffon cape floating from beaded shoulder straps. Her hair was still up, and her only ornament was a beaded sash around her hips. Lachlan, in an evening suit, followed closely behind her, glowing as he basked in her success.

Arriving at last at the table Forbes had booked for the four of them, Lena shook his hand, hugged Elspeth, then collapsed into a chair. 'My feet are killing me!'

Forbes was enchanted by her, but it was Lachlan who absorbed all Elspeth's attention at first. 'Lachie, where did you get those clothes?'

He grinned self-consciously, and put a hand up to the bow tie at the collar of his dazzlingly white shirt. 'D'ye like it? Lena made me borrow it from the wardrobe department.'

'I like it very much.' The formal clothes had transformed him from the Lachie she knew into a stylish young man. 'You look so handsome!'

'He is handsome,' Lena said. 'You've just been too used to looking on him as a brother.' She flicked a teasing sidelong glance at Lachlan, and he beamed back at her, comfortable in her presence. 'I saw him as he really is the first time I clapped eyes on him in that big room at Brodie's store where we all ate our dinners. He was a poor wee thin creature then, in an overall that was far too big for him, but I knew what he'd look like in different clothes – and I was right.' Then she leaned across the table, her eyes brimming over with laughter. 'D'ye mind those days, Ellie?'

Clearly, although the sewing room rebel had become a sophisticated and elegant artiste, Lena's zest for life hadn't changed. She entertained them all throughout the meal with her memories of the sewing room, followed by a string of stories about her life in the theatre, each one more outrageous than the last. Diners at the other tables glanced across enviously at the four young people rocking with laughter, so obviously enjoying their evening out. Finally Lena announced that she had said more than enough, and demanded to know all Elspeth's news.

'I knew you were wasted in that dreary wee sewing room,' she said when she had heard something of the new business. 'You wrote such lovely letters. Wait and see – we're both going to become very famous and earn lots of money.' Then, with a wicked gleam in her eyes, 'And we'll have our clothes made at Brodie's, and criticise every stitch, and drive Miss Buchanan and Miss Arnold mad.'

'Miss Arnold's in charge now. Miss Buchanan retired a month or so ago.'

'Then we'll invite ourselves to Miss Buchanan's for tea as well, and criticise her taste in crockery,' said Lena.

She called in at the office two days later, all work coming to an abrupt halt when she swept into the room in a loose-fitting calf-length black woollen coat with a wide collar and deep cuffs at the wrists. Her red hair was tucked under a small black hat with a wide brim turned up all round and trimmed with jet beads. A large white satin bow was pinned at one side.

'I admire you,' she said as the two of them stood in the smaller of the two upper rooms where, Elspeth had explained, she hoped eventually to install more typewriters. 'You've done so much in such a short time.'

'Not as much as you, travelling all over the place and appearing in front of hundreds of people.'

Lena shrugged, smoothing her black gloves. 'The life's not as romantic as it looks. There are a lot of nasty little boarding houses I'd not put a cat into, and a lot of audiences more interested in throwing insults than flowers. Anyway, I was lucky – I got the chance to climb up on to a stage and sing. My voice did the rest. Now you – you've changed your life right here in your home town, and that's far more difficult. I can be anyone I like when I'm far away from the folk who knew me before.'

'Your father must be pleased to see you home for a wee while.'

Lena threw her head back and laughed. 'Him? I'm not so sure. D'you mind old Miss Lambert that lived upstairs from us? The retired schoolteacher? It seems that she took to "keeping an eye on poor Mr Stewart when his daughter upped and left him"' – she imitated an elderly woman's dry, genteel voice to perfection – 'and now she's got her feet tucked very comfortably under his table. If you ask me, they'll be wed by the time I come back again.'

'At their age?'

'Love doesn't worry about birthdays,' Lena said blithely. 'She's not my choice as a stepmother, but if she's his as a wife, good luck to the two of them.' Then, her lovely turquoise eyes fixed on Elspeth, she said thoughtfully. 'Talking of marriage, Forbes seems a nice man.'

'He's helped me to set up the agency, and he's a good friend, but I'm not looking for marriage.'

'He is. I could tell by the way he looked at you. No need to put that face on, Ellie Bremner, you could do worse than marry money. I nearly fell over when he ordered champagne the other night!'

'I'd as soon earn my own fortune.'

'Then mebbe you should make that clear to Forbes before it's too late,' Lena advised, moving to the window to look down on the windswept cobbled street below. 'It's a grey old town this, isn't it? But I'm still fond of it.'

As Elspeth escorted her down to the door Lena said casually, 'Lachlan's working well in the theatre, you'd think he'd done it for years. The rest of the crew like him. He's fairly come on since I went away.'

'Your cards and letters helped.' Elspeth thought of Flora, hiding the cards, then decided to say nothing of that to her friend. 'It was kind of you.'

'Away with you – I've never been kind in my life. I did it because I like Lachlan. I always have and I always will,' Lena said, and left, her feet seeming to skim over the cobbles.

The local people, proud to know that one of their own had become a public performer, flocked to see Lena and the company played to packed houses throughout the week. Each night after the show there were crowds waiting at the stage door to speak to her, and by mid-week her photograph was on the billboards at each side of the theatre entrance.

'Dolly Costello's not pleased,' she reported gleefully to the girls in the agency. 'She's had star billing since before I was born – so mebbe it's time she got used to the idea of moving over for someone younger.'

'It must be hard for her, though,' Elspeth said, and Lena retorted, 'It's life. One day the same thing'll happen to me.'

She called in almost every day, perching on a stool in the corner, enthralling Peggy and Kirsty with her stories about theatrical life. Delighted though she was to see Lena again, Elspeth was secretly glad to know that she was only in town for a week. If it had been longer, she thought ruefully, reminding the other two yet again that there was work to be done, she might go out of business.

Despite the fact that Lena arranged free tickets for all the family, Flora steadfastly refused to attend the music hall. 'I've never approved of women flaunting themselves on a stage, and I never will,' she said coldly when Lachlan tried to coax her.

He reddened with suppressed anger. 'Lena doesn't flaunt herself. She's got a beautiful voice and folk love to hear it. Where's the harm in that?' he argued, but got nowhere.

Thomas refused as well, but civilly, and to Lena's face when she met him in the garage.

'I'm pleased for you, lassie, but I'm not ready yet for enjoyment.'

For once, Lena's pretty face was solemn. 'I can understand that, but would your Aileen want you to shut yourself away from the rest of the world and work yourself to death?' she asked bluntly.

Thomas didn't take offence. 'I've asked myself that, and the answer's no, she wouldn't. Nor would I have wanted her to mourn for ever if it had been me killed instead of her. But something inside me says I'm not ready to face things yet. Mebbe I will be, the next time you perform in Greenock.'

'I hope so,' she agreed, then put a hand on his arm. 'Don't punish yourself forever over something that wasn't your doing, Thomas.'

As they walked out on to the street, she said to Elspeth, 'When you see a decent man like your Thomas with all the life taken out of him, then look at some of the folk walking around that the world could do without, you wonder what God's thinking of at times.'

Janet Docherty and her neighbour, Mrs Begg, spent an enjoyable night at the theatre, and even Bob and Rachel took advantage of Lena's generosity. Elspeth looked after the little girls for them that evening. She was rarely in Rachel's home, and now that she had the time and the freedom to study her surroundings properly, she was struck by the dreariness of the place.

Everything was spotlessly clean, but the linoleum and the fireside rug were badly worn and the furniture cheap and uncomfortable. Mary and Pearl tended to be shy, though at the garage they usually blossomed in the warmth of Joe's kindness. But here, in their own home, both little girls seemed very withdrawn. Given the bleak atmosphere of the small flat, Elspeth could understand why.

Rachel and Bob didn't come home until about an hour after the show ended. When they did arrive Bob smelled of drink and Rachel's eyes were anxious despite the pretty flush that the chill night air had brought to her cheeks.

'I'm sorry we're late,' she burst out as soon as they arrived. 'We met some folks and got talking.'

'I'm in no hurry,' Elspeth assured her, although she had been nodding over the book in her lap for the past half-hour. 'Did you enjoy the theatre?'

'Oh, it was bonny! All those lovely clothes, and the music – and Lena was beautiful!'

Bob said nothing, but Elspeth was aware of his eyes on her as she fetched her coat. 'I'll walk ye home,' he offered.

'I'll manage fine on my own.'

He tried to insist, then lapsed into a huffy silence when she finally told him sharply that she could manage. Rachel accompanied her to the close-mouth. Someone had shattered the gas mantle, and the close behind them was pitch black.

'Don't mind Bob,' Rachel whispered as soon as they left the flat. 'He's tired.'

'How much did he have to drink on the way home?'

'Just the one wee glass, to keep the cold out. Just the one. You'll not say to—'

When Bob spoke his wife's name from just behind her, both women jumped and gasped.

'What're ye whisperin' about?' he wanted to know suspiciously, sliding an arm about Rachel's hips and glaring at Elspeth. In the dim light from the street, he looked menacing, and Elspeth edged towards the pavement as Rachel, chattering nervously, 'I'm comin' – just comin',' was drawn back into the close.

Once out on the pavement Elspeth broke into a run, and raced all the way to Mearns Street as though a pack of devils were at her heels.

*

Despite his mother's open dislike of Lena, Lachlan insisted on bringing her to Mearns Street for the midday meal on Saturday, the day of her final appearance at the King's Theatre. Out of deference to Flora the girl dressed demurely in a plain jersey and skirt, scrubbed her face clean of make-up, and tied her glorious hair back with a ribbon.

'Mrs McDonald, it's lovely to see you again,' she flattered as soon as Lachlan ushered her proudly into the kitchen. Flora murmured something unintelligible.

'And Mr McDonald. Did I not see you in the audience on Thursday night?' Lena asked, shaking Henry's hand.

'What?' Flora barked, while her husband's face drained of colour.

'No, no, lassie, it was never me – I've a union meetin' on Thursday nights.'

'If ye were at yer precious meeting last Thursday, how did the lassie come tae see ye in the theatre?' Flora asked ominously.

'I must have been mistaken,' Lena said before Henry could speak. 'With the lights shining on us it's difficult to see the audience – we just get wee glimpses sometimes.'

'But ye saw Henry clear enough.'

'I thought I saw someone like him. But now I look at you, Mr McDonald, the man was nothing like you at all. It was a right noisy audience that night—' Lena chattered on until Flora finally turned back to her cooking. Henry, relaxing visibly behind her back, winked at Lena, who winked back.

She did her best to dampen down her natural vitality during her short visit, but even so Flora's disapproval hung in the air like the smell of burned cabbage. She studiously ignored the angry looks Lachlan gave her from time to time, and by the time he and Lena left for the Saturday matinée his face was tight with suppressed rage.

Elspeth walked downstairs with them. 'Pay no heed to Aunt Flora, Lena, you know what she's like.'

'Stop makin' excuses for her, Ellie,' Lachlan burst out. 'She'd no right to be so cold!'

'Ach, don't fret, she doesnae bother me,' Lena assured him, then hugged Elspeth. 'Mebbe next time I'm back in Greenock you'll be a married woman with a bundle of weans round your knees.'

'And you'll be the top of the bill.'

'I will that,' Lena said, and left for the theatre, Lachlan in attendance.

Upstairs, Flora was already washing the dishes vigorously, as though trying to erase every sign of the recent visitor. 'Thank goodness the week's over,' she said as soon as Elspeth went into the kitchen. 'She'll be out of the town tomorrow and we can get back tae normal.'

Lachlan hadn't returned from the theatre by the time they went to bed that night.

'They'll be clearin' everythin' away, ready tae move on tomorrow,' Henry said placidly when Flora looked at the clock for the hundredth time. 'Mebbe havin' a bit of a party. He'll come home when he's ready.'

Elspeth was roused some time later by the sound of the outer door closing softly, and when she slid back into sleep a few minutes later Lachlan was still moving about his room.

When he came into the kitchen the next morning, shaved and dressed in his best clothes, Henry raised his brows.

'I thought ye'd be too tired tae go tae the church today.' The McDonalds weren't regular churchgoers, but since recovering from the effects of his shell shock Lachlan had taken to attending the Sunday service almost every week.

'No, I'm—' Lachlan hesitated, then said, looking at his mother, 'I'm off to Ayr, with the company. I've taken up a position with them.'

Henry, still tousled from a night's sleep, his unshaven chin black with stubble, gaped, while Elspeth almost dropped the

311

large teapot she was carrying from the cooker to the table.

'Don't be stupid,' Flora said crisply. 'Ye've got a good job here. There'll be no goin' off tae Ayr or anywhere else.'

'Mam, the train leaves in an hour's time and I'll be on it. I'd have told you two days ago, when they first asked me, but I knew you'd only start on at me to turn it down, so I kept my mouth shut.'

Flora spun away from the cooker, porridge ladle in hand. 'It's her – that woman. I knew she'd try tae entice ye away from us!'

'It's not Lena, Mam, not altogether.' Although he had had very little sleep Lachlan looked rested and confident. It was clear to Elspeth, at any rate, that he meant what he said and wouldn't be swayed from the path he had decided to take. 'Mebbe she's part of it, but it's mostly the work. I've enjoyed this week, and I like the thought of the travellin', too.'

'Ye're not goin'!'

'I am. I'll write to you, every week, and I'll send what I can afford—'

'Ye're not goin'!' his mother repeated, dropping the ladle, oblivious of the porridge spraying from it. She advanced on Lachlan and caught at the lapels of his coat. 'D'ye hear me? Ye're not goin' – I won't let ye go!'

Her voice began to rise, out of control. Henry pushed his chair back and got up, taking his wife by the shoulders. 'Flora, sit down and let's talk about it.'

She ignored him, and Lachlan himself had to loosen her grip on his coat, finger by finger. 'Mam, will you listen to me, just for once? I want to do this. I want to get on with my life!'

'He's got the right tae dae as he pleases, Flora.' Henry's voice was gruff as he drew his wife back against his own body, wrapping his arms about her in an attempt to confine her struggles. 'I don't want tae see him go any more than you, but it's his decision and we have tae abide by it.'

'We don't have tae do anythin' of the sort! She'll desert ye when she's done with ye, d'ye not have the sense tae realise that?' Flora spat the words at her son. 'She'll laugh at ye an' send ye crawlin' back home!'

'I told you, Mam, it's not Lena I'm doing this for, it's me.' Lachlan's face was pale but determined. 'Mebbe we'll end up together, mebbe we'll part, but that doesnae matter. What matters is me doin' what I want to do.'

'Ye've already got a job here! And ye've got family, and a home!'

'Ye'll tell Mr Brodie for me, Elspeth? Explain things tae him?' Lachlan said, and she nodded.

'I will. Write to us.'

'Every week.' He hugged her tightly, then glanced at his father.

'I've packed my clothes, they're waitin' at the door.'

Henry was still holding Flora. 'Best just go now, lad. And I hope everythin' goes right for ye.'

'It will, I'll see tae that,' Lachlan said, then, with a faint tremor in his voice, 'Take care of Mam for me.'

He went without a backward glance. Flora, fighting hard against her husband's iron arms, screamed out her son's name, but there was no answer.

The outer door closed, and Lachlan had gone.

31

Pausing on the landing to shift the weighted shopping bag from one hand to the other, Flora McDonald cast a sidelong glance at the smooth brown hair lying against Elspeth's cheek.

'Every time I look at ye I think ye're a stranger.' Her voice was heavy with disapproval. 'I don't know why ye did it – ye'd such bonny hair. Thinkin' of it on someone else's head gives me the shivers. It's like wearin' someone else's dentures.'

'There's plenty that do that, Aunt Flora.' Since taking over Mr Monteith's pawn shop books, Elspeth had seen and heard of many things.

'Aye, well, nob'dy in my family's ever done it, or ever will!'

'The braid was too heavy, and it took so much looking after,' Elspeth explained for the umpteenth time, 'And the money I got for selling it came in useful.'

'Ye'll be sellin' yer soul next.' Flora gave her familiar, last-word sniff, a sniff that indicated that Flora McDonald knew best and there was no sense in further discussion, then set off up the final flight.

When the shopping had been unpacked and stored away, Elspeth went into her own small room to change from her everyday skirt and blouse into a lemon cotton dress with brown trim on the crossover bodice and on the cuffs, for she was calling on a prospective client that afternoon. Glancing in the mirror as she fluffed out her bobbed hair she decided that whatever Flora might say, she herself liked the new style. It made her look older, more like the professional woman she had become.

Returning to the kitchen, she found Flora, who always made tea her priority after being out, filling two cups from the teapot.

'Aunt Flora, I've not got much time—'

'Time enough for a cup of tea and a scone.' It was waiting on a plate, already buttered. 'Ye don't eat enough these days. Too eager tae look smart for yer precious clients' – Flora said the word with contempt – 'and that Forbes Cameron.'

The accusation was unjustified. Elspeth's weight and shape were the same as two years before, when she had worked in Brodie's sewing room. It was true that the clothes she wore now were more fashionable and flattered her slim figure, but there was no sense in explaining that to Flora, for Elspeth knew very well that there was another reason behind the woman's carping.

After years of dominating her family, Flora McDonald had lost her main purpose in life now that they had all flown the nest, and was finding it very hard to come to terms with the situation she now found herself in.

Lachlan had been gone for six months, and despite his mother's dire predictions at the time, the letters that arrived every week were written by a man who had finally found his proper place in life, and was supremely happy. Flora always left it to Henry to open the letters, and looked as though she was sucking lemons as he proudly read each one aloud.

'You'd think she'd be pleased for Lachlan,' Elspeth had said to Rachel, who replied flatly, 'I sometimes think Mam can only be pleased for folk if they're doing what she wants them to do.'

Mattie and Kenneth had married at Easter, and had settled in Glasgow, where Kenneth was working in the Southern General Hospital. Thomas still drove himself on relentlessly, and had done so well that Forbes Cameron had made him his partner and there was talk of buying another garage. He had long since cut his mother's apron strings, and even Rachel's visits weren't so frequent now that she had her sewing to occupy her time.

Only Elspeth, the child Flora had taken in and never loved, remained. As she sat down at the table she flicked a swift glance at the clock on the mantel shelf. She and Peggy and Kirsty organised their work round the needs of their clients and their own domestic duties, each taking time off in turn when the office was quiet. Elspeth saw to it that the other two were always free on Saturday afternoons and Sundays, but she herself often worked at the weekends, enjoying the peace and quiet of the office when nobody else was there.

As she glanced at the clock again, someone knocked on the outer door. Flora, tutting, put her hands flat on the table and started to lever herself up. 'That'll be Annie from across the landing. That nose of hers can smell fresh-made tea through stone walls.'

Elspeth was already on her feet. 'I'll go.'

As she opened the door her eyes moved to the spot where she expected to find wee fat Mrs McGlashan's face, and saw instead the buttons on a smart grey morning coat. Startled, she lifted her gaze and saw a tall, elegantly dressed man in the act of raising his bowler hat.

'Good afternoon, is Mrs McDonald—' His voice faltered and his polite smile faded as their eyes met. Elspeth's knees suddenly started to tremble, forcing her to tighten her grip on the edge of the door in order to stay upright. The man was a stranger to her, and yet she recognised him after just one glance at the clear blue eyes set in a handsome, middle-aged face. She knew those eyes so well; she should, for she saw them every time she looked into a mirror.

'Elspeth,' Flora said impatiently from behind her, 'there's a terrible draught comin' intae the house. Who is it?'

The man on the landing tore his gaze from Elspeth's face to look beyond her shoulder. 'Good afternoon, Flora,' he said through pale lips, and Flora's hand clutched at Elspeth's arm, her fingers digging in painfully.

'Oh my God!' Her voice came out in a strange croak. 'You?'

'Yes, it's me.'

'What d'ye want?'

'I've come to see my daughter,' he said, then, throwing a glance over his shoulder as Mrs McGlashan's door gave a slight creak, 'Would it not be better if I came in?'

'I thought you were still a child,' Duncan Crombie said in the kitchen a few minutes later. 'Time passes so quickly.'

'Aye, 'specially when ye've turned yer back on yer responsibilities,' Flora said harshly. She hadn't mentioned the cup of tea that was always offered to visitors as soon as they stepped into any West of Scotland home. Instead, she sat on the edge of an upright chair, her face pinched, her hands clasped tightly in her lap.

'I'm not proud of what I did, Flora.' His voice was pleasant to the ear, his accent anglicised Scots. 'I can only say in my own defence that I was very young – mebbe too young to face up to my responsibilities.'

Although he was answering Flora, he spoke directly across the table to Elspeth. Since his arrival they had been unable to take their eyes off each other. 'And Maisie's parents didn't make things any easier. They were against me from the first.'

'With good reason – look what ye did tae her,' Flora said bitterly, and he flinched.

'Aunt Flora—' Elspeth, embarrassed, put a hand on the woman's arm but it was twitched off.

'This is my house, I'll say what I please!'

'You never liked me either, did you, Flora? Between you and Maisie's mother we never had a chance.'

'I didnae trust ye, and I was proved right – ye cannae deny that.'

He shrugged, then got to his feet and reached for his hat

and cane. 'I'd best go. I've no wish to upset anyone.' Dipping into a breast pocket he removed a small flat case and opened it to extract a slip of pasteboard. 'Here's my card, Elspeth. The address of my hotel's on the back. I hope you'll call on me there.' Then, as Flora got to her feet, clearly determined not to let him have a moment alone with Elspeth, 'I'll see myself out.'

'Let me see that wee bit of paper,' Flora demanded as soon as the outer door closed behind him.

Elspeth, knowing that it would be thrown into the fire immediately, curled her fingers about the card. 'It's mine, Aunt Flora.'

'Ye're surely no' goin' tae see him?'

'I have to. I can't just let him walk out of my life again.'

'Of course ye can, and ye must, if ye've got any sense at all. That man's no use tae anyone, you take my word for it. He's a sleekit, deceitful devil – look what he did tae yer poor wee mother!'

'He meant a lot to her, once.'

'Aye – and she died hatin' him. She'd no' want ye tae have anythin' tae dae with him!' Flora's eyes were slits, her lips drawn back in a snarl. Elspeth jumped up, suddenly desperate to get out of the place. 'I must go, I'm late as it is.'

'If ye see that man again ye'll be turnin' yer back on me and all I've done for ye.' Flora followed her out on to the landing to throw the words at her departing back, then, as Elspeth started down the stairs, she leaned over the wrought-iron railing that edged the landing. 'I'm tellin' ye,' she called down as Elspeth started down the stairs, 'ye'll be turnin' against me if ye as much as set eyes on him!'

Thomas McDonald, leaning against the door of the car he had been working on, took a large swallow of tea from the mug Elspeth had brought him, then wiped the back of his hand across his mouth. 'So – what are you going to do?'

'I don't know. What d'you think would be best?'

'You're a woman, Ellie, not a bairn,' he said implacably. 'You have to make your own decisions.'

She clenched her fists, longing to batter them on his chest. 'Thomas, this is important – help me!'

He emptied the mug and handed it over before turning back to the car that stood with bonnet raised, like a fledgling waiting in the nest to be fed by the parent bird. 'Don't bring me or anyone else into it, Ellie.' He tossed the words over his shoulder, his hands already on the engine. 'I've told you, it's your decision.'

Going back into the house, she met Rachel settling little Pearl in her perambulator while Mary and Sandra, Kirsty's little girl, bounded around the hall like little rubber balls.

'We're going to the park,' Mary announced, rushing to hug Elspeth's knees as she always did.

'Mind your Aunt Elspeth's nice dress,' Rachel ordered, tucking a blanket round the baby's waist.

'It's only a dress, and I've got my smock on anyway.' Rachel had made loose smocks for herself and the typists to wear over their clothes as a protection against oil and grime. With the garage yard so close, they frequently got stains on their clothes.

'I'd best get this lot out of your way. We'll be back by the time Kirsty's ready to go home.'

Rachel had been working for Elspeth for the past two months, ever since Kirsty, her face white with misery, had handed in her notice.

'I don't want to leave, for I've loved working with you, but it's the wee one.'

Sandra, a toddler with dark curly hair and a dimpled smile, was the reason why Kirsty had been unable to apply for full-time work after completing her typing course. Deserted by the child's father before Sandra was born, Kirsty had refused to consider giving her baby up for adoption, and the two of them lived with Kirsty's parents. When Elspeth had first set up her agency nine months before, Kirsty's mother, delighted at her daughter finally getting the chance to earn her own living, had agreed to care for the little girl.

But the woman had recently had a bad bout of pleurisy, and as there was nobody else to care for Sandra, Kirsty had no option but to leave.

Elspeth, distressed at losing a good worker as well as a friend, had had the idea of turning the room she had intended one day as a second office into a nursery, and asking Rachel to spend time at the garage every day, caring for Sandra and her own two.

'I'd pay you,' she told Rachel. 'And it would only be for the afternoons, because Kirsty doesn't work in the mornings.'

'Folk don't get paid to look after bairns,' Rachel protested.

'Nannies and nurserymaids do.'

'That's different. Anyway, why should you put out more money just for the one wee girl? Would it not be easier just to let Kirsty go and find someone else?'

'Kirsty's my friend,' Elspeth said firmly, 'and she's a good worker. She needs the little I can afford to pay her.'

Rachel's eyes brightened, and a touch of colour came to her pale face. 'It's a bonny room, right enough, and there's so much space for the bairns to play.'

'What about Bob? What would he say about it?' He had been getting moodier lately, and had lost his job after arguing with the foreman. Henry had managed to find a place for him in the shipyard where he himself worked. Elspeth didn't want to cause even more trouble for Rachel by crossing Bob.

'He'll not care as long as his dinner's on the table when he comes home from work – if he comes home instead of going to the public house,' Rachel added with contempt.

Elspeth had scoured the second-hand shops and pawn shops for furniture for the empty room, gaining two new clients in the process, and Sandra had quickly settled down with Rachel, who loved children and got a lot of pleasure herself out of the new arrangement.

PEBBLES ON THE BEACH

'It's such an easy room to keep nice,' she told Elspeth. 'Not like home, where everything's packed in like sardines in a tin. It minds me of the times we had, you and me and Mattie, playing at wee houses.'

She insisted on taking over responsibility for cleaning the whole upper floor, and keeping everyone – Thomas and his staff as well as the typists – supplied with tea. She organised the kitchen and even baked scones occasionally in the large old cooker, brushing Thomas's mild grumbles aside.

'This is a garage, not a restaurant,' he pointed out when the first plate of scones, light as feathers and smelling delicious, came from the oven.

'I've not set foot in your yard, nor do I intend to,' Rachel retorted, her face flushed with the heat, her curly fair hair escaping in wisps from the pins that were supposed to keep it in place. 'But there's surely no harm in a wee bit of baking now and then.'

'No harm at all,' Joe agreed enthusiastically, his voice muffled by a mouthful of scone. 'I've never tasted anythin' as good as this!'

Rachel slapped at Thomas's hand as it reached out towards the plate. 'Wash that first – I'm not having good food smothered in oil before it gets to your mouth.'

He gave her an exasperated look tinged with amusement, and did as he was told. From then on, Rachel ruled the kitchen. She had blossomed since starting work, Elspeth thought now as she helped her to lift the perambulator down the front steps, though she still tended to keep her sleeves rolled down, to hide her forearms.

Elspeth saw the little group off, then, glancing up to make sure that Rachel's back was turned, rubbed at an imaginary speck of dirt on the nameplate, 'Bremner Office Agency, First Floor', with a corner of her smock. Rachel polished the plate every day, but now and again Elspeth liked to find an excuse to touch it, just to make sure that it was real, and not a dream.

321

Later, she tried to concentrate on the long list she was typing, the rattle of Peggy's and Kirsty's typewriters providing a pleasant background as she painstakingly transferred scribbled notes on crumpled scraps of paper into neat, clear columns on a fresh white sheet. But her mind kept returning to Duncan Crombie. Discovering that she had typed 'father' on the list instead of 'feather', she ripped the half-finished page free with an exclamation of disgust.

'Something wrong?' Peggy asked cheerfully.

'I wasn't concentrating properly.' Elspeth glanced at the clock and pushed her chair back. 'It'll have to wait until later, I'm due to call in at that new bookseller's soon.'

As it happened, the bookseller's shop was almost directly across the road from the hotel where Duncan Crombie was staying. From where she stood explaining the services the agency offered, Elspeth could see the corner of the building; by the time the business meeting had come to a mutually satisfying conclusion her mind was made up.

When she left the shop, she crossed the road and stepped into the hotel.

32

'You're so like Maisie,' Duncan Crombie marvelled an hour later, as they faced each other across a small tea table in the hotel lounge.

'But I've got your eyes.'

He smiled. 'You have indeed. Maisie's were like trees in the autumn, golden brown – something like the colour of your own hair.' His face softened with memories. 'They were long-lashed and always laughing. She was so unlike her parents that I used to tell her she must have been a changeling, left in her crib by the little folk.' Then, returning to the present, 'I understand that her parents have both died.'

'My grandmother died two years ago. She'd been' – Elspeth hesitated, then said carefully, reluctant to entrust Celia Bremner's bitter betrayal to this man who was her own flesh and blood, yet a complete stranger – 'on her own for years, since I was very small. I never knew my grandfather.'

'I liked him well enough, but his wife ruled the roost,' Crombie recalled. 'Poor man, he must have been stifled, living with that woman year in and year out. As for me – Maisie's mother was convinced that I'd never come to anything. She wanted better for her daughter. I don't think anyone other than royalty would have pleased her.'

Two middle-aged women passing their table glanced back at him with interest. He was still a good-looking man; in his youth he must have been very handsome. Elspeth could understand why her young mother had fallen in love with him.

'Tell me about my mother. There was nothing of hers in Grandmother's flat, not even a picture.'

He looked down at his cup, taking the teaspoon from the saucer and stirring his cooling tea slowly. 'She was beautiful, and loving, and I treated her badly. I was an orphan, living with my uncle, a man with no time for human weakness. I took fright when she told me she was carrying my child, and I ran away. My uncle had apprenticed me to a legal office, and I wasn't earning enough to keep the two of us. I couldn't face him – or Maisie's parents.'

He put the spoon down and took a sip of tea. 'I thought that if I was out of the way her mother and father would help her. If I'd only known how wrong I was!'

They talked the afternoon away without noticing time passing. Crombie told of his life in England, where he had found a position in another lawyer's office, working his way up and eventually marrying his employer's daughter.

'My wife's health broke down and we moved to the Isle of Man. I've been very lonely since she died a year ago, and finally I thought of trying to discover what had happened to Maisie and to our child. I'd always assumed that she had married, and that you had probably been raised by her husband as his own. I knew that I'd already caused her great unhappiness – I didn't want to do so again. Then I discovered that she died all those years ago, and that you'd been raised by Flora and her husband.'

His mouth twisted wryly. 'Flora never had any time for me either, because I worked in an office. In her opinion the only real men are those who work with their hands.'

'She was opposed to me taking up office work.' Elspeth told him about her struggle to achieve her ambitions, and he listened with interest.

'I'd like to see this office of yours.'

'You will, on Monday,' she promised, then, her heart

quickening at the thought of half-brothers and sisters, 'Did you and your wife have a family?'

To her disappointment he shook his head. 'We would have liked children, but there were none – until now.' He reached out and covered her hand briefly with his, his eyes sparkling. 'And now I have a beautiful daughter – I can't believe that we're finally together.'

Smiling at him, Elspeth relished the thought of introducing this man to people with the words, 'This is my father.'

At last she belonged to someone who was truly her own flesh and blood.

Everyone who met Duncan Crombie took a liking to him, apart from Flora and, to Elspeth's surprise, Forbes.

'I hope he doesn't intend to try to interfere with your life.' He took her hands in his. 'You've got your own business, and folk who cared for you long before he came along. He's left it too late to start making demands on you.'

'For goodness' sake, Forbes, he has no intention of making demands. Even if he did I wouldn't give in to them.'

She had cause to remember his words a short week later, when Duncan Crombie rented a small but comfortable house in Greenock, hired a housekeeper, and asked Elspeth to live there with him.

'We've been apart for so long, my dear, and now I want to be with my daughter. We need to get to know each other.'

When she refused, as gently as possible, hurt flooded into his expressive face. She tried to explain, choosing her words carefully in order to avoid causing further pain. 'I've just begun to control my own life. I need to be free at the moment to get the business established.'

'But you know I would never stand in your way! I'm very proud of what you've achieved already.'

'I know you are, but in any case I can't leave Aunt Flora and Uncle Henry just now.'

EVELYN HOOD

'Now that,' he said explosively, 'is ridiculous! You've just been talking about controlling your own life, and now you tell me that you can't live where you choose.'

'Their own family's gone now and I know that Aunt Flora's missing them. If I left I'd feel that I was deserting the two of them.'

'You're too soft, Elspeth. How d'you expect to run a successful business when you're worried about hurting people?'

They were in the drawing room of his new home, facing each other across the fireplace after enjoying an excellent meal.

'Aunt Flora's not a client. I owe a great deal to her, and caring about her feelings is entirely different from doing business.'

He bit his lip. 'You're right, and I apologise. It's just that—' He got up and paced the floor for a moment, then turned. 'We've lost so much time, you and I.'

'It may take more time for us to get to know each other.' With an effort, she managed to rise fairly gracefully from the deep, soft armchair. 'I must go. Give me a little while yet.'

He put his hands on her shoulders and kissed her forehead. 'I won't mention the matter again. I'm just fortunate to have found you at all.'

As the summer passed, Duncan Crombie moved with ease into the town's social life, drawing Elspeth with him. Without quite knowing how it had happened, she found herself attending concerts and soirées and dinner parties, even acting as his hostess when he invited people to his new home.

She gained a few more clients at these social occasions, for Duncan, proud of his new-found daughter, bragged to all and sundry about her talents as a businesswoman.

Once, when the two of them attended a performance by the Carl Rosa Opera Company at the King's Theatre with Forbes and his parents, she came face to face with James Brodie and his wife.

The store owner looked at her, puzzled, as they were introduced. 'I've met you before, Miss Bremner.'

'I used to work in Brodie's sewing room, and did some typing in the accounts office when Theresa McCabe was ill.'

His jaw dropped. 'Good heavens, so you did. And you left because you didn't get the position when it fell vacant. I always regretted that – I felt that we had let you down.'

'On the contrary, I'm grateful to you. I set up my own agency after I left Brodie's,' she explained as the puzzled look came back. 'And the bonus you paid me for doing your typing came in useful.'

'I'm very glad to hear it, and to see you looking so prosperous.'

Mrs Brodie, an elegant woman, had been studying Elspeth with interest, taking in her smooth, shining cap of hair and her elegant, simply cut crimson dress.

'Tell me, Miss Bremner,' she asked carefully, 'did you buy your gown in Glasgow?'

'I made it myself.' She had bought the material only the day before, and had persuaded Flora to let her use her old heavy sewing machine. With Rachel's help she had made the gown in an evening.

The woman's eyebrows rose. 'To your own design?'

'I copied it from a sketch in a magazine.'

'Indeed?' Envy flickered across Mrs Brodie's face. 'You have more than one talent,' she observed, and Duncan and Forbes, flanking Elspeth, both glowed with pride.

'You can look better in a home-made gown than all the other women in the clothes that cost them a fortune,' Duncan murmured as they left the Brodies and returned to their seats for the second part of the opera.

Hurrying along Hamilton Street with a thick envelope of completed work under her arm, Elspeth noticed a 'For Sale' sign on the opposite side of the street. She hesitated, then crossed over during a break in the traffic to look more closely at the property – a double-fronted shop. Pressing her nose against the glass and holding the bulky envelope up to block the reflection from the street behind, she made out a spacious interior with a counter, and a door in the rear wall. Further investigation through the close by the side of the shop revealed a walled back yard.

Elspeth returned to the street and took another look at the empty property. Then, thinking hard, she went on her way.

During dinner that evening at the Camerons' – a frequent occurrence, since Mrs Cameron had taken to Duncan from their first meeting – Elspeth announced that she was thinking of moving the agency to new premises. She could tell by the way his brows drew together that Forbes disapproved.

'There would be more space for us in that shop than at the garage,' she hurried on before he had a chance to object. 'I was asked only a few weeks ago to supply a temporary typist to work in an office in Port Glasgow, but none of the three of us can be spared for that sort of thing, and I've not got the space to bring anyone else in.'

'That's because you gave the extra room over to a child minder,' Forbes pointed out curtly.

'If I hadn't done that I would've lost Kirsty, and she's a good worker. Now that I've got Rachel I could mebbe employ another young mother looking for part-time work. I've been thinking of going back to letter-writing as well – I'm sure there's still a demand for that. It would help to be nearer the centre of the town, too. As things are, the three of us have to walk quite a distance each time we deliver work to our customers. If I took over that ground-floor shop the clients could come to us.'

'I think it's a good idea,' Duncan Crombie said. 'Perhaps it's time for you to expand your business.'

She turned to him gratefully. 'The shop itself would make

a good-sized office and I'd not need to do much more than have it painted. The big windows would give us more light – I'd put some net curtaining over them to prevent folk gawping in at us from the pavement. And there's a back room with a cooker and a sink.'

'You sound as though you've already decided.' Forbes sounded hurt, and she turned to him apologetically.

'I know you've done a lot to the old house for my sake, Forbes, but you did say at the beginning that if I failed you could let the upper floor out to someone else.'

'If you ask me, it's too early for you to consider moving, Elspeth. You should harvest your resources for at least a year before making changes.'

'I don't agree,' Duncan Crombie said at once. 'There's nobody else in the area with a typing agency. If Elspeth expands now folk'll take that as an indication that she's doing well. Success builds on success – you should know that as well as I do.'

Forbes said nothing, but looking from his closed face to her father's bland, handsome features, Elspeth felt, not for the first time, like a bone being fought over by two dogs. The coolness between the two men and the way they tended to vie for her attention made her uneasy. She was quite sure that if Forbes had shown enthusiasm for her new plans, her father would then have opposed them.

On the following afternoon Duncan Crombie arrived at the garage when Elspeth was working on her own. He took a turn about the room, stared out of the window for a few minutes, then said, 'I've had a look at that property you mentioned last night.'

She felt a tingle of annoyance at his interference, but curbed it, asking mildly, 'What do you think of it?'

'I notice that there's a small upstairs flat included. Are you thinking of living there?'

She was, but knowing of Duncan's desire to have her living

under his roof, she avoided a direct answer to his question, 'If I take on the property, Rachel'll need somewhere to care for the children.'

'Ah.' There was relief in his voice. 'You don't want to pay too much attention to what young Cameron says, Elspeth. He's never had to worry about money. It's folk like you and me who've pulled themselves up by their bootstraps who know when to take our chances. What d'you plan to do about financing the move?'

'I've already seen the bank manager and I think I can get a loan large enough to set up the place and compensate Forbes for the move. He let me have these rooms for a low rent for the first year, and I'd like to reimburse him for that if I leave,' she explained as her father gave her a questioning look.

'I don't see why you should, if he made the offer of his own free will.'

'I'd prefer to set things straight. After all, he was very kind to me when I first decided to start the agency. I could never have done it without his help.'

'I'm sure,' Crombie said drily, 'that he had his reasons. The man's besotted with you, Elspeth, you must know that. It would only be natural for him to want to help you and place you under an obligation so that he could turn things to his own advantage.'

She felt herself tense with anger. Why did her father and Forbes always have to use her as an excuse to criticise each other? Why couldn't they be more like Thomas, who believed in giving others the right to do as they pleased, and had merely said when told of her new plans, 'You could do well with anything you tackled, Ellie. You've got the courage to fight your own battles.'

'I think you're being unnecessarily hard on Forbes,' she said. 'He's a good friend, and I'm very fond of him.'

'Fond enough to agree to marry him? That's what he's after, my dear. Make no mistake about it.'

'As to that, he hasn't proposed marriage – and if he does,' she said, letting a little of her growing irritation reveal itself, 'I'll be the one to decide what to say.'

He lifted his hands in swift apology. 'Of course you will. Forgive me if I'm interfering, my dear. I'm still learning how to be a father. In any case, I didn't come here to criticise Cameron. I came to say that I'd like to give you a personal loan for the new premises, instead of you having to go cap in hand to the bank. My terms would be more advantageous.'

'I can't let you risk your own money. What if something went wrong?'

'It won't. I have faith in you, and I want to show it in more than words. Please consider it, at least.'

Forbes, Elspeth thought, might say that now it was the older man who wanted to place her under an obligation. On the other hand, she had already hurt her father's feelings by turning down his invitation to move into his home. She owed him something.

'I accept. Thank you,' she said at last, and his face lit up.

'I'm so glad, my dear! I wish your mother could have known that we're together at last. It would have made her happy, I'm sure.'

33

Elspeth and Forbes almost fell out over her decision to lease the shop and the flat above with a loan from Duncan Crombie.

'You should have let me lend you the money!' he argued, his lower lip pushed out like a sulky child's.

'You've done more than enough for me as it is.'

'And how d'you repay me? By moving out of the garage house.'

They were down on the beach, still one of Elspeth's favourite places. She sat on a rock, while Forbes, sprawling on the ground, threw pebbles into the water, one after another. He had none of Thomas's expertise, she noticed, but on the other hand Forbes wasn't attempting to skim the stones across the water's surface, he was hurling them as though trying to punish the waves, which took no notice, but continued to break in lacy froth on the beach, absorbing the thrown pebbles effortlessly.

'I need more space.'

'I could have given you the other downstairs room.'

'You need it as an office – and I'd not put Thomas out of the only home he has.'

He tossed a final stone and sat up, linking his hands round his knees. 'Why expand the business anyway? You've proved your point – you've shown everyone that you can do it. Isn't that enough?'

'No, it's not. It's more important to me than that – it's my future.'

'I'm your future.' Forbes suddenly twisted round on to his knees, reaching out to take her hand. 'Marry me, Elspeth.'

'Forbes—'

'I'm serious. I want you to be my wife.'

She hadn't been prepared for such a sudden proposal. 'I'm too young for marriage,' she protested weakly.

'You're almost nineteen, the same age my mama was when I was born.'

'But I don't want to marry anyone just yet,' she said in a panic. Despite himself, he started to laugh, then gave a grimace of pain.

'Ouch! I wish I'd picked a better place to propose.' He got to his feet and bent to rub at his knees. 'I'm crippled – and you don't even have the decency to say yes and make it all worth the suffering.'

She rose and put a hand on his arm. 'I'm sorry, Forbes, but I really and truly don't want to think of marriage just now. Not yet.'

'It's not Crombie, is it? Is he turning you against the idea of marrying me?'

'Of course not!'

'He doesn't approve of me. I don't think he'd approve of any man who might come between you and him.'

Elspeth thought fleetingly of her father's comment that only royalty would have met with Celia Bremner's approval as far as her daughter was concerned. 'You're wrong, Forbes. I'm not the sort of spineless creature who would allow anyone to dominate her.'

'I know – that's why I love you, and why I'm going to keep on proposing until you say yes.' Then, as they turned together to walk back to where the car stood, 'You don't really know much about him, do you?'

'I know that he's my father, and he's a good man.'

'A wealthy man, too – yet he came from nothing. What d'you know about the way he earned his money?'

'He earned it honestly!' she snapped, breaking free of him and striding ahead to the road.

Hours later, lying in bed and staring up at the pattern thrown on the bedroom ceiling by the moonlight, she tried to understand why she hadn't accepted his proposal. Was it because of her father's attitude towards Forbes? she wondered, then decided that the reason lay in herself. She liked Forbes very much, and took great pleasure in their shared caresses. But surely there should be more than just a sense of pleasure between two people who genuinely loved each other?

On the following morning Rachel and her daughters were late arriving at the office. The children were unusually subdued when they got there, while Rachel, who claimed to have toothache, had tied a scarf over her head, half obscuring her face.

Once she had given her foster sister time to settle the children, Elspeth left her typewriter and went down to the yard. Thomas, in his dungarees, was working on a car and reluctant to leave it.

'If it's something that needs fixing upstairs, get one of the other men to see to it.'

'I doubt if you'd want any of the men to see to this problem,' she persisted, and finally, grumbling, he wiped his hands with a rag and followed her into the house and upstairs.

Leaving him in the corridor, she put her head round the playroom door and asked Rachel to come outside. When the other girl joined them her face was still wrapped in the scarf. At sight of Thomas she ducked away and tried to go back into the room, but Elspeth was too quick for her. She caught at the scarf and it fell away to reveal a livid black bruise covering most of the side of Rachel's face and puffing the tender flesh beneath one eye.

Thomas's breath caught in his throat. 'Good God, Rachel, what's happened to you?'

334

'I fell against a door.' His sister tried to turn her injured cheek into the shadows, but he forestalled her, putting one hand beneath her chin and turning her head so that the light from the window at the end of the hall showed up the ugly bruise.

'I think she fell against Bob's fist, and more than once by the look of it,' Elspeth told Thomas.

'Bob?' His voice cracked with disbelief. 'Did Bob do this to you?'

'He's been ill-treating her for a long time, but she wouldn't let me tell anyone.'

'You promised you wouldn't!' Rachel accused Elspeth, tears glistening in her eyes.

'I know I did, but I've held my tongue long enough, and so have you. He's never hurt you as badly as this, Rachel – what d'you think his next step'll be? You could end up in the hospital, or in a graveyard. And what about the bairns? When'll he start on them?'

'He won't – and he'll never touch my sister again,' Thomas said thickly, releasing Rachel and moving towards the stairs.

'Thomas!' She threw herself after him, clutching at the banisters. 'Where are you going?'

'To see Bob,' he said from the landing. 'He's not going to get away with what he's done!'

'No – please! Thomas!' Rachel tried to follow him, but Elspeth held her back.

'Rachel, he can't mark you like that and think that nobody'll see it. Sit down.' As Rachel's knees sagged, Elspeth eased her on to the top step and wrapped her arms about the banisters. 'I'll be back in a minute.'

She put her head round the office door and asked Kirsty to keep an eye on the children for a while. 'Rachel's toothache's worse and I'm going to make some tea for her,' she explained, then helped Rachel downstairs.

As there was a risk of Joe or the other men coming into the

kitchen and finding them, she led the distraught girl into the downstairs room that had once been the garage office, and was now Thomas's home.

'He'll not mind us sitting in here, I'm sure.' She settled Rachel in a chair and went to the kitchen, returning a few minutes later with two cups of strong tea.

'Bob'll kill me for this,' the girl said as Elspeth put a cup into her hand and folded the cold fingers of her other hand round it to hold it steady. Her voice was flat and listless and eerily certain of the truth of the words.

'He'll not.' Elspeth leaned forward and put her own hands round Rachel's. 'We'll see to that – Thomas and me.'

'I'm his wife, you can't stop him.'

'Yes we can. For a start, you're not going back to that house.'

'I have to – where else can I go? I'm not having my bairns sleeping in the gutter or the poors' hospital.'

'Aunt Flora and Uncle Henry'll take you in.'

Rachel laughed bleakly, then winced at the pain in her face. 'Mam? She's told me often enough that a woman's place is with her man, no matter what happens.'

'Uncle Henry wouldn't agree with that.'

'He's got little choice,' Rachel said wryly. 'I'll not be the cause of trouble between them – and I'll not live where I'm not wanted.'

She was right. If Flora McDonald was overruled, and forced to take Rachel and the children in, she would make their lives miserable. Elspeth thought briefly of her father, who had room enough in his rented house, but she couldn't see him agreeing to having two children he didn't know running round the place.

Searching for a solution, she glanced around the room Thomas had been living in for several months. It was immaculate and sparsely furnished, with nothing out of place. The chairs she and Rachel sat in flanked the fireplace, and the sagging old *chaise-longue* that she and Thomas had sat on, holding each other, on the night of Aileen's death had been replaced by a sturdier couch that acted as a seat by day and Thomas's bed by night. A marble-topped washstand in one corner of the room held a large basin and ewer, and a curtain had been hung across one corner as a makeshift wardrobe. The only other pieces of furniture in the room were a chest of drawers with a brush and comb and mirror on top, and a small bookcase.

The house had been designed and built to hold large, heavy Victorian furniture, and Thomas's few possessions scarcely began to use the available floor space. As a result, the room had a barren, cheerless air about it. Every time she went into it Elspeth longed to make it more comfortable, but knew that Thomas would resist such attempts. Since becoming a widower he had had no time for comfort and pleasure.

She sighed, cast a glance at Rachel, who was sipping her tea, then looked up at the ceiling and found the answer to their problems.

'You could live here, Rachel, you and the girls – in the playroom. It's big enough for the three of you, and there's the bathroom – and the kitchen downstairs, and Thomas here at nights, so you'd not be alone.' Now that the idea had occurred to her, Elspeth could see no barrier to it. 'We'll get some furniture easily enough, from second-hand shops. Mr Monteith might be able to help us, and some of my other clients.'

'It wouldn't work,' Rachel said, but there was a faint gleam of hope in her eyes. 'Thomas wouldn't agree – and what about Mr Cameron? It's his house.'

'Leave them to me. We could get something arranged today, then you'd not have to go back to Bob at all. And,' Elspeth added, regretfully relinquishing her secret hopes of moving out of Mearns Street, 'there's the flat above the shop. That'd be ideal for you once I move the office from here.' She got to her feet. 'Finish your tea and we'll see what we can do.'

*

Thomas was working in the yard when they returned, and at sight of him Rachel gave a squeal of horror.

'What happened to your mouth?'

Hampered by a cut lip and a blue knot on his jaw, he gave her a lopsided grin. 'I went to the shipyard and made it clear to Bob Cochran that the McDonalds don't take kindly to their womenfolk being ill-treated.' He looked at his bruised knuckles thoughtfully, then added, 'It took a bit of explaining, but I think he understood what I was trying to tell him.'

'You hit Bob?' Her eyes were dark with horror.

'It's the only language a man like that understands, Rachel. Don't fret – I'll mend, and so will he, for I let him off lightly.'

'And he'll not be able to take it out on you or the children, for you're not going back to the flat,' Elspeth put in, and explained to Thomas about the upstairs room.

He nodded. 'It's the best way, and I'll be here during the night to look after them. You'd mebbe better ask Mr Cameron's permission, though, since it's his property.'

'I've already done that, and he's agreed.'

Thomas gave her a look that Granjan would have described as 'old-fashioned'.

'He'd not deny you anything, would he?'

She flushed, but refused to rise to the bait. 'And I've arranged for some bits of furniture to be delivered, to tide Rachel over.'

'Bob'll not like this,' Rachel moaned. 'He'll mebbe come after us and make us go home.'

'He'll do nothing of the sort. Da was there when I went to the yard, and if I hadnae seen to Bob, he would've. He'll not let the man bother you again,' Thomas assured her.

'But my clothes, and all the bairns' things – they're still at the house.'

'Elspeth and me'll go down with you this evening to collect them. There'll be no more trouble, Rachel, I promise you. Men like Bob Cochran are cowards. They only hurt folk that can't hit back. Now that me and Da know about him, he'll keep well away from you.'

In spite of all their reassurances, Rachel was shaking with fear as the three of them walked to the flat that evening, and Elspeth herself, remembering the way Bob had looked at her in January when she had cared for the children while he and Rachel went to see Lena at the theatre, felt her stomach clenching as her foster sister turned the key in the door.

Thomas went in first, and the two girls stood quaking in the close, clutching at each other and ready to flee if necessary, until he reappeared, grim-faced.

'He's not here, but the place is in a bit of a mess, Rachel.'

'How can it be? I always clean it before I go to the gar—' Rachel, who had pushed past him as she spoke, stopped short, a hand flying to her mouth. Following close behind, Elspeth saw that the kitchen looked as though a whirlwind had passed through it, with drawers thrown to the floor, the curtains ripped from the window, and plates smashed. Clothes and the few toys that Mary and Pearl owned had been strewn everywhere, and a pretty little wall mirror, a wedding gift from Granjan, had been torn down and smashed.

Rachel fell to her knees, trying to gather everything up at once. 'Look at Mary's bonny wee dress that I made just last week!' She held it up to show them the great jagged rip where the skirt was almost torn away from the carefully smocked bodice. 'And Pearl's dolly—' The head had been wrenched off, and lay in a corner, half under a torn fragment of cloth that Elspeth recognised as part of Rachel's favourite skirt.

She knelt and took the other girl into her arms. 'Don't fret, Rachel, it'll all mend.'

Above their heads Thomas said grimly, 'We'd best just gather the lot up and take it all out of here. Then he can live on his lone in the pigsty he's created.'

34

They had to support Rachel between them back to Mearns Street, where Flora, tight-lipped, was looking after the children. To Elspeth's relief the little girls were sound asleep in the darkness of the curtained wall-bed, and were spared the sight of their mother's distress.

Granjan had arrived, and she immediately gathered Rachel into her plump arms and rocked her while Thomas upended the sack he carried and let the debris of Rachel's married life spill out on to the kitchen floor.

'There, there, pet, don't fret yersel', we're all here tae put everythin' right,' Janet Docherty soothed, while Henry, his shirtsleeves rolled up and his braces dangling round his hips, chimed in with, 'As tae that blaggard Bob Cochran, don't give him another thought, for he'll have more sense than tae come near ye after the lesson our Thomas taught him. By God, but it's been many a year since the yard saw such a fight!' He slapped his son on the back. 'Ye went at him as if he was responsible for all the ills o' the world.'

'He's been responsible for enough of them,' Thomas said shortly, his eyes on his sister.

'I didnae know ye were so handy with yer fists—'

'Bein' able tae hit a man hard's nothin' tae be proud of,' Flora broke in. 'And we'll have no more talk of fightin' in my kitchen. Elspeth, make some tea. Rachel, wash yer face and help me tae sort out this mess that's been dumped on my clean floor.'

Henry prudently took his son out for a drink while the womenfolk sifted through the pile of toys and clothing that Thomas had brought from Rachel's flat.

On closer inspection, the damage wasn't as bad as they had first thought. In the throes of his mindless rage, Bob hadn't taken the time to destroy each item individually, so quite a few of the garments and toys had simply been thrown down and were still intact. Some were repairable, and only a small percentage was beyond redemption. The four women settled down with needle and thread, putting things to rights.

'I'm sorry, Mam,' Rachel said meekly as they stitched.

'Sorry doesnae pay for food tae put intae yer bairns' bellies and clothes on their backs. It's menfolk that dae that.' Flora's voice was hard and unforgiving, and Elspeth felt sudden anger against her. Not once had the woman comforted her distraught, bruised daughter.

'If this is what Bob does to his children's clothes,' she held up the tiny skirt she was trying to mend, 'his children are better off without him.'

'And what dae you know about husbands – or fathers, come to that?' Flora asked crushingly.

'I know that Rachel would be better off earning her own money. At least she'd get the use of it, instead of seeing it all go in drink.'

Bright spots of colour flamed on Flora's cheekbones. She had been proud of Bob's teetotal background when he and Rachel first married, and had bragged about it to the neighbours. Now she would have to eat humble pie, something that Flora McDonald hated doing. 'Ye think our Rachel's goin' tae manage on the few pence ye hand over tae her every week like Lady Muck?'

'It's not just what I earn at the garage, Mam.' Rachel rushed to Elspeth's defence. 'There's the money in the—' She caught Elspeth's warning glance and subsided.

'What money?' Flora asked at once. 'What're ye talkin' about?'

The two young women exchanged glances, then Rachel said carefully, 'I've been doing sewing for folk, and Elspeth put the money I earned into the bank for me.'

'Bank?' Flora spoke as though her daughter had just admitted that she had been working in a brothel. 'What are ye doin', havin' truck with banks?'

'It was the only way to keep Bob from taking it, Aunt Flora.'

To Elspeth's relief, the menfolk returned just then, Henry jovial and Thomas his usual quiet, controlled self. The children were coaxed awake and tucked into their coats, and while Henry set off to walk Granjan home, Elspeth accompanied the others to the garage to settle Rachel and the children into the playroom.

'I'm sorry, Mam,' Rachel said timidly as she was about to leave.

'Sorry?' Thomas echoed. 'It's not your fault that Bob Cochran turned out to be such a poor excuse for a man.'

Flora's face was still stony. 'What's done can't be undone,' she said enigmatically.

Thomas carried Mary, the older and heavier of the two little girls, while Elspeth hoisted Pearl's solid, warm little body into her arms and Rachel carried the sack with the salvaged clothes and toys. They walked uphill through the darkness in silence, past the lit windows of tenements. Pearl, light enough when they first set out, seemed to grow heavier with each uphill step. Her head rested on Elspeth's shoulder and her breath was hot and tickly. Elspeth longed to shift her burden to her other arm, but didn't dare for fear of wakening the little girl, who had fallen asleep again.

'Are you managing?' Thomas asked as they neared the garage.

'I'm fine.'

'I hope Bob's not come after us,' Rachel said nervously.

'He's got other things on his mind. It's not just the hiding he got from me – now that Da knows what he's been doing to you, he'll be keeping a close eye on Mr Bob Cochran too,' Thomas told her confidently.

After the day's turmoil it was soothing to be out in the night. Thomas walked between Elspeth and Rachel, and the three of them had fallen into step, their shoes tapping down on the pavement to the same beat. Now and again their arms touched and Elspeth took comfort from Thomas's reassuring nearness.

Despite the fact that the furniture had been acquired so hurriedly, the playroom looked quite comfortable. Joe had set a fire in the grate, and when Thomas put a match to it, the flames took hold at once. Elspeth drew the curtains as Rachel turned slowly, wide-eyed, to take everything in.

'It looks so – cosy!'

They helped her to tuck the children into bed, then left her. 'I'll walk you back home,' Thomas said as they reached the front door.

'And leave Rachel and the bairns here on their own? You'll do nothing of the sort – you know that she's nervous in case Bob's around.'

'Him? He'll be licking his wounds in some public house.'

'Did you really give him a thrashing?'

'Not as bad as Da says, and not as bad as he deserved.' His jaw tightened. 'I could have killed him, Ellie, and I wanted to. I wanted to just keep on hitting until there was nothing left of him but I held back because I knew it wasn't just Bob Cochran I was lashing out at, it was Ian Bruce as well. I've been needin' to hurt someone for a long time, and today I got my chance.'

'Mebbe now that you've got it out of your system you'll be able to get on with your life.'

Although he didn't move she sensed his instant withdrawal. 'I'm fine as I am.'

'You should take some time off.'

He gave her a level look from beneath his brows. 'What would I do with it?'

'Go further down the river and sit on the beach, or walk up over the braes to Loch Thom. I'll come with you, if you like.'

He smiled slightly. 'You've already got your hands full with Mr Cameron.'

She poked him in the ribs. 'Do you want another punch in the mouth?'

His smile widened to a grin, then he was serious again. 'Mam didn't have much to say for herself tonight, did she? I thought she'd have been ranting on about Bob.'

'She already knew about him,' Elspeth said, then, as he looked puzzled, 'Bob's been ill-treating Rachel since Mary was small.'

'And Mam knew? Why didn't she say anything?'

'She didn't want to admit that Rachel had made a bad marriage.'

The anger was back in his face and his voice. 'She stood by and let her own daughter suffer just because she didn't want the neighbours to talk? I'll never understand that woman!'

'There are a lot of folk like her in Greenock – probably in the rest of the world too.'

'Aye – folk that let everything crumble about their ears just so's they can go on pretending everything's fine.' His voice was thick with contempt.

'I'll have to go, it's getting late.'

'What'll happen to Rachel when you move?'

'She'll live in the wee flat above the shop.'

'I thought you'd want that for yourself.'

'I was thinking about it, but Rachel's need's greater than mine.'

Thomas ran a hand through his fair hair. 'She's my sister, and it should be my place to find somewhere for her to live – especially after the way Mam turned her back when Rachel needed her most.'

'She's my sister too, and you're doing enough. She can sleep safely at night knowing that you're downstairs.'

He tried again to insist on walking back to Mearns Street with her, but she was adamant.

'Rachel needs to know that you're downstairs and she's not alone in the house. I can look after myself.'

'I never doubted that, but even so—'

'I mean it. I'll be home in five minutes.'

He gave a resigned shrug and reached for the front door latch. Elspeth too had begun to reach for it, but Thomas was swifter, and as her hand landed on his knuckles he winced slightly.

'Let me see—' She took his hand and turned it over, palm on palm, drawing him towards the glow of the gas mantle. His knuckles were bruised and torn and painful-looking.

'I'll find something to put on them,' she said, but Thomas put a hand on her shoulder as she began to lead him to the kitchen, where she had gathered together a box of ointments and salves to treat any cuts or bruises the men might suffer during their workday.

'Don't fuss, it'll be healed by the morning.'

She glared up at him, exasperated. 'You're such a difficult man to help.'

'And you care too much about folk.'

'Only some folk,' Elspeth said. His hand was warm against hers and his other hand still gripped her shoulder. As she looked up at him she saw that the dim light from the gas mantles touched the ends of his rumpled fair hair and his eyelashes with pale gold and cast shadows over his face, emphasising its strong planes and angles. His hazel eyes glowed, and she could smell a hint of the drink he had had earlier on his breath, mingled with the fresh outdoor air on his clothes. She felt slightly dizzy and confused.

'Only special folk,' she heard herself say, then the words died away into silence. Something was happening; it was as if the hallway where they stood was changing, becoming a magic place she had never been in before. Thomas, and her feelings towards him, were also changing.

Suddenly embarrassed in his presence, she dipped her head and found herself looking at the square, strong hand still resting on her own. Although he scrubbed his hands thoroughly after each day's work his trade was etched on them in a faint, permanent tracery of oil around the knuckles and dark shadowing beneath the fingernails, cut short and straight across. The sight of his bruised, painful knuckles struck her to the heart; she laid the palm of her other hand gently over the broken skin as though trying by touch to make him whole again.

The hand on her shoulder moved, the fingers landing lightly on her neck, just below the smooth line of her bobbed hair. The unexpected caress sent a blaze of warmth through her. His thumb moved across her cheek so gently that she scarcely felt it, to touch the corner of her mouth. Giving way to impulse, she turned her head so that her lips brushed the hollow of his palm, tasting the faint mixture of oil and soap that was Thomas's physical signature.

She heard him make a tiny sound in his throat, and as if it was a signal she had been waiting for all her life, she let herself sway towards him. His arms received her, closing round her, gathering her body against his.

She lifted her face, seeking and welcoming his mouth with parted lips. His hair was soft and springy beneath her hands, his kisses urgent, his arms strong and possessive. This was surely what loving felt like. It was far greater than the mere pleasure she knew with Forbes; it was a fierce hunger that, for her, could only be sated by one man. And at last she had found him.

When they drew back from each other she looked up into

his eyes and for just one fleeting moment saw what she had been confidently looking for. Then it was gone. His lids dropped to hood his eyes, his face went blank, his hands put her gently but firmly away from him.

'You'd best go, Elspeth.'

'Go? How can I just go after what's happened?'

'Because it should never have happened. I – forgot myself.'

'It seems to me that we've just found ourselves.' She couldn't believe that he was sending her away. 'Thomas—' She put a hand on his arm, which was hard and unyielding. 'You've been alone for almost two years now. That's long enough.'

'Long enough to realise that happiness has to be paid for, and the price is too high. I'll not walk that road again.'

'Do my feelings not mean anything to you?'

'They mean a great deal – too much for me to let you throw yourself away on me. I failed Aileen and I couldn't bear to fail you too.'

'You didn't fail Aileen – she loved you, and you never let her down.'

'Talk sense, Ellie,' he blazed down at her. 'I took her away from all she'd ever known and put her into a – a box! If I hadn't let her down she'd never have been in that car. She'd be alive today!'

There was no reasoning with him, she thought in despair. No way of convincing him that the blame for Aileen's death shouldn't be lying on his conscience. 'So you're going to punish yourself – and me – for the rest of our lives over what happened to Aileen?'

'You'll thank me, one day. Leave it, Ellie,' he ordered as she began to protest. 'I'll not discuss it again. Are you certain that you don't want me to walk down with you?'

She did, so much. She wanted to be alone with him in the dark night, just the two of them, but she knew by the set of his jaw and the steely note in his voice that he meant what he had said. She had found him and lost him in the space of five minutes.

All that was left to her now was her dignity – tattered, but still there. She gathered it around herself like a shield. 'I'll manage fine,' she said, and stepped out on to the pavement, feeling more alone than ever before.

35

When Elspeth told Joe about what had happened to Rachel he made no secret of his disgust and anger.

'How can anyone treat a bonny wee family like that so badly?'

'There are plenty around like Bob Cochran.'

'I hope I never come across them.' His big fists clenched. 'I'm glad tae hear that Thomas taught the man a thing or two.'

'You'll not say a word in front of Rachel? She's so ashamed of what's happened.'

'What's she got tae be ashamed about?' Joe demanded to know. 'We're all responsible for our own sins, but not for other folk's. Ye neednae fear, lassie, she'll no' hear a word about it from me. Mind you, I thought there was somethin' goin' on. The bairns were too quiet at times – wee ones shouldnae ever look worried, but there were days when Mary and Pearl seemed tae have the cares of the world on their wee shoulders. I can see the difference in them already.'

'Now you come to mention it, so can I. Why didn't I notice it before?'

'You were too close tae them,' he told her. 'We tend tae see what we expect tae see, an' it never occurs tae us tae take a fresh look at folk now and again.'

'I wish I had your understanding, Joe.'

'I learned the hard way.' His face took on a grim look. 'I lost a mate once, at sea. He deliberately put himself overboard, with his pockets weighted down so's we couldnae save him. A right cheery fellow he was, tae. It wasnae until he died that I discovered that he'd been nursin' all sorts of problems and never sayin' a word. I never forgave mysel' for not seein' the truth and doin' somethin' about it in time tae save him. How's Ra – yer sister goin' tae manage?'

'There's the wee bit I pay her, and she'll not be without a roof over her head. She does sewing for people, and that'll help.'

'I'll pass the word around our street,' said Joe. 'She'll probably be glad of some extra work.'

They were in the kitchen. The other mechanics had returned to the yard, but Elspeth had kept Joe back to tell him about Rachel. Now he glanced out of the window and moved away from the sink, where he had been rinsing his cup.

'There's the gaffer – I'd best get back tae work.'

A sense of loss swept over Elspeth as she stood by the window, watching Thomas stride across the yard and disappear into the garage. The night before he had talked of the heavy price he had to pay for Aileen's death, and now Elspeth felt that she herself was paying for the few moments she had spent in his arms. The closeness they had always shared had vanished, possibly for ever. She didn't know whether the ache of bereavement in her heart was due to losing the old Thomas, a dear and trusted friend, or the Thomas she had just discovered and known so briefly. The only thing she was certain of was that the pain of her loss was more than she could bear.

Drearily, dragging her feet, she went back upstairs and tried to get on with her work.

In the afternoon she walked down to Hamilton Street, where she had arranged to meet a local painter to discuss work to be carried out on her new premises.

It took an hour to agree on colours and terms for the work on the flat as well as the office; Elspeth had been looking forward to the task of redecorating the former dress shop to suit her own tastes, but now that the moment had come, she found herself unable to concentrate, and ended up agreeing to the painter's suggestions.

'Aye, ye've got yersel' a nice wee property here,' he said as they returned downstairs after going through the flat. 'Well placed, too.'

'Yes.' Elspeth looked round the spacious area that was to be the office, and wondered if she had done the right thing in renting it. She suddenly realised that the painter was looking at her as though expecting an answer to some question.

'Did you say something?'

'Twice, lassie. I wanted tae know about your name above the door.'

She looked at him blankly for a moment, then remembered that that had been one of the first things she had written at the top of her list – a list she had left lying on her desk at the garage.

'I'd forgotten about that.'

'I thought ye had,' the man said drily. 'Now – what sort of letterin', and what d'ye want it tae say?'

All the pleasure had gone out of the move, Elspeth thought when the man had departed after agreeing to start work the following day, and to call in someone he knew to put the back yard to rights. Rachel and the little girls would be happy in the snug flat, Kirsty and Peggy would enjoy the spaciousness of their new workplace, and now there would be room for another desk and another typist. Thanks to her father's generosity she had a loan large enough to accommodate her plans for expansion.

She looked out at the busy street, so unlike the quiet area where the garage was located, and knew why she had suddenly lost interest in the move. In Hamilton Street she might go for days or even weeks without seeing Thomas. She would have no reason to go to the garage, and that would probably suit him, for he hadn't as much as glanced at her since the previous night.

351

A church clock chimed as she was locking the door. She had stayed longer than she had intended, and it was too late to return to the garage. She might as well go back to Mearns Street.

Flora was crashing pots about in the kitchen, her features gathered into a tight knot, her body almost throwing off sparks. As soon as Elspeth went in, the woman rounded on her.

'You've got a nerve, walkin' in here as if ye owned the place!'

'What?'

'Don't play the innocent with me, miss. I can see through ye, even if others can't – breakin' up our Rachel's marriage and makin' her the laughin' stock of the town!'

'Aunt Flora, you saw the mess her face was in. Everyone saw it. You surely don't want her to stay with a man who'd treat her like that?'

'A marriage should only concern the two folk that's wed tae each other. "For better or for worse." Rachel made the vows, and it's her duty tae keep them.'

'Bob made vows as well. He vowed to care for her,' Elspeth pointed out, and her aunt glared.

'Bob Cochran was a decent enough man when our Rachel married him. If anythin's gone wrong between them she's tae blame as much as him.'

'Bob Cochran,' said Elspeth clearly, 'is a weakling who needs drink and a woman to bully before he can pretend to be a man.'

'Ye know an awful lot for someone who couldnae even keep her own sweetheart. Ye've never forgiven our Mattie for takin' Kenneth away from ye, have ye? Ye've been spoilin' tae cause trouble in this family ever since.'

'Aunt Flora, that's not true and you know it. I've never wished Mattie and Kenneth anything but well.'

Flora had worked herself up into a frenzy. 'Sniffin' round

that Forbes Cameron just because he's got money! I don't know what yer mother would say if she could see what ye've turned intae! She was an angel, and God knows I did my best tae raise ye tae be like her, but it's been an uphill battle all these years. And how dae ye show yer gratitude for all me and Henry's done for ye? Ye talk Rachel intae makin' fools of us in front of the whole town!'

'I'm grateful to you for taking me in, and I've always done my best to please you, Aunt Flora. But I've always known that you didn't want me.'

'That's what I mean – ingratitude!' Flora shrieked, her rage going out of control. 'It's that wastrel of a father of yours – he's turned yer head altogether since he's come here. Not that it was hard tae dae, for ye've always been his daughter, rotten tae the core!'

Years of resentment had broken through, and now her hatred filled the room, pushing against the walls and stifling the breath in Elspeth's lungs, so that she could only stare at the older woman in stunned silence.

'An' look at what's happened tae our Lachlan, runnin' off after that whore that flaunts hersel' on the stage for all tae see – it was you that encouraged him, and you that got the two of them together—'

At last Elspeth found the energy to turn and stumble from the room. Ranting on, Flora followed. Elspeth shut the bedroom door on the older woman's crimson face, then pushed the one and only chair beneath the door handle which twisted back and forth. Thwarted, Flora McDonald banged on the closed door, screaming abuse, the words running into each other. As Elspeth began to gather up her belongings with shaking hands and push them into the battered old case which one of the boys had used when they went off to the army, she heard the outer door open, then Henry asking, 'Flora? What's amiss?'

To Elspeth's relief Flora McDonald stopped banging on the

door. 'She's amiss – that ungrateful besom I took in when nobody else wanted her!' One single blow on the door made Elspeth jump nervously. 'Get her out of my house – tell her tae go!'

'Who are ye talkin' about? What besom?'

'That daughter of Satan that's destroyed my family,' Flora screamed.

There was a tentative tap on the door. 'Hullo?'

Elspeth's knees were shaking. She leaned against the door panels. 'Uncle Henry—'

'Don't you talk tae her!'

There was the sound of a scuffle, then Flora started to cry with loud, harsh tearing sobs. Beneath the noise, Elspeth heard Henry murmuring soothingly and coaxing her along to the kitchen. The door closed but Elspeth waited, afraid to venture out in case Flora came back.

Five minutes later knuckles tapped gently on the door. 'Ellie?' Henry McDonald whispered. 'Let me in, hen.' She had never been so glad to see his sturdy, stolid bulk. His hair was tousled, his face almost grey. 'Are ye all right, lass?'

'I'm fine,' she told him through chattering teeth. 'How's Aunt Flora?'

'I've never seen her like this – but I knew somethin' was comin' on her, for she's not been hersel' for a while. She's quietened down now.' His eyes fell on the bag in her arms. 'Ye're leavin'?'

'I can't stay here, can I?'

'Where'll ye go?'

If the quarrel had happened a few days earlier she would have gone straight to Thomas, but now that avenue of escape was closed. Nor could she involve Granjan – that would only force the old woman to take sides between her daughter and Elspeth.

'My father's got a spare room I can use. What'll you do?'

'I'll send a neighbour's bairn tae fetch Flora's ma. She'll

354

know what's best.' As Elspeth opened the main door he put a hand on her shoulder. 'Take care, lass.'

'It's you that needs to do that, Uncle Henry.'

'I'll be fine – and so will she,' he said sturdily.

Duncan Crombie himself opened the door, his eyebrows rising as he saw his daughter standing in the tiny porch, a battered old suitcase clutched in both arms, her face white as a sheet.

'My dear girl, what's happened?'

'I've come to live with you,' said Elspeth, and burst into tears.

Although her father and his housekeeper did all they could to make Elspeth feel at home, she found it hard to settle down. Her new room was bright and spacious and comfortable, but she couldn't forget that if things had gone as she had originally planned she would have been able to live alone in the flat above the shop. Now that the flat was earmarked for Rachel and her children, Elspeth had no option but to stay with her father for the time being, much to his delight.

After her outburst, Flora had alarmed the entire family by taking to her bed for the first time in her life. Janet Docherty moved into Elspeth's former bedroom to nurse her daughter, who lay flat on her back in the wall-bed, staring at the ceiling and taking no interest in life.

The doctor was called in and prescribed an iron tonic to build up her strength, and the removal of all her remaining teeth.

'He says they might be poisonin' her system,' Janet reported to Elspeth. 'But our Flora just gave him one of her looks, then shut her mouth tight and stared back at the ceiling. It'll take a better man than Dr McKee tae open that mouth and take the teeth from it.'

Lachlan, who was working near Glasgow that week, was contacted, and travelled to Greenock with Kenneth and Mattie for a family consultation. He bounded into Thomas's garage room and gave Rachel and Elspeth hugs that almost crushed them.

'It's good to see you both again – and to see Greenock, though I've got no regrets about leaving the place.' He had put on weight, most of it muscle, and had regained all his pre-war vigour, but now it was tempered with maturity and a purposeful air. Studying him, Elspeth saw that Lachlan looked as though he fitted perfectly into his own skin and his own personality, with none of the boneless gawkiness of his youth, or the heartbreaking timidity the war had stamped on him.

'Is Lena with you?'

'She wasn't able to get away – she's almost top of the bill now,' he reported proudly. 'I can only stay for two days myself, for we're moving to Edinburgh at the weekend and I'll be needed.'

'Have you seen Mam?' Rachel asked anxiously.

'We all went straight to the house from the station.' Mattie, bulky in the sixth month of pregnancy, cast an envious sidelong glance at Elspeth's royal-blue hip-length jacket over a slim-fitting cream dress.

The excitement and pleasure vanished from Lachlan's face, leaving it still and shadowed. 'Poor wee Mam – I never thought to see her looking so pathetic and helpless, lying in her bed in the middle of the day.'

Henry and Janet arrived just then, having left Flora in a neighbour's care so that they could join in the family conference, and the excitement of meeting up again abated as they settled down to discuss the reason for their gathering.

Rachel had taken her mother's illness badly. 'It's my fault,' she told the others wretchedly. 'It's me leaving Bob and defying her when she told me to go back to him that did it.'

'From what I hear, you did the right thing,' Lachlan said at once, while Mattie chimed in, 'The only thing. No man should be allowed to strike his own wife!'

356

Henry, his normally cheerful face suddenly old, put an arm about his elder daughter's shoulders. 'It's not your fault, hen. Ye were quite right tae leave him. If I'd only known about this sooner ye'd have left him long since.' He looked around the group. 'Bob's goin' from bad tae worse, drinkin' most of the time. If he doesnae watch out he'll be turned off from his job. I've tried tae get him tae see sense, but there's no talkin' tae him.'

'If anyone's to blame for Aunt Flora's condition it's me,' Elspeth pointed out. 'I'm the one she quarrelled with just before she fell ill.'

She found an unexpected ally in Thomas. 'I'd say that it's her own temper that's finally turned in on her. Mam's always been used to ruling our lives, and now that we've grown and gone our own ways she misses being able to dominate us. She's brought this on herself.'

'Thomas!' Mattie was shocked. 'It's your own mother you're talking about!'

'I know, but I'm only speaking my mind.' His glance at his father was half apologetic, half defiant. 'This is mebbe hard for you to hear, Da, but it's the way I see it.'

Henry nodded his grey head. 'I cannae deny that yer mam has a temper. It's somethin' I've always accepted, for it's just part of the way she is. It's mebbe the only way she has of showin' she cares. But I know it was hard at times on the rest of ye.' He looked round the circle of faces. 'Especially you, Thomas. I'll always regret that, but it's too late now tae do anythin' about it.'

'Far too late,' Thomas agreed, his face suddenly grim with bitter memories. There was an awkward silence, then Kenneth did his best to bring a note of optimism to the meeting.

'As far as I can gather from Dr McKee there's little physically wrong with her. What she needs most is a good rest.'

'I think she's on her way back to her old self already.' The mischievous smile that had been missing for so many years began to break through Lachlan's solemnity. 'She managed to rouse herself enough to tell me that it was time I settled down and got back to the shipyards.'

'Kenneth's right,' Granjan said briskly. 'All she needs is rest and looking after for a wee while. And some plain, nourishing food.'

Henry looked hurt. 'When did I ever deny her the money tae buy good food?'

'It's nothin' tae do with that,' his mother-in-law told him briskly. 'Women who raise families never eat properly – they're more inclined tae feed themselves from what's left on other folk's plates. They're like rubbish tips, but it's all part of bein' a wife and mother.'

'Are you all right, Da?' Thomas suddenly asked, reaching across the table to put a hand on his father's arm. 'There's nothing to worry about. Kenneth's right – she needs a rest, and once she's had that she'll be right as rain.'

'I know that. Don't worry about us, laddie, ye've got enough tae do with keeping this place goin'.' Henry looked at those who had been away for a while, and added proudly, 'Our Thomas has done a grand job. He'll be owner of his own garage afore he's finished.'

After that, the business over and everyone more at ease about Flora, they settled down to the serious work of catching up on each other's news.

Tomorrow, far too soon, Lachlan and Mattie and Kenneth would return to their own lives, but they would all, those who left and those who stayed, retain a little of the rekindled warmth of their relationships with each other, Elspeth thought, looking at their animated faces.

Flora McDonald's breakdown had served one very useful purpose – it had brought her family together again.

36

Two days after Lachlan and Kenneth and Mattie left Greenock, a horse-drawn wagon clattered to a standstill in front of the garage house to be loaded with furniture for Hamilton Street.

'I never realised we'd gathered up so much stuff,' Peggy lamented, opening yet another drawer to find it filled with papers and notebooks.

'Folk are like magpies,' Kirsty told her. 'Put it all into different boxes, so that it doesn't get mixed up.'

With Thomas's permission, Joe was pressed into carrying boxes downstairs to the waiting cart. Kirsty's daughter and Rachel's little girls, excited by all the activity, tried to accompany him, weaving dangerously round his legs, and Rachel was forced to round them up and remove them from under his feet.

'They're no trouble,' Joe assured her breathlessly, staggering out of the office under the weight of a pile of boxes. 'I'm just worried about their own safety, for I'd not like tae see them trip and fall down the stairs.'

'If you ask me,' Peggy remarked to Elspeth when Joe and Rachel were both safely out of the way, 'Joe's got a fancy for your Rachel – and she likes him too.' She tossed her head. 'After what she's been through she's entitled to some happiness with someone else.'

'But she's married. D'you mean she should get a divorce?'

Kirsty asked, wide-eyed. Not many people in Greenock got divorced.

'She's still young, and Joe's a good man. He dotes on those bairns too—' Kirsty swiftly changed the subject as Rachel returned, her eyes shining with excited anticipation. Even with her hair tied up in a scarf she looked pretty, Elspeth thought. It was understandable that Joe was attracted to her. And Peggy was right – surely Rachel deserved some happiness after what she'd been through. Mebbe a divorce wasn't out of the question.

Carrying down a box filled with pens and pencils and ink bottles and paper a few moments later she almost bumped into Thomas, who was ushering out a client.

'I'll take these.'

'I can manage. You don't want to get your good suit all dusty,' she pointed out, but he took the box from her arms.

As he stowed it on the wagon, she lingered in the doorway, using her handkerchief to remove a slight smear from the brass plate, which was to be unscrewed in the morning. There was no need for it in Hamilton Street, where her name was painted above the door, but she intended to keep it safe forever.

'A car sale?' she asked as Thomas returned.

'I hope so. How's the move going?'

'We'll finish it tomorrow.'

'The place'll be quiet without the lot of you running in and out.'

'I wish we weren't going, Thomas,' Elspeth said impulsively, and for a brief moment their eyes met. Then his were veiled.

'I think it's for the best,' he said quietly.

'I don't—'

He held a hand up. 'Ellie, I don't want to lose your friendship. Leave it at that,' he said, and after a long, difficult moment she bit back the rebellious words flooding to her lips and nodded.

'Neither do I.'

Then they went their separate ways, Thomas to his room to change into his working clothes, Elspeth to climb the stairs, the now-familiar ache, lodged uncomfortably somewhere near her heart, worse than ever.

The opening of the new office was marked with a party on the premises, followed in the evening by a dinner held in Elspeth's honour by Forbes' parents, and attended by Duncan and several of the area's businessmen.

'Forbes and his father thought of inviting them for your benefit, my dear,' Mrs Cameron murmured confidentially as she led Elspeth to a bedroom to take off her coat and brush her hair. 'They're all influential people – they may well bring business your way.'

'I hope so.' Elspeth sat down at the dressing table and studied her face critically. She had learned to use make-up discreetly – a very thin film of powder, a touch of pale pink lipstick to highlight her mouth.

'That's such a pretty dress. I like periwinkle blue – and it matches your eyes perfectly. I can't tell you how pleased my husband and I are about you and Forbes, my dear,' Mrs Cameron went on. 'Every mother likes to see her son settled.' Then, with an arch twinkle in her eyes, she added, 'As you'll find out for yourself one day.'

'Forbes and I are good friends, Mrs Cameron, nothing more.'

'There I go again, jumping to conclusions! I know nothing's been decided, Elspeth, but perhaps one day . . .?'

Elspeth smiled and murmured something noncommittal as she ran a comb through her hair, which now clung to the shape of her head and fell in soft feathers round her face.

As she and her hostess walked into the drawing room, Forbes came forward to meet them, his eyes signalling his approval of her simple tubular dress and its silver lace over-bodice.

'The best-dressed woman in the room,' he murmured. 'And without doubt the most successful. Come and meet everyone.'

The dinner was superb, but only part of Elspeth's mind was on the food she ate and the conversation around her. The other part was looking ahead to the following day, the first in the new office. She had advertised for another typist, and hoped that there would be at least a few applications.

While listening with apparent interest to someone enthusing over a play that had recently been staged in Greenock, she ran over the list of things that had been done that day. Everything was in order for the morning, and Rachel and the children were comfortably settled in their new home. As the dinner party prevented Elspeth herself from looking in on them that evening, Joe had promised to call on his way home from the garage to make sure that they had everything they needed. Not that Hamilton Street was on his way, but that wouldn't worry Joe, who lived alone and had little to go home to.

She glanced up the length of the table and saw her father talking animatedly to an attractive woman by his side, who hung on his every word. Duncan Crombie adored social events. He had so much energy and such enthusiasm for life that sometimes Elspeth wondered how long it would be before he tired of Greenock and wanted to move on. He had indicated to her several times his desire to travel, suggesting that she should accompany him.

'See something of the world before you settle down,' he had advised.

'I have settled down. I'm quite content here.'

'Nonsense,' he had retorted. 'How can you know you're settled until you've tried other places and met other people?'

Once, he had spoken like that in front of Forbes, who had flown into a panic in case Elspeth gave in to her father and went off with him. The gulf between the two men was gradually widening, and Elspeth was uncomfortably aware that she herself stood in the middle, courted by both of them.

After the meal the guests roamed the downstairs rooms freely, their voices rising and falling. Forbes escorted Elspeth round the drawing room to make what he called useful introductions.

The warmth and the wine she had had during dinner, coupled with the day's excitement, had made her sleepy. The curtains hadn't yet been drawn over the long drawing room windows and it was dark outside, the glass reflecting movement and colour from within the room. She smothered a yawn and glanced at a clock. It was almost ten o'clock. In another hour, she decided, she would make her excuses and leave.

Forbes was making his way over to her, a prosperous-looking man by his side. Elspeth pinned a polite smile to her lips, but before the two men reached her a maidservant touched Forbes on the arm, murmuring to him. He halted, frowned, asked a question. The woman shook her head and pointed to the hallway, and with a brief word to his companion Forbes turned away.

Elspeth followed, her curiosity roused. At sight of the police constable standing in the hall her blood froze and memories of the night the policeman had called at Mearns Street to tell them that Thomas had been beaten unconscious flooded her mind. This constable, like the other, looked solemn and carried his high helmet beneath one arm. She hurried across the carpet and caught at Forbes' elbow.

'What's happened?'

His face was dazed with disbelief. 'This fellow says the garage is on fire—'

'Thomas! Is Thomas there? Is he all right?' She let Forbes go and clutched at the policeman, who shook his head.

'I don't know any names, miss, but I b'lieve there was someone found on the premises.'

'I must go,' Forbes said. The maidservant was already on her way back from the cloakroom with his coat. 'Tell my parents that—'

'I'm coming with you.'

'Elspeth, you can't do anything to help!'

She was already running to the cloakroom, for there was no time to go upstairs to fetch her own coat. She took the nearest garment from its hook and struggled into it as she hurried outside. Forbes was already getting into his car while the policeman pedalled off down the driveway on his bicycle. Hampered a little by the borrowed coat, which was far too large for her and smelled of cigars, Elspeth reached the car and climbed in just as the engine roared into life.

A cloud of oily smoke shot through with streaks of fire hung above the garage. The red glow of flames nearer ground level flickered and danced over the street and the buildings beyond. A fair-sized crowd had gathered, and a fire wagon stood at the kerb.

'The house is standing – it's the garage itself that's burning,' Elspeth heard Forbes say as the car came to a standstill. She threw herself from it and pushed through the gawping people, her muscles and bones strangely lethargic, as though she was struggling through deep water.

'You can't come any closer, miss.' A policeman barred her way. 'It's too dangerous.'

'I'm the owner,' Forbes said breathlessly from her side.

'In that case, follow me, sir.' The man turned, and Elspeth hooked a hand into Forbes' coat pocket to make sure that she wouldn't be left behind. His own hand slid into the pocket to close over hers.

'It'll be all right,' she heard him say reassuringly, but in the red glow from the flames she saw that he was as apprehensive as she was.

They were led across the road to where a group of men huddled together a safe distance from the blaze. Elspeth glimpsed a fireman, axe in hand, running round the side of the house, and others handling a hose. From this vantage point she could also see an ambulance wagon waiting further down the street, well away from the conflagration.

'I'm afraid we're not going to be able to save your garage, sir, or any of the vehicles in it,' someone was saying to Forbes, 'not with all that petrol about. But the house is all right and the fire's beginning to come under control.'

'Damn the garage, man, my manager was in the house,' Forbes said impatiently. 'Is he safe?'

'My men searched the house, but there wasn't anyone there. They've found two men in the garage, though. I can't tell you yet what condition they're in. The medical people are with them now.'

Fear caught at Elspeth's throat and her grip on Forbes' hand tightened. 'Two?' she heard him ask, then his face, stained crimson by the flames, as though covered with blood, swung round towards her. 'Who—?'

'Joe.' To her own ears her voice sounded strange, as though someone else was speaking. 'He must have stayed later than he meant.'

'Oh my God!' Forbes said, just as a group of men appeared through the smoke, two stretchers being handled among them.

'Thomas!' Elspeth tried to run across the street, but someone held her back. 'Best to leave them to get on with their work, miss,' a voice told her, while Forbes said swiftly, 'We'll go to the hospital.'

As she followed him back to the car she realised that the fingers of one hand were scrabbling at the lapel of the thick leather coat she had dragged on during her rush from the Camerons' house. For a moment she couldn't understand why, then she remembered the pebble brooch, pinned to the collar of her own coat.

She had been trying to clutch at it for comfort, as she always did in moments of stress. But this time, the brooch wasn't there to reassure her that all would be well.

*

It turned out that when the fire started Joe was sitting in the flat above the Hamilton Street office, chatting comfortably to Rachel. Thomas McDonald, found in the yard where the blast from an explosion within the workshop had thrown him, had been badly burned. Bob Cochran, inside the workshop at the time, had died when it blew up.

Elspeth would gladly have spent all her time sitting by Thomas's bed in the hospital, but Flora, who had recovered with startling suddenness on hearing that one of her own had been hurt, was there each time Elspeth went into the ward, straight-backed and stony-faced in an upright chair. Uncomfortable in her presence, Elspeth was forced to cut her own visits back. There was plenty for her to do, but she went about all her tasks feeling as though she had been split into two people. One of them was in the hospital with Thomas, the other dealt with the office and with Rachel, shattered by sudden widowhood. Mrs Cameron, who loved children and had told Elspeth frequently that although she herself had not been blessed with the large family she had desired, she hoped to have a lot of grandchildren, took Mary and Pearl over to let Rachel cope with the suddenness of Bob's death.

'I never thought he'd – mebbe if I'd stayed,' she said to Elspeth and Granjan, her face blotched with tears. 'I should never have left him!'

'It was the only thing ye could have done, lassie,' Janet Docherty told her. 'Ye've heard what the polis said – the man was so drunk that he didnae know what he was doin'. An' he'd just been turned away from the shipyard. Ye might as well say that they were tae blame for takin' his work away from him. If that had happened, an' you were still with him, there's no knowing what he'd have done tae ye.' She shivered, holding Rachel close. 'It might be you and the bairns bein' buried at the end of the week, and not Bob, God rest him.'

Bob's drunken rage and his thirst for revenge had centred instead on Thomas, who had given him such a humiliating beating at the shipyard. Venturing into the ward on the day after Bob's funeral, Elspeth was startled to see Thomas's bed unattended, the bedside chair empty. He was lying back on the pillows, eyes closed, bandaged hands lying limply on the bedspread. She perched on the edge of the chair supplied for visitors, anxious not to disturb him. When he was first taken in almost all of his face had been swathed in bandages; now, only one side was covered, and the bandages had been removed from his neck and chest, revealing red but healing skin.

It was the first chance she had had to study him, and now her eyes devoured him as though trying to imprint the memory of him forever in her mind. His fair curly hair had, amazingly, been spared by the flames though his lashes and part of his eyebrows had been burned off, giving what could be seen of his face a strangely naked look.

With a twist of the heart she recalled the night he had kissed her in the garage house. Gaslight from the street outside had caught the tips of his lashes then, making them sparkle with gold light.

In repose he looked vulnerable against the crisp white of the hospital pillows. She desperately wanted to touch him, to brush her fingertips or, better still, her lips over his sleeping face, but she held the yearning in check. Which was just as well, since she found, on transferring her gaze from his mouth to his eyes, that they, in turn, were studying her.

'Did I wake you?'

'I wasn't asleep. I heard you coming and I thought it was Mam. She sits and stares and won't answer any questions. I'll be glad to get out of here.'

'When'll that be?'

'Next week, they say. I'll mebbe have a bit of scarring on my face and on the back of my hands, but I'll be fine.' A shadow came into his eyes. 'It was Bob's funeral yesterday, wasn't it?'

367

'Yes.' It had been a sorry affair, with only Rachel and Forbes and herself sharing the graveside with Bob's parents and his sister and brother-in-law. There had been no gathering afterwards; each group had gone silently away, with nothing to say to the other.

'How's Rachel?'

'She's taken Bob's death badly. Granjan's been staying with her.'

'It's a terrible thing to say about a man who's dead, but she's better off with him out of her life once and for all.'

'What happened?'

He wrinkled his brow. 'I don't mind much about it – I was in my room and I heard a noise round the back. When I went into the workshop Bob was splashing petrol around the place. I went for him, and he threw the can at me and knocked me off my feet. I must have hit my head when I fell, for the next thing I knew there was fire all round and someone was dragging me along the ground.' He shook his head. 'You'd have thought the man would at least have had the sense to get clear before he started the fire.'

'He was very drunk, seemingly. Mebbe he didn't know what was happening.'

'If so, it would be for the best, poor creature.'

She shivered, and changed the subject. 'Forbes says he's going ahead and buying that other garage he's thinking of, and you'll manage it.'

'Aye, I know. He looked in this morning to tell me.'

She began to say something else, but the words seemed to clump together into a large ball that stuck in her throat. Thomas's face misted then shimmered.

'What's amiss? Is there something they haven't told me yet?'

She swiped at her eyes with one hand. 'It's you. You could have died.'

'But I didn't.'

'You could have! And then I'd not have had the chance to tell you—'

'Ellie,' he said wearily. 'Nothing's changed, and nothing will change.'

'Of course things have changed.' Tears gave way to anger. 'Everything's changed. You almost died! Does that not make you give some thought to your future – our future?'

'My future lies in getting another garage started. Yours is with your agency, and mebbe with Forbes Cameron.' For a moment their eyes locked and to her despair she saw the same stubborn determination in his as before. Then his gaze slid past her and he gave a muffled groan then went limp, his lids closing as Flora McDonald arrived at the other side of the bed.

'I thought you'd be busy with yer fancy new office.'

'I just looked in. He's sleeping.'

'He's always sleepin',' Flora said with a sniff. 'It's this place – it doesnae agree with him.'

She looked pointedly at the chair, and Elspeth relinquished it and left.

37

To Flora's annoyance Thomas refused to convalesce at Mearns Street when he was discharged from hospital. He went straight back to his own home, beside the blackened ruins of the garage he had worked so hard to build up, and he and Forbes immediately became absorbed in plans for the new garage, on the shore road between Greenock and Port Glasgow.

Elspeth rarely saw him. She too had thrown herself into her work, taking on another typist earmarked for temporary work in offices. Her belief that the agency would do well in the heart of the town proved to be correct and her decision to return to letter-writing brought in a fairly steady stream of clients. Peggy, a good letter-writer, shared the task with her.

The rivalry between Forbes Cameron and Duncan Crombie continued as Duncan became increasingly bored with life in Greenock, and pressed Elspeth to sell the business and travel with him.

'Can't you see what he's up to, Elspeth?' Forbes asked. 'He wants you all to himself, and he doesn't care what sort of sacrifice you might have to make. You wouldn't be allowed to be your own person.'

'And could I be my own person if I stayed here and married you?' she asked drily, and he flushed.

'That's different – you know that I'd do anything to make you happy. And you've known me longer – I'm not a fly-by-night who's scarcely been here long enough to take my hat off.'

Often in the evenings she escaped from them both to Granjan's placid little flat, where there were no demands made on her other than making toast or buttering hot home-made pancakes. A month after the fire she found Thomas there one evening; the skin on one side of his face was still red and tender-looking and although the backs of his hands would always be scarred he had retained full use of them.

He didn't stay for long after she arrived. 'He's lookin' well, our Thomas,' Janet said as she returned from seeing him out. 'Havin' that new garage tae hold his interest has helped.'

Elspeth, staring into the fire and wrapped in her own thoughts, said nothing, and Janet lowered herself into her chair with a grunt of relief, turning her skirts back to let the fire warm her knees.

'The nights are fair drawin' in – the bairns'll be round the doors lookin' for their Hallowe'en next week.' Then, with a sidelong look, 'When are ye goin' tae stop pinin' for the man, lassie, an' do somethin' about it?'

'What?' Elspeth was startled out of her reverie. 'D'you mean Forbes?'

Janet Docherty tutted. 'Of course not! Oh, he's a nice enough laddie, but he's not for you. I'm talkin' about Thomas – an' don't try tae tell me I'm haverin', for I've seen the way of it ever since he came back from the army.'

'That's nonsense!'

'I mebbe talk a lot of rubbish at times, but never nonsense. I did think when he met Aileen, rest her soul, that that was an end tae it for you and him, but as it turned out I was wrong there.'

'Thomas has told me that he won't marry again. He means it.'

'So ye've discussed it?'

'No, we—' Elspeth stopped short and felt her face warm. She knew that it wasn't caused by the fire.

'He always was stubborn. So are you – that's what makes

the two of ye so suited.' Janet Docherty leaned across the rag rug and put a swollen-veined, work-roughened hand on Elspeth's knee. 'But it seems tae me that you've been short on yer usual stubbornness over this business. Lassie, if something's worth the havin', it's worth fightin' for.'

'I've tried.'

'Tuts – if ye havenae won it means ye've no' tried all that hard. You're the only person that can get ye what ye want. Nob'dy'll dae it for ye.'

Elspeth stared into the flames. 'Mebbe I'd be as well marrying Forbes, or giving in to my father and going away from here.'

'Have I not already told ye that he's no' the right one for ye? Oh, he'd make ye happy enough, and so would Duncan Crombie, for they both care for ye in their own ways and they've both got the money tae spend on ye. But will either one of them bring ye contentment? That's what ye've got tae ask yersel'. Contentment's gettin' what's right for ye, no' just gettin' by.'

Elspeth snuggled into her warm coat and watched the moonlight tracing a path across the dark, almost still river. On the opposite shore, houses and streetlights looked like jewels strewn over the black velvet of the hills. It was a clear, cold night in early December, and Forbes was driving her home along the coast road after an evening spent with friends of his.

As they drew up at the house and she moved to open the door he put a hand out to stop her. 'Let's just sit here for a minute.'

'D'you not want to come in for a cup of tea? My father'll be expecting us.'

'I want to say something, and it's not for his ears.'

Her stomach fluttered, then tensed. She had been expecting another marriage proposal from him, but had thought that he would choose Christmas or possibly the New Year. She hadn't been prepared for it to be so soon.

He sensed the slight withdrawal. 'What's the matter? Are you cold? There's a rug in the back. Or, even better—' He drew her towards him and kissed her, his mouth moving gently on hers, the moustache he had recently grown rough on her upper lip. The scent of the hair oil he used mingled with cigarette smoke and the car's leather upholstery to produce a familiar, pleasant, essentially secure aroma. Security, Elspeth thought, could be very important. Not that Granjan would agree.

When they finally drew apart he shifted slightly in his seat, clearing his throat and staring out through the windscreen. 'Elspeth, I've – heard something about your father.'

'Heard?'

'If you must know, I've been making enquiries. I know I'd no business to do so,' he added hurriedly as she started to speak. 'But he's only just come into your life and I felt it was right that somebody should look after your interests. I discussed it with my father, and he agreed.'

'But you didn't discuss it with me.' She was furious with him for interfering, and for broaching the subject in a voice so serious that it caused her flesh to cringe with apprehension and anxiety.

'You're still very young—'

'I'm old enough to run my own business, old enough to look after my own life!'

'D'you want to hear what I have to say?'

She didn't. She wanted to get out of the car and walk away from him and from Greenock and from everyone. She wanted to put her head under the blankets then wake up to find that the world had been set to rights. She reached up to touch the pebble brooch; she wanted to go back to the day Thomas had given it to her, the day of her thirteenth birthday dumpling.

Instead, reluctantly, she listened to what Forbes had to say, then crept quietly into the hall in the vain hope that Duncan Crombie might have decided, for once, not to stay up for her return.

He appeared from the drawing room as she eased the front door shut. 'Is young Cameron not with you?'

'Not tonight.'

'Come and tell me all about your evening.'

'I'd rather just go to bed. I've got a bit of a headache.' It wasn't a lie; there was a tight metal band round her temples.

'Do you want something for it?'

'I just need my bed.'

'Elspeth,' Duncan Crombie asked with an edge to his voice as she started to climb the stairs, 'Cameron hasn't upset you, has he?'

'No, I'm just tired. Goodnight.' She escaped to the privacy of her room, closing the door with relief. She had a great deal to think about before morning.

Crombie's handsome face wore a worried frown when the two of them met at the breakfast table.

'You don't look at all well. You'd better go back to bed and I'll call a doctor.'

'I'm fine, please don't fuss.'

He looked more closely, and his face darkened. 'Cameron did upset you last night. What happened?'

Elspeth poured herself a cup of tea with a steady hand. 'He asked me to marry him.' Then, as his eyes went blank, 'And I turned him down, once and for all, because he told me that he'd been making enquiries about you.'

'He did what? The young pup!' he exploded, half rising from the table.

'Sit down please, Father.'

He did as she asked. 'What did he tell you?'

'That when your uncle died six months after you went away he left you quite a lot of money in spite of what happened between you and my mother. In fact, it was because you went away – because you did as he told you – that he kept you in his will. Forbes says' – she set the teapot down gently –

'that you inherited enough to support my mother and me. But in spite of that you didn't come back to Greenock.'

The colour drained from his face and the piece of toast he was about to butter was put back on to his plate. 'I – I wrote to Maisie, at her parents' home, asking her to come to England. When she didn't reply I thought—'

'You must have known that her mother would intercept the letter and probably destroy it. You should have come back for her.' Elspeth fisted her hands on the table. 'For us.'

'I – you have to understand that I was very young, Elspeth, younger than you are now. I had no way of knowing if Maisie would take me back. I had no choice but to leave – my uncle held the purse strings, and he arranged the job in England for me with a lawyer he knew.' He swallowed hard, then went on, 'I don't suppose Cameron told you that my uncle had already arranged with the lawyer to buy a junior partnership for me once I'd served my time. The money left to me in his will was part of the arrangement. If I'd returned to Greenock I would have lost it all. I still wouldn't have been able to support you and Maisie.'

'So you put yourself first and kept the money, and left my mother to cope as best she could.'

'I told you – I thought that her parents would look after her – and you – if I was out of the way. And I did come back to look for you, to atone for what I'd done to the two of you all those years ago.'

He leaned across the table earnestly. 'Elspeth, we've only just found each other. Now's the time for us to start again, together. Don't let Cameron's mischief-making come between us – that's what he wants. Once he gets me out of your life, he'll marry you. That's what he plans. You deserve better than him, my dear. Sell the agency and come away with me.'

Elspeth had been making a pretence of drinking her tea. Now she put the cup down gently and got to her feet. 'I'm not my mother. She's dead, and nothing you can do for me will make up for the wrong you did her.'

'Elspeth—'

'I'll come and collect my things when I've found somewhere to stay,' she said steadily from the doorway. 'As for the loan you made me to rent the shop and the flat—'

All his confident charm had gone. He looked old and defeated. It would have been easy to pity him, but Elspeth knew of the dangers that lay in that direction. 'I don't want it back!'

'I wasn't going to offer it. I'm going to do as you wanted in the first place and accept it as a gift – for my mother's sake,' she said, and went out of the house without a backward glance.

She attended to her office duties as usual throughout the day, glad that there were no prospective clients to see, and worked on into the evening, until she was sure that Thomas would be home.

He answered the door in shirt and trousers, blinking his surprise. 'What are you doing here?'

'I want to ask a favour.'

'Did you forget your key?' he asked over his shoulder as she followed him into his room.

'I gave it back to Forbes.'

The room was neat and clean, as usual. An empty plate with knife and fork on it stood on the table, together with a mug.

'I was just finishing my dinner,' Thomas said, following her glance. 'D'you want some tea?' He reached for his jacket, hanging over the back of his chair.

'No, I want you to come to my – to Duncan Crombie's house with me to collect my things.'

He paused in the act of slipping one arm into a jacket sleeve. 'You're moving out? Have you found somewhere else to stay?'

'I'm sharing with Rachel and the bairns for the time being.' She told him, in detail, what Forbes had found out about Duncan Crombie, and he heard her out in silence, then said,

'It takes all sorts of folk to make the world, Ellie.'

'I know that, and mebbe one day I'll forgive him for what he did to my mother. But I'll not stay under his roof.'

'What're you going to do? Marry Forbes?'

She looked him in the eye. 'D'you think I should?'

His gaze dropped. 'You could do worse. He'd be able to give you everything you want, not like—' He paused, then said carefully, 'Not like most men in this town.'

'Money's not everything.'

A muscle jumped in Thomas's jaw, just below the livid scar that now bisected one cheek. 'Mebbe not, but it can be very important.'

'Aileen didn't think so, and neither do I. I'm not going to marry Forbes, for I couldn't marry a man who thinks he has the right to pry into other folk's lives. But I can do business with him.' She glanced round the room. The house windows had shattered in the heat from the fire, but they had been replaced, and the old building still stood steady as a rock. 'I'm going to ask him to sell me this place.'

His jaw dropped. 'What on earth—?'

'I need to live somewhere, and I've always liked this house. It should be lived in, properly, by a family. I'm going to see the bank manager tomorrow, then I'll have a word with Forbes. He might be quite glad to get the place off his hands now that he's got a new garage to finance.'

'And what about me?'

'I'd never turn you out on the street. There's room enough for us both, though I'd really like to see this room going back to being a drawing room. I'm sure we could come to some arrangement,' she said sweetly, and understanding began to dawn in his face.

'Ellie, if this is a ploy to force me to—'

'I've no intention of forcing you to do anything, Thomas McDonald, but I've had enough of accepting what other folk say. Granjan told me that if I wanted something badly enough

I should fight for it. And that's what I'm going to do.'

She held his gaze with her own, while her fingers nimbly unfastened the pebble brooch from the lapel of her grey jacket. 'I can never take Aileen's place, but I can give you a different kind of happiness. I want you to think over what I'm saying, and when you get round to admitting that I'm right, I'm going to sell the agency and buy a wee garage where you can look after the motorcars and I can see to your books. We'll mebbe even rebuild this garage, if that's what you want. Here—'

She crossed to where he stood, going up on tiptoe to fasten the brooch to the inside of his lapel, feeling his chest warm and solid beneath her fingers as she did so. 'You can keep it for the next five years if necessary,' she told him, stepping back. 'When you're ready to see sense you don't have to say so, you only have to return the brooch. Now – come and help me to collect my things and take them to Hamilton Street.'

'You're daft, Elspeth Bremner,' he said, as she reached the door.

She smiled at him over her shoulder, and saw his lips twitch in reply.

'I know I am, but I see no reason to change,' she said, and went through the door and out into the dark street, knowing without having to look back that he was just behind her.

She doubted whether it would be another five years before the pebble brooch came back to her, but even if it was, she could afford to wait.

Five years was such a small price to pay for an entire future.

Another Day

This book is dedicated to
Caitlin Rose Mitchell,
who allowed me to use her name,
and to her parents, Pauline and Rory,
with love.

1

As the train drew into Paisley's Gilmour Street Station pandemonium broke out in the Lennox family's compartment. Ewan had sulked throughout the journey because he had been made to travel with his parents and help with the luggage while his brother and sister, gloriously independent, had gone on ahead; now, impatient to be free, he lunged for the door and began wrestling with the handle. Kirsty, somewhat hampered by the weight of the baby fastened securely against her body by a large shawl, screamed at him not to open the door before the train stopped.

Stiff from a warm July day mainly spent sitting in crowded trains, Matt struggled to his feet and began scooping parcels and bags and a shabby, battered suitcase held together by half a ball of string from the overhead luggage rack.

'Lend a hand here, Ewan,' he barked, but the youth was more interested in the station as the train came to a standstill.

'There's Alex – and Caitlin.'

To her great relief Kirsty glimpsed her first-born's red head outside the window. 'They got here all right, then,' she said thankfully. She had fretted all day about Alex and

1

Caitlin, who had been sent ahead early that morning to collect the house key from the lawyer and buy in some bread and milk.

'Of course they got here,' Matt said irritably. 'You fuss too much. If Alex cannae manage at eighteen years of age, God help us all. Ewan!'

The boy, struggling to get the window down, paid no heed.

'I'll help,' Kirsty said, but as she reached up towards the rack the engine of a train about to leave for Glasgow on the adjacent line proclaimed the fact by releasing a blast of steam. The triumphant shriek startled five-year-old Mary, who let out a shrill scream of her own and tried to bury herself in her mother's skirt. Kirsty reeled and almost lost her balance as her daughter's small body slammed against her thigh. She just managed to save herself by clutching at the edge of the rack.

Fergus, eight months old, slumbered on in the folds of the shawl, oblivious to the chaos all around him. Having driven his mother almost frantic by refusing to sleep all day despite his obvious exhaustion, he had finally allowed his eyelids to droop on the last leg of the journey from Falkirk, lying against Kirsty's breast like a hot, limp, soggy, and somewhat smelly, stone.

Alex opened the door from the outside and Ewan immediately jumped down onto the platform, shouldering his stepbrother aside, and made for the engine, deaf to his father's orders to lend a hand.

By the time they had all descended from the train most of their fellow travellers were disappearing through the door where the ticket collector waited.

As her feet touched the platform Kirsty was caught unawares by the wrenching memory of the last time she had been in this station more than eighteen years earlier, banished from Paisley by her father. For a moment her husband and family and even the great noisy, steamy iron train ceased to exist as her mind swept her back over the years to another life. She felt the ache of the bruises her father had inflicted on her, knew again the desolation and sheer terror of being forced, at sixteen years of age, to leave everything she had known behind and go alone into an uncertain future.

'God save us, the train'll be away and the things not out of the guard's van yet,' Matt fussed at her side, and suddenly the wintry days of early 1888 vanished and Kirsty was back in the summer of 1906 with her husband and her family, the ache in her shoulder caused not by the beating her father had given her, but by Fergus's weight in the crook of her arm.

'Is Ewan down at the guard's van?'

'He's gone to look at the engine,' thirteen-year-old Caitlin informed her father as she helped Alex to gather up the parcels.

'He's got no more sense in his head than a sparrow,' Matt fumed at his wife. 'Now ye know why I'd not let him travel ahead with Alex – he'd have gone past Paisley and ended up down at Ayr at the very least. Mary, go and tell him tae get back here and give us a hand!' He snatched up the suitcase and started towards the guard's van, leaving Alex and Caitlin to deal with all the parcels.

'Go on, Mary – do as your father tells you,' Kirsty urged, anxious to save Matt's temper from further irritation. Mary's only response was to tighten her grip on Kirsty's skirt, burying her head in its folds.

'Ach, leave him be, Mam,' Alex advised, balancing the assorted parcels in his arms. 'He'll never hear us and we can manage without him.'

The shabby perambulator that had been second-hand when it was bought for Caitlin had been removed from the guard's van and stood on the platform. With some thought of putting wee Fergus into it so that she could take Alex's parcels and free him to help with the trunk, Kirsty hurried towards it. It wasn't until she reached the perambulator that she recalled with dismay that it had been filled with all the odds and ends that couldn't be accommodated in the trunk or the suitcase or the many bags they had.

Inside the van the guard and Matt were struggling with the large trunk that held most of the Lennox family's belongings. The guard, using one knee to give it a final nudge from his van, reached for his pocket watch. Doors slammed up and down the train's length as embarking passengers settled down.

The trunk thumped onto the platform so hard that Kirsty feared for the china packed in it. She had wrapped each piece carefully in brown paper and had tried to surround it with clothing and bedding, but even so . . .

Backing across the platform, dragging the trunk two-handed, Matt almost fell over the perambulator. 'Someone take that damned thing out of the way,' he snapped irritably, and Caitlin bumped it aside with her hip while Alex put his parcels down on the platform and went to the other side of the trunk. Although he was lean, with scarcely a pick of flesh on him, he was strong; even so, he and his stepfather had a

4

struggle to carry the large old trunk to the exit. Watching them, Kirsty fretted about the strain Matt was putting himself under. He had been troubled with rheumatism throughout the previous winter, and to her mind he still wasn't entirely fit.

'That's too heavy for you, Matt – I'll get a porter.'

'I'll not pay good money tae a porter when I've got lads that can do the job for nothin',' he told her through gritted teeth. 'Caitlin, go and fetch Ewan!'

As she obeyed, the guard, who had disappeared into his van, emerged with a furled green flag. Throwing a swift glance along the length of the train to ensure that the new passengers were safely on board and the doors closed, he consulted his watch again and raised his whistle to lips already pursing to receive it.

Its piercing blast made Kirsty's ears ring and startled Mary into a fit of hysteria. Then, as the train began to lurch forward, a piercing scream came from the opposite platform. A woman stood there, horror etched on her face as she stared across the gap left by the departing train.

'My God,' she shrilled, 'the wean!'

The people on both platforms swung round to look in the direction of her outflung, pointing arm, then from up and down both platforms came wails and cries of anguish as the battered, unattended perambulator rolled slowly but surely towards the edge of the platform, where it teetered for a breath-stopping moment before toppling over, showering the packages that had been packed carefully within its depths to right and left as it went.

It was halfway down when a small shawl-wrapped bundle soared from beneath the hood and spun into the air, shedding its covering as it went.

'The bairn! The poor wee bairn!' the woman on the opposite platform screeched.

A chorus of screams and shouts from the helpless onlookers rang out as the bundle landed on the rails with a sickening, soggy thud. The woman who had first raised the alarm collapsed into the arms of a porter, while the rest of the crowd rushed to the edges of both platforms to gaze in horror at the wreckage strewn over the tracks.

The pale, scrawny carcass of the chicken Kirsty had cooked the night before for her family's first meal in their new home lay on the cinders between the lines, its legs pointing pathetically towards the sky. Beside it the shawl it had been wrapped in for safekeeping flapped feebly in the air like a distress signal.

'Never,' said Matt grimly, limping alongside the cart, 'have I been so affronted! What sort of a way's that tae start a new life – makin' a spectacle of ourselves in front of everybody? And you laughin' like that.' His dark eyes scowled up at Kirsty.

'I couldn't help it,' she apologised for the third or fourth time, wishing, as the cart rumbled through Paisley Cross, that Matt had let her walk to their new home instead of insisting that she and the two little ones should travel in what he called 'comfort'. She felt like a tinker woman, with all her worldly possessions lashed on behind her. The curved handles of the perambulator, which Alex and a porter had rescued from the railway line, nodded above the trunk as though acknowledging the glances of pedestrians on the pavement.

The cart lurched again and she slid towards the end of the

bench until she was almost overhanging the drop to the street below. She clutched Fergus tightly in one arm, fearful that he might slip from her grasp, while the other arm encircled Mary who, when the cart rolled the other way, was in danger of being crushed between her mother and the silent, thickset carter.

Kirsty looked longingly over Matt's head at Alex and Ewan and Caitlin, striding along the footpath, laughing and chattering together in the sunshine and looking incongruous in their thick, heavy clothing. Despite the pleasant July weather Matt had insisted on them all wearing their heavier clothes to save space in the trunk. Kirsty could feel perspiration trickling down the length of her body; she yearned to take off her long grey woollen coat and splash her face and neck with cool water, then unfasten her stays and have a good scratch.

After that she would like to make a cup of tea and sit down with it in a chair that stayed still instead of swinging and swaying and rocking like almost every seat she had occupied during that long day.

Matters were made worse when they left the Cross and started descending the short stretch of St Mirren Brae. Now the cart took on a forward tilt, and Kirsty, convinced that they were all going to topple from the bench and onto the horse's huge swinging behind, had to push the soles of her feet hard against the footboard to maintain her balance. A sudden mental picture of herself and the two youngest finishing their journey on the carthorse's back caused a bubble of laughter to spurt from between her lips. She turned it into a cough then swallowed hard, knowing that Matt would never forgive her if she started giggling again. To subdue her unseemly mirth she cast about for more sobering thoughts and found, as the brae levelled out into Causeyside Street and she began to look around the once-familiar place, that her amusement had already vanished.

She had last travelled through Causeyside Street in a tramcar, but going the other way, towards the station. It had been January, a cold, wintry day that suddenly became so real in her memory that she shivered, caught up again in the heartbreak of her mother's sudden death and the subsequent daily struggle of trying to please her father.

She had known loneliness since, before Matt had come into her life, but it hadn't matched the terrible loneliness of those days, when there had been nobody to care about her except her maternal grandfather, Alexander Jardine, and Sandy, the orphan her father had taken on as his apprentice. In the months following her mother's death they had come to care for each other, she and Sandy, both too young and naive to realise the dangers of caring too much. When Kirsty had fallen pregnant with Sandy's child her father had beaten them both, his rage so great that Sandy had had to be taken to the infirmary, more dead than alive. What had become of him Kirsty didn't know; she herself had been packed off in shame to her aunt in Stirling to await the birth of her baby, which was then to be given for adoption.

She glanced again at Alex, tall and lean, laughing as he strode along the pavement. She had known from first sight of him that she couldn't let him be taken from her and given to strangers. She had run away, fleeing with only the clothes on her back and Alex, named for her grandfather as well as for his own father, in her arms. She had been very fortunate; instead of dying with her baby in a ditch, she had found work

8

with a kindly, childless couple willing to let the two of them live in. Five years later, she had met and married Matt Lennox, a widower with a son, Ewan, a little younger than Alex.

'Ye're away in a dream, woman!' Matt's voice jolted Kirsty back to the present and the heat of the sun through her clothes.

'What?'

'I'm askin' ye has the town changed much since ye were last here?'

'No, not much.'

He grinned up at her. 'We're goin' tae do well here, lass. I can feel it in my bones,' he said, then faced front again, tramping along the gutter by the side of the cart. He was elated – she could tell by the set of his chin and the way he held his shoulders back and his head up despite the exhaustion of the journey.

It was Matt who, when she had finally told him the truth about herself, had nagged her into writing to her father. She had resisted for a while, then, worn down by his insistence, had written a brief note. To her surprise Murray Galbraith had replied and in the ten years since they had exchanged a few scribbled words once a year. But to Matt's disappointment and Kirsty's relief, Murray Galbraith had not invited his daughter and her family to Paisley or expressed any interest in seeing them.

The news that he had died and had left his house and his cabinet-making business to Kirsty had come as an unwelcome shock to her. Paisley and the sad memories it held for her were locked away in her past, and she had had no desire to return to the place. But Matt had reacted angrily to her suggestion that her father's lawyer should be asked to sell the property.

'Of course we're movin' there. After all those years of workin' for other folk I'm finally gettin' the chance tae run my own business. I'd be daft tae let it slip from my fingers!'

'But you're a joiner, Matt, not a cabinet-maker.'

'What's that got tae do with it? Alex is a time-served cabinet-maker, and Ewan's only got another year tae go in the same trade. I'll learn tae be the master easy enough. Now d'ye see how right I was tae put both lads tae that trade?'

He had insisted on apprenticing Alex to a cabinet-maker when the boy left school in the hope that when Murray Galbraith heard of it he would offer the boy employment.

'It would only be right for him tae take his own grandson on and make him his heir,' he had told Kirsty, and had even apprenticed his own son, Ewan, to a cabinet-maker a year later. But to his disappointment, no invitation had come from Paisley. Secretly, Kirsty had been relieved, horrified by the prospect of her Alex suffering under his grandfather's domination as she herself had.

Now, though, just as Alex had finished serving his time, and Ewan had gone into his final year's apprenticeship, Matt had got his reward, she thought sadly. Just then he started sniffing the air. 'What's that smell?'

On the pavement, Alex and Ewan and Caitlin were also sniffing, their brows furrowed as they tried to identify the sweet, tangy, mouth-watering smell. To Kirsty, lifting her face to the sun, it was part of the smell of childhood. She felt her lips curve in a smile. 'It's Robertson's marmalade factory in the Neilston Road. That's Canal Street Station we're just passing – Causeyside Street turns into Neilston Road at the turning just ahead.'

'D'ye tell me? Marmalade?' Matt said, fascinated, and sniffed again. 'It makes me feel hungry. I'll be glad tae get somethin' in my belly.'

They had almost reached the wide junction where Causeyside Street gave way to Neilston Road, with Espedair Street off to the left and Stevenson Street and Calside coming in from the right. The carter pulled on the reins and as the horse swung round into Espedair Street the happy memories the rich aroma of orange marmalade had brought to Kirsty fled at the sight of the tobacconist's shop on the corner. It looked as it always had, but surely, she thought fearfully, Mrs Laidlaw, the scourge of the local children, couldn't still be behind the counter? The perspiration chilled on her at the mere thought of the woman, with the cold merciless eyes that had recognised sixteen-year-old Kirsty's pregnancy even before she knew of it herself and the vicious tongue that had given the news to Kirsty's father even as she and Sandy had feverishly been making plans to run away together.

'Mam, I want to go home,' Mary whimpered. 'I want a drink of water.' Kirsty pushed her fears aside, reminding herself that even if Mrs Laidlaw was still alive, she herself was a grown woman now, not to be intimidated, and she used a corner of her shawl to wipe the sheen of sweat from her daughter's upturned face.

'We are home, pet. See – there's our new house, the one with the pend at the far side.'

A strip of board was fastened above the pend, the writing on it so faded by time and weather that it was impossible to read unless you stood as close as possible. But Kirsty knew that the faint lettering said, 'M. Galbraith, Cabinet-Maker.'

Even after all those years everything was so startlingly familiar that she wouldn't have been surprised if her father had appeared at the mouth of the pend, wearing his sacking apron with its big pocket for tools, and ordered her to stop dawdling and make his dinner.

2

The cart stopped and Alex produced the key from his pocket while Caitlin reached up to take the baby. Kirsty had been holding Fergus for so long that when she handed him down to her daughter she felt oddly unbalanced.

Matt whistled softly as he surveyed the two-storey building. 'It's finer than we're used tae.'

'Are yez goin' tae take all day?' the carter asked from above their heads, and Matt, prodded into action, started barking orders at his family while Kirsty, clutching Mary's hand, went into the house. A waft of stale air, still bearing a hint of her father's strong pipe tobacco, met her in the narrow hall. She hesitated, and Matt, following behind with the roped, handleless suitcase in his arms, said impatiently, 'Let's inside, for any favour. The sooner we bring everythin' in the sooner the carter can get away.'

He nudged the case against her bottom, urging her towards the foot of the stairs.

'I want a drink of water,' Mary whined again, and Kirsty led her past the stairs and into the small, dark kitchen. Alex and Caitlin had brought some of the dishes with them and

13

had unpacked them; Kirsty found a cup and filled it from the tap over the sink. Mary buried her small face in it, drinking deeply and noisily as Kirsty looked around.

This was where it had happened. This was where her father, fresh from hearing her secret from Mrs Laidlaw, had slammed his way into the house and started beating her to make her tell him who had fathered the child she carried. She turned blindly to the door, wanting only to escape back into the street, and came face to face with Caitlin, who was carrying Fergus in at arm's length, her nose wrinkled against the strong smell of urine.

'He's wringing wet – and he stinks!'

The sight of her daughter, and of the baby dangling in midair blinking, his round little face still crumpled with sleep, calmed Kirsty. 'So did you when you were his age.' She took the baby and followed Caitlin out of the kitchen and into the front parlour.

'It's awful dark in here!'

'My mother used it for special occasions, and she kept the curtains drawn so's the sun wouldn't fade the carpet and the furniture.'

'I couldn't be doing with that.' Caitlin wrestled with the window shutters. 'When I'm grown up and married I'll let the sun flood in whenever it chooses. And if it spoils the furniture, I'll buy more.' The stiff shutters finally submitted to her impatient young hands and let the July daylight grope its way through the dirty windows. Caitlin looked about and again wrinkled her nose, this time against the air of neglect about the room. 'Let's go upstairs.'

In the main bedroom the double bed had been stripped and the sagging mattress and two yellowed pillows looked naked and obscene without covering. They would have to be replaced tomorrow, Kirsty thought, shivering at the prospect of spending the night on the mattress her parents had once used.

'Alex and Ewan'll have the room across the passageway, and you and Mary can have the wee room over the pend. It used to be mine,' Kirsty added, remembering how much she had loved that room, especially in the mornings when she had lain snugly in bed listening to the clatter of hooves and the rumble of iron-shod wheels as a cart passed through the pend below on its way to or from the workshop at the end of the yard.

Caitlin had put their own sheets and pillowcases on the washstand. Kirsty put Fergus, now struggling in her arms, down on the floor to crawl and made up the bed swiftly, then went to the window, which was thick with dirt. With childish pleasure she wrote her name in the grime, then added 'Lennox' to make it clear to the house and the street that although she might have left the town in disgrace, she had returned as a wife and mother, a match for Mrs Laidlaw and others of her ilk.

She heard the trunk thump onto the hall floor, then the boys' feet thundering up the stairs and onto the small, square landing.

'We've got a real bath!' Ewan whooped. 'And a privy inside the house!'

In Falkirk they had shared an outside privy with two other families and bathed in a hip bath in front of the kitchen fire. Kirsty, who had quite forgotten about the bathroom, her mother's pride and joy, picked Fergus up and arrived in the doorway in time to hear Alex say, 'There's spiders, too.'

Mary fled to her mother's skirts while Caitlin, who had been hanging over the edge of the claw-footed bath, retreated, shuddering.

'Is nobody goin' tae get some food ready?' Matt shouted from below. 'My belly thinks my throat's cut!'

Already, Kirsty thought as she went downstairs, the ghosts were being laid. Perhaps there was nothing for her to fear here after all.

The battered chicken had been rescued from the railway lines by Alex and a porter. Kirsty was doubtful about the wisdom of eating the bird after all it had been through, but Matt, brushing cinders and tiny stones from the carcass, shrugged her objections aside. 'It's not as if a train ran over it. In any case, it cost good money and I'm not lettin' it go tae waste.'

When the meal was over, they poured out of the back door to explore further. The tiny drying green resembled a small meadow, with the three metal poles that held the washing lines rising from the grass. The border where Eliza Galbraith had lovingly tended flowers as well as vegetables for the table was overrun with weeds, and the once low and well-kept hedge separating the drying green from the workyard was tall and shaggy. A stone building containing the wash house and coal store and outside privy, now used only by the men in the workshop at the end of the yard, stood at right angles to the house.

Kirsty, with Fergus jiggling about in her arms, followed slowly as her family moved beyond the hedge to the large cobbled yard where a sturdy sawhorse stood against one wall and a great pile of timber was stacked against another to allow air to get to all the planks. At some time in the past, beyond

Kirsty's memory, her father or perhaps his father before him had bought the end part of the yard belonging to the house on the other side of the pend so that the work yard could be enlarged to accommodate the delivery carts that came and went. In the L-shape thus created stood the two-storey workshop. Matt made for it at once, longing to explore his new domain. The interior, smelling strongly of glue and wood and varnish, was immaculate. The windows sparkled, and the tools were clean and oiled and well cared for, some laid out neatly on the bench, others hanging to hand on the wall. A half-made chair stood to one side, ready for the next day's work.

'We've met the journeyman – his name's Todd Paget,' Alex said. 'He's been looking after this place – and doing it well,' he added, his hands moving deftly over the tools.

'He's nice,' Caitlin put in, and Matt's mouth tightened.

'I'd as soon we'd the place tae ourselves. The four of us'll be fallin' over each other.' From the first he had criticised Murray Galbraith's stipulation that although the house and business would be owned by the daughter he hadn't seen for more than half of her life, his current journeyman should be kept on for a period of at least two years.

'It's mebbe as well to have someone here who knows the customers and the suppliers,' Kirsty said. 'I just wish the house had been as well cared for as this place.' She thought of the stained old mattress on the double bed and the dusty cushions on the shabby fireside chairs in the kitchen and shuddered. 'It'll need a deal of work.'

'We'll manage.' Matt looked around the place with satisfaction. 'Our own business!'

Kirsty saw Alex flick a glance over his shoulder at his stepfather. From the moment the lawyer's letter had arrived

Matt had felt slighted at not being co-inheritor of the business. Since that day he had resolutely referred to it as 'ours' and even, on occasion, 'mine'. Kirsty had not corrected him.

A sudden rapid tattoo of feet on the floor above made her jump. Caitlin's black-stockinged legs, then the hem of her skirt, appeared on the top step of the flimsy wooden stairs at one side of the room. Her face appeared next, upside down, the ends of her silky auburn hair drifting beneath it.

'There's a wee room up here—'

'Come down at once!' Kirsty knew by Matt and Alex's surprised faces that her voice was too sharp.

'Don't fret yerself,' her husband told her as Caitlin, subdued, came down the stairs, followed by Ewan. 'If she falls it'll teach her tae be more careful the next time.'

'If she breaks her neck on these rickety stairs there won't be a next time!'

'You fuss too much.'

It wasn't fear that had prompted her sharp reaction but memories. 'I'm tired,' Kirsty said by way of apology to her family. 'We're all tired, after the travelling. We'll have an early night.'

'But there's still that other room by the pend to look at,' Caitlin protested. 'There's some strange stuff in it.'

'Let me see.' Ewan was out of the door at once, Caitlin and Alex at his heels.

'Can it not wait till the morning?' Kirsty appealed to Matt, who plucked Fergus from her arms and carried him out of the workshop.

'It won't take long. Ye want tae see the storeroom now, don't ye, my wee mannie?' he asked the baby. 'One day ye'll

18

be workin' here along with yer brothers an' yer daddy. Lennox and Sons, eh?'

A door set in the wall of the pend led into the large storeroom that ran the full length of the dwelling house's parlour and kitchen. It was meant to be lit by two small windows, one at the front of the building, the other at the rear, but Kirsty had never seen the window shutters open. She recalled her mother telling her that in Paisley's heyday as a weaving town this very storeroom had been a weaving shop.

'There's a step down,' she suddenly remembered as her husband handed Fergus back to her and lifted the latch.

'Alex fell down it already,' Caitlin informed them with a chuckle as Matt probed about in the gloom with one foot.

'A man could twist his ankle in this place if he didnae know better. Is there a lamp?'

'There might be spiders,' Mary quavered, staying close to her mother.

'There was always a lamp on a shelf to the right of the door, and matches beside it.'

'I've got them,' Alex said almost at once, and they all blinked in the sudden spurt of flame from a struck match. Within moments the oil lamp's steady glow illuminated a collection of tables and chairs and two small chests of drawers neatly placed against one wall.

Alex ran a hand over a table. 'They're good pieces of work.'

'See.' Caitlin's voice came from the far corner. 'There's funny-looking strips of wood here, tangled up with string.'

'It's just rubbish,' Matt said dismissively.

'I don't think so.'

Carefully, Kirsty picked her way over. 'Alex, bring the

19

lamp here,' she said, then as he obeyed, 'hold it nearer.'

'And risk settin' the place on fire?' Matt wanted to know.
'I've told ye – it's just rubbish tae be thrown out.'

'Caitlin, take the bairn.' Once Kirsty's arms were free she
stooped to examine the jumble of timbers lying against the
wall, then straightened.

'It's not rubbish.' Her voice was thick with excitement and
emotion. 'It's a loom. It must have been brought here from
my grandfather's weaving shop in Kilbarchan.'

'A loom – like the one you told us about?' Caitlin asked
excitedly. She had always loved Kirsty's stories about her
grandfather's two-loom shop in Kilbarchan and the early
days of her childhood playing amongst the looms while her
grandfather and her mother wove cloth.

'It is the one I told you about. Look.' Kirsty dropped to
her knees, heedless of the chill of the hard-packed earthen
floor, and ran her hands over the timbers. 'Hold the light
closer, Alex. There, on this upright – AJ. That's him –
Alexander Jardine. And this rounded piece is the beam, and
this narrow strip that broadens out at one end's a treadle.
And that's not string – it's the web.'

'It looks like old rubbish tae me . . .' Matt began, then was
caught unawares by a massive yawn. 'Whatever it is, ye can
have a good look at it in the mornin', when the light's better,'
he decreed when he got his voice back. 'Right now, I'm for
my bed.'

For the time being, Fergus had to sleep in his perambulator,
while Caitlin and Mary squeezed together into Kirsty's old
narrow bed and Alex and Ewan made do with mattresses on
the floor of their room.

'We'll have to get a decent bed for the boys, and a crib for the wee one,' Kirsty said when everyone else was settled and she and Matt were finally free to go to their own bed.

'Ye can go out tomorrow and get what ye think best. Use the money we got from sellin' our own things. I told ye that'd be for the best, didn't I?'

Kirsty, anxious to sweep every trace of her father from the house, had wanted to refurnish it with the few pieces from their Falkirk home, but Matt had insisted on selling what they had, thus saving on the cost of moving.

He took his jacket off and opened the door of the big old wardrobe. 'There's still clothes in here.' His voice echoed in the wardrobe's depths. 'They must be yer father's.'

Kirsty, investigating, was enveloped in the stale smell of pipe smoke. 'It's his best Sunday suit and his winter coat. I'll sell them tomorrow.'

'That's good material.' Matt rubbed a lapel between finger and thumb. 'Ye could mebbe alter some of these things tae fit me.'

Kirsty said nothing but decided that she would find a second-hand shop first thing in the morning. She couldn't bear the thought of her husband wearing her father's clothes.

Her body almost cried out with relief as she unlaced her stays. She hated them but had no option but to wear them, for to her great sorrow Kirsty had never been slender, and motherhood had rounded and softened her body even further.

Although she was weak with fatigue she delayed the moment when she would have to lie down on her parents' bed, taking time to brush her long fair hair, hearing it crackle as she drew the brush through it. She had inherited her father's fair hair instead of her mother's rich auburn tresses, but when the light caught her hair a certain way there was just a hint of red. Murray Galbraith had had deep-brown, almost black eyes, while his wife's had been a brilliant, startling turquoise. Again, Kirsty had inherited her colouring from her father, though her eyes were lighter than his, more of a hazel shade.

Although he looked very like his true father, Alex's hair owed something to his maternal grandmother's colouring and was a deeper red than Sandy's had been. But Caitlin was the fortunate one, for she had inherited Eliza Galbraith's tresses as well as her beautiful blue-green eyes.

Matt started snoring, and Kirsty turned out the gas mantle and crept into the bed, deciding that she would replace it on the following day, no matter how much Matt might protest.

The knowledge that the very loom her grandfather had owned lay close by warmed and comforted her. Alexander Jardine had always represented warmth and love and security in her world, especially after her mother's death. She would never forgive herself for leaving Paisley without saying goodbye to him, but during her final days at home her father had turned a deaf ear to her pleas to be allowed to see the elderly weaver, and Mrs Laidlaw had cruelly given it as her opinion that, since the old man was already ill and frail, a visit from the granddaughter who had brought such shame on him would probably kill him.

Kirsty had written to her grandfather from her aunt's cold, comfortless house in Stirling. She had longed to spill out all her fear and anguish and worry about Sandy but had smothered her instincts in order to spare the old man further grief, sending only a brief explanation of why she had been sent

22

away. She had begged his forgiveness and promised to do all she could to see him again, if he so wished.

She still had his reply and would always treasure it, a small scrap of paper with a few words scrawled over it, assuring her that he would ask God every day to watch over her and her child. Six days after giving birth to her son, she had received a second note, this time from one of her grandfather's neighbours, telling her that he had passed away. She had taken Alex from her aunt's house on the following day.

Even if the loom couldn't be put together again, she thought as sleep began to close over her, she would keep it. As long as it existed, even in its present sad condition, her grandfather and her mother wouldn't be forgotten.

3

Kirsty woke to the sound of a cart rumbling along the road-way outside and the whistling of an errand boy on his rounds. Matt still slept soundly, close against her back, and the house was silent. Even Fergus, worn out by the previous day's excitements, hadn't stirred all night.

She slid quietly out of bed and gathered up her clothes then went downstairs, avoiding the treads that creaked just as she had years before in order to keep from disturbing her father when she rose to prepare his breakfast and heat his shaving water.

She could have wept at the sad picture the kitchen presented in daylight. The wooden fireplace, large table and big dresser badly needed polishing. The varnish that had once protected the two wooden fireside chairs was worn away and the spars and arms looked shabby and neglected, while the cushions were stained and torn.

In her mother's time the kitchen had been fragrant with the mingled smells of fresh baking and the promise of a good meal in the making, and the hearth had always been swept clean and the fire well tended. 'My Eliza could make a home out of four bare walls and a wooden crate,' her father had been known to say of his wife in a rare moment of affection.

After Eliza Galbraith's death Kirsty had done her best to keep the place bright and welcoming in her memory, but it was clear that once she had left her father had made no attempt to look after it.

She blinked, realising that she was staring at the corner where she had last seen Sandy, motionless on the floor, his face a mask of blood. He had burst into the room to save her from her father's rage but, thin and undernourished as he was, he had been no match for Murray Galbraith's iron-hard fists once the man realised that this was the lad who had got his daughter 'into trouble'.

Wrenching her gaze away, she was calmed by the sight of the cups and plates still lying on the big table from the previous evening's hurried meal, reminders that the past was over and the present had need of her attention.

After filling the kettle and putting it on the greasy gas cooker, she dressed swiftly before washing the dishes and resetting the table. She had brought enough oatmeal with her to make porridge – a lot of it, she decided, tossing generous handfuls of meal into the pot, since there was only enough bread for Matt. She and the children would have to make do with porridge and tea, both without milk.

The debris of the last fire her father had built still lay in the grate. Down on her knees, cleaning it out, Kirsty suddenly noticed his pipe and tobacco pouch on the little wooden table by his fireside chair. She snatched them up at once and threw them into the bucket she was using, hurriedly piling more ashes on top to hide them. If this must be her new home – and Matt was determined that it would be – she would at least remove every trace of her father from it.

Outside the morning was still and cool, the sky a soft pearly grey with a flush of warm peach over to the east heralding the sun's approach. Kirsty emptied the bucket into the big metal container that stood, as ever, against the outhouse wall, then set it down and walked through the long grass, which soaked her feet and legs and skirt with dew, and round to the yard behind the hedge. There were still ghosts to be laid, and it was best to deal with them while she was alone.

In the workshop, she went up the wooden staircase leading to the garret. Lit only by a skylight, it was a place of shadows and secrets, even on a clear morning. This was where Alex had been conceived, where she and Sandy had discovered the comfort of loving and being loved and had briefly escaped from the misery and loneliness of their lives. Standing in the middle of the room, she half expected to hear his voice saying, 'Kate,' the name that only he and her mother had given her, and to feel his bony hands, marked with the scars of his trade, drawing her down onto the pile of sacking used to protect completed furniture from harm while it awaited collection.

There was no voice, no Sandy – but there was still sacking in the corner. She knelt beside it then sat back on her heels, grunting a little. She was thirty-four years old now, and the passing of time and the birth of four children had made her less agile than the sixteen-year-old she had been then. Laying a hand gently on the rough sacks, she knew from memory how they would cushion the hard floor a little if she lay on them and that if she rested her cheek against them they would smell of linseed oil and wood and dust.

'Sandy . . .' She shaped the name soundlessly with her lips. At first, in the long weeks and months between her last sight of him and Alex's birth, she had hoped and prayed that he had recovered from the terrible beating her father had given him and would come looking for her. But the pain of seeing day after empty day pass by without any word from him had become too much to bear, and she had let hope go. Remembering how he had looked when the passers-by she had summoned frantically from the street had carried his limp body out to the ambulance wagon, she accepted that he had probably died from his injuries.

Below her feet the workshop door opened. Kirsty froze, her mind scrabbling for the right words to explain to Matt why she was in the garret when she should be in the kitchen, seeing to his breakfast.

She must have moved slightly, for a plank creaked beneath her foot and a voice from the workshop below said sharply, 'Who's there?'

It wasn't a voice she knew. The journeyman must have arrived.

'It's only me,' she called back, hurrying to the top of the steps, embarrassed at being caught. The man in the workshop was tall and well-built, with smoky grey eyes looking up at her from under a thatch of dark-brown hair.

'I'm Kirsty Lennox,' she said from halfway down the stairs. 'I was just looking round. You'll be Todd Paget.'

His face was lit by a smile, and his hand, hard and calloused from work, clasped hers firmly for a few seconds as she stepped off the final tread. 'I met yer lad Alex yesterday – and his sister.'

'They said. Have you been managing on your own since . . .' she paused, then said carefully, 'my father's death?' The word, rarely spoken aloud since she had last seen her father, felt alien in her mouth.

'Aye, mistress.' Like many local people, he still used the old title when addressing a woman. 'There were some orders that had tae be seen tae, so the lawyer told me tae keep workin'. There's more orders come in since.'

'You've kept the place neat.'

He glanced round the workshop. 'It's a good wee business, Mistress Galb— Lennox.'

'The old loom in the store by the pend – when did that come here?'

'It was there when I started as an apprentice. Mr Galbraith talked of throwin' it out, but he never got around tae it.'

Kirsty nodded, then remembered her domestic duties. 'I must get back to the house. Come to the kitchen in a wee while for a cup of tea and meet my husband and my sons,' she invited, and he ducked his head in agreement.

'I left some kindlin' by the back door yesterday, and there's wood waitin' tae be chopped in a corner of the yard. I'll see tae it now and bring it tae the house.'

She found the neat bundle tucked into a corner by the door and carried it into the kitchen, then dealt with the neglected kettle, which was filling the place with steam. Footsteps and voices could be heard overhead, followed, just as Alex and Ewan came down the stairs and into the room, by the panic-stricken wail of a baby newly wakened to find himself in an unfamiliar place.

Leaving the boys to see to the porridge and the fire, Kirsty went up to the bedroom where Caitlin, still in her nightdress, walked up and down with Fergus roaring over her shoulder, outraged tears pouring down his scarlet face. Mary trudged by her sister's side, clutching a fistful of Caitlin's nightdress, still unsure of the house and unwilling to venture downstairs on her own, while Matt, in shirt and trousers, sat on the side of the bed, seemingly oblivious to the noise, carefully turning one of his socks the right way out.

'Here – I'll take him.' Kirsty laid the baby over her own shoulder and the roars eased to a damp wail, then stopped as she sat by Matt's side, unfastening her blouse and easing her petticoat down to give Fergus's hungry mouth access to her breast. 'Caitlin, get yourself and Mary dressed then see to the breakfast. Todd Paget's coming in for a cup of tea.'

'The journeyman? Comin' in for a cup of tea?' Matt propped one ankle against the other knee so that he could pull on his sock. 'Is the man a worker or an honoured guest?'

'I met him in the back yard,' Kirsty said glibly. She couldn't tell the truth, for then he would have wanted to know why she had been in the workshop instead of in the kitchen, getting the breakfast ready. 'I thought he might as well come in and meet everyone. It'll not be happening every morning.'

'I should hope not.' He dusted the sole of his foot before reaching for the second sock. There had always been something about her husband's long naked feet, narrow and pale skinned with delicate toes, that pulled at Kirsty's heartstrings. They were the most vulnerable part of him, not rugged like his face, or calloused like his hands or muscular like his lean body.

'We'll have to go and see the lawyer,' she remembered.

'We'll do that this afternoon – that'll give me time to brush your good clothes and iron a shirt.'

Matt slid his feet into his boots and stood up, stamping hard on the floorboards as he always did to settle his feet in place before tying the laces. 'I'd best get downstairs, then, and be ready tae meet this man.'

Kirsty had fed and dressed Fergus and gone down to the kitchen before Todd Paget arrived. 'I left a pile of logs in the store for ye, mistress. Any time ye need more, just let me know.'

He had removed his canvas work apron with its tool pocket and donned his cap for the short journey between the workshop and the house. As soon as he stepped indoors he took the cap off, rolling it up and twisting it between his hands.

Matt didn't get up or offer his hand to his new employee. He eyed the young man thoughtfully from where he sat, then said shortly, 'Sit down. The wife'll give ye some tea.'

Todd nodded his thanks as Kirsty put a cup before him. 'We've no milk,' she apologised. 'I'll have to get some provisions in.'

'Ach, it's no hardship,' Matt said brusquely. 'Milk's for bairns.' Startled, she looked along the table at him then realised, from the way he gripped the handle of his knife as he scraped the last of the margarine on to the last slice of bread, that he was as tense and nervous as the young man facing him. Matt had never been an employer before, and at that moment he was floundering in deep water.

Alex and Ewan had no such problems. By the time the four men went off to the workshop the two of them were talking easily with Todd, while Matt, working hard at being a master, was still aloof.

Once they had gone Kirsty started making plans. The whole house needed cleaning, Alex and Ewan needed a new bed, Fergus would have to have a proper cot – the list grew as she moved from room to room, leaving Caitlin, always reliable, to wash the dishes and see to Mary and Fergus.

The large drawer beneath the wardrobe was filled with spare sheets and blankets, just as her mother had left them. Kirsty spread a sheet over the bed then emptied the contents of the wardrobe onto it, the smell of stale pipe smoke almost choking her. She tossed all her father's clothing on to the sheet then she knotted its corners together, just as determined as she had been the night before that she wasn't going to let Matt wear clothes that had been on her father's back.

Kirsty's best friend at school had been Jean Chisholm. Jean's widowed mother had owned a second-hand clothes shop in Causeyside Street, and to Kirsty's surprise the shop was still there. When she lifted the bundle of clothing from the perambulator and went in it was like stepping back into the past. The same cracked bell gave a flat clang as the door opened, and she remembered the one step down into the dim interior. Even the clothes hanging on the walls and the overflowing boxes left on the floor for customers to hunt through seemed to be the same.

'Yes?' A woman hovered in the shadows behind the wooden counter, itself covered with clothing. It wasn't Mrs Chisholm, who had been elderly when Kirsty knew her.

'I was wondering,' she negotiated her way between boxes and put her bundle down on top of the things already on the counter, 'if you'd be interested in these?'

'Mmm.' The hands that sorted through Murray Galbraith's clothing wore woollen gloves with the fingers cut off at the knuckles. The shopkeeper was smaller than Kirsty, and with her head bent over the bundle, all Kirsty could see was the top of a felt turban pulled well down over the woman's hair. 'I don't usually deal with men's clothing. What price would you be lookin' for?'

She glanced up, fixing large brown myopic eyes on her customer. With a sudden stab of astonishment, Kirsty recognised her.

'Jean? Jean Chisholm?'

'Aye, that's me. Who wants tae know?'

'I'm Kirsty Len— Kirsty Galbraith. D'you mind me?'

'Kirsty?' Jean Chisholm stared, then scuttled around the end of the counter, moving with a familiar rolling gait. Her body was solid and quite squat, her legs bowed. Jean had had rickets as an infant and would carry the legacy to her grave. She peered up at Kirsty, then her round face broke into a wide grin. 'Kirsty Galbraith, back in Paisley at last!'

'It's Kirsty Lennox now.'

'You got married? I thought you would, for you were a bonny lass. I was that upset when you left without a word,' Jean said. 'Your father said you'd tae go and look after an aunt, but he never said when you were comin' home again. D'you have any weans?'

'Five – though one of them's my stepson. The youngest's outside in his pram.' Kirsty beamed down at her former friend. 'Oh, Jean, I'm so glad you're still here!'

'Where else would I be? I took over the shop when my mam died five years back, and I still live upstairs. Where've you been? Are you back tae stay?'

32

'I've been living in Falkirk. My father left the house and the business to me, so we've moved to Paisley.'

'Let me see the bairn.' Jean waddled towards the door. 'Oh, he's bonny,' she crooned a moment later, bending over Fergus, asleep in his perambulator. 'Like a wee angel! Come and have a cup of tea and tell me what's been happenin' tae you.'

'I haven't time,' Kirsty said regretfully, following her friend back into the shop. 'I've got things to buy for the house, but I'll be back as soon as I can.'

She left Jean's shop equipped with advice on the best second-hand furniture shops to visit, and a suspicion that Jean had paid her more for her father's clothes than she would have given a stranger. Promising herself that she would make it up to the woman for her kindness when she could, she set off along Causeyside Street.

Half an hour later she turned towards home, well pleased with her purchases. She had bought a cot and bedsteads, complete with mattresses. None of her purchases was new, but everything was in good condition. And there was just enough money left to buy some pipe tobacco for Matt.

She hesitated, tempted to go back down Causeyside Street in search of a tobacconist's, then gripped the perambulator handles and advanced on the corner shop. It was time to lay another ghost to rest.

The name 'Laidlaw' was still over the door and the interior of this shop, too, was just as she remembered it, but to Kirsty's relief the young woman behind the counter looked nothing like old Mrs Laidlaw.

She was breathtakingly beautiful; beneath arched brows her

eyes were a clear, pale green, with an almost Eastern slant to them. Her glossy black hair was drawn back to lie in a coiled plait at the nape of a long, slender neck, and her skin was creamily flawless. When Kirsty went in, the girl was dealing with a male customer, laughing up at him. The hands wrapping the man's purchase were small and dainty, the nails perfectly rounded. She watched him leave the shop before turning to Kirsty, the smile vanishing as though it had never been.

'Yes?' she asked crisply.

Kirsty scanned the shelves and saw Matt's favourite pipe tobacco. The girl unwrapped the solid black cake and put it on the chopping board Kirsty had always admired.

As she handed over the money she summoned the strength to say casually, 'Old Mrs Laidlaw used to run this shop, didn't she?'

'My grandmother.' The girl rattled the coins into a drawer and picked out change. 'She died a while back.' Then, as a wave of relief broke over Kirsty at the news, 'My father owns the shop now.'

Kirsty looked closely at her, remembering the pretty little girl, the joy of Mrs Laidlaw's life, who had often been in the shop when she went in to buy her father's tobacco. 'You're never Beth, are you?'

One perfect eyebrow was raised in cool surprise. 'I am.'

'I mind you as a wee girl, when I lived across the road. My father was Murray Galbraith,' Kirsty explained.

The girl's head snapped up and for the first time she looked fully at Kirsty. The eyes that had smiled at the last customer were hard and cold, and so was her voice when she said, 'Is there anything else?'

Outside Fergus wakened and gave a loud impatient wail. 'Nothing else,' Kirsty said, and left, suddenly chilled by the girl's attitude. Bumping the perambulator across the cobbled street and onto the footpath, she puzzled over the coldness in the girl's lovely eyes. Surely, she thought uncomfortably, Beth Laidlaw couldn't know anything about what had happened to Kirsty all those years ago?

4

When she and Matt returned from their visit to the lawyer that afternoon, Kirsty enlisted Caitlin and Mary's help and set to work in the house. They carried all the rugs into the back yard and hung them over the clothesline, beating years of ancient dust out of them, then leaving them to air while they marched upstairs. Fergus was wedged with pillows and blankets into an empty drawer from the big cupboard in the main bedroom, and Kirsty tied a rope to the handle so that she could drag him from room to room as she worked. He clutched at the sides of the drawer as he was pulled along the oilcloth, screaming with excited laughter and well pleased with this new form of transport.

All the curtains were stiff and sticky with grime. They would have to be taken down and washed; some of them would disintegrate in the washtub, which meant that Kirsty would have to make new ones. Fortunately her father had left some money – not much, but enough to buy what was needed to make the house habitable again, if she was careful.

The lawyer hadn't had much to tell them, other than that her father had died in the Royal Alexandra Infirmary in

Neilston Road. Kirsty was grateful for the information, relieved to know he hadn't died at home.

Looking through the chest of drawers in the small room over the pend, she found that everything she had had to leave behind when she was banished to Stirling – a few precious books, her favourite wooden doll, the teddy bear that had been hugged almost bald – had disappeared. Her father had stripped the house of her presence, just as she was now stripping it of his.

The room was lit by two small windows, one overlooking the street, the other overlooking the work yard. Kirsty recalled standing at that one after her mother's death, hoping to see Sandy come out of the workshop. She rested her forehead on the glass and narrowed her eyes, half convinced that if she looked hard enough she might manage to magic him into being there, glancing up at the window as he usually did and smiling at the sight of her.

'The beds have arrived,' Caitlin shrilled from downstairs, shattering the moment.

'Go and ask your father if he and Alex and Ewan can spare a few minutes to help the carter,' Kirsty called back, turning away from the window. There was work to be done.

Within a few weeks the house was well on its way to becoming a home again. Every inch of the place had been scrubbed and polished, and new curtains hung in the bedrooms.

Murray Galbraith's sign had been taken down and Alex, who had some artistic talent and enjoyed drawing and painting, made a new square board to set on the wall by the pend. Against a yellow background, 'Lennox & Sons, Cabinet-Makers' stood out in bold white edged with black. After reading about the art of decorating furniture in a book borrowed from Paisley Library, he volunteered to refurbish the shabby old fireside chairs in the kitchen, painting them a deep oyster colour and finishing each one off with a spray of intermingled flowers and leaves along the top bar of each backrest to match the new cushions Kirsty had made from a large floral-patterned skirt bought from Jean Chisholm's shop.

Kirsty was delighted with the result, for it not only gave the chairs a new lease of life but helped to brighten the kitchen. But when she suggested to Matt that some of his customers might be interested in painted furniture he huffed into his moustache then retorted, 'We make good solid furniture and that's what folk want – not fancy nonsense.'

Todd Paget, who saw the chairs when he brought in some logs for the fire, was as impressed as Kirsty had been. 'They're bonny. I know my Beth'd like somethin' like that for our house, when we get one.'

'Beth?'

'My intended,' he told her proudly. 'Ye'll have seen her, surely – she works in her father's shop at the corner.'

Kirsty gaped at him. 'You're marrying Beth Laidlaw?'

'Aye, though I cannae see what a lass like her sees in a big lump like me when she could surely have any man she chooses. There's times I have tae pinch myself tae see if I'm dreamin'.'

'That's not what I meant at all,' Kirsty hurried to assure him, though it was true that she couldn't see Beth Laidlaw's cold beauty as a match for gentle, likeable Todd. 'I just thought that you were young for marriage.'

'Young? I've just turned thirty.'

Again, she stared at him, taken aback for the second

time. 'I'd thought you to be a good few years less than that.'

'So do most folk,' he said ruefully. 'My mam always said I was tryin' tae hold on tae childhood, and mebbe she was right.'

'Why don't you bring Beth here on Sunday afternoon to see the chairs?' Kirsty said on an impulse.

'Ye mean that?'

'Of course I do.' After he had gone, beaming with pleasure at the invitation, she recalled the girl's cool demeanour each time she went into the shop and wondered if she had spoken too swiftly. Then she reminded herself that the invitation had been extended for Todd's sake, not Beth's.

But on Sunday, pouring tea for her visitors in the parlour, Kirsty wished that she had never made the invitation. Beth, in a green muslin dress elaborately trimmed with primrose-yellow ribbon and small knots of artificial primroses, was cool and reserved, twitching her full skirt aside ostentatiously whenever Fergus crawled within a yard of where she sat. A wide-brimmed straw hat lavishly decorated with more artificial primroses and yellow ribbons was tipped elegantly over one eye.

She had admired the painted chairs, studying them with a gleam of avarice in eyes that matched the colour of her gown, but since then the conversation had faltered. Beth Laidlaw seemed to be more interested in the house and its furnishings than in the people who lived there, Kirsty thought, willing the hands of the clock to move faster.

Todd, dressed in his Sunday best and uncomfortable in a stiff, high-collared shirt, was perched on the edge of an upright chair, his large hands dwarfing the china cup they held. He had tried to persuade Beth to visit the workshop, but she had declined, protesting that the rutted lane was too difficult to negotiate.

Matt, horrified at the prospect of entertaining his own journeyman, had retired upstairs before the guests' arrival, leaving Kirsty to make excuses for him. At that moment, she thought enviously, he would be stretched out on the bed, enjoying the Sunday afternoon doze he usually had in his chair. Ewan and Alex had opted for a walk over the braes beyond Paisley; only Mary and Caitlin had stayed to greet the visitors. They were both fascinated by Beth's elegance and entranced at the sight of Todd in his Sunday best.

'Mary, offer Miss Laidlaw another sugar biscuit.'

Mary, who had been sitting on the floor, scrambled to her feet and very carefully lifted the plate of biscuits, mincing across the floor with small steps in order to avoid spilling her precious cargo. Beth watched her approach unsmilingly then said, when Mary arrived by her side and offered the plate, 'No, thank you.'

Mary swung round to face her mother, and the biscuits almost fell to the floor. 'She doesn't want one – and I carried them all that way, too!'

'Put the plate back on the table – and have a biscuit yourself,' Kirsty said hurriedly, then, to Beth, 'and when do you and Todd hope to marry?'

For some reason the question appeared to offend the girl. Her chin came up sharply and as she opened her mouth to speak, Todd, shifting uncomfortably on the edge of his chair, broke in, 'Mebbe next year. We're savin' towards gettin' someplace to live.'

Beth's green eyes shot a cold look at him, and he freed one hand from the saucer he clutched so that he could run a finger round his collar to ease the pressure on his neck.

'What sort of place would you like?' Kirsty asked, and was taken aback when Beth retorted, 'This house would have suited us fine.'

'This house?'

'Beth . . .' Todd almost dropped his cup in his agitation, and Caitlin rescued it just in time.

His fiancée swept on, ignoring him. 'Did Todd not tell you that we'd hoped to live here?'

'No.' Kirsty shot a puzzled look at the journeyman, who had gone scarlet.

'When Mr Galbraith took ill it was Todd who did all the work and kept the place going.' Beth's voice managed to put a sharp edge on every word, as though flicking small knives across the room at her hostess. 'And when Todd visited him in the infirmary Mr Galbraith told him that the business was to be left to you, but he'd made sure that Todd would be kept on because of all he'd done to help.'

'Beth, will ye—'

'It's as well spoken of, Todd,' the girl snapped. 'Folk should know the truth.' Then, turning back to Kirsty, 'Mr Galbraith said that he didn't think you'd want to come back to Paisley, so Todd would probably manage the place for you and live here, in this house.'

'I see,' Kirsty said faintly. And now she did. No wonder Beth had been cold towards her – she had taken over the house that the girl had coveted as her own.

'It was only in the master's mind, Beth – I said so all along,' Todd protested to his betrothed. 'Mrs Lennox had every right tae—'

The door opened and Ewan came surging into the room,

jacket and tie discarded and shirt collar open, his handsome face flushed with exercise and fresh air, and his thick brown hair tousled. At the sight of the visitors Alex, following his stepbrother, hurriedly ran a hand over his own hair and rolled his shirtsleeves down, but Ewan merely said, 'I didn't realise you still had company, Mam,' and scooped up a handful of small sugared biscuits, surveying Todd, who had scrambled to his feet, with amusement. 'You must be hot in that outfit,' he said, and stuffed the biscuits into his mouth, mumbling through them, 'any tea left?'

'Ewan, don't speak with your mouth full,' Kirsty scolded, annoyed with him but at the same time relieved that he had arrived just in time to put an end to a difficult scene.

His mouth was still full, but his blue eyes, darker than Alex's, laughed at her. Although he was only seventeen, Ewan could charm the birds from the trees if he so chose, and he knew it.

'Caitlin, go and make a fresh pot of tea – and bring two of the big cups,' Kirsty said, then, to Beth, 'you'll have to forgive my sons' sudden intrusion.'

'Not at all.' The girl rose, smiling, and advanced on Ewan, one gloved hand outstretched. 'How do you do, Mr Lennox? I thought that your painted chairs were delightful. I shall insist on having some made and decorated for me once Todd and I find a home of our own.'

He swallowed down the last of the biscuits, jerking his head in Alex's direction. 'They're not mine – he's the artist in this family.'

'Oh – I was so sure . . .' Her smile faltered slightly, then rallied as she withdrew her hand from his and turned to Alex. 'They're quite charming,' she said, then, picking up the half-empty plate, laughingly offered it to Ewan. 'Do have another biscuit.'

It was just like the shop, Kirsty thought, watching him grin cheekily down at her as he swept the few remaining biscuits up in one hand and tossed them into his mouth. She had seen it happen more than once on her visits to buy Matt's tobacco. When Beth was serving her, or any other woman, she was expressionless and businesslike, but let a man enter the premises and the girl immediately became charming and flirtatious.

It was a relief when Beth, having decided that she would like to see the workshop after all, went away with the others in attendance, leaving Kirsty on her own. Putting the empty biscuit plate on a tray with the cups, she wondered if Todd knew what he was taking on.

'I can't see what she sees in the likes of Todd,' Ewan said flatly once the visitors had gone. 'She's too lively for him.'

'That's for Todd to worry about, not you.' Alex's voice was heavy with meaning. 'She's his sweetheart.'

'I know that – no need tae fret,' Ewan said easily, a smirk playing round his mouth. Since leaving school at thirteen he had been 'walking out' with girls. Alex, who had his fair share of feminine company, had stopped bringing his girlfriends to the house because on more than one occasion they had been charmed away from his side by Ewan.

'She's very beautiful, but . . . I'm not sure about her,' Caitlin's voice was thoughtful. 'She's more like a doll than a person.'

'She didn't like the biscuits.' Mary was still suffering from rejection.

Ewan ruffled her hair. 'I did, pet – lucky you kept them for me. Are there any more, mam?'

On the following morning Todd came to the back door, nervously twisting his hands in his canvas apron. 'About what Beth told ye yesterday,' he began as soon as Kirsty opened the door. 'She shouldnae have—'

'It's all right, Todd. I'd no idea that my father had given you reason to think that you might live here.'

'He didn't, not really.' The man couldn't meet her eyes. 'He was failin' fast by the time he went intae the Infirmary and I didn't think seriously of anythin' he said then, though I'm grateful tae him for seein' that I was kept on. I should never have told Beth, though.'

'I can understand her disappointment when we decided to come to Paisley and spoiled your plans.'

'Ye didn't,' he said at once. 'I just wish she hadnae said anythin', after you makin' us so welcome, too.'

'Put it out of your mind, Todd. You'll get a suitable place soon, I'm sure.'

'Aye, and when we do,' he said, cheering up, 'Beth'll be wantin' some of these painted chairs. She was right taken with them.'

Watching him stride down the lane, Kirsty wondered if it was the prospect of getting the house that had prompted Beth to agree to marry him. She dismissed the thought as unfair, but it lingered. The house was certainly finer than the three small rooms she and her father occupied above the tobacconist's shop, or anything that Todd's wages could buy or rent.

*

Jean's shop, untidy and disorganised as it was, had turned out to be a treasure chest. As she regularly collected unwanted clothing from the big houses in the area, everything in the shop was of good quality and in good condition, though mainly old-fashioned and far too elaborate for the women who frequented the shop. During one visit, Kirsty unearthed two very large gowns, one in flowered silk, the other of fawn velvet with a voluminous waist-length cape.

'These belonged tae old Mrs Naismith,' Jean told her as the two of them spread the velvet gown out between them. It took up all the space in the shop, and little Mary stared up in wonder at the rich canopy it made above her head. 'She was that big she'd tae have a special carriage made for her with wide doors.'

Kirsty stroked the velvet. 'It's beautiful. How much d'you want for this – and the flowered silk, too?'

Jean eyed her doubtfully. 'Ye're mebbe a wee bit on the sonsy side, Kirsty, but three of you'd be lost in one of they dresses.'

'There's some lovely material there. I could make a dress for Caitlin from the silk and bonny winter coats out of the velvet for Mary and Fergus, and have plenty left over for cushions or the start of a patchwork quilt.'

'I mind you were always good with a needle – not like me. You can have them both with my blessin',' Jean said, 'for there's nob'dy round here big enough tae wear them. I only took them because I couldnae refuse. Imagine the likes of me turnin' up her nose at the chance tae get pickins from the Naismiths – they'd be fair scandalised. I'd never get as much as a rag from them or their neighbours again if I did that!'

Kirsty insisted on paying, and they haggled amiably for a few minutes before coming to an agreement.

'Would ye be lookin' for a wee sewin' job?' Jean asked, bundling the purchases into crumpled brown paper.

'I could do with the money. I'd expected to do the books for Matt the way I did them for my father, but he's insisting on seeing to them himself.' Kirsty had strong doubts about Matt's ability as a book-keeper but kept them to herself, knowing that it was his constant sense of insecurity that had made him insist on taking the books on in the first place. 'D'you know of someone looking for a sewing woman?'

'I've heard that Mrs Hamilton's sewin' woman's off tae Ayr tae look after her old father, and she's not been replaced. You mind the Hamiltons, surely – you worked there after we both left the school.'

'Is Mrs Hamilton still alive? She was a nice old lady, a good employer.'

'The one you knew's long dead. It's her son and his wife that have the house now. It might be worth yer while havin' a word with her.'

Kirsty thought it over as she walked home. With the children growing so fast and continually needing clothes and shoes, it would be useful to have some money of her own. Although Matt was a good provider he felt that he had the right to know how every penny of his money was spent, and sometimes Kirsty longed to have even a few coppers of her own to spend as she wished.

A year after Caitlin's birth Matt had been badly hurt in an accident at work, and Kirsty had had to take on a cleaning job in order to pay the rent and keep food on the table. Although the work was hard, she had enjoyed the independence and had insisted on keeping the job when Matt was fit again, much to his annoyance. His opposition had been vindicated when Kirsty suffered a miscarriage, then a few months later, although she had stopped work by then, there had been another loss.

'Ye see?' he had harangued her each time as she lay in bed, weak from the loss of blood, 'This is what happens when ye try tae take on too much. Your place is in the house, looking after me and your bairns.'

The heartbreak of losing the children had been hard to bear. On the advice of an older and wiser neighbour, Kirsty had resorted to various ploys to avoid any further pregnancies for a year or two to give her body a chance to recover. Matt, who believed in letting nature have its way, would have been furious if he had known, but Mary's uncomplicated birth, followed, after a secretly planned wait of a few years, by Fergus's safe arrival led Kirsty to believe that she had been right to take control over her own body.

Matt would probably object again to her going out to work, but there was no danger this time. As far as Kirsty was concerned, five children between them was enough. Her child-bearing days were over.

5

'Mistress Lennox – what're ye doin'?' Todd Paget asked in astonishment.

Kirsty sat back on her heels. 'I'm cutting the grass,' she said, and a chirrup of agreement came from Fergus, crawling about the back yard.

Todd came in from the lane and dropped to crouch before her, putting the box he had been carrying on the ground and taking the scissors from her. 'With those?'

'The mower and the shears are all rusted.'

'Ye should have told me. I'd've oiled an' sharpened them.'

'You've got enough to do.' She had spoken to Matt once or twice about the shears, but nothing had been done. Knowing from the tension round his mouth that he was finding it hard to grasp all the facets of running his own business, she hadn't pressed him.

'I'll see tae them before I go home,' Todd said, then lunged after Fergus, crawling at surprising speed towards the lane. 'Not yet, my mannie,' he told the baby, swinging him above his head then depositing him in Kirsty's arms. 'Ye're too wee tae go out intae the world on yer own.' He

48

tickled Fergus's neck, then said, 'Ye should mebbe get a wee fence put up tae keep him away from the road and the work yard. I'll see tae it for ye, when I've got a minute.'

He must have arrived for work early the following morning, for when Kirsty went into the wash house to use the copper, the shears and the lawnmower were gleaming with oil and, as she discovered when she tested them cautiously with the tip of one finger, well sharpened. Todd and Ewan were alone at the bench when she went to the workshop to thank him.

'It was no bother. I brought a scythe with me, for the long grass'll have to be cut down before you do anything else. I've got a minute or two free now, I'll just start on the grass for ye.' The curved blade flashed as he lifted the scythe from a corner.

'I'll do it,' Ewan offered at once. He had served most of his time with a large and successful workshop employing quite a number of men and was finding the Paisley business restricting. He also disliked working with his father and stepbrother. 'I feel like a wee laddie when they're beside me all the time,' he had complained to Kirsty. 'I can't be myself.'

Now he reached eagerly for the scythe, his face falling when Todd shook his head. 'If ye've never used one before it could have the legs off ye, laddie – then what would Mr Lennox have tae say?'

'He'd find a low bench for me and make me work on my stumps,' Ewan muttered, scowling.

'I don't want to take you from your work,' Kirsty protested as they went up the lane.

'It'll take but a minute or two. Is the wee lad in the house?' he asked. 'This thing could cut him in two.'

'Him and Mary both, with the door latched.' She stood back as Todd took a firm two-handed grip on the scythe handle, setting his feet apart. He swung the blade smoothly along at ground level, and a swath of grass toppled and fell. A step, another swing, and more grass was laid low by the shining blade. It was fascinating to watch.

'Where did you learn to do that?'

'I've got a wee allotment,' Todd explained without breaking the rhythm of his work. 'It means I can help my sister with fresh vegetables. I bide with her and her man now that my mam and da are gone,' he explained as another strip of grass fell before the blade. 'I like tae do what I can tae pay them back for their kindness.' He had reached the far side of the patch in no time. 'There's nothin' like new tatties cooked in their jackets. I'll bring ye some if ye want.'

'That'd be kind.'

'When Beth and me get wed we'll be able tae eat our own home—'

'What's this?' Matt asked from the pend.

'I'm takin' the worst of the grass away for the mistress,' Todd told him easily, flipping the scythe around with practised ease to bring the wicked-edged blade uppermost. He ran one broad hand carefully over the metal to clear away strands of grass and nodded at the lane. 'And I'll put up a fence tae keep the bairn safe by the house now that he's gettin' around so well.'

'I'll see tae that,' Matt's voice was sharp. 'It's my concern – yours is in the workshop.'

Todd shrugged easily. 'I'd a minute while I waited for the glue pot tae heat. It'll be ready by now,' he said, and went off whistling, the scythe over his shoulder.

That night in the privacy of their room, Matt gave his wife a lecture on how employees should be treated.

'He was just trying to be helpful,' Kirsty protested. 'And that scythe made a difference to the grass.'

'But he's my journeyman.' She noticed that Matt's stiffening fingers were having some difficulty unfastening the buttons on his shirt.

'Let me do that,' she suggested, but he twitched away, in no mood to accept it. 'I can manage fine. As I was sayin', how am I expected tae keep the man's respect if my own wife treats him like one of the family?'

'I don't think Todd Paget's likely to stop respecting you that easily.'

'Just tend tae the house, Kirsty, and let me tend tae my workshop and those in it,' Matt said huffily, wrenching one of the buttons so hard that it came off and bounced against the washstand. He muttered a curse. 'The thread can't be up tae much.'

Kirsty retrieved the button. 'I'll sew it tomorrow morning.'

Her father, she thought, as she released her hair from the bun she kept it in during the day and began to brush it, had objected just like Matt when her mother had taken an interest in Sandy, fresh from the orphanage and alone in the world.

'The laddie's never known a mother or father, or a proper home,' Eliza Galbraith had protested. 'And he's that thin. If you'll just let me give him his dinner every day it'll strengthen him, then he can work all the harder for you.'

Her husband had been adamant. He would not, under any circumstances, allow his apprentice to share his table, but Eliza had finally persuaded him to let her send the occasional bowl of hot soup to Sandy in the workshop on cold days.

'Men seem to need self-respect more than women do,' she had explained to her daughter. 'Women have the comfort of knowing who and what they are, but for some reason men have to keep proving that they're men. It's best to humour them.' Then, her lovely turquoise eyes lighting up with amusement, she had added, 'And even though it means letting them win the big battles, we women can aye use the wits the good Lord gave us to make sure that we always win the wee ones.'

Eliza Galbraith was never to know it, but her efforts on behalf of the shy, undernourished apprentice had set in motion events that would reach far into the future. It was during her visits to the workshop at her mother's request, carefully negotiating the stony lane without spilling a drop of the hot soup, that Kirsty had got to know Sandy, first as a friend, then later, after Eliza' s early death, as a confidant and lover.

It was strange, Kirsty thought as she put the brush down and got into bed, how even an occasional bowl of soup could alter people's lives.

Caitlin and Mary jostled for a place at the window as the tramcar rocked its way through Paisley. Even Fergus, who normally fell asleep when in motion, sat bright-eyed on Kirsty's knee as she pointed out the handsome library and museum and, a little further along, the Coats Memorial Church.

'Look at all these steps up to the door,' Caitlin marvelled. 'I've never seen so many steps!' While Mary wanted to know, 'Why do they have a church just for coats?'

'It's named after the Coats family. They own big mills in Paisley, and they built the church – and the library and the museum. See that hill we're passing? That leads up to the John Neilson School. If you squeeze against the window and look up above the trees you can see the dome on top of it, like a porridge bowl turned up side down.'

The tram rocked through the town and out into the countryside, past the big tramcar workshop at Elderslie, then through the tiny village itself before rattling downhill into the engineering town of Johnstone.

They were fortunate; until two months before, the terminus had been in Johnstone's main square, and travellers wanting to get to Kilbarchan had faced a three-mile walk. Now, much to Kirsty's relief, they were transported in comfort to the foot of Steeple Brae, the hill that linked the village's two levels.

Instead of walking up the brae, Kirsty started up a narrow, steep road off to one side. It rose a little, then levelled off into a cool, shaded lane running between the high walls bounding two small estates. At the other end of the lane, where it opened onto a green, sun-filled park, Caitlin and Mary raced ahead while Fergus chattered in a language of his own, pointing at everything with his chubby little hands. At the other side of the park the path rose again, towards double gates leading to a road. Kirsty called the girls to her, pointing at a row of neat two-storey stone houses facing the park.

'One of these houses used to belong to my grandfather. The rumbling noise comes from the stone quarry on the other side of the park.'

A few minutes later they had reached the house. The minute patch of grass in front of her grandfather's former home, the pansies edging the stone path, the rambling roses smothering the trellis by the door were just as they had been. Kirsty went up the path and, from force of habit, lifted the latch. The door swung open to reveal a long, cool, dark hall, running from front to back of the building. From behind a door halfway along the hall she could hear the steady familiar beat of looms at work, the click of the treadles beneath the weavers' feet, the rattle of the overhead harness, the rhythmic crack of shuttles speeding back and forth, carrying the warp thread.

The place and the sounds were so familiar that when Kirsty opened the door she fully expected to see her grandfather's sturdy body swaying on the saytree – the weaver's bench – his bald head shining in the sun from the window behind him. But the man at the big loom was as thin as a rake, with spiky dark hair, well dusted with grey, thick over his narrow skull.

The dark-haired girl operating the smaller of the two looms was the first to see Kirsty and the children hovering at the door. 'Faither,' she said in a soft, pretty voice, and the man looked up, then stopped work.

'Aye, lass ?'

'I'm—' she stumbled over the words. 'My grandfather, Alexander Jardine—'

'You're never Mr Jardine's grandwean! Come in, come in – and welcome!' Beaming, he got to his feet.

'You knew my grandfather?'

'Knew him? I was his 'prentice once.' Like the girl, he had a soft, lilting Highland accent. 'When I became a master weaver I went back home tae work in the islands.'

He caught up a broom handle from its place against one

54

whitewashed wall and thumped the end of it against the ceiling. 'I'm just callin' the wife,' he explained, putting an arm about the girl, who had come to his side. 'This is Ellie, my daughter, and these'll be your own bairns.'

'There are another two at home.'

He nodded at Caitlin. 'This one's got the look o' Mr Jardine's daughter. She used tae work that wee loom when I first came here.'

'She was my mother.'

'Aye, well, she would be.' His smile faded. 'I heard she'd passed on.'

'Nineteen years ago.'

'And awful young tae be taken.'

'Now what is it, Geordie Bishop?' a voice demanded from the doorway. 'Can a body never have a minute's peace?'

'Morag, ye mind me mentionin' Mr Jardine that I was 'prentice tae? Here's his daughter and grandweans come tae visit.'

'Mentionin'?' Mrs Bishop's smile almost split her round face as she shook Kirsty's hand. Her voice had the same lilt as her husband's, and although she radiated energy, her hair, wound round her head in a long plait, was white as freshly fallen snow. 'In all the years I've kenned him Geordie's never stopped talkin' of Mr Jardine. I'm pleased to meet ye, Mrs . . .?'

'Mrs Lennox – Kirsty. I wanted the children to see where my grandfather used to live.'

'It's not changed since then,' Bishop said, 'though the loom's my own. I don't know what became of yer grandfather's.'

'It's in a storeroom at the house we're living in now,' Caitlin told him. 'But it's all broken.'

'Now that's a great pity, for a loom's only content when it's working.'

Caitlin looked puzzled. 'How does it know? It's only wood.'

'Some folk'd agree with ye, pet, but looms are more than they seem.'

'Can we see yours working?'

'To be sure ye can.' The weaver moved back to his saytree as Mary tugged at Kirsty's sleeve and said in a loud, clear whisper, 'Mam, I need to go to the privy.'

'I'll see tae the wee one,' Mrs Bishop took Fergus from Kirsty, 'while you take the lassie to the privy at the back. Then you'll come upstairs and have some refreshments.'

The kitchen above the weaving shop was warm and bright, with patchwork cushions on the armchairs by the fire and copper pans and spotless hand-painted dishes set in rows on the dresser shelves. Fergus was chewing contentedly on a crust when Kirsty and Mary arrived, while Mrs Bishop buttered warm scones.

'My Geordie thought the world of your grandfather – and his daughter,' she said as they drank tea. 'That'd be your mother?' She fed a piece of scone to Fergus. 'He said she was always lively.'

'She was.' Kirsty thought of her parents, one brimming over with her love of life, the other dour. Perhaps folk were attracted by opposites. Perhaps that was the secret of the romance between Todd Paget and Beth Laidlaw.

'Is Ellie your only child?'

'Dear me no, she's the youngest of eight. The others are all over Scotland, all wed and with bairns of their own. She's a grand wee weaver – Geordie's pleased that she's still workin' with him.'

Fergus fell asleep and they put him on the Bishops' big bed, wedged in with pillows and cushions, then went to the weaving shop, where Caitlin was still watching the looms at work.

'Mr Bishop says he'll come to Paisley to see the broken loom,' she announced as soon as her mother appeared.

'I'd said I'd like tae have a look at it, if yer mam and da don't mind,' the old man corrected her mildly.

'I'd be very pleased if you would, Mr Bishop.' Kirsty was certain that sooner or later Matt would throw out the remains of the old loom, and she wanted to know, before it was too late, if it could be saved.

Listening to the beat of the looms, she recalled playing on that same earthen floor while her mother and grandfather worked. There were usually others in the weaving shop – local men who looked in for what her grandfather called 'a good crack'. He loved taking part in the nonstop talk and the arguments, which usually centred round politics or religion.

'My mother used to make clothes for me from the dumps – the ends of cloth that weren't needed,' she told the Bishops. 'Good, sturdy cloth it was too. It wouldn't wear out, no matter how roughly I treated it.' She laughed, memories flooding back. 'I remember telling her that I didn't want to wear dumps any more – I wanted clothes bought in shops, like the other girls at school.'

Morag chuckled. 'Ellie knows what you mean,' she said, and as her shy daughter laughed and agreed, she lifted a pile of cloth from a shelf in one corner. 'Here.' She handed the material to Caitlin, 'These are dumps. Mebbe you and your wee sister can use them to make clothes for your dollies.'

Caitlin fingered the cloth, her eyes round with pleasure. 'Was this made on these looms?'

'Every bit of it, lass,' Geordie assured her.

A carter called to deliver pirns and collect finished cloth, and Kirsty, reminded of the passing time, announced that they must go home.

'Jamie'll take ye back tae Paisley on the cart,' Geordie Bishop said. 'Will ye not, Jamie?'

The carter nodded. 'If ye don't mind cuddlin' up beside the cloth I'm takin' over tae Barrhead.'

It was an improvement on the last time Kirsty had been on a cart, bumping uncomfortably through Paisley Cross. They were tucked snugly in among large bales of cloth, a bag filled with home-baked scones and a piece of fruit cake beside them.

'Mind and come back soon,' Mrs Bishop called from the gate, while her husband waved his pipe at the departing guests.

'Can we?' Caitlin asked as the cart jolted off.

'If you want.'

Caitlin hugged her precious cloth. 'I'd like to be a weaver when I leave school,' she said, and Kirsty put an arm around her. She herself had wanted to take up weaving, and eventually work with her grandfather, but her father had refused to consider it.

'Weaving's a dying craft,' he had said. 'Best tae go into service an' get a trainin' that'll stand ye in good stead. If ye're not fortunate enough tae find a man willin' tae marry ye,' he had added, 'there'll always be a rich woman wantin' a servin' lass.'

6

'It's fit for nothin' but firewood,' Matt said, indicating the ruckle of timbers and yarn lying in a pathetic heap against the store's stone wall.

Geordie Bishop stooped and put a hand on one of the wooden rollers, touching it gently, as though soothing a sick animal.

'It's worth trying to make it better, isn't it?' Caitlin asked anxiously, then, as her father gave a soft snort of derision, said, 'Mr Bishop says that looms are more like people than machines.'

'I think it'd be worth tryin' tae get it together again,' Geordie said slowly. 'There's not that many looms left, though once they numbered in their hundreds in this very town. It's a shame tae let this one go without tryin'.'

'I've no room for it in here,' Matt told him impatiently. 'I've got orders tae fill – I need the space.'

Geordie sucked on his pipe, and its tobacco fragrance floated through the air. 'There's an old weavin' shed in our back yard. It's got bits an' pieces in it, but I can clear them out easy enough.'

Caitlin's face shone. 'Could we send it there, Father?'

'One of the carters could mebbe bring it over tae Kilbarchan when he brings pirns,' the weaver went on placidly. 'He'd need payin', mind.'

'I'll see to that,' Kirsty offered.

'Father?' Caitlin went to Matt, standing before him, taking his hands in hers. 'Please?'

His face softened as he looked down into her pleading eyes. He had always had a soft spot for Caitlin, though he would have been the first to deny it. 'As long as I get it out of here, I don't care where it goes.'

'I don't know what ye think ye're at,' he grumbled to Kirsty that night, 'payin' out good money tae get a clutter of old wood taken tae Kilbarchan. Ye're daft, woman, that loom'll never work again.' He slid his nightshirt over his head, pulled his trousers off and sat on the edge of the bed, rubbing at one of his knees.

'It matters to Caitlin.' It mattered to Kirsty as well, but she kept quiet about that. 'If Mr Bishop can't restore the loom, at least she knows he tried. Is your knee sore?'

'Aye, confound the thing. I cannae understand it, it's not as if the weather's cold.'

'It'll be the rain we've had over the past few days.' Kirsty fetched the jar of wintergreen. 'That's why the west of Scotland suits textile manufacturing; the dampness in the air is good for the yarn.'

'It's not so good for folk, though,' Matt said as she knelt before him and began to rub the strong-smelling ointment into his knee, working at it until her palm burned with the friction.

'I'll wrap a piece of flannel round it to keep it warm.' The strong smell of wintergreen stung at her eyes and caught her throat as she put the lid back on the jar and washed her hands thoroughly in the basin before wrapping the flannel round his knee.

He rolled into bed with a grunt of satisfaction. 'That stuff can warm like a dram of whisky in yer belly,' he said, and was asleep and snoring before she got into bed.

In September Caitlin and Mary started attending the South School in Neilston Road. For Caitlin, it was the beginning of her final year, while it was Mary's first taste of education. She clutched at her sister's hand as they left the house and hurried along the pavement, her plain little face set with the sheer effort of leaving babyhood behind and becoming a 'big lassie'.

Until then, Kirsty had been too busy to apply for the post of sewing woman that Jean had mentioned. On the day the schools started she walked to the Hamiltons', where she discovered to her surprise that the cook was Bessie MacIntosh, who had been a kitchen maid when Kirsty worked for the family. She recognised Kirsty at once and insisted on giving her a cup of tea and bringing her up to date with all that had happened since.

'I've not done all that much,' Kirsty said evasively. 'I married and raised a family – and here you are, in charge of these big kitchens!'

Bessie simpered and smoothed her apron and launched into her own story. While Kirsty had travelled along a road beset with disgrace, banishment, motherhood and marriage, Bessie had stayed on with the Hamiltons, gaining the post of cook when the only son of the house and his new bride had taken over as master and mistress.

'It's fortunate that you came when you did,' she finished. 'Another sewing woman was taken on, but she didnae suit the mistress one bit, and she's just been dismissed.'

'Is this Mrs Hamilton difficult to get on with, then?'

Bessie shrugged massive shoulders. 'She's no' easy, but ye just don't let her bother ye. If ye're good at yer job, she leaves ye alone. And as I mind, you were always the best seamstress in the class. If ye'd stayed on here, ye'd probably have been Mrs Hamilton's lady's maid by now. I'll let her know ye're wantin' a word and I'll keep the wee chap company while ye're talkin' tae her.'

The present Mrs Hamilton, plump and fussy and not at all like her late mother-in-law, who had been both elegant and serene, agreed there and then that Kirsty should spend two mornings a week in her sewing room.

'It's difficult to get good reliable servants these days, and I need someone as soon as possible. You'll be on trial, of course, for a month.'

'Yes, Mrs Hamilton.'

'The last sewing-woman claimed to be good, but she was quite impossible, and there's a lot of work waiting to be done. Can you start this week, Mrs er . . .?'

Her face fell when she heard that Kirsty would have to bring Fergus with her each morning.

'He's very well behaved,' Kirsty pleaded. 'He'll be no bother.'

'Well, I really do need a sewing woman. You can bring him,' Mrs Hamilton said reluctantly. 'But if he makes a noise or gets into the rest of the house, you'll have to go.'

'Daft woman,' Bessie scoffed when she heard. 'The bairn can play in the sewin' room, and if he gets tired of that, or milady's in talkin' tae ye, I'll see tae him.'

As it happened, Fergus coped with the new arrangement very well. For most of Kirsty's time at the big house he played contentedly in a corner of the room, and when he tired of that, Bessie was happy to take him into the kitchen, where she and the rest of her staff made a fuss of him. Sometimes one of the yard staff took him out to see the horses. Fergus adored animals and had no fear of them, not even the large horses that drew Mrs Hamilton's carriage. Soon he was a favourite with the entire staff, who became adept at whisking him out of sight when the master or mistress happened to appear.

Mrs Hamilton didn't believe in paying her servants well, but even so there was enough, with what was left of the money inherited from her father, for Kirsty to buy an old sewing machine from a second-hand shop. She carried it home triumphantly, and after cleaning and oiling it she used it to make a stylish winter coat and bonnet for Mary from the huge velvet gown she had bought from Jean Chisholm's little shop. There was enough material left over to make a little coat for Fergus, too, and for two velvet cushions for the chairs in the front room. The remaining scraps were cut into shapes then sewn into a ball for Fergus, who celebrated his first birthday in November with a traditional home-made dumpling.

By that time he was toddling about the house, drunk with the sense of power that his newly learned method of transport brought. In order to curtail his travelling Kirsty knitted a harness to go round his chest and back and over his shoulders, with long reins that could be used to tether him to her sewing table when she was working at Mrs Hamilton's or, in the house or the wash house, the table leg or the leg of the deep stone sink used for rinsing clothes. If she was hanging up her washing in the back yard, she tied him to the clothespole furthest from the pend, for he knew that it led to the street and was continually making a bid for freedom.

'He's an adventurous one,' Jean said in the shop one day as Kirsty stopped him from making yet another dash for the door. 'He's going to grow up to be a sailor or a soldier.'

'A tinker, more like,' Kirsty said in despair.

'This is bonny enough tae grace a lord's bairn.' Jean was examining the velvet coat and bonnet Kirsty had brought in to show her. She turned the coat over in her work-reddened hands, holding it close to the window so that she could study the lining. 'Where did ye get the pattern?'

'Out of my own head. I can't afford patterns, but I've learned a lot just trying to keep all of us dressed on Matt's wages.'

'What about the other gown ye took?'

'I've not had time to start on that, now that I'm working at the Hamiltons'. It'll make a dress and jacket for Caitlin and the bits left over'll make more cushions.' Kirsty peered round the small dim shop, wishing that there was more light. 'D'you have any bits of fur I could use to trim the coat and bonnet?'

The old bell fixed above the shop door signalled a customer's entry with the toneless clack that was all it could muster. 'Have a look for yersel' in the back shop,' Jean said.

The tiny room behind the shop was crammed with boxes

and bags of clothing. Kirsty began to rummage through a box while Fergus plunged into a great pile of clothes stacked in one corner.

By the time Jean came in Kirsty had found a fur stole. 'This might do. There'll be enough left over to make a nice wee muff once I've done the trimming. And I'll take this too.' After a tussle she pulled out a fawn and blue striped dress. 'I could make it over for myself.'

'Ye'd need tae take the whole thing apart.'

'That's no trouble.' Kirsty set the things aside and went to untangle Fergus, who was squalling for help after burrowing into skirts and blouses and jackets and getting lost. 'You should sort all this stuff out properly, Jean. You'd probably sell most of it if the folk could just see it. What you don't need could be sold to the ragman. It'd bring in some money and make space for the better stuff to be hung up properly.'

Jean looked round helplessly. 'I know, but there's so much of it. I don't know where to begin.'

'You'll have to make a start one day, for it'll not sort itself out. Before you give anything to the ragman you should cut off the buttons first, for some of them are bonny. They're probably expensive too. And take off any ribbons and bits of fur or lace you find,' Kirsty went on, her enthusiasm rising. 'You could put them into wee boxes in the front shop. Folk who make their own clothes would be glad to buy them.'

'It all sounds like more trouble than it's worth.'

'I'll help you,' Kirsty said without stopping to think. Jean brightened at once.

'Would ye? I could never do it all on my own – I'd not know where tae start.'

It had been a rash promise, made on the spur of the moment. Kirsty already had enough to fill her time, but her fingers itched to set the place to rights and to find any treasures that might be lurking undetected among the untidy piles of clothing.

When they started work on the back shop Kirsty began to understand why Jean had put the task off and thus let the stock get out of hand. The place was so full of clothing that there was no room to sort out what was to stay and what was to go to the ragman. Finally they resorted to tossing the contents of every box and bundle into one corner, a method that gradually cleared half the room, while creating a colourful mountain of muslins, tarlatans, flannels, taffetas, silks, bombazines and velvets against the opposite wall. The sturdier boxes were retained and the others banished into the tiny back yard.

The hours they spent together revived the close friendship they had once shared, until finally Kirsty felt comfortable enough with Jean to tell the truth about her sudden departure from Paisley. She half expected the other woman to react with shock and perhaps censure, but instead Jean said, 'I'd not have wanted tae lose a bairn if I'd been fortunate enough tae have one.' Then, an edge to her voice, she added, 'If ye ask me, yer father treated ye cruelly. Ye were little more than a bairn yersel'. I wish ye'd thought tae come tae my mother, Kirsty. I'm sure she'd have helped ye.'

'I didn't have time to think of that, but even if I had my father would have fetched me back. He'd not have wanted me to stay in Paisley, where everyone knew that I was his daughter.'

'Still,' Jean said, 'it all worked out for ye, and I'm glad ye finally found yer way back.'

It took a week to empty all the boxes. Kirsty and Fergus returned home each afternoon sneezing from the dust and fluff they had inhaled. When the first rough sorting was over, the boxes that had been retained were each assigned to a different type of garment, with RAGS crayoned on the largest. Then the two women began to dismantle the great pile of clothes, garment by garment.

Buttons were snipped from clothes deemed to be too stained, torn or worn to be of use, and at Kirsty's insistence other forms of ornamentation, such as ribbons and flowers and strips of velvet and lace were also kept back.

'We could mebbe use them to improve some of the clothes you're selling,' Kirsty told Jean when she tried to argue. She paused to mop her face and fold her sleeves back. It was a bitterly cold day in November, and chilly draughts blew into the unheated shop through the ill-fitting doors and windows, but the two of them were working so hard that perspiration stood out on their foreheads.

'I'm not in the business of improving things, Kirsty. I just take in stuff that folk don't want any more and try tae sell it tae other folk that do want it.'

A customer came in and she bustled into the front shop while Kirsty, glad of a respite, sank down onto the pile of clothing still awaiting attention. If the shop was hers, she thought, she wouldn't settle for just receiving and selling castoffs. There was surely more to running a business than that.

7

By the beginning of December Jean Chisholm's back shop
was cleared of the tumbled mass of bundles and boxes that
had annoyed Kirsty. A row of boxes against one wall held
stock to be sold, and Jean was a few pounds richer, having
struck a lucrative deal with one of the town's ragmen.

As far as Jean was concerned, matters could be left like
that, but Kirsty, fearful of seeing the little back shop slowly
fill up again, tried to persuade her to turn her attention to the
shop itself.

'It's too cluttered, Jean.'

'How else dae folk know what I've got if they cannae see
it?' Jean argued.

'You can always bring other things from the back shop if
they ask to see more.'

They were standing together behind the counter, watching
as two women picked their way through piles of clothing,
tossing each rejected article aside. One of them had taken out
several pretty but impractical gowns, then dropped them on
the floor. Now she held a more serviceable dress up in front

of her scrawny, undernourished body and asked Jean, 'D'ye think it's too big for me?'

Jean narrowed her eyes thoughtfully. 'A wee bittie, mebbe – but if ye put a belt round it and fold the sleeves back it'll do ye fine. It's good material and it'll last for a long while.'

'I suppose ye're right,' the woman said doubtfully. Kirsty knew that she was probably younger than she looked, still young enough to like pretty clothes and to want to look her best, even though she had been prematurely thrust into middle age by hard work.

'What's it for?' she asked.

'I wanted somethin' nice for the kirk on Sundays. My best frock's that worn ye could spit peas through it. It'll no' take another washin'.' The woman looked again at the dress, chewing at her lower lip, then said, 'I thought I could mebbe find somethin' in here.'

'That'll hang on you like an empty sack,' Kirsty told her bluntly and heard a sharp intake of breath from Jean. 'Here, let me look.'

Well aware that Jean was seething silently at her for throwing away a possible sale, she went through the box herself and found a sturdy cream-coloured dress. 'This'd fit better.'

Disappointment spread over the once-pretty face. 'It's awful plain, though.'

'There's a nice bit of red velvet in the back shop, enough to make a collar and put a strip of velvet down each side of the bodice – here and here, see?' Kirsty suggested, then, as interest dawned, 'Mebbe the velvet could stretch to a narrow belt and strips round the wrists and the hem. You've got a nice slim waist; a narrow belt would suit it. Come into the back shop and try the dress on while I look for the velvet.'

By the time she found it in the box of pieces saved from rejected clothes, the woman had stripped off her shabby blouse and skirt. The skinny body beneath her much-darned petticoat bore indications of the fullness it would have had if its owner had not been born into a life of drudgery and malnourishment. She had probably never had pretty clothes, Kirsty thought with compassion. She deserved one nice dress.

'Here it is.' She held the velvet up. 'There's just enough to do everything I suggested. And here are some pretty wee pearl buttons – a row of them down the velvet strips on the bodice would look bonny. Try the dress on and I'll hold the velvet against it.'

The different colours and materials went well together. Kirsty looked round in vain for a mirror, then led the customer through the shop and out onto the pavement. Jean's small-paned window was no use, but the large window in the butcher's shop next door provided quite a good reflection.

'If you sewed the velvet on here, and here . . .' Kirsty held the ribbon against the dress, ignoring the stares and sniggers of passers-by. The woman nodded eagerly, her face flushing with pleasure.

'It'd look braw,' she agreed. 'I'm no' a great hand at the sewin', though. I'd probably spoil it.'

'I'll do it for you – for threepence more than the price of the dress.' Kirsty already had more than enough to do, but she was eager to see what the altered dress would look like. When they had returned to the back room she ferreted around for a pair of scissors and a box of pins then started pinning the velvet to the dress.

'You could pay half now and the other half when it's finished,' she said through a mouthful of pins, 'and I'll try to have it ready next week.'

The customer was glowing when she left, but Jean's mouth was tight with annoyance.

'There was nothin' wrong with the first dress she picked out. It would've done her fine. And it was hard-wearin'.'

Kirsty was picking up the scattered clothing, grunting slightly each time she stooped. She straightened up, easing her back. 'Just because folk are poor it doesn't mean that they can't look nice, Jean. If you showed the clothes off to better advantage on rails folk wouldn't need to dig into the boxes and make such a mess.'

'Ye were never as bossy as this when we went to school together, Kirsty Galbraith!'

'I've learned an awful lot since then,' Kirsty said dryly.

The red velvet and pearl buttons made all the difference to the dress. When the young woman saw her reflection in the butcher's window a week later her stooped shoulders seemed to lift and straighten.

'It's the bonniest gown I've ever had,' she whispered, touching the velvet gently with the tip of a finger, basking in the inquisitive, interested glances of the women queueing in the shop. 'Even bonnier than my weddin' gown was!' Pleasure smoothed years of hard work and worry from her face, giving a glimpse of the pretty girl she had once been.

'You need a good mirror, Jean,' Kirsty said when the customer had departed, walking on air, her new Sunday dress in a brown paper package beneath her arm. 'It's not seemly for folk, standing on the footpath and trying to see themselves in

. a window reflection mixed up with cuts of meat and plucked chickens.'

'Ye should have used the window of the empty shop on the other side,' Jean told her. 'Anyway, most of the folk that come in here don't need tae try the clothes on. This isnae a dress shop.'

'It is, for the folk that live round here. Mrs Hamilton's maid sometimes brings fashion papers she's done with down to the kitchen for the servants to read, then they're thrown out. I'll ask if I can have them. We could hang them on the counter to let folk have a look through them.'

'You're going to be the ruination of me,' Jean said in despair.

While Christmas was celebrated in England, north of the border Ne'erday, the arrival of the new year, was considered to be the more important of the two festivals. To mark the family's first New Year in Paisley, Kirsty invited Jean and the Bishops to share in their New Year dinner.

'The place'll be a madhouse,' Matt grumbled when he heard her intentions. 'It's supposed tae be my holiday – I cannae be doin' with all those folk in about me.'

But Kirsty was adamant. Jean had nobody else to celebrate the New Year with, and the Bishops had been good to Caitlin, who had taken to visiting the weaving shop every week to watch the looms at work, sometimes taking Mary with her. Geordie and his wife always made them welcome, and as often as not the girls returned with gifts of garden produce or home baking or pots of honey from the bee skeps Morag kept in the long back garden behind the house.

Kirsty would have liked to invite Todd as well, but that

would mean asking Beth too, and she was in no hurry to repeat the experience she had gone through on the girl's last visit. She asked Jean's advice and told her what had happened during Beth's last visit.

'She always was an uppity lassie, that Beth Laidlaw,' Jean said with a disparaging sniff. 'Her grandma spoiled her, and so does her father.'

'I never see him behind the counter.'

'That's because he believes himself tae be a religious man.' Jean gave another sniff. 'He doesnae believe in drinking, gambling or smoking. He's a worshipper – he worships the Lord three times every Sunday, and worships Mammon all the time. You can laugh, but it's true. That's why he kept the shop on instead of sellin' it. But Beth works behind the counter so's his hands can stay pure. How can the lassie be anythin' else but uppity, raised by folk like her granny and her da?'

'Poor Todd! He's a decent man who deserves a good wife.'

'Beth may not be the wife you'd want for him, but she's bonny, an' sometimes men cannae see the wood for the trees. As tae invitin' her for Ne'erday dinner – I'd leave it be, Kirsty. She'll only spoil the day for the rest of us.'

With Caitlin's help, and a little assistance from Mary, Kirsty cleaned the entire house in readiness for the New Year, paying particular attention to the parlour. During her childhood the room had only been used occasionally, when her mother entertained friends to tea. But there had never been visitors at Ne'erday because Murray Galbraith, like Matt, disliked having other people in his home.

Jean was the first to arrive on the day, in her best dress of grey watered silk with a pale lilac turban in the same material covering her grey hair. The Bishops knocked on the door just as she was accepting a small glass of sherry, their arms full of gifts including pipe tobacco for Matt, who thawed noticeably as he accepted it.

Ewan had made no secret of his interest in meeting Ellie Bishop, who was his own age, but the girl's natural shyness was even more evident among strangers, and he soon gave up his attempts to start a conversation. He lapsed into a sulky silence as he saw that Alex, with his more gentle approach, fared better with the girl, and once the meal was over and everyone had settled down in the parlour, he slipped out and went off to seek the company of his own friends.

'That Bishop lassie was awful quiet,' he complained the next morning. 'Ye get more crack from our Mary than from her.'

'She's nice enough,' Alex said defensively. 'Just young, and not used to meeting folk.'

'Going tae see her again, then?' Ewan teased, and Alex flushed slightly.

'She said she'd go out walking with me next week.'

'Can I come?' Caitlin asked at once.

'No, you can't.'

'Might as well let her, since the two of you'll only be walking,' Ewan jibed, and Alex flared up.

'There's nothing wrong with just walking and talking. You should try it some time.'

'And mebbe you should try—'

'Ewan!' Kirsty said sharply, while Matt rumbled, 'That's enough – I'll not have talk like that in my house.'

Ewan laughed and shrugged, but the exchange made Kirsty

74

feel uneasy. Although Ewan and his father were very similar, and the boy's good looks showed what Matt must have been like as a youth, their natures were completely different. Ewan was more adventurous than his father had ever been, and he certainly hadn't inherited Matt's strong views on morality.

Since coming to Paisley the youth had been restless, though he had made many friends among the young men in the area and rarely spent any of his free time at home. He liked dancing, and visiting the theatre in Smithhills, and Kirsty knew from the smell of his breath when he came home most evenings that he enjoyed a drink, though he held it well and she had never seen him the worse for it.

He was very popular with the girls. There were plenty to choose from; Coats' and Clark's huge mills mainly employed female workers of all ages, and it was a common sight, particularly at the end of the mill shifts, to see great numbers of laughing, chattering girls and women march along the streets, arm in arm, their clothes and hair flecked with white clumps of cotton from their workplace.

Recalling Alex's words and reminding herself that Ewan had reached eighteen years of age in October and was no longer a mere boy, Kirsty began to worry. If he ever got into trouble or, worse still, got a girl into trouble, Matt's fury would know no bounds.

She was glad, on reflection, that Ewan had found Ellie Bishop uninteresting.

During January the front shop was cleared and tidied and more of the clothes were hung on the walls instead of being left in boxes. Kirsty had coaxed some fashion papers from Mrs Hamilton's personal maid, and Jean insisted on boring holes in the corner of each one so that they could be hung on a string from the counter.

'Some folk round here have sticky fingers,' she explained, watching Kirsty push the string through the rough holes. 'Best not tae put temptation in their way.'

'I wish there was a bit more room. Then folk could try on the clothes.'

'God save us, Kirsty Lennox, what'll you think of next? I'm not givin' up my room upstairs for anyone, so you neednae think it!'

'I'd not expect you to. That shop next door's still empty,' Kirsty said slowly. 'It's a shame you can't take it over.'

'Have you gone clean daft? Where would I find the money to rent another shop?'

'You could mebbe get a loan from a bank.'

'And lie awake at nights worryin' about bein' in debt – no, no,' Jean said firmly. 'I'd not consider it.'

'I suppose you're right,' Kirsty agreed, and concentrated on getting another magazine onto the string. If the shop was hers, Kirsty would have ventured to try for a loan to improve it. But it wasn't, and Jean had already given in to so many of her ideas. She resolved, since it was the start of the new year and the right time for resolutions, to guard her tongue in the future, and she cast around for a change of subject.

'There's ructions in the Hamilton house just now. The youngest daughter, Rose, is home for the holidays from that finishing school of hers, and she and her mother don't see eye to eye on anything.'

'I thought I saw the lassie at the Cross the other day. She was always the cuckoo in that nest. Tall and gangly, and dresses more like a man than a woman.'

'She likes her clothes to be plain,' Kirsty agreed. 'But that's because she's mostly outside anyway, walking or bicycling. Mrs Hamilton's maid says that she's determined to get Miss Rose into pretty clothes now that she's almost old enough for marriage, but the lassie hates frills and ribbons.'

'Her two sisters were the pretty ones. They were both married off with no trouble, but Mrs Hamilton's goin' tae have trouble with this last one,' Jean said sagely. 'You wait and see. When does she finish that fancy school she's at?'

'In the summer. The maid says she's dreading it, for the girl'll be home all the time then. There.'

Kirsty tied several large knots in the end of the string and pulled it to make sure that it was well nailed to the counter. 'Folk'll enjoy looking through them.'

'And if they don't,' Jean said, 'the papers'll always come in useful in the privy.'

8

Contrary to Jean's prediction, the fashion papers attracted so much attention that she herself began to ask for more at the houses she collected clothing from. The box of bits and pieces cut from discarded clothes also proved to be popular; as often as not women who bought a dress or jacket then went on to choose ribbons or buttons or artificial flowers from the box to embellish their purchases.

Some of the women now sought Kirsty out to ask for her help in choosing clothes or her advice on alterations. Kirsty enjoyed it, and Jean no longer objected, realising that the new service offered by her friend was encouraging more women to come into the shop.

'You've got a rare way with the customers,' she said admiringly. 'You should've been a shop assistant instead of a maidservant.'

'I'd not have been able to care for Alex when we were on our own if I'd been working in a shop.'

'I suppose not, but what's meant'll no' go by, and you were meant for this sort of work.' Jean hesitated, then said tentatively, 'I don't suppose you'd be willin' tae work here with me?'

Kirsty was tempted, but common sense prevailed. She had become dependent on the little she earned at the Hamiltons', and Jean couldn't afford to match it. 'I've not got the time, what with the house and my wee sewing job.'

'Right enough, I couldnae expect you tae give that up. But mebbe you could do some sewin' if it's needed,' Jean said hopefully, 'the way you did for that woman. You could make a wee extra charge for it.'

'Ye've got enough tae dae without takin' on more,' Matt grumbled when Kirsty told him that she had agreed to Jean's suggestion.

'It'll just mean an hour each day in the shop, and I can do some of the sewing in the evenings when I'm seeing to the darning anyway.'

'If the house or the bairns suffer it'll have tae stop.'

'They'll not suffer, and neither will you.' Kirsty was determined not to let this chance slip by. To her mind, there was potential in the little second-hand clothes shop, and she was keen to develop it in any way she could.

Snow fell in early February, turning the industrial town into a different world overnight. Even the work yard was beautiful, with the piles of timber like mountains beneath a spotless white blanket and sunlight glittering on the icicles suspended from the workshop roof. Horses' hooves on the road and in the pend, where snow had been blown during the night, scarcely made a sound.

Fergus, enchanted, wanted to spend the entire day outside, and Kirsty was hard put to keep him indoors so that she could get on with her work. Another heavy snowfall came as she made the midday meal, so she filled an extra bowl with hot soup and handed it to Alex when he and his stepfather and stepbrother came in.

'Take this to the workshop for Todd before you sit down to your own meal.'

'Todd's got bread and cheese tae eat,' Matt growled as Alex, snow still clinging to his hair and eyelashes, went out again. 'There's no need for you tae feed him.'

Kirsty lifted Fergus onto her knee and started spooning soup into him. 'It's bitter cold in that workshop.'

'There's the stove that keeps the glue-pots goin'.'

'That doesn't make much difference, as you know from your rheumatics.'

'Todd's a good bit younger than me,' Matt snapped. 'He doesnae feel the cold the same.' Without thinking, he rubbed at the ache now gnawing continually at his knee joint.

'And where d'you think your rheumatism started? Working in cold shops when you were his age. One bowl of soup's not going to turn us into paupers.'

While Kirsty washed the dishes and made preparations for the evening meal, Fergus clamoured to get out to run about in the soft white world.

'If you're a good laddie and play with your bricks for a minute we'll go to Auntie Jean's shop later,' Kirsty promised, settling him on the rug with his wooden blocks and making sure that the guard was secured in front of the fireplace. Gathering up some clothes to be soaked in the wash house, she hurried out of the back door before he realised what she was doing. Ignoring the howl of realisation and rage, she pulled the door shut behind her, listening for the click of the latch falling into place. The snowfall had passed, but a few flakes drifted down from the lightening sky, and the footprints she and Fergus had left that morning in the back yard had almost been obscured beneath the new fall.

Kirsty had built a fire beneath the copper that morning and the whitewashed room was pleasantly warm. Dropping the last garment into the bubbling water, Kirsty pushed it well down with the wooden tongs. As she went out again, shivering as the sudden cold hit her, she heard a cart rumble into the pend from the street and saw that the ghostly footprints beneath the previous snowfall had been replaced by a line of small, fresh hollows leading in a wide curve from the back door, now swinging open, to the pend. Even as she took in their meaning, a man's hoarse shout came from the pend and was drowned out almost at once by the shrill squeal of a frightened horse.

Kirsty, screaming Fergus's name, dropped the empty basket and started to run. A stone hidden beneath the snow tripped her and threw her to her hands and knees. Pain stabbed through her ankle as she fell. Plunging her hands into the snow to the wrist, she tried to get up, but her body had locked with cold or fright or both, and she could only crouch like an animal, screaming Fergus's name over and over again while within the hidden recesses of the pend the horse kept squealing, and the man kept shouting.

Alex and Todd Paget came running from the yard, staring into the pend at something Kirsty couldn't see and shouting, their eyes and mouths gaping wide.

Ewan followed, a hammer still clenched in one fist, with Matt limping behind as fast as he could. Ewan forced his way between the two men in front of him, his shoulder slamming into Alex and sending him flying. Kirsty, still kneeling in the snow, still screaming, heard the dull thud as his forehead collided with one of the metal poles holding the drying line.

Tossing the hammer away with such force that it clanged on the wall, dislodging stone chips as well as a shower of snow crystals, Ewan threw himself into the pend, his hands reaching forward and down towards something on the ground, something that Kirsty couldn't see. Todd leaped out of her sight too, reaching up instead of down, while Matt, panting, half fell against the wall dividing the lane from the adjoining property. Later Kirsty was to learn that the journeyman had managed to catch the terrified horse's bridle, saving Ewan, at least, from the animal's slashing ironclad hooves.

Alex lay motionless where he had fallen, a line of red blood spreading across his forehead and spilling into the white snow beneath, while Matt, his face grey and his eyes glazed with horror, cast a glance into the pend, then folded in the middle like Mary's favourite rag doll and vomited on to the dirty, slushy lane.

Matt carried Fergus's small coffin through the streets in his arms, followed by Ewan and Alex, who insisted on going although he was still white and shaken, his badly cut and bruised head bandaged.

Kirsty, following tradition, stayed at home with her daughters. Jean was with her, and Morag; Caitlin helped the two of them to prepare food for the mourners who would return to the house, while Kirsty sat by the fire, Mary huddled in her lap. She was unaware of the warmth of the coals, or the others' hushed voices or Mary's face, wet with tears, against her neck. All she could see was the windswept cemetery and the open grave, a slash of bitter black earth against the white snow. All she could hear was the thud of cold wet earth falling on the wooden casket that cradled her bairn.

She blamed herself bitterly for not crediting Fergus with the wit to open the latched door. It was clear from the way the sturdy box that housed his wooden bricks had been found lying empty on its side that the little boy had clambered onto it in order to lift the latch.

Mary whimpered, and Kirsty automatically rocked her to and fro. 'I knew he never liked being shut in the house,' she said aloud. 'I should have thought . . .'

'Nobody can read a bairn's mind.' Morag came to sit opposite, putting a work-worn hand over Kirsty's.

'Did you ever lose a child, Morag? I don't mean a stillbirth or a death before you got to know the wee soul, but a child you had long enough to know?'

'Two of mine went that way, hen. One from the diphtheria, the other drowned in a burn. I know how it is, and I know that ye'll survive it. My Geordie believes that looms have souls,' Morag said with a faint, affectionate smile. 'As for me, I think folk's lives are as true and as sure as patterns on the woven cloth. What's meant tae happen's already planned, and what's planned'll happen.' She got to her feet as the street door latch was lifted. From the hallway came the shuffle of feet and the subdued murmur of voices.

'Ye'll not make much sense out of what I'm sayin' for now, lassie, but one day ye'll know that I'm right. Now,' Morag lifted Mary from her mother's knee, then helped Kirsty from the chair, 'come and greet your visitors.'

*

In the weeks following the funeral Kirsty threw herself into work in the house, at the Hamiltons' and in Jean's shop, where she willingly took on more alteration work. She felt as though Fergus's death had somehow made it essential for her to find, or to make, new purpose in her life.

Although the house had been cleaned thoroughly when they had first moved in, she started again, first the bedrooms, then the parlour, and last, on a mild day heralding the end of winter and the arrival of spring, she dragged the chairs and rugs from the kitchen out to the drying green.

She had hung the rugs on the line and was attacking them with the carpet beater when a deep voice said from the lane, 'Aye, ye're in fine fig the day, Mrs Lennox.'

Startled, Kirsty swung round. 'It's yourself, Mr Gregg.' Embarrassed at being caught in such a mess, with her hair wisping about her face and her working apron on, she waved the beater. 'I thought I'd take advantage of the better weather and give the kitchen a good turnout.'

As a little girl, she had regarded Thomas Gregg, the merchant who had always supplied her father with timber, as a giant of a man, heavily built and loud voiced. Now, although he must have been nearing seventy, his voice still boomed, and his back was as straight as ever, though he had lost some weight and furrows had dug themselves into his face as the fat had melted from beneath the skin. She had heard that even though he was now a wealthy man he still worked alongside his employees when he had the time.

'Ye sound just like my wife – and my daughters,' he said, then, with sudden interest, asked, 'what have we here?'

Stepping off the lane, he examined the kitchen chairs, running his blunt, work-calloused fingers over the painted sprays on the back of one of them. 'That's bonny. Who did it?'

'The chairs are old, but Alex – my son – painted them and decorated them for me.'

'A pattern like that'd fairly brighten a room,' Gregg said thoughtfully. 'Yer man's already makin' a kitchen set for me. I think I'll ask the lad tae paint it when it's done, for I know the wife'd like fine tae have some pretty pictures like that in her kitchen. Is he asked tae do many?'

'These were done just for me, Mr Gregg. I don't think he's given a thought to decorating furniture for anyone else – though I know he'd be happy to do it for your wife,' she added hurriedly.

'Hmmm.' The man ran a hand thoughtfully over his chin, his eyes still on the chairs. 'I was hearin' recently about a big furniture exhibition comin' up in Glasgow this summer. He should exhibit some of his work in it.'

'D'you think folk would be interested?' Mr Gregg was known to be a shrewd businessman, with a good eye for anything that might make a profit.

'The womenfolk certainly would. I'll have a word with yer man – and the lad.'

The sun glanced on his bald head for a moment as he lifted his hat to her, then he strode off down the lane.

Alex was exultant when the men finished work for the day. 'Mr Gregg wants me to paint the furniture we're making for him – and put it into an exhibition!'

'What I want tae know is who put him up tae it?' Matt glowered.

'He saw our chairs in the passing. I'd put them out on the

green to get room to wash the kitchen floor. Are you not pleased for Alex?' Kirsty asked.

'Pleased tae see good wood painted like a loose woman? The man's gone daft. He's a timber merchant himself; he should know better than tae encourage such nonsense.'

Alex flushed. 'It's not nonsense. I've told you, it's popular all over the world. There's no reason why we shouldn't supply it if it's what folk want.'

'If it was what folk wanted they'd ask for it – and they don't.'

Kirsty could tell that Alex was holding in his temper with an effort. When he was angry, his red hair seemed to take on added colour. Tonight it almost lit up the kitchen.

'They don't ask because they don't know we can provide it. That's why Mr Gregg wants us to put his furniture into this exhibition when it's done.'

'Where's the harm in it, Matt?' Kirsty asked, and Matt, who had been taking his jacket off, shrugged it back on again.

'I'm away out for a breath of fresh air.'

'But what about your dinner?'

'I'll have it when I get back.' He threw the words over his shoulder, slamming the door behind him.

Mary, who had been jumpy and suffering from nightmares since Fergus's death, burst into tears and ran to her mother, while Caitlin, who had just come in to the room, asked, 'What's Father angry about?'

Alex gave a short, mirthless laugh. 'He's angry because someone likes something that I did.'

'Alex.' Kirsty glared at him over Mary's head. 'That's no way to speak of your father!'

Alex made for the door to the hall. 'I'm only telling the

truth, Mam. Nothing any of us does in that workshop pleases him!' he said, then he too stormed from the room, while Ewan, who had taken no part in the argument, asked plaintively, 'Are we never to get our dinner?'

When Mary had been soothed and soup had been ladled out, Kirsty took a bowl upstairs for Alex. He was sitting on the edge of the bed he shared with Ewan, staring at the opposite wall and clenching and unclenching his fists.

'I brought your soup, and some bread. You can come downstairs for your next course.'

He looked up at her, and for a moment, it was like looking at Sandy. 'I don't want it.'

'Of course you do. You've put in a day's work and there's no sense in punishing your stomach just because your head's angry.'

He shrugged, but accepted the bowl and the hunk of bread.

'You should have seen his face when Mr Gregg said he wanted that furniture painted and shown to folk,' he said at last, when the edge had been taken off his hunger. 'But there was nothing he could do but agree to what the man wanted. Mam, what's wrong with a wee place like ours branching out and trying something different – something that might bring in more work?'

Kirsty thought fleetingly of Jean's shop. It seemed that she and Alex were more ambitious and adventurous than Jean or Matt. 'I don't see anything wrong with it.'

'He's not even a cabinet-maker,' Alex said through a mouthful of food. 'If he'd just be content to see to the ordering and the customers and leave the work to the rest of us we'd manage fine. But he's always poking his neb into everything we do and treating us as if he's the craftsman and we're the 'prentices. There's no reason why he should be so opposed to me decorating furniture, except that it's another skill that I have and he hasn't.' He dug the spoon into the soup again. 'Todd's as tired of his pettiness as I am. I'd not be surprised if he found work elsewhere.'

Kirsty felt a flutter of alarm. 'Todd wouldn't do that.'

'I'd not blame him if he did,' Alex said bluntly.

'Mebbe your father needs to feel important. Is that so wrong?'

Alex stuffed the last hunk of bread into his mouth. 'If he does,' he said indistinctly, 'he can't be much of a man.'

She put a hand on his arm; beneath her fingers it felt strong and hard. 'He'd be upset if he knew how you feel.'

'Would he? I'm not his blood kin, remember.'

'He never thinks of that!'

Alex gave her a long, level look. 'Lennox and Sons. It's not me he wants to take over after him, mam. It's Ewan. The thing is,' his mouth took on a wry twist, 'Ewan can't wait tae get out of that workshop. It's me that'd like to take it over one day, not him. But it's him that'll get it.'

'That can't happen.'

'Can it not?' He got up and went to the door. 'We'd best go downstairs.'

9

As usual, Ewan went out after his evening meal, and when he finally returned Matt was with him. The two of them had obviously met in a public house, for they were cheerful and swaggering, more like drinking companions than father and son, and the stink of alcohol was strong on their breath.

Without comment, Kirsty set out Matt's dinner, now dried out from the oven. He wolfed it down without complaint, then settled into his usual chair by the fire with his pipe and the newspaper.

'You should see the doctor about that knee,' Kirsty said later in the bedroom. The business of rubbing wintergreen into his bad knee had become a daily routine, but tonight the swelling was worse and the skin of his knee was hot against her palm. 'Is your hip as bad as ever?'

'Aye, but I'm managin'.' His hand landed on her head, trailed down over her ear and her cheek to cup her chin and raise her face to his. His open mouth, still tasting strongly of drink as well as tobacco, lingered on hers for a long time while his free hand fumbled with her blouse buttons.

She drew her head away from his. 'Matt . . .'

His breathing had quickened, his eyes were half closed, his mouth slack. 'Hush, bonny bird,' he whispered. He had unfastened the first two buttons, and his fingers were rough against her skin as they probed beneath her blouse and petticoat then moved lower. She heard the pop of a button giving way and felt the sudden lack of resistance in her clothing as his fingers gained their objective, curving round below her left breast, then lifting.

'No, Matt . . .'

He stopped mouthing at her neck and drew his head back to survey her blearily. 'Why not?' he wanted to know, a belligerent note creeping into his tone.

'It's too soon.'

'For God's sake, Kirsty, it's been more than a month. How long am I supposed tae wait? I'm a married man – I'm used tae my comforts. I cannae just go without at your whim!' He caught at her wrist, pulling her hand down, forcing it against his groin. 'Ye cannae deny that I've strong need of ye.' Beneath the nightshirt he was hard, pulsing. He buried his face in her throat, nuzzling her, his lips hot on her skin.

'At least let me put my nightdress on and get into bed.'

'An' hope I'm asleep by the time ye're ready?' he mumbled against the curve of her breasts. 'No, no, bonny bird. I know yer tricks, and ye're not tryin' them tonight.'

'But it's not seemly this way!'

'There's a ring on yer marriage finger that says whatever way I want it's seemly,' said Matt, pushing her back onto the bed, following her down, stopping her mouth with his.

When Matt finally rolled away from Kirsty he fell into a deep sleep with the suddenness of a child, his arm lying heavily across her breasts, his unshaven face scratching her neck. Carefully, Kirsty eased out from beneath his embrace and got out of bed, locating her nightdress and feeling her way downstairs in the darkness to the kitchen.

She lit the gas mantle then hastily stripped off her disordered clothing, noting that two buttons would have to be found and sewn back on before she could wear that blouse again, and slipped the nightgown over her head. Working quickly and silently, she gathered together the things she needed – a bowl of clean water, a small dish of vinegar, a towel, and the carefully cleaned sponge she kept hidden away from the family's sight. She dropped the sponge into the vinegar, then lit a candle and carried everything out into the night.

The flagstones were cold beneath her bare feet and so was the cold stone floor of the wash house. Shivering, Kirsty closed the door then set the candle by the sink and put the bowl on the flagged floor. Squatting over it, she pulled her nightdress up to her waist and sluiced herself with clean water again and again, crouching like some primitive witch in the flickering, dancing shadows. She could have used the bathroom instead of going out into the cold night air but, being unused to such a luxury, none of the family felt comfortable there. In any case, Kirsty needed, that night, to be right out of the house where her children slept and to be sure of privacy.

Finally, after dabbing herself dry, she squeezed out the vinegar-soaked sponge and inserted it into her body. It should have been put in place earlier, but there had been no warning, and no time. She could only hope that as it had protected her against unwanted pregnancy before, it could still do so.

For the present, at least, she couldn't bear the thought of conceiving and birthing, and possibly losing, another child.

'What've ye done tae yer hair?' Jean asked in surprise a week or so later. The usual loose knot at the back of Kirsty's head had gone, and instead her fair hair was rolled up all around her head and knotted loosely on top.

'I got tired of wearing it the same way. And I finished making this blouse last night,' Kirsty took her coat off to display the plain white blouse, high necked and with deep cuffs. She had tied a piece of black silk round her throat as a cravat. 'I'm going to wear it and this black skirt in the shop from now on – and I'm making a blouse and skirt like them for you.'

'I keep tellin' ye – this isnae a high–class gown shop!'

'The customers'll enjoy seeing us both look a bit smarter.'

'I'll admit that ye suit havin' yer hair piled up like that,' Jean acknowledged. 'An' the blouse is smart. Ye look very . . . capable.'

Kirsty eyed herself in the full-length mirror Jean had bought. The severity of the blouse and black skirt did give her an efficient air, and the new hairstyle made her hold her head high, which was all to the good.

When the spring–cleaning was over, Kirsty still felt restless and filled with untapped energy. Turning her attention to the shop, she persuaded Jean to let her whitewash the back room, then the shop itself. She experimented, buying some red dye and stirring it into the bucket, so that the walls took on a faint but warm blush of colour.

Once that was done, it was easy enough to coax Jean, who

was impressed by the difference the whitewash made, to go with her round the pawnshops. In one they were fortunate enough to find some rails to hang dresses from, and in another they wrangled over a section of garden trellis Kirsty discovered in a corner.

'We can whitewash the outside wall and fasten this to it. Then we can hang clothes outside in the good weather,' she explained to Jean, who replied witheringly, 'What good weather? It's more often wet than dry in Paisley, summer or no'!'

'We have our good days. A few nice dresses hanging outside'll tempt folk to come in and look around,' Kirsty coaxed.

'I've got a pot of green paint ye can have for tuppence if ye buy the trellis,' offered the shopkeeper, who had been listening with interest.

'We'll take the both,' Kirsty said, while Jean groaned and raised her eyes to heaven.

The tobacconist's shop was busy when Kirsty went in. Todd Paget and Beth faced each other across the counter, while Ewan, who had recently taken to smoking a pipe, lounged at one side of the shop, idly eyeing a selection of tobaccos.

Beth's mouth was sulky, and drooped even more when she saw Kirsty, though Todd greeted her with a smile. 'I was just sayin' tae Beth, I've heard of a wee place nearby in Mary Street for rent. We're goin' tonight tae look at it.'

'We're mebbe going.' Beth sliced off a piece of Matt's favourite tobacco with a vicious slam of the knife.

'If we don't go tonight we'll mebbe lose it.'

'You don't want that to happen, Beth,' Ewan put in, and the girl shot him an irritated look.

'It's only two rooms, and Mary Street's not what I had in mind at all.'

'It'd do tae start with,' Todd said hopefully. 'We'd look for somethin' better once we were in.'

'And have to keep moving from one place to another? Where's the sense in that?'

He shuffled his feet. 'But if we find somewhere tae live, even if it's not what we really want, we could fix the weddin' date.'

'Settle for Mary Street and have the wedding,' Ewan drawled. 'I'd like to dance at a good wedding.'

'What makes you think you'd be invited?' Beth snapped at him, and he laughed and clapped Todd on the shoulder.

'We're workmates, me and Todd. He'd want me to dance at his wedding. Wouldn't you, Todd?'

'I'd want ye all tae come,' the journeyman agreed, beaming at Kirsty.

'You see? I'd wear my best clothes, Beth. I'd not shame you.'

'We'll see.' Beth spread the coins Kirsty gave her over her palm, counted them, then threw them into the brass bowls in the till drawer contemptuously.

'Ye'll meet me in Mary Street at eight o'clock, then?'

'Aye, I suppose so.' The girl shut the drawer with a bang. She asked Ewan tartly, 'Are you in here tae buy or just tae make a nuisance of yourself?'

'To buy, but I'm not sure which mixture I should use. I'm new to pipe-smoking.'

'And I don't do it at all, so there's no use in asking me, Ewan Lennox. I just sell the stuff.'

Kirsty put the small packet in her bag. 'Come away, Ewan, and stop bothering the lassie.'

'I'll come over when I've bought my tobacco. If the old man starts his complaining, Todd, tell him I'll not be a minute.'

'I'll see tae yer basket, Mistress Lennox,' Todd offered when the two of them paused on the footpath to allow a large brewery cart piled with barrels to lumber past. He took the heavy basket and put a guiding hand beneath Kirsty's elbow as they crossed the road.

'You're quite the gentleman, Todd.'

'I got intae the way of helpin' my mam across roads, for she was near blind before she died,' he said, then added hurriedly, 'not that I'm sayin' you're old and helpless, of course.'

'Women of all ages appreciate a gentleman's assistance,' she assured him, amused. 'I'm certain that Beth does.'

'My Beth knows what's what,' he agreed proudly. 'I know Mary Street's not where she'd like tae live, but it'd be a start for us.'

'If we hadn't come to Paisley and claimed the house you'd be wed by now.'

'No, no, you've got far more right tae this place than I have.' Todd paused at the street door.

'I'll come through the pend with you,' Kirsty said. 'Todd, are you content working for us?'

'Of course I am. It's where I served my apprenticeship, where I've always worked.'

'Alex tells me that sometimes things can be . . . difficult. I'm sorry if you're finding that too.'

She hadn't mentioned Matt, but glancing up at the journeyman, she could tell by the look in his steady grey eyes that he knew what she meant. 'I'm no' complainin', Mistress Lennox,' he said. 'It must be awful hard on the master, with his hands gettin' tae be so bad. Bein' in pain all the time'd make a saint bad-tempered now and again.'

'He probably shouldn't even be in the workshop at all now, but he'll not listen to me.'

'The rheumatics might get better.'

'I don't think they will – not now.' The pain had been going on for too long, and Matt's hands were so misshapen now that Kirsty suspected that they would never improve.

'He's best left tae make the decision himsel'. It's hard for someone who's worked all their lives tae feel that they're no longer able.' Todd followed her into the kitchen and put the basket on the table. 'There ye are. We'll just have tae look out for him all we can, me and the lads,' he said as he turned back to the door. 'As for mysel', I've no mind tae leave.'

'I'm glad of that, for we need you – all of us.'

He coloured and shrugged the compliment off awkwardly. 'I'm right pleased about young Alex gettin' that order from Mister Gregg.'

'You approve of painted furniture, then?'

'I like well-made furniture, painted or not. The laddie's got a skill there, an' he deserves tae be free tae use it,' Todd said.

Watching him go past the window, Kirsty wished that Matt could realise how fortunate he was to have Todd and Alex working for him.

10

'I'm not wearing that!'

'You are.'

'You can't make me!'

'Indeed I can.'

'We'll see what Father says.'

'Your father,' Mrs Hamilton told her daughter icily, 'will agree with me, Rose – and he will be very cross if he hears of this disobedience. I don't know what that finishing school taught you, but it certainly isn't good manners.'

The girl's vivid blue eyes flashed. 'If you don't approve of it, you and Father should never have made me go there.'

'Rose, don't be impertinent!'

Kirsty longed to shout at both of them to be quiet and behave themselves, but instead she had to sit silently at her sewing machine, looking from one to the other of the squabbling women, one on either side of her, like a child at a Punch and Judy show.

Once, the Hamiltons' sewing room had been a quiet haven, but with Rose home for good, and on the verge of her eighteenth birthday, her mother was bent on launching the youngest, most difficult and least attractive of her daughters into society as soon as possible. Discovering that her sewing woman could do more than darn and patch and sew on buttons, Mrs Hamilton had shamelessly decided to save money by getting Kirsty to make a dress for the girl to wear at some social occasion. Since Rose and her mother could never agree on anything, Kirsty's former refuge had become a battleground.

'Look at it!' Rose scooped up the paper pattern from among the mass of pink silk lying on the cutting table and thrust it under her mother's nose. 'It's the wrong shape entirely – and the colour's dreadful! I'm not a pink silk person. I shall look like a – a French doll!'

'Nonsense! Phemie Sanderson's Margot looked very fetching in this exact colour at her engagement party.'

Rose tossed the pattern, mercifully still intact within its packet, at her mother's feet. 'Margot Sanderson only comes up to my shoulder, Mother. And she's plump – and she has curly black hair and dimples and a silly simpering face. Of course she looked fetching, but that doesn't mean that I will!'

Mrs Hamilton made an attempt to retrieve the pattern, then realised that her girth prevented her from bending. 'Pick it up, Mrs, er, Lennox, there's a dear,' she said airily, then to her daughter, 'take off that blouse and skirt. You can't be measured in those clothes.'

'Mother . . .'

It was difficult for Kirsty, too, to pick up the pattern, but she managed to get to her knees, wincing as her stays dug into her ribs.

'The more you protest, the longer the task will take. For myself,' Mrs Hamilton said, ignoring the fact that it was almost time for Kirsty to go home, 'I'm willing to stand here all day, and so is Mrs, er, Lennox.'

There was a moment's silence, during which Kirsty had to bite her tongue, then Rose said sulkily, 'Oh – if you must!'

Now that Kirsty was on her hands and knees, the hem of Mrs Hamilton's skirt swung just before her nose, and she could see the woman's fat ankles and the tops of her feet bulging over the stylish strapped shoes she wore. No wonder she always walked with little mincing steps, Kirsty thought as she groped for the pattern. Each step in those tight shoes must be agony for the woman.

Just as her fingers brushed the packet Rose's brown skirt collapsed into a pool on the floor, creating a puff of air that wafted the pattern beneath the big cupboard that held bolts of cloth and drawers full of needles and thread and thimbles and tape measures. Only a corner of the pattern was left poking out.

Rose stooped effortlessly and picked it up, then put her free hand beneath Kirsty's arm and hauled her to her feet. 'Let's get it over with,' she said in a voice heavy with gloom.

The girl was quite right, Kirsty thought as she started work while Mrs Hamilton wrote down the measurements in the tiny notebook she carried wherever she went. That pattern was all wrong for her. She was taller than fashion decreed for a young woman of her social standing, and thin to the point of gawkiness, with practically no bosom.

She held herself rigidly throughout the measuring, forcing Kirsty and her mother to move her around as though she was a jointed wooden doll. Resentment emanated from every pore. As soon as the ordeal was over she slid swiftly into her clothes then stalked from the room.

'I'll not wear it!' Her voice floated back as the door closed.

'You will!' her mother screeched after her, then said to Kirsty, 'Now then, Mrs, er, Lennox, do you think there's enough material here?'

'Yes, madam. If you don't mind, madam,' Kirsty ventured, 'it's time for me to finish for the day.'

Mrs Hamilton glanced at the clock. 'It's only ten minutes to noon!'

'When I agreed to change to three mornings instead of two, we arranged that I could go home in time to see to the midday meal for my family,' Kirsty reminded her. The woman frowned; she hated to pay servants a penny more than she had to, and at the same time insisted on getting full value for what she did pay. This meant that all members of her staff usually had to work at least five minutes over their correct time.

'Can't your family see to their own meal?' suggested Mrs Hamilton, who had never in her life had to boil a kettle. 'Or eat bread and cheese?'

'My husband works hard, and he's used to eating a proper meal. That was our arrangement,' Kirsty said again, anger clenching like a fist inside her.

'Oh, very well, though I'm sure that there are plenty of sewing women who would be glad of the chance to work here without making such a fuss about stopping times!'

It was people like Mrs Hamilton, Kirsty thought as she walked home later, that caused working-class resentment towards the wealthy. The woman was shallow, selfish and had no idea of life outside her own pampered existence. In Kirsty's view it was unfair that someone like that should have so much while others, decent and honest folk like Matt or the customers who came into Jean's shop in the hope of finding something nice for themselves among other people's cast-off clothing, had to struggle all their lives simply in order to survive.

'You'll get yourself into trouble with that sort of talk, Mam,' Alex teased when on occasion she voiced such thoughts.

'But it's true! Folk that don't have to work for their money don't appreciate it.'

'And folk that do have to work for it are supposed tae be humble and keep their thoughts to themselves,' he pointed out, while Ewan often chimed in, laughter in his voice, 'Think of the shame you'd bring on us, Mam, if you were taken off to prison for stirring working folk to rebellion!'

Waiting her turn in the grocer's, Kirsty recalled that once, when she had been particularly incensed about what she had considered to be mindless extravagance on the part of the Hamiltons, Alex had made her a paper hat like those the French revolutionaries had worn in the last century. He had painted it red, white and blue and pinned a pleated cockade in the same colours to one side. She smiled at the memory as her turn came.

'That's what I like tae see,' the bearded shopkeeper boomed as she stepped up to the counter, fumbling in her pocket for the shopping list she had written out that morning, 'a happy, smilin' customer!'

She arrived home from Jean's shop that afternoon to find a dark-haired girl hesitating before the door. As she and Kirsty came face to face the girl burst into speech.

'Are you the lady o' the house? Would ye have a wee morsel o' food for the bairns, ma'am?' Although she looked little more than a child herself, a baby was tied to her body by a shawl and a toddler clutched her hand. 'Just a crust or a bit of broken biscuit would do, for we've been walkin' all the day, and me with nothin' tae give them.'

Her voice was soft and wheedling, the words flowing in a singsong way into each other. It was a speech she repeated day after day, hour after hour, Kirsty knew, for she had heard it often enough before from the great band of tinkers that roamed the country in all seasons.

The baby stared solemnly at Kirsty with large wondering eyes, and so did the little girl, from under a thick mop of matted hair.

Matt, like Kirsty's father, strongly disapproved of encouraging tinker folk, claiming that they were shiftless and lazy. But her mother had never turned any of them away empty-handed, nor could Kirsty, especially when there were children involved.

'Wait here for a minute,' she said, and went into the house, prudently closing the front door behind her. When she opened it five minutes later the girl-woman was sitting on the scrubbed white step, the baby suckling at her breast, while the little girl squatted patiently beside her.

As soon as the door opened the tinker readjusted her clothing and rose gracefully. The baby was clearly used to interrupted meals, for it accepted the situation without complaint, a trickle of milk at one corner of its small soft mouth. When Kirsty handed over a bag containing a few vegetables, some hastily made slices of bread and jam and a bottle of milky tea, a radiant smile lit the girl's face, revealing a gap where a tooth had fallen out, or been knocked out. 'Bless ye, lady,' she said, and began to turn away.

'Wait – could you do with some clothes for the wee ones?'

The girl's eyes narrowed for a second, then opened wide. 'I could that, lady. Ye've bairns of yer own?' The singsong plaint returned. 'Ye'll know then how hard it can be tryin' tae clothe them and them growin', growin' every day the good Lord sends.'

'Is your man nearby? Has he a cart?'

'He has, lady, in the next street, just.'

'Go and find him and tell him to fetch it here,' Kirsty said, and closed the door. She ran to the wash house, noting with relief that Mary was still playing happily with her doll in the back green, and fetched a clean sack from the pile that lay in a corner, then hurried back into the house and up the stairs. Bundling Fergus's clothes into the sack willy-nilly, she was keenly aware that part of her, like another self, was standing by and watching with horror.

Even so, everything went into the sack – the soft woollen shawl she had knitted while waiting for Fergus's birth, the larger shawl used to bind him to her body so that she could carry him about, his flannel gowns and tiny shoes, and even his toys. It was time for them to go; she knew that instinctively. Fergus would never be out of her thoughts, but the continual hard work of the months since his death had blunted the immediate pain of her loss and made it bearable. As Morag would say, Fergus had been woven into her life's pattern; he was – and always would be – part of her. Because of this she no longer needed material reminders.

Scooping the bedding from the cot, Kirsty stuffed it in on top of the clothing, then, hearing the clop of a pony's hooves in the roadway she ran downstairs to the front door, motioning to the man on the cart.

'Up here,' she said when he came to the door, and ran up the stairs before him, driven on by a fever that suddenly consumed her. 'Take that cot downstairs and put it onto your cart,' she ordered when the tinker came into the bedroom, fumbling nervously with the cap he had pulled from his black greasy hair and ill at ease within the room's confines.

Nervousness faded and avarice lit his eyes as he looked at the sturdy cot, then suspicion washed over his features. 'Are ye certain, missus? I'd no' want for the polis tae throw me intae the jail for theft because ye'd changed yer mind.'

'I'll not change my mind,' she told him impatiently. 'Will you just do as I say?' Responding automatically to the sudden snap of authority in her voice, he hurriedly moved towards the cot as she dragged the sack to the stairs, anxious, now that she had made her mind up, to get the matter over before Matt discovered what was going on and put a stop to it.

All was calm in the back yard. The sound of hammering could be heard from the workshop, and Mary, deeply involved in some game of her own making, paid no heed as Kirsty wrestled the shabby perambulator from where it had been stored in the wash house. She tossed the full sack into it before wheeling it hurriedly through the pend and out onto the pavement.

The tinker woman was waiting by the horse, her baby in her arms and the little girl clinging to her skirt. 'Where's my man?' she wanted to know anxiously.

'He'll be out in a minute. See.' With trembling fingers Kirsty pulled the mouth of the sack open. 'There's clothes for the bairns, and some toys – and the perambulator too.'

The girl's eyes rounded. Just then the man struggled out of the front door, laden with the cot. Kirsty went to help him, certain that at any moment Matt would burst through the pend and make her take everything back. Her tension and sense of urgency communicated itself to the tinkers, already uneasy about her orgy of giving. They were more used to closed doors and unwelcoming faces than to having goods pressed on them.

'Missus, are ye sure?' the man said again.

'I've no need of the things now. Take them.' Kirsty swung the full sack up onto the back of the cart as she spoke, and to her relief he followed suit with the cot without any further argument.

Once everything was lashed on, he bundled his woman and their children up onto the bench and leapt up beside them.

'God bless ye, lady,' the girl said as the tired, thin horse, startled from its reverie by the sting of reins on its back, burst into action.

Watching the roped perambulator nodding and shaking as the cart rattled along the street, Kirsty suddenly remembered their own arrival a year earlier. For a moment her arms seemed to be weighted down, as they had been on that day, by Fergus's warm, solid, soggy little body, and such a rending pain came into her chest that she felt as though her very heart was struggling to tear itself loose so that it could follow her dead baby's possessions.

Then the cart made the turn that took it out of sight and the pain eased away, replaced by a great calmness and a sense of acceptance.

11

'Ye've done what?' Matt's voice was low, but his fury was so strong that for a moment Kirsty thought that he might strike her.

'I've given all Fergus's things to some tinker folk,' Kirsty repeated as calmly as she could. To her surprise, she had managed to keep her secret all evening, until Matt decided to go to bed. She had followed him up within the minute, to find him staring in confusion at the spot where Fergus's cot had stood that morning.

'Tinkers!' Her husband spat the word out as though it was a foul-tasting stone he had found in his mouth. 'Tinkers! How often have I told ye never tae give those scoundrels anythin'?'

'They'd two wee bairns, Matt. They were in more need of the things than we were.'

'In need?' He gave a derisive laugh. 'Ye don't think their bairns'll get the good of the things you handed over, do ye? It'll all have been sold by now tae buy drink!'

'Mebbe, and mebbe not. It's their business what they do with what I gave them. They were of no more use to us.'

'Those things belonged tae our Fergus!' She was astonished to see sudden and unexpected tears sparkling in his eyes. He turned away quickly to hide them. Matt rarely showed such signs of weakness; involuntarily, appalled by his reaction, Kirsty went to him and put her arms about him, her face pressed close to his back.

'Fergus has gone, Matt,' she said into his heavy work shirt. He turned to face her, breaking her hold, blinking rapidly and fighting against his tears.

'There'll be another bairn tae take his place.'

'No!' The word was so hard that they were both startled. 'No,' she said again, this time softly. 'No more children, Matt.'

'But we're young enough yet . . .'

'It's not that. I couldn't bear to lose another child.'

'It wouldn't happen again, pet.' He reached for her, but she stepped back.

'I mean what I say, Matt. We've still got four bairns – we should be content with that,' she said, and saw his expression change as he grasped her meaning.

'So it's like that, is it?'

'It's like that. We're not old, but we're not young either. I'll not risk another child – or myself. You shouldn't ask that of me, Matt.'

He bit his lip, thinking, then his anger began to return. 'Ye'd no right tae give the wee lad's things away!'

'I had the right. I made the clothes, and the bedding, and most of the few toys he had. I bore the bairn and I cared for him.'

'Ye werenae carin' for him that day, were ye?' Matt asked deliberately. He might as well have pushed a knife into her chest.

For a moment the pain was so strong that the breath went out of Kirsty. When it returned, she took no time to consider before she rapped back, hurting as she had been hurt, 'And if you'd put up that wee fence as you promised he might still be here!'

The blood drained from his face, and he picked up his nightshirt then went out of the room without another word.

Kirsty lowered herself carefully, like an invalid, onto the edge of the bed. She couldn't believe that after all they had been through together they could have injured each other with such deliberation and such malice. At some point during their short angry exchange, Fergus had stopped being the issue; all they had wanted to do from then on was cause pain in whatever way possible. And they had both succeeded.

Changing into her nightgown, Kirsty wished with all her heart that she had never given in to Matt's coaxing to write to her father. If she had kept silent as she had wanted and intended, Murray Galbraith wouldn't have left the house and business to her. She and Matt would still be living in Falkirk, content enough in their marriage, and Fergus would still be alive. Now, by giving away all Fergus's things, she had come to terms with her loss – and had neglected to think of Matt's loss.

When Matt finally returned from the bathroom she was in bed, pretending to be asleep.

He put the light out and she felt the mattress dip as he slid beneath the covers, settling as far away from her as he could.

The tension between the two of them the following morning seemed to permeate the house like an acrid smell. The rest of the family couldn't miss it; Caitlin was puzzled, looking from one to the other of her parents, unspoken questions in her vivid eyes, and Mary was silent and ill at ease. Ewan was indifferent, while there was concern in Alex's gaze when he looked at his mother, and censure when he looked at his stepfather.

Kirsty was glad to escape to Jean's shop in the afternoon. Walking along Causeyside Street, she remembered an ornament owned by the woman she had worked for before Matt had come into her life. It was a ball of very fine glass, sitting on a stand, a fragile thing that caught the light on its curved surface and reflected it in rainbow colours. Kirsty had loved that beautiful thing. When she lifted it carefully from its stand to dust it, it was as light as a feather within the careful cradle of her palms, almost as though it was a figment of her imagination. Today she felt strangely like it – brittle and weightless and dreamlike and fragile. In her case, though, she was certain that should she break, the shattering would release not trapped air, but a multitude of tears.

It was a warm, bright summer's day, so she set herself to hanging clothes outside the shop on the trellis, which Alex had secured to the shop frontage. When it was done she stepped back and considered it, head to one side. It looked very fine, but there was something missing.

On an impulse, Kirsty fetched an old tailor's dummy she had found during their excavation of the back shop and dressed it in an elaborate cerise and gold striped costume from among the stock. When she stood it outside the door, passers-by immediately stopped to look at it.

Jean was scandalised. 'Ye're makin' a laughin' stock of me!'

'Not a bit of it. With luck, it'll bring some of them in to see what else we have. It's attracting attention already. See?'

she finished as the broken bell clacked and the door opened to admit a woman wreathed in smiles.

'I like yer new assistant,' she said blithely, 'the one standin' outside havin' a crack with all the folk.'

Jean glared. 'It's her doin', not mine,' she snapped, jerking a thumb in Kirsty's direction.

'I call her Aggie,' Kirsty informed the woman from the corner where she was sewing a new hem on a skirt.

'It's a grand idea – folks need a laugh now and again,' the woman said. 'Ye'll need tae keep an eye on her, though, or some laddie'll be runnin' off with her her bein' so bonny,' she added, going into a peal of laughter at her own wit.

'She's right,' Jean said gloomily when the woman had gone, after making a purchase. 'The wee rascals round here cannae keep their hands off anythin'. It'll disappear within the hour – and the dress, too!'

'If it does, it'll be a small loss. It's old, Jean, and not many folk round here'd want the outfit it's wearing. That's why I chose it.'

Jean looked at her closely. 'Is somethin' botherin' ye?'

'What could be bothering me?' Kirsty asked brightly. She could tell Jean a lot, but never about the destructive quarrel between herself and Matt.

'Ye're . . . different. It's as if ye're tryin' tae cover up bad news.'

'It's just that terrible dress I'm making for poor Rose Hamilton,' Kirsty lied. 'I'm so sorry for the girl, for she'll look a right fright at this party she's going to.'

The bell clacked again, and again, and for most of the afternoon. Every customer came in to ask about the dummy, and not one of them left empty-handed.

'Mebbe that dummy wasnae such a bad idea after all,' Jean admitted grudgingly as Kirsty brought it in before going home. 'I suppose ye might as well put it out again tomorrow, if ye've a mind tae.'

'I'll dress her in a different outfit then. Mebbe it should be something folk might want to buy.'

'And have good clothes stolen along with it when it goes?' Although the ever-changing small crowd around the dummy had kept thieves at bay, they had had to go and rescue it from barefoot, ragged urchins twice during lulls.

'I'll try to think of a way of tethering it tomorrow,' Kirsty promised.

'You might be in much better condition than poor old Aggie, and have a better pedigree than her,' Kirsty said to the dummy in the Hamiltons' sewing room the next morning, 'but I must say, milady, that she's got better taste in clothes.'

She laughed aloud, then composed herself hurriedly and set the sewing machine whirring as she heard footsteps in the corridor.

Rose Hamilton must have been out bicycling, for she wore a grey flannel skirt and mannish jacket, and a peaked cap was jammed over the brown hair. 'I thought my mother was here.'

Kirsty, sighing inwardly, stilled the machine. 'She's not been in this morning, Miss Rose.'

'Did I not hear voices as I came along the corridor?'

'No, Miss Rose,' Kirsty said blankly.

'Oh.' The girl's eyes fell on the dummy, swathed in pink silk. 'Are you still wasting your time on that?'

'Mrs Hamilton says it must be finished for next week, miss.'

'You might as well save yourself the trouble,' Rose said shortly, pulling the cap off.

'But it's nearly done, Miss Rose. I'm working on the over-skirt now, then there's only the rib—'

'I – won't – wear – it!' Each word was snapped out, sharp and clear, as though she was talking to a small child, or a cretin. She had rolled her cap up and used it to underline the words by slapping it against her thigh.

'I must take my orders from your mother, Miss Rose.'

Kirsty's head began to ache, the result, she knew, of sitting in a stuffy room for two hours, watching the needle flash in and out of the material travelling beneath it.

'Here.' The girl fished in her skirt pocket and brought out a banknote. It fluttered from her hand onto the mass of silk frothing across the sewing machine table. 'This'll help you to make some sort of mistake, so that I can't possibly wear the dress.'

As Kirsty stared at the note, sudden rage at the girl's con-descending audacity swept through her. It was all she could do to hold it in check. 'I don't take money I've not earned, Miss Rose.'

'You will earn it, by doing what I ask,' Rose pointed out, then, suddenly shedding her usual arrogance, 'have a heart, woman. You must know that I'll look like a – a parcel in that dress,' she said, in genuine misery. 'I'll be a laughing stock!'

Anger gave way to sympathy. The girl was right, and it was unfair of her mother to put her in such a difficult situa-tion. 'It might be possible to do something with the gown,' Kirsty said slowly.

'The only thing anyone could do with that,' a long bony finger pointed at the dummy's finery, 'is burn it.'

'I'd something else in mind,' Kirsty said, going over to the cupboard covering one wall. Mrs Hamilton, blessed with more money than sense, was addicted to buying yards of any material that took her fancy just in case she might need it one day. Kirsty often looked longingly at the bolts of cloth that might never be used, wishing that she could have such riches in the shop.

She found the dark-blue lace she was looking for and took it to the dummy, unrolling a yard or two so that she could hold it against the skirt.

'An overdress of this lace would tone the pink down,' she explained. 'I could do a cummerbund of the pink and a short cape of the lace round your shoulders. See . . .' She gathered an edge of the lace between her fingers and held it against the bodice. 'Artificial flowers in this same dark blue would look well on the bodice in place of that knot of pink ribbons. And the blue matches the colour of your eyes.'

Interest began to temper the anger in the girl's eyes. 'You're right. How clever you are.'

'I'm used to matching materials and trying to think what's best for folk. I help a friend who runs a second-hand clothes shop in the town.'

'You mean she sells clothes that have already been worn by someone else?' Rose's nose wrinkled with disgust. 'Why would anybody want to wear someone else's clothes?'

'There are plenty women in Paisley who can't afford new gowns, Miss Rose. My friend Jean sells good second-hand clothing that comes from—' Kirsty stopped suddenly, realising that she would have to choose her words carefully, 'from rich folk that don't want them any more.'

'Really?'

113

Aware that the girl's interest had been caught and that she was on the brink of accepting the offered compromise, Kirsty hurried on. 'Most of the clothes need to be altered to suit, so I've got used to matching materials and colours and mebbe—'

The words died in her throat as the door opened and Mrs Hamilton bustled in. 'What are you doing in here, Rose? And what,' she added sharply, taking in the dark-blue lace, 'is that?'

For once Rose was enthusiastic rather than mutinous in her mother's presence. 'Look, Mamma – an overdress of this lace would be a great improvement to the gown. Don't you think so?'

The older woman's eyes narrowed and she drew her breath in sharply. 'I most certainly do not think so! Whose idea was this?'

'Mine, Mrs Hamilton. I thought—'

'My good woman, if you had the capacity for thought, you would know that dark lace is far too mature for a girl of my daughter's age!'

The animation immediately drained from Rose's face. 'Mamma, I am not an empty-headed ninny like most of your friends' daughters. I want the overdress.'

'It would look ridiculous on you,' Mrs Hamilton snapped. She was a head smaller than her daughter and considerably rounder. Their confrontation looked almost comical, but Kirsty had no desire to laugh.

'Not as ridiculous as that will look!' Rose's outflung hand smacked against the dummy so hard that it rocked precariously on its solid circular stand. 'Mamma, you're treating me like a child, and I'm not – I'll be eighteen in September, and then I'll have my inheritance from Grandmamma and be independent.'

'That is not a subject to be discussed before servants, Rose! As you say, you can choose your own clothes once you are eighteen, but until then you will be guided by me.'

'I will not wear that nasty, ugly dress, and you can't make me!' In her rage and frustration the girl was rapidly reverting to nursery behaviour. Her mother immediately reacted in the same way and began to treat her like a child.

'Go to your room and change for luncheon. You look like a – a hobbledehoy!'

For a moment it looked as though Rose was going to refuse, then she shrugged and spun towards the door, head held high, just as Kirsty, smoothing out the folds of material on the sewing table, found the treasury note that the girl had tossed at her.

'Miss Rose.' She held it out, 'This must be yours.'

Blue eyes, blazing with anger, surveyed the money then flicked up to hold Kirsty's gaze. 'You're mistaken.' Her voice was heavy with meaning. 'It's your money.'

Kirsty held the look, refusing to submit. 'I know it's not, miss. Mebbe you dropped it when you came in.'

'For goodness' sake, Rose.' Mrs Hamilton plucked the note from Kirsty's hand and pushed it into her daughter's. 'Clearly the money is yours. You shouldn't be so careless with it – you know how hard Daddy has to work to earn it for us.'

Rose cast an angry, unforgiving glance at Kirsty. 'I won't wear that pink monstrosity,' she said, and swept out.

'You will!' Mrs Hamilton said just before the door slammed. Then, rounding on Kirsty, 'And as for you, Mrs, er, Lennox, I don't know what you think you were doing, encouraging my daughter to defy me.' She held up a podgy

hand as Kirsty tried to speak. 'All I require of you is to
follow the pattern I gave you. If you find that too difficult
you need only say so. I'm sure I could find plenty women
willing to take your place.'

She paused, her raised eyebrows inviting comment. Kirsty
closed her lips tightly over the tongue that longed to speak,
and stared at a point just beside the other woman's left ear.

'Very well,' Mrs Hamilton said triumphantly, consulting
the little enamelled watch pinned to her bosom. 'You've
wasted a good fifteen minutes this morning. I shall expect
you to make that up before you go.'

12

As the door closed behind her employer, Kirsty spun the wheel and set the treadle rocking furiously and the pink silk racing beneath the needle. She had been hired as a sewing woman, not a seamstress; she shouldn't have to spend more time here than she could afford – and more than she was being paid for – making clothes for a spoiled brat. She seethed as she stitched, turning the material, turning it again, the machine whirring beneath her deft fingers.

There was a brisk tap at the door, and one of the kitchen maids looked in. 'Cook says d'ye know it's gone quarter past, Mrs Lennox?'

'Already?' Kirsty stopped treadling, and the wheel whirred into blessed silence. When she eased herself from the chair she enjoyed the luxury of a good stretch then covered the sewing machine and tucked a white sheet over the pink silk to protect it until her return. Then she left the room without a backward glance and made her way to the kitchen.

Despite the bustle as the kitchen staff prepared the family's midday meal, Bessie MacIntosh had a cup of tea waiting for Kirsty.

'I've no time to drink it, I'm late as it is.'

'Get it down ye before ye set off,' Bessie insisted. 'Ye've been workin' hard all mornin' without a bite or a sup. What kept ye?' she wanted to know as Kirsty swallowed the tea down in quick gulps, one eye on the kitchen clock. 'Ye should have been gone a good twenty minutes since.'

'Miss Rose and her mother had one of their spats about the new gown.'

Bessie clicked her tongue. 'That lassie! Her sisters werenae half the trouble she is. We'll all be glad when she finds herself a man and a place of her own. Here.' She thrust a bulky brown paper parcel into Kirsty's shopping bag. 'There's half a roast chicken and a pair of chops for ye.'

'I can't take the Hamiltons' food!'

'Away ye go,' the cook said vigorously. 'She owes ye for the extra time ye put in. Since she'll no' pay ye what ye're worth, ye're surely entitled tae some of her food.'

When Kirsty got home Matt and Alex were confronting each across the big kitchen table, which was strewn with the debris of a makeshift meal.

'I'll decide what happens in that workshop, not you,' Matt was shouting. 'I'm the master, and by God ye'd better—'

'What's going on here?'

'A lot of noise about nothing,' Alex said tightly, then ducked back as Matt swiped at him across the table.

'Ye cheeky bugger, ye – ye're not too old tae get a good hidin'!'

'But I'm old enough to hit back – and I will, make no doubt about that!'

'That's enough!' Kirsty dropped her shopping bag on the

table. She had already been forced to witness one domestic quarrel that morning, and she was in no mood to suffer another. 'Will one of you tell me what this is about?'

For a moment the two men glared at each other like dogs being held back from a fight, then Matt said contemptuously, 'Let him be the one tae dae it, seein' as he's always got so much tae say for himsel'.' He threw himself down in his usual chair and hawked deeply in his throat, then spat a gob of phlegm into the kitchen fire. It sizzled noisily on the red hot bars.

'Matt!' Kirsty protested, then as he ignored her asked, 'Alex, what's happened?'

Alex glanced at his stepfather as though expecting to be interrupted, then when Matt remained silent said, 'It's Mr Gregg's furniture. The exhibition's coming up soon, and if the order's not finished within the next two weeks I'll not have enough time to paint it.'

'But surely you've already started.' Kirsty knew that Matt had refused to let Alex carry out any decorating during normal working hours, claiming that the workshop was too busy to spare him. Instead Alex had been working on the furniture in the store by the pend every evening.

'I've started, but I can't paint furniture that's not been made yet,' Alex said impatiently. 'The order should have been finished by now.'

'That's Gregg's fault,' Matt said at once. 'He got it intae his head that he wanted a dresser as well, so it's takin' longer.'

'That's because you've put us onto an order that came in since Mr Gregg's. His should have been seen to before the other!'

Now that they were back at the nub of the argument, the tension in the air began to thicken again. 'It's me that decides these things,' Matt barked at his stepson. 'And you work for me, not for Gregg. You do as I say!'

'But surely finishing Mr Gregg's order in time for the exhibition is for the good of the business, Matt,' Kirsty offered.

'You mean it's for the good of Master Alex here. That's all he's thinkin' of!'

Hot colour flew to Alex's long face. 'Ye're haverin'!'

Matt scrambled to his feet and lunged across the table, pushing his chin belligerently at Alex. 'Am I? You're the only one in that workshop that decorates furniture. Ye think if ye dae well in that fancy exhibition and we get enough orders for yer rubbish, it'll be easier for ye tae edge me an' Ewan out an' take over yersel'. And that's the truth of it!'

The skin seemed to tighten on Alex's face. He started to speak, but Matt drove on, emphasising the words with stabs of one thick-knuckled finger in the air.

'But yer plottin's not goin' tae work, lad. My Ewan's got as much right tae be master here as you . . . mebbe even more.'

For a moment Kirsty thought that Alex was going to throw himself across the table at his tormentor. Matt thought it too – she could tell by the way his broad shoulders tensed in readiness. Then with a disgusted snort, Alex whirled away and slammed out of the back door.

'Leave him,' Matt ordered as Kirsty made to follow him. 'He's upset.'

'He's no' the only one. What sort of time d'ye call this tae come in? We'd tae get by on bread and cheese for our dinners because you weren't here.'

'I had to stay behind to finish some work.'

'It's not good enough, Kirsty. Your place is here, not working at that big house . . .'

She went out, unable to listen to his ranting any longer, and caught up with Alex in the work yard, catching at his sleeve so that he had to turn towards her. 'Your father didn't mean what he said, Alex.'

'He's not my father!' She could feel him trembling with rage beneath her fingers.

'He's the only one you've ever known. And he's been good to you – to both of us.'

He wrenched himself free. 'When I was wee, mebbe, but now I'm in his way. You heard him, Mam – it's Ewan he wants tae leave this place tae. I might as well get out of it now.' He paused, breathing heavily, glaring at the kitchen window, where Matt stood watching them. 'It'd be safer for him if I did go,' he said at last. 'For if I don't, I'll mebbe end up swinging for the bastard!'

In the morning every joint in Matt's body was locked with pain, and he couldn't stir from his bed. Caitlin was dispatched to fetch the doctor while Ewan and Alex helped Matt, groaning through gritted teeth every step of the way, to the bathroom. When he had been settled back in bed Kirsty sent the others downstairs to break their fasts while she eased her husband's nightshirt off and replaced it with a clean one.

'The doctor'll be along soon.'

Though grey with pain, Matt was mutinous. 'I don't need a doctor. Fetch the wintergreen ointment and some hot flannels and I'll be fine by noon.'

121

'Matt, you've never been so bad before. This is what comes of working in that cold workshop,' Kirsty fretted. 'I've told you time and again that you don't keep yourself warm enough.'

'Ach, stop fussin'!' He couldn't even hold a spoon or a cup. Kirsty fed him as if he was a baby, then left him to rest while she poured herself a cup of cooling tea in the empty kitchen.

Only Todd and Ewan were in the workshop when she went down the lane a little later.

'How's the master?' Todd asked at once.

'The doctor gave him something to ease the pain.'

Ewan shrugged. 'We'll manage well enough without him,' he said indifferently, and made for the garret.

'Did the doctor say how long Mr Lennox'd have tae stay in his bed?'

Kirsty looked round the workshop that had been the realisation of Matt's dream just one year earlier. 'No, but I doubt if he'll be working in here again, Todd,' she said, then pushed the unacceptable prospect from her mind. 'I meant to ask you about that house in Mary Street. Are you and Beth taking it?'

He was at the bench, dipping a small brush in the glue pot. 'It didnae suit, so I'm lookin' for somethin' else now.'

'I hope you find something soon.'

'So dae I,' Todd said fervently as Kirsty wandered over to a sturdy broad-seated fireside chair in the corner. It had been painted pale yellow, and bright cornflowers and poppies rioted along the length of one armrest. The flowers seemed to stand out from the wood, real enough to be picked.

'Is this one of Mr Gregg's chairs?'

'Aye. With the master not comin' in today, Alex thought he'd do some paintin' in here where the light's better.'

'It's bonny.'

'The design's from Mrs Gregg's best china. She's goin' tae set it all out on the dresser.' Todd drew the glue brush carefully along one edge of a shaped piece of wood. 'I'm goin' tae get Alex tae paint a dresser for my Beth once we've found the right house.'

'What do you think about Alex exhibiting the furniture in Glasgow?'

He tossed a sidelong glance at her, then went back to his work. 'I'm no' paid tae have opinions, Mrs Lennox.'

Kirsty moved to stand beside him at the bench. 'I'm asking you as a friend, not an employee.'

Todd laid the wood aside carefully, then replenished the brush. 'Since ye ask, I think it's a grand idea.'

Kirsty nodded slowly. 'We're of the same mind, then.'

Silence fell between them. The wooden beams above their heads creaked, measuring Ewan's movements in the garret. Todd ran his brush along a second piece of wood, then fitted it to the first and carefully put both pieces into a vice. He moved unhurriedly but with confidence in his ability. Kirsty, her eyes on his hands, was reminded of something she had once heard her father say about wood needing to be treated with respect and never hurried.

The tension brought on by worry about Matt began to drain from her. Todd was a craftsman, and it was such a pleasure to watch him at work. Alex was a craftsman too – he should be allowed to display his talents.

He came in just then, the sawdust rippling over the floor

123

like waves on a beach as the door opened. 'The doctor's been, then,' he said at the sight of his mother.

'He's given Matt some laudanum to ease the pain. It seems that he's got arthritis, not rheumatics. It's some kind that can get worse all at once for no reason.'

'No reason?' Alex shrugged out of his jacket and took his apron from the hook where it hung. 'The man's filled to the brim with malice and it's started poisoning him. That's the reason.'

'Alex!'

Todd carefully laid down his brush and left, mumbling some excuse about checking the timber piled outside.

'You shouldn't speak like that in front of Todd,' Kirsty said as soon as they were alone.

'He knows full well what's going on in this family.'

'The doctor says Matt'll not be back at work for a good while. Mebbe never. That means you'll be running this place.'

'Aye, I know.'

She hesitated, then said, 'Give your father his place, Alex. Talk to him about what's happening and let him give orders. If you don't, he'll just lie in that bed and fret and make himself worse. Do it for my sake if not for his.'

He gave her a level look. 'And am I supposed tae follow his orders to the letter – for your sake?'

'As to that, you must do as you think best. I just want Matt to feel that he's still master.'

He shrugged, then called Ewan's name. When his step-brother appeared on the stairs, Alex said, 'You can stop what you're doing – we'll be working on Mr Gregg's order now.'

*

Matt's illness meant that Kirsty was forced to spend more time in the house and less at Jean's shop. She kept going to the Hamiltons' because she needed the work and the hated pink silk dress had to be finished. She saw to it before she left for work that Matt was comfortable and that everything he might need was to hand, and while she was away Todd and Alex and Ewan took it in turns to look in at the house and make sure that he was all right.

To Kirsty's relief, Rose Hamilton stayed away from the sewing room, so there were no more tantrums and no more attempts to bribe her. The family were about to leave for their six-week summer holiday within days of the party at which Rose was to wear the dress, and as a result the big house was in turmoil.

'How's yer man?' Bessie asked, as she always did now, when Kirsty arrived that morning.

'He still can't get down the stairs, but at least he can manage to get himself to the bathroom with the help of a walking stick.'

'It's an improvement. Mebbe things'll get better week by week.'

'I hope so, for he's not taking kindly to being an invalid. When he's not grumbling, he can be so quiet that I worry about him, Bessie. It's not in his nature just to sit about and be looked after. I think not being able to do things for himself hurts him more than the swollen joints. At least,' Kirsty added, cheering a little, 'Miss Rose's dress'll be finished today. I'll be glad to see that over and done with.'

'And I'll be glad when the whole jing-bang of them go off tae the seaside next week.'

'Are you going with them?'

125

'No, no. They hire some other poor soul tae cook for them when they're away. I'll get a holiday with my cousin in Dumfries, then I'll be back in time tae get the kitchens all readied for them comin' home.'

Kirsty, too, was going to have two weeks free of her duties in the sewing room before returning to repair bed linen while the Hamiltons were out of the house.

'I hope the mistress is goin' tae give ye a bit extra for all yer hard work,' Bessie said as Kirsty left the kitchen.

'I doubt it.' But as Kirsty went along the corridor leading to the sewing room she wondered if Mrs Hamilton might, after all, decide to be generous for once. An extra shilling or two would help to pay for the delicacies she had been buying in an effort to tempt Matt's flagging appetite.

'What's the sense in a man eatin' when he's not earnin'? he had started asking, turning away from the meals she and the girls carried up to him.

To her surprise, the sewing room door was ajar, although she was certain that she had closed it behind her when she had last been there. She pushed it open, then stared in horror.

The window, which she had also closed, was partly open, and the protective cloth she always used to cover the silk material lay on the floor. A small bottle of oil on the sewing table had tipped over, its contents spilling out to cover the pink silk overskirt on the table with a dark, ugly stain.

13

'Carelessness!' Mrs Hamilton's double chin shook with rage. 'Sheer carelessness! How could you have allowed such a thing to happen?'

'I left the silk well covered. I don't see how the covering could have fallen off.' To her own ears, Kirsty's voice sounded distant and unreal. The sight of the terrible stain on the half-finished overskirt seemed to have taken the wits from her and she couldn't think straight.

'Look at the window, woman! You should have known better than to leave it open and the door ajar. Clearly a gust of wind blew the covering off – if it was ever on in the first place,' her employer added scathingly, 'and blew the bottle over. You didn't even put the stopper on properly!'

'Mrs Hamilton, I always make sure that the door and window are latched when I leave this room. And I would never leave a bottle of oil so close to material—'

'Don't argue with me! What else could have happened? This is what comes of being more interested in rushing home to your family than in remembering your duty to the people who pay your wages! Now what am I going to do?' the

127

woman moaned. 'The party is tomorrow evening and the gown's ruined – ruined!'

'The dress itself is unspoiled, ma'am,' Kirsty ventured. 'It could still be used. There's the blue lace I showed Miss Rose—'

'Will you be quiet about the blue lace?' her employer shrieked, then reeled dramatically against a cupboard and fumbled in the small cloth bag that always hung from her wrist.

'Ma'am?' Kirsty, moving forward to help her, staggered and almost fell when Mrs Hamilton pushed her away, showing surprising strength for a woman on the verge of fainting.

'Don't come near me!' She produced a small bottle of smelling salts, opened it, inhaled deeply, then went into a fit of coughing. 'Out!' she choked. 'Out of my house! Out of my sight!'

'But Mrs Hamilton—'

'One more word and I'll make you pay for the material you've ruined. Get out!'

There was no reasoning with her. Kirsty gathered up her things with shaking hands and went. Mrs Hamilton's final words, 'And I shall see to it that nobody else in this town employs you as a sewing woman!' followed her down the narrow passageway.

In the kitchen Bessie looked at her in surprise. 'What are you doin' back here?'

'I think you'd best fetch Mrs Hamilton's maid to the sewing room.'

'Has the mistress taken ill?

'No, there's b-been an accid-dent.' Kirsty's tongue stumbled over the words. 'Some oil spilled on Miss Rose's new g-gown. I don't know how it could have happened. Oh Bessie – I've been d-dismissed.'

'Sarah, ask Miss Hastie to go to the sewing room at once,' Bessie ordered one of the maids, then as the girl disappeared through a door in a whirl of black skirt and white apron strings, the cook pulled a kitchen chair forward.

'Sit down before ye fall down, woman,' she ordered, 'ye're as white as a sheet.' Then to the others, who had stopped what they were doing and were listening, agog. 'Well? The work won't do itself – get on with it!'

Kirsty was desperate to get away from their inquisitive eyes to somewhere where she could be alone to try to make sense of what had just happened. Ignoring the proffered chair, she said, 'I have to go,' and blundered towards the back door, bursting out of the house just as the hot tears started spilling down her cheeks.

She tried to dash them away as she half ran round the side of the huge house towards the tradesmen's drive, but they kept coming, blinding her, so that halfway down the drive she was forced to step in among the trees and lean unseen against a sturdy trunk and give way to them. When the worst of the weeping was over she started walking back to the town, her body shaken with involuntary hiccuping now and again, like a child's after a paroxysm of weeping.

She couldn't face the thought of returning home and admitting to Matt that she had been dismissed. Instead, keeping her face averted from the people she encountered, she went to the only refuge she knew – Jean Chisholm's wee shop.

*

Jean, busy with a customer, looked up in surprise. Knowing that if she tried to speak she might start weeping again, Kirsty lifted the hinged section of the counter and pushed past her friend and into the back shop without a word. She was rinsing her face with cold water when Jean hurried in a few minutes later.

'What's wrong? Is Matt worse – or has something happened tae one of the bairns?'

'No, it's—' To her horror, Kirsty felt the tears well up again. 'Oh, Jean!'

The Paisley folk weren't ones to touch or embrace each other, but on this occasion Jean took Kirsty into her arms without hesitation. Her tenderness reminded Kirsty of her mother's comforting arms years before and sent a wave of self-pity through her. By the time she had brought it under control her face was in ruins again. Jean put her into the big chair that had to be used with care and respect because of its broken spring and wrung a cloth out in cold water.

'Hold that tae your eyes while I make us a cup of tea. I've locked the door, so we'll not be disturbed.'

'But folk won't get in,' Kirsty objected, her voice muffled by the cloth.

'That's why I locked it. I don't want tae be bobbin' in and out all the time.' Jean settled the teapot on the gas ring. 'We'll let it mash for a minute tae get nice and strong.' As it began to boil briskly, throwing out a steady plume of steam, she took a chair opposite Kirsty's, surreptitiously wiping wet tears from her neck. 'Now, tell me what's happened.'

Her sympathy changed to fury as the story came out in a series of gulps and chokes and broken sentences. 'The nerve of the woman, speakin' tae you like that after all you've done for her! Money doesnae always bring good manners with it!'

'It was the humiliation that hurt the most, Jean.'

'And no wonder. She's treated you like a dog, with not even the chance tae defend yoursel'.' Jean dashed strong hot tea into their cups so vigorously that drops and splashes flew in all directions, then added two spoonfuls of sugar and a generous dollop of condensed milk, which she adored, to each cup. 'Drink that down,' she instructed.

The tea was scalding, and very sweet, but it was also comforting. Drinking it down as she had been commanded, nearly burning her mouth in the process, Kirsty felt strength flow back into her rubbery limbs.

'I'd never have left that silk uncovered, Jean – never!'

'Of course you wouldnae!'

'And I'd never have left the bottle of machine oil beside it, or forgotten to put the stopper on securely.'

'Or left the door and the window open,' Jean agreed. 'You'd be as likely tae cut your own throat as tae do that.'

'I haven't even used the oil for a week. It should have been on a shelf in the cupboard, where I always keep it. But she'd not listen when I tried to explain.'

'God forgive me for sayin' this about another human bein', but that woman's a right cat.' Jean refilled both cups. 'Now listen, there's no sense in frettin' about it, for it'll no' change what's happened. Best put your mind tae what you're going tae do next.'

'I'll have to find more work.'

'D'you think she will tell her friends not tae take you on?'

'Probably, knowing Mrs Hamilton. If she does, I'll have to

look further afield – Barrhead, mebbe, or Johnstone. There
are some big houses there too.'

'I wish there was enough work for you here. I'd like it fine
if there was, but I couldnae pay as much as you got at the
Hamiltons.'

The broken spring had been pressing painfully into
Kirsty's backside for the past few minutes. She rose and
began to rinse her cup out at the single-tap sink in the corner. 'Something'll turn up, I'm sure.' She sniffed, scrubbed
at her nose with the back of her hand and forced a smile at
her friend. 'My mother always said that tomorrow's another
day. Mebbe tomorrow'll bring something better than working
for Mrs Hamilton.'

'It's for the best – ye've got enough tae do here,' Matt said
when told of his wife's dismissal. Ewan, always caught up in
his own interests, shrugged the news off without comment,
while Caitlin, who had left school in April and was now
working behind the counter of a grocer's shop, promised to
keep her ears open for any word of an opening in one of the
big houses.

'Sometimes the cooks or the housekeepers say something
when they're in the shop. You'll find work easily, Mam, for
you're the best sewing woman in the town.'

'Will you be sent to the jail for spoiling the dress?' Mary
asked anxiously. Mary had always tended to be a worrier, and
she had got worse, Kirsty knew, since Fergus's death.

Alex, who was fond of his timid little half-sister, scooped
her up and deposited her on a seat at the table. 'Of course
not. It's more likely to be Mrs Hamilton in the jail for tellin'
wicked lies. Mam didn't spoil the dress, it was someone else

that did it. Here.' He tore a sheet of paper from his sketch pad and gave it to the little girl along with some coloured pencils. 'Draw me a nice design to paint on a chair. Mebbe it was that girl herself that damaged the frock,' he added to Kirsty as Mary settled down happily to her task.

'Miss Rose? She'd not do a thing like that.'

'Would she not? You told us yourself that she didn't want to wear it. I'm certain it was her. She got into the room and ruined it, then left you to take the blame. Mrs Hamilton should set herself to finding out the truth instead of turning you off when she's got no proof at all!'

'What's done's done, Alex,' Kirsty said wearily, sick of the entire matter. 'I'll start looking for another place next week.'

'You shouldn't have to go out to work, Mam. You've done your fair share already.'

'I like to be independent,' Kirsty told her first-born, and meant it.

He said no more, but as he passed behind her chair later she felt his hand touch her hair in a swift token of affection. The small, unexpected gesture sent a warm flood of pleasure through her. She would have laid her life down for Caitlin and Ewan and Mary, and she would always miss wee Fergus bitterly, but there was something special about Alex.

She reached up, and for a brief moment their fingers met.

On Monday Kirsty visited three of the big houses in Carriagehill Road, which was closer to home and ran along the back of the Royal Alexandra Infirmary's imposing redstone structure. It had occurred to her over the weekend that as Mrs Hamilton and her family were leaving Paisley in a day or two for six weeks, the woman might not have time before then to make good her threat to blacken Kirsty's name among her friends. If she could find work quickly, Mrs Hamilton would probably have forgotten the matter by the time she came home again.

There was no work available at the first two houses, but at least, Kirsty thought as she walked down the second drive-way, the ladies she had spoken to showed no indication of having heard anything amiss about her. But the mistress of the third house, who interviewed her in the drawing room because, she said, she had need of a good sewing woman, suddenly cooled when Kirsty gave her name.

'You worked for Mrs Hamilton at Thornly Park, didn't you?'

Kirsty's heart sank. 'Yes, Mrs Brodie.'

'And she dismissed you.'

'Because of an accident that wasn't my doing.'

Mrs Brodie's face suddenly looked as though it had been carved from marble. 'I would prefer to seek elsewhere,' she said, and pulled the bell rope hanging close at hand. A uni-formed maid arrived almost at once, and Kirsty was shown out, humiliated and close to tears.

There was nothing else for it, she thought as she went to the butcher's and the grocer's, she would have to look fur-ther afield, though the cost of a tram or bus fare to and from Barrhead, Elderslie or Johnstone would eat into her wages.

'Mebbe ye should try the west end of the town,' Jean suggested. 'There's big houses there too.'

'I'd not thought of that.' Each district in Paisley tended to keep itself to itself, and folk from one area rarely had friends or interests in another, as though the town had split itself up into a collection of villages.

'You'd only need tae walk up the length of George Street then, instead of payin' fares tae get tae work. An' mebbe if you worked there,' said Jean, with gathering interest, 'you could start collectin' old clothes for the shop.'

14

'You there, is this where Mrs Lennox lives?'

Alex, about to go into the house, turned as a young woman in a plain, tailored costume marched up to him, taking strides almost as long as a man's. She was tall for a woman, her eyes on a level with his, and beneath a straw boater clamped over a severe hairstyle her features were sharp and uncompromising.

There was something about the girl that he disliked at once, and his own voice was curt when he said, 'Who wants tae know?'

Her eyes narrowed with irritation. 'My business is with Mrs Lennox. Is she at home?'

He suddenly realised, from her arrogance and her educated accent, who the caller was. 'She's out,' he said abruptly.

'When will she return?'

'I don't know. I don't own her – nobody owns my mother.' Her clear blue eyes blinked. 'You're her son?'

'I am. And you're Miss Hamilton.' He took satisfaction in knowing that he had managed to discomfit her twice.

'How did you know?'

Alex looked her up and down, making no attempt to hide his dislike, and she reddened. Normally he wouldn't have dreamed of embarrassing anyone in this way, especially a female, but to his mind, this particular female didn't deserve to be treated with courtesy. 'It wasn't hard tae guess.'

She gathered herself together. 'When your mother returns, perhaps you would be so good as to tell her that I would like to see her.'

Alex folded his arms across his chest, standing straddled before the door as though protecting his home. 'You may want tae see her,' he said bluntly, 'but I doubt if she'll want tae see you.'

'How dare you speak to me like that!'

His temper began to spill over. 'I dare, Miss Hamilton, because my mother's a hard-working woman, and the most honest person I know. She's been treated unfairly by you and your family, and she doesn't want tae set eyes on any one of you again. I'm telling you this,' he added, 'because she's too much of a lady tae tell you herself.'

The girl's high, strong cheekbones were glowing and her eyes snapping with rage during his tirade. 'I'm aware that she's been treated . . . unfairly. That's why I have to see her.'

'What's done's done.' Alex used his mother's own words. 'Just leave it at that.'

'As you said yourself, you don't own her.' She began to lose her self-control. 'Nor do you have the right to make decisions on her behalf!'

Alex was more than ready to have a full-blown row with her, right there on the pavement. 'Folk like you believe that folk like us shouldn't have any rights at all, don't you? But we do, and I'm speaking for my mother when I tell you tae

just go away and leave us alone. Goodbye, Miss Hamilton!'
he said, and turned his back on the girl, stepping into the
house quickly and shutting the door in her face. He leaned
back against it, listening, and released his breath in a long
sigh as he heard the click of well-shod feet fading away along
the pavement.

Rose Hamilton, he thought as he went along the hall, was
as pleasant as a mouthful of vinegar. He hoped that she had
taken heed of what he had said and would stay away. In his
view, the girl was nothing but trouble.

'There.' Kirsty settled the dummy against the shop wall.
'Behave yourself and you'll be quite safe.' Today Aggie was
matronly in an elderly brown silk two-piece dress, complete
with bustle. She had already become a familiar sight on the
pavement, and whenever the weather was fine enough for
her to be outside people made a point of passing to see what
she was wearing. At least once every day someone came in to
ask about her, and most of them stayed to look around and
buy.

Kirsty now tied a rope round the dummy's ample waist
beneath the clothes. The other end was looped to a hook once
used to hang clothes on inside the shop. After a particularly
determined raid by a small clutch of lads, she had bought a
bell in a pawnshop and fastened it to the pedestal beneath the
skirt. The entire street had been alerted the first time boys
tried to make off with Aggie after the bell was installed, and
the culprits had almost collapsed with the shock. Now the
other shopkeepers looked out for Aggie as well, and the
would-be thieves had more or less given up.

Once Aggie was well anchored, Kirsty stepped back into

the shop to collect the basket of clothes waiting just inside the door and began hanging them on the trellis, humming under her breath. The sting of Mrs Brodie's haughty rejection faded away. It was a lovely day, far too nice to fret about stuck-up women in big houses.

'Mrs Lennox, may I speak with you?' Startled, Kirsty turned to see Rose Hamilton hovering by her side. All at once, the day stopped being lovely. Her first impulse was one of flight, then, realising that if she ran into the shop the girl would only follow, she said coolly, 'I'm very busy.'

'Let me help, then you'll be free to talk to me.' Rose swooped down at the basket and brought out a skirt, holding it fastidiously at arm's length and trying, using only the tips of her gloved fingers, to locate the waistband. Two women passing by on the pavement nudged each other and grinned.

'It wouldnae fit ye, hen,' one called, and Rose swung round, fixing her with a cold look.

'I beg your pardon?'

The women yelped with laughter and moved on. Rose stared after them, the skirt still dangling from her hands. 'What did they mean?' she asked Kirsty, who snatched the skirt from her and tossed it into the basket. Tucking the basket against her hip, she urged the girl towards the shop with her free hand.

'We'll go inside.'

'But the clothes . . .'

'I'll do them later. Mind the step,' Kirsty said just as Rose stumbled and almost fell down it, arriving in the shop at a clumsy run. Jean and the customer she was serving turned to gape, their faces like pale moons in the dim interior.

'We'll go into the back shop,' Kirsty said hurriedly, and as

139

Jean, mouth still open, automatically lifted the counter flap for them, she steered her unwelcome visitor through the gap and into the back, where she put the basket down. 'What are you doing here?'

'You sound just like your son.'

'My son?'

'A . . . person,' Rose said coldly, 'with red hair. I went to your house first and met him there.'

'Was it him who told you I'd be here?' If it was, Kirsty thought, she'd have a word or two to say to Alex when she got home.

'He wouldn't tell me anything.' Rose's face was stiff with disapproval. 'He was most rude to me. He even said that you wouldn't want to see me. Then I recalled you telling me once about helping in a friend's shop, so I looked for it, and it was easy enough to find.' She looked round with open curiosity at the old sewing machine on its rickety table in the corner and the clothing hanging on the walls or stacked on every available surface. 'You've not got much room here.'

'We manage.' Kirsty was beginning to lose her patience. This girl had caused her nothing but trouble. She had had to suffer in silence at work, but why, she asked herself, should she have to put up with Rose Hamilton on her own ground? 'Mebbe you'd be best to go back home, Miss Hamilton, and leave me in peace.'

'At least listen to what I have to say.' Rose's eyes had become accustomed to the poor lighting. Fastidiously, she lifted a pile of clothing from a chair, laid it on top of another pile on the table and sat down in the chair with the broken spring.

'What could you have to say to me?'

'I only discovered this morning that my mother had dismissed you because of what happened to the gown you were making for me.' Rose took a deep breath, and looked at her intertwined fingers, then at Kirsty. 'It was I who spoiled it,' she admitted. 'I only wanted to make sure that I wouldn't have to wear it. I thought my mother would believe it to be an accident. I opened the window and the door and laid the bottle down to make it look as though a breeze had knocked it over.'

She stopped, then said feebly as Kirsty kept silent, 'It didn't occur to me that Mamma would blame you and dismiss you.'

'If I'd left the bottle of oil beside the material, and if I'd left the door and window open as well, I would have deserved dismissal,' Kirsty said stonily. 'I was responsible for everything in the sewing room. That meant that if anything went wrong, I'd be the one held to blame.'

'I – I didn't think of it that way. I'm sorry, Mrs Lennox. Truly very sorry.' The words came out jerkily. Clearly Rose Hamilton wasn't used to apologising – especially to her social inferiors. 'I'll tell Mamma the truth, of course, and you'll get your job back.'

Without stopping to think, Kirsty heard herself say, 'You needn't trouble yourself, Miss Rose. I don't want to work for your mother any more.'

The girl's head lifted sharply. 'But I've said I'm sorry – you must come back now!'

Kirsty's curt reaction had surprised herself as much as Rose, but now that the words had been spoken, she realised that she meant them. Much as she craved the independence of earning her own money, she loathed the thought of submitting to Mrs Hamilton's narrow-minded bullying again.

'Your mother will find another sewing woman easily enough. She told me so several times during my employment.'

The spring must have discovered Rose, for she shifted uncomfortably in the chair. 'Please.' She had probably never pleaded with anyone in her life. 'If you don't come back you'll be on my conscience for the rest of my life!'

'I'm sure you'll have forgotten the whole matter by next week, Miss Rose. I know I will. I've no wish to be at your mother's beck and call again, always wondering if I'm going to be turned off because of something that was no fault of my own.' Kirsty could scarcely believe that she was talking like this to Rose Hamilton of all people.

'But what will you do?'

'Mebbe I'll just work here, doing something I enjoy. At least I'll be among friends and helping my own kind.' Kirsty turned towards the door. 'If you'll excuse me . . .' She had made her decision, and now she wanted the interview to end.

Rose struggled out of the armchair's clutches. 'If you won't come back to work for us, at least let me give you some money to make up for . . .' Her voice faltered into silence as she met Kirsty's eyes.

'I wouldn't take your money before, Miss Rose, and I'll not take it now. Good day.'

The girl's face flamed. She dipped her head, and fled from the room.

'Was that not Rose Hamilton?' Jean asked, hurrying into the back room to find Kirsty busy with kettle and teapot.

'It was. She wanted me to go back to work for her mother.'

'They've realised you weren't at fault?' Jean's face lit up. 'That's grand news! Now you won't have tae worry about findin' another position.'

'I will, for I told her I wasn't going back.'

Jean's jaw dropped. 'You said no?'

'I said more than that,' Kirsty admitted. 'I think I might have said a bit too much altogether.' She squared her shoulders. 'But on the other hand, it was grand being able to speak my mind for once.'

'Will you sit down and tell me what she said – and what you said – and let me try to make some sense of it before I lose my wits altogether?' Jean screeched.

'Och, Kirsty,' she protested ten minutes later when she had heard the whole story, 'should you not just change your mind and go back? There's still time – think of the wages Mrs Hamilton paid!'

'That's not much to think about.' Kirsty poured a generous dollop of condensed milk into her cup and discovered, when she lifted the hot drink to her lips, that her hand was shaking. 'Think of the misery the woman's caused. I'd rather do without than work for her again.' She took a second sip of tea, feeling stronger already. 'Sometimes it does you good to face up to folk instead of letting them have their own way. Morag Bishop says that folks' lives have patterns. If so, mine's just taken a new turn.'

Alex flushed with anger when he heard about Rose's visit to the shop. 'I told her tae leave you alone!'

'Rose Hamilton was never one to take a telling. Anyway, she wanted to get a confession off her mind, for it was her that spoiled her own gown.'

'Did I not tell you that?' he exploded. 'Her sort have more money than decency!'

'At least she said she was sorry. It cost her dear to have to say such a thing to the likes of me.'

'Not as much as she cost you in the first place. I'm glad you sent her away, Mam. We can manage without the likes of the Hamiltons.'

15

Matt had refused from the beginning to let Kirsty handle the firm's books, despite her protests that her mother had done them for her father and she herself had taken them over after her mother's death.

'You see tae the house, and I'll see tae the business,' he had insisted all along. It had hurt to watch him toiling over the ledgers and the order books, knowing that he didn't understand book-keeping but that any offer of help would be spurned. She could only try to concentrate on her own sewing work while he sucked furiously at the end of his pen evening after evening, alternately mumbling and staring into space. Every now and again he laboriously wrote something, hunching over the book and holding the pen clumsily in his fist.

But illness had broken his resolve. At first he was determined to keep that part of the business, at least, under his control, ordering her to bring the books to the bedroom and making a show of working on them. But holding the pencil hurt his fingers, and the weight of the ledgers on his knees was more than he could bear. Then there was the worry of the inkwell toppling and spilling over onto the bedclothes.

When Kirsty tentatively suggested that she should do the books for him, 'Just until you're able again,' he finally agreed.

'Ye might as well keep them for the time bein' – but just till I'm better, mind.'

Turning the pages was like looking back over her family history. First came her paternal grandfather's faded copperplate writing, then her father's hand, clumsier but legible and meticulous. This was followed by more copperplate, indicating the point where her mother had taken over the books. Much as she would have liked to write as well as her mother, Kirsty had never quite mastered the art, and her own earlier contributions to the ledgers were in the round, childish style that she still used. After her banishment to Stirling, Murray Galbraith had taken on the task again. Kirsty turned those pages quickly, then gave a soft exclamation of dismay at the sight of Matt's work, a confusion of scrawls and blots and scoring out. Reaching for the workbook, which itemised incoming materials as well as outgoing orders, she found the same mess and confusion.

'What are you doing?' Alex wanted to know that evening when he came in to find his mother at the table, surrounded by ledgers.

'I'm writing the figures from the ledger into this exercise book I've bought, so that I can see things properly.'

He glanced over her shoulder and whistled softly. 'He's made a right mess of them! No wonder he's so jealous of me being able to draw neatly.'

'Alex,' she indicated an entry in Matt's handwriting, 'I think you should start buying your nails from Jackson's again, instead of that shop in the Back Sneddon.'

'I didn't even know we'd changed merchants. We've had

no need to order more since he fell ill, though I'll be ready to put in an order by the middle of next month.'

'Look.' Kirsty indicated an entry she had made in the exercise book. 'The new people must have made Matt a special offer to get his business. They gave good value at the beginning, but once we started ordering regularly from them, they began adding a penny or two each time, not enough to be questioned—'

'Unless the book-keeper knew what he was about,' Alex put in, but she ignored him.

'But enough to help their profits. Now they cost more than Jackson's ever did.'

'And we've been payin' it over without a word. I'll go and see them tomorrow,' Alex said grimly. 'They're not gettin' away with that. You'd think he'd have noticed!'

'It's easy enough to overlook wee things,' Kirsty said in swift defence of her husband. 'And a man should have a right to trust folk he trades with regularly.'

'Nobody's got a right to trust anyone in business, Mam. It's a lot to ask when you've got enough on your hands, but would you see to all the paperwork for me? It'd be a help, and I'd pay you for it.'

'Of course I'll do it, but I'll not take money for it.'

'And I won't have you working for nothing just because you're blood kin,' he said firmly. 'It'll not be much, but I'll see that you get something.'

The small gardens fronting the terrace where the Bishops lived were brilliant with colour and poured a heady mixture of fragrances over the low stone walls as Kirsty, Caitlin and Mary passed by.

Morag and Ellie were working in their little front garden. They waved when they saw their visitors, and Morag called in at the door to her husband. Caitlin ran ahead, Mary at her heels, and they were all waiting when Kirsty arrived, delicate blue smoke from Geordie's pipe mingling with the perfume of the red roses climbing over the front of the house.

'We've interrupted your evening, but Caitlin was so insistent—' Kirsty began, and was interrupted by Geordie.

'We were expecting ye, lass. It was all arranged with Caitlin.'

'Was it?' Kirsty raised an eyebrow at her daughter, who had the grace to look slightly embarrassed.

'Come and see what we've done with the loom, Mam.'

'Mebbe yer mother would like a cup of tea first,' Morag suggested, but Kirsty, seeing her daughter's face fall, opted to visit the weaving shed first.

The old shed lay almost at the end of the long, narrow back garden. Her grandfather had loved gardening in his spare time, and most of the plants and bushes growing there – the redcurrant bushes with their clusters of small, shiny, bead-like red berries, the hydrangeas he had so loved, the raspberry canes – had probably been planted by him. The very sight of the raspberry canes reminded Kirsty strongly of the fruit's perfumed flavour bursting in her mouth when she had been Mary's age.

Geordie and Morag had green fingers too, and the rich black earth had been well tilled and well planted with vegetables and flowers. Bees hummed around the flowers, gathering the day's last pollen collection before returning to their skeps at the far end of the garden. Some of the bushes blossomed with shirts and sheets. Morag liked to dry her washing in the old way, spreading it over the bushes and leaving it there for days at a time so that the rain could soften it and the sun bleach it.

Kirsty knew that when it was finally gathered in it would be spotlessly clean and soft, with the mingled scents from the garden held fast in every fibre.

'Come on, Mam,' Caitlin shouted impatiently from the shed, where she and Ellie waited hand in hand.

'I wish Alex and Ellie had taken more of a liking to each other,' Kirsty said thoughtfully. To her disappointment, the romance that she had hoped would blossom between the young couple had come to nothing. They had gone walking over the braes above Paisley several times and enjoyed each other's company, but Ellie was too shy and Alex too caught up in his interest in art for the relationship to develop.

'They took pleasure in each other's company for a while, and that's what matters,' Morag said comfortably. 'Ye've got a fine lassie in Caitlin. We've all enjoyed her visits.'

'She's wasted in that grocer's shop. I'm hoping to get her into Cochrane's sewing room when she's older.' Kirsty was referring to the large and very grand shop opposite Paisley Abbey, patronised by the wealthy members of the town.

'Whatever she turns her hand tae, she'll do it well – like her mother. That lassie's pattern's strong and bright.'

At the shed, Caitlin drew Mary to one side and motioned to Kirsty to go in first. She did, then stopped short, staring. 'Is that—?'

'It's great-grandfather's loom, Mam, all mended.' Caitlin almost sang the words in her excitement. 'That's why I wanted you to come here tonight. Go on in and look at it.'

The loom almost filled the shed; Kirsty walked round it,

stopping to touch a beam here, fondle the curve of a roller there. It was solid beneath her hand, solid and strong and brought back from the dead. When she sat on the saytree her haunches settled exactly into the hollow created through the years by her own grandfather's backside. She stretched her feet out towards the treadles, remembering, as she felt them beneath the soles of her shoes, that her dearest ambition as a child had been to reach those same treadles.

Caitlin could contain herself no longer. 'Are you pleased, Mam?' she wanted to know, sliding onto the saytree beside her mother. Mary, not to be outdone, came scurrying to the other side.

'Pleased?' Kirsty put her arms about both girls, holding them tight. 'I've never been so pleased about anything in my life!'

'I didn't tell you how it was coming along because we wanted it to be a surprise. Mr Bishop found a man who used to repair looms, and another man who used to be a weaver himself helped. A lot of folk helped.'

'And they all had a grand time.' Morag gave a rich chuckle. 'All men that used tae be in the weavin' business, an' that pleased tae be dealin' with a loom again.'

Despite Caitlin's optimism, Kirsty hadn't really believed that the broken loom could ever be made whole again. But here it was, proof that miracles could happen – or rather, proof that faith and determination such as Caitlin's, coupled with the skill of dedicated craftsmen, could make miracles happen.

'Can it – will it work?'

'There's no reason why not,' Geordie told her placidly. 'There's a man in Houston who used tae be a dresser, and he's goin' tae try tae set it up. If he can, I'll try a bit of weavin'.'

Caitlin stroked the loom lovingly and took a deep breath. 'It's come back to life,' she said, and Geordie beamed down on her from behind his pipe.

'Didn't I tell ye that it would, lass?'

A faint mist rose from the basketful of warm, damp clothes as Kirsty carried it from the wash house. The air was cool, but a pearly grey sky with a rosy flush to the east promised a warm day, though it was almost September. A hush lay over the still-sleeping town, and she felt as though she was the only person awake.

She hummed a tune and even broke into a little dance step as she pinned one of Ewan's heavy work shirts on the line. A bird foraging in the vegetable bed halted and cocked its head at her.

'Aye, I'm daft, but sometimes it's allowed,' Kirsty told it. Apparently deciding that, daft or not, she was harmless enough, the bird continued its search, keeping a bright eye on her as it worked.

When the basket was empty she began emptying the copper. Todd Paget, a canvas sack dangling from one hand, came whistling through the pend as she brought out the first pailful of warm water, and he hurried along the path by the house to put the sack down and take the pail from her.

'Here – let me.'

'I'm not in my dotage yet,' she protested.

'It never hurts tae get a wee hand from someone. Were ye goin' tae put it on the vegetable bed?' When she nodded, he began to trickle the water, a little at a time, around the plants. 'I brought ye some vegetables from the allotment.' A nod of the head indicated the bag by the back door. 'There's more than my sister can use.'

'That's good of you, Todd, but what about Beth?' Todd's allotment was thriving, and he had supplied almost all the vegetables the household needed over the past few months.

'She's got some,' he said, and went into the wash-house to fill the bucket again.

'What's happened about the flat you found?' Kirsty wanted to know when he returned.

A shadow passed across his normally cheerful face. 'Beth didnae like it, though I thought it was just right, myself. She said the close was too dark.'

Kirsty opened her mouth to say something, then closed it again. Todd was tireless in his hunt for a suitable place that he and Beth could rent, but every time he found one, there was something about it that Beth disliked. It seemed to Kirsty that Beth just didn't want to get married, but even if that was the truth, it was no business of hers.

'So, you'll be looking for something else then?'

'It's the only way. One of them'll be just right for us, you'll see. Is Alex all set for the exhibition?'

'I'm just going to waken him now.'

'Then I'll not hold ye back. Give him my good wishes,' Todd said, and went off to work.

Alex was already in the kitchen when Kirsty brought in the sack of vegetables, wearing only his drawers and washing himself at the sink.

'I was just going to wake you.'

'I scarcely slept,' he confessed, glancing vaguely around, droplets of water cascading from his chin and dripping from his fingers onto the floor. 'I forgot to bring the towel over.'

'Here.' She handed it to him, then mopped at the floor as he dried himself vigorously. 'It's a grand day.'

'Just the right sort of day for success,' Alex agreed. He was rubbing at his wet hair, the smooth skin on his chest and arms moving easily across the sheet of interlocked muscles overlying his skeleton. He had grown to full manhood, his formerly thin, boyish body now lean and sinewy.

'Are you nervous?'

'No,' he said briskly, then followed the denial almost immediately with, 'and that's a lie if ever I've told one. Mam, I'm scared tae death. What if the Glasgow folk don't like what I've done with the furniture?'

'Of course they'll like it.'

He ran his arms into the shirt she had carefully ironed the night before and buttoned it, then tried several times to get his tie to lie correctly, tutting and muttering annoyance at it. 'I'll do it,' Kirsty offered at last, unable to stand by and watch any longer. He was much taller than she was, and she had to reach up. His teeth were worrying his lower lip, a sign of inner anxiety stretching back to his earliest childhood.

'I hope the furniture arrived safely.' The pieces being put on show had gone off to Glasgow the day before on one of Gregg's carts, and Alex was following by train.

'I'm sure Mr Gregg's seen to that very efficiently.' Kirsty gave one final tug to the tie then stepped back to study the overall effect.

'How do I look?'

'Grand – and you'll look even better when you cover your shirt-tail with your trousers,' she said, and he glanced down at his legs, puzzled, then gave a muffled exclamation and hurried upstairs.

16

The other three were eating their breakfast when he came back and asked anxiously, 'Will I do, Mam?'

Glancing up from the stove, Kirsty experienced a glow of maternal pride so strong that she was sure it must be radiating from her like beams from the sun.

He was wearing a grey flannel suit that she had found in Jean's shop and had carefully altered to fit and steamed and pressed. His shirt was snowy white, with a high cellulose collar, and the tie, also from Jean's, was soft blue speckled with grey. His curly red hair had been plastered to his skull with oil; the severe style gave his longish face a distinguished look.

'Mam?' he prompted, panic beginning to glitter in his eyes. 'Is there something wrong? Is it the tie, mebbe, or—'

'You look just right,' she said simply, and he relaxed, then laughed when Mary, whose mouth had fallen open to reveal a half-chewed lump of bread to all and sundry, swallowed hard then said in a breathless squeak, 'You look just like a gentleman! Can I walk to the station with you before I go to school?'

'I'd be honoured by your presence, my lady!'

After a swift glance at his stepbrother, Ewan returned to his breakfast without comment. Kirsty, who had happened to catch his look, recognised a sudden flash of jealousy in it. Ewan made no secret of the fact that he was bored by his work and by everything else in his life. He would no doubt have given a great deal to be going to Glasgow in Alex's place, Kirsty thought, feeling sorry for the boy.

'I never realised how handsome you are, Alex,' Caitlin said. 'Now I know why Ellen Forsyth likes you.'

'Who's Ellen Forsyth?'

'One of the girls in the shop. She's talked about you quite a lot.'

'Ellen Forsyth's easily pleased, then,' Ewan jeered, and Kirsty's sympathy shrivelled somewhat. Caitlin turned on her half-brother with a sudden and rare flash of anger.

'She must be – she's walked out with you often enough,' she snapped.

He glared at her, then at Alex, who said, 'Is there a lassie in this town who's not walked out with our Ewan?'

'That's more than anyone can say about you.'

'Has your father seen you?' Kirsty broke in swiftly.

Alex shrugged. 'He'd not be interested.'

'You must go up to him before you leave, Alex. He'll be offended if you don't.'

He gave her a sidelong look. 'D'you think so?'

Too excited to eat, he only managed to swallow half a cup of tea and a slice of bread and margarine before going upstairs, at Kirsty's request, to see Matt.

'I was right,' he said tersely when he returned. 'I needn't have troubled myself. He just grumbled about me expecting the workshop to run on its own while I'm gallivanting in Glasgow.' His face was shadowed.

'Me and Todd can manage fine,' Ewan said at once. 'He knows that.'

Alex ignored him. 'I'd best go,' he said, then offered his arm to Mary and forced a cheerful note into his voice. 'Her Royal Highness's coach awaits – and if her prince doesn't catch the train and get to Glasgow in time he'll turn into a toad for ever. Come on.'

'You might have wished the laddie well,' Kirsty said when she went up to give Matt his breakfast.

'Wish him well when he's jauntin' off on some daft ploy and leavin' Todd and Ewan on their own?' Matt had aged noticeably in the past month or so. There were more lines on his face and more grey in his hair and in the stubble over his chin.

'They can manage fine.'

'I wish I wasnae stuck here, of no use tae anyone,' he railed.

'There's no sense in fretting; it'll only make you worse. D'you want to come downstairs? I'll fetch Todd and Ewan. You should come down, Matt,' she added when he shook his head.

'What's the point in exchanging one prison for another?'

He was in continuous pain, and at night he still needed laudanum, which Kirsty carefully measured out, to help him to sleep. But now he could manage the stairs with assistance, although once down them he was more or less confined to his chair in the kitchen. Kirsty worried over the way he seemed less and less inclined to make the effort.

'It'd be a change of scene. If it gets warm enough, you could sit out at the back.'

'And have everyone who goes up and down the lane stoppin' tae pity me? Ye can tell Ewan tae come up tae discuss the day's work.'

'D'you not mean Todd?'

'I said Ewan, and I mean Ewan,' he flared at her. 'It's my bones that've gone wrong, woman, not my brain. If one son isnae interested in how the workshop's doin', then I must depend on the other.' He tossed his newspaper aside petulantly and it slid over the side of the bed to land on the floor like a broken-winged seagull. 'Ewan can fetch Todd if I decide tae go downstairs.'

Kirsty walked round the bed to pick the paper up and folded it properly. 'I'll fetch Ewan,' she said.

Going out to the workshop, she thought longingly of the peaceful days when Alex and Ewan, growing up together and much the same age, had been close friends. As often happened with brothers, the friendship had weakened as they neared maturity and developed different characteristics – Alex quiet, Ewan with his love of activity and companionship. But even so, there had never been any antagonism between them. That had come after the move to Paisley. Kirsty didn't know why or when it had first appeared, but she felt that Matt, with his habit of favouring Ewan over Alex, had had a hand in it.

Alex shifted the chairs, table and dresser from one position to another, wishing that Mr Gregg had stayed with him instead of hurrying away to see to other business he had in the city.

Most of the exhibits in the large hall were attended by two or three or even four people who had, he suddenly realised with alarm, brought various items with them to highlight their wares. Lengths of material were being pinned to the walls as backcloths, or draped over stands. Bright Spanish shawls with long silky fringes were tossed over the backs of handsome chairs, and lush green pot plants or vases of dried flowers were being placed on polished surfaces. One exhibit even boasted a live model, a smartly dressed young woman stretched nonchalantly on a chaise longue with a magazine in her lap.

If only, he thought in despair, he had asked Mrs Gregg to lend him the china he had copied the design from, to display it on the dresser. But it was too late now, and his work would have to speak for itself.

He studied it, trying hard to see it with a stranger's dispassionate gaze. The poppy and cornflower spray had been painted across the top bar of each of the four chairs that went with the table, and the same flowers swarmed up the table legs. They appeared on the dresser as formal posies on the doors and the drawers, and in a spray along the top. On the two fireside chairs they covered the armrests generously, as well as decorating the backrest.

Mr and Mrs Gregg had been delighted with the furniture, but what, Alex wondered with a clenching feeling in the pit of his stomach, would other folk think? Was it all too much, too garish?

Strolling casually to the far side of the hall he glanced across and saw with relief that the cream-coloured plaster walls in the corner allocated to him displayed the furniture well enough, though an extra splash of colour would have helped. He returned to move the pieces around for the last time, then, for want of any other embellishment, dug into his bag and brought out the large book of patterns he had brought with him to study if time permitted. Opening it at a favourite page, he propped it on the dresser, then tore some half-finished pages from his sketch pad and scattered them carefully over the table.

Another stroll to the far wall satisfied him that the sketch-book and drawings fitted into the overall picture. There was nothing more he could do, and in any case, the exhibition was about to be opened to the public. Returning to his corner, Alex sat down at the table and brought out the crayons he always carried in his pocket. He might as well work as sit there doing nothing.

The day passed fairly swiftly. Alex became quite intent on his work, relaxing as he began to get used to the place and the people. Now and again someone came over to look at his furniture and ask him about it. He got one small order, which elated him, and another two people said that they would return later.

During a lull, he became so involved in the sketch beneath his hand that when one of the organisers approached he had to give a little cough to attract Alex's attention. Crimsoning, he jumped to his feet, almost knocking the sketchbook to the floor.

The man referred discreetly to the list in his hand. 'May I introduce Mr Alexander Lennox, Miss MacDowall? Mr Lennox, this is Miss Fiona MacDowall . . .' He paused, then added with subtle emphasis, 'whose father owns one of the city's most successful furniture emporiums.'

'Mr Lennox, I am most taken with your furniture.' Fiona MacDowall held out a gloved hand, and Alex took it carefully in his own. She was the most beautiful woman he had ever seen. Her face, small and neat, was dominated by wide brown eyes flecked with gold and thickly lashed. Beneath her corn-flower-blue hat – the same blue as the flowers on the furniture, he noted – her hair was a smooth sweep of pale gold.

'And this is . . .' The official looked at the older woman, then said again, 'This is . . .'

'Mrs Dove, our housekeeper.' Fiona MacDowall's voice was as clear and as pure as spring water. Alex suddenly realised that he was still clasping her hand and released it hurriedly as the housekeeper bowed her head in acknowledgement, her own gloved hands remaining folded at her waist.

'Will you sit down, Miss MacDowall, Mrs Dove?' he invited.

'If you'll excuse me, Miss MacDowall?' the official said when both women were seated.

'Of course. You must have a great deal to do, and I'm sure that Mr Lennox will look after us very well.' As the man hurried off Fiona MacDowall spread her fingers wide over the painted rests of her chair. 'I feel as though I'm dipping my hands into a field of flowers,' she said with delight.

'That was my intention. You don't think it's too much?'

'Oh no, not at all.' This girl, Alex thought, was the best embellishment his furniture could have; better by far than china, or Spanish shawls or vases of flowers. The deep blue of her dress and neat-fitting bolero jacket and the pale-blue straw hat with its froth of creamy feathers round the brim, almost the shade of the furniture itself, were quite perfect.

'Do you always decorate your furniture with flowers?'

'I can do any pattern the customer asks for.' Alex dipped

into his bag and brought out a smaller sketchbook. 'Perhaps you would care to look through some of my ideas.'

She and Mrs Dove bent together over the pages, while Alex went on to explain that the furniture was made in his father's workshop.

'These are beautiful,' Fiona MacDowall said, 'but I think that I like the flowers best. My father has just bought a new house, Mr Lennox, and I'm furnishing my own bedroom. Could you make a set of furniture for me?'

'It would be my pleasure, Miss MacDowall.' Alex turned to a blank page in the sketchbook. 'Tell me something about the rooms and the style you would like,' he invited, while the hall and all the people in it, including the housekeeper, faded into the background, leaving only the two of them – Alex Lennox and the exquisite young woman who had just walked into his life.

Kirsty jerked awake and scrambled to her feet, the darning she had dozed over falling from her lap to the floor, as the latch was lifted on the back door and Alex came in.

'I thought you'd be in your bed, Mam.' Although it was late, he didn't look in the least tired. Instead he was glowing and filled with energy, the hair he had oiled so carefully that morning framing his face like a blazing halo.

'I wanted to find out how—' The words ended in a muffled squeak as he surged across the little room and swept her into his arms, spinning her round. 'Alex, put me down, you'll have the two of us on the floor!'

'Not a bit of it, you're light as a feather,' he said breathlessly, setting her back on her feet. 'Mam, I'd a wonderful day! There was so much tae see, and so many folk.'

'Did they like the furniture?'

'I got three orders, and some other folk showed an interest.' He pulled his jacket off and wrestled with his high shirt collar. 'I wasn't the only one with painted pieces, but those that looked at mine seemed tae like them well enough.'

'I'm glad – not that I'd any doubts that you'd do well,' Kirsty added hastily. 'I kept some dinner hot, but it'll be dried up by now.'

'I'm not hungry.' He dropped the collar on the table then stretched out in Matt's chair, rubbing at his neck where the collar had chafed. 'That's better – I couldn't be doing with having tae wear one of these things every day. It made me feel as if my head was being cut off.'

'You'll have some tea, at least. I thought you'd be home earlier than this,' she said over her shoulder as she picked up the teapot.

'I walked about Glasgow for a while tae see something of the place while I was there. Mam,' he suddenly burst out, 'there was a lassie – I mean, a young lady – that was awful taken with my work. She's given us an order for chairs for her own bedroom, and a washstand and two chests of drawers and a wardrobe.'

She handed him his tea. 'That'll cost her a fair bit.'

'Her father can afford it.' He lifted the cup to his lips, then lowered it untouched. 'He owns one of the big furniture shops in Glasgow, yet she wants us tae make the furniture and me tae decorate it. She's called Fiona MacDowall.' He said the name reverently, as though reciting a poem.

'Oh aye?'

'She invited me to her house when the exhibition ended, so's I could see the room for myself.'

163

'Just the two of you, on your own?' Kirsty asked, shocked.

'No, no, her housekeeper was with her.' Again the cup was lifted then set down. 'It was the grandest house I've ever been in.'

'And what does her father say to her ordering furniture from us instead of using his own shop?'

'Not a word, for he's away somewhere just now, seeing to a new shop he's opening in another town. Anyway, she says he doesn't sell decorated furniture, and that's what she wants.'

'Alex, son, are you sure of this order?' Kirsty asked gently, reluctant to spoil his elation. 'Her father'll mebbe get her to change her mind when he comes home.'

'I'm quite sure. She's not the sort of lassie tae say a thing if it's not true, and the housekeeper seemed tae think that it was all right.' He got up and emptied his untouched tea into the sink, saying as he rinsed out the mug, 'You'll meet her yourself on Monday, for I've invited her and the housekeeper tae come and see the workshop.'

'Monday?' The shock of his announcement brought Kirsty upright in her chair. 'This Monday coming?' Then, as he nodded, she cried, 'Oh, Alex, could you not have given me more warning?'

'What for? She only wants tae see where her furniture's going to be made.'

'But they'll expect to be invited into the house and given refreshments!'

'Just a cup of tea after their journey, and mebbe a bit of shortbread. I'd tea and sandwiches at her house,' Alex said happily, oblivious to his mother's dismay. 'Wee dainty things they were, not even big enough for a decent bite at them.'

'Alex Lennox! Men have no idea of what's right and proper! I'll have to turn the place out – and do a baking . . .'

Surprised, he cast a look round the crowded, shabby kitchen. 'It looks fine to me, and she's not one to fuss. You'll see that for yourself when you meet her. You'll like her, Mam – you'll not be able to help but like her,' Alex said, then went off to bed, beaming as though he didn't know how to stop, leaving Kirsty to panic over the impending visit.

17

Matt reacted with predictable derision to the news that his stepson had done well at the exhibition, and when he heard that one of the customers was coming to the house, his temper flared.

'I've never heard such nonsense – if we start allowin' everyone who puts in an order tae come an' see the workshop first we'll never get anythin' done!'

'This is a special matter, with the lassie's father selling furniture himself,' Kirsty tried to soothe him. 'You never know, we might get orders from him one day. Anyway it's been arranged, there's nothing we can do about it now.'

'One thing's for sure – I'm havin' nothin' tae do with it. I'm staying in my bed while she's here!'

The decision was a great relief to Alex, who, Kirsty knew, had been worried about what his father might say in front of the visitors. But on Monday morning Matt suddenly changed his mind.

'When all's said and done, I'm still the master here, even if that laddie is puttin' on airs an' graces an' tryin' tae make folk think otherwise,' he announced, sitting up in bed, his grey hair awry and his chin thick with stubble. 'I'd best be there, tae keep an eye on things.'

Kirsty, worn out after a weekend of cleaning and baking, looked at her husband in despair. The visit would be a lot easier for her as well as for Alex if Matt stayed where he was. 'Are you sure? It'll mean getting shaved and washed, and having to wear your good suit . . .'

'In my own house? And me an invalid? A shirt and trousers, and a blanket about my shoulders'll do.'

'If you come downstairs while we've got visitors, Matt Lennox, you'll be dressed in your best and that's final. I'll press your good suit.'

'Can you not make him change his mind?' Alex asked in despair when she went downstairs with Matt's suit over her arm.

'You know your father – once he's decided on something he'll not be moved from it.'

A broad grin split Ewan's face. 'That'll spoil your nice wee afternoon tea with your young lady.'

'She's not my young lady, she's a customer!'

'I've never seen you put on your best suit and oil your hair for Mr Gregg,' Ewan retorted. He himself was annoyed because he was expected to work as usual instead of being included in the welcoming party.

'At least you'll see Miss MacDowall when she visits the workshop. She'll not be coming to the grocer's shop,' Caitlin said. 'Remember, Mam, I want to know all about what she wore.'

'I'm going to wear my best dress and say please and thank you,' Mary said smugly. She wasn't due to return to school for the new term for another two days, so she would be there to see the visitor. Ewan and Caitlin both glared at her.

Alex had arranged to be at nearby Canal Street station that afternoon to meet Fiona MacDowall's train and escort her and the housekeeper to the house. By the time he left, in his good grey suit, Matt had been washed, shaved, dressed and settled in an armchair in the parlour.

'He'll ruin everything,' Alex said gloomily on the doorstep. 'He'll say – God alone knows what he'll say, but it's sure to be something tae embarrass me!'

'It'll be fine – your father wouldn't spoil things for you,' Kirsty soothed. Then, nervously, her hands smoothing her brown skirt and fluttering among the frills on her pale-green blouse, she said, 'D'you think I look all right? I'd not want to let you down.'

His worried frown melted into a smile. 'You look fine, Mam. You'd never let me down,' he said, and strode off to the station, holding his shoulders back stiffly, like a brave soldier marching to possible doom.

Fiona MacDowall disarmed Matt from the start by saying, as she took one of his swollen hands gently in both of hers, 'I was so sorry to hear that you suffer from arthritis, Mr Lennox. I can feel the inflammation's heat in your poor joints – it must be a great trial to you.'

'It comes an' it goes,' Matt said gruffly, making no attempt to draw his hand from hers. 'There's no' much I can do but thole it.'

'That's very brave, but courage doesn't make the pain any easier to bear.' The girl gave his hand a final pat before releasing it. 'My poor grandmamma had very bad rheumatics,

I remember. There was an ointment that she swore by. I'll ask our housekeeper about it when I go home, and send it to you.'

Kirsty could understand why her serious, level-headed son had been captivated by this girl. Although everything about her indicated wealth and comfort, her manner was natural and friendly, and her expressive brown eyes sparkled. Instead of the housekeeper, she was accompanied by a smartly dressed middle-aged man who was introduced as Mr George Gavin, the manager of her father's furniture shop.

'Mr Gavin was interested in hearing more about your painted furniture, and he's willing to stand witness to the fact that although I'm a mere woman I have the authority to order furniture for my own use. I felt that you were unsure about that,' Fiona MacDowall said solemnly to Alex, then laughed when he began to splutter out denials. 'I know how men's minds work – my father would have thought just the same.' She laid a hand on his arm, and Kirsty saw her son's eyes glow at the brief contact.

'What d'you think of her?' he whispered when the two of them left the room, Kirsty to bring the tea tray from the kitchen, Alex to fetch some sketches to show to the visitors.

'She's a nice lassie – and a pretty one, too. Best not to leave Matt alone with them for too long, though,' she warned, and they went about their business.

To Kirsty's relief the atmosphere was still calm when she returned to the parlour. Matt, more animated than she had seen him for a long time, was talking to George Gavin about the business, while Mary showed Fiona MacDowall her doll.

'Her drawers can't come off, but her dress can – and her petticoat,' she was saying in her clear, composed little voice. 'And her bonnet. My sister, Caitlin, made them all. She makes lots of clothes for my dolls.'

'Your sister must be very clever.'

'She is. She makes her own clothes, and some of mine. She made this.' Mary stepped to the centre of the floor and turned round to display her square-necked cotton dress, frilled at the neck and sleeves and hem.

'It's very pretty.'

'It's my best.' Mary eyed the guest's yellow jacket, decorated with bands of dark-green lace, and her dark-green skirt trimmed with yellow rosettes. 'Did you make your clothes?'

'No, I didn't. I'm afraid I'm not good at sewing.'

'Princesses like you don't have to sew, do they? They have servants to do that for them.'

'I'm not a princess, dear,' Fiona said.

'You look very like the princess in my book. P'raps you really are, but you don't know it yet,' Mary suggested.

Kirsty, listening and watching, saw Fiona glance up at Alex, who had just come into the room, from beneath long thick lashes. 'Perhaps I won't know it until the right prince comes along,' she said.

The conversation flowed easily enough while they drank their tea, but when George Gavin showed a keen interest in Alex's sketches of decorated furniture and expressed his view that his employer might take a professional interest in them, Matt stiffened.

'Tae my mind, Mr Gavin, a chair's a chair an' a chest o' drawers is a chest o' drawers. Furniture's made tae be used.

170

If ye want something nice tae look at, ye can put pictures on the wall.'

Alex shot to the edge of his chair, his lean body tense. 'What's wrong with furniture that's serviceable and looks bonny at the same time?'

'Turnin' a good piece of work intae a sideshow's an insult tae the man that made it,' Matt snapped.

'It's not an insult – it's just a way of helping the furniture to fit in better with the decor of the room!'

Matt took in a noisy mouthful of tea, shooting a withering glance at his stepson over the top of one of Kirsty's good china cups. 'Decor, is it? That's a word for lassies, no' skilled craftsmen!'

Alex, scarlet to the tips of his ears, opened his mouth to reply, but Fiona spoke first. 'I can understand your meaning, Mr Lennox, but isn't it usually the woman who chooses furniture for her home? And women put great value on pretty things. What do you say, Mr Gavin?'

'I'll admit that in my experience the ladies usually have the last word.'

'Although my father sells very fine furniture,' Fiona added, with a warm smile at Matt, 'I know full well that he has no great idea of how to make a place homely. That task has fallen to me.'

'Aye, well,' Matt humphed, determined not to give in but reluctant to offend her.

'I knew that you'd understand my meaning.' She gave him another sweet smile and put her cup down. 'I would so like to see your workshop, Mr Lennox. Would you allow your son to take us there?'

*

Kirsty took advantage of the visitors' absence to wash and dry the cups and make a fresh pot of tea in case it was needed. She was putting the last dried piece of china back on the tray when the door from the yard opened and Alex ushered his guests into the kitchen, announcing cheerfully, 'Miss MacDowall wants to see the chairs I painted for you, Mam.'

While the visitors enthused over the chairs, Kirsty glared at her eldest son, who looked back at her with puzzled innocence, quite unaware of any wrongdoing.

An hour later Alex swung out of the station and turned towards the Cross, too elated to think of going back to Espedair Street. He knew full well that he should return to the workshop, but he needed to walk, to be free to dwell on every moment he had spent in Fiona MacDowall' s company that afternoon.

She had liked his family, and the chairs he had painted for his mother, and the workshop. She had invited him to call on her on Thursday evening with preliminary sketches for her furniture. And Mr Gavin had said, shaking Alex's hand before stepping onto the train, that he was certain that his employer would be interested in meeting Alex and seeing his work when he returned to Glasgow.

At that moment Alex Lennox wouldn't have changed places with any man on earth except George Gavin, now sitting opposite Fiona – in his most private thoughts, he allowed himself to call her by her Christian name – in the enclosed intimacy of a railway carriage, free to look at her lovely face, hear her voice and, at the end of the journey, able to take her hand in his and help her to alight from the carriage.

Remembering the touch of that small gloved hand against his palm as he had assisted her to board the train, Alex's heart sang, while the fingers of the privileged hand curled slightly by his side as though enfolding hers again.

At the foot of St Mirren Brae he came face to face with Beth Laidlaw, who inclined her head slightly and swept past. Now there was a stuck-up besom, Alex thought. He'd seen Beth often enough to realise that her smiles and her charm tended to be reserved for men she considered to be blessed with either looks or money. He hoped that Todd might come to his senses before he went to the altar with Beth, for the man deserved better. Not that there was any sense in trying to say so to Todd, who was too besotted by the woman's looks to give much thought to the calculating creature beneath the surface. She was pretty enough in her own way, but not a patch on Fiona when it came to beauty and good manners.

Fiona. As he crossed the road to walk up through the public gardens that ran alongside St Mirren Brae, Alex gloated over the way Ewan's eyes had widened when Fiona had walked into the workshop. Because young women tended to forget Alex when his handsome, charming step-brother was around, he had been nervous about bringing the two of them together. But Fiona had been different from the rest – pleasant enough towards Ewan, as she was pleasant towards everyone, but staying by Alex's side throughout the visit, asking questions of him and not of Ewan.

He emerged from the gardens into Paisley Cross and turned along the side of the imposing George A. Clark Town Hall, built with a handsome donation from a member of one of the town's leading textile-manufacturing families. At the corner he turned right again along Abbey Close, the narrow thoroughfare between the town hall and Paisley Abbey.

The close was quite busy on that pleasant afternoon, but because of her height he saw Rose Hamilton almost at once, walking along the pavement towards him, a step or two behind a middle-aged couple. Even in his euphoria Alex felt his hackles rise at the sight of her and saw, by the way she drew herself upright, that she had seen and recognised him. Stepping aside to let the couple pass, he gave Rose a brief nod, which she acknowledged with a dip of the head.

A sharp voice floated in his wake. 'Rose, did I just see you acknowledge that . . . that person? Who . . .?'

Alex smiled to himself and strode on.

'How could you?' Kirsty stormed at Alex when he finally arrived home. Matt, worn out by the afternoon's events, had gone back to bed and Ewan, his day's work finished, was washing his hands at the sink, his sleeves rolled up to the elbows.

Alex looked at his mother, confused. 'How could I what?'

'You know fine and well what! Bringing these people into the kitchen, and it in a mess!' Kirsty wielded the potato masher vigorously in the big pot. 'I didn't know what to do with myself when they walked in without warning.'

'They only wanted to see the chairs I'd painted for you – and there's nothing wrong with the kitchen.'

'Alex Lennox—!' she began, just as Caitlin burst in at the back door, wanting to know all about the afternoon's visitor.

'She was like the princess in my story book.' Mary spread a handful of cutlery on the table and began to set it out. 'She was the most beautiful lady I've ever seen.'

'If you like those sort of looks,' Ewan drawled, reaching for a towel. Alex stiffened.

'What does that mean?'

Ewan turned, resting his backside on the edge of the sink, a slight smile on his face as he dried his fingers one by one. 'I'm just sayin' that a glass of spring water can be pleasant now and again, but I prefer somethin' with more bite to it, myself. Like a good whisky.'

'You keep your tongue off Fiona MacDowall.'

'I never mentioned her name,' Ewan protested. 'I was talking about different drinks – wasn't I, Mary?' His eyes were wide and innocent, but there was a smirk at the corners of his mouth.

'That's enough,' Kirsty said sharply, sensing trouble.

Alex ignored her. 'We both know who you were talking about,' he said tightly to his stepbrother. 'You're jealous because Fiona MacDowall wouldn't bother herself with the likes of you!'

'What makes you think she'd look at you either?'

'Nothing – Miss MacDowall's a customer, that's all.'

'Oh aye?' Ewan's faint smirk broadened into a grin. 'I've never seen you simpering and blushing when Mr Gregg comes into the workshop.'

Caitlin gave a yelp of laughter at the thought, and Mary started to giggle. Alex, his face almost as red as his hair, stared at Ewan for a moment, then said slowly and clearly, 'Going back to what you were saying about drink, at least I'd not stoop so low as tae sip from another man's glass when his back's turned.'

The grin vanished from Ewan's face as though it had been struck off by a blow. He whitened, then tossed the towel down. 'You . . .' he began, all the amusement gone from his voice as he advanced on Alex, who moved willingly to meet him.

A swift step brought Kirsty between them. 'I'll have none of this in my kitchen!'

'We'll go outside then.' Alex's voice was hard and flat.

'You'll do nothing of the sort! If there's any blows being struck today, they'll come from me – and this!' Kirsty brandished the heavy wooden potato masher at them. 'Ewan, pick up that towel and sit at the table. As for you, Alex, go upstairs this instant and take that good suit off. The food'll be on the table in a minute.'

For a moment she thought that she might have to carry out her threat and use the masher, then Ewan threw himself sulkily into a chair and Alex, the threat over, marched from the room. Looking at her daughters, Kirsty saw that the merriment had flown. Caitlin was ashen faced, and Mary's eyes were bright with frightened tears.

'Caitlin, you put the soup out while Mary helps me to finish these potatoes.' When Mary came to her, she lifted the little girl onto a chair and put the heavy masher into her hands, covering them with her own so that her arms were about her daughter.

'You're getting to be too heavy to lift, milady – you've been eating too many potatoes. Now, push down hard, that's it . . .'

She realised that she was shaking inside. Ewan and Alex had always had squabbles, even fights on occasion. That was only to be expected from two boys growing up together and less than a year apart in age. But this had been different – this had been a confrontation between two grown men. It had blown up so quickly, too. She was confused as to exactly what they had said to each other, but it was clear that they both understood it.

Something had gone wrong between them, and she hoped that it could be resolved before it went too far.

18

It was to be a full month before Angus MacDowall, Fiona's father, returned to Glasgow. By that time Alex had completed the first piece of furniture for the girl, a chest of drawers painted a light stone colour, with a design of roses in all hues – cream, yellow and every shade of pink and red from shell-pink to crimson – edging the top. A full deep-pink rose decorated each drawer, its heart the brass handle.

'It's lovely, Alex,' Kirsty said when he showed her the finished piece. 'Mr MacDowall'll surely be impressed.'

'We thought – Fiona and me – that it was best tae complete a small piece first, tae let him see it. The rest should be finished by the turn of the year.' He started to rewrap the chest of drawers carefully in sacking. 'Mr Gavin's cart should be here within the hour tae take it to the house.'

Detailed technical drawings of each of the other pieces of furniture had also been completed, with the planned decorations clearly shown. Alex had worked hard at the sketches in his own time – when he wasn't in Glasgow with Fiona.

After the quarrel with Ewan, he hadn't invited the girl back to Paisley but visited Glasgow at least once a week, sometimes calling on Fiona in her home, sometimes going out walking with her or listening to band music in one of the city's many parks. From what Alex said, Kirsty gathered that the housekeeper was always in attendance; from what he didn't say, she had a shrewd idea that he and Fiona managed to spend a fair bit of time on their own.

'It'll end in tears,' Matt prophesied gloomily. 'That lassie's father'll be lookin' for a wealthy son-in-law, not a cabinet-maker who has tae work hard for every penny he can get.'

'It's just a friendship between the girl and Alex,' Kirsty protested, and her husband gave a disbelieving snort, then winced and barked, 'Will ye watch what ye're about, woman!'

'I'm sorry. It's hard to rub the stuff in properly without hurting.' Matt's health had deteriorated again, and Kirsty was rubbing the ointment Fiona had sent into his swollen knuckles, trying to loosen them.

'Just good friends?' he returned to the subject when the pain in his hand had eased. 'A lad and a lassie their ages don't just have friendships. If ye've got any sense ye'll warn him tae put an end tae it before there's trouble.'

'Does that feel any better?'

'Aye, a bit.'

When he nodded, she went to wash her hands in the bowl of water on the stand, breathing in the rose-scented fragrance of the small tablet of soap she kept on the washstand. It made a pleasant change from wintergreen. She was sick of the smell of the ointment; the bedroom reeked of it these days.

It had been agreed between Fiona and Alex that he should wait until her father had settled back home before their meeting. To his surprise, when the summons finally arrived, it

179

was an invitation to call on Angus MacDowall at his office, and not in his home.

'You're discussing business,' Kirsty pointed out, although she herself was surprised. 'He'll want it to be man to man, without Fiona there. Mebbe it means that he's going to give you an order for his big shop. Perhaps he'll ask you to the house afterwards.'

'Mebbe.' Alex's teeth worried at his lower lip, then he shrugged. 'I'll not know till I get there, will I?'

Bathed, and dressed in his good suit, his hair oiled down and his sketchbook under his arm, he went off to Glasgow and returned three hours later.

'He doesn't like the furniture,' Kirsty said as soon as she saw the look on his face.

'Oh, he liked it well enough – it's me he didn't like.' Alex tossed the sketchbook on the table and sank into a chair.

'You? Did you have words with the man?'

'I didn't spend enough time with him to have words about anything. Most of the time I was with George Gavin, being shown round the place.'

Kirsty sat down opposite him, confused. 'Start at the beginning. What did he think of the furniture?'

Alex kept his gaze fixed on his clasped hands. 'He said he liked it, and so did Fiona, and it was fine to go ahead with the rest of the order. He asked me about the workshop – if it was a big place, and who I worked for, and if I'd served my time there. I told him about Falkirk, and your father leaving it tae you, and I invited him over tae see it.'

'When?' Kirsty asked nervously, and he looked up at her, smiling faintly.

'You've no need tae worry, Mam, I've not landed you

180

with a visitor again. He said that he'd like tae see the place
sometime, but he said it in that sort of way that tells you a
person's not telling the truth.' He suddenly slammed a fist on
the table. 'Mam, I don't know what I've done tae annoy the
man, but it seems that I must have done something.'

. A cold feeling in Kirsty's chest hinted that she knew what
Alex had done, even if he didn't. 'Was Fiona mentioned ?'

'He said that she'd been taken with my work, and she'd
apparently enjoyed visiting my home.' He gave a short laugh.
'That's just the word he used – "apparently", as if he didn't
believe that she really had enjoyed coming here. Then he said
that she'd been invited to visit friends in Fort William and
she'd be gone for a while. And that was that. George Gavin
was waiting in the other office. Mr MacDowall said he'd a lot
tae see tae, after being away, and he'd asked Gavin tae show
me round the shop.' He turned his right hand over on the
table, uncurling the fingers and staring down at his palm. 'He
could scarce bring himself tae shake hands with me when I
left, Mam. It was as though he thought I was a leper!'

'Alex,' Kirsty began tentatively, 'have you thought that
mebbe it's something to do with this friendship that's grown
between you and his daughter while he was away?'

His head came up. 'What's wrong with friendship?' he
asked at once, on the defensive. 'The lassie was lonely on her
own with her father away. We like each other, that's all.'

'Mr MacDowall might have thought that you were becoming more than just friends.'

'You mean he's decided that I'm not good enough for his
daughter?' he said bitterly. 'We've already talked about that,
her and me. She told me that her father came from ordinary
stock himself and he believes in judging folk by what they've

done with their lives. She was certain he'd like me, and instead of that—'

Again he banged a fist on the table, then got to his feet abruptly. 'I'd best change into my work-clothes.'

The dull thump of the stick Matt kept by the bed echoed through the ceiling.

'One of these days,' Alex said, 'he'll come right through and you'll not have tae bother going up tae see what he wants.'

'Did I hear Alex?' Matt asked as soon as she went into the bedroom.

'You did. He's getting ready to go back to work.'

'How did he get on with the man?'

'Fine,' she lied, rescuing the newspaper, which had fallen off the bed, and restoring it to him. She didn't feel strong enough at that moment to tell him the truth and have to put up with his inevitable gloating.

'I'll have tae visit the wee room soon.' Matt hated having to use a chamber pot, but when his hips and knees were bad, as they were that day, it was almost impossible for him to get to the bathroom unaided. He refused to allow Kirsty to help him, preferring to rely on his sons and on Todd, who had helped to nurse his own father in his final illness and, big as he was, had revealed a talent for providing steady and reliable support without causing added pain. He had taught the rest of them how to handle Matt more gently.

'I'll get Alex to give you a hand before he goes along to the workshop,' she said. But when Alex came downstairs and she passed the request on, he said abruptly, 'I'll send Todd and Ewan,' and went out.

*

A letter arrived for Alex on the following morning after he had gone to the workshop. Kirsty, seeing the Glasgow post-mark, waited until after the midday meal, then called Alex back as he and Ewan prepared to leave for work.

'This came for you.' She handed the envelope over and was glad that she had waited until they were alone when she saw the naked emotion and hunger in his face as he took it from her. Alex had lied when he had claimed mere friendship with Fiona MacDowall. Kirsty turned quickly away and bus-ied herself at the table, giving him privacy to tear it open and scan its contents.

'She's not going away tae Fort William at all!' His voice was exultant.

'I thought her father said—'

'He was right about her getting an invitation from friends there, but she's not going. She says it was him that wanted her tae accept.'

'Does she say anything about him being cool towards you?'

'Only that she had expected him tae invite me to the house after our meeting. She's as confused by the man's behaviour as I am – and she's known him all her life.' Beaming, he folded the letter and put it back into the envelope.

'Are you going to see her again?'

'Why not?'

'But Mr MacDowall—'

'As Fiona says, if he can't give either of us good reason why we should stop being friends, then why should we do what he wants? She says he's always wanted them tae be truthful with each other, and now he's the one who's broken his word.'

'Alex—'

'It's between me and Fiona, Mam,' he said, tucking the letter into his shirt pocket. 'I'd best get back tae work.'

Kirsty fretted about the matter all the way to the shop and would have gone on fretting if Jean hadn't been waiting for her on the pavement, rocking from one foot to the other in an ungainly dance of impatience.

'I'm that glad you've arrived at last!' She seized hold of Kirsty's sleeve. 'It's that Hamilton lassie – she's back again.'

'Rose Hamilton? Am I never going to get rid of that girl? Tell her I'm not interested in going back to work for her mother,' Kirsty said in a panic, and turned to flee. Jean's fingers held her, digging painfully into her arm.

'I've already said you'd be here any minute. She's in the back shop. She's your problem, Kirsty, not mine. You cannae leave me with her!'

Rose Hamilton had avoided the chair with the broken spring and was perched on the edge of an upright chair. She bounced to her feet as soon as Kirsty appeared.

'I've had an idea.' Until then, Kirsty had only seen her animated by anger, but today the sparkle in the girl's eyes and the set of her shoulders spoke of excitement and a sense of purpose rather than frustration.

'What has any idea of yours got to do with me?' Kirsty was too worried about Alex and Fiona, not to mention Matt's health, to care what she said to this nuisance of a girl.

Rose didn't seem to notice the rudeness. 'It has everything to do with you – you're the reason I had it in the first place.' She sat down again, but Kirsty stayed on her feet to indicate to the girl that her unwelcome visit was going to be brief. 'When I came here to ask you to come back and work for my mother again I noticed that this place was too small for all the clothes you have in store.' Rose indicated the garments hanging on the walls and the pile of clothing Jean had brought in that morning, waiting on the floor to be sorted out. 'I also noticed that the shop next door's for rent.'

'I cannae afford tae rent that one as well,' Jean immediately chimed in.

'I could.'

'You?' Kirsty and Jean spoke together, and Rose beamed and settled herself more comfortably in her chair, sure now of their attention.

'When I reached my eighteenth birthday a few weeks ago I inherited some money from my grandmamma. I want to do something useful with it – and what better than helping you to expand this place?'

Jean gasped and sat down abruptly on the arm of the broken chair, while Kirsty said at once, 'It's out of the question!'

'Why? You told me yourself that this shop is popular with the local women. It would make sense for them and for you to improve it.'

'Your parents would never agree to it.'

The girl's chin jutted in an all too familiar gesture. 'The inheritance is mine, to spend as I wish. It has nothing to do with my parents.'

'Even so, I'm sure your father'll expect you to save it towards your future.'

'He wants me to invest it.' With a sweeping movement of the arm, Rose indicated the small room. 'I could invest it here.'

'I doubt if that's what he meant,' Kirsty said irritably. She had alterations to see to, and after all that had happened at home, she had been looking forward to a quiet hour or so with her needle. 'And what about your mother? She'll say you should spend your money on yourself.'

'This would be for myself. I'm not just proposing to hand the money over to you and go away. I would become a partner, and I'd hope to make more money out of it eventually. That's what investments are all about,' Rose explained smilingly.

'But you could just as easily lose every penny of it,' Kirsty argued, keeping one eye on Jean, who had slid from the arm into the chair itself and flopped there, mouth open like a fish.

'My dear woman,' a flash of the old, arrogant Rose came through, 'I didn't just wake up this morning with the idea in my head. I still feel guilty about what happened to you. After you refused to take your job back, or let me give you money to make up for my . . .' she paused, then said flatly, 'my childish, selfish stupidity, I started thinking of other ways to make up for what I did to you. And one day the answer just came to me. I've come down here every day this month, ever since we got back home, to watch the people coming in and out of the shop. You do quite a brisk trade. If the place was larger you might very well do better. I'm sure my father would call that a sound investment.'

'But this isnae a dress shop, miss,' Jean quavered. 'We only sell second-hand clothes. The folk don't pay much for them.'

'A shilling here and a shilling there can mount up,' Rose Hamilton said briskly. 'I've taken advice on the matter. I spoke to the junior partner in my father's lawyer's office, and he has confirmed that my inheritance is mine to use as I wish. He took the trouble to listen to what I had to say,' she added pointedly, 'and he would like to speak with you both.'

She paused, looking from one of them to the other, then when they said nothing, 'Please don't turn my suggestion down without considering it,' she said, her voice suddenly losing its force and shaking slightly. 'Think what you could do to this place with a little money behind you.'

'I don't know what tae say,' Jean faltered, and Rose nodded.

'It's all very sudden, I know.' She got to her feet, gathering up her bag and her gloves. 'I should leave you to talk about it. I'll come back tomorrow afternoon for your answer.'

At the door she turned and said directly to Kirsty, 'You probably think that I'm just looking for another toy to play with, but that's not true. I know that my parents think I'm fit for nothing but marriage then running some man's home, like my sisters. But I want more than that. I want to do something with my life while it's still mine.'

19

'Have you got any brandy?' Kirsty asked when the girl had gone.

'No.' Jean was still lolling in the chair, heedless of the way her skirts rode up to expose her short, bowed legs.

'In that case I'm going to the public house along the road to buy a wee bottle of the stuff.'

Jean shot upright. 'You can't go intae a pub! Someone might see you!'

'I don't care, I need something to steady me. I've heard that spirits are a good help for shock.' Kirsty turned to the door, wondering if her shaky knees would carry her as far as the public house.

'Wait – if you're that determined, there's some whisky in the wee cupboard by the grate in my room. For hot toddies,' she added hastily. 'I get terrible throats in the winter.'

When Kirsty had located the small bottle and returned down the dark, rickety staircase, she poured a generous amount into two cups then topped them up with tea.

Jean downed half a cupful in one swallow, then erupted into a bout of coughing. She banged her chest with a clenched fist and said, when her voice returned, 'It seems tae do the trick.'

The sharp sting of the whisky made Kirsty's throat muscles contract, and for a terrible moment she thought that she was going to vomit. Then the contractions eased and a warm glow began to spread through her stomach.

'What d'ye think we should do about the lassie's offer, Kirsty?'

'It's your shop.'

'Mine?' Jean snorted. 'It stopped bein' my shop the day you walked in with all yer fancy plans about hangin' the gowns up an' puttin' them on display outside an' doin' alterations. You cannae leave me tae decide things for myself now!'

'Rose Hamilton can't be trusted. Look what she did to that gown I was making for her birthday party.'

'Give the lassie her due, Kirsty. She apologised for that, an' tried tae put things right.'

'You're right,' Kirsty had to admit. 'But even so, you'd be taking a terrible risk, letting her get her hands on this place.'

The broken bell over the shop door indicated the arrival of a customer with its usual dull 'chunk', and Jean drained her cup then got to her feet. 'She doesnae seem tae be as empty-headed as most of her kind.'

'Even so, I'd not trust her.'

'You're probably right,' Jean said, and disappeared into the front shop.

*

189

When Kirsty arrived the following afternoon, though, Jean had changed her mind. 'I think we should go and see Rose Hamilton's fancy lawyer.'

'I thought we decided against it yesterday.'

'I know what we decided,' Jean interrupted with unaccustomed asperity. 'But I couldnae sleep a wink last night for thinkin' about it. My mother, rest her soul, worked herself tae death tae scratch a livin' out of this shop, and after she went I was doin' the same until you came along with all your daft ideas.' She grinned at Kirsty. 'That's when I began tae enjoy myself instead of just workin' tae keep a roof over my head and food in my belly,' she said. Then the grin faded. 'Now this Hamilton lassie's offerin' me the chance tae make a proper livin' out of the place instead of just scrapin' by. And you could do with more money too, with your man an invalid. If her plans work out the way she seems tae think they will, you'd never need tae beg for work again from the likes of her mother.'

'Jean, it's too much of a risk. What if Rose gets tired of helping us? She'll marry soon; most rich girls do. I don't see any husband agreeing to let her spend her money on a business like this.'

'The only way tae find out the answers is tae ask the questions. When the lassie comes back today I'm going tae tell her we'll talk tae this lawyer of hers.'

'We?'

Jean's determination dissolved. 'You'll have tae be with me, Kirsty, for I couldnae face him on my own. I've given in tae all your ideas. You should be willin' tae stand by me for once, just in case this notion of hers turns out tae be better than we realise. Will you?'

Kirsty hesitated, then nodded. It was true that Jean deserved her support, but at the same time she was wary of trusting Rose Hamilton. She felt that she and Jean were both taking a risk.

John Brodie, a junior partner in the legal firm that handled the Hamiltons' business, had been given responsibility for Rose Hamilton's finances. He was young, efficient and, to Kirsty's surprise, enthusiastic about his client's new venture. He listened patiently, quelling Rose with a glance whenever she tried to break in, while Jean outlined the shop's history, haltingly at first but gaining confidence as she went along.

'And the proposal is that the three of you would be partners in this development?'

Kirsty began to explain that she herself had no money to put into such a venture, but Jean promptly overruled her. 'Kirsty does the alterations, and she's the one that's come up with all the ideas about improvin' the place. I'd not want tae make any changes without her agreement.'

Brodie smiled at her. 'I can understand that, Miss Chisholm. The partnership I referred to would be based on the strengths and abilities of each partner; Mrs Lennox would qualify in terms of her past and, it is hoped, future contributions to the success of the business, you yourself would continue to be the owner and senior partner, and Miss Hamilton's main asset is her ability to provide financial investment.'

'As Kirsty already knows, I can't be trusted near a sewing machine,' Rose Hamilton admitted with a grin. 'But I'd like to do more than just contribute the money.' She sat forward in her chair, looking hopefully at Jean and Kirsty. 'I know I wouldn't be of much help in other ways, but I was good at arithmetic and English at school. I could see to the books for you, and any writing that might have to be done.'

'You'd have to be given a trial first,' the lawyer said promptly, and she shot upright in her chair, glaring at him.

'John Brodie, you've known me all our lives. If I say I can keep books, then I can!'

He smiled blandly at her. 'I don't doubt your word, Rose – as a friend. But this is business. Miss Chisholm and Mrs Lennox have already proved their worth, and you must prove yours. If they are in agreement, I can arrange for a fictitious set of accounts to be drawn up to find out if you can balance them.'

Rose scowled at him then, realising that he was not going to be moved, she muttered, 'Oh – very well.'

'Ladies, are you in agreement?'

'We've not even decided on the partnership yet,' Kirsty objected, feeling that matters were hurrying along too quickly.

'You're quite right, Mrs Lennox. But if the matters under discussion do go ahead, would you be willing to let Miss Hamilton see to the books and any administration that might be required – if a trial proves her fit to do so? We would, of course, appoint a financial auditor to make sure on an annual basis that everything was being done properly.'

Jean and Kirsty exchanged glances, then Jean nodded. 'That'd be fine – if we get tae that stage.'

'And a fair and agreed system of sharing out the profits would be drawn up.'

'Profits? There's never been any of those!' Jean squawked.

'There will be now,' Rose told her confidently.

'If all goes as we hope there most certainly will be,' John Brodie agreed. 'I'll have a look at the place tomorrow, if that suits.'

'That Hamilton lassie'll be the ruin of both of you, Mam,' Alex stormed when he heard the news. 'She had you dismissed from your position as her mother's sewing woman, and now she's out tae spoil the pleasure you get from working in the shop.'

'It's Jean's decision – and Jean's shop.'

He ran a hand through his red hair. 'Could you not have persuaded her tae say no?'

'Jean has a mind of her own, and she can stick her heels in when the mood takes her. The lawyer seems sensible enough,' Kirsty said hopefully. She had fully expected John Brodie to be a male version of Rose but instead had been favourably impressed by the young man.

'He's one of her own kind, Mam,' Alex argued. 'No doubt he lives in a fine big house himself. How d'ye know he's not just as irresponsible as she is?'

'He's got his reputation to think of. I don't think he'd allow Rose to destroy the shop.'

'I'm telling you, she'll ruin everything. I've met the woman – I know what I'm talking about.'

Kirsty's temper began to fray. 'D'you not think I'm worried enough about how it's all going to turn out without you fretting me as well?' she snapped at her son. 'It's what Jean wants, and we'll just have to hope for her sake that it doesn't go wrong!'

*

'It's been that long since the place was opened up,' the factor's man said apologetically, struggling to turn the large key in the lock. When it finally gave way, John Brodie was first into the vacant shop's stuffy dark interior. Rose was about to follow when Jean warned, 'There'll probably be rats.'

'Nae harm if there is, missus,' the factor's man said cheerfully. 'They'll be more scared of us than we are of them. But it's best for ye tae wait till we get the shutters down from the windows and let a wee bit light intae the place.' He stamped his feet on the dusty boards as he went to the window, and the three women huddled in the doorway, Rose included, gave out muted squeaks as they heard scuttering sounds from below the floor.

Brodie, looking a trifle apprehensive, rattled a sharp tattoo on the boards with his cane. 'We'll bring in the rat-catcher – and get all this cleared out,' he added as the shutters came away from the large window and autumn sunlight flooded in to reveal discarded rubbish scattered over the floor and the long counter. 'Then we'll get some cleaning women in.'

The factor's employee went into the back shop as the potential partners, keeping close together for comfort, ventured in from the pavement. There came the sound of nails being wrenched from wood, then light broke through the dark oblong of the inner doorway. He reappeared, dusting his hands together.

'I'll just take the upstairs shutters down, then yez can all have a good look round,' he announced.

Twenty minutes later they arrived back in the main shop, dusty but exhilarated. 'It's a grand size.' Jean ran her hand over the long sturdy counter. 'Much bigger than my wee place.'

'We could use this as the shop, and your shop next door as the sewing room,' Rose suggested. 'You'd have better light in there, Kirsty.'

'And if Jean's back shop was cleared it would make a fine wee place for folk to try on the clothes,' Kirsty put in, then they all started talking together.

'What about this back shop and the wee scullery next to it?'

'They'd be for our own use—'

'And there's more storage space upstairs—'

'And more space in here to display the clothes—'

'The first thing we must do,' Rose said firmly, 'is find a laundry.'

'A laundry?' Jean was bewildered. 'What for?'

'To get the incoming clothes cleaned before we offer them for sale.'

Jean and Kirsty gaped at each other, then at their proposed partner. 'But folk can wash them after they buy them from us,' Kirsty pointed out.

'They ought to be clean when we hand them over. It would be better for the shop and for us if they were dealt with right away. You'd surely prefer to know that the clothes you were sewing were clean, Kirsty.'

'Most of them havenae even been worn much,' Jean argued. 'And they come off the backs of moneyed folk that take baths.'

'Just because people have money it doesn't mean that they bathe regularly,' Rose told her sweepingly, then glared at John Brodie when he turned away and made a strange choking noise. 'Some of the garments hanging in your back shop are badly in need of a good washing, and all the others are dusty. Do stop making that silly noise, John!'

The factor's man obligingly banged the young lawyer on the back.

'But we cannae afford tae have them washed, or tae do it ourselves!'

Rose was adamant. 'We'll find the money.'

John Brodie, his choking fit over, turned back to face them. 'The important question is, do you want to rent this place?'

'Do we?' Rose asked the others, her eyes pleading, her voice hopeful. The moment of decision had come. Jean and Kirsty, taken aback by the suddenness of it all, glanced uncertainly at each other, then Jean gave a faint nod.

'We do,' Kirsty said, and Rose squealed like a child and clapped her hands together.

'Then I'll draw up an agreement for your signatures and see about renting this shop,' Brodie said briskly. 'The next step will be to obtain permission from the landlord to carry out the necessary refurbishment in both premises, but I don't anticipate any problems since this place has been empty for so long.' He beamed round the circle of faces. 'I'm sure, ladies, that your new partnership will do very well for itself.'

'Laundry, indeed,' Jean muttered as they stood together on the pavement five minutes later watching the factor's representative lock the door again.

'It might be a good idea.'

'But think what it'll cost!'

'She's the one who'll have to worry about that – and Mr Brodie. He'll keep an eye on Rose.'

'We'll all have tae keep an eye on that lassie. She's a bossy one.'

'Are you sure you're doing the right thing?'

Jean studied the empty shop then glanced at her own little place. 'I'll tell you better in a few months' time,' she said, her voice sharp with nerves. 'But for now – I just have a feelin', Kirsty, that this is worth the tryin'.'

20

Espedair Street was all but empty, Kirsty and a man loitering a few yards further along the pavement being the only people out and about on this wet and windy day. Crossing over from the tobacconist's and walking the last few yards to her door, head down against the wind and a basket in each hand, Kirsty felt that despite the miserable weather the street was cheerier than the shop she had just left, with Beth Laidlaw presiding behind the counter.

The girl's sullen, cold mood never seemed to change – as far as Kirsty was concerned, at any rate. She had just dashed poor Todd's hopes of renting yet another home, on the grounds that it wasn't comfortable enough.

His usual cheerfulness was beginning to fade and might disappear altogether if Beth continued to be so finicky. The truth, as Kirsty saw it, was that Beth had set her heart on Kirsty's house, and nothing less would satisfy her.

The man, well dressed against the weather in a bowler hat and caped raincoat, was glancing in at the mouth of the pend now. She thought of offering her assistance, but just then the rain started to come down harder, so instead she put down one of the heavy baskets and lifted the latch, anxious to get indoors. She pushed the door open and stooped to her basket, then froze as a voice said, 'Kate?'

She straightened and turned to look at the man who had been by the pend. The face was that of a stranger, but she knew the blue eyes that looked out from it. She saw these same eyes every time Alex looked at her.

'Sandy,' she said, the past twenty years tumbling away from her as though they had never happened.

'You've not changed, Kate.' He took off his bowler, letting the rain fall on hair that was still thick and curly, but silver now, with no trace of red. Then, glancing up at the sky and blinking against the fast-falling rain, he said, 'Can I talk with you – away from this downpour?'

Her mind jumped into action. Alex and Ewan would be in the workshop, and Matt, who had had a restless night, was still in his bed and, with any luck, asleep. It would surely be safe for a little while.

She nodded and led the way as he picked up her basket then took the other from her hand. She had meant to take him into the parlour, but while she closed the door he walked ahead of her to the kitchen, the only room he had ever been in.

When she arrived at the door he was setting the baskets on the table and glancing around. 'I mind this place as if it was yesterday,' he said. 'But I don't mind it being so small. We're alone?'

'My sons are in the workshop. My husband's in his bed; he's not well.'

'I know.' He put his hat on the table and unfastened his long raincoat to reveal a well-cut suit. 'You look as if you've seen a ghost, Kate.' His voice was deeper than before, and his speech cultured.

'I have. I thought you were—'

'Dead? Killed by your father? I very nearly was.' He indicated the coat. 'D'you mind if I hang it up? I'd not want it to drip all over your kitchen.'

She nodded, moving automatically to light the gas beneath the kettle as he hung the coat on the back of the yard door.

'How did you know I was here?'

'From Alex.'

'Alex?' She felt as though she was caught up in a dream.

'Your son.' He turned from the door to face her, pausing behind Matt's chair with both hands resting on the back. 'Our son.'

'When did you see Alex?'

He stared at her, as confused as she was, then said, 'I'm sorry, I expected you to know, though I don't see why you should. Alex is making some furniture for my daughter.'

The kitchen seemed to blur for a moment. 'Fiona? You're Fiona's father?'

His head dipped slightly. 'Angus MacDowall.'

'But – surely Sandy's short for Alexander?'

He gave a soft bark of a laugh. 'Red-haired lads are always called Sandy in Scotland – you know that.'

'All these years,' Kirsty said wonderingly, 'and I didn't even know your real name.'

'I was only an orphan, Kate,' he said with sudden bitterness in his voice and his gaze. 'Orphans aren't supposed to own anything, including names. I always had one, though. I suppose that at that time I must have been the only person who knew it. A lot of people know it now.' His fingers had been running over the raised pattern on the back of the chair. Now he looked down at it. 'Is this his work?'

'Yes.'

'He's a talented laddie. You should be proud of him.'

The kettle came to the boil and she made tea, grateful for something ordinary to do. Sandy drew out a chair by the table and sat down, watching her.

'What have you told him about me?'

'I said you'd died.'

'Died? You left him with no hope of ever meeting up with me?'

'I thought you had. Nobody would tell me what had become of you.'

'You could have come to the infirmary and found out. I looked for you, but you never came.' For all his confidence, she heard, for just a few seconds, a trace of the lonely, frightened boy he had once been.

'I wanted to.' The grief she had suffered all those years ago swept back, putting a tremor into her own voice. 'But my father sent me to his sister's in Stirling.'

Pouring tea for them both, she told him briefly about running away from her aunt's house with Alex only days after his birth and about her marriage and, finally, about her return to Paisley. Talking gave her a chance to look at him; although he couldn't be more than thirty-seven years of age, and moved like a young, active man, his hair had nothing left of the original fiery red other than just a hint in his eyebrows and well-trimmed moustache. Prosperity had filled his body out and rounded his features. His mouth was firm, with a slight droop at the corners. Deep lines etched round it, and his nose gave his face a look of severity in repose.

'I'd no knowledge of what had happened to you – or to the child,' he said when she had finished. 'I'd only the one visitor in the infirmary – the old woman that ran the tobacconist's shop at the corner.'

'Mrs Laidlaw? She visited you?'

'She'll be dead now?'

'A long time ago.'

'And rotting in hell, I hope, alongside your father,' Sandy said evenly, and she shivered at the chill in his voice. 'She said that the shock of what she called my attack on your father had caused you to lose the bairn you'd been carrying and that there wasn't an employer in Paisley who'd give me work. She said that if I valued my life I'd get as far away from Paisley as I could.'

He paused, looking back down the years, then went on, 'When I was discharged from the infirmary I walked to Glasgow and found work.'

The tea cooled untasted in both cups as he listed the events in his life as though they had happened to somebody else – hard work and study, clawing his way up the ladder of self-improvement, marriage, the birth of his daughter, the death of his wife.

'I was fortunate enough to find a good employer who taught me everything and left his small business to me when he died. I built it up into a success, for Fiona as much as for myself. Then she brought Alex into my life, and I looked at him and saw myself at his age. That was when I knew that that old bitch had lied to me.'

He looked down into his cup, then across the table at Kirsty. 'He and Fiona are still meeting, aren't they?'

'He's not said anything, but I think they are.'

'I suspected it.' For a brief moment his gaze softened. 'Fiona's like her mother – she needs good reason before she'll agree to anything. And I was so confused with the shock of seeing him after all those years of believing that he had never existed that I couldn't think of any reason to give her. I let her believe that it was a matter of him being working class, while she – I should have known that my own daughter would never accept that,' he said, pushing the cup away, angry with himself. 'That's why I came to see you. It has to be stopped, Kate. We have to stop them meeting each other. D'you not see? They're both my children. They're brother and sister.'

The words stifled the breath in Kirsty's throat. She had been so caught up in seeing Sandy again that the real reason for his visit hadn't occurred to her.

'Oh – dear God!' she whispered.

'Nothing but the truth will do for her – and for him, I've no doubt.' He spread his hands wide on the table. 'We must end this friendship before it goes any further. I'm not saying that it will turn to love, but we can't take—'

'It already has, on Alex's part at least.'

'What?' He blinked at her, then said impatiently, 'No, no – they've only known each other for a short while, and they're too young for strong feelings. It's the future we have to worry about.'

'They're older than we were, Sandy.'

For a long moment they stared at each other, then Kirsty jumped up guiltily as a muffled thumping came from the upper floor.

'My husband – he'll be wanting to come downstairs.'

Sandy got to his feet at once and collected his coat and hat. 'I'll go. Things are bad enough without making them worse. You'll tell him, Kate?'

'I'll tell him. And the Lord only knows how he'll take it.'

'He'll have to take it. So will Fiona. At least,' Sandy said with a glimmer of cold amusement in his voice as he went into the hall, 'you have the consolation of knowing that he'll not be beaten half to death as I was for looking at a lassie he can't have.'

As usual, Ewan went out as soon as he had eaten his dinner and Caitlin, who found her work in the grocery tiring, went to bed not long after Mary. As soon as she had gone, Kirsty laid her sewing down and said bluntly, 'Alex, Mr MacDowall came here today.'

He was in his usual seat at the table, studying books. His red head jerked up at once. 'He was here? Why didn't you fetch me?'

'It was me he came to see.'

His eyes narrowed. 'About me and Fiona?'

'You're still meeting each other, aren't you?'

'We are, and if he has anything to say on the matter it's me he should say it to, not you!' She could see his temper beginning to rise.

'Alex—'

He scooped the books up and got to his feet. 'He's got no right tae bring you intae it, and he's got no right tae treat me and Fiona like two bairns!'

'He's got every right!' Kirsty scrambled out of her chair and snatched at his sleeve as he brushed past on his way to the door. 'Every right, Alex. He's your father.'

'What?' His eyes widened then glazed with shock. 'What?' he said again.

'He's your father,' she repeated, and saw the colour drain from his stricken face. Slowly he turned back to the table, pulling himself free of her grasp, and put the books down. Then he drew out a chair and lowered himself into it gently, as though his bones had become as brittle as glass and he was afraid of breaking them.

'You said that my father had died.'

'I thought he had.' The wind had died down late in the afternoon, but now it had returned. She could hear it whistling down the chimney and moaning through the pend, a fitting background to the story she had to tell her son about herself and Sandy and her father's vicious assault on his apprentice in that very room, and about her banishment and the cruel lies her lover had been told while recovering in the infirmary. Alex's burning gaze never left her face.

'All those years I was certain that he had died – and he thought that you'd never been born. Then he met you and recognised himself in you.' She waited for a moment, then as he said nothing, 'Alex,' she said gently, 'you and Fiona—'

'Fiona!' Shock suddenly blazed into his eyes and he clapped his hands over his face. 'Dear God – me and Fiona! Wantin' her's the same as lustin' after Caitlin, or wee Mary!'

'It's not like that at all!' Kirsty reached out to touch his hand, but he jerked away, his throat muscles pumping as he swallowed hard.

'Leave – me – be!' he said, and lunged out of his seat and towards the back door, wrenching it open and disappearing into the darkness.

The wind swooped in, setting the curtains at the window

into a frenzied dance, sending Matt's discarded newspaper flapping beneath the table, wrapping Kirsty's skirt about her legs. She followed Alex, afraid to leave him on his own.

He was a humped silhouette at the corner where the pend opened into the lane, supporting himself with one hand on the wall as he bent over to vomit on the ruts and grooves carved into the mud by the cartwheels. She waited, the wind's cold bite, more like winter than October, sinking almost at once through clothes and skin and flesh, striking her to the bone, until the paroxysm was over and he had straightened, wiping his mouth on his sleeve. Then she stepped up beside him.

'Come inside – you'll freeze out here.'

Before he could answer, Ewan came whistling through the pend. 'What's going on?'

'Alex's stomach's troubling him,' Kirsty said swiftly.

'Cannae hold your drink? Here—' Ewan protested as Alex pushed him aside roughly, making him stagger, and strode through the pend and out into the street. He made to follow, but Kirsty held him back.

'Leave him – he's not well.'

She urged Ewan towards the back door and he went reluctantly, grumbling. Kirsty followed him upstairs and lay awake by Matt's side, listening. After about an hour, she thought she heard Alex in the kitchen, but he didn't come up the stairs.

When she went down in the morning he was sprawled in Matt's chair, fully dressed and sound asleep, reeking of drink and clutching an empty whisky bottle in his arms.

21

Matt, with little else to occupy his mind, picked at Alex's moodiness and his silence as if trying to unravel a tangle of wool.

'He'll be frettin' over that lassie,' he told Kirsty, a thin thread of satisfaction in his voice. 'She's sent him off with a flea in his ear. Didn't I tell ye he was settin' his sights too high?' His voice went on and on until she could scarcely bear to be in the same room with him, while she held her tongue, determined not to make matters worse by lashing out at him and perhaps, in her exasperation, letting slip more than she should.

Ewan complained about his stepbrother's bad temper in the workshop, and on one occasion when Kirsty went to get help to bring Matt downstairs she heard angry voices, which cut off as soon as she opened the door, and found Todd standing between Ewan and Alex, who were scowling at each other from separate ends of the shop.

'What's going on here?'

Alex swung towards the workbench without answering, while Ewan muttered, 'Nothin'.'

'Just a wee argument about work, Mrs Lennox,' Todd

said. 'Is the master ready tae come downstairs? Come on, Ewan, we'll give him a hand.'

Once Matt was settled in the kitchen she followed them outside, detaining Todd for a moment. 'Were the two of them fighting?'

'No, no,' he assured her, shifting from one foot to the other, his eyes refusing to meet hers.

'Todd—'

'I've got tae get back, Mrs Lennox,' he said, and slid away before she could say another word.

The shop was Kirsty's rock in the midst of all the domestic turmoil. Whenever she stepped through its door the growing weight of family problems seemed to slide from her shoulders, and for the short time she was there she felt like a different person in a different life. She said nothing to Jean about Sandy coming back into her life; she could tell by the concern in her friend's eyes that Jean knew that something was wrong, but the woman was too loyal a friend to pry. One day Kirsty would tell her, but not yet.

John Brodie had obtained permission to make alterations in both shops and found a builder. At the end of October the 'For Rent' sign came down in the shop adjoining Jean's, and on the same day the partnership papers were signed. Rose, the last to affix her signature, did so with a flourish, then beamed at her new partners. 'A door has just opened,' she announced in ringing tones.

'I've a wee bit of a feelin' that it's opened beneath my two feet,' Jean confided to Kirsty as they left the office.

'It's still your shop. It says so on the papers Mr Brodie drew up, and it'll say so above the new door. We'll stand together, you and me.'

Reluctantly, Jean had had to agree to the temporary closure of her little shop, so that both premises could be refurbished. It had been decided that an archway would be broken through the wall between the new main shop and the former shop, which was to become Kirsty's sewing room, and doors installed between the two back shops and the rooms on the upper floor.

Once Jean's shop was closed, the two of them worked alongside the women who had been hired to clear everything from the new shop before the builders came in. To their surprise, Rose helped as well, wrapped in a large apron and with a scarf tied around her head.

'I want to be more involved with the place than just providing the money. I mean to do something with my life.'

'Your mother won't be pleased,' Jean ventured, and Rose, wringing out a filthy cloth with deft twists of her strong young wrists, grinned at her. 'She's not, but I'm of an age to do as I please.'

Despite her sheltered upbringing the girl wasn't afraid of hard work. Her inexperience caused considerable amusement among the other cleaners, but Rose, fully aware of her own incompetence, was quite willing to be the butt of their jokes and soon earned their respect with her dogged determination and willingness to tackle anything, even the removal of a dead mouse found behind a pile of rubbish. While Kirsty and Jean and the other women pressed themselves in a shuddering, squealing mass against the walls, Rose carried the tiny body out into the overgrown back yard at arm's length by the tail and dropped it into the metal rubbish container, saying, as she returned to the shop, 'Poor wee thing, what a terrible place to die in.'

The restless, mutinous girl Kirsty had known in the Hamilton house had matured overnight. As promised, she found a laundry willing to take on the entire contents of Jean's shop. Despite Jean's protests, everything was whisked off in batches to be washed and ironed.

'She's that forceful I don't know if I'm goin' tae be able tae stop her from takin' over entirely.' Jean's small round face was puckered with concern.

'You've got a good sharp tongue in your head,' Kirsty urged. 'You'll just have to use it.'

'It's a plain-spoken tongue, though, and she's such a lady,' Jean fretted. 'I know she's worked alongside the rest o' us, and I couldnae have done what she did with that mouse,' they shuddered in unison at the thought, 'but she's that bossy at times.'

Todd and Alex were easing Matt into his chair when Sandy MacDowall arrived at the back door. Kirsty's heart almost failed her when she opened it and saw him standing there. She stared up into his set face and he looked back at her stonily.

'I'd like to see Alex. The lad in the workshop said he was here.'

'Who is it, Kirsty? Bring them in, for there's the devil of a draught,' Matt shouted peevishly, and she had no option but to stand back and let Sandy walk past her into the house.

Alex's face tightened when he saw the visitor. 'What d'you want?'

Matt had taken in the newcomer's good clothes and confident bearing at a glance. 'Alex, that's no way tae talk tae—'

210

'Angus MacDowall. And you, I take it, are Matthew Lennox. Don't try to get up – I know from my daughter that you're not so able.' Sandy took Matt's twisted hand in his and shook it gently, careful not to cause any pain. Behind his back, Alex's blazing eyes asked his mother silent questions, and Kirsty shook her head helplessly, unable to supply the answers. Todd, after a swift glance from mother to son, slipped quietly out of the back door.

At Matt's invitation, Sandy sat down on Kirsty's usual chair. 'I came about the work that's being done for my daughter.'

'A bonny lassie, an' kindly, tae.'

'It's good of you to say so, Mr Lennox.' A faint smile touched Sandy's mouth. 'I'll admit to agreeing with you, but perhaps I'm biased, being her father. She's . . . gone away to visit friends in Fort William,' he added, turning to look at Alex, who stood motionless by the table. 'She'll be gone for some considerable time.' He reached into his pocket and brought out an envelope. 'She asked me to give you this. I promised that it would be delivered, and I thought it best to bring it myself to make certain that it reached you.'

Alex's gaze flickered briefly to the envelope being held out to him, but he made no move to take it. Sandy tossed it onto the table close to the younger man's hand.

'I wanted you to know that the fact that she has gone away will make no difference to her order. We both want you to complete it. When d'you expect that to be?'

The question was directly addressed to Alex, who answered through white, set lips. 'By the year's end.'

'Good. Let Mr Gavin know when it's finished, and he'll arrange to have it collected,' Sandy said, then produced a

211

second, bulkier envelope. 'I'll pay for the entire order now. It's my own experience that folk prefer to wait until the goods are delivered, but I know that you're trustworthy and that you'll no doubt be glad of the money to buy timber and the like.'

Matt took the envelope, his eyes brightening as he felt the weight of it. 'That's generous of ye, Mr MacDowall.'

'I've put something extra in, to show my appreciation.'

'There's no need of that.' Alex's voice cracked through the air like a whiplash. 'I agreed a fair price with – with your daughter, Mr MacDowall,' he almost spat the name out, 'and I've no wish tae take a penny more from you.'

'But I've put you to a great deal of inconvenience,' Sandy told him quietly. 'I want to do what I can to help.' Then, as Alex said nothing more, 'And I'm also here to ask if you'll make more furniture, and decorate it, when Fiona's is done. The new order would be for my shop. I'd like to see what my customers think of it.'

Matt's eyes gleamed. 'We'd be happy tae—' he began, just as Alex rapped out, 'No!'

'Alex! The man's offerin' us more work!'

'The order book's full,' Alex snapped at his stepfather.

'We'll see about that. Kirsty, fetch the book!'

'I said we're too busy. Find someone else tae make your furniture, Mr MacDowall, and tae paint it,' Alex said icily, making for the door. 'Good day tae you!'

As the door slammed behind him, Kirsty noticed that the envelope Sandy had tossed onto the table was gone.

Matt struggled to his feet, gobbling and spluttering like a turkey. 'Come back here! Alex!'

He tottered and almost fell as his bad knee gave way

Sandy and Kirsty both jumped forward to support him and ease him back into his chair.

'Fetch him back this instant, Kirsty!'

'I'll do nothing of the kind. It's Alex who's in charge of the workshop now, and he has the right to decide what orders can be accepted.' She glared at Sandy, who had the grace to look slightly ashamed.

'He'll not be runnin' it for much longer if he cannae learn tae mind his temper!' Matt fumed. 'Ye see what I have tae put up with, Mr MacDowall? That laddie's impossible tae deal with when the mood comes over him.'

'Matt, you know that's not true.'

'Don't you start defendin' him again. Just because he's yer first-born ye think the sun shines out of his arse – beggin' yer pardon, Mr MacDowall,' Matt said, suddenly remembering their caller. 'It's just the way he angers me at times. If I didnae need him so badly because of no' bein' able tae work mysel', I'd take him by the scruff o' the neck and run him out!'

Sandy reached for his hat, his face suddenly wiped of all expression. 'In my opinion, Mr Lennox, he's a very talented young man, who has probably, as he said, got more than enough work to do for the moment. Don't distress yourself; my furniture can be ordered another time – mebbe next year.'

'I'll show you out, Mr MacDowall – by the street door.' Trembling with rage, Kirsty led him through the hall.

'What did you think you were doing, coming here and upsetting the boy like that?' she stormed at him when they were on the footpath, with no danger of Matt hearing them. 'Have you not done enough harm to him?'

His eyes blazed blue fire down at her, just as Alex's did. 'I've done nothing. I wasn't the one who let him think all those years of his life that his father was dead. I promised Fiona that I'd make sure he got her letter, and heaven only knows I've let her down badly enough without breaking my word on that promise too. And I wanted him to see for himself that I hadn't withheld it, or tampered with it. And . . .' he hesitated, then said with a shrug of the shoulders, 'I wanted to see him again.'

'In God's name why?'

'He's my son,' Sandy said icily. 'Just because I knew nothing of his existence it doesn't mean that he's of no importance to me.'

'And now you've handed the letter over and—' Kirsty stopped and turned, hearing footsteps on the pavement at her back. 'Beth.'

'Mrs Lennox.' The girl swept by, nodding curtly to Kirsty, running her eyes appreciatively over Sandy, smiling sweetly at him when he raised his hat to her.

'Does it not matter that you've upset the boy?' Kirsty asked when Beth had gone out of earshot.

'He'll recover from it. He's got steel in him,' Sandy said, glancing beyond her to the pend. 'A lad to be proud of, Kate. Good day to you.'

Watching his straight back stride away from her, Kirsty knew that there was nothing left of the Sandy she had remembered fondly during all their years apart. The struggle to make his way in a harsh world had taken away the warmth and compassion that had once been at the very core of his nature. She wondered if the death of the lad she had once known had begun with the first blow of her father's fist.

When she went back into the kitchen Matt was counting the envelope's contents clumsily. 'God, Kirsty, the man's been very generous.' His eyes were shining.

'He must like Alex's work a lot more than you do,' she said tartly.

The sarcasm was lost on him. 'He couldnae like him for his manner, that's for certain. Did ye hear the way he spoke tae the man? I'll have somethin' tae say tae the bold laddie about that when he shows his face in here again.'

'Matt, let it be.'

'Are ye daft, woman? What'll happen tae the business if he starts talkin' like that tae every man that wants tae place an order?'

'Mr MacDowall wasn't bothered, and I'm sure Alex'll do his furniture when he's got more time.'

'I'll see tae that. I'm still the master when all's said an' done, and I decide what orders we make. If Alex doesnae like it, Ewan can take over.'

'Ewan can't decorate furniture,' Kirsty pointed out, almost at the end of her tether. 'And it's painted furniture Mr MacDowall wants.' Then, taking advantage of his sudden silence, she said, 'Just be content with the extra money and let the matter end here and now, Matt. Now, is there anything you need before I go to help Jean?'

This was the day the builders started work. When Kirsty arrived, still furious with Sandy for invading her home and her family, Jean and Rose and John Brodie, who was taking a keen and enthusiastic interest in everything that went on, were gathered in the new shop together with the builders.

'There should be a ceremony,' Rose said when the outline

of the new archway had been drawn on the grimy plaster wall.

'Like launching a ship?' John Brodie raised his eyebrows while the builders waiting to get on with the work glanced at each other, smirking.

'Mebbe.' Rose, used by now to being laughed at, shrugged her slender shoulders.

'P'raps Mr Brodie could say a few words,' Jean suggested, but the girl shook her head.

'No, no, it should be something that comes from one of us. Something . . . dramatic!'

'Like this?' Kirsty marched forward and grasped a large sledgehammer that had been propped against the wall. It proved to be unexpectedly heavy, and she couldn't raise it beyond knee level. For a moment she thought she would have to let it drop and admit defeat, but determination and the anger still smouldering after Sandy's visit provided the necessary energy. She managed to raise the hammer, clinging with both hands to the shaft and scared to lift it too high in case she toppled over onto the floor in an undignified heap of petticoats and stockings and drawers, then let it fall in a swinging arc.

Jean yelped, and a workman standing by the wall leaped to safety as the hammer head hit the wall with a thud that reverberated up Kirsty's wrists and arms to her shoulders and rattled the teeth in her jaw. Plaster cracked and pattered to the floor, exposing the lathes behind. Jean yelped, Rose cheered and Brodie applauded.

'Here, missus,' the building foreman said respectfully, 'I'd no' like tae go home tae you wi' an opened pay packet.'

Kirsty's arms felt as weak as strips of paper, and her

216

shoulders and wrists and elbows would surely be painful in the morning, but even so she was elated. Letting the man relieve her of the hammer, she turned to beam triumphantly at her partners.

'Another door has just opened,' she said.

22

The inevitable quarrel between Matt and Alex erupted that night while Kirsty was tucking Mary into bed, something she still did every night, even though Matt disapproved of what he called 'mollycoddling'.

'This is a grand chance for our workshop – mebbe makin' furniture for a big Glasgow shop,' Matt was saying when she went back downstairs, his voice low but the anger already heating it. 'And you stand there and look the man in the face and say no, just like that?'

'You're not in the workshop – I am, and it's me who knows what we've got tae do.' Alex's voice was equally low. There was something frightening about the fact that these two, who normally yelled at each other, were being so controlled. Caitlin, who hated quarrels, washed dishes at the sink, her slim back tense with misery.

'Caitlin, pet, away upstairs and tell Mary a story. She's restless tonight,' Kirsty lied, and the girl hurried from the room.

'I'm still the master!' Matt said, as he always did when he and Alex clashed.

'Aye, and you were the one that jeered at the painted furniture. I thought you'd be pleased to hear me refusing to do more.'

Matt was purpling with anger. 'Ye didnae turn it down for my sake – an order's an order, even if it is for spoiled furniture. The man might put in orders for plain furniture afterwards.'

'We're too small tae satisfy the likes of MacDowall. Let him go somewhere else.'

Kirsty interrupted. 'Mr MacDowall said he'd be content to wait until the spring, so there's nothing lost. Matt, d'you not want to go to your bed now?'

'He'll not have tae wait until the spring. As soon as the lassie's furniture's completed, Alex, ye'll find out what Mr MacDowall wants and start on it.'

'And leave the other customers high and dry?'

'For pity's sake, man, there's three of ye in that workshop, an' all time-served. Ye can manage more than one order at a time.'

Alex, too, was angry; Kirsty could almost see fire sparking from the ends of his red hair. 'I'll not do his furniture before others, and that's an end tae it.'

'Ye don't own that workshop yet, my lad, and I'll make damned sure ye never will if ye don't grow up.'

'Matt—'

'Keep out of this, woman,' he snapped. 'It's high time someone told this upstart the truth about himsel'. Can ye not see,' Matt said to Alex, leaning forward and thumping his fist on his knee in emphasis, 'that the man feels sorry for ye?'

'Sorry?'

'Aye. Ye made a fool of yersel' with his daughter, thinkin'

she'd fancy ye, forgettin' that when it comes down tae it ye're only an ordinary workin' man. And he could dae nothin' else but put a stop tae it, the way I would if some scoundrel from the gutter started payin' court tae our Caitlin.'

'Matt, for pity's sake leave it!' Kirsty begged, and was waved aside. Matt's temper had eased; clearly he was impressed by what he saw as his own diplomacy and was too taken up with himself to see how white Alex had become.

'An' he's decent enough tae want tae make it up tae ye for yer disappointment, so he's givin' ye this order.'

'You think so?'

'I know so. I'm a businessman, same as him only not so grand. And I've got daughters. I can understand how his mind's workin'. The thing is,' Matt forged on, 'he was awful generous with the payment for his lassie's furniture, for all that she's gone away and doesnae need it just now. That means that we could dae well out of keepin' the man happy.'

Alex's face was now chalk white, contrasting sharply with the brilliant blue of his eyes and his bright hair, and the skin seemed to have tightened over the bones.

'You've told me the truth the way you see it. Now it's my turn tae tell it tae you.'

'Alex, leave it. Just go to your bed and let things be!' Kirsty was beside herself with fear.

'No, no,' said Matt, 'ye've said often enough that ye wish me and Alex could just speak tae each other without losin' our tempers. I've had my say, let him have his.'

'The truth is,' Alex said, his eyes never moving from his stepfather's face, 'that Angus MacDowall isn't being kind to us because he feels bad about coming between me and his daughter or even because he likes the way I paint furniture.

It's because the man's riddled with guilt. It's because he's my real father, and he's Fiona's father, and she's my half-sister, and neither of the two of us knew until he came back tae Glasgow.'

He went to Matt's chair, putting a hand on each of the wooden arms, bending over so that his face was only inches from Matt's. The older man stared up at him, mouth agape, trying to make sense of what he had just heard.

'That,' said Alex softly, 'is the truth of it. And if you ever speak of it, or of him, to me again, so help me God I'll take you apart bone from bone, invalid or not.'

He turned away, caught up his jacket from the nail on the back door and went out, closing the door very gently at his back.

'You knew.' Matt's voice was frail, the voice of a very old man.

'I've only known for a week.'

'Ye should have told me.'

'There was no sense in hurting you. I didn't know that San— Mr MacDowall would come back.'

'He's been here before?'

'Just the once, to tell me that – to tell me who he was, and that Alex and Fiona had to stop seeing each other.'

Matt was beginning to rally his thoughts. 'Are ye sure it was just the once? Are ye sure he's no' the reason ye were keen tae get back tae Paisley?'

Kirsty felt bone weary. 'I wasn't the one who wanted to come to Paisley, it was you.'

'Ye didnae try tae stop me.'

'I did. I didn't want to come back.'

'Because ye knew he was nearby. Because ye—'

'I'll not hear any more of this,' she blurted out. 'D'you hear me? I thought the man was dead; I told Alex he was. I never thought to lay eyes on him again – I wish to God I never had!'

There was a long silence, during which they didn't look at each other, then Matt said, 'I think I'll go tae my bed.'

'I'll fetch Al—'

'Ye'll not!' Strength came back into his voice, and he began scrabbling at the chair arms, seeking for a good grip so that he could haul himself to his feet. 'I'll manage alone, without him and without you, if I have tae crawl every inch of the way!'

He reached for the walking stick that was always close at hand now, found that it couldn't give him sufficient support, and threw it aside. While Kirsty watched, not daring to touch him, he got out into the hall. Clutching at the back of his chair, the door frame, the banisters, he managed to get to the foot of the stairs unaided. It took some time, and she could tell by the grunts and stifled moans that it cost him a lot of pain.

The stairs defeated him. Grasping the newel post with one hand and supporting himself on the wall with the other, he made several attempts to put a foot on the first step. Finally, unable to bear his struggles any longer, Kirsty went forward and put an arm about him.

'For pity's sake, Matt,' she said when he tried to push her away, 'is it worth killing yourself just for a bit of pride?'

Realising that he couldn't manage without her help, he gave in and let her ease his crippled body up the stairs, tread by painful tread, then along the corridor and into the bedroom, where he collapsed on the bed. He kept his eyes tightly shut.

'Matt,' she said when she had drawn the blankets over him, 'it all happened years ago. It's been over long since.'

His lids fluttered but remained closed, and he made no answer.

As she reached the top of the stairs Ewan came in at the street door, too late to be of help, Kirsty thought wearily.

'D'you want something to eat?'

He shook his head and began to mount the stairs, bounding up the treads his father had had so much trouble with. 'I'm away tae my bed.' His hair was rumpled, his shirt collar open. His mouth looked slightly swollen – from kisses, she thought – and as he passed her, brushing against her for a brief moment, she was shocked and embarrassed to discover that she was keenly aware of the strength and virility of the young body so close to her own. Even the smell wafting from him was exciting – a mingling of youth and masculinity and drink, and something else, an underlying whiff of cheap flowery perfume, telling that he had been with a girl.

To her embarrassment and disgust, Kirsty felt colour rush to her cheeks as she continued on down the stairs.

The workshop door creaked beneath her hand. Inside it was pitch dark, and she was frightened to move in case she fell over something.

'Alex?'

There was no answer, but she could tell that he was there. There was a listening, human quality to the air that didn't belong to empty space.

'Did you have to tell your father?' she asked the blackness pressing against her face and body. 'Did you have to hurt him so badly?'

'My father's in Glasgow,' he said from the stairs.

'Matt's been a father to you for most of your life.'

'It was you he wanted, not me. You should have let them take me when I was born.' Her eyes were becoming accustomed to the dark now, and she could just make him out, a hunched shape curled halfway up the stairs.

'I couldn't have done that. You were so wee – there was no knowing what might have become of you.'

'Whatever it was it couldn't have been as bad as what's happened tae me now.'

'If we hadn't come back to Paisley,' she said wretchedly, 'if we'd stayed in Falkirk none of this would have happened.'

'If – if – if!' He almost spat the words out. 'If you and that man in Glasgow had never met, if I'd never been born – I wish tae God I never had!'

'You don't know what's ahead of you. You've got talent, Alex, you can do a lot with your life.'

'Go away, Mam.'

'You'll freeze if you stay here.'

'There's sacking in the loft I can use if I want it.'

Kirsty winced. She knew well enough that there was sacking in the loft, and that it made a passable bed. She'd lain there herself, with Sandy. And because of that one coupling, Alex would lie there tonight, more alone than he had ever been in his young life.

'Go back to the house, Mam,' he said in the darkness. 'If you care for me at all, you'll just let me be!'

The next day Alex was out of the workshop for some time, and at the evening meal he announced that he had found lodgings nearby.

'You don't need to do that,' Kirsty protested, while Matt, who had scarcely said a word to anyone all day, kept his eyes fixed on his plate.

'Don't worry, I'll come to the workshop every day. I'll not let my own family down.' Alex's voice was heavy with sarcasm. Within the hour he had gone, leaving Mary in tears and Caitlin white faced and miserable.

Once he had recovered from the shock, Ewan was envious. 'I'm less than a year younger than Alex – mebbe I should think of movin' out too.'

'You do that,' Matt told him harshly, 'and ye'll have tae find somewhere else tae work as well!'

'Ye never said that tae Alex,' the young man protested.

'Never mind him, we're talkin' about you, an' ye're not movin' out of this house till I say so,' his father bellowed, with a brief return to his old self.

Ewan, his handsome face sulky, pushed back his chair and went out, while Mary promptly burst into tears again, 'I don't want Ewan to g-go too!'

'He won't, pet,' Kirsty soothed the little girl, lifting her onto her knee.

'Ye're damned right he won't,' Matt muttered into his tobacco pouch. 'There's one at least that knows which side his bread's buttered on.'

With her once-secure family life disintegrating around her, the shop continued to be Kirsty's anchor. Despite all her worries, she felt a small thrill of excited anticipation every time she went into her new work room, the original shop. The archway that was to be curtained off from the new shop had been completed and the walls painted, and there would be net curtaining over the small window to ensure privacy. The room was still empty, but a good-sized work table and a second-hand sewing machine, together with a smaller table to put it on, had already been purchased. It was far superior to the stuffy little cupboard she had had to use at the Hamiltons' and, best of all, there would be no Mrs Hamilton sweeping in to harass and harangue her. This was her domain.

Even Jean's modest little single-roomed dwelling above the former shop had been repainted and the crumbling window sashes renewed to keep out the winter winds.

'Why shouldn't your own home be seen to as well?' Rose had asked in answer to Jean's half-hearted protest about the cost. Then, the businesswoman in her coming to the fore, she had added, 'Besides, it's all part of the building, and we need to keep that in good order.'

Rose had passed the book-keeping test John Brodie had set for her with flying colours and had been officially given the job of seeing to the shop's ledgers. She planned to set aside a corner of the back room as her office.

Standing in the empty sewing room, listening to the other two chattering beyond the archway, Kirsty knew that the first strands of the new three-way partnership had begun to inter-weave. Morag Bishop was quite right – life was a series of patterns, some able to merge into new and larger designs, while others, like Matt's, remained stubbornly independent. For the sake of the new business, the pattern made up of herself, Jean and Rose Hamilton had to work.

Jean was still in awe of Rose. As well as possessing a strong and confident personality, the girl dominated Jean physically, her tall, lean shape towering over the other's short, dumpy figure. Jean, Kirsty knew, would have to learn to assert herself – after all, she had the most to lose if the new venture failed. The shop was her livelihood, the room above it her home.

The first real confrontation between Rose and Jean came when the second-hand clothing returned from the laundry. Unpacking it, Jean and Kirsty had to admit that there was a considerable improvement. The colours were brighter and the folds free of dust, and when they began hanging the clothes on the rails Rose had bought, their hands were no longer sticky and grimy from contact with the fabrics.

'They look much more attractive, too,' Rose said with satisfaction. 'Folk'll be willing to pay a bit more for them now.'

Jean immediately bristled. 'They're not goin' tae pay more.'

'Only a few pence, or maybe a shilling for something made from really good material.'

'I've told ye before, this isnae a dress shop. It's always been for folk with little money tae their names.' Jean's shoulders squared and her chin came up.

Rose gave her a condescending smile. 'Jean, business is never for the benefit of anyone but the owners and managers – and partners,' she explained.

'Your kind o' business, mebbe, but not mine.'

'But there's the cost of laundering everything.'

'It's nice that the clothes are cleaner, but that was your idea. You never said the cost'd have tae come out of the customers' pockets. If you had, I'd not have agreed tae it.' A faint tremor had come into Jean's voice, and she gripped the jacket she had been unfolding so tightly that her knuckles shone white. Kirsty opened her mouth, then closed it again. If Jean didn't learn now to fight for what she believed in, Rose would always dominate her.

'Surely you realise—'

'This shop was set up by my mother for ordinary folk who cannae afford tae buy themselves new clothes,' Jean interrupted. 'It's true that she made a livin' from it, an' so must I, but if we start puttin' prices up just tae make a profit we'll drive folk away, and that wouldnae be right. They've come tae rely on me for some decent clothes. I've never let them down in the past and I won't start now!'

Kirsty, knowing the effort it had cost Jean to speak her mind like that, could have hugged her friend.

'But if you'd just think about—'

'The prices are goin' tae stay the same, Rose,' Jean said flatly, 'an' that's an end tae it.'

Kirsty, seeing Rose's lips press together, held her breath. Rose was in danger of reverting to the way she had been with her mother. If she gave way to her anger the partnership could end there and then.

Rose appealed to her. 'What do you say, Kirsty?'

'I think Jean's right. We'd be letting our clientele down if we started charging more money.'

Slowly, the light of battle faded from Rose's long face and she nodded. 'I suppose you're both right. It wouldn't be fair.'

Jean's pent-up breath eased from her lungs in a tiny sigh as another strand, fragile but important, was added to the new three-way pattern they were weaving between them.

23

Alex, concentrating on the pink rose he was painting, didn't look round when Kirsty went into the workshop. As she had hoped, he was alone. She had left Ewan eating his midday meal with his father, and she knew that Todd usually went along to the tobacconist's to see Beth during the break. Ewan, who often went to buy tobacco after he had eaten, had frequently jeered about the way the journeyman leaned against the counter, watching Beth at work with, according to Ewan, a look of cow-like devotion on his face.

Kirsty waited patiently while Alex finished what he was doing. He was still working on Fiona's furniture, in this instance a small bedside table. On a chair close to hand stood a half-empty bottle of cold tea together with a half-eaten sandwich. It looked clumsy and unappetising, a thick slice of hard yellow cheese between two pieces of bread hacked, rather than cut, from a loaf.

Since moving out of the house Alex had refused to eat any meals there. He had found lodgings with an elderly widow in the tenement next to where Todd lived with his sister and her husband and family. According to Todd, the woman was a kindly soul.

'Alex'll be all right with her, for she keeps a clean house – not like some of the folk ye get round our area. She'll look after him, and my sister says she'll have him in for his dinner now and then,' Todd had assured her. Even so, Kirsty's heart was broken for her much-loved first-born, living in a rented room, eating alone in a cold workshop, painting roses on furniture he had made for the girl he loved and could never have.

He laid down his brush, balancing it carefully on the edge of the paint pot, and got up from his knees to take the sandwich and bottle from the chair. 'Sit down, Mam.' He didn't smile, but his voice was mild enough.

'How are you?'

'I'm grand,' he said levelly, settling on the stairs, taking another bite of bread and cheese. 'And I'm busy, so if that's all you came tae ask—'

'It's not. There's a whole rack of shelves behind the counter in the new shop, but they're falling down, and some of them are broken. Jean was wondering if you'd put them right for us?'

'Me? You need a joiner for that, not a cabinet-maker.'

'I know, but Jean sees it as putting business your way. It'd be a kindness to her.'

His eyes darkened. 'You've not told her about—'

'I've not said a word to her or anyone else. As far as Jean knows you're still living at home – where you belong,' she couldn't help adding.

He gave her a long look, and she felt as though his eyes were boring into her mind and reading the truth there – that

230

instead of pointing out to Jean that Alex wasn't the right person to repair the shelving, she had seized on her friend's request because it was one way of seeing him, talking to him. Then he shrugged. 'I'll look in at the shop tomorrow.'

Alex had forgotten that Rose Hamilton might be in the new shop. To his surprise, she was talking to a painter and laughing at something the man had said. He stared, surprised to see her looking so animated – and with an ordinary workman, too.

'Alex, it was good of you tae come!' Jean Chisholm called from the other side of the shop, and Rose's head turned swiftly in his direction. The speed with which the warmth vanished from her face at the sight of him amused Alex. It wasn't often, these days, that anything amused him, he thought, as Jean swooped over to lead him to the shelving behind the counter. It was a sorry mess, but the brackets were still usable.

He took measurements, made notes. 'We've got some timber in stock that'd do.' Glancing over his shoulder, he saw that Rose had gone. 'Some of the shelves can be saved. I'll take them back tae the workshop and work on them. Then I'll cut new timber tae the right size and varnish it.'

He was wrenching the shelves free when his mother arrived and insisted on showing him round the place. Despite his doubts about the success of the new venture, Alex was impressed by what had already been done and by the spaciousness now that the two shops had become one.

He was pleased, too, to see his mother so enthusiastic and happy. She had had a lot to contend with since the move to Paisley – probably even before then. She deserved her fair share of happiness, and despite his strong mistrust of Rose Hamilton, he hoped for Kirsty's sake, and Jean's, that the shop would turn out to be a success. Not that he could find the words to say so. His utter despair and soul-destroying misery over the loss of Fiona and the way he had lost her had begun to ease, and he had stopped blaming his mother. She had only been a child when it all happened, little older than Caitlin. She had fought to keep him safe, and it wasn't her fault that he had met and fallen in love with Fiona. But although the first keen edge of the pain had blunted, it was still with him, locking him into a dour silence that prevented him from speaking openly to her. That was why he had agreed to try to do something about the shelving. He had seen it as a way of helping her rather than Jean.

In one of the back shops he spied a battered corner cupboard that had been pushed to one side.

'That's a good piece of furniture.' He squatted down to examine it. 'It's been ill-treated, but it's been bonny in its day.'

'We found it lying here,' Kirsty said. 'We were thinking of just putting it out.'

'Don't do that. It's got a nice shape to it.' Alex studied it from all angles. 'And that's good glass in the doors. It's a wonder it's not been broken.' He straightened up, dusting his hands. 'This would look bonny in a corner of the front shop. You could mebbe use it for displaying wee things like gloves and ribbons.'

Jean had joined them with a mug of tea for Alex. 'It's badly scratched,' she said doubtfully.

'That can be put right. I'll repair it then French polish it and reset the doors with new hinges, if you like.'

232

Jean beamed up at him. 'You'd not mind givin' the time tae it?'

'Not if it's for you,' he told her, and she giggled girlishly, slapping his arm.

'You're a terrible man, Alex Lennox!'

'Only with beautiful women,' he said, grinning, and she went into another fit of giggles.

Kirsty and Alex looked over her turbaned head at each other, smiling, and for a moment there was a lightness in the air, then it burst like a bubble as Rose swept down on them, a challenge in her voice as she asked, 'Well now, Mr Lennox, what do you think of the place?'

The laughter went from Alex at once and he buried his face in the mug, taking a long swallow of tea. 'It looks well enough,' he told her coolly, 'but the test's yet tae come.'

'You doubt if the shop'll be a success? Does that mean that I have more faith in your mother than you have?'

'Of course not,' Jean protested, but the smile went from her face as she looked from one young person to the other, puzzled by their antagonism.

To Alex's mind, Rose was reminding him of the day he had told her to leave his mother alone. But she hadn't and she had won. He stared at her, the anger he had been feeling against the entire world ever since Angus MacDowall's first visit to Espedair Street settling back into his heart. 'I've got faith in my mother and in Jean.'

'But not in me.'

'Not from what I've known of you so far,' he said deliberately. Colour swept into her face and her eyes narrowed.

'Rose,' Jean broke in hurriedly, 'Alex says he can repair this cupboard for us.'

'We'll pay you for it, of course.'

'There's no need. I'm doing it as a gift for Jean.'

Her eyebrows rose. 'I thought workmen considered their time to be valuable?'

'I'm not a workman, Miss Hamilton, I'm a craftsman. And friendship's got its value, too – but mebbe you've never learned that.'

'What's amiss?' Jean asked in confusion as Rose flounced away, her narrow back rigid with anger.

'I cannae abide that lassie!'

'Alex feels that after the way Rose lost me my place with Mrs Hamilton she can't be trusted,' Kirsty explained hurriedly.

'Och, that! It was naughty of her, but she's made up for it since, hasn't she, Kirsty?' Jean patted Alex's arm. 'I wasn't too sure of her myself at first, but when you get tae know her, she's a nice lassie at heart. You'll see.'

'I doubt if I will, for she's got as little time for me as I have for her.'

'Why can't you just be civil to the lassie if you should meet her?' said Kirsty when Jean had moved away. 'She's one of my partners now.'

Alex took a final swallow of tea then returned the mug to her and wiped the back of his hand across his mouth. 'Mebbe so, but that's no reason for me tae like her. There's somethin' about that lassie that I can't abide, and never will.'

'Mebbe it's because she's as stubborn as you are,' his mother said.

Rose's suggestion that every customer calling in on the shop's opening day should be given a small glass of sherry was quashed immediately by her new partners.

'But my uncle did that when he was auctioning off the contents of his late brother's house, and it worked wonderfully well. It brought in a lot of buyers.'

'It worked for him, mebbe, but round here it'd bring in every drunk in the town,' Jean protested. 'We'd see the same faces comin' through the door time and again!'

'It would help to spread the word that we'd reopened,' Rose explained, and Jean laughed.

'You've no need tae worry about that, hen. Word of anythin', be it good or bad, spreads faster in Paisley than lice on a mongrel. In any case,' she added firmly when the girl showed signs of arguing, 'I signed the pledge years ago and I couldnae possibly permit hard drink on my premises.'

Kirsty shot a startled look at her friend. It was met by a flat stare that defied her to open her mouth.

'You've never signed the pledge,' she challenged when they were alone. 'I mind that whisky we both drank the day Rose came up with the idea of a partnership.'

'I nearly signed it once, but there's been times like that day when I've been glad I didnae take the step. I was just givin' the lassie a wee reminder that she's not goin' tae get everything her own way,' Jean said blandly. 'An' when it comes down tae it, handin' out drink tae every creature that comes in through the door's a waste of good money and a daft idea anyway!'

The shop's reopening in December caused quite a stir. A steady stream of women flowed through the place, some there only to gawk and stare, others intent on buying.

'It used tae be that the only customers were folk who knew where I was,' Jean marvelled, wrapping a jacket for a satisfied customer. 'Now look at the size of the place – and there're women comin' in from all over the town today. The dear Lord knows what my mother'd say if she saw this place now.'

'She'd say that you've made a good move,' John Brodie assured her. He had insisted on attending the opening. 'I'm hoping that this is the way it'll be from now on, Miss Chisholm. I believe that this shop will do very well for itself.' He bowed to the customer and sprang to open the shop door for her. 'Thank you for your custom, madam. We hope you'll call again.'

'You've got a way with the ladies,' Jean said as the woman went off, blushing and simpering. 'If you're ever turned away from your own place of work we'll mebbe give you a position here.'

He grinned and said, 'I'd enjoy that,' as she scurried away to help someone else.

Thanks to Alex, the shelving behind the counter was broad and sturdy and glossy with brown varnish. Now that the clothes were laundered before going on display, the place had taken on the look of a real dress shop instead of a second-hand clothes store. That, Kirsty thought as she watched the women, most of them shabbily dressed, who milled about the place, would help the customers' morale. Every woman, whatever her situation in life, liked to feel well-treated.

Behind the counter, to her delight, was a drawer just like the one in Mr Laidlaw's tobacconist's shop, fitted with metal bowls to hold the takings. She took great pleasure in dividing a handful of coins into the appropriate bowls. 'There's plenty buying, but in this part of the town you'll find that most of the money coming in's just coppers.'

'Coppers have a way of becoming pounds.' Brodie nodded towards a corner where Rose, in the crisp white blouse and black skirt they had all agreed to adopt as their uniform, was earnestly trying to sell something to a customer. 'I never thought to see Rose Hamilton working in a shop.'

'She insisted, and we're so busy today that we need her help, even though she has to ask Jean or me the cost of everything.'

Brodie watched the long and earnest conversation between Rose and the other woman with interest. 'D'you think they can understand each other?'

Kirsty knew what he meant. Most of the women coming into the shop had shied back in alarm on hearing Rose's clear, confident voice with its finishing-school accent. Some had fled, some had made a point of always being in another corner of the shop to avoid having to speak to her, some had sniggered – although Rose gave no indication of noticing – and some, braver than the rest, had joined verbal battle.

Although Kirsty and Jean had both found those encounters between the two levels of society amusing, Kirsty was quite offended by John Brodie's attitude. Rose, after all, was her partner. Her voice was sharp when she said, 'I'm sure they can. She's sold quite a few things already. I've come to admire her over the past weeks. She's not afraid of getting her hands dirty – or of being laughed at.'

'My dear Mrs Lennox, I wasn't laughing at her! On the contrary, I share your admiration.'

'Will she get into terrible trouble with her parents, being here?'

'She already has,' he said blithely. 'To their minds it was bad enough that she insisted on putting her inheritance into

237

this place. When they heard that Rose herself intended to spend at least part of her time in the shop her mother had an attack of the vapours and her father threatened to turn her out of house and home. I know because my parents are friends of hers.'

Kirsty felt an unexpected twinge of sympathy for Mrs Hamilton. She well knew, now, what it was like to see a child moving out of the family home. 'Jean and me wouldn't want to cause trouble between Rose and her family.'

'Don't worry about Rose, she can take care of herself. When she told her father that she'd be delighted to find a place of her own he gave in at once, for he knew that she meant it. He's really very fond of her. I think he secretly admires her independence. I understand from my mother that the Hamiltons have decided to let her have her own way in the hope that she'll eventually lose interest in the whole idea.'

'D'you think she'll lose interest?' Kirsty said nervously. She couldn't bear to contemplate what might happen to herself and Jean if Rose withdrew her financial support.

'Absolutely not. Rose isn't the type, and in any case she herself made sure that the papers were worded in such a way that even if she were to walk away from this place she couldn't take her original investment with her for several years. You have to admire her,' John Brodie mused, his eyes still on the tall, thin girl, who looked well in the plain blouse and skirt. 'When it comes to courage and determination there are few women as strong as Rose Hamilton.'

Kirsty looked at him with interest. If there was a romance in the air, it would be a very good thing, she thought. The young lawyer would make an ideal husband for Rose.

'Indeed,' she said encouragingly. 'She's a quite remarkable young woman.'

'Kirsty.' Jean beckoned from another part of the shop. 'Could ye mebbe shorten a skirt for this lassie, and perhaps do somethin' different with these sleeves?'

As she moved away from the counter Kirsty was disappointed to hear the lawyer, his eyes still on Rose, murmur, 'A pity the girl's as plain as a pikestaff.'

24

Although Matt was in no mood to celebrate New Year, Kirsty insisted on inviting Jean to share their Ne'erday dinner as before.

'She's got nobody but us, Matt.'

'Och, have it yer ain way,' he said peevishly. 'Ye always do, these days. I'm not master of my own house any more.'

'That's not true.' Since Sandy's last visit Matt had retreated into his own world, only emerging from it now and again when they were alone to ask questions about the days when Sandy had been her father's apprentice. Kirsty had done everything she could to convince him that the past was the past, but Matt refused to believe her.

'The man's widowed, with a fine house needin' a mistress. Ye'd like that, wouldn't ye? Servants tae follow yer biddin', and money tae spend, the things,' he said bitterly, 'that I've never been able tae give ye.'

'I'm content where I am. I'm not interested in San— Mr MacDowall, and he's certainly not interested in me.' She knew as she said it that she wasn't being entirely truthful.

She pushed the memory away and went on briskly, 'As to

a mistress for his house, from what I've heard the man's got a very good housekeeper.'

Caitlin, disappointed at the Bishops not being invited this year, took gifts to them from herself and Kirsty and brought back tobacco for Matt and Ewan, a necktie for Alex, a rag doll made by Morag for Mary, and two bottles of raspberries from their garden for Kirsty. Radiant with happiness, Caitlin displayed her own gift, a length of soft, light cloth in checks of misty green and purple, the colours of heather.

'It was made on great-grandfather's loom.' Her slim hands stroked the cloth gently. 'I'm going to keep it for now, and one day I'll make something special from it.'

To Kirsty's disappointment, Alex refused to eat his Ne'erday dinner with his family. 'My sister'll invite him tae eat with us,' Todd assured her. 'He'll not go hungry for food or friends.'

'But she's got enough to do without taking Alex under her wing as well,' Kirsty protested. She knew that Todd's sister, a cheerful, motherly woman, was also entertaining her husband's parents as well as her own children, Beth, Mr Laidlaw and Todd himself.

'She can always find room for another one. We have a grand time at Ne'erday – it's just like the times we used tae have when my own parents were alive.' His eyes sparkled at the memory. 'We usually had that many folk in for their dinner that we'd tae take it in turns tae sit at the table.'

Since Jean was coming to the house, Kirsty had to explain to her in advance about Alex's absence. She didn't mention Sandy, saying only that Alex and Matt had fallen out.

Jean nodded sagely. 'It happens with grown laddies. They say you cannae do with too many women in the one house, but to my mind it's just the same with men. Fathers are used tae rulin' the roost and they take it hard when their sons become men an' start havin' opinions of their own.'

It was a difficult meal. Ewan, fretting to be free like Alex, wasn't good company, nor was Matt. Kirsty wished that, like Alex, she could be in Todd's sister's busy, happy kitchen instead.

As soon as the meal was over Ewan helped Matt to settle in the parlour then went out to meet his friends. Jean offered to help with the dishes, but Kirsty shooed her back into the parlour, where Matt was reading his newspaper and Mary played on the rug before the fire with her new doll.

When she went into the parlour to ask if they were ready for a cup of tea, she found the pair of them sound asleep, and looking like bookends on either side of the fire. Jean's head was lolling on her left shoulder, Matt's on his right. Jean's snores were little ladylike puffs of sound, while Matt's were deeper, longer but, mercifully, lacking the guttural harshness that often kept Kirsty awake at nights. Mary, oblivious to the noise on either side, was holding a long whispered conversation with her doll.

Smiling, Kirsty closed the door quietly and returned to the kitchen.

'They're both sound, but make the tea anyway.' She suddenly realised that Caitlin was standing motionless by the stove, tears rolling silently down her rounded cheeks. 'What's wrong, lassie? Did you burn yourself?'

'It's wee Fergus,' Caitlin's tear-filled eyes were like clear blue-green rock pools, 'and Alex. They were both here with us last Ne'erday, and now – oh, Mam, I want them both back and Father well again. I want everything the way it was!'

Kirsty gathered her daughter into her arms and rocked her gently, noticing for the first time that Caitlin was her own height now. 'Hush, pet. We all want things to go back to the way they were, but it can't happen.'

'D'you think Alex'll come home, at least?' Caitlin mumbled into her neck.

'Mebbe, in a wee while.'

'Why did Father quarrel with him?'

'It's the way of things, Caitlin. Alex is grown up now. He has his own ideas, and sometimes they're not the same as your father's.'

The girl drew away, dabbing her eyes with the dish towel. 'If growing up causes trouble and unhappiness for everyone, I don't want it to happen to me.'

'It's already happening, pet. You're out of school and earning a wage, but even so,' Kirsty said guiltily, remembering that she herself had been too busy with the shop to think of the Ne'erday celebrations, and it was Caitlin who had prepared most of the meal they had just eaten, as well as cleaning the house from top to bottom, 'you're young yet. I expect you to do too much in the house.'

'I don't mind.'

'I'll need to make certain that you get out with your friends more in the future.'

'I see them often enough.' Caitlin unrolled the sleeves of the high-necked pink blouse Kirsty had brought from the shop for her. The slight swell of her young breasts nudged against the blouse, and beneath her well-cut dark-blue serge skirt, also from the shop, her hips flared sweetly from a small waist. Her hair, looped back with a pink ribbon long enough for the ends to hang halfway down her neat straight back, was like bronze silk, touched here and there with gold in the light from the gas mantle.

Peering at herself in the small mirror, she asked anxiously, 'D'you think they'll know that I've been crying when I go through?'

'Not a bit of it. Crying just makes you look prettier.'

Her soft mouth curved into one of its frequent smiles. 'Pretty? Me? I don't know about that.'

'I do,' Kirsty said. It was true. Instead of reddening the girl's dark-lashed eyes and puffing her oval, neat-featured face, the fit of weeping had merely touched her skin with a pearly sheen and given added lustre to the striking turquoise eyes.

Caitlin was well on the way to becoming a beauty. And while she was proud of the fact, Kirsty found herself hoping that it wouldn't mean more trouble as her daughter ripened into maturity.

Fiona's furniture was completed early in January and collected by a motor vehicle with Angus MacDowall's name painted on the sides in large letters. The sight of the van standing in the street outside while the furniture, carefully wrapped, was carried through the pend, sent Matt into a flurry of questions about Kirsty's past and caused a quarrel between himself and Ewan.

'Just because Alex has managed tae get away from him he's started pickin' on me,' Ewan complained to Kirsty that night. 'I'll not have it. And I know he's in pain and frettin' about not bein' able tae work any more,' he added impatiently as she opened her mouth to speak, 'so don't bother tellin' it all tae me again. It's not my fault that he's got arthritis, and it's

244

not my fault that he's gettin' older. I'm still young – I've got my own life tae think of.'

He thrust his hands into his trouser pockets and scowled at the sink. 'I've got Alex goin' on at me in the workshop and that old bugger narkin' at me in the house – it's no fit life for a dog. I've a good mind tae up and off, and tae hell with the pair of them!'

'That would be daft, and you know it. Your father needs you, and one day you and Alex'll own the business between you.'

Ewan gave a contemptuous laugh. 'What's so grand about ownin' a place like that? A wee wooden shed an' a yard – an' Alex bossin' me around because he's the eldest? I'm goin' out.' He made for the door.

'You've not long come in – it's past time for bed!'

'Don't you start on me now,' he said, and strode out, leaving the door swinging open behind him.

A month after its opening the shop was still thriving. All the regular customers had returned, and now that the place was larger and able to hold more stock, women from other parts of the town had started to call regularly. As Jean was too busy to go round the big houses collecting clothing, a woman had been hired to do it in her place.

The partnership still survived, and Kirsty was pleased to see that having won at least two small battles, Jean was more comfortable with Rose, who was still coming in for a period of time every day and seemed well settled in her new life, with no sign of boredom or regret.

Once, leaving to go home, Kirsty had almost bumped into Mrs Hamilton, hovering outside. The woman, crimsoning when she recognised her former employee, had hurried away without a word.

'I know,' Rose said airily when Kirsty mentioned the meeting the following day. 'I've seen her out there a few times, trying to look as though she's just passing by. I haven't the heart to let her know that she's been spotted, much as I'd like to.'

'Does she still try to get you to give the shop up?'

'All the time, poor thing. They've all had a go at me – Mamma, Daddy, my sisters and their stuffy husbands, but they should all know by now that once I set my mind to something I'll not be talked out of it.' She grinned. 'I hear that poor Mamma has stopped mentioning my name in front of her friends. I think she'd rather see me in prison for committing a crime than behind the counter of a shop selling second-hand clothing. At least there would be no chance of any of her friends seeing me in prison!'

Once Fiona's order was completed Alex turned his attention to the corner cabinet he had agreed to refurbish for the shop. It became a handy excuse for Kirsty to visit the workshop now and again, supposedly to see how the cabinet was coming along but in reality to see Alex and reassure herself that he was all right. He was still cool towards her, and she wondered at times if he would ever forgive her for not telling him everything she knew about Sandy from the start, but at least he didn't make her feel unwelcome.

Almost at once, though, her interest was caught by the work he was doing on the cabinet. She watched, fascinated, as he cleaned and repaired it, then started the long and laborious task of French polishing it, mixing the polish then patiently distributing it evenly over the entire surface, bit by bit, over and over again, building up the layers.

One day he even entrusted the polish-soaked pad to her and let her do some work on the cupboard. Thrilled, she moved the pad over the surface in small even circles as directed, Alex occasionally putting his hand over hers to demonstrate the pressure and movement needed. When she finally handed the pad back, flushed with success, he smiled down at her.

'You did well, Mam.' For a blissful minute he was her Alex again.

'We'll turn ye intae a cabinet-maker yet,' Todd chimed in, while Ewan, glancing up from his own work, said sourly, 'Once is fine – try doin' it day in and day out and ye'll soon wish ye'd taken up another craft.'

To Jean's delight, Alex brought the completed cabinet to the shop one dark February afternoon and set it up in the front shop.

'Oh, Alex, it's lovely – I'd no idea it could be made so nice! And tae think we were goin' tae throw it out!'

'It's as well you didn't, for it's made from good oak and worth a bit of money,' he told her.

He stood watching while Jean and Kirsty fussed over the cabinet, trying different items in it and finally deciding that it should be used to display gloves.

'You've done a grand job with this place.'

'I never thought I'd see the day when I'd have a shop like this,' Jean told him. 'It's all thanks to Rose. She's a fine lassie,' she added, then, seeing his smile dim slightly, 'I forgot – you don't like her, do you?'

'I don't dislike her, I just don't trust her.'

'That's because you don't know her, Alex. Mebbe the two of you should get to know each other better. Two young things like you might have a lot in common.' Jean burbled on, then, peering up into his face and seeing that the smile had gone entirely, 'Well, mebbe not. So what about yoursel'? Are you happy away from home, or are you missin' bein' looked after by your mam? I know she's missin' you.'

'I'm doin' fine where I am. I'll walk home with you, Mam, if you're leaving soon,' he said abruptly. 'I've got work to finish off before I'm done for the day.'

'Jean means well,' she apologised as they set off. 'I had to tell her at Ne'erday that you were in lodgings, but I didn't say why.'

'I just wish folk didn't always have tae interfere. How can she say you miss me when you see me every day? I'm a man now, Mam, I can't be tied to your apron strings for ever.'

'I know,' she said wretchedly. 'I've never said a word to Jean about missing you. It was her own idea.'

He let the matter drop, but as they crossed the road he guided her with a hand beneath her elbow, as though trying to make up for his sharp tone. At the corner of Espedair Street their eyes were drawn to the tobacconist's lighted window. Above the low partition separating the window display of pipes and packets of tobacco and cigarettes from the main shop they could see Beth Laidlaw handing change to an elderly man, dimpling and smiling at something he had said.

'I don't know what Todd thinks he's about, courting that one,' Alex muttered. 'She's just turned down another place he found for them. She's got no intention of marrying him yet he doesn't see it.'

'She'll agree to some place eventually. She's young yet.' Beth was only twenty-two, eight years younger than Todd.

They had reached the street door. 'Goodbye then,' he said, and went on towards the pend, waving a hand in acknowledgement when she called after him, 'Thank you for doing the cabinet.'

As she stepped into the hall, lit only by the glow of a gas street lamp through the fanlight above the door, a voice hissed, 'Mam,' from halfway up the stairs.

Kirsty peered into the gloom, and saw Mary sitting halfway up, clutching the rag doll Morag had given her for Ne'erday. 'What're you doing there, pet?' She held her hand out. 'Come on into the kitchen.'

Mary's brown head waggled vigorously from side to side. 'Daddy's talking to a man in there.'

'What man?'

'Just a man. I'll come down when he's gone,' Mary whispered loudly.

'You can't stay—'

'Is that you, Kirsty?' Matt called from the kitchen.

Kirsty looked helplessly from the closed door to the stairs. 'I'll come and get you in a minute,' she told her daughter, and went into the kitchen, where Matt sat in his usual chair and Sandy MacDowall stood by the table.

Her heart sank at the sight of him. 'What are you doing here?'

'I've come to see Alex. I'm told he doesn't live here now.'

'No, but he's still working here,' Kirsty said, and Matt darted an angry look at her, then glared defiantly back at the visitor.

'I . . . hadn't realised that,' Sandy said slowly.

249

'Matt—'

'He's caused enough upset in this family,' Matt snapped. 'Why should we tell the likes of him about our affairs?'

'I regret the trouble.' Sandy's voice was cold. 'But I have the right to talk with Alex.'

'Ye've got no rights! Tell us yer business, if ye must, and we'll tell Alex – or his mother will, for the stubborn fool'll not speak tae me.'

Sandy's eyelids flickered. 'All the more reason why I should say what I have to say to his face, in front of both of you, to make certain that I'm doing nothing underhand. I'm not going until I see him or find out where he is,' he added, his voice still mild but with a steely obstinacy creeping in.

'I'll fetch him,' Kirsty said as Matt opened his mouth to argue. The sooner Sandy stated his business and left them all in peace, the better.

'You can tell him to go, for I'll not talk to him,' Alex said as soon as he heard about Sandy.

'You'll have to.' She had called him outside so that they could speak without being overheard by Todd or Ewan. 'The man won't go until he's said his piece.' Then, as he half turned to re-enter the workshop, she added, 'D'you want me to send him down here where the other two can listen to every word he says? I will if it's the only way to get him out of our house.'

He hesitated, gnawing at his lower lip, then shrugged. 'I'll come to the house, but he'd best be quick, for my patience is short,' he said, and together they turned away from the workshop and went along the lane.

25

Alex took up a belligerent stance just inside the kitchen door, his gaze on Sandy. 'I've things tae do,' he said shortly. 'I've not got much time.'

'Then I'll not waste any. I want you to come and work for me.'

'What?' Matt's knotted hands clutched at the arms of his chair.

Alex's expression flickered, then held. 'Why should I?'

'Because you're a fine artist as well as a good cabinet-maker. Because,' Sandy flicked a sidelong look in Matt's direction, 'you should be where your talents are properly recognised and used. And because you're my son. Who else would I leave my business to?'

'You have a daughter,' Alex said harshly.

'I have, but I don't see her wanting to take over a furniture store, and after all the years I've spent building it up I've no wish to leave it to whoever she may choose to marry.'

Alex's face darkened, and Kirsty saw his Adam's apple bob as he swallowed convulsively. Sandy swept on.

'I'll see that Fiona's very well provided for, but MacDowall's matters to me almost as much as she does. I've cherished and nursed that business into what it is now, and when my time comes I want to know that I'm passing it on to someone who cares about it as much as I do. I never thought I'd see the day, but now I've got the chance of leaving it to someone of my own blood.'

'I make furniture, Mr MacDowall. I don't sell it.'

Sandy's silvery head inclined slightly. 'I'm well aware of that. I've had it in mind for a while now to buy over a cabinet-making business so that we can manufacture some of the furniture we sell, possibly to customers' own specifications – as you did for Fiona.'

'By God, ye'll not have my business!' Matt snarled, and Alex took time to flash a cold look at his stepfather.

'It's my mother's, not yours.'

Matt's face flamed and he gurgled with rage before managing to spit out, 'And she's my wife. And I'm tellin' the both of ye, this place is not for sale, so ye neednae think ye can get yer hands on it!'

'I've no intention of making an offer for this place. I already have my eye on a small factory in Glasgow,' Sandy told him without moving his gaze from Alex. 'The owner's looking for a buyer, and I think the business might do very well in the right hands. I'd like you to run it for me.'

'What makes you think I'd want to work for you?'

'From what I can gather you're stifled here. If you agree to work for me the place will be yours to run as you think fit. You'll have the right to make the decisions and deal with the customers yourself.'

A faint cold smile quirked one corner of Alex's mouth

252

'And you think you could trust me to do what's best for your precious emporium?'

'I'm sure of it. You're not a fool; you'd not destroy a business that'll be yours one day.'

'You could be making a stick tae lash your own back with in other ways, Mr MacDowall.'

'If you're referring to Fiona, she's settled down well in Fort William and means to stay there for several months at least. I'm told,' Sandy said slowly and deliberately, 'that she's already taken a liking to a most suitable young man.' Then, as Alex drew his breath in sharply and half turned towards the back door, one hand groping blindly for the latch, his voice sharpened. 'I said you were no fool, lad – don't prove me wrong. Before any decisions are made you have to face the truth. You cared for Fiona more than she cared for you. My daughter's young for her age, and I'll admit that I've probably spoiled her, for until now she's been all that I had. She's more like her mother, God rest her soul, than me, in temperament as well as in looks. She's a butterfly, as any girl of her age and her background has a right to be. But you – you're like me,' Sandy said with a satisfaction that made Matt wince in his chair. 'You're ambitious, and too level-headed to let the past get in the way of what you want.'

Kirsty, who had stayed silent because she well knew that she had no part in the scene being played out before her eyes, moved to stand by her husband, a protective hand on his shoulder. Neither Alex nor Sandy seemed to notice the movement; they were still locking gazes, Alex bone white, his hair a brilliant beacon, Sandy calm and collected.

'I shall make certain that when Fiona visits me there'll be

no danger of a meeting between the two of you. George Gavin has a comfortable home – he and his wife have offered you lodgings there until such time as you find a place of your own. For the time being, Fiona won't even know that you're working for me.'

'Alex already has work here!' Matt rasped.

'But is he content with what he has?'

'I raised him as my own – I've fed him and clothed him . . .' Matt's temper began to boil over. Frightened for his health, Kirsty tried to hush him, but he waved her aside. 'For God's sake, woman, think! The man fathered a child on ye and left ye tae take the consequences alone—'

'He didn't know—'

'And now, when he walks intae my house bold as brass and talks of taking Alex from us, ye want tae treat him as a guest? I've had enough of this. Get out of my house,' he roared at Sandy, who calmly picked up his hat and cane.

'I've had my say, and I'm going. Take a day or two to make up your mind,' he told Alex. 'When you have, come to the shop and ask for me.'

'I might – and I might not.'

'Whatever your decision, I surely deserve to be told man to man.'

'Out!' Matt erupted, struggling from his chair. 'Or by God I'll—'

'Leave it.' Alex went to his stepfather and eased him back down. 'It's no business of yours.'

'No business? After all I've done for you?'

'I can understand your anger, Mr Lennox,' Sandy said from the door. 'But at least I made the offer in front of you and not behind your back.'

Leaving Alex to deal with his stepfather, Kirsty followed Sandy into the hall. 'Why have you done this to us?'

He loomed above her, the silver of his hair haloing his face in the light sifting through the fan window. 'I want to help Alex.'

'You want to have your own way – and you'd hurt a sick man to get it!'

'Kate, I've already heard from your husband's own lips that he doesn't give a damn about the lad's ability, let alone encourage it,' Sandy's voice was low and fierce.

'There's more to it than that.'

'Of course there is. I want my son.' The words dropped from his lips with cold deliberation. 'That man's called Alex his son for most of his life, and he has a lad of his own besides. I've had none, and now I want what's mine. D'you not see, Kate – I have a right to him!'

'He's a person, not a possession. Nobody has any rights to him.'

'At least I have the right to try to make up for all those years. As to whether or not I'll succeed, let the lad decide that. I'd not want him to come to me unwillingly. It has to be of his own free will.'

'M-mam?' Mary quavered from the stairs, and they both whirled, startled.

'It's all right, pet – everything's all right. I'm coming.'

'It's only fair,' Kirsty heard Sandy say as she moved towards the stairs, 'to let him make the decision.'

The street door opened and closed, letting a breath of chill air into the hall.

When Kirsty reached Mary she had to coax the little girl to let go of the wooden balustrade she clutched tightly with both arms. In the kitchen, Matt and Alex's voices were raised in argument. For once she felt no desire to intercede and try to stand between them. They must each come to terms with this latest situation in whatever way they could. And so must she, for she knew that Alex would choose to follow Sandy. It was the only road for him.

Sitting on the stairs, holding Mary's trembling body tightly, she wondered if life would ever settle down instead of whirling around their ears like the cold wind Sandy had let into the hall, and into her life.

It started to snow heavily on the day Alex went to live in Glasgow. When he came to the house to say goodbye to his mother, white flakes lay thickly on his shoulders and tangled in his eyelashes and his fiery red hair. He had said his farewells to Caitlin and Mary the day before.

'You've got everything?'

He glanced at the bag on the floor. 'All my worldly possessions.'

'I made you some sandwiches.'

'I'm only going to Glasgow, Mam,' he protested, laughing. 'I'll not starve.'

'Take them anyway,' she insisted. She had known while making them that it was foolishness, but to her mind he wasn't just going to Glasgow; he was setting out on a journey that was taking him from her for good.

Perhaps he sensed this, for when he had stowed the packet in his coat pocket he said, 'You know I have tae go, Mam.'

'I know.'

'It'll make things easier for you in the long run. No more quarrelling between him and me, and he'll get his own way about Ewan inheriting the business. It'll be for the best all round.'

'Are you not going up to see him?' Matt had taken to his bed since Sandy's visit.

'Best not.'

'You can't just leave without a word.'

'Mam, you know he'll only snarl at me, and I'll snarl back. And I'm sure he won't want to see me any more than I want to see him.' Then, glancing at the clock, 'I'll need tae go in any case, or I'll miss the train.'

For a few seconds Alex hesitated, embarrassed and unsure of how to say goodbye, then Kirsty opened her arms and he went into them. For a moment his cheek was pressed to hers, the snowflakes in his hair icy against her warm skin, before the contact was broken and he picked his bag up and opened the back door.

'I'll not be far away. I'll write and let you know how things go, and I'll see you often.'

'Yes, I know.'

He stepped out into the whirling snow, and was gone.

Matt made no mention of Alex when she took his midday meal upstairs. 'Tell Ewan tae come up. There's things we have tae talk about.'

'He's just started on his own food.' She spread a clean towel over the bedclothes then laid a tray holding a bowl of soup and a plate of bread on his knees. 'He'll come upstairs when you've both eaten, and not before.' She held out his spoon, which had strips of cloth bound round the handle to thicken it and make it easier to grip. 'Take your soup before it gets cold.'

He picked up the spoon, dipped it into the plate, then muttered a curse as his hand jerked and some of the soup splashed back into the dish before it reached his mouth. Kirsty wiped the splatters from his nightshirt and the covers, then laid the cloth by his other hand and left, knowing that he hated anyone, even her, to see his clumsiness.

'Mind now – you've not to say anything that'll worry him,' she instructed Ewan when he went up to his father later.

He scowled. 'I wish he'd just leave us tae see tae the business and stop interferin'.'

'Listen to him and agree with him, and if necessary, just go your own way,' she said wearily. 'It's what Alex did to keep the peace.'

'If Alex did it, then it must be right,' he snarled, and trudged off.

With Matt upstairs and not knowing what was going on in the kitchen, she had insisted on Todd coming in for his mid-day meal with Ewan. Now he got up and reached for his jacket.

'That was a grand dinner, Mrs Lennox. My thanks tae ye.'

'You're welcome, Todd. I want you to eat in here every day with Ewan, during the winter, at least. I won't have you sitting out in the workshop in this weather.'

'It's no hardship, but there's nothin' like a cooked meal.' She was stacking dishes at the sink, and he came to stand behind her, peering out at the snow. 'It's comin' down hard again,' he observed, then fumbled in his pocket and laid a parcel wrapped in greaseproof paper down on the draining board.

She opened it to find some neatly cut sandwiches. 'Don' be daft, Todd!'

'Since you've given me my dinner it's only fair that you have the food I brought to eat, Mrs Lennox. I don't like tae take yer hospitality and give nothin' in exchange,' he added as she began to refuse. 'Ye'll mebbe be able tae use them.'

Perhaps it was Todd's kindness, perhaps it was because the little parcel was so like the one Kirsty had given Alex not two hours ago; she would never know. All she did know was that she tried to say something but instead, to her horror and embarrassment, started to weep.

'What's wrong? Is it the master?' Todd asked in alarm. 'Has he got worse?'

'It's – it's Alex—' She turned blindly, reached out for the dish towel. It wasn't there.

'Here.' Todd thrust his own handkerchief into her hand. 'It's all right, it's clean.'

'I know I'm making a fuss about a grown man,' she said shakily. 'It was time he went off on his own. It's just – it was a year ago today that we lost Fergus, only with all that's been going on nobody's remembered.'

Mention of her dead baby's name was her undoing. She lurched forward towards the comfort and security of Todd's shoulder, and felt his arms go around her. He held her, one big hand patting her back, as she wept for Fergus and for Alex, and for poor crippled Matt, and for herself.

'I'm such a fool,' she said shakily when she finally drew back.

'No ye're not. Everyone needs tae have a good cry now and again.'

'But I shouldn't have landed you with it all, Todd.'

'Of course ye should. What else are friends for?' He peered down into her swollen face, then said awkwardly, 'If ye're all

259

right now, Mrs Lennox, I'd best get along tae the workshop.'

'Of course – on you go, Todd, I'll be fine. And thank you,' she said, as he opened the door. He gave her a quick smile and stepped out into the snow.

She barely had time to thrust his handkerchief into her apron pocket and rinse her face before Ewan clattered downstairs and erupted into the kitchen, muttering under his breath. Kirsty pretended to be busy with the dishes in the sink so that she could keep her face hidden, but she needn't have worried, for he stormed through the room and out of the back door without a glance or a word.

From the window she watched his broad back disappear into the whirling snow, shoulders hunched and hands thrust deep into his jacket pockets.

26

Once the snow melted, pools of dirty water were left on the shop floor each time customers came in, and a mop and bucket had to be kept in a corner at all times. Whenever any of the staff had a moment free they ran the mop over the muddy, dirty floor. Jean was shocked the first time she saw Rose wield the mop.

'I'll do that.' She tried to take the mop from Rose, who held onto it.

'I can manage fine.'

'But it's not seemly, you cleanin' up after folk.'

'It's perfectly seemly. Anyway, I enjoy it.' Rose pushed the mop vigorously around the floor. 'There's something pleasurable in doing things that I know would shock my Mamma.'

She had lost none of her enthusiasm for the venture and continued to spend time in the shop every day despite her mother's opposition. To everyone's surprise, including her own, she had begun to reveal a hitherto hidden sense of humour, sharp as a honed blade, which made her popular with the regular customers.

'There's always been things I've wanted to say, but I couldn't, for they'd have shocked everyone,' she admitted to Kirsty and Jean. 'But here it's different. I can say whatever comes into my head, and people know what I mean. Ordinary folk have a much better sense of humour.'

Winter gave way to spring and spring to summer, and Kirsty was kept busy between the shop and the house. She was surprised, in June, to realise that it had been four months since Alex's departure. He had never been back, but he wrote now and then, brief letters indicating that he had settled down in Glasgow and was busy reorganising the small factory Sandy had bought. Matt professed to be uninterested in the letters, but Kirsty made a point of telling him of their contents, and he didn't stop her.

'I think he's sorry now that he let Alex go so easily,' she said to Jean, who had been told long since of the reasons behind his sudden departure, 'but it's too late now, so he'll not admit it. He quarrels with Ewan just as much as he did with Alex – probably more, since Ewan's heart isn't in the business at all.'

'He's young yet.'

'There's more to it than that, Jean. Ewan's restless, and he doesn't like the responsibility, or having to answer to Matt all the time. And we've lost some regular customers since he took over. I notice these things now I'm doing the books.'

'Did you ask the laddie about it?'

'He just shrugged it off, so I asked Todd.' She smiled faintly. 'Poor soul, he hated having to talk about Ewan. He squirmed as if I'd been trying to pull a tooth from his jaw.'

'So it's Ewan's fault?'

'He gets impatient easily, and folk who're willing to spend

good money to get what they want don't take kindly to being treated harshly.' Ewan, she thought, was too like his father.

'Are you going to say anything to Matt?'

Kirsty shook her head. 'It would only make him worry, and cause another row. It's Ewan I'll have to—'

The door flew open and Rose burst in, glancing round the empty shop. 'Thank goodness there's nobody here!' She began to haul her jacket off.

'What's wrong?'

'Everything. John's sister's engaged to be married, and her parents are holding a party for her.' She tossed the jacket over the end of a rail. 'And John's asked—'

'Rose,' Kirsty said patiently, 'your jacket belongs in the back room.'

'I'll put it there in a minute. I'm trying to tell you—'

'You know what happened the last time you left it there for a minute.'

Jean's lips twitched at the memory. They had had a sudden rush of customers that day, and a determined woman had tried to buy the jacket, which was expensive and almost brand new. Even worse, she had wanted Kirsty to alter it for her. They had had quite a bother rescuing it.

'Oh, very well!' Rose snatched the jacket from the rail and flounced into the back room.

'She's burstin' tae tell us somethin', poor lassie,' Jean whispered. 'Sometimes you're awful hard on her.'

'I'm just reminding her that she has to follow the rules like the rest of us.'

Rose shot back into the shop, smoothing her black cravat. 'As I was saying,' she took a second to glare at Kirsty, who smiled back, 'John's invited me to be his partner at this party for his sister.'

Jean beamed at her. 'That'll be nice for you.'

'That's what Mamma said when I told her.' Rose paced the shop. 'But it's not nice at all, it's terrible. She wants to help me to choose a gown, and I know that she'll choose some dreadful, silly, fussy thing.'

She looked at them both, her eyes tragic. 'And I can't bear the thought of embarrassing poor John in front of his family and friends after he's been kind enough to invite me.'

'You make it sound as if he's doin' you a favour,' Jean said.

'Of course he is! He knows that nobody else will invite me.'

'Mebbe he just thinks that he'd enjoy your company.'

'Good heavens, no,' Rose said at once. 'We've known each other for years, and believe me, it's kindness and nothing else. And as a kindness to him,' she reverted back to her former panic, 'I have to find something to wear before Mamma does. She's still got this bee in her bonnet about marrying me off, and she's quite certain that if she leaves it to me to find something to wear I'll look a fright and spoil my chances completely – not that there are any.'

'Why not?' Kirsty asked, and Rose gave her a withering look.

'I'm not wife material, you know that. If I ever do marry, it will be to some old and ugly man from mutual despair.' She scanned the nearest rail, then detached a dress and held it against herself. 'What about this?'

'You can't wear something from here,' Jean said, shocked.

'Why not?' asked the girl who had once shuddered at the thought of people wearing second-hand clothes.

'Because it might be recognised. What if the woman it used tae belong tae was at the party?'

'I never thought of that.' Rose put the dress back reluctantly. 'What a bind!' Then, brightening, she said, 'There's that little cream gown I brought back from France. The one Mamma hated because it had no frills or ribbons. D'you remember it, Kirsty?'

'I do, but you'd need something more elaborate than that for an engagement party.'

'I have to think of something!'

'That dark-blue lace your mother refused to let me put over the pink silk,' Kirsty suddenly remembered. 'Is it still in the sewing room?'

'Probably. I haven't dared to set foot in there since . . .' Rose stopped suddenly and gave Kirsty a sidelong look. 'Since that day.'

'P'raps it would do over the cream.'

'I'll bring it in,' Rose said at once. 'And the dress too.'

The cream satin dress, Kirsty recalled as she lifted it from its wrappings the next day, was the very garment that had set off the first quarrel she had witnessed between Rose and her mother. Mrs Hamilton, maintaining that it was far too old for her daughter, had made Kirsty add a frill round the skirt, puffed sleeves, and a bunch of flowers at the low rounded neck. The result had ruined the simple lines of the gown and made Rose look, as she herself said at the time, like a carthorse decked out for a parade.

'I couldn't take all that rubbish off by myself,' she said, stepping out of her skirt in the fitting room. 'I'd probably ruin the material if I tried, and the sewing woman Mamma hired after you left knows nothing.' The cravat was draped over the back of a chair and her long fingers seemed to flow down the front of her high-necked white blouse, leaving buttons undone in their wake. Watching, Kirsty thought of poor Matt, scarcely able to hold a newspaper.

The blouse was whipped off to reveal a round-necked sleeveless petticoat in snowy white nainsook, with narrow lace round the bodice, armholes and hem. Watching Rose reach for the cream gown, Kirsty realised that although the girl was gawky and normally strode about like a man, her bare arms and black-stockinged legs were nicely rounded and her movements, controlled by the size of the little room, were surprisingly graceful as she lifted the gown over her head and let it fall into place down the length of her body.

The shop door bell gave its melodious chime, so unlike the former flat clang, and Jean came into the room. 'How are you gettin' on? Here, Rose – you've got a nice figure.'

'Nice? I'm a beanpole! No hips to speak of,' Rose clamped her hands over her chest, 'and I'm flat as an ironing board.'

'But you've got nice lines,' Jean said, then nodded approval as Kirsty unrolled the blue lace and held it against the gown. 'That'd make a bonny overdress.'

'One that follows the simple lines of the gown itself—'

'With wee sleeves,' said Jean, 'and a rounded neckline, following this one—'

'And just a little fullness in the skirt, and perhaps a short cape of the lace at the back.'

'You'd want a narrow sash—'

'But not too high – mebbe coming down low at the front, to a point—'

'And little crystal beads down the front of the bodice,' Jean said. 'Or wee pearls.'

'Or both.'

Rose was looking from one to another. 'I'd not want anything too fancy,' she warned anxiously.

'Just enough to make the gown a wee bit more . . . interesting,' Kirsty assured her, reaching for the box of pins. 'Hold that lace at her shoulder for me, Jean.'

'There's not much time before the party.'

'I'll manage. I'll work on this dress at home as well as here.'

'You shouldn't have to do shop work at home,' Rose protested.

'I can't give more time to the shop because of Matt being the way he is,' Kirsty said through a mouthful of pins. 'I don't mind taking work home with me. You'll have tae stand still if you don't want a pin stuck in you.'

'D'you not think we should bring in another seamstress?' Rose asked. 'There's enough work now to warrant one. Someone who could do some of the plain work under your instruction, Kirsty.'

'There's Teenie Dunbar in Mary Street,' Jean said thoughtfully. 'She's a widow woman, a respectable sort of body, and good with a needle. She'd be glad of a wee job that'd bring in some money. She could help behind the counter too, when we're busy.'

'But it'd mean another wage,' Kirsty protested, removing the pins. 'And another sewing machine.'

'You have to put money into a business to get it going, just like priming a pump,' Rose told her. 'We'll find the money, John and me. Business hasn't been too bad in our first six months. Ask your friend to come in and have a word with the three of us, Jean.'

Teenie Dunbar, a scarecrow of a woman with anxious brown eyes, was waiting in the shop when Kirsty arrived a few days later.

'I've brought samples of my work.' She delved into a large carpet bag and pulled out several items of clothing, a clean, nail-bitten finger indicating the small neat stitches on this hem and that seam. 'They've all been done by hand.'

'Can you use a machine as well?'

'I can that.'

Kirsty led the woman into the sewing room and found a blouse that needed taking in for the undernourished woman who had bought it. Teenie whipped off her coat, revealing a neat apron over a grey blouse and black skirt, and set to work, spinning the wheel and pumping the treadles until Kirsty feared that she would send the machine whirring free of the screws that held it down.

The woman was accomplished, there was no doubt of that. She was also a dedicated worker; on being told that Jean and Kirsty would have to wait for Rose's arrival before making a decision, she turned down the suggestion that she might like to return in an hour.

'I'm not doin' anythin' else. It'll save the walk home an' back again if I just get on with some work here while I'm waitin',' she said, and off went the sewing machine again.

By the time Rose arrived Teenie had shortened one skirt and was working on a second. It was agreed, on Kirsty's recommendation, that she should be hired for two hours every afternoon.

When Teenie had departed, beaming from ear to ear, the three partners looked at each other.

'Well,' Rose said at last. 'We've just engaged our first employee!'

'Don't start on me,' Ewan said when Kirsty brought up the subject of the fall in orders. 'I've got enough of that with Father naggin' away at me day after day.'

'He only wants to make sure that everything's going well.'

'Everythin's fine. We've got enough work tae keep the two of us busy.'

'But you've not got many orders in hand.'

They were sitting at the table; Kirsty pushed the opened order book over to him, but he only glanced at it and said, 'There's enough, surely.'

'I thought Mr Wilson was supposed to put in an order for another two chairs last month. He said he would when his last order was completed a year ago.'

'Two chairs won't bring in much money.'

'It's better than nothing.'

Ewan shrugged. 'He's forgotten.'

'He's given the order to someone else, Ewan. He told me that when I spoke to him the other day.'

His handsome face flushed. 'So you're spyin' on me now? Goin' round askin' folk why they're not rushin' tae give us their business?'

'I met the man in the street and I reminded him about his promise, that's all.' She hated having to confront him like this, but there was no other way. 'He says he came to see you about the chairs, but you didn't seem to be interested.'

Ewan pushed his chair back abruptly. 'I've got my father

269

goin' on at me, and Todd, and now you. Alex did the right thing when he walked away from this place!'

'Ewan—'

'I've got work tae do,' he said, and slammed out of the back door, almost knocking Mary over as she came in.

'Get out of my way,' he snapped at her, and she stared up at his angry face and said at once, 'It wasn't me that told.'

He swept on without a word and she came into the kitchen, her face wrinkled with concern. 'You know it wasn't me that told you, don't you?' she demanded of her mother.

'Told me what?'

'About seeing Ewan walking in Brodie Park with Beth when he should have been wor—' Mary stopped abruptly, with one hand flying to her mouth. 'Now I've told,' she said between her fingers, her eyes wide with horror. 'Will he want the penny back?'

'What penny?'

'The one he gave me when I promised not to tell. And I didn't, but now—'

'Sit down, Mary.' When her daughter had obediently perched on the edge of a chair, Kirsty said 'Now, tell me what all this is about – you might as well, now,' she added as Mary began to argue, 'since you've already said so much.'

The story came out reluctantly, a few words at a time. Mary, playing in Brodie Park with friends the previous week, had seen Ewan out walking with Beth Laidlaw.

'He was probably in the park alone, and so was she, and they met up with each other.'

'That's what he said, and I pretended that I believed him because he was angry about me seeing him. But he was holding her hand, and you don't do that when you're alone,' now that she had started confessing Mary seemed to be unable to stop, 'so I promised not to tell in case Father gave him another row because he should have been working and not in the park at all and he gave me a penny.' She stopped and sucked in a great lungful of air, then finished, 'And now he might want it back and I've spent it!'

When the little girl had been reassured and sent out again to play, Kirsty closed the order book and put it away. Her mind kept returning to Mary's story as she peeled the potatoes for the evening meal. Ewan had an eye for a pretty girl, but he knew well enough that Beth Laidlaw was promised to Todd. They must have met by accident, she decided, and Mary was confused as to what she'd actually seen.

But even so, why had Ewan been walking in Brodie Park when he should have been at work?

27

Thanks to Teenie, who freed Kirsty by taking over most of the alterations, Rose's dress was completed a few days before the party. She gasped as she looked at herself in the full-length mirror.

'It's beautiful!'

Kirsty felt her mouth curve in a satisfied smile as she saw how well the dress and its wearer complemented each other. There were no ribbons, no flowers, no frills. The cream satin underdress showed as a pearly glow through the blue lace overdress, which followed the lines of Rose's long, slim body. A slightly gathered bodice led the eye down to a skirt just full enough to allow for easy movement, with a slight flare at the bottom, where Kirsty had inserted a deep panel of flower-patterned lace in the same shade of blue. Flowered panels had also been inserted at each side of the bodice, and seed pearls scattered over the flowers echoed the undergown's pearly sheen.

'I must let Jean see it.' Rose made for the main shop.

'There might be a customer in.'

'Then we'll give them a treat.' But the shop was empty,

giving Rose room to parade up and down while the other three watched.

'You're striding out too much,' Kirsty said. 'Take smaller steps. That's better.' The small steps made Rose look as though she was gliding across the floor, and set the dress floating easily around her feet.

'It feels so . . . free!' She spun round, and the flare at the bottom of the skirt swung out, then fell back. 'It's as if I'm not wearing any clothes at all!' she exulted, and Teenie blushed.

'Long gloves – dark blue, not cream,' Kirsty suggested. 'And a necklace round your throat.'

Jean disagreed. 'A blue velvet ribbon'd be better. She's got bonny shoulders – a ribbon'd show them off better.'

'You're right.'

'Mamma has a nice sapphire brooch I could fasten the ribbon with – and earrings to match,' Rose said eagerly, caught up in the excitement of the moment. 'I'm sure she'd lend them to me.'

'Yer hair's too tight,' Teenie put in. 'Here.' She whisked the girl back into the fitting room and sat her down in front of the mirror. 'Let me have a try at it. I used tae be a lady's maid,' she added, her fingers already busy with the grips and combs that strained Rose's hair back from her face. 'There now.'

The last grip came out and a cascade of reddish-brown hair tumbled down to fall softly about Rose's shoulders. It curtained both sides of her face, softening the strong bony features. All at once she didn't look much older than Caitlin.

'It's a sin tae treat bonny hair so badly, like tyin' a dog up an' never lettin' it run free.'

'I don't like my hair loose.'

'At least ye could put it up in a more kindly way,' Teenie lectured, no longer in awe of the girl and her money now that she was able to use some of her own skills. 'Someb'dy find me a hairbrush.'

Five minutes later her nimble fingers had swept Rose's hair into a soft, full roll framing her face then sweeping back into a single thick plait that sat snugly at the nape of her neck.

'Oh, Rose, you look lovely,' Jean said, awed, while Teenie studied her own handiwork critically from all sides, then nodded.

'Yer maid'll need tae use pads tae get the right fullness, but that's the general idea. Let's see ye walkin' up and down again.'

The overall effect was much improved, but once again Rose had broken into her usual long stride. They all tried to show her the right way, mincing up and down the empty shop and scattering each time a customer came in, but it didn't work.

'You're ruinin' the line of the dress,' Jean lamented.

'I can't help it – it's the way I've always walked. I'll never remember to take short steps!'

'We could mebbe tie each end of a ribbon round her knees under the dress so's she can't take long steps,' Teenie suggested.

'And what if I forget about it and try to step out? I'd fall over!'

'Your Caitlin moves like a princess, Kirsty,' Jean said. 'It's half-day tomorrow – d'you think she'd mebbe come in and teach Rose the right way of it?'

*

274

Caitlin did indeed move well, Kirsty realised as she watched her daughter walk easily up and down the shop on the following afternoon, hand in hand with Rose so that she could hold the older girl back each time she tried to stride ahead.

'I feel like a gun dog being trained to walk to heel,' Rose said, starting to giggle.

'Now try it on your own.' Caitlin stood back, watching. 'You're stepping out again.'

'It's no use, I'll never get it right.'

'Music,' Caitlin said suddenly. 'If you could learn to walk to music, you could sing it to yourself in your head.'

'"The Man Who Broke the Bank at Monte Carlo",' Teenie said at once. 'I like that one.'

Caitlin shook her head. 'That'd just encourage her to stride.' She thought for a minute, then suggested, '"Two Lovely Black Eyes". Come on.'

She seized Rose's hand again and then started to walk her up and down, singing. The others joined in. 'Two lovely black eyes, oh, what a surprise . . .' they carolled, Jean sweeping Teenie into a dance around the room.

The song seemed to do the trick. Within ten minutes Rose was gliding up and down on her own, the lace overskirt flaring out neatly with each step.

Rose beamed at them all. 'It's all going to work, thanks to you. You're the best friends anyone could ever have, and I'm lucky to have found you. And never mind the maid, Teenie. If I get the pads, will you come to the house to do my hair for me on the night?'

'Your house? I couldnae do that!'

'Yes you could – you must, Teenie!' Rose took the woman's work-worn hands in hers. 'If you don't, Mamma will get her maid to do it, and she's sure to get it wrong. Please! Kirsty knows the house; she'll come with you,' she added as Teenie began to shake her head. 'Won't you, Kirsty?'

The thought of going back into the Hamilton house made Kirsty's knees feel weak, but Rose's eyes were begging her to agree. Against her own will, Kirsty nodded.

'Oh, thank you! I'll send the new car for you,' Rose promised, and Teenie almost fell apart again.

'I couldnae go in one of those things – don't make me do that! I'd be much happier walking on my own two feet!'

'Rose is nice,' Caitlin said as she and her mother walked home. 'Nicer than I expected. It just goes to show, moneyed folk can be just as friendly as anyone else when they put their minds to it.'

Kirsty sent word ahead to Bessie, the Hamilton's cook, and she and Teenie were given a warm welcome when they arrived in the big kitchen. Teenie, clasping a worn bag holding all that she needed and looking anxiously back over her shoulder at Kirsty, was led off to Rose's room by a maid, while Bessie, waving to one of the two comfortable armchairs in the room, said, 'Sit yerself down and tell me what ye've done tae tame Miss Rose.'

The chair was deep and soft and comfortable. 'You should try to get a sight of her in her party gown tonight,' Kirsty told the cook as she sank into its welcoming depths. 'She's far prettier than she allows herself to be. And she's done well by the shop. She's not afraid to do her share of the work.'

Bessie chuckled. 'Ye should have heard the rows when she first came up with the idea. Her and her parents went at it hammer and tongs, then finally the master gave in and said that Miss Rose could do whatever she wanted as long as she took the consequences – only he put it more strongly than that. Between ourselves, Kirsty, I think that lassie's the one he likes the best, because she's got more backbone in her than the other two. She was his mother's favourite an' all.'

'She was a lovely lady – a real gentlewoman.' Kirsty thought of her first employer with fondness. Slender and elegant, her back as straight as a stair rod, the woman had been firm but fair with her servants and had earned and held their respect and loyalty.

'She was that. Not in the least like that . . .' Bessie glanced round to see if any of her staff were within listening distance, then elaborately mouthed, 'that bitch,' before reverting to her usual speaking voice. 'As I was sayin', old Mrs Hamilton aye had a soft spot for Miss Rose when she was a bairn. That's why she left money in trust for the lassie – an' that caused quite a stramash when the will was read, I can tell ye. This Mrs Hamilton and her older daughters made such a fuss, but Mr Brodie – that's Mr John's father – said there was nothing they could do but accept it.' She gave a sudden bellow of laughter. 'I cannae tell ye how pleased I was when I heard what she'd decided tae dae with it. Her grandmother would've approved.'

'I'm not so sure about that – but I'm glad it happened, for my sake as well as Jean's.'

'It's worth all the money if it keeps Miss Rose happy, I can tell ye.'

Although it was a warm evening and the kitchen was hot after a day's cooking, Bessie, who felt the cold keenly, always had a fire going in the grate. Now she turned her skirt back to let her knees have the good of it. 'The mistress must have

277

bought out Paisley's entire stock of smelling salts, and at one point she took tae her bed and said she wasnae gettin' out of it until Miss Rose saw sense. That was a nice few days for us, for it meant she couldnae come down here and make a nuisance of herself. But she soon got tired of bein' an invalid – and she soon saw that she wasnae goin' tae win that way.'

'Has she accepted it?'

'No' entirely, but she's havin' tae live with it. Young Mr Brodie bein' involved helps, for the mistress is very friendly with his mother, and she's got faith in him. She was fair excited about him askin' Miss Rose tae this party. Now, how's that poor man of yours?'

'No better, Bessie. Worse, if anything. He scarcely comes downstairs at all now.'

'Poor soul. I've got some things for ye tae take home tae him.' Bessie nodded at a bag on the table.

'You can't—'

'Now don't start talkin' with yer conscience instead of yer tongue again, Kirsty Lennox! It's just a wee mouthful here and a wee mouthful there. Ye'd not grudge an invalid a few tasty bites, would ye?'

Kirsty smiled at her old friend. 'You've got a good heart, Bessie.'

'Not a bit of it! There's a cake I baked with my own hands too. It must be hard tae see yer man in a state like that.'

'It is. I think the fight went out of him when Alex left.'

The cook's eyebrows shot up. 'Yer eldest? He's away from home?'

Kirsty had forgotten that Bessie knew nothing of what had been happening. 'Alex got the chance of a good job in

278

Glasgow,' she said casually. 'He's been gone four months now.'

'Ye'll miss him, but I suppose the business is a bit wee for him and his brother. An' how're the lassies? Is Caitlin growin' up tae be a beauty like I said she would?'

In no time at all Teenie was back, flushed and fluttery and too excited to bother with a cup of tea. After the warmth of the kitchen it was pleasant to walk down the tree-lined driveway in the cool evening air.

Now that her ordeal was over, Teenie chattered like a parrot all the way back to the town. 'Mind Rose said her mother had a sapphire brooch she could use? I've never seen anythin' like it. The gems sparkled that much they could have put yer eyes out. It looked just right on a blue velvet ribbon, and the earrings were dangly. She's got just the right neck for them, long and slim.'

'You didn't have any trouble doing her hair?'

Teenie shivered. 'There was this woman that turned out tae be Mrs Hamilton's maid fussin' round the place all the time and givin' me black looks. Rose told her more than once that she could go, but she'd not budge – just kept makin' excuses about things she was doin' for the lassie. She was fair eaten up wi' jealousy because it was me doin' Rose's hair and not her. Oh – and ye should have seen the look she gave me when I called Rose by her name the way we do in the shop, without the "Miss" in front of it. I just gave her a nice smile back, and she flounced her head in the air and looked as if she'd been suckin' on a lemon.'

'Did you see Mrs Hamilton herself?'

'A fat woman that looks as if someone had let off a bad smell right under her nose? She came in when I was nearly

finished and said, "Not like you at all, Rose."' Teenie did a
good job of mimicking Mrs Hamilton. 'So Rose says, "I
thought that was the idea, Mamma," and Mrs Hamilton went
red. Then Rose made me wait behind tae see how she looked
in the dress, and – oh, Kirsty, she was a picture!'

'What did her mother say?'

'Her eyes nearly came out her head. She said, "Very
nice, Rose," and Rose said, "Thank you, Mamma," as if
butter wouldnae melt in her mouth. Then when her ma
turned her back Rose winked at me in the mirror and that
snide maid saw it and nearly swallowed her own teeth. And
Rose gave me a pound note for my trouble – imagine, a
pound!' Teenie said as they turned out of the gates and onto
the road. She halted and began to fish in her large bag.
'That's ten shillin' for me and ten shillin' for you, when I
get it changed.'

'You keep it, Teenie; you earned it.'

'But you walked there and back with me. I'd never have
had the courage without you.'

'Even so, I spent a nice hour with an old friend, and I'll
not take a penny of – what's amiss?' Kirsty asked, startled, as
Teenie, who had found the note and was smoothing it out
carefully, gave a sudden scream.

'Kirsty – it's five pounds, not one!'

'That shows how pleased Rose was with her hair.'

'But – but . . .' The woman was gabbling, her agitated
hands screwing up the note she had just smoothed out. 'It's
too much!'

'It's what she wanted to give you. Put it in your purse
before you tear it.'

'But you made that bonny dress for her—'

'And I was well paid for it,' Kirsty assured her. 'So we're all happy.'

'Happy?' Tears stood out in Teenie's eyes. 'I've never had so much money in my life!'

They didn't expect to see Rose the next day, but she swept in at her usual time, looking radiant. Her hair was no longer strained back tightly; instead she had piled it on top of her head in a soft bun, similar to the style Kirsty had adopted.

'It was the best party I've ever attended, and everyone admired my gown – and my hair. John's eyes almost fell out of his head when he first saw me, and even Mamma thought I looked passable for the first time in my life. Several of the ladies asked where I had had the dress made.'

'What did ye tell them?' Teenie asked.

'The truth, of course.' Rose gave a gurgle of amusement. 'It caused quite a stir. I'm surprised your ears weren't burning, Kirsty, for your name was being passed around quite considerably.'

'What did your mother say to you telling the truth?' Kirsty was half amused and half horrified.

'She didn't care for it, but she herself raised me to be honest, so she couldn't object.' Rose giggled again. 'I overheard her tell one friend that she had employed you at one time, and found you to be a skilled dressmaker.'

'And you managed to keep yourself from striding out?'

'Oh yes. Your Caitlin's a genius, Kirsty. That song worked very well, though I haven't been able to get it out of my mind since!' Rose broke into 'Two Lovely Black Eyes', sweeping Teenie into a waltz round the empty shop. Then, sobering for a moment, she said, 'I was thinking when I looked at the ladies gathered there from all round the town, we should be spreading our net and collecting used clothes from other districts. We've got enough room for them now, and two seamstresses.'

'You were thinking about that while you were enjoying yourself at a party?' Kirsty asked, and Rose's vivid blue eyes sparkled at her.

'Why not? I'm a businesswoman now. Anyone object to the idea? No? Then I'll draw up a notice asking for collectors and put it in the window.'

28

In September Beth Laidlaw's father decided that since Beth and Todd still hadn't found a place to live, they should share his flat above the tobacconist's shop.

'It means that we'll be gettin' married at long last,' Todd told Kirsty exultantly. 'And I'll be just across the road from my work.'

'I didn't think Beth would want to stay in her own home, since she's turned down all the other tenement flats you've found.'

'She'd as soon have somewhere with her own front and back door,' he agreed, 'but that'll come one day.'

Todd seemed to be the only one who approved of the plan. 'The man's clean daft, agreein' tae it,' Jean said flatly. 'Andra Laidlaw's never done somethin' for nothin' in his life – this'll be him makin' sure there's someone there tae look after him in his old age.'

'I don't see Beth doing that.'

'She's probably got little choice. From what I hear, Andra's romised that if she stays with him she'll inherit the shop when he goes, instead of havin' tae share it with her sister that

283

lives in Glasgow. That'd be enough tae bring her tae heel, for she's got his love of money.' Jean sniffed and shook her head. 'Her and Todd'll pay a heavy price for the inheritance, bein' at that old miser's beck and call for as long as he lives. The day might come when she'll wish she'd not done so much hummin' and hawin' and turnin' her nose up at all those places Todd found.'

'D'you think Todd knows what he's letting himself in for?' Caitlin asked that evening. 'I'd not want to live with Mr Laidlaw. Have you seen the way he counts out the money when you pay for something?'

'I have.' Kirsty hated it when the man was in the shop. He always counted her money out carefully at least twice before tucking it tenderly into the till, as though suspecting her of trying to cheat him.

'You can see the pain on the man's face if he has to give you change.' Caitlin shivered. 'I don't know how Todd can think of living in the same house as him.'

'It's because the man knows which side his bread's buttered on,' Ewan broke in. 'He'll do very well for himself, marryin' a woman who'll have her own wee business one day.'

'That's nonsense,' Kirsty said. 'All Todd wants is to be married to Beth. Goodness knows they've been engaged long enough.'

'Only because he's a fool. A lassie like Beth needs a man who'd just make the decisions and tell her about them afterwards. Todd's not got the first idea of how tae treat women.'

'And I suppose you have,' Caitlin jeered, and he gave her a long cool look.

'I certainly know a lot more about them than the likes o

Todd Paget. He's just a carthorse without a brain between his ears.'

'He is not,' Mary flared. She was devoted to Todd, who always had time to talk to her when they met. 'He's the nicest person I know – nicer than you!'

Ewan laughed and reached out to pull the ribbon from her long brown hair, something that he knew infuriated his little sister. 'You're a trustin' wee soul, aren't you? Goodness knows what you'll end up walkin' down the aisle with.'

'That's enough!' Kirsty caught at Mary's arm as the little girl flew at Ewan. 'Stand still, Mary, and I'll put your ribbon back in. And you should have more respect for Todd,' she added to Ewan as Mary, scowling, snatched the ribbon from her half-brother and handed it over. 'He does a grand job in that workshop. I don't know where we'd be without him.'

Ewan got out of Matt's chair and tossed Matt's newspaper down on the floor. 'He's certainly not lost for admirers in this family,' he muttered, then grabbed his jacket from the nail on the back of the door and went out.

'There.' Kirsty gave the ribbon a final tweak and patted Mary's arm. 'As good as new.' As she picked up the newspaper and folded it, she fretted about Ewan. Matt had been convinced that once Alex was out of the way his own son would enjoy taking control of the workshop. Instead Ewan had made no secret of his boredom and his resentment of the way Alex had, as he saw it, escaped from the family business.

Matt, who knew nothing of the way Ewan's lack of interest was beginning to affect the order book and the ledgers, and who would never know, if Kirsty could help it, had recently begun to depend more on Todd, summoning him for consultations rather than Ewan.

Perversely, Ewan resented his father's growing dependence on the journeyman and seemed to blame Todd for it. When it was time for the midday meal, they arrived in the kitchen separately and kept their eyes on their plates, not looking at or speaking to each other, their mutual dislike thickening the air. The situation had become so fraught that when Todd had found a lame reason for spending the midday break in the workshop again Kirsty had accepted it without protest.

Only the other day, going to ask if Todd would help Matt to get to the bathroom, she had heard the two of them in the workshop, voices raised in anger. Silence had fallen as soon as she put her hand to the door latch, and when she went in both men were busy at opposite ends of the shop. She was convinced, though, that they had sprung apart when they had heard her at the door and that she had unwittingly prevented a violent confrontation.

There was nobody to confide in. She didn't want Matt worrying about something he couldn't control, and she was afraid that if he did get to hear of it he would solve the matter by dismissing Todd. Without him, she was convinced that the business would collapse within weeks.

When she tried to find out the truth of the situation from Todd, he was evasive and so uncomfortable with her questions that she gave up. She could only watch, and wonder and worry.

She thought, briefly, of confiding her fears in one of her letters to Alex, then discarded the idea, realising that it was no longer his concern and that he probably had enough on his hands forging a relationship with his real father and establishing himself in the new business.

*

The wedding dress came into the shop a few weeks later, a great billowing mass of oyster satin and corded silk with knots of orange blossom scattered over the vast skirt. Rose spent some time wrestling it onto Aggie, the dressmaker's dummy, who had been rescued from her precarious existence on the pavement and given her own corner in the front shop.

'It's probably the sort of gown my mamma might have worn. Isn't it frightful?' She lifted a great armful of satin train, then let it fall. 'Such a weight to drag around.'

'There would have been several pageboys carrying the train.' Teenie stroked the skirt. 'I wonder what happened tae the bride it was made for?'

'She's probably a grandmother by now. We'll never be able to sell this,' Rose said dismissively. 'We might as well let the ragman have it.'

Teenie was shocked. 'But it's beautiful material!'

'It's served its purpose – and lain in a trunk for about thirty years,' Rose scoffed. 'Nobody round here's going to want it.'

'Beth Laidlaw will be looking for a wedding gown,' Kirsty said thoughtfully. 'She'd look lovely in something like this.'

'You'd need to do a lot of work on it, Kirsty,' Jean warned. 'Why go tae all that bother for a lassie that'd pass you in the street without a glance if the mood took her?'

'I'd not be doing it for Beth, I'd be doing it for Todd.' Kirsty could imagine the pride on the journeyman's face as he saw Beth come up the aisle in a beautiful gown like this. 'It could be my wedding gift to them both.'

Beth came to the house reluctantly, but her green eyes filled with avarice when she saw the gown Kirsty had brought from the shop. It fitted her slim figure almost perfectly, and the ivory satin emphasised her smooth creamy skin. Studying herself in the long mirror Kirsty had brought down from the bedroom, the girl became almost animated.

'None of my friends has ever had such a bonny gown.' She moved a few graceful steps about the room, twisting her head so that she could continue to watch her mirrored reflection.

Kirsty studied gown and wearer from all angles. 'The train and the bustle will have to go, of course. I'll use some of the material to make a back panel with a wee train to it, and I'll take away some of the fullness in the sleeves and use the extra lace from the skirt to make a higher neckline.'

'Will that not spoil the dress?'

Kirsty shook her head. 'Its lines could be seen better without all the frills and fuss.'

Beth's cheeks glowed and her eyes sparkled. 'I cannae – can't,' she corrected herself swiftly, 'wait to see folk's faces when they see me in this!'

It wasn't until the girl had gone and Kirsty was carefully wrapping the dress in an old linen sheet to keep it safe from harm that she realised that not once, in all her prattling about how much she would be envied for her fine wedding gown, had Beth made any reference to what Todd might think of it.

Beth's dress took up all the spare time Kirsty had. There was so much of it that she took her old sewing machine into the parlour rather than having to carry the great bulk of the dress from room to room. Caitlin helped in the evenings. Together they stripped the bustle and train away and

288

removed the elaborate bows on the bodice and the knots of orange blossom scattered over the skirt.

'It looks prettier already,' Caitlin said as they surveyed the result. 'A girl with Beth's looks doesn't need all those additions.' She rescued the train from Mary, who had wrapped it around her shoulders and was walking about the little floor space left, her head twisted back over her shoulder to admire the great stretch of satin trailing behind. 'Don't spoil that; we'll be able to make something else out of it.'

'My dolly wants a wedding dress.'

'She'll get one, when I've got the time,' Caitlin promised. Ever since Mary's babyhood, Caitlin had made doll's clothes for her from scraps that Kirsty didn't need.

'I thought I'd take this deep lace frill off the skirt altogether and gather it into a high neck using some of the material I'll take from the sleeves. It'd look better than this round neck.'

Caitlin nodded. 'Much better.'

Once the gown had been stripped of all its embellishments it was easier to work with. Rather than ask Beth to come in to try it on as it went through the various stages of alteration, Kirsty used Caitlin, who was about Beth's height and just as slender. For the final fitting before Beth herself was invited back to the house, Caitlin brushed out her hair, normally hanging down her back in a single plait, and pinned it up out of the way before slipping into the gown.

Kirsty fastened the row of tiny buttons that ran up the length of the spine and hooked the high, severe satin collar, then shifted the sewing machine to one side so that Caitlin could move about.

'You're like a fairy princess!' she heard Mary say in awe.

Caitlin laughed. 'What d'you think of it, Mam?'

Kirsty glanced up, then stared. 'You look beautiful!'

'It's worked out well, hasn't it?' Caitlin agreed, all her attention on the dress. She was oblivious to the picture she herself made with her glowing auburn hair piled on top of her head and her turquoise eyes sparkling. 'It feels grand, too.' She moved a few steps, and the skirt seemed to flow around her. 'It's just a wee bit too long. She might trip over the hem when she's walking into the church.'

'I'll finish off the hem when Beth herself tries it on. Turn round and I'll unfasten the buttons.'

Studying herself in the mirror, Caitlin said almost wistfully, 'Beth's lucky, marrying in such a lovely gown.'

Kirsty swallowed the lump in her throat and wondered what on earth she'd be like when Caitlin's own wedding day arrived. 'I'll see that you get one just as nice when your turn comes,' she promised.

Caitlin flashed a wide smile at her over her shoulder. 'Oh, that'll not be for a while yet,' she said.

Two weeks before the date set for the wedding, Beth came to the house for another fitting. Her eyes widened when she saw the dress spread out over an armchair, and she gasped when she put it on. 'It's the most beautiful gown I've ever seen!'

'You look lovely in it.' But not, Kirsty thought, as lovely as Caitlin had. She had a fresh innocence that complemented the gown, whereas Beth's beauty was already slightly flawed by the discontent round her mouth and a hardness in her green eyes. 'I've still to get the hem right. I'll fetch a stool for you to stand on.'

Lifting the skirt delicately in both hands, Beth followed her. 'It'll save you bringing the stool through,' she said, looking openly about the kitchen while Kirsty brought the stool from the corner and moved one of the armchairs back to make room.

Glancing at her, Kirsty saw the girl's lip curl contemptuously as she took in the worn chenille table cover, the old chairs set round the table, the shabby rug before the grate. She knew fine and well that Beth was thinking of the way she herself would have furnished the room if she had achieved her ambition and become its mistress.

'Can you step up here?' she asked levelly, picking up the old tobacco tin she kept her pins in. As she worked, Beth kept up a constant chatter about the wedding gifts she and Todd had already received and those she still hoped to get. Kirsty had pinned up a third of the hem, shuffling uncomfortably round the stool on her knees, when the door burst open and Ewan came in.

'Mam, show me that order—' He stopped suddenly. Peering round folds of oyster satin, Kirsty saw him framed in the doorway, motionless, staring at Beth. After her first surprised squeak, and a sudden start that almost toppled her from the stool, she too was as still as a statue.

Kirsty tried to speak, and almost swallowed the pins between her lips. She spat them into her palm and scrambled to her feet. 'Ewan, did you have to come bursting in like a – a bull in a china shop?'

He shut his mouth, swallowed, then said, 'I didnae know – I wanted to see Rab Leitch's order.'

'No harm done,' Kirsty said as she fetched the book from its drawer. 'It's the bridegroom that's not supposed to see the bride in her wedding dress. Not a word to Todd, mind.' She leafed through the book. 'This is the order you want.'

'What?'

'Rab Leitch's order. You can take the book to the workshop, but don't let it get dirty.'

'I'll do that.' He turned to go, then looked back at the girl on the stool. 'I'm sorry if I frightened you, Beth.'

'D'you like the gown?' she asked, preening, and he ran his tongue round his lips before saying huskily, 'Aye. It's . . . very grand.'

'Mind now,' Kirsty called after him as he left, 'not a whisper about it to Todd.'

To Kirsty's relief, Beth's nonstop chatter dried up after Ewan had gone. When the hem was pinned, she hurried back into the parlour to change into her own clothes.

'I'll have it ready by Sunday,' Kirsty said, and the girl nodded. She looked pale, and there was a worried frown between her well-shaped eyebrows.

'Are you all right?'

'I'm fine,' Beth said swiftly.

'Did Ewan upset you, bursting in like that?'

Beth shook her head. 'I'm just in a hurry to get back to the shop. My father doesn't like being behind the counter.'

Going back into the parlour to cover the dress with its protective sheet, Kirsty thought uneasily about the way Ewan had gaped at Beth in her finery, and the way Beth had gone quiet afterwards. It occurred to her that it was just as well that Todd was finally about to claim his bride.

29

Someone was banging on the street door, an ominous pounding that reverberated through the house and sounded like an attempt to smash through the panels. Kirsty, setting the table for breakfast, let a handful of cutlery clatter to its surface, her mouth dry and her heart fluttering at the urgency of the racket.

'I'm coming!' she called as she hurried through the hall, but the words either weren't heard or weren't heeded, for the pounding continued until her trembling fingers managed to raise the latch.

'Where is he?' Todd Paget demanded to know, bursting into the hall, almost knocking her down.

'Who?'

'Ewan – who else?' His face was distorted with rage.

He pushed her aside and started for the kitchen, then swung round when she said, 'He's not up yet. It's Sunday – he always lies abed on a Sunday.'

'Is he in the house at all? Have ye seen him?'

'Of course he's in the house. Where else would he—'

He was already halfway up the stairs, taking them two at a

293

time. As she followed she heard him say, 'Where's Ewan's room?' and arrived in the upper corridor in time to see him throw the door open so violently that it banged against the small chest of drawers behind it. Caitlin and Mary, still in their nightclothes, were huddled together at their own door, Caitlin white as a sheet, Mary dissolving into frightened tears.

'Mam, what's happening?'

'Take Mary into the room and shut the door, Caitlin. Wait there till I come to you.' Kirsty could hear Matt calling from the front bedroom, but she went on past the door. For once, he would have to wait. Todd must have taken some sort of seizure, she thought in a panic. She had to get him downstairs and out of the house and away from her family.

He erupted from the room just as she reached it, almost knocking her down for the second time. Only his hands, fastening hard on her upper arms, saved her from falling to the floor.

'Where is he?' He shook her, his face, suffused with blood, close to hers.

'He's not in his room?'

'See for yersel'.' He thrust her through the door. It was true – Ewan wasn't in bed after all. He hadn't risen early, because the bed was still made. She pulled back the curtain that shut off one corner as a wardrobe, then looked through the little chest of drawers while Todd watched, filling the doorway with his body and the entire house with his smouldering rage.

'His things are all gone.' She stared at the journeyman, trying to make sense of the situation.

'When did ye last see him?'

'Last night, when he came in late and went to his bed.' Pretended to go to his bed, she thought, looking again at the smooth coverlet, the plumped pillow. He must have packed his clothes and crept out once the rest of the household was asleep. 'But why—?' she began, then, sharply, 'How did you know?'

'Beth's gone too.'

'Beth?' For a matter of seconds, Kirsty couldn't think why Todd should link his fiancée with her stepson; then the truth hit her, and she had to sit down suddenly on the bed. 'Beth and Ewan?'

'Ye didnae know?'

She shook her head, but already her mind was filling with pictures – Ewan lounging against the tobacconist's counter, Ewan's expression a few days earlier after he burst into the kitchen and saw Beth standing there in her wedding gown, Beth's sudden silence afterwards. She remembered Mary, too, calling after Ewan, 'I didn't tell!'

Todd was still speaking, his hands running through his hair, over his face, continually moving as if they couldn't, daren't, be still for one second. 'I guessed about him – the things he said, the sly wee glances at me, the grins when he thought I wasnae lookin'. He thought I hadnae the wit tae know what he thought of me, but just because I'm easy-goin' it doesnae mean I'm daft!' He slammed one fist hard against the doorframe, oblivious to pain. 'I faced him about it – I warned him that I'd kill him if I ever got proof of anythin'.'

'Did Beth . . . was she—?'

'Beth flirts with every man she sees,' Todd said bluntly. She swore tae me it was never anythin' more than that, an' believed her. I thought with us gettin' wed at last that there

295

was nothin' tae fear. But I was wrong!' Again his fist thudded at the frame. 'Where d'ye think they might have gone?' he demanded of her.

'I don't know.'

'Because it's not over,' Todd said thickly. 'I'm goin' tae find them, and I'm goin' tae kill him for this!' Suddenly he turned and went storming along the corridor and down the stairs. By the time Kirsty was halfway down to the hall, he had gone, slamming the door hard behind him.

The smell of burning porridge was beginning to seep into the hall from behind the closed kitchen door. Mary was screaming with fear now, and Matt was bellowing, demanding to know what was happening. 'I'm coming!' Kirsty shouted for the second time that morning, and took time to hurry into the smoke-filled kitchen and heave the burning pot out into the yard. Back in the kitchen she halted and took down the old ginger jar from the mantel shelf. She always kept some emergency money in there, but now it was empty.

Upstairs, she put her head into the girls' room, where Caitlin was hurriedly dressing herself and Mary was huddled on her bed, curled into a ball, rocking herself to and fro, the screams pouring from her.

'Take her downstairs, Caitlin, and try to quiet her while I see to your father. It's Ewan and Beth,' she added quickly to the girl's questioning face. 'It seems that they've run away together.'

Matt had got out of bed and was standing clutching the bedhead, trying to find the courage to attempt the few steps across the linoleum to the door. 'A body could die in here and still never get help,' he started raging as soon as Kirsty went in. 'Is the house on fire? Is it the workshop? For God' sake, woman, will ye tell me what's goin' on? Who was that bangin' at the door and chargin' about the house?'

She pushed him back onto the bed and sat beside him, taking his hand in hers. 'It was Todd. He's gone now.'

'Todd Paget? Right, that's the end of it — he'll not ever work for me again after makin' all that stramash an' frightenin' the lives out of us.'

'Matt, he came about Ewan.'

He stopped his blustering at once, the colour draining from his face. 'Has he been hurt? Is he—?'

'He's fine, as far as I know. He's gone, and so has Beth Laidlaw. That's why Todd was so upset.'

He stared at her, the angry colour draining from his face as he took the words in. 'Ye mean . . . our Ewan's run away with Todd's woman?'

'It looks as if he's done just that.' For a moment she thought that he was going to collapse completely. He turned from pale to a sickly grey colour, and she ran to fetch the bottle of sal volatile that she kept in one of the two smaller drawers in the tallboy. He pushed her away when she unstoppered the bottle and tried to hold it under his nose.

'Get that filthy stuff away from me,' he said, his voice weak and thready. 'And for pity's sake bring out the chamber pot before I wet this bed.'

Kirsty felt as though she was living through a nightmare.

Ewan hadn't left so much as a note, and nobody seemed to know where he and Beth might be. When she went down to the workshop on the following morning hoping against hope that Todd might be there, the place was empty, the tools stacked neatly where they had been left on Saturday, a small table abandoned half finished in the middle of the floor.

At the flat where Todd lived with his sister and her family the door was opened by a woman who bore a striking resemblance to him. She had his thick brown hair and grey eyes set in a face that, like his, was naturally cheerful, though on that day it was drawn. A flicker of a smile appeared when Kirsty introduced herself.

'Todd's talked a lot about you and your family, Mrs Lennox. I'm his sister, Marion Lang.' Then she asked hopefully, 'Did he turn up for work today?'

'No, I thought he might be here.'

'Ye'd best come in,' Marion said. 'Let the lady in the door, Tommy,' she added to the toddler clinging to her skirt, sweeping him up and stepping back to let Kirsty pass. The door opened into a fair-sized kitchen, warm and comfortable and spotlessly clean. A little girl slightly older than Tommy played with a kitten on the rug before the grate.

'These are my two youngest.' She put the little boy down. 'Ella, take Tommy and Tinker intae the bedroom tae play, there's a good lassie. Sit yourself down, Mrs Lennox. You'll have some tea?'

When Kirsty explained that she had very little time, Marion seated herself opposite and said, low voiced, 'Todd's not been home all night and I'm worried out of my mind about him. I thought he might have gone tae work but Archie – that's my man – said he didnae think so.'

'You've no idea where he might be?'

'Archie went round all his friends last night, and one of them says Todd was with him till mid-evening, then he left. He'd had a fair bit tae drink by then, and that's not like Todd at all. I've never once seen him the worse for drink.'

'D'you think he's out looking for Beth and Ewan?'

'That's what I'm afraid of,' Marion admitted. 'Normally I'd say that he'd never hurt a fly, but this time . . .' She had taken up some knitting when she sat down; now she glanced at it and saw that several stitches had slipped off one of the needles. 'He worships Beth. I've never seen him as happy as he was when she agreed about the two of them stayin' with her father. Not that I was happy about him havin' tae live under old Mr Laidlaw's roof, but Todd was all for it, for it meant bein' married tae Beth at long last.'

'What happened? Todd was in such a state when he came to the house that I couldn't get any sense out of him.'

Marion gave up her attempt to salvage the dropped stitches and put the needles aside. 'He was supposed tae see Beth on Saturday night as he usually did, but she sent word round that her father was poorly and she was stayin' in tae see tae him. Then on Sunday mornin' when he went round as usual tae walk with her tae the church for the mornin' service he found Mr Laidlaw in a fine takin' because he'd got up and found the lassie gone.'

'He'd not been ill at all?'

'Not a bit of it. Beth had gone out as usual and let him think she was with Todd. She came back and went to her bed just like any other Saturday, but she must have slipped out when he was asleep.'

'They'd planned it all, then.'

Marion nodded. 'All Beth's clothes were gone, and some jewellery belongin' tae her grandma and her ma that was tae go tae her on her marriage. And some money, seemingly, that Mr Laidlaw'd put by for the weddin' too. She must have packed her clothes and hidden them in the shop ready tae pick up on her way out. They'll likely have caught the train tae Glasgow. They could be anywhere by now.' The woman got up and went to the window, peering out into the street below. 'I just wish I knew where our Todd was. I'm sorry he's let ye down, Mrs Lennox, it's not like him at all.'

'It's us that have let him down by the sound of it.'

'Folk cannae be held responsible for what their grown weans do. If he'd just come back, so's I know he's all right.' Marion Lang turned back to the room with a shamefaced smile. 'Here's me sayin' folk cannae be responsible for other folk, and I'm frettin' about Todd as if he was one of my own weans.'

'Have you gone to the police office? They might be able to help you to find him.'

'We cannae do that,' Marion said at once. 'What if he's found the pair of them and—' She broke off abruptly, then said, 'If he's done somethin' wrong, even out of grief, he might end up in trouble. I'd not want tae be the one tae bring him tae the law's attention in the first place.'

Kirsty got up. 'I must go, my husband's not well. You'll let me know when he turns up? Just so that I know he's all right?'

'I will that. And I'm sorry,' the woman said as she opened the door, 'for all yer own trouble, Mrs Lennox.'

To Kirsty's surprise, the tobacconist's shop was open, and Mr Laidlaw, looking even more pinched and skeletal than usual, was behind the counter.

'Ye can just get out of my shop,' he said as soon as Kirsty went in, 'for I'll no' serve ye.'

'I'm not here for tobacco, Mr Laidlaw, I came to ask how you are.'

'How I am? How d'ye think I am?' he said harshly. 'I'm grievin', that's how I am. Grievin' because I've been robbed of my daughter. Grievin' because she's been thieved away from me by your son – and you come in here and ask me how I am?' His voice, which had been rising with each word, ended in a falsetto shriek.

'Mr Laidlaw, we knew nothing about—'

'Get out!' He moved to the end of the counter. 'I mind you – don't think I don't, just because I held my tongue like a good Christian and said nothin' when ye came back! I know all about yer whorin'!' He had rounded the counter now, and was advancing on Kirsty as she backed away. 'My mother said this town was well rid of ye, and now ye're back, bringin' yer spawn with ye tae curse my family . . .'

He raved on, out of control, while Kirsty groped for the door handle, turned it, and escaped from the shop, running across the street and into the house, pushing the door closed and leaning against it until her heart stopped pounding in her ears and her breathing slowed. Matt was shouting for her.

'I'm coming!' she called, and started up the stairs, climbing slowly, clinging to the banister and dragging herself from step to step.

She couldn't go out that afternoon, for there was nobody to look after Matt. Not that she wanted to leave the house; the scene with Mr Laidlaw had so unnerved her that for that day, at least, she couldn't face the prospect of leaving the safety of her home. When Mary got home from school, Kirsty sent her to the shop with a note for Jean briefly explaining what had happened and promising that she would

301

call on her friend on Tuesday afternoon. That was the town's early closing day, and Caitlin would be at home to see to Mary and Matt.

Matt had retreated from the world. He scarcely said a word to anyone, and Kirsty had trouble coaxing him to eat that evening. Gloom hung over the house and seemed to seep in beneath the doors and through every crack in the window frames.

'I want Alex,' Mary said suddenly as her bedtime approached. 'I want him to come home!' Tears sparkled on her lashes.

'Mary . . .' Kirsty stopped ironing and sat down, pulling her youngest onto her lap. Mary was growing so fast that it was like trying to cuddle a daddy-longlegs, but they both needed the closeness and the comfort. 'Alex's all grown up now, pet, and grown-up folk need to go away from their mams and their dads and find places of their own and meet other folk.'

'Is that why Ewan went away?'

Over the brown head, Kirsty's eyes met Caitlin's. 'That's why.'

'And Todd? He's not in the workshop; I looked when I came home from school,' Mary sniffled.

'Todd's just taking a wee rest. He'll be back.'

'Can you be certain about Todd coming back?' Caitlin asked when Mary, reassured, had trotted upstairs to get ready for bed.

'I can't be certain about anything any more. But I hope he will.'

'If he doesn't, we'll have to close the workshop, won't we?'

'Unless you've been secretly learning how to be a cabinet-maker all this time,' Kirsty said, and surprised a spurt of laughter from her daughter.

'I only know how to weigh lentils and slice ham. Mebbe we should tell Alex about this, Mam.'

'Where's the sense in that? He has his own life now. He's not going to be able to come home and take over the work-shop.'

'What're we going to do?'

'We'll manage. We always do.'

'Ewan never was one to think of the way the things he does might hurt others, was he?' said Caitlin.

30

'Everyone knows about Ewan and Beth,' Caitlin burst out as soon as she came in the back door on Tuesday afternoon. 'Folk have been staring at me and pointing me out to their friends and whispering all morning.' She bit her lip to hold back the tears glittering in her eyes. 'I'm sure that some folk came into the shop just to look at me!'

'It'll pass, pet. Empty-minded folk always behave like fools when something like this happens. They'll be off gawping at some other poor soul soon enough.'

'If Ewan was here right now I'd – I'd smack his ears for him good and hard for the trouble he's causing us!'

'If Ewan was here right now folk wouldn't be gawping at you, would they?'

'I can't understand why Beth went off with him – from what I've heard of her, all she wants is money and a nice house and nice things. How can the likes of Ewan give them to her?'

'He probably gave her more attention than Todd did.'

'Todd worshipped her,' Caitlin protested.

Kirsty reached for her coat. 'Mebbe Beth needed somethin

more than worship. I'll try not to be long. Will you wait in for Mary coming home?'

'I've got no notion to go out again – not until folk find something else to talk about.'

'Your father's had his dinner and I think he'll sleep for a wee while. I've put something in the oven for you. You'll be all right?'

Caitlin nodded, but glancing back from the door, Kirsty was struck to the heart by her wan face. It wasn't right that Caitlin or any other innocent soul should have to suffer just because Ewan had taken what he wanted.

Although the shop was shut for the afternoon, Rose and John Brodie were crowded into Jean's tiny living room.

'We agreed that it was best not to come to your house,' Rose said, 'but we wanted to find out what we could do to help.'

'Jean's told you?'

'There was no sense in keepin' it from them with all the folk comin' intae the shop knowin' the story,' Jean said defensively. 'And Rose is our partner.'

'I know.' Kirsty was glad to see the three of them.

They represented an increasingly important part of her life, and it was comforting just to know that they were there. 'I'm not going to be able to come to the shop for the time being. Matt's taken Ewan's disappearance hard, and I'm worried about him.'

'If it would help, I'd be happy to pay for a private nurse,' Rose offered.

'It's kind of you, but he'd not hear of it. Nor would I, for that matter. It's my duty to look after my own husband. I'd

305

not feel right if someone else was being paid to do it.'

'What about the business?' John wanted to know.

'The workshop's closed at the moment, but I'm hoping that Todd might come back. Nobody knows where he is – it was his fiancée Ewan ran off with,' she explained as John looked puzzled.

'I didn't realise that. Quite a mess.'

'And one that we have to help Kirsty to sort out,' Rose told him firmly.

'I could do some work at home. I've got my own old machine, and I'll have time in the afternoons. I just have to be there in case Matt needs me. We can trust Teenie to take folk's measurements.'

'That's what we'll do, then,' John said. 'Perhaps the woman who bring in the clothes could deliver work to you.'

'I've already got work in hand at the moment. It's just a case of going downstairs to collect it. I brought this.' Kirsty unwrapped the parcel she had brought with her and lifted out Beth's wedding gown. Jean helped her to spread it out over the table.

'It's bonny!'

'It's beautiful,' Rose corrected Jean.

'The bride it was made for won't be needing it now – she' the one who eloped with my stepson.'

'Poor bridegroom,' Brodie murmured, his eyes travellin over the detail of the gown. 'It's a lucky man who'd hav watched his bride coming up the aisle in a gown like this.'

As soon as the evening meal was over Kirsty left Caitlin i charge again and set off to call on all the customers on th workshop books. She was exhausted when she got back.

'I've managed to persuade them all to wait a wee while longer for their orders, but if the workshop's not opened by next week I'll have to ask another cabinet-maker to take them on. It'd not be fair to keep them waiting any longer than that.' She eased her shoes off and groaned with pleasure at the relief. 'Did Mary get off to sleep all right?'

'It took a while, but she went over at last. And Father's sleeping too. I had to give him some of his laudanum. Archie Lang came to see you – Todd's sister's man. He said to let you know that Todd came home this evening.'

'Is he all right?' Kirsty sat upright, glancing at the clock, scrabbling for her shoes. 'I'll go round . . .'

'He said not to, not tonight. Todd was very drunk, and they had to put him to his bed. Archie says you could try him in the morning, though.'

Todd came to Espedair Street before Kirsty was ready to visit his sister's house. She had settled Matt and was washing her face at the kitchen sink before fetching her coat when she saw a man pass the window on his way to the kitchen door, then almost immediately pass back again towards the pend. She snatched up a towel and dabbed the water from her eyes, then looked again.

At first she thought that the figure standing in the lane, shuffling from one foot to the other, wavering very slightly, was a tramp who had wandered in from the street. Then he half turned and she got a glimpse of the side of his face. Running to the back door she threw it open. He jumped, then swung round guiltily to face her.

'Todd!' His face was unshaven, his eyes bloodshot and his clothes looked as though they had been dragged on.

307

'I thought . . .' He stopped, then tried again, pointing down the lane, his outstretched arm wavering so that the stiff index finger drew patterns in the air. 'I thought I'd just go down tae the workshop . . .'

'You'll do no such thing. You'll come in here.'

He shuffled over to her like an old man and said almost pleadingly, 'I'm no' decent for visitin'.'

It was true. His clothes and his hair and even his skin stank of stale tobacco smoke and stale drink and other things she preferred not to try to identify.

'Never mind about that. Come on in,' Kirsty said mercilessly, pointing to Matt's chair when she had got him into the kitchen. 'Sit down, Todd.'

He flinched away from the chair and had to catch at the edge of the table for balance. 'Tha's th' master's chair.' His voice was still slurred with drink. 'I'm no' fit tae sit in th' master's chair.'

'Sit down before you fall down, man!' In the past, Matt had been fond of a drink, and on more than one occasion he had come home the worse for it. Kirsty had learned then that some inebriates responded, like children and dogs, to a sharp command. Luckily Matt was one of them and Todd apparently another, for he collapsed untidily into the chair without further argument.

Kirsty threw a handful of leaves into the teapot, asking, as his stomach rumbled noisily, 'When did you last eat?'

He waved his hand vaguely. 'Yesterday – mebbe. I've no had the stomach for food.'

She cut some bread and buttered it, then thrust it into his hand. 'Eat this.'

'I'm feared I'll mebbe—'

'You'll keep it down – and if you can't there's a privy just outside the back door.'

She bullied him into eating the bread in small, reluctant mouthfuls, and swallowing down hot strong tea. He managed to keep it all down, and a tinge of colour came into his grey stubbly cheeks.

'Now, what have you been up to, Todd Paget?'

He looked up at her pathetically. 'I cannae mind, but it had somethin' tae do with drink. Then I woke up in a ditch outside of the town, and a carter brought me back.' He belched hugely, clapped a hand over his mouth, and said through his fingers, 'I didnae mean tae disturb ye. I just came for my tools.'

'What d'you want your tools for? You're in no fit state to use them.'

'A craftsman needs his tools, Mrs Lennox. How else am I tae get work?'

'You've got work here.'

He blinked at her, then began to shake his head, stopping immediately and wincing with pain. 'I cannae come back here – no' after the way I behaved, shoutin' at ye an' all.'

'I'd have shouted myself if I'd been in your place. And of course you'll come back.'

'Ye mean ye'd still employ me?'

'Todd,' Kirsty said patiently, 'right this minute I'd employ Beelzebub if he was a time-served craftsman.'

'But what'll the master say?'

'I'm afraid the master's not well enough to decide what's to happen in the workshop. I'm having to do it for him, and I've got orders waiting to be filled. You'll be on your own, but we'll talk about getting help for you later.'

'I'm grateful.' He struggled to his feet, beginning to look better already. 'I'll just away down tae the workshop, then.'

'And gash your hand with a chisel and be no use to me for weeks? You'll do nothing of the sort, Todd Paget. You'll get yourself back home and get a decent meal in your belly. Then you'll have a good sleep and tomorrow you'll wash and shave and make yourself presentable. Then you can come back to work – but not until then.'

Muttering his thanks, he made for the door, looking back at her before going out. 'I didnae find them,' he said, 'but I have tae tell ye – if I had, I'd've killed Ewan for what he's done.'

'Then I'm glad you didn't find him, Todd, for your own sake as well as for his.'

When he had gone she propped the door open to let the cool wind scour the smell of him from the kitchen and poured herself another cup of tea, her spirits beginning to rally. The workshop, at least, had been taken care of and the customers assured of their orders. And Todd, who had begun to matter to her just as much as any member of her family, was home and safe.

Kirsty waited until Todd returned to work the next day washed and shaved and penitent, before telling Matt that the journeyman was back in the workshop. As she had expected his temper erupted.

'D'ye mean tae tell me that he's workin' down there as if nothin' had happened after the way he came chargin' in here wakenin' the whole household and threatenin' tae do harm tae Ewan? I'll not have that rascal on my premises, and ye can just go out this minute and tell him tae take himsel' off!'

310

'Matt, we've got orders to fill and customers waiting.'

'We'll employ someone else!'

'We've not got the time to interview men, and even if we had, I know nothing about the work and you can't go down to the shop to keep an eye on them. Todd knows the business – he's the one who kept it going before we got here. He cares about the place.'

'Cares? He wasnae doin' much carin' when he went off after . . .' he paused, searching for the right words, then said, 'after that woman of his. Two, three days he was away from the place. He wasnae carin' then about what happened tae it, was he?'

'He was upset – what man wouldn't be with his bride running away the week before their wedding?'

'More fool him for ever havin' trusted her. I knew from the start, that time you insisted on them visitin', that she was a sleekit lassie. Did I not tell ye at the time that no good would come of treatin' an employee like a friend?'

Kirsty opened her mouth to point out that Ewan had some blame in what had happened, then closed it again, realising that they were on dangerous ground. Matt was in a mood to blame everyone – Beth Laidlaw for tempting Ewan away, Todd for letting it happen, Kirsty herself for trying to be friendly towards Beth. But never Ewan, his beloved son.

'What's done's done, Matt,' she said instead. 'I had to try to keep the business going, and Todd's the best man to do that just now.'

'If Alex hadnae gone waltzing off—'

'But he did, and there's no sense in crying over spilled milk.'

He tried to clench his hands into fists, but couldn't. 'D'ye mind when these hands were able tae do a good day's work?'

'I mind it fine.' She touched one hand gently. 'You did your share of work, Matt. There's no shame in not being able to do it any more.'

'Don't talk nonsense, woman,' he told her roughly. 'When a man like me loses the ability tae work, he loses everythin' that makes life worth the livin'. Damn this arthritis tae hell!' And he turned his face away and closed his eyes against her and against the entire world.

Going downstairs, she suddenly recalled those same hands of his, gentle enough for their size and the rough skin, fondling and pleasuring and rousing her. Their marriage had come about for practical reasons rather than love. Matt had wanted a mother for Ewan, she had wanted security and a father for Alex. They had both wanted a home, a hearth, the comfort of marriage.

But through the years it had become more than that – for a while, at least. A yearning she hadn't experienced for a long time stirred deep inside Kirsty – a need to be held and touched and loved again before it was too late.

'This business of you working at home isn't any use,' Jean said on the following Tuesday. 'Teenie's willing, but she hasn't got your flair for knowing what suits folk and what can be done tae make the clothes look right for them.'

'And you're looking strained, Kirsty,' Rose butted in. 'You need to come here and meet folk and be yourself for a few hours.'

They were both right. Kirsty was missing the shop, and she hated being in the house all day, but she couldn't see any way out of the problem.

'Matt can't be left on his own, and I can't ask Todd to keep an eye on him, for he's working alone.' Matt had finally had to give in and let Todd help him into the bathroom every day, but it went against the grain, Kirsty knew. Ewan's ghost seemed to stand between the two men, and always would. Matt certainly wouldn't agree to being left in the journeyman's care, and she'd not ask Todd to take on the added burden in any case.

'What about Caitlin?' Rose asked tentatively.

'She's got her job at the grocer's shop, and her own friends. I'll not ask her to give up either to look after an invalid. And Mary's very good at starting the dinner and seeing to her father's needs when she comes home from school, but she's too wee to take on more responsibility. There's only me.'

'What sort of help does he need ?'

'It's mostly just being there to fetch and carry for him, or pick up his newspaper or his tobacco pouch if they fall off the bed. And making tea, and sometimes just giving him a bit of company.'

'I could do all those things.'

Jean and Kirsty both gaped at Rose. 'You?'

'The shop can manage without me better than it can manage without you, Kirsty. I could fetch and carry for your husband and give him a bit of company if he wants someone to talk to.'

'But . . . you and Matt don't even know each other.'

'Every friend used to be a stranger. And if it's . . . the more personal side of things that you're worried about,' Rose said delicately, 'we've got a commode at home that you could borrow. I've been meaning to offer it to you. And there's the man in the workshop to call on if I need help or advice.'

Jean and Kirsty looked at each other, then Kirsty said, 'I couldn't ask you to do a thing like that for me.'

'Why not? We're partners.'

'But you're – you're—'

'Upper class?' Rose asked with a wry grin. 'Maybe I am, but I've got two arms and legs and hands like you, and a brain – and a good Scots tongue in my head. And you'd not be all that far away if you were needed.'

'What would your parents say if they found out?'

Rose batted the words away with a wave of one hand. 'They stopped trying to tell me how to live my life a while ago.'

As far as Kirsty and Jean knew, that was true. John Brodie had told them that Mr and Mrs Hamilton had grown weary of continually arguing with their daughter and continually losing. Since his sister's engagement party, the young lawyer had frequently invited Rose to be his escort at various social occasions. As he was an eligible bachelor, her parents took some comfort from her relationship with him.

'Let's see what your husband thinks before we make any decisions.' Rose unfolded her tall and lanky body from the chair she had been sitting in. 'I'll call round tomorrow morning, and the three of us can talk it over.'

31

The commode Rose had promised arrived in a chauffeur-driven car on the following morning, to Kirsty's embarrassment. It wasn't the commode that worried her, for Rose had had the forethought to have it carefully wrapped, but the handsome car and its uniformed driver.

A group of stragglers hurrying along Espedair Street on their way to the South School just as the vehicle drew up at her door immediately forgot about their teacher's wrath and their teacher's cane in their delight at being so close to a motorcar.

The chauffeur insisted on carrying the commode upstairs and into the bedroom, where Matt sat up in bed staring, his hair awry.

'What in the—'

'I'll be back in a minute,' Kirsty told him hurriedly, sweeping the man out of the room. In the hall, overwhelmed by his smart appearance and his experience with motor vehicles, she asked timidly, 'Will you have a cup of tea?'

'Best not, missus, not with these wee toerags out there up tae God knows what wi' the master's precious motorcar.'

Outside on the footpath the youngsters, who had been admiring but not daring to touch, scattered like flies as he emerged and touched the shining peak of his cap to Kirsty. 'Miss Rose asked me to tell you that she'll be along in the middle of the afternoon, madam,' he said, reverting to his official working voice, then gave her a huge wink and left.

In the bedroom Matt was squawking and fussing like a shedful of hens. 'It's a commode,' she told him as she started stripping off the wrapping paper. 'Rose Lennox thought it might be of help to you while you're in bed.'

'We don't take charity!'

'It's not charity; it's a loan made out of kindness. She's – oh, my!' She broke off as the last of the paper fell away to reveal a handsome carved wooden chair. 'I didn't realise it'd look so grand.'

She stepped back, as intimidated by the chair as she had been by the chauffeur in his finery. 'Bring it closer,' Matt ordered, and when she had summoned up the courage to do as she was told he leaned across the pillow to touch it. 'It's oak – an' made by a craftsman. Lift the lid.'

She did, and withdrew a large, deep, cream-coloured chamber pot, tastefully decorated with painted strands of ivy

'I'd be feared tae pee in a pot like that, let alone shit in it,' Matt said, awed.

'You'll have to – that's what she sent it for. And think how useful it'll be instead of always trying to get to the bathroom.'

'Right enough,' he said thoughtfully. She could tell by his expression that he had realised that the commode would mean freedom from dependence on Todd's strong, gentle arm. 'I suppose it was a kindly thought,' he acknowledged and she seized the chance to break her next piece of news.

'Rose was talking about coming round for a wee while this afternoon, to see what we think of the commode.'

'Comin' here?'

'She'd like fine to meet you, Matt. She'd not stay long,' she added as he started to object. 'I'd best get you settled, just in case she does come.'

By the time Rose knocked at the door he was washed and shaved and in a clean nightshirt. His hair had been brushed, his moustache combed and the bed remade.

'Did the commode arrive?' Rose asked in her clear voice as soon as the door was opened.

'It did – we're both very grateful. Come on in.'

'I decided to wait and walk round this afternoon instead of coming this morning in the car.' Rose stepped into the hall. 'I thought it might be too much for your poor husband, me and the commode arriving together.'

'He's nervous about meeting you.'

'I'm nervous about meeting him,' Rose confessed. 'Should we both get it over with at once?'

At first Matt treated the visitor as though she came from a far land and spoke a foreign language. But when Rose launched into an amusing and faintly bawdy story about the commode's history he began to thaw, and even to smile a little. Kirsty left them together while she made tea, and when she went back upstairs with the tray Rose, using her ability to laugh at her own faults, was deep into another story, this time concerning some confusion she had caused in the shop because of her ignorance of the local dialect. Matt was listening closely, and even chuckling now and again.

Rose had more sense than to outstay her welcome. 'I was wondering,' she said casually as she got up to go, 'if I could call on you again, Mr Lennox – mebbe on Friday afternoon?'

'If ye like.'

'If I'm going to be here, Kirsty, you could go to the shop. We'll be fine together for an hour or so, won't we, Mr Lennox? I'd like to hear all about the trade you were in,' Rose swept on as a flicker of uncertainty came into Matt's eyes, 'and about the training you had to do.'

Before Rose left, Kirsty took her to the workshop to meet Todd, then led her back into the house through the kitchen without thinking twice. To her, Rose was a friend, not a visitor who should only see the parlour and visit the workshop via the pend. Mary, who had just arrived home from school, was introduced, then before leaving Rose paused to admire the fireside chairs.

'These are very pretty – the flowers look real enough to pick. Who did them for you?'

'Our Alex,' Mary said proudly, and Rose shot her an astonished look, then said, 'Oh.' It was a flat, negative sound.

'He's a decent lad, Alex,' Kirsty said at the front door. 'I think you and him got off on the wrong foot the first time you met.'

'Maybe we did,' Rose said distantly. 'Why isn't he here helping you to manage everything?'

Kirsty hesitated, aware of Mary in the hall behind them. 'It's a long story,' she said at last. 'I'll tell you about it one day.'

'Father's agreed to let Rose sit with him?' Surprise sent Caitlin's voice soaring up the scale when she heard the news that evening.

'He's willing to give it a try. I've not said to him about next week, though, we'll just take each day as it comes.'

'She was asking why Alex wasn't here to help us,' Mary chimed in, 'but Mam wouldn't say.'

'There's nothing to say, lady. Alex is grown up and off leading his own life, that's all.'

'I want to see him again. I've nearly forgotten what he looks like!'

'You'll see him one day, Mary. But we don't want to bother him just now when he's so busy.'

Caitlin shot a look at her mother and opened her mouth to speak, then closed it again. Later, when Mary had gone to bed, she said quietly, 'Mam, I wrote to Alex today, to tell him what's happened.'

'Wrote to him? Have you posted it? Why?' Kirsty asked as her daughter nodded.

Caitlin looked guilty but defiant. 'He's got a right to know what's happening here, Mam – about Ewan and Beth, and Father being worse. He's still part of this family.'

And a fast-shrinking family it was, Kirsty thought. All three sons had gone for one reason or another. Apart from Matt, the house had become a place of women. Aloud she said, 'Alex has his own life now, and his own work to do. We can't expect him to come back and run the workshop for us.'

'You never know – he might think of something,' Caitlin argued.

As soon as Kirsty stepped into the shop on Friday afternoon her domestic worries seemed to drop from her shoulders. She revelled in it all – the sewing room, the demented whirring of Teenie's hard-worked machine opposite her own, the frequent summonses to the front shop to give advice, the customers' chatter, the cups of strong tea, the stolen moments when the shop was empty and Jean came into the sewing room to perch on a stool and talk.

'You look the better for your outin' already,' Jean commented when Teenie had gone off home and the two of them were alone together.

'It's been grand, being back. I've never seen anyone work as fast as Teenie. I keep thinking that she'll end up with crooked seams, going at that rate, but she never does.'

'You and me can put in a peck of work ourselves, when we put our minds tae it.' Jean looked round the shop with satisfaction. 'D'ye realise it's near enough a year since this place opened? I couldnae sleep at nights at the time for worryin' about what I'd let myself in for, but it's turned out well.'

'I was certain that Rose would lose interest long before the summer and be off on a new ploy.'

'Not that lassie. You have tae give her credit for her determination.'

'D'you know what she brought with her this afternoon?' Kirsty asked. 'A big blanket made into a cape thing that one of her uncles brought back from South America. There's a hole in the middle for your head, and slits to put your arms through. She says there's a lot of bits and pieces in their attic that were brought from foreign parts.'

Jean's eyes widened. 'She's never expectin' you tae wear the thing!'

'Not a bit of it – it's for when Matt's on the commode.' Kirsty felt a broad smile begin to spread across her face. 'By her way of it, when he puts this thing on it covers him and the commode, so's he can attend to his business without fretting about being seen. She thought it would make it easier for

320

him to let her help him on and off the thing if Todd wasn't to hand.'

'Fancy,' Jean said weakly. There was a pause, then she caught Kirsty's eye and the two of them went into peals of laughter.

'I'm quite sure it'll work, too,' Jean said when she had sobered up. She pulled a handkerchief from her sleeve and mopped at her eyes. 'Once that lassie makes up her mind tae somethin' she'll make it work. She'll not let anythin' put her off.'

'I just hope,' Kirsty said as she made for the door, 'that Matt hasn't been the one to finally put a dent in her determination.'

But in fact Rose's first afternoon with Matt had been quite successful. They both seemed to have enjoyed their time together, and it was agreed, before Rose left, that she would return on Monday to let Kirsty go to the shop again.

It seemed to Alex, as he turned the corner from Causeyside Street, that Espedair Street was smaller than before. So was the house. He smiled faintly, remembering the first time he had seen it and how large it had appeared to him then. But that had been before he knew Glasgow, with its broad, busy streets and its handsome, airy buildings. He hesitated at the door, and almost turned towards the pend instead, then, deciding that he no longer had the right to go round the back, he put a hand to the latch.

The hallway, too, had shrunk, and was darker and narrower than he remembered. As he closed the door the kitchen door opened.

'Who's there?'

'It's me, Ma—' He stopped halfway along the hall, staring at the girl framed in the doorway. 'What are you doing here?'

Rose Hamilton was clearly as dismayed to see him as he was to see her. 'You'd best come in. Your father's asleep and we don't want to disturb – oh!' She whisked back into the kitchen, and he followed in time to see her snatch a flat iron from where she had left it, on one of his father's shirts. She examined the material anxiously. 'Thank goodness, it's not burned,' she said, then wet one finger and dabbed gingerly at the flat of the iron. 'It wasn't hot enough to burn.' She put the iron on the lit gas ring.

'What are you doing here?' Alex asked again from the doorway. His abrupt tone was enough to bring her head up sharply.

'I'm looking after your father.' The hostility that always came between them sparkled in her eyes.

'You? But where's my mother?'

'At the shop.'

'She should be here,' Alex said without thinking. He had come home eager to see his mother again after all those months apart, and he was almost childishly disappointed to find that she wasn't where he had expected to find her, where he had pictured her during his self-imposed exile – in the kitchen, the heart and the core of the family.

Rose interpreted his sense of loss as masculine selfishness. 'She's not a prisoner.' She smoothed the shirt she had been ironing on the blanket-covered table with angry sweeps of her hands. 'As you once told me yourself, nobody owns her. She surely has the right to go out now and again. I'm trying to help because nobody else seems to be willing to share the burden she's having to carry.'

Alex coloured angrily. 'Why else d'you think I'm here?'

'It took you long enough.'

'I didn't know about Ewan until the other day!' he snapped, then wondered why he was justifying himself to this arrogant intruder.

For a moment they scowled at each other, then Alex asked, 'When will she be back?'

'In an hour, maybe.'

'I'll look in at the workshop,' he said, and escaped outside.

When he returned to the house he had simmered down. 'Todd tells me you've been doing what you can to help my mother. I'm . . . grateful.'

'I've made some tea,' Rose told him stiffly. She was still ironing, her movements clumsy and uncertain. He filled a cup for himself, grimacing when he saw how weak it was, then lit another gas ring and put the teapot on it.

'You'll boil it.'

'That's what it needs. It's far too weak as it is.'

'I've never heard of boiling tea.'

'You've probably never made tea before,' he said dryly. 'Or ironed. Here.' He went round to her side of the table and took the iron from her. 'Longer strokes and a bit more pressure. And this end's pointed so's you can push it into the gathers. See?'

'I've never met a man who could iron clothes,' she said, faint respect creeping into her voice, as he relinquished the iron. He drew a chair out from the table and sat down.

'I had to learn when I moved into lodgings in Glasgow. That's when I learned how to make tea too,' he added.

In the silence that fell, he stared at his clasped hands on

the table, sneaking brief glances at her from beneath lowered lids. Her face was flushed from the heat of the room, and her hair was different – softer round her face instead of being scragged back. It improved her looks.

'There.' She finished the shirt and shook it out. In places she had ironed creases in instead of removing them, but Alex, who had heard a glowing report about the girl from Todd, held his tongue. Her effort reminded him of his own first attempt, but at least she hadn't burned the material, as he had.

She folded the blanket and put it away, then poured tea for herself, grimacing at its strength.

'I'll take that one,' Alex offered, 'and you can have mine. I've not touched it.'

He watched her adding milk and stirring in a spoonful of sugar, liking the deft, feminine movements of her hands now that she was doing something familiar. It occurred to him for the first time that he missed feminine company in his new life. Until then he had been too busy to think of it.

A thumping on the ceiling brought both their heads up. 'That's your father wakened. He'll be ready for a drink.' Rose put her cup down and got up to pour more tea. She put some biscuits on a plate, then settled cup and plate on a small lacquered tray Alex had never seen before. 'Are you coming up to see him?'

He hesitated, then shook his head. 'Best not.'

Censure came back into her eyes. 'He's a sick man, and he's your father.'

'My stepfather.'

Her lips tightened. 'From what I've heard he's the man who raised you. You owe him the courtesy of a visit.'

'He'll not want to see me any more than I want to see him.'

'You should let him decide that for himself instead of skulking down here out of sight.'

The open challenge brought warmth to Alex's face. He pushed the chair back noisily and got to his feet. 'Give me the tray,' he said, and followed her from the room.

32

At the top of the stairs Rose halted and turned. 'He's taken your brother's disappearance very hard,' she said, low voiced. 'You have to make allowances for that.' Then before he could answer she whisked round and went off along the corridor, carolling, 'You've got a visitor. Mr Lennox. Someone you'll be pleased to see.'

Alex's first sight of his stepfather gave him a shock. The man had aged far more than the nine months since they had last met, and he seemed to have shrunk in on himself. But his glare was still the same, and so was the antagonism in his voice when he said, 'What're you doin' in this house?'

'I came to see how you were.'

'Came tae gloat, ye mean.'

Alex almost gave an angry reply, almost walked out of the room and out of the house to wait for his mother on the footpath, but just then Rose moved between him and the bed to take the tray from his hands. With her back to Matt she stared up into Alex's face, shaking her head very slightly. He took a deep breath and moved past her to look down at the man in the bed.

Pain had used a blunt knife to carve deeply into Matt's forehead and cheeks and round his nose and mouth. His eyes were dull and the clawed hands lying on the bedcovers were little more than lumps of bone enclosed by shiny red skin stretched tightly, as if it was having a struggle to contain them.

'No,' Alex said, pity tempering his dislike of the man. 'I just came to see you.'

'I'll sort your pillows.' Rose had laid the tray down on the bedside table; now she put an arm behind Matt's shoulders and eased him forwards, using her free hand to rearrange the pillows. When they refused to go where she wanted, Alex went to the other side of the bed and freed her by supporting his stepfather's shoulders. The man felt like a bag of bones. When he was settled, Rose wrapped some cloth round the cup to make it easier to hold, then placed it carefully into Matt's hands.

'Drink it while it's hot. Kirsty'll be home in a wee while.' She had a special voice for Matt, soft and light and reassuring; a voice Alex had never thought to hear from the likes of Rose Hamilton.

Matt slowly lifted the cup, bending his head until his lips touched the brim, and sucked the strong tea in noisily. 'That's a good cup o' tea. Ye're learnin', lass,' he said, and Rose blushed.

Alex stayed in the room for five minutes, during which, with Rose's help, he and Matt managed to make conversation of a sort. It was a relief to him – and, he was sure, to his stepfather – when Rose sent him back downstairs while she washed Matt's hands and face and made him comfortable.

'You're very good with him,' he acknowledged when she came into the kitchen.

327

'I feel sorry for him, having to end his days like this. And I like him,' she said, then added, with a sidelong glance, 'I've got the freedom to like him, for I've not had the experiences of him that you've had.'

'You know about it all?'

'Kirsty told me as much as I needed to know. Thank you for not losing your temper upstairs. He's not strong enough to manage a quarrel, and there's no sense in it anyway, is there?'

'It wasn't easy.'

'Doing the right thing's never easy,' Rose told him briskly. 'I'll be off now, since you're here to see to things.'

'You don't have to go on my account.'

She shook her head. 'They'll all be pleased to see you. I'll just get in the way.'

Mary, who got home from school before Kirsty arrived from the shop, met her in the hall, her small thin face glowing. 'Alex is home!'

He appeared behind her, laughing, scooping her out of the way so that he could take his mother's bags from her. 'I've not come home, Mary, I told you that. I've come for a visit to see you all – hey!' he protested as Kirsty threw her arms round him, 'You're crushing me!'

'I've got every right to crush you – I'm your mother. Let me look at you.' She drew back, drinking in the sight of him in his good suit and white shirt and neat tie. 'You look . . all grown up!'

'Mother, I'm twenty years old now!' That wasn't what she had meant. There was a new maturity about him, an air of confidence. His hair, normally tousled, was shorter than it had been, well cut and almost smooth, with just enough of wave to break the perfection. It was as red as ever, though, and the colour was echoed in his new, neatly trimmed moustache. Even his speech was different, just a little more refined. Most important of all, the pain and bitterness of Fiona's loss had gone from his eyes, and they were clear and steady, the eyes of a man who had found himself and liked what he had found.

Caitlin arrived home, and Kirsty left brother and sisters together while she went up to see Matt.

'Yer prodigal son's returned, then,' he said as soon as she went in.

She refused to rise to the bait. 'It's nice to see him after all this time.'

'And lookin' so prosperous.'

'You've seen him?'

'Rose brought him up.'

'Come downstairs and eat with us, Matt. Todd'll still be in the workshop and he and Alex could help you.'

'I'm no' able,' he said, and turned his head away.

'He's gone downhill fast,' Alex said later when they had eaten and Mary had gone to bed.

'It's losing Ewan that's done it, and the way he lost him.'

'Has there not been any word? You'd think,' Alex said angrily when Kirsty shook her head, 'that he'd at least write to let his father know he was all right.'

'Ewan's always acted without thinking of the consequences,' Caitlin put in.

'He's taken on a deal of consequences this time. D'you think he and Beth'll stay together?' Alex wanted to know, and his half-sister shook her head firmly.

'They're too like each other. And Ewan's not got what Beth wants. He's helped her to escape from her father, and from poor Todd, but to my mind she'll be off with the first man who offers her more than Ewan can give her.'

He laughed. 'You seem to know a lot about how folk work.'

'You learn a great deal behind the counter of a grocer's shop,' Caitlin told him solemnly, then leant forward. 'But never mind Ewan and Beth – tell us all about what's been happening to you.'

He launched into the story, glowing. 'It's been hard work, but the wee business I took over's beginning to show results. I've got two men in the workshop making the furniture – both good at their trade and able to take responsibility – and we've taken on an apprentice. We've just finished our first big order, and there are others waiting their turn.'

'You're doing the decorating yourself?'

'For the moment, but we're talking of bringing in an artist to free me for the office work. There's a deal of that. I'm going to night school to learn about book-keeping and the like. And I'm in lodgings now. Two nice big rooms, and the landlady's a decent enough body.'

'She seems to look after you,' Kirsty said, and he laughed.

'I'm learning to look after myself. You'd be proud of the way I can iron my own clothes, Mam, and do a bit of cooking.'

'D'you get on well with . . . with Sandy?'

He nodded. 'Better than I thought I would. We're alike in many ways, and he's pleased with my work.' He hesitated and stared for a moment at his hands, then looked up. 'I've got something to tell you, Mam. I'm changing my name from Lennox to MacDowall.'

'Oh.' She couldn't think of anything else to say.

'It's what he – my father –' he said, flicking a swift glance at her, then looking back at his hands, 'wants, and it makes sense, for all going well I'll be made a partner when I'm twenty-one. He'd like to make it public knowledge now that I'm his heir.'

'Did you say anything to . . .' she hesitated, about to say 'your father', then realising that to Alex the title no longer meant Matt.

He understood at once. 'I didn't, and I don't think you should.' He looked from her to Caitlin. 'He'll never know, and it's best that way, for it'd only hurt his feelings. I just hope,' he touched Kirsty's hand lightly, swiftly, 'that it doesn't hurt yours.'

'It doesn't. You're as entitled to call yourself MacDowall as Lennox.'

Kirsty wanted to ask about Fiona, but couldn't bring herself to. It was Caitlin who finally said baldly, 'What about Fiona?'

Something flickered across Alex's face and was gone. 'She's still in Fort William, and engaged to be married to a man who lives there. We've not set eyes on each other, though she knows now that I'm working in Glasgow, and that I'm changing my name. She wrote to wish me well. Now,' he said briskly, without giving either of them time to comment, 'I spoke with Todd this afternoon. You'll need to get another journeyman in, Mam, for he can't manage for long on his own.'

'I know. The orders are beginning to pick up again, and with the shop doing quite well, and Caitlin earning, we could manage to pay another wage.'

'You should let Todd pick a man for himself,' he advised.

*

331

When he left, Kirsty walked through the cold November night to Canal Street Station with him, their breaths rising into the air in white clouds that met and mingled as they spoke, then dissolving into the darkness.

'The old man's deteriorated a lot. I don't see him getting better, Mam,' Alex said as they waited for the train.

'I know that. He's in such pain now that he can't sleep without laudanum. I have to dole it out carefully.' Kirsty sighed. 'It's hard to see him suffering like that.'

'I'm glad you've got the shop, and Jean.'

'We're doing well. Rose's daft idea worked after all.'

He gave a short laugh. 'She's changed too. I couldn't believe my eyes when I walked into the kitchen and found her doing the ironing.'

'I've lost a few garments since she decided to try her hand with the flat iron. But her heart's in the right place.'

'I mind you telling me once that you needed some independence, and I couldn't understand it because I thought that having the house and us to look after should be enough.' His eyes glittered in the gaslight as he looked down at her. 'I know better now. I'll try to visit more often, but it's not easy with so much to see to.'

She patted his hand as the train hooted in the near distance. 'You've got your own life, Alex, and I'm glad it's a success. We'll be fine, me and Caitlin and Mary – and Matt. And there's Todd in the workshop if I ever need him.'

'I'm glad he came back to work for you. He'll never see you lost for a friend.'

The train came charging into the station, huffing steam impatient to be on its way to Glasgow. Alex gave her a brief

332

peck on the cheek. 'You know where I am if you need me,' he said.

Heedless of the cold, Kirsty stood on the platform and watched the train's lights until they vanished before walking slowly home.

33

Kirsty ran out of the shop without stopping to fetch her coat or hat, heedless of the March rain soaking her hair and her blouse. The child who had been sent to fetch her pounded along at her side, pointing as they turned into Espedair Street. 'There, missus,' he gasped, 'the house where the car is, and the folk standin'. That's where the lady is that sent me tae fetch ye.'

She fumbled in her skirt pocket and found a coin to press into his hand, then pushed through the small knot of people who had gathered at the door, drawn there by the sight of the doctor's car.

Todd was in the hall, his arms about Rose, who was white faced and shaking. 'Oh, Kirsty . . .' At the sight of her, Rose broke free and ran to take her hands. 'I thought he was just having a good sleep for once. He said he didn't want to be disturbed, so I just left him . . .' She started to weep, and Kirsty put an arm round her.

'Come into the kitchen and sit down.'

Todd followed them in, his face drained. 'I'd have fetched ye mysel', Mrs Lennox, and tried tae save ye some of the shock, but I felt I was needed here.' He nodded at Rose.

'You did the right thing, Todd.' Kirsty eased Rose down into her own chair, then asked the journeyman over her bowed head, 'Is he—?'

He nodded, then swiftly pulled a chair out from the table. 'You should sit down too. You've gone white as a sheet.'

'He said he was tired and I was just to leave him be,' Rose said. 'Then I began to wonder . . .'

She began to cry again, and Kirsty was comforting her when the doctor came downstairs.

'I'm very sorry, Mrs Lennox. He just slipped away in his sleep.'

He offered to take Rose home, and Kirsty managed to persuade her to go. 'I'll manage fine, with Todd's help, and you've had a bad shock. I'll see you tomorrow.'

The doctor went ahead to open the car door for Rose, and Todd stayed in the kitchen. For a moment the two women were alone in the hall. 'Kirsty, I found this by the bed and put it into my pocket before I went to fetch Todd.' Rose slipped a small bottle into Kirsty's hand.

'It's all right, I gave him the last of it before I went out because the pain was bad,' Kirsty said, and relief came into Rose's reddened eyes.

'I didn't say anything to the doctor because I wasn't sure if it . . . I wondered . . .'

'There's nothing to worry about,' Kirsty soothed, walking with her to the pavement.

'About the layin' out,' Todd said awkwardly when she went back into the kitchen.

'I'll see to it myself.' Once or twice she had helped her mother to prepare bodies for burial, and she herself had assisted neighbours in Falkirk when the need had arisen.

'My sister could give ye a hand if ye want. She knows about these things.'

She thought of Marion's calm warmth. 'I'd be grateful for her help. Could you fetch her, Todd – and notify the undertaker while you're at it?'

'I'll send Davie.' Davie was the new journeyman he had hired to take Ewan's place.

'I'd as soon you went yourself, being as near to one of the family as anyone could be.'

Concern came into his smoky eyes. 'I'm not leavin' you on yer own at a time like this. If I must go, I'll ask one of the neighbours tae sit with ye while I'm away.'

'I'll be fine, Todd. I just need to have a minute on my own with him before—'

'I should've thought of that,' he said gruffly. 'I'll not be long.'

'Todd,' she said as he headed for the back door. He turned, and she stepped forward into his arms, resting her head on his shoulder, as she had done just over a year ago, on the anniversary of Fergus's death. He stood rigid for a moment, then his body relaxed and his arms enfolded her. She leaned her weight against him for a full minute, drawing strength and comfort from his support, then drew back and looked up into his face, her hands on his chest.

'You're a good friend, Todd Paget,' she said gently. 'On you go now. Mebbe you could look in at the grocer's and tell Caitlin to come home,' she added as he turned away. 'It would help me if she was here for Mary coming home from the school.'

When she was at last alone she went upstairs to a bedroom

that was strangely empty now that everything that had been Matt had gone, leaving only his body behind. After opening the window to release his soul, she went to the bed and lifted the sheet back from his face. He lay on his back, his eyes closed as though in sleep, but when she bent and kissed his forehead the skin was cold against her lips. His hands, which had been feverishly hot from the arthritis for the past few years, were also cold. She smoothed a strand of grey hair back from his forehead then took from her pocket the small brown bottle Rose had given her.

It hadn't been completely empty when she had left for work; there had been some laudanum left in it; just a few drops, but enough. Only she and Matt had known that the bottle was in the bedside drawer instead of in the bathroom, out of his reach. At Matt's request, she had put it in the drawer on the first day of the new year. It was his key to the final door, should the pain become too much for him. Their final pact, their secret, and something nobody else would ever know about.

She put the bottle back in her pocket and drew the sheet over his face. Clearly he had hoped that Rose would leave him to sleep until Kirsty came home. Instead the poor girl had caused herself anguish by trying to make sure that he was all right.

In the back yard she pushed the bottle deep into the rubbish container then stood for a moment, breathing in the cold air. The rain had stopped, but there was more to come. The skies were grey and lowering, the wind heavy with moisture.

She had left the house that afternoon a wife and returned to it a widow. Kirsty rubbed a finger over the broad gold wedding ring she had worn for the past sixteen years. It would take a long time to get used to the change in her status.

Matt's funeral was well attended, and the house was packed with mourners after the burial. There was a buzz of interest when people realised that the tall, thin, brisk young woman helping to prepare and serve the refreshments was none other than Rose Hamilton, from one of the big houses in Thornly Park, and another buzz at Alex's smart and prosperous appearance.

'My . . . Angus MacDowall would have liked to attend,' he told his mother at the gathering afterwards, 'but he felt that it might not be proper. He sends his deepest condolences.'

'Thank him for his thoughts – and his consideration.'

'I'm surprised to see him here.' Alex nodded over at Mr Laidlaw, standing in a corner devouring a plate of ham sandwiches.

Kirsty had been surprised, too, in view of the way the man had ordered her out of his shop, but nobody else knew about that. 'He's a local businessman, and so was Matt. It's the done thing for them to attend each other's funerals.'

'And get a good feed,' Alex commented. 'Who are the two sour-looking folk with him?'

'That's Annie, Beth's older sister, and her husband. They came back to Paisley to live with Mr Laidlaw after Beth went away. Annie's taken over the shop, and when Mr Laidlaw's time comes she'll inherit it instead of Beth.'

'If Ewan's wed Beth he'd be well advised to stay right away from this place,' Alex murmured. 'Imagine marrying into a family like that. You'd think they were trying to stock up their bellies before a famine.' Then, voicing Kirsty's own thoughts, he said 'It doesn't seem right, Ewan not knowing his father's gone. If we only knew where he was . . .'

Morag Bishop had hurried over from Kilbarchan as soon as she heard of Matt's death, and she and Todd's sister, both strong and caring women, had done a lot to help Kirsty and her daughters through the days before the funeral. All three members of the Bishop family were present that day, although they had only met Matt once.

'The arthritis is beginnin' tae bother Geordie's hands now,' Morag told Kirsty. 'It happens as often as not with weavers when they get tae his age. I doubt he'll be able tae work his loom for much longer.'

'What'll you do?'

'We'll go back north, tae our own folk, when the time comes,' Morag said.

The hours dragged by, and at last the mourners departed. Rose and Jean would have washed all the dishes, but Kirsty, wearied to the bone, dissuaded them.

'We'll see to it in the morning – me and the girls. For tonight I just want to be quiet for a while.'

John Brodie, who had also attended, offered to take Jean and Rose home in his new motorcar. Alex would have escorted Jean on the short walk to her home above the shop, but she shook her head at him and went on tiptoe to whisper in his ear, 'No offence, laddie, but I've never been in a motorcar before and I'd fairly like tae try the experience!'

Todd would have left with his sister and her husband, but Kirsty detained him with a hand on his arm. 'We'll be talking about the future, and I'd like you to stay,' she said, and his face, already flushed from the warmth of the small crowded house, the funeral whisky and the pressure of his tight high collar, reddened a little more.

Kirsty had decided that Mary, tearful over the loss of her father and yet another bewildering change within her family circle, should be allowed to participate in the funeral gathering. 'Mary needs to say goodbye to her father,' she said when Alex and Caitlin argued with her. 'If she's shut out of what's going on, she'll mebbe feel cheated in later life when she thinks of him.' She knew what she was talking about – she herself had suffered, and always would, because she hadn't been able to take part in her beloved grandfather's funeral.

Dressed in a black dress her mother and sister had hurriedly made for her, Mary had worked hard, scurrying to and fro among the guests like an ant in a patch of tall grass, burdened with plates of sandwiches and sausage rolls and biscuits and cake. Now, with the visitors gone, she was white with exhaustion and could scarcely keep her eyes open.

'Bed for you, miss.'

'Can I not stay up . . .' Mary began, but was interrupted by a jaw-cracking yawn. 'Will you be here in the morning Alex?' she wanted to know when she had regained the power of speech.

'No, pet, I've got work to do tomorrow,' he said, glancing apologetically at his mother and other sister. 'I'll have to take the train back to Glasgow tonight.'

Fresh tears were added to those brought into her eyes by the yawn. 'But you'll have to come back now that Ewan's gone and Father's . . .' Her voice began to wobble, and he picked her up and hugged her, his face drawn with misery and guilt. 'Mary, love . . .'

'We'll be fine, you and me and Caitlin.' Kirsty patted her

young daughter's hand. 'You're old enough to do your share of looking after the house, and Todd's never far away.'

'I'll carry you upstairs,' Alex offered, and Mary blinked the tears away and nodded, wrapping her arms round his neck and laying her head on his shoulder. He well knew that ever since babyhood she had loved the sensation of being carried upstairs, her head bumping and rolling against some adult's shoulder at each lift and step.

He lingered while Kirsty helped Mary, now stupefied by fatigue, out of her funeral clothes and into her nightdress. She was asleep before the two of them reached the bedroom door.

'I want to stay, but I have to go back, Mam,' Alex said as they began to descend the stairs. 'I've to see an important customer tomorrow morning and he's off to Carlisle at midday, so . . .'

'You've got your own work, Alex, and your own life. We'll manage fine.'

'Are you sure? I'm not all that far away if you need me. And Father,' he said the word easily without even noticing that he had used it, 'says that if there's ever anything he can do to help you, he will.'

'Don't forget to thank him for his kindness – and say I'll not hesitate to accept his offer if I need him,' Kirsty told him, knowing that the time when she had most needed Sandy, and he had needed her, was long past. She would not ask for his help.

Caitlin had made a fresh pot of tea, and she and Todd had made a start on gathering up the cups and saucers and glasses and plates scattered over the kitchen and parlour.

'What's to be seen to?' Alex asked when the four of them were seated round the table.

341

'Nothing much, to tell the truth. Poor Matt was house-bound for so long that we all got into our own ways of coping. I just wanted to make sure that you knew how well we could manage. Then you'll be able to get on with your own business without fretting over us.' Kirsty stared at her cup, realising with a stab of guilt that life without Matt would in fact be easier, since she would no longer have to worry about him being left on his own. 'I've got the shop, Caitlin has her work, and when Mary's on holiday from school she can come to the shop with me. She's a good lassie, and the others won't mind.'

'What about the workshop?'

'I'm going to keep it on. We've got our regular customers and I'd not want to let them down.' She smiled across the table at the journeyman. 'Todd's been the master there since Ewan left. Since you left, Alex, if the truth be told. Now the title's his, for all to see, for as long as he wants it.'

Todd glowed with pleasure. 'I'll be there for as long as y need me,' he said, and for a moment Kirsty thought of Beth who had so wanted Todd to become the master of the little workshop. Now it had happened, and she knew nothing about it.

'The new man's good?' Alex wanted to know.

'I picked Davie mysel'. He's a fine craftsman, and a reliable worker.'

'If there are problems, you'll both let me know?' Alex looked from Todd to Kirsty.

'We will, if we need you. But there'll be no problems,' she told him firmly. 'If there are, I'm sure we can see to them, Todd and me.'

34

...ose, who, thanks to Caitlin, had learned how to walk prop-
...ly in an evening dress, had still not mastered the art of
...alking like a young lady at other times. She burst into the
...op in her usual way to announce excitedly that John
...rodie's mother wanted Kirsty to call on her.

'Me? What for?'

'She's having problems with some outfit she bought. She's
...ke me, entirely the wrong shape for clothes, and she
...membered the nice dress you made for me for her daugh-
...r's engagement party. Please, Kirsty,' she hurried on as
...irsty began to shake her head. 'It's not like Mrs Brodie to
...k for our help, and she'd pay you well – I'd see to that.
...nd since she's a close friend of Mamma's, it would give me
... much pleasure,' she added with a wicked grin. 'Do it for
...hn if you won't do it for me. Think of all he's done to
...lp us.'

She and John Brodie were now spending quite a lot of
...ne in each other's company, so much so that they were
...ually linked in the minds of the local hostesses when they
...ued invitations. Kirsty had made or adapted a number of

outfits for Rose in the past few months, and from what she heard, each one had been well received.

'She's right about John. You should go and see the woman, Kirsty,' Jean said, and Teenie nodded vigorously.

'Oh, very well.'

Rose hugged her. 'Bless you! She's a dominating woman but quite nice in her own way,' she added casually, to Kirsty's alarm. 'Assert your authority if you must – she caves in if she's challenged.'

Carriagehill Road, where the Brodies lived, was familiar. So when Kirsty reached it, was the Brodies' gate. She looked along the length of the driveway to the house and remembered all at once that she had indeed walked along that road before, and in at that gate and up to that door.

On her last visit to the house she had been shown from the back door into the sitting room. This time the uniformed maid led her upstairs and into a large carpeted front bedroom, complete with a hand basin and vast wardrobes along two walls.

'Mrs Brodie will be along in a moment,' the maid said, and withdrew. Nervously, Kirsty took her jacket off and studied her hair and her clothes in the full-length mirror. Although only four months had passed since Matt's death she had recently decided that she and her daughters should dispense with the usual year of wearing nothing but black. To her mind it served little purpose, and heavy mourning had a depressing effect on the wearers and all those who came in contact with them. She had reverted to the shop uniform of white blouse and black skirt, but today, since she was outside the shop, she wore a grey skirt and jacket over a lilac blouse.

with slightly puffed sleeves and a high neck with a flounce of lace at the throat. She nodded approvingly at her reflection and had just moved to the window when the door opened.

'Mrs Lennox?' Mrs Brodie swept into the room, followed by another uniformed maid, presumably the servant who helped her to dress and attended to her clothes and her hair. 'Miss Rose Hamilton assures me that you will be able to assist me with a slight problem.'

'I'll do my best, Mrs Brodie.' Kirsty took a step or two away from the window, and the woman's eyes narrowed as she saw the caller's face more clearly.

'Don't I know you?'

'We met once before, Mrs Brodie.'

'Where?'

'Here in your home, almost two years ago. I was looking for work as a sewing woman, but I didn't find it here.'

'Good heavens!' Red patches flared high on the woman's cheekbones. 'You're the woman who used to sew for Mrs Hamilton.'

'Yes.'

'And now you're working for Rose? What a small world.'

'Now Rose and I are partners, together with Miss Jean Chisholm.' Kirsty corrected the woman gently but firmly. Then, as Mrs Brodie, taken aback, blinked and stuttered, she introduced a businesslike note to her voice. 'You mentioned a problem?'

Mrs Brodie managed to collect herself. 'It's this costume.' She indicated the outfit she wore – a flowery silk-taffeta dress, the skirt embellished with two deep frills of the same material, and a matching bolero jacket thick with dark-blue braid. 'I'm accompanying my husband on a business trip next month, and I planned to wear this at an important afternoon gathering. For some reason he doesn't care for it.' She twisted and turned before her full-length mirror, frowning at her own reflection. 'The question is, can something be done with it?'

'Perhaps your own dressmaker—'

'She made it, and she thinks, like me, that it looks quite all right as it is. Then dear Rose suggested that I should consult you. I must say that she has been looking quite elegant recently. Something of a revelation, in fact. I'm hoping that you can do as much for me.'

Glancing at the maid, Kirsty read the slight flicker of the woman's lips accurately. It was one thing dressing Rose's long, angular frame and quite another dealing with Mrs Brodie, who was built like a box – square and solid and quite wrong for the frills and flounces and cummerbunds of modern fashion.

Kirsty took a deep breath. 'To begin with, Mrs Brodie, I think you should replace the bolero jacket with something longer, perhaps, and looser.'

'But that would require more of this patterned material. It may not be easy to find now.'

'I would suggest a jacket in one colour that picks up shade from the dress – grey, perhaps, to match the background of the dress material.' The background could scarcely be seen behind the large, rioting flowers, but it was there.

'Grey?' Mrs Brodie was shocked. 'How dull!'

'Grey can very fetching, and excellent for offsetting colour and patterns. A grey sash too – not a cummerbund, something narrower . . .'

Mrs Brodie clasped both hands protectively over the broad

sash about her generous waist. 'I insist on retaining the cummerbund. It's very fashionable.'

Kirsty began to wonder how a nice man like John Brodie could be the son of this overbearing woman with not the slightest understanding of colour or style. 'Mrs Brodie, you asked for my advice, and that's what I'm giving you,' she said as politely as possible.

'My dear woman, you must bear in mind that she who pays the piper is allowed to call the tune.'

For a moment they eyed each other, then Kirsty, remembering Rose's advice about asserting her authority, shrugged and picked up her jacket and bag. It took all her courage, but she managed to do it with an air of finality. 'Then I'm afraid I can't help you, Mrs Brodie. I'm a seamstress and, as you say, you pay the piper. Perhaps a piper can be of more help to you than I am.'

'Wait,' said Mrs Brodie.

It took an hour, and all the tact and firmness Kirsty possessed, to persuade the woman to allow her to strip the outfit of its cummerbund and puffed sleeves and bolero jacket. Even the starched maid was wilting by the time Mrs Brodie conceded defeat.

'Oliphant, help me off with these things so that Mrs, er, Lennox can take them away,' she commanded. Kirsty watched, fascinated, as the servant removed the dress and jacket to reveal a meaty torso so well corseted that it was a wonder that Mrs Brodie could draw breath, then eased her employer into a pretty lacy tea gown, fastening the buttons and tying the sash. She had never before seen a grown woman being undressed and dressed like a doll. Mary was far more capable than this woman when it came to looking after herself.

'If I don't care for the changes you've suggested once they're done,' Mrs Brodie said as the maid carefully packed the clothes into a small travelling bag, 'I shan't pay one penny.'

'As you wish, Mrs Brodie.' Kirsty had used up a month's supply of firmness and was too drained to argue.

'And if you spoil the dress I shall expect you to reimburse the cost. It was very expensive. In fact before you start cutting into it I want to see a sketch of your proposed changes.'

'Certainly, Mrs Brodie,' Kirsty agreed. Anything to escape from this house and get back to Causeyside Street, where folk were able to do up their own buttons.

Although it was half-day, the others had all waited in the shop to find out how she had got on. 'I'll never forgive you for this, Rose Hamilton,' she said when she arrived back.

'Oh dear, was she in one of her ladylike moods?'

'I'd say she was in one of her Queen Victoria moods.'

'She can be quite a nice woman really,' Rose said helplessly, then went red when Kirsty retorted, 'Mebbe so – if you've got money and you're walking out with her son.'

It was generally agreed that Kirsty's ideas would be a great improvement. 'We'll charge her for the time you spend on it,' Rose promised. 'She can afford it, and she'll pay happily she likes the changes.'

'If she doesn't, it'll cost us money.'

'That's my problem, not yours.'

'The thing is, I've agreed to let her see a sketch first, and I can't draw.'

'Nor can I,' Rose said at once, while Jean added, 'I mind I was good at drawing wee houses at school, with daffodi in the yard and chickens scratching about. But not dresses.'

Kirsty began to fold the dress and jacket up. 'I'll have a word with Caitlin. She was quite good at drawing at school.'

'Here.' Rose snatched up a handful of fashion papers and put them on top of the clothes in the travel bag. 'Perhaps these will help her.'

'But I was going to spend the evening working on my new jacket,' Caitlin protested. She was walking out with the new apprentice Todd had recently taken on and had started making herself a jacket from the length of woollen cloth the Bishops had given her almost two years earlier.

'I'll do some work on the jacket for you if you'll try the drawing,' Kirsty coaxed, and the girl shrugged and agreed. She spent some time frowning over the fashion papers strewn across the kitchen table, then trying out some sketches on an old sketch pad Alex had left behind, working with colouring crayons borrowed from Mary. Kirsty, busy at the sewing machine, glanced up at her now and again. Caitlin, at fifteen years of age, had all but blossomed into womanhood and was nearly going to be beautiful in another year or so. Bryce, her new sweetheart, was a year older, which meant that they were the ages Kirsty and Sandy had been when Alex was conceived.

Strongly aware of that from the first, and remembering how mutual loneliness and lack of security had catapulted her and Sandy into each other's arms, Kirsty had made certain that Bryce, a likeable lad, was made welcome in her kitchen. Caitlin was going to be given all the time she needed to make decisions about her future.

'I went to Kilbarchan this afternoon,' the girl said just

then. 'Mr Bishop's going to give up work in November, and they're all going back north.'

'You'll miss them – we all will.'

Caitlin nodded, then said, 'I think I can start trying the sketch now. Come and tell me what it is you want.'

'This is very well done,' Rose said, awed, when she saw the sketch the following day. 'I'd no idea that two of your children were artists, Kirsty.'

The sketch was good, but Kirsty did her best to conceal her maternal pride, saying casually, 'Caitlin's scribbled out ideas from time to time for clothes she wanted to make, but that's been all up until now.'

Rose herself took the sketch to show Mrs Brodie and returned to report that the woman was impressed by it and had agreed to let Kirsty proceed.

'We'll need to buy material for the jacket.'

'We can hardly make it out of something from the shop,' Rose agreed. 'We'd best go shopping.'

After a lifetime of unpicking and remaking second-hand clothing it was a joy to Kirsty to see so much virginal cloth in all patterns and colours, and of all materials. She moved from one shelf to the other in the draper's shop, drinking all in while Rose watched her, amused.

'You look like a child let loose in a sweet shop for the first time.'

'It's – it's like being in heaven!'

'We should buy new material sometimes for the shop.'

'Our customers couldn't afford to pay for it.'

'Then we'll think of other ways of using it,' Rose said, light in her eye.

Kirsty finally settled on a pale-grey silk taffeta for Mrs Brodie's jacket. She bore it almost reverently back to the shop, where the first cut was a nerve-wracking moment.

'What if she doesnae like it once it's finished?' Teenie quavered. 'Ye'll have tae pay the full price of it.'

'If we must, we must – but she will like it,' Rose told her firmly as they stared at each other over the expensive material. 'Look at us – we're like the witches in Macbeth. For goodness' sake, Kirsty, start cutting!'

'Well begun,' Kirsty said with a bravado she didn't feel, 'is half done.'

'Or you could say, another door opened . . .' Rose put in as the scissors plunged into the material and started snipping.

35

Mrs Brodie was delighted with her new outfit and almost at once asked Kirsty to alter another dress for her.

'Please,' Rose coaxed when Kirsty firmly refused.

'It's not what we're supposed to be doing, Rose! I've got enough work on my hands without becoming Mrs Brodie's personal dressmaker. Isn't that right, Jean?' Kirsty appealed to her friend.

'Well, the thing is . . .' Jean said evasively, and Kirsty looked from one partner to the other.

'What have you two been plotting behind my back?'

'Not behind your back, Kirsty, it just came up in conversation when you didnae happen tae be in the shop . . .'

Rose grasped the nettle with both hands. 'To tell you the truth, Kirsty, I knew from what Mrs Brodie said after her first fitting that she was delighted with your ideas for the outfit, and I was certain she'd want to use your talents again. And you know how much pleasure it gave you to buy the material for her jacket. So Jean and I thought that if she did ask you to do more work—'

'It wouldnae be a good idea tae turn the likes of M

Brodie down,' Jean broke in. 'We think you should do it, Kirsty.'

'As a sort of sideline.'

'It wouldnae take away from the other customers.'

'But it would,' Kirsty protested. 'It would take up too much of my time . . .'

'Not if we brought in another employee,' Rose said. 'Not if we asked Caitlin to come and work for us.'

'Caitlin?'

'I first thought of employing her when I saw that drawing she did for Mrs Brodie. And I made up my mind the day she came in wearing that bonny jacket she had made for herself. She's wasted in that grocery shop, Kirsty.'

'I had it in mind to try to get her into Cochrane's sewing room one day.'

'And let someone else get the good of her when she could work for us?' Rose almost exploded. 'With us she could sew, and mebbe even try her hand at some designing—'

'And help behind the counter if she had the time,' Jean broke in. 'Say yes, Kirsty.'

'Can we afford another wage?'

'Yes we can – and Caitlin would more than pay her own way,' Rose assured her.

'We'll need to see what Caitlin thinks of it,' Kirsty said, already knowing the answer, and already looking forward to bringing her daughter into the business that had come to mean so much to her.

pale autumn haze was lying over the park and the quarry and the row of old terraced houses when Kirsty walked up the park on her last visit to the Kilbarchan house that had once belonged to her grandfather. Mary ran ahead, scuffing her booted feet through the gold and red and brown leaves by the side of the path, while Caitlin and Kirsty followed behind, talking about the shop. Caitlin had just completed her first month there and had already settled in and become an integral part of the place.

Geordie and his daughter, Ellie, had completed their final orders, and the two looms on the ground floor were silent, waiting to be taken apart and crated for the journey north.

'There'll be work for Ellie, for the weavin's still goin' on up north,' Geordie said as they stood in the silent shop. 'And I'll still do some work, but not so much. There'll be others ta take over if my hands decide they cannae keep goin'.'

'I'll be sad to see you go.'

'There's nothin' sad about it,' Morag said robustly. 'It's only another change, and life's full of those – as you should know, Kirsty.'

They walked up the garden, still rich with autumn fruit and flowers, to the shed where the old loom stood, its roller empty of cloth. Geordie took a parcel from the shelf. 'This for you, Kirsty. I made it specially on this loom.'

Kirsty unfolded the wrapping and found herself looking at all the colours of the Scottish moorland – russet and gold and yellow, and every shade of brown, all intermingled in a pattern that seemed to flow like a burn purling its way down through the bracken moors to the river.

'Geordie, it's beautiful!'

He nodded with justifiable pride. 'I think it's one o' the best pieces of cloth I've ever woven. Caitlin here helped me tae decide on the colours.' Then, laying a hand on the loom, he said, 'The thing is, lass, what's tae be done with the

354

machine? I cannae take it with me, for the two I already have are more than enough. And if it's left here it'll mebbe end up the way it did before.'

'We have to think of somewhere to keep it, Mam,' Caitlin said anxiously. 'I couldn't bear to think of it being abandoned again, not after seeing it working.'

'We won't let that happen,' Kirsty assured her, stroking one of the big rollers gently. 'I'll speak to Todd about it.'

It seems only fitting to bring it back to the store by the end,' she explained to Todd the next day. 'After all, that was once a loom shop, before my father's father started up his cabinet-making business. But I'll not allow the loom to be put into a corner in pieces the way it was. I want it to be set up properly, even if it's never used again.'

'Ye never know, ye might be able tae find a weaver one day.'

She smiled at him, struck by the way their minds often seemed to be in tune. 'I'd wondered about that myself. Caitlin's got an idea in her head about making clothes from material woven on it, but we'll have to wait and see. For the meantime, I just want to know that it's safe and it's being looked after properly. It would mean you losing some of your storage space,' she added anxiously.

'We can manage without it,' he said easily. A year had passed since Beth had run away with Ewan, and for Todd, the wounds appeared to have healed. He had thrown himself into his work and had reverted to his usual cheerful self. 'It's just a matter of makin' certain that the finished furniture's moved right away so that it doesnae have tae be stored. There's no worry about that.'

'Are you certain? I can try to find somewhere else for the loom if you want.'

'You own the place, Mrs Lennox,' he said simply.

'Mebbe I do, but you're the master.'

'Even so,' he said, his eyes holding hers, 'it's what you want that matters tae me.'

Geordie arranged to have the loom taken apart, delivered to Paisley and reassembled, while Todd and Kirsty cleared the store out and prepared it.

There was an air of celebration about the place on the frosty November day the loom arrived back in Paisley. Even Alex had arranged to be there. Once it had been reassembled and settled, they held a gathering in the kitchen to celebrate – Todd and the other two men from the workshop, Alex and Kirsty and Caitlin and Mary, and the Bishops.

In the evening, when all the visitors had gone and the workshop was closed for the day and Caitlin was out with Bryce, and Mary in her bed, Kirsty took a lamp into the store to look again at the loom, strong and sturdy in the store that had, in a way, become a loom shop again.

It was true what some folk said, she thought, running her fingers over the timber. Things did have a way of coming full circle. The storms of yesterday were over, and today here she was, back in her old home, reunited with her grandfather through the loom that had been an almost lifelong companion to him. Alex was well settled with his father; Ewan, wherever he was, had chosen his own road; and she and Caitlin and Mary were at peace with their lives. As for tomorrow, it would take care of itself, for as her mother had always said, tomorrow is another day.

Morag had had the right way of it with her sayings, too. Kirsty felt that this very loom had somehow woven her own life pattern, a pattern that brought together all her children, and Sandy, and Matt, and Jean and Rose and the shop.

A step sounded in the pend and the door creaked slightly at her back.

'Come on in, Todd,' she said without looking round.

'I'm not disturbin' ye?'

'Not a bit of it.'

'I just wanted tae have another look at it, without all those folks around,' he said, coming to stand by her side, his big hand landing gently on the loom close by hers. 'It's a beautiful piece of machinery.'

'It is.' His presence, in the flickering shadows of the shed, was comforting as always, but at the same time being alone with him in the calm darkness sent a very faint tingle of pleasure dancing along her veins. It was a sensation she had first noticed only weeks earlier while talking alone with him in the workshop. She suspected that it had been with her, unnoticed, for much longer.

Kirsty was well aware that she was nearing her fortieth year and that Todd was a few years her junior, and that she hadn't been widowed a full twelve months yet. But something whispered to her that one day, perhaps quite far in the future, Todd might just become an important part of her own particular life pattern.

Then again, she thought, standing by the loom, Todd close by her in the store's silence, it might not happen.

But the possibility that it might, distant as it was, filled her with happiness.